For my father, who served on submarines in the Far East during World War Two.

And for my mother, who waited.

Also in dedication to the memory of Bill Coenen's dear friend, Mike Timpani, as well as all Chinese dissidents who, over the years, have risked persecution and imprisonment in their fearless pursuit of political freedom and basic human rights.

Terence Strong was brought up in south London, after the Second World War. He has worked in advertising, journalism, publishing and many other professions. His bestselling novels (which have sold more than one million copies in the UK alone) include *Rogue Element*, *The Tick Tock Man*, *Wheels of Fire*, *Cold Monday* and *White Viper*. He lives in the south-west of England.

Visit www.twbooks.co.uk/authors/tstrong.html

Acclaim for Terence Strong

'An expert miasma of treachery and suspicion building to a thrilling climax' *Observer*

'Belongs to the action-man school of writing, backed up by hands-on research' *The Times*

'Tension ratchets up wickedly – a strong sense of reality is reinforced with powerful emotion and gritty characters' *Daily Telegraph*

'An edge-of-the-chair thriller with the chilling grip of authenticity' *Independent on Sunday*

'Well plotted and genuinely exciting' *Sunday Telegraph*

'An extremely good topical thriller' *Jack Higgins*

Also by Terence Strong

Author's Note

Collaboration in developing the storyline of this book with my American friend (and a previous technical adviser to *Stalking Horse*) Bill Coenen began by happy coincidence.

When he telephoned a couple of years ago to thank me for a copy of an earlier book, I mentioned the new idea I was working on. I had the concept of a Special Forces' stealth submarine, inspired by my father's wartime exploits, and was thinking of China for the setting. It transpired that Bill was a seasoned 'Far-East hand' and within days plot ideas were being thrashed out between us over the Internet. After numerous computer crashes and e-mails lost in the ether, this was the result.

I am also grateful for Bill's input on US intelligence and military matters, American dialogue and his numerous useful suggestions.

Appropriately enough, given the hi-tech nature of elements of the story, e-mail was to provide a fast and vital link with many of those who generously gave of their help and advice, including former senior members of Britain's Special Air Service Regiment and Special Boat Service.

Very special thanks go to Ed Evanhoe (Intelligence Editor of *Behind-The-Lines* Magazine, USA, and a veteran Far East expert) for his kind interest and invaluable input about exactly how to bring down the government of totalitarian China.

Likewise, I owe an immense debt of gratitude to my 'man in Beijing', the lovely Carol Harper, a fellow member of the Crime Writers' Association, who tirelessly and enthusiastically investigated locations and provided hilariously descriptive reports by e-mail, clearly sent late at night and under the influence of too much *tsingtao*.

My submarine was designed by merging the brilliant ideas of marine engineer Steve Becket B.Sc. M.Sc. MBA CEng MIMechE and long-serving submariner and naval engineer Pat Drummy. Military advisers were old friends Dave Abbott, Hugh Wiltshire and Neil Roberts. Aircraft bomb by Kevin Callaghan GM OGM and Richard Prangnell.

A final word of thanks goes to the editorial team: my respective past and present editors on the book, Tom Weldon and Maria Rejt, my wife Linda for her eagle-eyed first edit, typist cum miracle-worker Judy Coombes and my diamond-polisher, copy editor Anne Scott.

Due to the topicality and importance of this story about China, all have worked at fever pitch to turn the finished manuscript into the final book in just six weeks from a standing start. I am grateful to them all.

Terence Strong
London 1998

Prologue

The sonar operator's hunched shoulders stiffened suddenly.

'I've got somethin'.' He studied the display screen in front of him. 'Yeah. Faint, but definitely somethin'.'

His laconic Tennessee drawl belied the surge of adrenaline he felt; this was not a man to break sweat easily.

The tactical action officer moved through the air-conditioned red twilight of the combat information centre, deep in the bowels of the anti-submarine frigate USS *Knox* and peered at the console display. 'You sure, Crosby?'

'Only that it's *somethin'*, sir.'

Crosby was good. Crosby had bat's ears, they all knew that. But even Crosby could be wrong. They were running on USS *Knox's* ED passive towed-array sonar because the target was one hell of a mother. Her state-of-the-art stealth hull would simply absorb active sonar signals pinging out of the bow-mounted Western General Electric rig and give away nothing. So they were reduced to passive listening. Because, however dampened, you could never fully eliminate engine noise and however slick the design, you could never stop water rushing over a submarine's bow.

USS *Knox* had only a bearing. You needed at least three bearings from separate sources to get a fix. And so far, they had only one.

The tactical action officer made his decision, silently vowing to give Crosby a bad time he'd never forget if he'd screwed up on this one. 'Bearing?' he snapped.

'Zero-eight-five degrees, sir,' Crosby snapped back.

'Get the wax out your ears – track and report.'

'Sir.'

The officer turned to the communications suite. Time to stick his neck out and pray he wouldn't be left with more

1

egg on his face than on his cap. 'Signal OPREP 7th Fleet. Include current position. Unconfirmed contact. Bearing zero-eight-five.'

Forty-five seconds later Vice Admiral Ross Harding was handed the message aboard the USS *Theodore Roosevelt*. Wearing tropical whites, he sat in a bridge high chair which gave him a perfect view of the carrier's floodlit flight deck below.

His was the appearance and build of a man who had not been born in the normal way, but hewn fully grown out of limestone. Flinty eyes scrutinised the piece of paper in his huge fist.

After reading the signal, Harding took time to relight the well-chewed cigar butt before acknowledging the anxious faces of the small group of VIP visitors to the exercise. A bunch of grey suits. Politicians and spooks, he wasn't sure which he detested most. And he had them all here on the carrier's bridge in equal measure. In Harding's strictly private view, each was as overconfident in his abilities and as untrustworthy as the next.

Hal Katz, Deputy Assistant Secretary of Defense for Special Operations was one and Frank Aspen, CIA, Assistant Deputy Director of Operations, another. Both, he knew of old, had the smooth charm and all the backbone of a rattlesnake. Katz wouldn't agree to anything that he might have to explain away in bodybags, while Frank Aspen didn't mind any number of them as long as no one could pin the blame on him directly.

Obviously the vice admiral wasn't familiar with his British visitors from across the pond, but he doubted they were much better. Their spook was Piers Lansdowne, a thirtysomething high-flyer with a schoolboy's face and a pronounced Adam's apple. The trendy foppish cut of his blond hair and round-rimmed swot's spectacles were anathema to Harding. But he had to admit the boy's mind seemed as sharp as the broken shards of his cut-glass accent. That told Harding everything: privileged

2

background, English public school and now Far East Desk of the Foreign Office.

At least that was the fiction that the British junior defence minister insisted on maintaining.

But then Jim Hudd was new to the high echelons of his government, the Armed Forces in general, and ships in particular. Even as Harding had received the signal from USS *Knox*, Jim Hudd was throwing up his guts into a plastic bucket out on the flying bridge. The sea was mill-pond calm.

Harding didn't bother hiding his irritation as he addressed Piers Lansdowne. 'You wanna see if your Minister is well enough to join us yet? I don't wanna go over all this again.'

Lansdowne had the grace to blush. 'I'll check on him, Admiral.'

The American grey suits and Harding shared expressions of silent exasperation: the entire US war machine held up for a bucket of British puke.

Moments later Lansdowne reappeared, helping Jim Hudd as he stumbled through the hatchway, wiping his mouth with a stained handkerchief.

'Feeling better?' Hal Katz asked brusquely.

Hudd's watering eyes, set in a meaty bloodhound face, couldn't disguise the embarrassment he felt for displaying such feebleness before these men of iron. He smiled weakly. 'Thanks. Better out than in, eh?'

That drew no response, so he tried to look businesslike, straightening his back and hiking up the trousers of his crumpled off-the-peg suit to cover his beer belly. 'Piers says something's happened?'

Vice Admiral Harding nodded. 'One of our destroyers picked up an unconfirmed passive sonar contact two minutes ago.' He strode across to the wall chart that showed the small island off Saipan. The surrounding area of the Pacific was ringed by ships of the Carrier Task Force. Harding jabbed a finger at one of these. '*Knox* puts

3

the contact bearing at zero-eight-five. That's a bearing but no fix. Any number of miles along that trajectory. So it could still be outside *or* inside our protective ring.'

Jim Hudd looked concerned. 'Surely that couldn't be *Manta*. All this stealth technology stuff, it's supposed to be foolproof.'

'That's what we're here to find out, Frank,' Hal Katz reminded patiently. 'To separate the shit from the shinola.'

Vice Admiral Harding cut in: 'We're ordering up three Sea Kings – they're anti-submarine helicopters with dunking sonars. We'll attempt to get a confirmation and triangulated fix on the contact.' Behind him, through the bridge windscreen, the three sea-grey shapes could be seen lifting off into the clear night sky. 'Now we're finally all together, let me bring you up to speed.'

He tapped again on the map of the island. 'Tim-Wan is an island some two miles in diameter. It is deserted except for a small detachment of electronics engineers and US Marines who maintain and guard a small listening station. The destruction of its antennae is the ultimate objective of the intrusion force.

'The exercise is to evaluate the technical abilities of an experimental submarine and the efficiency of the crew and on-board assault team which combine to make up Project Deadwater.

'As you will be aware, the sub began development in Britain as a joint private and Royal Navy venture in the last few years of the Cold War. Under the designation SCUBA – Secure Clandestine Underwater Basing Apparatus – the sub employs state-of-the-art stealth technology to allow it to operate close to shore in enemy waters and remain undetected. Its function is to provide an operational base for clandestine activity – from the launch of commando raids to supporting agent networks – for up to a month's duration.'

Jim Hudd still felt queasy but forced his mind to concentrate. 'Er, Admiral, since Project Deadwater became a joint British–American development after our Options for Change cutbacks at the end of the Cold War, we've had little detail of progress. What we have had, I'm afraid, is pretty incomprehensible.'

Hal Katz frowned. 'You have a Royal Navy liaison officer assigned?'

Hudd smiled sheepishly. 'Oh, yes. I'm afraid it's me who's the problem. I used to be a coal miner. Don't know one end of a gun from the other.'

'Old Labour,' Piers explained kindly.

'All that technical jargon is gobbledegook to me,' the British Defence Minister added. 'And I've had no sight of naval architects' plans, or even a snap.'

'Snap?' Vice Admiral Harding queried.

'Snapshot, photograph. I've begun to wonder if Britain *really* still owns the half it pays for.'

The CIA man, Frank Aspen, spoke in his usual flat and deadly serious tone. 'That's down to my department, Minister; we tend to be a little overzealous on the secrecy front. Especially where new technology's concerned.'

'But we do have an artist's impression here,' Katz added. 'Don't we, Admiral?'

'Sure do.' Harding moved to the flip chart next to the map and threw back the cover.

'This is *Manta*,' Frank Aspen said. 'And I hope this is something no one outside naval operations will *ever* see.'

Hudd fumbled for his spectacles and as he focused on the drawing his mouth dropped. It was like no submarine he had ever seen before. His first impression was of a sort of black underwater flying saucer. But rather than being perfectly symmetrical, it was a teardrop-shape which tapered towards the stern. And he could see now where the name had come from. The wide stabilising 'wings' running the full length of each side of the craft gave it an uncanny resemblance to a manta ray. There was no obvious conning-tower, or 'fin', as Lansdowne had taught him to call it, just a four-foot smooth hump amidships from which twin masts protruded.

'The hull shape's been streamlined considerably since the original conception,' Aspen explained. 'She may look like something out of *Star Wars*, but inside she's still a one sixty-tonne cigar tube carrying a four-man crew and sixteen combat swimmers.' He grinned. 'Maybe a few more if they all breathe in. As you can see, the outer is covered with sonar-absorbent panels. In layman's terms, they prevent any hostile sonar signals pinging back to give away the sub's location.' He pointed to the X-configured rudder and hydroplane control fins at the stern. 'Each arm operates independently under computer control for high manoeuvrability. More like an aircraft than a conventional sub. Plus port and starboard thrusters, so she can turn in her own length. GPS navigation and communications via satellite.'

The British Junior defence minister was lost. 'Of course.'

'Silicon Valley's best,' Aspen continued proudly. 'But when it comes to putting an assault team ashore, we embrace *appropriate* technology. High-tech stealth sub, but the men go ashore by good old tried-and-tested means as required.'

'Quite incredible,' Hudd murmured.

'It will need to be,' Piers Lansdowne observed, 'if the project is to fulfil the role we have in mind.'

Vice Admiral Harding's face remained inscrutable, only the fractional narrowing of his eyes indicating that his analytical mind was humming like a computer. Piecing together fragments of knowledge, linking them with threads of logic. Specialist submarine, Special Forces, intelligence experts on China, joint American–British interests. . .

But when he spoke there was no curiosity in his voice. It was typically matter-of-fact. 'Whatever you have in mind, gentlemen, this exercise should tell you whether the sub and the Project Deadwater team are up to it.

'We have the island of Tim-Wan surrounded by a ring of ships from the 7th Fleet, deploying the most efficient anti-submarine technology in the world, including ASW aircraft from our Rota base. *Manta* will have to penetrate that ring undetected, their assault team destroy the dummy aerial, return to the mother ship and escape the ring of ships again.'

Hudd was enthralled, not conscious that he was chewing his thumbnail. 'And do *you* think they can do it, Admiral?'

Harding's back stiffened. 'A personal view, Minister?'

'Of course.'

'Not a snowball's.' He ignored Frank Aspen's withering glare. 'Looks like *Knox* is already on to them.'

The signals officer approached the vice admiral. 'Sorry, sir. *Knox* reports it's lost the contact.'

'Thank you.' Harding did not bother hiding his annoyance. Fleet reputation was on the line here. 'When are our AS helos due on station?' he checked with the carrier's captain.

'A couple of minutes, Admiral.'

'Then it won't have gone far. I've every confidence.'

But Harding's confidence was apparently misplaced. After fifteen minutes of hovering while they lowered their sonar buoys into the water, the flight commander reported negative to contact.

Hudd felt a small rush of pride. After all, the initial concept of the SCUBA had been British, even if the Yanks had tinkered with it. 'If it's slipped through the net, Admiral, when might we expect them to reach the target?'

'At least another hour.' Harding indicated the CCTV monitor installed above the control console. It showed a hazy green monochrome picture of a patch of land and the base of the dummy radio mast on Tim-Wan. 'That's being relayed direct from the target. Low-level light camera, so we'll be able to see when the assault team gets there.'

'*If*,' reminded Hal Katz. 'And there are a dozen Marines on patrol.'

'Maybe it's time to take a break instead of hangin' round waiting for nothing to happen,' Frank Aspen suggested.

'The wardroom's at your disposal,' Harding said.

Hudd looked relieved. 'I could do with a stiff drink. Might settle the old tum.'

Harding gave the British minister a curious look as he showed the way.

Piers Lansdowne explained quietly. 'Sorry, Jim. It's a dry navy.'

'Oh, God, I was forgetting.'

'No problem.' He held something concealed in his hand. 'Take this.'

'What is it?'

'My hip flask.'

Coke, Fanta and coffee were on offer in the wardroom and a range of snacks was spread on the gleaming table. The plates bore little flags describing the contents, most of which were unfamiliar to Jim Hudd and awfully American. Almond pretzels, bagels with blue cheese, pastrami on rye, pecan pie slices. . .

'A pot of tea would be nice.'

The steward smiled stiffly, sure he would find an old box of teabags hidden *somewhere* in the galley.

They had barely settled in their seats when the officer of the watch put his head round the door. 'Admiral Harding, sir, message from the captain. Thought you'd want to know that that Chinese naval vessel the Hawkeyes have been monitoring is now a hundred and ten miles north of the fleet. Identified as destroyer *Luhu*.'

Harding's left eyebrow lifted a fraction. 'Makin' this way?'

'No, sir,' the officer replied. '*Luhu*'s remaining on station, but she's put up two helos to see what's going on. Otherwise her stance is non-aggressive.'

'And what's our counteraction?'

The officer smiled tightly. 'Two F18s are buzzing the helos to warn them off, and we've signalled *Luhu* this is a private party, invitation only.'

Harding nodded. 'Keep me posted. We don't want an international incident by accident.'

'Sir.'

As the officer withdrew, Hudd looked across the table at Vice Admiral Harding. 'What does all that mean?'

Harding offered one of his rare bleak smiles. 'It means the Chinese Navy is monitoring the exercise and it's playing a long way from home.'

'That's what we in the CIA have been warning,' Frank Aspen added darkly. 'We've had evidence for a long time that China has serious territorial ambitions. It's the only major power in the world that doesn't accept the geographical status quo and it's got major territorial disputes with all its neighbours. That's why Beijing is determined to project its influence with a modern blue-water navy.'

Hal Katz swallowed the remains of his first bagel. 'I've seen those reports, Frank. The assessment is it'll be at least fifteen years before the Chinese have an operational navy good enough to allow them to cause real trouble. And anyway, that assumes causing trouble would be in their interest. To my mind they're too far down the capitalist road for that.'

'Sorry, sir,' Admiral Harding interrupted, 'but that's not what I'm seeing. Despite the friendly face they've been offering the world media, there's been a subtle but distinct shift towards aggressive nationalism and they've been flexing their muscles. Two years ago you'd never have seen *Luhu* out here, nearly two thousand miles offshore and aggressively poking its nose into an American exercise.'

Katz shrugged dismissively, but Piers Lansdowne from the British Foreign Office, added: 'Things have changed since the Hong Kong handover. Restored national pride went to the heads of the leadership. Since President Deng Xiaoping's death, there's been an ongoing power struggle and at the moment the hard men are holding sway. Two hundred years ago China was the most powerful nation on earth, and now they see the economic miracle as the key to restoring them to their former position in the world.'

'Nothing wrong in that,' Katz said defensively. 'Every nation has its aspirations.'

'Nothing wrong,' the vice admiral agreed, 'as long as we in the West don't help them there by selling them all our latest weapons technology.'

'That's not how State or the White House sees it,' Katz snapped back. 'They see it as the greatest investment opportunity for America that the world will ever see. A fifth of mankind and the second largest economy on earth.'

Admiral Harding did not respond. No point in reminding the Defense Department official that far from being a great market opportunity, China had actually become the largest source of trade deficit to both the USA and Europe. He just wouldn't listen, because the President wouldn't listen and Hal Katz was the President's man. If the President said jump, he'd ask how high. So Harding would save his breath to cool his porridge. Besides, as the old saying went, it wasn't his job to ask how or why.

The boy Lansdowne accepted a coffee cup from the steward. 'Have you noticed how the slogans have changed?' he asked absently, his cultured English accent sounding oddly out of place.

'What?' Katz asked, bewildered.

A politely patronising English smile. 'If you read the Chinese newspapers, you'll notice the old 'To Get Rich is Glorious' slogans have gone. No more stories of business-men successfully risking all to turn round ailing factories. The new slogans are full of reference to hostile forces abroad. Accusing them of using economics to democratise China in order to divide and control it.'

Hal Katz looked blank. 'I don't read Chinese.'

Piers Lansdowne sipped delicately at his coffee. 'Perhaps you should learn, sir.'

Jim Hudd nearly choked on his tea. Beautiful! A stiletto straight between the shoulder blades. Young Piers was everything the ex-Nottingham miner thought he hated about the old Establishment right wing, but he'd warmed to the young man quickly during the long flight out from Heathrow. He wasn't in the least bit patronising as the newly appointed minister struggled to absorb the complexities of the briefing. Piers was friendly and witty, explaining that the main obstacle to their secret mission was the President of the United States himself.

Hudd noticed that across the table Admiral Harding and Frank Aspen of the CIA were looking at Piers Lansdowne with undisguised admiration. Then Hudd's eyes met theirs and the Americans' expressions said it all. The boy from the British Secret Intelligence Service – sorry, Foreign Office – had put into words exactly what they thought.

For the first time since being flown aboard the carrier USS *Theodore Roosevelt*, Jim Hudd felt that he was among allies, if not yet friends.

An hour later, they returned to the bridge. Hudd was feeling much better, fortified by the tea he had surreptitiously laced with whisky from Piers's flask.

The carrier's captain informed them that nothing had happened during their absence. It was good from one point of view, thought Hudd. The stealth submarine was *still* undetected. But, as he could see from the CCTV monitor, there wasn't much point in that if the mission itself was unaccomplished. And no sign of life had been seen at the island aerial site so far.

Meanwhile the Chinese destroyer *Luhu* remained watching and listening on station, its helicopters now returned to the aft flight deck to refuel.

When thirty minutes had passed, Admiral Harding cleared his throat. 'Well, gentlemen, I have to tell you that it looks as though we are faced with mission failure. The US Marine detachment report no sign of activity on Tim-Wan and *Manta* has only thirty minutes left to return undetected to the outside of the cordon.'

'But the sub hasn't been found. . .' Hudd began.

Harding couldn't conceal his disappointment. 'That is true, Minister, and I'm sorry my boys haven't located it yet. That may be because of some mechanical failure. If the sub is lying doggo on the bottom, it would explain why the AS sonars haven't picked her up.'

'And why they haven't reached their target,' Frank Aspen added.

Concern clouded Hudd's face. 'They're not in any danger, are they?'

'Highly unlikely,' Harding replied. 'In about thirty minutes they'll make themselves known to us, wherever they are.'

Hal Katz said: 'I expect it's the new computer software. They've been having trouble with that.'

'You're probably right.'

Hudd felt suddenly depressed. It just underlined what the military sceptics back at the Ministry of Defence in London had told him. The concept was fatally flawed. And if it was, so was the entire mission that Piers Lansdowne and Frank Aspen had set themselves. To set free the largest nation on earth. A thousand million people.

Piers sensed his disappointment and placed a reassuring hand on his shoulder.

'Sir!' It was the communications officer. 'Signal from *Knox* again. Contact bearing zero-eight-one.'

'Inside the cordon,' Piers said instantly.

Shit, Hudd mouthed.

'Picked up on active this time,' the officer added. 'Strong signal and they have a fix.' He rattled off the reference. It was barely a mile off *Theodore Roosevelt's* bow.

'Odd,' Harding thought aloud as the CTFC scrambled the anti-submarine Sea Kings again. 'Active sonar's usually hopeless against *Manta*.'

Frank Aspen from Langley said: 'Maybe she's lost some of her tiles. That happened in earlier trials.'

'The anachoic tiles absorb sonar signals,' Piers explained to Hudd. 'If some tiles are lost, then an active sonar signal will hit the bare surface and bounce back to give a contact and approximate position.'

'So what happens next?'

Harding answered. 'We're dropping dummy depth charges. If they go off close enough, *Manta* will surface. That will represent a kill or SD. Severe damage.' He turned towards the bridge windscreen and vast flight deck beyond, crammed with rows of naval fighters. 'If you look off our starboard bow, you should be able to watch the floor show.'

The group craned forward to watch the helicopters speed across the sluggish swell of the Pacific, the surface glistening like hammered silver under the full moon.

Suddenly the bridge was filled with the squawk and static hiss and rapid radiospeak of the pilots as they assessed and confirmed their positions above the submarine.

'*Fired one, fired two,*' intoned the first helicopter.

He was joined by the second, forming a pattern. '*Fired one, fired two.*'

Hudd saw the dark shape of the charges falling like birdshit from the helicopter pods. He held his breath, expecting an almighty roar and the great geyser of displaced water he'd seen on war movies.

Stupid, of course, because these were only dummies. So the small fountains of spray were a bit of a disappointment and they couldn't even hear the detonations at that distance.

A tense silence followed, Hudd aware of his heart's slow and steady thud from somewhere deep within his crumpled shirt.

'*We got somethin'* ,' broke in one of the helicopter pilots, followed by a hiss and crackle. '*Stand by, stand by. Contact about to surface.*'

Hudd's spirits sank and he turned to Piers in search of consolation, but the eyes behind the glasses were fixed and concentrated, showing no emotion. A cold fish and no mistake.

Off the starboard bow, where the Sea Kings circled like vultures in the night sky, the sea began to ferment and bubble. Suddenly the frothing surface was illuminated by two fierce blades of light from the Nitesun lamps.

On the carrier's bridge, each VIP leaned forward, hoping for a clearer view and their first sight of the mysterious craft. Hudd tried to focus the binoculars he'd been issued with.

'Good God,' Aspen murmured. The slippery grey-blue hull was breaking through the cauldron of disturbed water.

'Holy Cow!' gasped Katz.

'What the hell?' Hudd began.

'*Negative, negative,*' crackled the nearest pilot. '*False contact. Repeat false contact. Anyone fancy a fish supper?*'

'A fucking sperm whale,' Vice Admiral Harding growled.

Hudd breathed again, looking at Piers and this time seeing the big wide grin that made him look more like a schoolboy than ever.

'Sir, sir!' It was one of the duty watch officers who constantly scanned from the carrier with night-vision aids. 'Unidentified contact bearing one-eight-one. Repeat one-eight-one.'

'What?' Hudd was totally bewildered.

'Aft,' Piers translated. 'Behind us.'

Outside the cordon, Hudd told himself, as Harding led the group across the bridge for a better view over the stern end.

Scarcely a half-mile off, a white froth was forming on the blue-black surface of the ocean swells. Piers helped his minister focus the binoculars.

It was bizarre, like something out of science fiction. The strangely globular monster rose from the deep, seawater spilling from her sides.

'USS *Manta*,' Aspen murmured in awe.

Then, barely without hesitation, it began gliding into the night. A fine wall of spray burst from the water jets around the hull's winged edge. They created an envelope of wet mist that broke up the craft's shape and merged it into the surrounding sea. Even as Hudd watched, it melted away before his eyes like an illusionist's trick.

'Cocky bastards,' the admiral growled, but there was no mistaking the admiration in his voice.

Hal Katz grunted. 'They've no grounds for being cocky. They failed to reach the . . .'

The end of his sentence was drowned out in the noise of the explosion relayed from the island over the loudspeaker. Everyone turned as the TV monitor pulsed momentarily with white light. As the picture settled and the smoke cleared, they could all see the collapsed wreckage of the dummy mast and bewildered US Marines running in all directions.

'They can't have done,' murmured the officer charged with watching the monitor. 'I didn't see a thing.'

'We'll rerun the tapes later,' Harding said dismissively. 'See if we can spot when they planted the delayed charge.'

But Jim Hudd was no longer listening. They'd done it and that was all that mattered. A British concept backed with Yank know-how had managed to defeat the technology of the world's finest anti-submarine force. Then put a joint assault group of American SEALs and British Special Boat Service troops ashore, succeeding in planting the explosives even while being watched by CCTV cameras.

And they said it would never work. Well, it had. And now Jim Hudd, ex-Nottingham miner and one-time CND protester, was going to claim his place in history – ironically, by freeing a fifth of humanity still yoked and shackled by the political philosophy he himself had once espoused.

Out there, silent beyond the horizon, the Chinese frigate *Luhu* rose and fell gently between the long Pacific swells.

One

John Dancer was not aware of her watching him from the park pathway. Or the nine-year old boy by her side, who was pointing at the *t'ai chi* group exercising with strangely elegant and restrained movements beneath the willows in the cool, early morning air.

They were too far away for the American to hear the boy remark to his mother, in giggling Mandarin. 'See, I tell you. A big nose in the park, doing *t'ai chi* with Chinese people! How funny he looks!'

'Don't point,' his mother chided. 'And so what? It is good that he takes exercise. You could do with taking more yourself. Come on, young man, you'll be late for school.'

She did not tell her son that she recognised the American. Nor that she thought he looked far from funny. He was tall and athletic in the silk jogging pants and sweat-stained T-shirt. She had seen him several times when he had visited the office where she worked and she had thought then how distinguished he looked. The way he walked with such a lazy grace – and now she realised why. He had the natural poise and movement of the seasoned *t'ai chi* practitioners. And of course she had noticed his fair hair, a pale coppery gold which was muted by the grey of early middle age. What Chinese woman living in a world where everyone had crow-black hair would not be fascinated by such a feature? Just like the eyes, not brown but a piercing cobalt blue.

Oh, yes, she had noticed him. And remembered the time she had shyly turned away when their eyes had met and he had given her a warm and ready smile.

But he would not remember her, she realised, as they walked away across the park towards the frenetic bustle of the Beijing streets. She was only one amongst so many.

As she and her son disappeared from view, the martial arts instructor ended the session and the class dispersed. Dancer waved farewell to the fellow pupils who had become his friends over the years. Mr Xuan the grocer, Mr Ren the butcher, 'Shanghai Joe' the market trader and Mr Liu the new-wave entrepreneur whose pager would always bleep during the *t'ai chi* class and drive the instructor mad.

As Dancer sauntered towards the park entrance, Mr Ren scurried after him and proffered a plastic carrier bag. Dancer peered inside. Four chicken breasts. Just a few *yuan*, said the butcher with a sly smile. The Chinese had a peculiar disregard for white poultry meat, much preferring to gnaw and suck on such delicacies as the feet. Now Mr Ren had discovered a way of making a little extra money out of leftovers that would otherwise have been consigned to a humble family stir-fry. The capitalist enterprise economy had even reached Mr Ren's family butchery in an Xidan backstreet.

Dancer wasn't complaining; in a city where even Kentucky Fried Chicken served only battered feet, locating plump breasts was like discovering the Holy Grail.

'I have plenty more,' Mr Ren said, pocketing the money. 'Corn-fed like Mother makes. Tell your friends, Mr Dancing, please.' As he smiled, Dancer could almost see the *yuan* signs clocking up behind the man's eyes.

'I'll do that. Thank you.'

He continued on his way, tugging a pack of Camel from his pants pocket and lighting one as he walked. It was eight o'clock now and already the heat and humidity were rising. Summer in Beijing was hell on earth. A layer of light cloud lay over the city like the lid on a pressure cooker, slowly broiling its citizens until they became limp and listless before the day had barely begun.

His Seagull bicycle was in the rack by the park entrance. After stuffing the packet of prized chicken breasts into the saddlebag, Dancer mounted and wobbled his way into the

17

never-ending stream of fellow cyclists. He had long ago discovered that this was the only sane way to move around the capital, avoiding the heaving mass of pedestrians on the pavements, the sardine-tin buses, or even the claustrophobic carriages of the Underground Dragon subway. Freedom, exercise and fresh air. Well, air anyway, considering the choking fumes from the battered and neglected vehicles in the grid-locked streets. That was another reason to avoid taxis. Why pay good money to sit in a decrepit, stifling cab just for the dubious pleasure of going nowhere fast? And certainly nowhere you wanted to go. Because, as Dancer had learned the hard way, Beijing taxi drivers knew as much about the streets of London or Washington as they did about their own city. In short, nothing.

He picked up a welcome cooling breeze as he weaved his way through the lines of jammed traffic, progressing speedily towards the Hua Thai Apartment Hotel in the south-east. The place was unusual in that it actually provided proper apartments with a kitchen and bathroom, unlike most of the others. For a long stay it at least allowed you to have a place that almost felt like home. The private market for accommodation was hopeless for non-nationals. Even if you could find a decent flat not snapped up by the Chinese Communist Government cadres, getting telephones installed, a plumber to call, or even the garbage collected, was a bureaucratic nightmare. Even the overseas Chinese gave up, threw money at the problem and made their long-term homes at the Beijing, the Chinese World or the Friendship hotels and apartments. At least at the Hua Thai 'foreign devil' journalists, businessmen, diplomats and Third World graduate students could form an impromptu club and commiserate with each other about life in China.

But for Dancer that morning the reliable flow of hot water was good enough reason for his choice, as he showered, shaved and changed into a denim cotton shirt, chino suit and loafers. He took a moment at the mirror to straighten his tie with its tiny winged motifs of Stonedancer Couriers.

It had been his partner's idea. Abe Stone believed in marketing from the bottom up. If Dancer recalled correctly, it had been the man's very first decision. Silk ties in every conceivable colour, made up in Shanghai and given as gifts only to their very top Chinese Communist – or Chicom, as Stone always liked to abbreviate things – customers and government ministers. He said he'd got the idea from Onassis who'd marketed his hand-made cigarettes in the beginning by *not* selling, but only giving them as gifts to the opera-house élite in Buenos Aires back in the 1930s, until everyone in chic society was begging for them.

Well, no one was actually begging for the ties, but they proved popular because their distribution was carefully restricted. That might not have been the case if Dancer hadn't insisted on a *discreet* motif and dropping the 'You Call, We Haul' slogan Stone had wanted to include.

He smiled to himself in the mantelshelf mirror as he donned his broad-brimmed fedora and glanced at the silver-framed portrait on the shelf.

Debs smiled back at him like she always did, like she always had. That zany Californian smile and laughing eyes. The freckles and wild ginger hair. A face that would never grow old. That would be frozen like that for all time. Just like the ache that still lurked somewhere deep inside his being.

'I think I've been here too long, Debs,' he murmured. 'What do you think?'

'I think if you don't stop talking to photographs you're going to be late,' he could hear her say. 'And Abe's going to be climbing up the wall.'

She could always make him smile, even now. 'It doesn't take much.'

And as he remounted the Seagull and began pedalling

towards the Wangfujing district, he mused that at least today Abe Stone would have every reason to rant and rave. With the huge Pacific Rim Trade Development Conference down in Macao in just two days' time, it would be the courier service's busiest time since the Hong Kong handover. It was billed as the biggest international show on earth, destined to launch the future of the Far East into the new millennium. Everyone would be in town. Senior sales teams from all the main Western and overseas Chinese conglomerates in telecommunications, computers, transport, arms and international retail. Entire diplomatic communities and political leaders from around the world. If you weren't there, then you weren't anywhere.

But all those from Beijing who intended to be there seemed to be sending their documents and sales material through Stonedancer Couriers rather than risk the post. Or else flying them with Dancer's relatively new ExecFlight service to avoid the unspeakable horrors of Chinese airlines.

Even as he dismounted in the teeming clamour of the hot and dusty street, he could hear Stone's gravelly foghorn voice from the open window of their offices on the first floor. Leaving his trusty Seagull in the corridor, Dancer took the stairs two at a time.

'In the name of dear Confucius, Mr Pu,' the operations manager was saying as Dancer opened the glass-fronted door, 'there are tens of thousands of troops in Xinjiang province. There is no *earthly* reason why your cousin should be amongst the casualties!'

The packed office of Chinese and American clerks and executives had momentarily become a frozen tableau in the dusty yellow bars of light that poured through the window shutters. Each was motionless at his or her desk, bemused by the vision of Abe Stone showing sympathy and compassion. It was something of a novelty, as was the compelling silence. It was a rare moment in the hectic office when no one happened to be speaking or tapping a keyboard, the telex had stopped chattering and even a telephone didn't ring. People say it's the moment when the angel of death is flying overhead.

It was that strange second's silence that made Dancer aware of the tinny background babble of the newscaster issuing from the little transistor radio on the top of Mr Pu's in-tray.

Abe Stone's ample backside, with billowing trousers suspended from bright red braces, had a precarious half-perch on the edge of the man's desk. His huge, hair-matted arms were folded across his chest. The body language was clearly supposed to signal understanding to his clerk, but Dancer suspected it was Stone's attempt to restrain himself from the temptation to strangulate.

The posture certainly did nothing to mollify Mr Pu any more than the rictal smile on the American's fleshy face, as he perspired in his effort at self-control. Nothing was going to pacify the underfed-looking clerk who was lost in a starched but frayed white shirt that was two sizes too large for him. His lank hair flapped as he shook his head, rolled his eyes and wailed.

'It is no good, Mr Abe. I know it is my cousin. I know! *Joss* is no good for my family this year. It is a bad time.'

Stone's patience was cracking. 'Never mind about your *yin* and *yang*, Mr Pu. If you don't get back to work pronto, your personal luck is going to run out along with your job!' He snapped off the thin sound of the radio and looked at the rows of faces gazing in his direction. 'And what are you lot gawping at! We've got a business to run. No business and we're *all* out of a job!'

A telephone trilled suddenly and the spell was broken. A voice answered the call and the shirt-sleeved clerks and executives reluctantly began to resume their duties.

'What's the problem, Abe?' Dancer asked.

Stone turned, noticing his partner for the first time. 'Oh, mornin', John. Oh, it's nothing, just a news bulletin. Been more trouble with the Muslims in Xinjiang province. An attack by separatists. Some Chinese troops were killed.'

Mr Pu still hadn't put pen to paper; he looked miserable. 'My cousin is a soldier there.'

Dancer knew all about the desolate north-eastern province of Xinjiang. It was China's trash bin. An empty dustbowl of a place over three times the size of France, where the indigenous Uighur inhabitants have shared a mutual hatred of their Chinese 'guardians' on and off for over two thousand years. It was the province where the Chinese tested their nuclear weapons, where they built their *laogai* gulags and to which the intellectual classes were banished during the upheaval of the catastrophic Cultural Revolution. The Beijing Government might well have abandoned it centuries before had it not been for its strategic position as a 'buffer zone' and its vast reserves of oil.

It was quite clear to Dancer that the disconsolate clerk would not have his mind on the job until he'd established that his cousin was still alive and well. 'Take the rest of the day off, Mr Pu. Speak with the People's Liberation Army and see if you can't telephone your cousin's barracks. Put your mind at rest. I would like you back here tomorrow. You really are an important little screw.'

Mr Pu liked that. Liked being allowed home, and appreciated the jokey compliment that likened him to Lei Fang, the legendary worker of Maoist propaganda. Fang's reputed saying, 'A man's usefulness to the Revolution is like a small screw in a machine. Though small its use is beyond measure – I want to be a screw', was as widely quoted as it was privately despised and ridiculed.

'Oh, thank you, Mr John,' the clerk gabbled, a wide grin plastered to his face as he gathered up his jacket from the chairback and stuffed the offending radio into his ancient battered briefcase along with his lunchbox filled with cold steamed pork dumplings.

As he scurried for the door, Stone led the way back to his office. 'Not sure that was setting a good example, John. You're going soft in your old age.'

'Mr Pu would have been a liability, Abe. His mind wasn't on the job. And I don't want any of our precious little screws fouling up on work for the conference.'

Stone flopped into the swivel chair behind a massive desk choked with dispatch notes, delivery and consignment documents. All around, boxes with the distinctive blue-wings insignia of Stonedancer Couriers were stacked to form a second wall to the office.

'You're ruining my reputation as a tyrant, John, but – yeah – I guess you're right. Pu's elevator wasn't stopping at every floor.'

'What sort of attack was it in Xinjiang?'

Stone shrugged. 'The bulletin said something about an ambush. A PLA convoy.'

'It must have been serious,' Dancer said thoughtfully. 'If Beijing thought they could have kept it quiet, it wouldn't have been mentioned.'

The manager fished a half-smoked stogie from his desk drawer and poured a can of Coke as he lit it with his free hand. 'Things must be heating up there, what with those two bombings last month.' But despite his words it was clear that Stone regarded Xinjiang as did most Chinese, as somewhere on the far side of the moon, and just about as relevant.

John Dancer knew differently, but forced his mind back to more mundane matters.

'Any problems with the conference I should know about? Anything I can help with?'

One of Stone's rare thin smiles glinted through the gathering clouds of smoke, momentarily twitching his heavy cheeks and scowling eyebrows. His bleak humour was to be detected more subtly in the amusement behind his pale grey eyes.

'It's the usual Chinese fire drill.' He pulled on one of the lobes of the jug ears that protruded from the mass of curls that surrounded his thinning crown. 'But we're keeping on top.'

23

They'd started as partners and become firm friends. Dancer would have been surprised had Stone given any other answer. There had never been any doubt about the man's ability since Dancer had picked him up from skid row in the Laotian capital of Vientiane six years before. With a broken marriage and shattered career behind him, Stone, the former high-flying air freight management expert from Kansas, had sought oblivion in a country that time had forgotten.

But if time had forgotten, Abe had not. Had not forgotten the magical time spent there in his youth on a posting with the CIA's covert Air America operations. And he had never forgiven his fellow countrymen for later bombing the shit out of the country, dumping more ordnance on its eastern provinces than was dropped in the entire Second World War in a futile and pointless attempt to sever the Ho Chi Minh trail where it ran across the border.

Stone remembered other things. The calming tranquillity of the air, the floating scents of frangipani and opium pipes, the beguiling and friendly people, the teak houses and crumbling French villas that overlooked the lazy Mekong river. And, of course, Suzy, star of the famous White Rose, who stole young Americans' hearts with her cabaret skill of smoking a cigarette between her legs.

That was where he'd met his first love, in one of the little cubicle rooms above the bar. Little Lindy-lou, a happy, almond-eyed teenage sprite who would laugh and giggle and teasingly strip for a dollar and make unforgettable love for just a couple more. She had stolen his heart. Within a week they were no longer whore and punter, but tentative lovers. One night she took him home to a clean but dingy backstreet flat. When he awoke he was lying naked and alone on the sheets. His clothes had gone and with them his wallet.

In an instant, Abe's light heart was filled with darkness and his rage boiled over. The cheap trickster, how could she? After all they'd done and said, after all the murmured words of how the rest of their lives would be spent together. He smashed what little furniture there was in the room, ripped the sheet from the bed and tore the tatty curtains from the rails.

Only then did he hear the light-toed movement behind him and turn to see the expression of bewilderment on her face. In her hands she held out his clothes, all freshly laundered, ironed and neatly folded. And, balanced on the top, his wallet.

It was a miracle the relationship had survived that, but it had. For nearly a year, until he was posted elsewhere. He wrote once or twice, but she never wrote back. Or, if she did, her letters never reached him.

His career with Air America was followed by a career in commercial air freight management, working in developing countries where his experience counted most. Africa, South America and the Far East. He married a Kansas girl whom he'd known since childhood. She was beautiful and adored him, but she was a home-bird, like a fine wine that didn't travel well. Eventually the long separations took their toll and Abe's wife found someone else. He sought comfort in the bottle and lost interest and concentration in his work. Having taken his eye off the ball, he allowed a bad deal to go through that almost bankrupted his company. When he was fired, it made trade press headlines. No one would touch him.

No one, that is, except John Dancer. He had been in China since 1984, when the Chinese Communist Government had begun quietly to drop its Maoist excesses and encourage an enterprise economy. Seven years on, Dancer Courier Services was well established, but now there were new opportunities and objectives. Dancer needed someone reliable to take over existing operations while he built up a new venture, ExecFlight, VIP passenger services for top businessmen and Chinese government officials.

He was given Abe Stone's name.

He found him back in Laos, living in the mist in a riverside pontoon house at Luang Prabang. Stone never had been able to find the whereabouts of his teenage passion; he guessed Lindy-lou had made the journey to Bangkok to seek her fortune in the fleshpots there. If anyone knew for certain, they weren't saying.

Instead, he'd settled with a delightful creature with Bambi eyes who was young enough to be Lindy-lou's daughter. She was a 'second-hand girlfriend', considered sullied because her first spotty adolescent admirer had not been persuaded to marry her. Abe had no such qualms about the 'second-hand' market. He had drowned out his self-pity in an orgy of self-indulgence.

She and the timeless Mekong had done their healing. Stone was off the booze, well, virtually, and content. But getting bored with fishing. The timing of Dancer's offer of a junior partnership could not have been more perfect. The downside was that history was to repeat itself. His girlfriend would not even consider moving with him to China, a country whose name she barely recognised; she moved back in with her family. Abe still sent regular small cheque payments which were cashed. But like Lindy-lou before her, Bambi was not one for writing letters.

Once in Beijing, Stone had gone to work with the energy and fervour of a television evangelist, kicking Dancer's somewhat chaotic operation into shape. There were hirings and firings, a move of office, new computer systems and a marketing campaign to drum up new business. Time and again he had proved his worth, just as Dancer's confidential adviser had said he would.

So Dancer was not in the least surprised that the great Pacific Rim Trade Development Conference workload had not even caused a blip on his partner's erratic stress chart. Bluff and bluster were his stock-in-trade, never panic.

'What about you, John?' Stone asked. 'You still going?'

Dancer smiled lightly. 'You bet. Got to fly our flag. I thought I'd join our midday ExecFlight tomorrow.'

'Who's on it?' He winked. 'Knowing you, some big bananas.'

'A couple of Chicom officials I've wanted to get the chance to talk to for some time.'

Stone understood. Relaxing in the flying hospitality suite, sinking into luxurious leather chairs and being served such delicacies as snake and crispy stir-fried scorpion with rare Napoleon Augier cognac by pretty and gregarious hostesses, put the sternest Communist cadres in the mood to talk and do business.

'And Wang,' Dancer added.

His partner grunted. Wang was a cross they had to bear. As assistant deputy director of the Civil Aviation Administration of China, Wang Fu's influence had to be bought in order to get ExecFlight off the ground and accepted as an official wing of the state-owned China Southern Star Lines, which was quoted on the New York Stock Exchange.

In order to meet the requirements of Chinese law, Wang arranged with Dancer for his brother to join the board of the official joint venture. This was also necessary as non-Chinese were not allowed to run aircraft or helicopters.

There was, however, another motive for this. While Wang made it his business to keep Chinese bureaucracy at arm's length from the Stonedancer operations, he could rely on his brother to keep an eye on things and ensure that he received a fair cut of the profits. *Hou-men* or 'backdoor business' was what oiled the wheels of the new entrepreneurial China and when it came to oil, Wang was never happier than when up to his neck in the stuff.

Mercifully, Xin-Bin was the complete antithesis of his older brother. He was quiet, almost bashful, and thoughtful. A former business management graduate from Nanjing University, he had even studied at Harvard for a year where he'd perfected his English with a decidedly American accent.

Even this didn't endear him to Abe Stone, who was deeply suspicious, probably because in his own mind he couldn't separate Xin-Bin from his brother. Moreover, he would blink, unmoved by Stone's ravings, so that the American manager could never quite fathom him. Because Xin-Bin was a very unusual character in real life – a genuinely inscrutable Chinaman. In his frustration, Stone's suspicions deepened. And it made no difference that the young man dedicated long hours to ExecFlight business which left little time for the wife and child to whom he was clearly devoted. It even meant doing something almost unknown in Beijing – forgoing lunch. It confirmed to Stone that there was something deeply wrong; it was just that he wasn't quite sure what.

'Why's Wang going to Macao?' he asked.

'Same reason he goes anywhere,' Dancer replied with a smile. 'It's a free perk and he wants to party.'

'And what about ExecFlight? You want me to go over and keep an eye on things while you're off partying with Wang?'

Dancer had been expecting that. It was a regular routine whenever he went away. 'No need, Abe. Xin-Bin is quite capable of running things.'

Stone's lips formed a disgruntled straight line. 'Sure he is, John. It's just that two heads and all that.' There was an accusing glint in his eyes. 'We should never have set up the ExecFlight office on the other side of town.'

That old chestnut. 'It made sense. It was suitable and the rent was a giveaway,' Dancer reminded.

'Wang family property.'

'So what?'

'It makes it difficult for me to drop over, keep them on their toes, that's what!'

Dancer didn't tell him that had been one of the main attractions. The less Abe Stone knew about ExecFlight the better. For his own good. Keep everything separate, that was the philosophy.

'We'll discuss it at our next board meeting. I've got to get over there now.'

Stone gave him a meaningful stare. 'See what I mean?'

But Dancer just laughed as he turned to leave the office for another cycle ride. 'The exercise does me good, Abe. Keeps me young. You should try it some time.'

His partner's expletive reply was cut off as the door swung shut.

'The Stonedancer courier is here,' announced the embassy clerk, a cool too-tall blonde called Suzy whose upright posture and accent marked her out as the daughter of a British Army officer.

'Shit!' Iona Moncrieff hissed, glaring up from the computer screen, cigarette clamped between her teeth, lank hair falling over her face. 'He's early.'

Suzy was unfazed. 'He's efficient.'

'Balls,' snapped Iona. 'On time is efficient. Early is a pain in the arse. No point being an army brat if your dad didn't teach you anything.'

'Late is a capital offence,' the girl replied with a lofty smile. 'He taught me that.'

'Okay, smarty pants, the printer's packed up. I'm on the last document and it's printing blind.' She smiled sweetly, ribbons of smoke drifting out between her teeth. 'Help me.'

'You're a Luddite, boss.'

'Okay, so you know big words. Help me.'

'You're out of ink. You need a new cartridge.' Suzy sighed at the sight of the second secretary trying to look angry and appealing at the same time. It didn't fit well with the lived-in features and amused, seen-it-all-before eyes. 'Okay, boss, I'll do it.'

'You're an angel.'

'I thought I was an army brat.'

Now that Suzy was deftly fitting the new cartridge, Iona felt safe to add: 'Yeah, that too.'

The scurrying of officials between departments, the hectic comings and goings and frantic preparation of documents was the nearest the British Embassy ever got to bedlam. And coping with computers was the only thing that brought Iona Moncrieff remotely close to breaking sweat. She'd been in the game a long time. Too long, she sometimes thought.

Diplomats were used to living at a measured pace, allowing only modest variations between embassies according to national culture and tradition. Certainly similar scenes of last-minute panics and glitches would be repeated, she knew, at all the other embassies in the two compounds of Jianguomenwai and Sanlitun. It was a legacy of Chinese xenophobia that all 'foreign devil' diplomats were kept together in the same place where they could be kept an eye on.

The last pages stuttered out of the printer. 'By the way,' Suzy said, 'your boyfriend's waiting in reception.'

Iona scowled. 'By that, I suppose you mean Bill. Why didn't you tell me?'

'I'm improving your chances.'

'What do you mean?'

'He fancies you rotten.'

Iona blinked for a second, pursing her lips. 'Balderdash.'

'Oh, yes, he does.' Suzy cocked her head to one side. 'That's why you've got to play hard to get. Keep him waiting.'

Her boss stubbed out her cigarette butt in the ashtray and straightened her jacket. 'That's your expert advice, is it? And you barely out of nappies.'

'Nearly thirty years out of them, boss,' came the typically cool reply. 'And you must be fifty. Time you landed yourself a bloke.'

'Not interested,' Iona said, quickly dabbing lipstick at her reflection in the mirror. 'I've got my cats and my origami. What do I want with men?' She didn't wait for a response. 'Now, Suzy, be an angel and get that document down to the courier while I see Bill.'

Suzy arched one finely plucked eyebrow. 'Only if you promise to vamp it up. Get his pulses racing.'

The diplomat paused by the door and peered back alluringly over her shoulder while fluttering her eyelids. 'Like this?'

'On second thoughts. . .'

Bill Dawson had not come far. The United States Embassy was sited conveniently on the next block of the compound. Therefore he was a frequent visitor. He was waiting in the lobby amid the piles of diplomats' luggage awaiting transportation to the airport on route to the Macao conference.

'Your Majesty,' the American greeted as Iona Moncrieff negotiated the bullet-proof glass of the security door. As always dressed immaculately – today in a pale grey mohair suit artfully cut to trim his thickening waist – Dawson took her hand and pressed it to his lips. '*Enchanté*, my dear Iona.'

She was aware of the mischievous glint in his flinty eyes as they smiled up at her from over her knuckles. 'My assistant says you are madly in love with me,' she challenged, straight-faced.

Dawson gently released her hand. 'Out of the mouths of babes. . .'

'I'll have none of it, do you hear.' She wore her best aloof expression, averting her head. 'I'm saving myself.'

The American couldn't suppress his grin. 'Alas, so I've noticed, Your Majesty.'

Several years older than Iona, he had known her for more than twenty years since his first posting to Beijing after the Viet Nam War where he'd served on detachment to the CIA. They'd met at an embassy party and it had not been a promising start. She had made some choice remark about the Americans' defeat in Viet Nam – in retrospect witty and perceptive – and he had mocked her accent and likened her to Queen Victoria. The 'Your Majesty' tag had stuck. But there was something about their antagonistic quick-fire repartee that signalled something else beneath the surface. They shared the same sense of dry, cynical

31

humour, sparking off each other like flintstones and had flirted outrageously ever since.

Dawson never had quite figured her strange allure. He was fond of saying she was the most beautiful ugly woman he'd ever met. Convent and public school educated, Iona was tall and gangling with a lazy posture which did little for her slim figure and rather shapeless legs. There was a constant look of weariness about her, as there was with her frequent smiles and her clothes. Her straight fair hair always looked as though it had been cut by a trainee in a poodle parlour and that she had forgotten to shampoo it the day before. Her face had had the slightly crumpled, lived-in look ever since he'd first met her.

So, what was it about her that always lifted his spirits if never quite stirring his loins? The smoky voice – hardly surprising given her consumption of tobacco and brandy – could have something to do with it, together with those expressive eyes that always hinted she was seeing the joke when you didn't, and that the joke was probably quite obscene.

Despite two decades of verbal flirtation, there had never been a hint of serious romance between them. How, Dawson asked himself, could there ever be with a woman like Iona Moncrieff? Was it possible to bed a personality rather than a person?

So he had taken the path to penury with three unsatisfactory marriages followed by three financially crippling divorces. Meanwhile, Her Majesty had settled contentedly into spinsterhood with her cat, her origami and her crochetwork. Or so she claimed.

'Come in,' she invited. 'Have some Earl Grey.'

Dawson shook his head. 'Thanks, but I'm flying down to Macao this evening. Just checking if you're still going?'

'Most definitely. I'm travelling down tomorrow.'

'Good. I want to have a chat.' He jerked his thumb back towards the main door. Iona looked out into the street and saw the young Chinese man in the polyester suit and

32

shades leaning against the lamppost, pretending to read a newspaper. 'It'll be good to get away from the Bureau kids for a few days. That jerk just followed me from the embassy. I wouldn't mind, but they really *believe* we can't spot them.'

Iona smiled in sympathy. The omnipresence of the Public Security Bureau could be a little claustrophobic at times. Like their counterparts in the former Soviet Union's KGB, its members weren't too clever at concealment. They were too used to making their presence obvious to intimidate their own people. But she and Dawson both knew that some more secretive elements within the Chinese security apparatus and the Ministry of State Security could be a lot more invisible and efficient than the man outside in his polyester suit.

'Which hotel are you staying at?' she asked.

He told her. 'Perhaps we could meet up tomorrow evening, around eight. Our President should be arriving then – an ideal time to slip away.'

'Remember the Silver Dragon? I'll meet you there. I understand Piers Lansdowne will be in town.'

Dawson's bushy eyebrows rose in unison. Piers Lansdowne. British Secret Intelligence Service. From 'Riverside', London. Iona's young chief officer. 'I hope he's got something on developments.'

'So do I, Bill. The suspense is killing me.'

He nodded. 'You heard the news?'

'Xinjiang? Yes.'

'We're doing our bit.'

'And we're doing ours.'

'Time I met Piers again.'

She gave her best coquettish look. 'A *ménage à trois*?' she asked provocatively. 'I'll see what I can do.'

A smile hovered on his lips. 'Macao's a hotbed of hormones. So you be careful.'

Iona feigned mock horror. 'I'm too old for that sort of thing. And so are you.'

He regarded her for a moment, wondering. Then his laugh cut in. 'Nonsense. Macao's just the place for a tired old divorcee.'

The evening rush hour was going full tilt as John Dancer cycled alongside Xin-Bin. Traffic was log-jammed to a cacophony of motor horns and an accompaniment of bicycle bells, the baked air laden with toxic fumes.

Despite the thousands of cyclists crisscrossing the city, he had little difficulty in picking out the Bureau tail. The man was wearing an unsuitably heavy quilted jacket as he pedalled his yellow Flying Pigeon, at the same time gabbling into a mobile phone.

What would Hollywood make of the Chinese spying game, Dancer wondered? A snail-pace bicycle chase through Hongqiao Market and a swordfight with chop-sticks hardly had the visual impact of high-speed cars, shoot-outs and explosions.

He wondered if Xin-Bin had spotted their shadow; probably, but he didn't ask. There was no point. Just lately there always seemed to be an obvious plain-clothes Bureau man about, and no doubt there were others who weren't as obvious. The only question was why? He just hoped the answer wasn't as obvious too. What he really suspected was a gradual, inch-by-inch shift in power behind the scenes in the Politburo. That was the way of things in China. It was the smallest of changes that indicated the really big ones. And since the British had handed back Hong Kong, there had been a lot of small changes.

They reached the Holiday Inn Lido, padlocked their bikes and made their way to the Pig and Whistle bar on the ground floor. It was the nearest thing in Beijing to an English pub and was popular with many European expatriates. Despite the exorbitant prices and the long ride to get there, it remained one of Dancer's favourite watering holes. At least they appeared to have lost their shadow on the journey.

Abe Stone was already in the mock-Tudor bar, hunched on a stool and watching CNN news on the television, mounted high on the far corner wall. He glanced round as they approached. 'Hi, John, usual?' Then to Xin-Bin: 'And you?'

The Chinaman gave a smile that said Stone always made him feel nervous. '*Jianlibao*, thank you.'

No emotion showed on Stone's face. 'You can manage something a little stronger, can't you? Day's over. Put hairs on your chest.'

Another smile said that he really wanted a soft drink, but he was prepared to relent to please the senior partner. 'I suppose sun is over the yardarm, Mr Abe. A ginny T, thank you.'

Stone waved a fifty *yuan* note at the sour-faced barmaid. 'A glass of *tsingtao* and a gin and tonic.'

'How was the day?' Dancer asked casually, lighting a Camel and taking his beer from the counter.

'We coped.' Stone added pointedly, 'despite being short-handed. Everything got off to Macao, although the British Embassy caused a panic when their pack wasn't ready for the courier.'

'Iona Moncrieff?' Dancer guessed.

Stone nodded his head. 'My grief, more like. She does that to me damn near every time.'

'Enjoys sailing close to the wind, that one,' Dancer agreed. 'Quite a character.'

'Customers, I like. Characters, I can do without.'

A group of new-wave Chinese businessmen had entered wearing flash suits and weighed down with expensive attaché cases and mobile phones. They were noisily ordering drinks at the other end of the bar. A couple of Mongolian hookers in red plastic skirts observed them with deep interest from their seats in the partitioned 'snug'.

Suddenly the businessmen broke into excited chatter, arguing with each other as they watched the CNN newscaster on the corner television.

35

'. . . *from Xingjiang province of China. Unconfirmed reports suggest upward of one hundred-twenty troops of the People's Liberation Army may have been killed or injured in the convoy ambush. Uighur secessionists calling themselves the Flames of Aktu are being blamed for the attack.*'

'Holy Cow,' Stone murmured. 'Maybe Mr Pu had good reason to be worried about his cousin after all.'

Another man had joined the group of Chinese business-men watching the television. He was short with a pock-marked face which was half-hidden by dark glasses. Angrily he began berating them and yelled at the barmaid to switch off the set.

'It is a disgrace to show that Imperialist American propaganda!' he shouted. 'You are unpatriotic and a snake spirit! You should be ashamed of yourself!'

The barmaid was unmoved; no one was going to tell her what television station she showed; she knew what her 'foreign devil' customers wanted to watch. Then the newcomer started waving a plastic wallet containing some sort of ID card. This time the barmaid's face paled visibly, a distinctly worried look in her eyes. She reached for the remote control, the picture flickered for an instant and CNN was replaced by a Chinese opera.

Xin-Bin leaned towards Dancer. 'He is PSB. Security Bureau. It is he who followed us here.'

It was only then that Dancer recognised the dark blue quilted jacket that the man on the yellow Flying Pigeon had been wearing.

'You were followed?' Stone asked. 'Why on earth should the Bureau want to follow you?'

His friend shrugged. 'No idea, Abe, but it's been happening quite a bit lately.'

'You never mentioned it.'

'Not relevant. Has anyone been tailing *you*?'

'I haven't looked.' Stone's eyes narrowed. 'What's going on at ExecFlight, John? Is that why the Bureau's taking an interest?'

Dancer's laugh was light. 'Nothing's *going* on, Abe. But you're right, that's probably the reason they're watching. We're flying a lot of Chicom cadre people nowadays and a few PLA generals are regulars. Someone at the Bureau's decided to do some positive vetting.'

That seemed a fair assumption to Stone. 'Then there's good reason for me to base myself at the ExecFlight office while you're away.'

Xin-Bin looked offended. 'There's no need, Mr Abe. I can handle things. There's no problem.'

'He's right,' Dancer agreed. 'I've already told you that.'

It was Stone's turn to look affronted. 'For God's sake, John, we don't have secrets from each other. We're supposed to be a partnership.' He spared Xin-Bin a withering sideways glance. 'All three of us. But if the Bureau pays a visit, they'll ride rough-shod over any Chinese. They just won't listen. But they *will* if a foreigner's there.'

'The Bureau will not come,' Xin-Bin insisted. 'My brother always makes sure of that.'

Mentioning Wang to Abe Stone was like a red flag to a bull. 'Since when can your brother control the Bureau? He's Civil Aviation Administration. All he can do is protect us from his own bureau-crats – when it suits him.'

Dancer tried to defuse the argument. 'Let's not blow this out of proportion. So the Bureau's given us a couple of tails. Fine, it's their job and we've nothing to hide.' He turned to Xin-Bin. 'If you have any trouble while I'm away, you get straight on the phone to Abe. Agreed?'

But before the man could reply, another voice interrupted. 'Hi, you guys, is this a private row or can anyone join in?'

It was Bill Dawson from the US Embassy.

Dancer raised his hand in greeting. 'Hi, Bill, take a pew. We were just talking business.'

'Thought it was serious,' Dawson said jokingly. 'You sounded like a couple of Greeks discussing the weather.'

'Have a beer.'

The newcomer sat on the edge of a spare barstool and gave an acknowledging nod to Abe Stone, who returned the gesture with obvious reluctance. 'No thanks, John, I've gotta scoot to get down to Macao.'

'You flying with us?'

'I can't afford your fancy prices. I'll leave the Chicom cadres to do that.' An earnest note crept into his voice. 'Just wanted to check you're still going?'

Dancer nodded. 'Tomorrow.'

'Then let's make sure we meet up. Might have some business to steer your way. I'll be at the Lisboa Hotel.' He was already on his feet.

'Okay, Bill, I'll make sure I see you.'

Dawson gave a cheery 'Ciao' and was on his way.

Stone scowled after him. 'I don't trust that guy, John. Watch yourself with him.'

'He's our commercial attaché, Abe.'

His partner grunted. 'He's our resident spook, John, and you know it. *Everyone* knows it.'

Dancer drained his beer. 'Then I'll wear rubber gloves next time we shake hands.' He rose to his feet. 'Now, I've got packing to do. I'll grab a burger on the way home. Either of you want to join me?'

Of course, he knew Xin-Bin wouldn't; as always he'd be anxious to get back to his wife and young child.

'You hate burgers,' Stone said accusingly.

'I'm learning to be a real American. Now, you coming?'

Stone shook his head. 'Ding's doing an anniversary steak supper. Celebrating three years together.'

Ding was the successor to Lindy-lou and Bambi-eyes; whilst she shared the diminutive stature of the Laotian girls, she was, in fact, an overseas Chinese from Singapore and was a petulant dragon. Dancer would joke with Xin-Bin that he could light a Camel off her breath when she was in one of her regular moods.

Abe Stone was right about one thing, Dancer mused as he cycled on towards the Hard Rock Café on

Dongsanhuan Beilu. He hadn't been a lover of Western food since he'd been behind the lines with the Green Berets during the Viet Nam War. Eating the simple peasant fare with friendly villagers had caught his imagination and re-educated his adolescent taste buds. At least the Hard Rock didn't have queues of Chinese waiting to have their photographs taken with a giant plastic Ronald McDonald.

But, of course, that wasn't the reason. It was common-place for both Westerners and Chinese to visit the Hard Rock; it was expected and would not raise suspicions.

Instead of the grinning burger clown, he had to endure the kinetic thud of heavy metal as a tribute to all the Western evils of which Chairman Mao had warned. But everyone was clearly too deafened to hear, he mused, as he watched the brisk trade in Hard Rock T-shirts at the merchandising counter. It occurred to him that the Chinese should be running courses in Basic Capitalism at the Harvard Business School; they really were the lousiest socialists he'd ever come across.

Watched over by a poster of Elvis, he mainlined on cholesterol with a Philly Steak sandwich, heavy on the cheese and piled high with onion rings. After washing it down with an iced bottle of Bud, he made his way to the toilets. He wasn't expecting to see a sign, let alone the small cross in yellow chalk on the wall above one of the urinals.

Yellow meant it was "Hunan". A cross meant there was something at the drop. Usually it would be a scrap of paper containing a line of numbers which, read in a certain order, suggested a date and time to meet. The venue had been decided at their last face-to-face encounter.

Life was a little simpler with "Hunan"; there was no great need for secrecy. It was one of the fallacies that secrecy was the prime requisite of the spying game; openness worked far better. The best spies were hearty, gregarious types with a wide circle of friends and acquaintances. Cover and alibis worked best when they were as close as possible to the truth. And where possible, meetings were best held in public places with obvious good reason.

The obvious good reason with "Hunan" was that he was a fanatical golfer. Dancer had quickly overcome his loathing of the game. He was even getting to like it – something he never admitted to Debs's photograph – and had driven his handicap down to twelve. There had even been another benefit of his new-found recreation; he discovered that it was especially popular with the highest echelons of Beijing's ruling cadres.

The only precaution with "Hunan" was not to play too frequently. He was by nature a subdued, even sullen character on first acquaintance and would not have been the type to strike up a close sporting friendship with a 'foreign devil'. So their games were played at lengthy intervals, often following seemingly chance encounters in mid-week mornings when the links were relatively empty.

In truth, the last thing Dancer needed was a visit to the drop. There was still packing to do and preparations to make for his trip to Macao. He was in half a mind to postpone it until his return. But then the Philly Steak sandwich seemed to have formed a doughy lump in his gut and he decided the exercise would do him good.

It was an ideal location, a park bench in a secluded area of shrubbery. By sitting at one end, Dancer could reach back over a low ornamental fence to the base of the metal lamppost sited just behind it. At its rear, out of view of casual passers-by, was a small junction box.

Dancer had made it himself from a plastic traveller's soap case. He'd carefully drilled and fitted a magnetic plate to the base before spraying it with metallic grey paint to match the lamppost. Then he'd stencilled a small lightning flash – the international warning for live electricity – in red on the lid.

When he reached the bench, he propped his bicycle

against the fence, took a newspaper from his saddlebag and sat down to read for ten minutes. Even a trained observer would have been hard pushed to recognise the moment when he reached back one arm, removed the soap-box lid and extracted the piece of paper. A few minutes later he began his return journey.

It wasn't until he reached his apartment that he examined the note from "Hunan". To his surprise, it wasn't the encoded numerals for a suggested rendezvous. It was a folded A4 sheet containing lines and lines of carefully hand-written numbers in groups of five digits.

Dancer frowned. "Hunan" had used his one-off cipher pad for only the second time in their relationship. This was going to take some time. The first line of "Hunan's" message told him which pad had been used, which pages and which lines. He poured three fingers of bourbon into a tumbler and sat at his desk, retrieving a two hundred carton of Camel from an unlocked drawer. In the pool of light cast by a brass lamp, he opened one of the packs and pulled out the cigarette from the right side of the back row. Close examination would have shown that it was not regular cigarette paper but matt laminated for extra strength. Using a pair of tweezers he extracted the tightly rolled plug of scrolled paper that formed the first inch of the cigarette.

The scroll was printed by a form of photographic reduction on inflammable cellulose nitrate material that was as thin as rice paper. Half-way through the scroll the colour of the thousands of numerical groups changed from black to blue, indicating the enciphering and deciphering sections. It was going to be a long and tedious job with a magnifying glass.

He wasn't at all sure what he was expecting. Fairly routine operational stuff. Problems with the network organisation and requests for assistance or equipment. To his surprise there was none of that. By the end of the fourth paragraph he found that his hand was trembling.

41

Three times he read the contents of his deciphered note, not even aware that his bourbon was untouched and that his cigarette had burned out in the ashtray.

His mind was reeling, his thoughts suddenly a confused jumble. Feeling slightly off balance, he hauled himself to his feet and paced the room a couple of times to help him concentrate. Then he noticed the glass of bourbon and, as he went to reach for it, caught sight of the photo frame on the mantelpiece. Debs was staring directly at him, seeming to be asking: 'What is it, John? What's shaken you like this?'

'You don't want to know,' he mouthed.

'I'm your lover and your friend. For eternity. We have no secrets.'

The corner of his mouth curled up in that lop-sided half-smile she had always loved so much. Thank God, sometimes when he was alone and it was quiet, he could still hear her voice.

'Taiwan,' he said silently. 'The Chinese are going to invade within the next four months.'

Two

Even if Macao's most famous landmark, the Hotel Lisboa, is a circular, post-modern architectural monstrosity with white blobs on its orange façade, the view from its bedroom windows is nevertheless spectacular.

Bill Dawson watched the scattered beads of ships' lights moving slowly to and fro in the inky void of the Pearl River estuary as he pulled on his jacket in readiness for his rendezvous with Iona Moncrieff.

It took him by surprise when the telephone rang; he half-expected she was phoning to say she'd been delayed. All flights and ferries from Hong Kong were overbooked with delegates and media teams attending the conference. In fact the tiny peninsula of Macao seemed as if it were in danger of snapping off from mainland China and sinking without trace under the weight of visitors.

'Bill, it's John Dancer here. You had some business to discuss?'

'Sure, John, but I'm just on my way out. Let's fix a time for tomorrow –'

'Something's come up. Urgent business. Give me five minutes.'

Dawson frowned at the receiver. It was unusual for Dancer to be so insistent or to sound so concerned. Normally nothing short of an earthquake would get him rattled.

'Where are you?'

'My hotel. I can come over.'

'No, don't do that.' As both Americans moved in the same social and commercial circles in Beijing, it would seem implausible to Chinese security if they were not on nodding acquaintance terms, but they kept any open chance encounters short and to a minimum. The CIA station chief glanced at his watch. Five to eight. 'Remember the church? I'll see you there in thirty minutes.' He hung up, checked he had a fresh pack of cigars, then left the room.

As the main body of the conference was being held at the Lisboa, most of the seven hundred and fifty rooms had been seized early by the Chinese and American delegations. The British had pointedly settled for the colonial grandeur of the Bella Vista, while the Taiwanese with their flourishing tiger economy, cocked a snook at Beijing by opting for the aptly named Fortuna on rua da Cantao. Such were the unspoken subtleties of international diplomacy.

With the hotel lobby teeming with Chinese delegates, it was virtually impossible to know if he'd picked up a tail. Although Macao had not yet followed Hong Kong in rejoining the motherland, he had no doubt that someone somewhere from Chicom counter-intelligence would be making a note of everyone he met. That didn't matter in itself. As commercial attaché he had good reason to talk with virtually any diplomat or businessman without arousing undue suspicions.

With precision timing the President of the United States was due to arrive at eight o'clock for the 'Grand Reception' – cocktails followed by a formal dinner – which would launch the Pacific Rim Trade Development Conference. It would be the perfect opportunity for him to slip away quietly while everyone was distracted. Gawpers and rubbernecks were already lining the red carpet in the lobby. There'd been muted handclaps as the ageing Chinese leadership had passed by, protocol demanding that, as hosts, they arrive first to greet the heads of visiting nations.

An advance guard of burly US Secret Service agents – crop-haired, pointlessly mean-looking, hyperactive and wired-to-sound – signalled the approach of the limousine carrying the President and First Lady. A murmur of interest rippled through the onlookers as, slightly off key, the bandsmen of the People's Liberation Army struck up the American national anthem. News frontmen for several global networks cued the TV teams and began their baying introductions to camera, trying to make themselves heard above the rising level of noise. On the steps outside, flash-guns began popping in a demented pocket thunderstorm.

The sound of triumphal brass rose to fill the lobby along with the muted, self-conscious cheers and handclapping.

Dawson hovered for a moment, just long enough to glimpse the familiar plastic smile, perfect bouffant hairstyle and those eyes glistening with sincerity. Then the First Lady and entourage of key advisers. And yes, there he was. Mr Terry Tan. Smiling, waving, a sheen of perspiration on a face that looked twenty years too young for a man in his fifties. At his side his petite wife, who had escaped Maoist China with her husband years before to build a business empire and make a fortune in the land of the free.

Dawson's spirits sank. If Mr Terry Tan was here it meant only one thing. The President still wasn't listening.

As the entourage passed, the CIA officer slipped into the adjoining shopping arcade, down the steps and away into the night.

Dancer hung up the receiver in the telephone booth in the hotel foyer and sauntered back to the casino. It was the smartest in Macao and the plethora of fake Armani suits as well as the flimsy Versace numbers the women were nearly wearing made him feel decidedly underdressed. Never-theless, the place hardly had the sparkle and fun of Las Vegas. There were no cocktail waitresses plying the punters with free drinks, the dealers didn't talk to their customers, and no one smiled. Must be against house rules, he mused, as he made his way to one of the blackjack tables.

He played a couple of games, busting twenty-one on both occasions, but it gave him time enough to identify his shadow. It wasn't difficult – you didn't find many people reading a newspaper in a casino. Either his department wasn't willing to allow gambling 'expenses' or else he'd pocketed it as an operational perk.

Nevertheless, Dancer felt irrationally miffed to be allocated such a low-grade tail – no doubt a cheap rent-a-spook from the plain-clothes police Bureau rather than one of the real professionals from the Ministry of State Security. But then, he reasoned, in true Chinese tradition, the MSS wouldn't want to lose face with the Chicom Party big boys by admitting that they were overstretched and underfunded for such a 'target'-rich environment as the Macao Conference. Yet, on second thoughts, he shouldn't really complain at the lack of resources levelled at China's most potent, but unrecognised, enemy.

Throwing in his hand, he made his way to the toilets in the knowledge that the tail would follow. Sure enough, moments later, the man entered and made a great play of just washing his hands. Dancer left the urinal and joined him at the adjoining basin. Talking to the image next to him in the mirror, he said, 'I've seen you watching me. I've been watching you. We seem made for each other. Who'd have thought the two of us could have met like this instantly recognised out of mutual need?'

The tail said nothing, but froze. Dancer smiled sweetly at him, fully aware of the extreme homophobic nature of the Chinese male. The man vanished, and when Dancer emerged into the casino moments later, he was still nowhere to be seen.

Grabbing the opportunity, Dancer left and took a cab outside the hotel. It dropped him by a bus stop in the old quarter. He then did a classic counter-surveillance run, doubling back in the direction from which he'd come. Satisfied that his tail had been well and truly lost, he took a four-stop bus ride and a half-mile walk to the old Portuguese church.

He checked his watch before entering. Inside it was dark,

ambient light gleaming dully on the dark mahogany pews between which ran an aisle of minuscule mosaic tiles. The smell of must and beeswax mingled with a hint of incense. Tapestries hung on the stone walls – the raising of Lazarus, Rachel by the well, and others – but they failed to deaden the hard echo as he walked towards the old priest who was rearranging the vase of roses and violas beside the candlestand. Only one was lit, its flame fluttering as if trying hard to breathe.

'I'd like to make my confession,' Dancer said.

He couldn't see the priest's eyes, the fitful light casting pools of shadow in the sockets of his skull. 'Over there. But first I *expect* you'll want to light a candle.'

'Pardon me? Oh, yes. Of course.' He reached for his wallet. What denomination, he wondered?

The priest seemed to read his mind. 'Dollars will be fine.'

Dancer extracted a twenty bill. The priest didn't move. The American pulled out another and, folding both, pushed them through the slit in the small steel moneybox. Then he lit the candle.

'For anyone in particular?'

Dancer hesitated. 'My wife.'

'Maybe you should also light another.'

'Another?'

'For China.'

The priest moved away then, seeming to melt into the velvet gloom.

Dancer walked towards the left-hand cloister of stone pillars and small rosette windows where the ancient confessional box stood. As he drew aside the velvet curtain, it was a tense moment.

'Bill?'

He smelled the thin trail of cigar smoke escaping through the ornate iron grille from the adjoining cubicle. 'Bless you, my son.' It was followed by a throaty chuckle. 'Because God knows you need all the help your sorry ass can get.'

A sense of relief flooded through Dancer and he grinned. 'Up yours, Father. I think it's me who should be forgiving *your* sins.'

'Most probably,' Dawson rejoined. 'In fact almost certainly. But forgetting how I'm more sinned against than sinning, I'm in a bit of a hurry. So what's gone and gotten a pure soul like you so excited?'

'I've had a contact from "Hunan".'

More smoke tumbled through the grille. 'He's not due.'

'I know. It was just a routine check after I saw you last night. I went to the emergency drop.'

'And?'

'Information. He'd obviously taken a helluva chance to get it.'

'He's too impetuous, that one. Can't you get it through to him? He's too important to us to take risks.'

'Having read his report, I think he did the right thing.'

The CIA man grunted. 'Subject?'

'Taiwan,' Dancer replied simply. 'Your worst nightmare.'

'C'mon, John!' Incredulous.

'Within the next four months. It'll coincide with the Phase Two opening of Hong Kong Airport. A big Chinese Navy regatta is planned. They'll use that as cover to get the fleet into position. The Amphibious Task Force at Shantu has already begun preliminary exercises and fifth columnists are functioning in all major centres in Taiwan.'

Dawson was stunned into silence for several moments. 'You're absolutely certain?'

'This is "Hunan",' his friend reminded, and pushed a rolled copy of the *South China Morning Post* through the grille. I've slipped a copy of his report in there. Take it with you. I'm in Macao for three more days. If you want to get hold of me, I'm at the Mandarin Oriental, Room 540.'

For a moment Dawson could hardly concentrate, hardly get his head round what he had just been told. He was aware that his pulse had begun to race and as he

48

watched Dancer walk away it was not reality, more like a scene from a half-forgotten movie. Surely this wasn't really happening . . .

Dawson was late now, his mind preoccupied. So he didn't read the directions properly and got lost trying to remember how to find the backstreet bar off the waterfront. For once Macao's natural air-conditioning system, the sea breeze that made it so much more pleasant than neighbouring Hong Kong, had broken down. The humidity cocooned him, sweat soaking his shirt as he hurried over the damp cobbles past the small grocery stores and pavement foodstalls, the still air filled with the sound of sizzling woks and the smell of frying seafood.

It was almost by accident that he stumbled into the narrow entrance of Jorge's Silver Dragon Bar.

The wooden staircase plunged steeply into the basement, pink-painted bulbs dimly showing the way. A mixed collection of tatty posters lined the walls: from Oriental-flavoured movie musicals like *South Pacific* and *Suzy Wong* to a jazz concert given by Chet Baker and – an incongruous late addition – the Spice Girls. Thankfully, no music emanated from the subterranean dive with its rough-plastered walls, bamboo bar and rattan furniture that was past its glory days. There was just the low background murmur of conversation and clatter of dominoes from an earnest group of Chinese playing *pai kao* in a far corner. An ancient baby grand piano had been squeezed into a tiny recess between two brick pillars on which posters announced the night's coming entertainment. The air, churned listlessly by two giant ceiling fans, smelled of stale tobacco and marijuana.

Two jailbait Thai hookers in shiny clingfilm microskirts eyed him from their barstools but lost interest when Iona Moncrieff from one of the shuttered alcove seats lifted her empty beer glass.

The morose Portuguese owner was absorbed, watching the multiscreen TV images behind the bar of the Conference reception. A line of elderly Chinese leaders shaking hands with the sandy-haired British Foreign Secretary who was dwarfed by the fixed-smiling Prime Minister beside him.

'Two beers, please.'

Jorge dragged his attention away from the screen, took a couple of glasses from the shelf and poured from a brass draught tap on the bar.

The screen image had cut to an American reporter in the Lisboa's lobby. *'This ambitious conference, aimed at reconciliation and re-establishing financial stability of Far Eastern nations as well as promoting world trade with the region, has experienced its first political upset,'* the man said in the irritatingly overdramatic manner of CNN. He was clearly hoping for more of them to break up the monotony of events. *'The President of Taiwan has refused to be greeted by the Chinese leadership hosts. And his delegation has refused to take its place at tomorrow's opening session until it is given a separate table from that of mainland China.*

'A spokesman for the Taiwan team said that the People's Republic of China was trying to make the point that it considered Taiwan to be a mere wayward province that was properly part of China. But history cannot be undone. Taiwan is now a free and independent democratic nation and is one prodigal son who will not return until its parents mend their authoritarian, corrupt and bankrupting ways.'

Beer slopped over the bar counter as Jorge carelessly presented the two glasses and took Dawson's money without bothering to say a word. He resumed his seat and his silent study of the screen. Expensive drinks, Dawson decided, when no change was forthcoming.

'No trouble finding it?' Iona asked as he joined her in the alcove.

'None, Your Majesty,' he lied. 'Just got held up. Sorry.' His voice lacked its usual light-hearted tone.

'You look tired, Bill, distracted.' She indicated the

50

hookers, now gossiping together. 'Hormones playing you up, are they?'

A breakthrough at last; his smile was almost real. 'Never stop when I'm in your company.'

'Sweet man.' Her gaze held his for a second. 'But I don't believe a word of it.'

He glanced around, taking in his surroundings. It was his habit to examine the shadows, to isolate the people and their faces. To assure himself there was no danger before he dropped his guard. 'This still a favoured haunt of yours, Iona?'

She lit a cigarette; there were already three squashed butts in the ashtray. 'It's about the only one left in Macao that doesn't have karaoke.'

Her voice trailed as she realised he was listening but not hearing. 'What is it, Bill? What's wrong?'

He came back into her orbit with a jolt. 'Sorry? Oh, nothing, a lot on my plate, that's all.'

'You sure? A trouble shared is a trouble halved.' Her eyes were serious, seeming genuinely concerned.

Not for the first time, he found himself unnerved by the Scotswoman's perception. Should he tell her? He certainly wanted to, but this was strictly for Langley's ears only. They made the decisions, he just did what he was told. Well, usually. Instead, he made a joke of it. 'Not a good maxim in the secrets business. Which reminds me, just how is your favourite project going?'

Her response was needle sharp and mischievous as always. 'Show me your secrets, Bill, and I'll show you mine. You're getting as mean as the boys from Tel Aviv.'

'Never!' he protested, appreciating the intelligence community joke – that the Mossad were past masters at apparently swapping information without giving a thing away themselves.

'Okay,' she relented. 'Just to prove how much I love Americans.'

His eyes narrowed a fraction, or was it her imagination?

Hell, she'd always been crap at the body-language game. She sometimes wondered if that was really why she'd never landed herself a man – or at least one who stayed for more than a night or two.

'Just *this* American,' he said, winking.

'You forced it out of me.' Game over. 'The PM had a secret meeting with the President of Taiwan this afternoon. Everyone is hopeful we've clinched the deal.'

Dawson inclined his head towards the multiscreen that Jorge was still watching impassively. 'Maybe you have. Taiwan's taking an aggressive public stance.'

'I'll know soon enough. My chief's coming to join us here as soon as he can get away.'

'The boy Lansdowne? I'd like to meet him again. No one at Langley seems to be able to make him out.' Upper crust chinless wonder, he didn't bother to add, knowing that Iona knew full well what CIA headquarters thought.

'He may get his shirts from Pink's and his bowler from Lock's,' Iona said. 'But he's got attitude. Don't jump to conclusions. I did and I was wrong.'

Dawson sipped thoughtfully at his beer. 'My chief met him a couple of weeks back with your Defence Secretary. Some joint naval exercise? Thought the boy Lansdowne was another of your inbred aristos – until he got to know him. Said he couldn't believe some of the things he was saying. Hardly the usual appeasing pro-Chinese kow-towing we're used to from your Foreign Office.'

'Things have changed since the handover of Hong Kong,' Iona said. 'A lot of it down to Piers Lansdowne.' As they talked, her thoughts were drawn back over the years, her mind's eye settling on the pink-walled villa like an old photograph faded by time and memory.

Iced drinks on the terrace under a blazing Cyprus sun. She, hot and perspiring, in a limp summer dress after the flight from London and taxi ride from the RAF base at Akrotiri, confused and excited by the mysterious call. Secrecy within secrecy in the secret world.

And then her surprise at being greeted by Davenport, Lansdowne's predecessor. The boy Lansdowne there too, almost ten years ago. *Really* just a boy then, a fresh graduate learning the ropes. Hovering, his mouth firmly shut, but eyes and ears wide open. Serving the drinks and batting phone calls from Washington and London. Especially London. That's where Davenport should have been, why she hadn't expected him to be here. Back in London he'd only have to ring down and she'd have been at his desk in four minutes. Three, if she didn't make a muck of applying lipstick before she went. So why all the way to Cyprus?

'Some people for you to meet,' Davenport had said.

The Americans were at the pool, of course. Frank Aspen with his neat hair dyed black to match his trunks sitting on the edge, feet dangling in the cool liquid. The other like a porpoise, head buried in the exploding water as he butter-flied towards her. And she remembered her surprise as he had surfaced, grinning like a kid, water streaming from the soft pelt of body hair.

'Bill! I thought you were in Manila.'

She recalled the effortless ease with which he'd hoisted himself clear of the pool, how he'd caught her eyes momentarily examining the flex of muscle showing beneath the middle-aged spread, the close cut of the seer-sucker shorts in blue check.

Remembered the diamond twinkle in his eyes. 'Your Majesty. Seems everyone thinks everyone here is some-place else.'

'And that's how we intend to keep it,' Davenport had confirmed.

And that was exactly how it had been kept from that day to this. Looking back, no one on the outside would ever have been able to pinpoint exactly when it had all begun. In fact, it was 1989. Exactly one week after the Chinese Government had murdered hundreds of unarmed student protesters in Tiananmen Square before the eyes of the global media.

The American and British Governments had reeled under the shock, the promise of a flowering democracy in Communist China cruelly snapped off below the bud. Nothing would ever be quite the same again.

It was then that Davenport had made his startling discovery which he revealed as Dawson towelled himself dry beside the villa pool. 'Britain signed away the six million inhabitants of Hong Kong to Communist China in the Joint Declaration of 1984. But it had promised the early establishment of a democratically elected Legislative Council, so that it would be deeply rooted and have matured well before the Chicom take-over. During his research last week, my assistant Piers Lansdowne unearthed a highly classified internal Foreign Office document. It was not meant for our eyes, possibly not even for the cabinet office. Tell them, Piers.'

Piers Lansdowne had blinked in the bright sunlight and cleared his throat, a schoolboy making his first speech in a debating society. That had been her first impression the first time she had set eyes on him.

'The memorandum is dated two years ago. 1987. In short, it confirms the Foreign Office has bowed to Beijing pressure and has agreed to use delaying tactics in the establishment of an elected democratic assembly in Hong Kong.'

'What exactly does that mean?' Iona had asked.

Lansdowne gained confidence, his voice deepening an octave. 'It means that, by stalling but not exactly reneging on the deal, democracy will barely be established in Hong Kong before the Communists take over in 1997.'

'No roots, you see,' Davenport had added with contempt. 'Not a baby oak, but a sapling. Barely more than an acorn. By 1997 democracy should have been established for around seven years. It's a betrayal of monumental proportions. Put this new revelation alongside the events in Tiananmen Square last week and you can see there is now no chance of a virtual reverse take-over of China by Hong

Kong, of democracy spreading *into* the mainland. That burning hope has all but been snuffed out.'

Frank Aspen said grimly. 'The US is committed to democracy in China.' Spoken by a man in swimming shorts, Iona thought the words sounded rather pompous.

'So what's to be done?' Dawson had asked.

'The only thing we *can* do,' Davenport replied. Whatever Iona was anticipating he'd say, it certainly wasn't what followed. 'Frank and I are agreed that we lay long-term plans to topple the existing Chinese Communist leadership and replace it with a quasi-democratic regime of the West's choosing. A regime that will follow the principles of human rights and the free market economy.'

At that point, Dawson's jaw dropped in surprise. But before he could speak, Davenport continued: 'I don't have to tell you this is a long haul and, at this stage, is very unlikely to receive official sanction in either London or Washington.'

'Both are mesmerised by the idea of profiting from trade with China,' Frank Aspen added helpfully.

'What exactly do you expect us to do?' Iona remembered asking.

'Pretty much as now,' Davenport said, 'but with a change of emphasis and more concentration of effort. We know already the Chicom are purging the student unions and pro-democracy movements. We must cultivate those people, both in China and abroad if any manage to escape. Provide funds and assist generally where we can. We already have agents in mainland China. What we have to do is gradually turn them into an effective network that operates in every key stratum of society.' He paused to smile. 'There is a song from the musical *Half A Sixpence*; it goes: "Can't go to jail for what you're thinking". Likewise, every action we take in general intelligence duties in China we'll be thinking: how can this further our ultimate goal?'

'And what do *we* do?' Dawson asked Aspen.

His chief poured some fresh orange juice from a jug.

'Much the same. But Langley will be looking at the wider picture too. There's an embryonic resistance movement in Chinese-occupied Tibet and simmering demands for separation in Xingjiang province. That's stuff the CIA's best qualified to handle.'

Iona hadn't exactly been sure about that, but there was no denying Langley had the clout and, more importantly, access to cash. And if Congressional Committees started probing too deep, the CIA would be happy to pay SIS to give them a helping hand. Public accountability in the United States had served British intelligence well in recent years.

'One day,' Davenport had concluded, 'I believe that politicians in London and Washington will finally realise that China will never change without outside influence. And when they ask what can be done, we will not be found wanting. Or needing to wait.'

But Davenport himself never saw that day. He had died of a coronary four years later while running to catch his homebound train from Waterloo. Just fifty-five years old.

His legacy, however, lived on. Lansdowne took it over, overhauling and refining the growing secret network of Chinese dissenters and pushing the SIS station in Beijing to identify Chicom government officials who might, one day, be willing accomplices in the overthrow of the leadership.

Meanwhile, Frank Aspen had been as good as his word. Using former US military, the CIA began training and equipping the Tibetan guerrillas and smuggling arms from Pakistan over the mountains for the Muslim separatists of Xingjiang province.

But it had taken the 1997 handover of Hong Kong to the Chinese and a new government in London for the politicians finally to persuade themselves that the totalitarian Chicom regime would remain as intransigent to political reform as ever. As Davenport's revelation at the Cyprus villa had predicted all those years before, diplomatic stalling had meant that the 1984 promise of a Legco legislative assembly, voted in by the people, had barely been in place a year. In the first hours of renewed Chinese control, it was outlawed and a replacement appointed under direction from Beijing. Any voice the elected politicians ever had was guaranteed to be minuscule for all time. The voice of freedom was silenced.

So bitter had been the row between Britain and Beijing that politicians from London boycotted the Chinese part of the handover celebrations along with the equally disapproving Americans. Within six hours, four thousand Chicom troops, with the same armoured cars that had been used at Tiananmen Square, poured into the tiny island territory to stamp their authority for the whole world to see.

The new British Prime Minister and his Foreign Secretary had returned home with the ex-governor crestfallen and crushed with a sense of sorrow and helplessness. Hong Kong's vibrant, happy inhabitants had always won the hearts of most British people. Now those inhabitants felt betrayed and the British Government knew it. And knew they were right.

Iona had heard the story of how, a week later, during a private audience with the chief of SIS, the Prime Minister had recounted his experience and emotions at the handover ceremony. The Chief sympathised.

'To be honest, I feel this country's let the people of Hong Kong down,' the politician confessed. 'I only wish there was something we could do about it.'

After a measured and solemn pause, the SIS chief said: 'Well, actually, Prime Minister, perhaps there is. You should meet one of my chaps, Piers Lansdowne. Perhaps informally over supper?'

And there it was. Two weeks later Lansdowne was telling the Prime Minister in private: 'Britain has had a long and fruitful affair with Hong Kong. It was good for both of us. But now we are filled with remorse that we ever agreed to relinquish our lover back into the hands of the legitimate husband who is known as a tyrant and a wife-beater.'

Iona smiled as she remembered the relish with which Lansdowne had recalled the important encounter. How the Prime Minister had been sadly amused by the analogy.

And how his eyes had begun to glaze and a frown began to gather as he learned that, of course, SIS had a network of dissidents in mainland China, some of them in government and the military. That, of course, Taiwan would want to rejoin the motherland *if* the old Chicom leadership could be toppled. That, of course, the CIA had been working for years now with the freedom fighters in Tibet and the separatists in Xingjiang. And, of course, everyone in the intelligence world knew that Communist China was rearming massively to emerge as a new menace to global peace.

Then one more 'of course'. Of course, if that happened, we would not only be setting free the people of Hong Kong but one whole fifth of the world's community from totalitarian repression.

The Prime Minister's eyes had flashed momentarily with an evangelical zeal before his frown returned as he turned over the difficulties and repercussions in his mind.

But, as he'd left the Prime Minister's private apartment in Downing Street, Piers Lansdowne knew in his water. Knew he'd landed the big one.

Sitting now in the sultry heat of the Silver Dragon Bar, Iona found it strange to think of that dream moving falteringly towards fruition.

'In the end the new Foreign Secretary had to drag the Foreign Office to heel,' Iona said. 'He'd been shocked to learn that China's annual defence spending has tripled in the past decade and the extent of its territorial ambitions.'

'As you and I've been predicting for years,' Dawson pointed out acidly.

'Be fair, Bill. We knew Beijing would be buoyed up by

getting back Hong Kong, but none of us thought it would take an aggressive stance so early.'

He had to agree with that. 'Up to fifteen years we said. Fifteen years to make its air force effective and to sort out its blue-water navy. Thought we were playing a long game.'

'Now they've got Russian Sukhoi Su-27 fighters and may soon have an aircraft carrier in Hong Kong harbour,' Iona mused. 'The military's own Great Leap Forward – now they're making a nuisance of themselves throughout the South China Sea.'

'If only it stops at nuisance.'

She studied her friend's face. 'Meaning?'

Dawson shrugged dismissively. 'Nothing.'

Her eyes narrowed. 'You're being very enigmatic. You're a bad liar, Bill, for a spook.'

The American had been watching the stairs. 'That's him, isn't it?'

Lansdowne looked every bit as adolescent as Dawson remembered. Hardly aged a day. There was no sign of British arch formality here, not the way he carried himself in a lazy slouch that emphasised his height and gangly limbs. Nor in the blue-striped shirt which he wore loosely outside his cotton trousers in the untidy style of current youth culture. Cool Britannia, Dawson thought. In a slightly girlish manner, Lansdowne tossed his head to clear the rain-flattened fringe of fair hair from his eyes before ambling to the bar.

He ordered a drink from the proprietor, then, as he waited, began chatting to the Thai hookers.

Irrationally, Dawson felt a wave of irritation as a joke in fluent Cantonese had them giggling and making moon eyes. He seemed in no hurry and it was several minutes before he left them, still laughing, and drifted across to the alcove table.

'Do you remember Bill Dawson?' Iona introduced. 'And, Bill, of course this is Piers.'

Lansdowne's hand was damp and cool, but his grip firm. 'Heard a lot about you recently, Bill.' His gaze was cool and appraising behind spectacles that were too heavy and old-fashioned for the delicate young face and the American was surprised to find himself unsettled by it.

'All of it true,' Dawson said, more aggressively than he'd intended – a tone he used when he felt he was being put on the defensive. He backtracked with a gruff laugh. 'Well, most.'

The Englishman's smile was disarming. 'I'm sure most of it is. Your co-operation with Iona here is much appreciated. This is not something we can ever hope to achieve alone. Without your people's work in Tibet and Xingjiang, it would never have got thus far.'

Dawson liked that. Getting the Brits to pay compliments to Americans was like drawing teeth. 'I'm just surprised to find London so enthusiastic for this, Mr Lansdowne.'

'Piers, please,' the Englishman insisted quickly. 'Well, as your own late lamented John Wayne might have said, sometimes mankind has to do what mankind has to do.

'I'm no child of Empire, Bill. But we handed over Honkers to the Chinese in good faith and that faith was betrayed even before the transition was complete. And suddenly the new British Government began to see it that way too. Realised that Beijing could never allow democracy and free speech to flourish because, inevitably, it would infect the mainland and destroy Communist rule. Ministers were not unhappy to discover that we had contingency plans in place.'

Dawson had pulled the pack of cigars from his pocket and picked thoughtfully at the cellophane wrapping. 'And you think they'll run to the wire with this?'

'As long as British involvement can be denied,' Lansdowne answered. 'The PM's taken a personal interest. He was at the handover ceremony. Told me there were tears in his eyes when the choir of boys and girls sang in the monsoon rain, the happy, innocent smiling little faces as they sang "All the Children of the World". And even as he watched them, he realised they'd already been betrayed by Beijing. Touching, eh? Perhaps he wasn't aware they'd also been betrayed by our Foreign Office.'

'British enthusiasm counts for nothing without Taiwan,' Iona interjected. 'Without the Taiwan leadership to front this operation, it just won't happen.'

Dawson understood that. Taiwan was the free and democratic face of China. However much America's and Britain's political expertise and pressure might be needed, it had to be seen by the world as a reverse takeover of Beijing by its own people.

'So, the Prime Minister's meeting with the President of Taiwan this afternoon, Piers – did it go as expected? Do we have the green light?'

A smile appeared hesitantly on Lansdowne's lips. 'Ah well, rather more amber than green, I'm afraid.'

Iona felt her heart sink. 'How can they possibly object? It doesn't make sense.'

Lansdowne arched one eyebrow. 'It does to them, when you consider they'd be taking on the biggest military power on earth. The stakes couldn't be higher. If we get it wrong and it backfires, then they'll pay the price. They're terrified of Beijing's wrath. Missile attacks, invasion, even a nuclear strike – they see no end to the ramifications. China's riding high on a wave of nationalism and patriotic fervour and Taiwan is afraid it could be wiped off the map with a single swipe of the dragon's tail.'

'A poetic turn of phrase,' Dawson muttered despairingly.

'But very apt,' the Englishman came back quickly. 'So they're insisting on safeguards.'

Dawson finally lit his cigar. 'Like what?' he asked, streams of tobacco smoke escaping through the gaps between his teeth.

'Like demanding the personal backing and reassurance of the President of the United States,' Lansdowne replied evenly. 'A secret treaty committing the US to defending Taiwan to the hilt if anything goes wrong. Even if that means air strikes against PLA units on the mainland.'

'Ouch,' Dawson said. 'That's some commitment.'

Lansdowne shrugged. 'It's a litmus test, Bill, that's all. The Taiwanese want to be sure they're not going to be left in the lurch if it all goes pear-shaped. So we'll have to see what reaction we get from the White House.'

Dawson's eyes followed the trail of blue tobacco smoke spiralling towards the ceiling fan to be dispersed by the spinning blades. In his mind's eye he saw the American delegation's arrival at the Hotel Lisboa, Terry Tan walking at the President's side.

Iona frowned. 'What is it, Bill? Something troubling you?'

The American looked uncomfortable. It wasn't easy to tell a long-term friend and professional rival that you'd shit your pants. He took a deep breath like a man about to dive from the high board. 'The President doesn't know.'

'About what?' Iona was confused.

'The whole thing. Operation Motivator. Our work to bring down the Chicom regime.'

Lansdowne stared at him in disbelief. 'This isn't real, Bill. Tell me it isn't.'

'Oh, it's real all right. That's why you Brits have been told to have *all* dealings with the US through Langley.'

'Why?' Lansdowne asked.

'We have a problem with the President.' He allowed himself a private joke. 'Several in fact, but one that affects our operations. You'll remember the FBI discovered the Chinese secret funding for the President's re-election campaign. . . Well, truth is, the man is in the thrall of the current Beijing leadership. You've noticed, no doubt, that Chinese-American entrepreneur called Terry Tan at the President's side during the opening ceremony of this Conference. Well, Tan is Beijing's man. He's been networking Washington since the early nineties and has the

President's ear. He's convinced him and half of Capitol Hill that Chinese political reform is inevitable so long as the West is patient and keeps pouring money in. Explained how important it is for the leadership not to lose face. The usual claptrap that lets China get away with murder – literally. Push too hard and rock the boat, Tan warns, and the US will blow monumental investment opportunities in addition to political reform.'

Lansdowne understood. 'So, like most of his administration and the Wall Street investment markets, the President's blind to the economic realities?'

The American nodded. 'That China is actually the largest source of trade *deficit* to both the US and Europe. They've a blind belief that'll change, but Beijing will make sure it won't.'

'So now the President will *have* to be told,' Lansdowne surmised.

'I guess so, and he's not going to like hearing what's been going on behind his back.' Dawson paused thoughtfully for a moment. 'But then I expect we'll approach the matter from another angle now. Give him the bad news first to soften the blow.'

'Bad news?' Iona asked.

'You said earlier that I seemed distracted,' Dawson said with a forced smile, and glanced at Lansdowne. 'Always trust a woman's intuition, Piers. Something I've just learned. Even Frank Aspen doesn't know yet.'

Momentarily the downdraught of humid air from the fan felt chill on Iona's neck and she was aware of an involuntary shiver. 'You're getting me worried, Bill. You sound serious.'

'Sure. Serious serious. I got news tonight. Chicom's planning to take Taiwan within the next four months – to coincide with the Phase Two opening of Hong Kong Airport.'

Iona was speechless, Lansdowne momentarily thrown. In the brief shocked silence between them, the rattling of ivory and the excited chatter of the *pai kao* players rose to fill the vacuum. 'C'mon, Bill, don't mess around.'

He lowered his voice to a hoarse whisper. 'Yeah, I know. That was my first reaction. Except that the source is impeccable.'

She leaned forward, her gaze penetrating his. 'Do you want to share that with me?' Her voice was tense, challenging.

Dawson withdrew a fraction to defend his space, naturally cautious. Hesitantly he said: '"Hunan."'

'"Hunan,"' she repeated breathlessly. Dawson's agents were given names of Chinese provinces, so they'd mean nothing to anyone if overheard in casual conversation. 'Shandong', 'Shaanxi', 'Fujian'.

Lansdowne was on to it like a terrier. '"Hunan?"' he said. 'The same one?'

The American nodded slowly. 'The same source that told us Chicom's Central Military Commission created that élite corps to develop computer virus systems to disable the West's command and control systems.'

Iona's eyes screwed into fierce slits. 'So it can't be dismissed as idle speculation.'

'I don't think so. "Hunan" also warned us that China would be orchestrating opposition to US forces in South Korea and the Jap island of Okinawa. And that Thailand would be under pressure to refuse the US Navy its traditional facilities. All have proved to be correct.'

Lansdowne was silent for a moment, but Dawson imagined he could hear the hum of his brain at work. 'Bill, both my people and yours have always assessed that China hasn't the military shipping for a seaborne invasion of Taiwan. That hasn't changed in the latest reports I've seen.'

'Satellite surveillance would have. . .' Iona began.

Dawson's jaw stiffened. 'Yeah well, satellites can be fooled like any form of aerial recon. Especially if we don't know what we're looking for. Or we're looking for it in the

64

wrong place. The shit'll hit the fan when this report gets to Langley. The boys at Fort Belvoir will have to restudy everything they already got and start taking a fresh look.'

'Four months,' Lansdowne repeated softly.

The American suddenly looked anxious. 'You didn't hear this from me, Piers. This is for Langley's eyes only. If they see fit, they'll pass it to you through the usual channels.'

'Of course,' the SIS man said, knowing Dawson meant Langley might also sit on it. 'I'm grateful. I think it might just give our PM the leverage he needs. It's not something Taiwan can afford to ignore.' The hint of a grin on his face suggested he thought it might be enough to clinch the deal, get the go-ahead for the reverse take-over of the greatest nation on earth.

Dawson read the expression. 'It's not enough, Piers. Time's too short. Shit, I mean, *four* months – I ask you. So Taiwan's on board, but we can't pull it off without major support from within the People's Liberation Army. I mean, it's coming. We're making progress. Our assets have identified many likely collaborators within the PLA and Chicom intelligence, but we've got to haul them in slowly. It's like fishing shark – slow and dangerous.'

Iona lay back in her wicker chair and cocked her head slightly to one side, a mischievous smile on her lips. 'You're not the only player in town, Bill,' she said enigmatically as she lit a fresh cigarette from the butt of her last.

'But I'm not playing games,' he came back pointedly.

'Nor is Iona,' Lansdowne intervened. 'You've been straight with us, Bill, so I'll be straight with you. Your news means we haven't got time for the usual horse-trading of information between Langley and "Riverside".'

Dawson frowned in Iona's direction. 'Something I don't know about?'

She blew a smoke ring and watched it being dragged jerkily towards the fan. 'A breakthrough. We've identified a powerful military clique that may be prepared to join in and play.'

The American couldn't disguise his surprise, and she knew him well enough to know he'd resent her having pulled off such a major stroke. Dawson was a competitive player and a poor loser, although he hid it well. 'No kid, Your Majesty? Want to share it with me?'

Her eyes met his. 'Not yet, Bill, but soon.'

'Well, don't leave it too long, Your Majesty. Support from the PLA is still the major problem. Without it the plans don't stand a snowball's chance in hell. We thought we had a three-year time-frame – or even longer – to achieve a palace coup in Beijing. Now, assuming my source is correct, we've barely got four months.'

Piers Lansdowne was unaware that he had been wringing his hands together in an unconscious display of anxiety. 'And whatever we do, we can't afford to get it wrong.'

Iona knew what he meant and understood why he couldn't bring himself to spell it out. Get it wrong and the people of Hong Kong would remain shackled to a Chinese totalitarian regime for eternity, and would probably feel the hot breath of Chinese wrath. And, as for the West's network of activists and agents-in-place, the aftermath didn't bear thinking about. The purge would be so relentless and so vicious it would be surprising if the rivers of China weren't running black with blood.

'There's only one way,' Iona said as she and Dawson walked back towards the Lisboa Hotel along the dark, deserted streets. 'Cleanly. Leaving no hostages to fortune.'

He nodded. The flashing neon sign of a night-club doorway was reflected on his face, giving him the gaunt blue pallor of an alien. 'No survivors. No one to provide a focus for opposition. No politicians waiting for trial, stirring up old loyalties.'

'One fell swoop,' she said emphatically. 'The entire Beijing leadership.'

A kiss of a breeze had picked up, carrying flecks of rain in off the Pearl River delta. The aroma of stir-fried seafood spun in invisible coils from the street stalls. 'Hungry?'

'I was. Not now.'

He understood. 'Too late, and got the taste for booze. Want to talk?'

'Maybe we should.'

'Have a nightcap. I've got a bottle of brandy in my room.'

'Five star?'

'Six.'

She smiled. 'If I was twenty years younger, I'd consider that a proposition.'

'If I was twenty years younger, it would have been.'

She nudged him, linking her arm in his. They walked on, slowly, as they entered busier streets bustling with Chinese doing late shopping, eating snacks or making their way to drinking-dens or discos. The noise of traffic mingled with the beat and strangulated efforts of karaoke singers. The sights and smells, she thought, the never-ending, exotic promise of the Orient. It gave her the same buzz this night as it always had. 'Where have they gone, Bill?'

'What?'

Her voice was little more than a whisper. 'The years. Where did they all go?'

She was aware of him shaking his head. 'I don't know. Just that they have.'

So fast, she thought. 'Just yesterday I was a young girl. Finished university. One year as a secretary at the Foreign Office and then posted to the British Consulate at Shanghai. Such excitement, such times.'

'I bet you were a beauty.'

'No, not me. That's one thing that passed me by.'

'Well, that's strange, because your beautiful now.'

Her elbow caught his rib. 'Don't say that, Bill.'

'Why?'

She averted her head, trying not to see the slender young

Chinese girls with their microskirts and pretty pert faces. 'Because it hurts.'

He stopped walking and half turned towards her. 'But it's true.'

His eyes seemed very close to hers, glinting fiercely like they did when he was angry. Yet she knew he wasn't angry. 'Don't be cruel, Bill. I'm not as tough as I look. I know what I look like.'

'Okay.' Playing along. 'Then maybe it's in the eye of the beholder. And you can't see what I can from where you are.'

She giggled, too deep to be girlish and coarsened by years of two packs a day. 'I suppose I can't argue with that.'

He looked pleased with himself. Ever competitive, she told herself, Dawson had scored a point. They walked on.

They were silent for a while until the extravagant and ugly rounded shape of the Lisboa came into view. Out of the blue, he said: 'I retire next year.'

His words jolted her. 'What?'

'The big six-zero. I get pensioned off.'

She felt shocked. 'You?'

'Put out to grass.' He saw her expression and decided suddenly that he couldn't bear to endure her sympathy. 'Out to stud in reality. Think I should settle in California. All those beach babes.'

Iona's banter tripped out without thought; it always did in Dawson's company. 'You'd hate it.'

His eyes glistened. 'Yeah, I would, wouldn't I? I've always gone for the maturer woman.'

'I mean retirement. You'd hate retirement.'

'Tell me something I don't know.'

'At least if this business goes ahead, you'll have something to remember.'

They were approaching the hotel entrance. 'Yeah,' he said, 'while I'm fishing.'

From force of habit, Dawson never handed in a room key to reception until he was checking out. No point in letting an enemy know when you were in residence or not. No point inviting him to search your room.

So they were able to go straight to the elevator to speed them to his floor. Once inside, she said suddenly: 'We need to get them all together.'

'What? Who?'

'The Chinese leadership.'

'Er, yes, right,' His mind back on track. 'Easier said than done. They're not often all together. The annual Chicom Party Conference, of course. But security's always tight.'

She stared at the floor indicator light, momentarily distracted. 'Hong Kong Airport,' she said suddenly.

'What about it?'

'The timing of the planned invasion – coinciding with the opening of Phase Two.'

Dawson nodded. The biggest engineering project in the world. Being built on land reclaimed from the sea, Phase One alone cost twenty-two million dollars. Started under the last years of British colonial rule, but now being claimed by Beijing as if it was their baby. 'And so all the leaders will be there,' he said aloud.

'And all the China-watchers will be studying to see who's there.'

The CIA man understood. Who was winning and who was losing in the ever-shifting Chicom power struggle. Winners go to Hong Kong, losers stay behind like Cinderella.

The elevator sighed to an asthmatic stop.

'So it all happens in four months,' Iona said thoughtfully. 'Beginning of October. It's going to be a tight-run thing.'

They stepped into the corridor and along to his room. It was twice the size of her own at the Colonial and sumptuously appointed with a spectacular view of the waterfront.

'Make yourself at home,' he invited, using the remote to switch on the television. Frantic coverage of the conference still going on. He adjusted the sound level to a pitch where it would drown out their conversation should anyone have bugged the room.

When he turned he found her propped up against the pillows of the king-sized bed, her legs outstretched as she eased off her shoes. 'Bliss.'

He grinned as he reached for the brandy bottle. 'Why is it women are obsessed with their feet?'

'Same reason you chaps are obsessed with your dicks,' she replied quickly. She patted the bedspread beside her. 'Come and join me.'

'Majesty!' he rejoined in mock disapproval.

'Don't be silly, Bill. We're much too old for that sort of thing.'

He clambered awkwardly on to the bed, balancing a glass in each hand. 'Welcome to my honey-trap?'

She gave a sly, pouting sort of grin. 'Are you sure it's yours, Bill? Perhaps it's mine.'

He rested on one elbow beside her and looked down over the bed at the television. 'I guess we'll never know.'

There was a brief silence before she said: 'How long have I known you, Bill? Over twenty years?'

'On and off. I think it was a diplomatic trade reception in Nanjing thrown by the French.'

'Ah, yes, I think you're right – I'm sure you are. Yes, I didn't like you much.'

'How old was I? Mid-thirties. In my prime. Straight back from Viet Nam, with a body like Sly Stallone.'

'Cocky and conceited was what I noticed.'

'I was just wanting to get to know you. I'd just trashed the first of my marriages. Perhaps my chat-up line was—'

'Brash,' she helped.

'The impetuosity of youth,' he returned with a defensive smile.

A sadness crept into her eyes. Brash Bill Dawson had come into her life over two decades ago. Cocky and conceited. And she hadn't been able to keep her eyes off him. 'If only we had been,' she said hoarsely.

'Been what?'

'Impetuous. You chatted me up and I told myself I didn't like you, yet deep down I wanted you like crazy.'

'We became pals. Still are.'

Idly she swilled the brandy around her glass and savoured the aroma. 'But I wasn't impetuous. And I should have been when I had the chance.' Her voice was low, reflective and melancholy. 'Might not have spent a lifetime of spinsterdom.'

He watched her keenly, fascinated by the flawed looks that had denied her beauty or even prettiness. 'Better than having been the fourth Mrs Dawson.'

She chuckled at that, a warm and throaty sound. 'If I'd been number two, maybe three and four wouldn't have had a look in.'

Maybe it was her voice he had always been in love with? Or the words that voice spoke. 'Very possible,' he said.

Turning her head, she found him studying her closely, his eyes just inches away. 'Really?'

He nodded. 'Nearly sixty. A bit late in the day to realise I've wasted over twenty years. Now we're both the same, lost and lonely.'

Another chuckle. 'That's the drink talking.'

'It's not,' he said and held her gaze. She had a sad questioning look in her eyes as the gap between them closed. Slowly, a quarter inch a second, until she was so close her features became a blur. Just skin and pores, lips and glittering eyes. He'd forgotten about her eyes. They were what gave her her strange beauty.

The kiss left her stunned, rigid and unmoving. She was surprised by the passion with which his lips delivered, the catch in his breath. And if that were not enough, there came the shock as she realised his fingers were plucking at the top buttons of her long summer dress.

'Bill, no,' she breathed.

There were a lot of buttons running from the neckline to the hem. 'Get undressed,' he said. 'I'd like to see you undress.'

'Bill, please.'

'Call it the impetuosity of old age. Before it's too late.'

She was in a daze, drifting in a dream as she stood beside the bed and let him take her glass. With eyes downcast, she continued what he had begun. Slowly, shyly, unsure like a teenager on her first serious date.

And she was aware of him watching, the curiosity in his eyes caught out of the corners of her own. She fumbled and a button spun free, landing at her feet. She hesitated.

'Go on,' he murmured, then watched until the dress fell open. He made no comment that she was totally naked underneath, just appraised the white body. It was remarkably slim for a woman her age. Her breasts now with a slightly pendular droop, but the nipples dark and alive, the swell of her belly, the thickening at the hips. The dusky thatch. Hyacinths, he thought, he could smell a faint scent of hyacinths.

'Bill—' she said. Suddenly she felt foolish, standing naked before him, uncertain what to do.

He raised his arm and took her hand, drawing her gently towards the bed.

The Chinese Government delegation walked on to the television screen. 'The walking suits', she called them, the sombre home-made suits seeming to glide on castors, some mechanical contraption bringing their hands together, fingers of the left playing a three-beat tattoo on the palm of the right. That weird Chinese custom of clapping yourself as they turned towards the camera, unaccustomed awkward smiles on the plastic faces of emotionless androids.

The mouth of the President split stiffly open like a ventriloquist's dummy and a strangulated, low-key babble of Mandarin tumbled out. The final welcoming address.

Dawson grinned as Iona snuggled her head contentedly against his chest. 'It's bizarre this,' she said. 'Us lying here in bed, planning how to kill them.'

He kissed her forehead where a comma of hair was plastered damply. His lips tasted of salt. 'Ssh.'

She nodded, lowering her voice. 'We'll need knowledge of their travel arrangements when they attend the airport opening. An insider.' Her mind was drifting back, now recharged and revitalised. 'If only I had someone.'

After a moment's contemplation, Dawson said: 'Maybe I can help there.'

'Really?'

'I'll tell you later.'

She looked up into the eyes that had fascinated her for so long. 'We would have made a great team, Bill.'

'We *are* a great team.'

Three

The offices of ExecFlight were in an unimposing two-storey concrete block set within a dusty wire-fenced compound in a rundown eastern sector of Beijing.

A large red flag hanging limply from a pole on the roof provided the only splash of colour, along with two smaller flags – the Stars and Stripes and, diplomatically, the newly designed emblem of Hong Kong. The building's very anonymity was its only obvious security feature along with the coils of razor wire that topped the perimeter fence. But at night steel shutters could be rolled down over every window, the front door was triple-locked and every room had been alarm-wired by an expert from the US Embassy. There was a nightwatchman on the gate and an amenable Rottweiler who was temperamentally unsuitable for his job as guard dog. The greatest danger any intruder would face would be that of being licked to death.

As John Dancer's airport taxi pulled up outside, he wasn't quite sure what to expect. Xin-Bin's radio message to the executive jet during the return flight from Macao had been garbled and barely coherent. One thing was certain, there had been a break-in at the office. Exactly how serious it was had been impossible to determine. That it had happened at all had deeply perturbed the imperturbable Xin-Bin.

Dancer found his flight co-ordinator and right-hand man standing in the compound puffing on a *Badaling* cigarette in an agitated manner, as he talked to Abe Stone. At their feet was the dead Rottweiler.

Dancer motioned them to join him outside the compound on the empty street corner where they could not be the target of any planted electronic bug.

'What happened?' he asked, dropping his travel grip to the ground.

Stone dispensed with any greeting. 'Well, Running Dog won't be doing any more running, that's for sure.'

Xin-Bin looked embarrassed as though the whole thing was his fault; he had been in charge. 'He was poisoned, we think. Very quick.'

'Strychnine, I reckon,' Stone added.

'When did this happen?'

'Sometime last night.'

Dancer glanced back into the compound, trying to make some sense of it. 'What about the watchman?'

'He is gone,' Xin-Bin replied miserably. 'He is not here when I come this morning. I go to his home. No one sees him.'

'But he's been with us for five years,' Dancer recalled aloud.

'Well, the old boy isn't with us now,' Stone said. 'Lives in a rented room. When Xin-Bin visited, his few clothes and possessions were gone. His neighbours knew nothing or weren't saying.'

Dancer turned to his flight coordinator. 'But he was here when you locked up last night?'

'Sure, boss.'

'So he's our prime suspect,' Stone pointed out unnecessarily.

'He didn't have keys,' Dancer said. 'So it must have been forced entry.'

'That is funny thing, boss,' Xin-Bin said. He looked sheepish, fully aware that only he and Dancer held keys. 'The door is opened, not forced. Maybe these criminals have – er, what you call? – skeleton keys. They take cash box and document files.'

'Did they manage to get upstairs?' He meant the second floor which was guarded by a steel security door with a coded keypad.

Xin-Bin shook his head.

'Maybe they panicked when the police arrived. Did the alarm go off?'

Stone gave a guffaw of disgust. 'Oh, the alarm went off all right, John. Direct line to the local cop shop. One of their cars turns up an hour later. They frowned a lot and muttered about capitalism encouraging criminals and did fuck all else. Made a few notes, but they clearly weren't interested.'

'I'd better take a look round,' Dancer said and Xin-Bin nodded, starting to walk towards the building.

'Fine, I've got to be getting back,' Stone replied, then restraining his partner by the arm, he lowered his voice. 'Something like this was begging to happen, John. You're too trusting, especially with Xin-Bin. He's got the only keys and he's Wang's brother, the same blood.'

Dancer hid his irritation. 'Xin-Bin's a partner, Abe. He doesn't have to break in. He works here.'

'Then it'll be Wang. Probably doesn't trust his own brother, probably suspects he's not getting his fair cut. Or else he was trying to dig some dirt on you.'

'Why, for God's sake?'

The big man shrugged. 'Maybe he wants to take over the business, I don't know. You know how these Chinese minds work.'

Dancer gave his partner a reassuring pat on the arm and a disarming smile. 'I know how *your* mind works, Abe, it's all part of your charm.'

Stone grunted. 'Well, don't say I didn't warn you. See you later.'

As the Kansas bison shambled across to his parked automobile, Dancer beckoned Xin-Bin to rejoin him outside the compound. When he arrived, Dancer asked, 'So?'

'It must be Bureau.'

'That's exactly what I was thinking. The Bureau or the Ministry of State Security. Which documents were taken?'

'Only the client lists.'

Dancer thought for a moment. There was nothing incriminating there; in fact if Chicom officials had asked, he'd have been happy to pass them across. 'What about the computers? Did they mess with them?'

'Someone tried,' Xin-Bin confirmed, 'but without passwords they not get in. At least not easily. Maybe they make disk copies for government laboratory. Their computer experts . . .'

'Sure,' Dancer interrupted, lighting a Camel to aid his concentration, 'but even if they do, data on individuals is well dispersed.'

Xin-Bin nodded, smiling suddenly at the realisation that the world was not about to collapse on their collective heads after all. 'Nothing to connect anyone, boss,' he agreed.

Dancer knew it wasn't that simple. Even without names, Ministry experts might be able to match his anonymous personality files with names on the clients lists if there were enough clues. They might even latch on to the open code that referred to clients as 'smokers' – 'heavy' or 'light' – if they were Chicom supporters. Those privately judged to be pro-democracy and free trade were described as liking 'beer', 'rice wine' or 'spirits', depending on the strength of their views. Its in-built security was good, although not infallible. But then what was? With so many Chinese contacts needing to be identified as potential allies or enemies, the use of a database was essential. At least nothing was ever entered on his key agents like 'Hunan'. Not even Xin-Bin knew about them.

'There could be another reason for the visit,' he said. 'Bugs.'

The man nodded. 'Yes, I organise an electronic sweep first thing this morning. Nothing shows up.'

'Well, that's something.' He smiled, feeling considerably more relieved, and turned back into the compound. 'Now, let's get to my office and I'll bring you up to date.'

There were some twenty staff working at ExecFlight,

split roughly fifty–fifty between the sexes and nationality, half being national Chinese and half American or American-Chinese. Most had airline or travel industry experience and worked on the lower floor. The upper floor was the reserve of Dancer and five Americans, two of whom had overseas Chinese parents. All spoke fluent Mandarin and Cantonese and had been individually selected by the Central Intelligence Agency.

Dancer gave a wave of greeting as he passed their desks to reach his office where he closed the door, opened a window and switched on his desk fan. His aversion to paperwork showed on the clutter-free desk in oiled teak with its empty out-tray and near-empty in-tray. Xin-Bin would have dealt with everything that didn't require his personal attention or his signature.

The only other items on the desktop were a cut-glass ashtray and a leather blotter pad which had been a present from Debs whose photograph smiled across at him from the bookshelves on one wall.

'Five names of interest,' he said as he settled in his swivel chair and passed the slip of paper across. 'Three were passengers on our flights. The other two I met in Macao. All cadre, except the last who's a bit of a wheeler-dealer from Wuhan. Get the guys to run the usual computer checks and do some digging. You'll get the audio and video tapes from the aircraft later.' It was all routine stuff, his special staff would phone the recent passengers on some pretext or other, asking if they knew about ExecFlight's luxury gifts for frequent flyers or offering some special travel package or some form of market research. They all had an excellent and relaxed telephone manner, all adept at luring the most reticent Chinese into conversation. The promise of something for nothing was the usual hook.

With a few simple facts gleaned, it was then on to various computer databases to unearth more facts and figures before arranging for them to meet Dancer or Xin-Bin again. If they had no immediate travel arrangements in hand, some sort of exploratory business meeting would be set up or else they'd be invited to one of the company's quarterly drinks parties for special 'customers'.

'There's something else,' Dancer added. 'I had an inquiry in Macao. Not really our line, but you never know. A joint venture perhaps. A businessman who's interested in setting up a network of river ferries for cars. It would be a big order to have them built, so he'd want a good price.'

Xin-Bin frowned. 'Shipbuilders?'

Dancer smiled, waving his cigarette. 'Little ships, specialist stuff. Companies that make landing craft for the PLA would be ideal. You know, shallow draught and hydraulic ramp, that sort of thing.'

'How urgent is it?'

'Well, he was talking to other people in Macao. I wouldn't want them to steal a march.'

'Okay,' Xin-Bin shrugged, clearly thinking this was an unnecessary diversion from their other activities. 'How many items, boats?'

Dancer plucked a figure from the hot, smoke-laden air. 'Twenty to start. Anything up to fifty eventually. Production to begin immediately or sooner.' He added with a grin, 'And a ten per cent cut for you.'

It was a bribe and Xin-Bin knew it, but it brought a smile to his face nonetheless. If the Americans failed to get rid of the Chicom regime, the money would be a welcome boost to his nest egg so he and his family could eventually emigrate to the United States.

As he reached the door, Dancer said: 'By the way, your brother was on the outward flight. Said he wanted me to join him for supper soon.'

'As his guest?'

'That was the idea.'

'No such thing as free supper, boss.'

'That's what I thought. Any ideas?'

'Maybe ten per cent not enough any more. Wang enjoys the good life. Has expensive tastes.'

Dancer wasn't surprised. 'It had to happen, I suppose.'

Then the door shut, leaving him alone with his thoughts. He must contact 'Hunan' through the dead drop. Set up the next meet. Arrange better and quicker communications as he'd discussed with Dawson in Macao. There was no time to lose.

His eyes idly crossed the room to meet Debs's immobile face staring back at him. Was it his imagination? Did the eyes look unusually serious, questioning?

What is it, John, what's wrong?

The shadows, Debs, he almost said. I can feel the shadows closing in.

Lily Cheung was half-way through tapping the assistant deputy director's report onto her PC when the intercom buzzed. Mildly irritated at the interruption, she flicked the switch. 'Mr Wang?'

As usual with Wang there were no pleasantries, no preamble. 'Is my report finished?'

She unhooked her spectacles from her small elfin ears. 'No, Mr Wang, you only gave it to me an hour before lunch. It is a *very* long report.'

Just in time she stopped herself from adding that, anyway, she was his personal assistant, not a pool secretary. By rights it was a job for one of them, but then as far as Wang was concerned no one had any rights except him.

His wheeze of impatience was clear over the intercom. 'Very well. Come in immediately, will you, and bring your dictation pad with you.'

'Yes, sir.' Lily flicked off the switch. Damn. And that crawling lizard Yan Tao was still with him. No doubt her boss would make a show of humiliating her in front of him. He seemed to relish that sort of thing; vaguely she wondered how Wang's wife endured life under such a tyrant. Like most wives in China, she guessed, she would just do as she was told without complaint. Despite an upsurge in the call for women's rights in recent times, it was difficult to change a culture that had existed for five thousand years.

She glanced in the dusty mirror above the unlit fireplace and quickly ran her hands over the straight black hair that hung to her shoulders on either side of an almond-shaped face. Wang insisted on impeccable smartness in his staff, especially the women. Should she reapply her lipstick? Hell, no, why should she? She bared her teeth at her own image, a snarl of anger at Wang, then giggled at the ferocity of her expression. What would her boss make of that? Momentarily light danced in those dark, sable-coloured eyes, a light that had been suppressed for so many years that others rarely saw it now. Her hands flew briefly to her slender hips, smoothing the material of the simple black flared skirt, before she picked up her pencil and pad and headed for the door.

The deputy assistant director's office was not in the main building of the Civil Aviation Administration of China on Xichang'an Jie, but a couple of blocks away in an unnamed annexe.

Once it had been an institute of something or other, the home of some élite Communist Party social scientists whose idealistic masterplan had faded and ultimately failed under the weight of reality and human nature. Now it was a remnant, a mausoleum of aesthetic Stalinist architecture, its severe puritanical grandeur cold and uninviting.

Wang had once confided in her that he liked it because it was away from his immediate superiors, but she wondered if he just enjoyed lording it in the austere surroundings of a faded people's palace.

As she approached the main staircase, her heels clattered on the dusty marbled floor, reverberating up the high walls to the vaulted ceiling with its cobwebbed chandeliers. As she climbed she was aware of the ornamental stone bas-relief panel above the varnished first-floor doors: heroic Chinese Communist peasants toiling on the land.

'Slaves to their own dogma,' she muttered under her

breath as she swung through the doors and into Wang's huge office.

In the former conference room, the gloom was relieved only by the tall narrow windows that allowed in thick bars of light which were blue with tobacco smoke and drifting particles of dust.

She felt his eyes on her as she approached, feeling insignificant and intimidated by the long walk that took her to the huge mahogany desk with its legs carved to look like roaring dragons. Averting her eyes, Wang's face became a pale blur at the periphery of her vision, yet she knew exactly what expression she would see on his face. She cursed her high heels for their seductive crack as they echoed on the mosaic tiles and wished that she could prevent her hips from swaying.

And Yan, how would he be looking? No doubt wearing the same impassive opera-mask face he always wore. Straight-lipped, and his eyes as emotionless and hard as ball-bearings glinting behind the steel-framed spectacles, his brushed-back quiff immaculate. The crawling lizard never changed, never would. How had she ever got it so wrong? In her mind's eye she could imagine the forked reptilian tongue darting out between the thin unsmiling lips.

Wang was a big man for a Chinese and gave the impression he had melted into his chair behind the desk and spilled over its arm rests. His mid-blue suit was very smart and cut to disguise his spreading gut. Whilst Politburo members looked as though their suits had been run up by their wives at home, Wang had always favoured the bespoke tailors of Shanghai.

His broad face wore the thin-lipped smirk he put on every morning before leaving home. Those who did not know him well remarked to Lily how lucky she was to work for such a congenial man. Clearly the thick bottleglass lenses of the tortoiseshell glasses prevented them from seeing there was no humour in the permanently laughing eyes.

'I am most disappointed in you, Lily. I had promised

Yan here a copy of the finished report.' He indicated the slim, solemn-faced man in his early thirties who stood rigidly beside the desk clutching an imitation leather document case.

Lily gave a small bow of acknowledgement in his direction, but avoided eye contact. 'I am sorry, sir. I worked all through my lunch break, but it is a long report.'

It was a stout defence; both Wang and Yan understood that lunch was sacrosanct to all Chinese people.

'Perhaps you should be sent for retraining,' Wang said softly. 'To improve your speed.'

She inclined her head with a shy smile and a small dimple formed beside her mouth. 'Perhaps, sir, if you had given it to me first thing this morning, it would be ready now. I saw it on your desk before you arrived.'

Wang's sallow complexion deepened to an orangey hue and his chin began to jut forward from his heavy jowls.

It was then that Yan intervened, speaking for the first time. 'Sir, it really is of no consequence. We at the Information Office are not in urgent need of it.'

This time Wang's anger was directed towards the young press secretary. 'I decide what is of consequence here at the Administration. A promise is a promise and my promise to you has been broken.'

Yan hesitated. Lily allowed her eyes to settle on him for the first time, not quite believing what she had just heard. Was the crawling lizard actually coming to her defence? She studied the stern, gaunt lines of the young *apparatchik*, seeking some humanity in the man who had once been a fellow student and who had once been a friend – who had always been serious but who would sometimes laugh and share a joke. But that had been a long time ago before he had become a crawling lizard.

Light from the window gathered on one side of his face, emphasising his hollow cheeks and the bluish hue of his chin, glinting on the lenses of his steel-edged spectacles so that his eyes were no longer visible.

He selected his words carefully. 'The Information Office would be pleased to accept your document first thing tomorrow, sir, if that is agreeable to you.'

Wang grunted and directed his gaze back to his PA. 'Well, Lily, can you finish it this afternoon?'

She hesitated, visualising the mountain of papers. 'I have to collect my son from school at five. It will be tight.'

'Ah, yes, your son.' He said it slowly, as though the words had deep significance. 'Some children are always a problem.' His sentence hung as though not quite finished. 'Is there not someone—?'

Lily sighed and nodded. 'Yes, of course. My mother. But we are not on the telephone.'

Yan coughed lightly. 'I am leaving the office early and go past the door. I can give her a message.'

'There you are!' Wang said, suddenly in a jovial mood as though some switch had been thrown.

Lily averted her eyes as Yan Tao looked in her direction and she gave a small nod of acknowledgement. '*Xièxie.*' It was hardly audible to the press secretary as it stuck in her throat to thank a crawling lizard.

'Your effort to make amends for your inefficiency is appreciated,' Wang said. 'When you are finished it will be late, and no doubt, having missed lunch, you will be hungry, Miss Cheung. As a gesture of my appreciation you will join me for a business supper.'

A frown fractured the porcelain-smooth surface of her brow. 'But, sir, I cannot.'

Heavy brows lifted like drawbridges above the tortoise-shell glasses. 'Oh, you can and you will, Miss Cheung. I have been looking at your file from Personnel and I see that you have a very unpatriotic history. Now I find that you are proving technically incompetent for the position you hold. If you wish me to allow you another chance, then at the very least you can indulge me by taking notes over a business supper.'

Lily felt like a trapped animal; she would be damned if

84

she did and damned if she didn't. She glanced across at Yan, hoping vainly for some measure of support. But this wasn't his province. He was Public Information Office and Wang was assistant deputy director of the CAAC. His mouth was firmly shut and his eyes hidden by the reflective sheen of his glasses.

She swallowed, her pride choking like a lump in her throat. 'There is someone else at this supper?'

Wang's laugh was deep and frothy. 'Of course, you don't think I want you as a concubine, do you?'

Even to joke about such a thing was deeply insulting to a Chinese woman, but her boss knew when he held all the aces. 'I think you've seen the American here at the office.'

'Yes?'

'Mr Dancer. A business associate of mine.'

There was an instant snapshot in her brain. One morning quite recently. Taking the shortcut to school across the park. Little Bao tugging at her skirt, pointing at the *t'ai chi* class. The fair-haired American with the deep-blue eyes.

John Dancer was not surprised at Wang's choice of restaurant. It was expensive. And, although he was ostensibly the guest of the assistant deputy director, he had no doubt that he would end up picking up the tab himself. Wang was a past master at such manoeuvrings.

He paid off the dilapidated taxi outside the Rising Moon restaurant in one of Beijing's more expensive residential suburbs. Pausing to light a cigarette, he took in the freshly painted rough stucco wall, the brass-framed menu and candy-striped awnings. It reeked class and high prices, although that wouldn't necessarily mean good service. But *why* had Wang chosen it? Normally he enjoyed seeing and being seen by his cadre chums in the exclusive central restaurants; this was a little tucked away for Wang's usual liking.

The answer became apparent when he found the man seated at a table in a secluded candlelit alcove. At his side was the most delightful-looking creature he could imagine. Her glossy black hair was drawn back off an expressive, delicately boned face into a soft bundle at the back of her head, held in place by a blue ribbon and decorated with a flower bloom. Late twenties, he guessed, her body obviously still youthful beneath the sheath of embroidered turquoise satin with its demure mandarin collar.

Wang's large hand covered hers on the starched white tablecloth. As the woman's eyes flickered briefly at seeing Dancer approach, the man noticed too and withdrew his hand. He rose to his feet, a mountain of wasted sartorial elegance that hid his female companion from sight.

'Mr Dancer, my old friend.' The fat smug smile appeared genuine as he greeted him in English.

'Mr Wang,' Dancer replied in English, accepting the outstretched hand. 'I am most honoured to be invited.'

'Bah!' Wang chortled dismissively. The sheen of perspiration on his face suggested he was well into his first bottle of *mao-tai* firewater. 'Let us not stand on formality! We know each other for a long time now. And I think maybe you meet my personal assistant at the office. Lily, this is Mr Dancer. Mr Dancer, this is Cheung Mei-ling, or, as we English speakers know her, Miss Lily Cheung.'

Her offered hand was cool and seemingly weightless in his own. Despite her frank, steady gaze, he noticed that she was blushing furiously. In that brief moment he was aware of certain striking features: the sad expression in her eyes set off by long curling lashes, the whiteness of the shy smile and her slender swan-like neck.

He was momentarily distracted, almost forgetting to speak as he habitually unscrambled her name. Given name Mei-ling meaning 'beautiful intelligence' and, not so usual for a mainland Chinese, an adopted Western name of Lily. 'My pleasure, Miss Cheung. I do indeed recall we met briefly in the corridor at your office – about a month ago?'

Her eyes widened a fraction in surprise, perhaps even flattered that he remembered. 'I believe so.'

Wang quickly inserted himself into the brief silence between them. 'Sit, sit, Mr Dancer. Over *there* if you please.'

The American took the chair, quickly aware that Wang had noted and hadn't liked the brief exchange between his two table companions. He was keeping Dancer at arm's length and Lily Cheung by his side. 'Lily is a rising star in the department, John. Let me call you John.' Dancer nodded. 'And you call me Hu, like old friends. You will notice how Lily speaks good English, no? A very smart lady. University graduate. She is good to me.' He leaned forward, winking behind the heavy spectacles. 'Looks after my *every* need – just like a personal assistant should. Isn't that right, John?'

Lily's eyes and mouth were downcast, her skin almost glowing with the rush of embarrassment. 'I'm sure,' Dancer murmured noncommittally.

Wang's arm was instantly around her shoulders in a consoling hug. 'Now, now, Lily, don't be shy. You should be proud your boss is so pleased with you. It's the way to get on in life, isn't it, John?' He looked to Dancer for confirmation, and when he didn't get it, continued: 'Be good to your boss and your boss will be good to you. See, after your hard work today, this is your reward. So let me see a little smile, eh?'

Her lips fluttered in a brief attempt to oblige before Dancer plucked the menu from the table and changed the subject. 'I really am famished, Hu, shall we make our choice?'

Relief showed clearly on her face as Wang moved on to the next most important interest in his life after money and women. Food. Like most Chinese he didn't eat to live, but lived to eat and then some. As usual he went for a banquet that even the three of them would have no hope of demolishing. Wang was heavily into tangy, peppery Sichuan cuisine, ordering dishes with gay abandon.

Dancer settled in to enjoy the meal as best he could. He knew the form. They would pick at different dishes, Wang insisting on Lily sampling titbits offered with his chopsticks, which was clearly making her squirm with silent embarrassment. He was never happier than when stray juice trickled down her chin and he could use his forefinger to wipe it off and then lick it away with his tongue. The enforced seduction technique was as crass as it was gross, but it was pure Wang.

They would all discuss each dish like gourmets and recall appropriate anecdotes and swap recipes like old women, leaving the business side of things for later. That suited Dancer who would pace his drinking while Wang raced for the finishing post – it was always debatable whether or not he'd remember why he wanted to meet in the first place.

'The reason for endangered species of animal in China is usually very simple,' Wang opined with a mouthful of stewed turtle. 'They tasted good.'

When the plates were finally cleared and bowls of fruit placed, Wang was obviously more interested in sweet-talking Lily Cheung than he was in discussing business with Dancer. As he watched the girl recoil while trying not to give offence, he wondered how he might come to her rescue. Then he remembered the gift.

'My dear Hu,' he said suddenly, fishing in his jacket pocket. 'I almost forgot. When you travelled with ExecFlight to Macao, you won a special bonus.'

Wang blinked, trying to concentrate. 'Yes?'

Dancer plucked the idea from the air. 'The two hundredth passenger on our new Challenger 601.' He slid the smart leather presentation case across the table. Wang fumbled with the tiny clasp. Momentarily Lily's eyes met Dancer's and held them with a slightly quizzical look, sensing something. The American said: 'A his and hers fountain-pen set, Hu, for you and your dear wife. Very exclusive. Mother-of-pearl finish. By the way, how is Mrs Wang?'

The assistant deputy suddenly looked as though he'd swallowed too much Sichuan chilli. His face reddened as he clamped shut the case with a loud snap. 'She is fine, Mr Dancer, thank you!'

At that moment Dancer noticed the light of laughter behind Lily's eyes as she struggled to prevent a smile, just a dimple deepening at the corner of her mouth.

'Waiter!' the American called. 'A bottle of your finest cognac to celebrate my client's good fortune!'

Wang blinked and his irritation evaporated quickly at the prospect of such a prestigious end to the meal. His eyes were slightly unfocused by the time the first glasses were poured. He even accepted Dancer's toast 'To Mr and Mrs Wang's future happiness together!' with a limp smile. For the moment at least, his amorous advance on Lily Cheung had been halted; it was no longer appropriate to attempt a drunken fondle.

'It's getting late, Hu,' Dancer said, steering the man's attention in a different direction. 'We are enjoying ourselves so much we will forget all about business. What did you want to discuss?'

Wang looked momentarily bewildered, as though someone had hit him over the head. 'Oh, er, yes, of course.'

'You want me to keep notes, sir?' Lily asked quickly.

The assistant deputy shook his head irritably. 'No, no that won't be necessary.' He tried to concentrate and refilled his glass, spilling half in his fumbled attempt. 'Old friend, Mr Dancer. John! How long is it we have been partners?'

Dancer smiled. 'Nearly seven long and happy years, Hu.' He raised his glass, turning it into a toast.

Wang drank and dribbled. 'And as a partner I have a percentage of the gross profits.'

'You do indeed, Hu, as my accountants are always pointing out. To our continued mutual profits!' Another toast.

'Ah, but John, old friend. What is that percentage?'

'Twelve and a half per cent.'

'Exactly, and I ask myself recently, is that fair?'

Dancer played along. 'You would like to reduce it? What, to maybe ten?'

Wang wasn't *that* drunk. 'Reduce! You joke with me! Am I not an equal partner?'

'No, Hu, you are a sleeping partner. I put all the money in and, when we set up, you gave generously of your expertise on China.'

The assistant deputy considered that. 'Yes, I did, didn't I? Very generously.' He could see a link there somewhere, but it took a moment for his befuddled brain to find it. 'Er – and maybe twelve and a half per cent isn't such a generous return after seven profitable years.'

Dancer smiled gently. 'It's what we agreed.'

'Ah, but times change, old friend.' He studied his glass as he nursed it between the fat palms of his hands. 'The airline business becomes more commercial, more competitive. There are new friends on the scene who may return to become old friends like you, John, if they are given the right encouragement. '

Lily was watching Dancer closely, her face deadpan but her eyes filled with curiosity. He felt he could read so much into those eyes. They were incredibly expressive, he thought – just a change of light, a sudden sparkle, a fractional lowering of the lids or a slight dilation of the pupils. Having barely exchanged a word, he was sure he knew how she thought about so many things.

His gaze darted sideways to the cognac bottle and he gave an almost imperceptible nod of his head. He was drawing her into a silent conspiracy and they both knew it. Knew they liked each other, knew he was trying to rescue her.

'More cognac, sir?' she piped up chirpily. Wang didn't object.

'So I've got competition, have I?' Dancer asked. 'Also seeking your generous advice?'

'Quite so.' Wang hesitated, losing his thread of thought again. 'The internal airline business is booming. I have

British, Germans, Japanese all knocking on my door. Some offering me a twenty per cent partnership.'

Inwardly Dancer winced. Twenty per cent of gross would be crippling. 'Maybe we should review the situation, Hu. Yes, times change. Maybe to fifteen per cent.'

Wang became momentarily more animated. 'Indeed.'

'Of net.'

He frowned and leaned back in his chair, such mental calculations now far beyond his capabilities. 'Fifteen,' he murmured.

'You drive a hard bargain, Hu. A toast to the best negotiator in Beijing!'

Wang's head slumped forward, his treble chins concertinaed on his chest. Lily's eyes widened in dismay as she leaned anxiously towards him. 'He is dead!'

If only, Dancer thought. 'No, just sleepeth. It often ends like this. He'll be all right.' He looked at her and saw her radiant smile for the first time that evening. 'If you're here when he wakes up he may – er – want you to have a nightcap at his office.'

She frowned a furious little frown. 'Why do you think that, Mr Dancer?'

He smiled: 'Because you are very beautiful and Wang is an old rogue.'

'Old rogue,' she repeated, tilting her head to one side. She liked that.

'And he's done it before. Usually with Silver Bullets.'

Her hand flew to her mouth in horror as he used the old Maoist euphemism for prostitutes – on the basis that their trade of temptation could be used as ammunition against the Party's cadres. 'He thinks of me like that?'

'No,' Dancer assured kindly, 'I'm sure he respects you. But when he gets drunk he gets confused.'

She understood and smiled, embarrassed. 'Old rogue.'

Dancer called for the bill and asked the maître d' to have Wang put in a taxi, giving the man's home address.

'I'll get a separate taxi,' he told Lily. 'Allow me to drop you home on the way.'

'Thank you, Mr Dancer. But my boss—'

He laughed. 'He'll remember nothing in the morning, and if he does he'll only regret it.'

They watched until Wang had been lifted bodily into the cab, protesting and flapping his arms around like some beached fish, but he had no strength or inclination to keep it up. As the taxi drove away, Dancer took Lily's arm and began walking towards the nearest main road. The night was becoming warmer by the minute, storm clouds pushing down on the city. Thunder rumbled like distant surf along a beach.

'I see you the other day,' she ventured timidly. 'Actually my son points you out. In the park.'

'Ah, my *t'ai chi* class,' he said, pausing to light a cigarette. 'I'm not very good.'

'You looked all right to me. Moving like water, isn't it?' She gave a little laugh. 'But then I do not do *t'ai chi*.'

'How old is your son?'

'Little Bao? He is nine, nearly ten.'

'And Mr Cheung, does he work in Beijing?'

He detected a small gasp of hesitation as she looked away, as though searching for a taxi. 'There is no Mr Cheung.'

Oops, Dancer thought. He could almost feel the shutters coming down. 'I didn't mean to pry.'

She gave a little nod of the head. 'Yes. Mr Wang knows I have no husband. That is why he gives me a bad time.'

'Does he?'

'Today he gives me much work to do – work that is for secretaries, not PAs. As it is I do all the work that he himself should do.' Dancer could well believe that. 'When the job is not finished, he says I am no good. He will have me sent for re-education or allocated a job in a factory.'

Dancer smiled. 'There's a saying in the States. You don't throw snowballs at the girls you don't like.'

'Pardon me?'

'He seemed pleased enough with you tonight.'

She shook her head. 'I do not understand. He says he is angry that the work is late, then happy that I catch up. So he forces me to come tonight with threats about my job. It is a punishment for being bad and a reward for being good!'

'Wang likes to cover all the angles.'

'He tells me I am to take notes. But as you see, he did not mean it.'

Dancer hailed a taxi. 'Like I said, snowballs.'

She laughed shyly. 'Yes, I think I see.'

The taxi was a bad choice. Its floor was covered in cigarette butts and watermelon seeds and glazed with spittle. The driver had his seat jammed back and refused to budge despite Dancer's request. But Lily took it in her stride, sitting behind the driver sideways on the back squab with her knees folded up beneath her chin. Dancer tried to resist the natural temptation to glance at where her thighs melted into tantalising shadow.

He tried to open the window, but it was jammed shut; they were travelling in a mobile steam cooker.

He said: 'Lily's your adopted name? That's unusual for a Beijing girl.'

She regarded him carefully, as though weighing up how much she should say, how far she could trust him.

'It was when I was in the student movement at university. We heard Chinese people adopt Western names in Hong Kong, Singapore and Malaysia and thought it was a smart idea. Very cosmic-politano – is that right?'

'Cosmopolitan,' Dancer helped out.

'Ah, yes, it was a trendy thing to do.'

'Why Lily?'

She blushed prettily. 'I want to be called Jo for Joanna – like the actress in the *New Avengers* TV films I see. A tough, brainy cookie. But there is this boy who likes me, always asking me to go out with him. He says I have the beauty and fragrance of a lily flower, and calls me Lily. He tells everyone this, and the name sticks. It was all very embarrassing to me.'

Dancer smiled. 'It could have been worse; he could have called you Lotus Blossom.'

She frowned very seriously. 'Is that a joke?'

'Sort of. I'm afraid I must agree with your admirer. Lily suits you very much.'

It had started to rain, heavy drops splattering on the windshield. The erratic wipers smeared the myriad squashed insects gathered there into a thick gooey film that obliterated visibility. Although the washers didn't work, it didn't deter the driver from racing through the ill-lit streets. Then Dancer became aware of the flashing light behind them and the wail of a siren.

Seconds later the police car was overtaking them and cutting across the front of the taxi. The driver stamped on his brakes. There was a thud of worn pad rivets scoring on drums as he went into a squealing skid. They jolted to a halt within millimetres of the police car's rear fender.

'Lizard's spittle!' cursed the taxi driver.

Now the two cops, dressed in summer khaki uniforms and peaked caps were out of their vehicle. Their faces looked pale and mean in the downpour. One argued briefly with the taxi driver before reaching into the window and snatching away the ignition key. The other jerked open the rear passenger door and shrieked at Dancer to get out. 'Come on, come on,' he jabbered. 'And the woman too!'

Dancer hunched in the teeming rain, thankful for the protection of the fedora as he took Lily's hand as she struggled to manoeuvre herself across the seat. The policeman yelled and brusquely broke their grip. 'Don't touch the Chinese woman! You'll only make your position worse!'

'What position?' Dancer replied in perfect Mandarin. That surprised the officer for a moment before he declined to answer with a twitch of his head and grabbed Lily's wrist himself.

'Leave me alone, you pig!' she protested.

'Shut up, woman, and show me your identity card.' As she fumbled in her bag, the rain dismantling her hair so that it started to hang wetly over her face, the policeman turned to Dancer. 'You are American, yes? Where is your passport?'

Despite the rain, a crowd was starting to gather, standing in the steaming humidity, fascinated by the drama being played out in the rain-streaked beams of car headlamps. Another police car pulled up, and more officers climbed out. These were in plain clothes, all wearing raincoats over remarkably similar, stiffly cut dark polyester suits.

Dancer looked around for Lily, realising suddenly that she had been deliberately separated from him. He squinted through the torrential downpour towards the first car. A policeman was screeching at her, the angry veins stretched taut in his neck and rainwater dripping from the peak of his cap. Her mascara was running and she was crying, her dress now a sodden second skin, her body heat causing vapour to rise into the hot wet night.

The passport was snatched from Dancer's hand and given a cursory examination. 'American national, yes? You stay here many years?'

'Yes.' But Dancer wasn't listening; he was watching as Lily Cheung was roughly manhandled into the first police car.

'Then you know it is an offence to insult Chinese women!' the policeman declared.

Dancer was well aware of the xenophobic Beijing idiom for having casual relations. It was why few Westerners risked inviting ethnic girls, even professional hookers, to their hotel rooms. There was always a Bureau informer around to tip them off. Despite that, a few relationships had blossomed, only to be crushed when the newly wed brides were refused permission to join their foreign husbands abroad.

'Don't be preposterous,' Dancer replied evenly. '*Where* am I supposed to have insulted her?'

The policeman jabbed a finger at the offending taxi. 'There. I even see the whore's legs up on the seat. It is obvious.'

'Her legs were up because there was no room,' Dancer said, restraining his growing temper. 'Ask the driver.'

Not such a good idea, he suddenly realised. Years of Chinese history and culture, reinforced by the Maoist years, had taught the Chinese to look after number one. If the taxi driver thought it would help him to back the Bureau's version of events, he would.

But before the policeman could respond, four plain-clothes men from the second car intervened. As they approached, Dancer thought he recognised the one who hung a little back from the group. The man had entered the Rising Moon restaurant a little after he himself had arrived and had dined alone.

The group leader wore a grey mackintosh and a trilby hat, the crown of which barely came to Dancer's chin. As he looked up, his eyes remained within the shadow of the brim. With a cigarette glued to the corner of his mouth, he spoke in a voice so low that the American had to strain to catch the words above the hiss of the rain. 'Mr Dancer, I am placing you under arrest.'

'On what charge?'

'We will discuss that later. Insulting a Chinese woman who is a government official can be a serious offence. It can lead to other charges. . .' There was an air of menace in the way he let his whispered words float away half-finished.

'Have you anything to say before we go to the station?'

Dancer took a deep breath, remembered his *t'ai chi* and forced himself to calm down, to go with the flow. As Lily had said earlier, like water. 'You've been watching too many Bogart movies.'

'Boogey?'

'Nothing, forget it.'

He couldn't make out exactly where he was. Somewhere

within a sensitive Public Security Bureau complex within the high-walled Zhongnanhai compound.

From the car he was led by his four-man escort into a grimy sixties building of long corridors with bare concrete floors, nicotine-yellow walls and flickering fluorescent strips. They passed rows and rows of numbered grey doors, around bends, more corridors and down steps to a lower level. The air smelled faintly of cabbages and stale urine. An iron-barred door led into a holding area, cells on both sides of a short passage.

Dancer was pushed through one of the open steel doors. The unpainted concrete cell was barely nine feet square with no window, the light coming from a single fluorescent strip which blinked intermittently. A thin mattress had been laid alongside one wall beside a galvanised bucket. In the middle stood a small trestle table with a steel, plastic-seated stacking-chair on each side.

His arresting officer pointed to the first chair with its back to the door. 'Sit, please.'

He obliged, dumping his sodden fedora on the table top. As the officer removed his grey raincoat, but incongruously still wearing his trilby, sat opposite, Dancer noticed the mirror on the wall facing him. It had a pretty obvious function as there was no need for a mirror in an interrogation cell. He wondered vaguely who was sitting on the other side.

'First, you empty your pockets,' said the policeman.

Dancer smiled. 'No, first you tell me who you are.'

The trilby tilted upward a fraction and for the first time he saw the little raisin eyes drilling into him. A brief, hostile pause, then came a low, tobacco-coarsened whisper.

'I am Inspector Xia, Public Security Bureau, Foreigners' Section. Now, empty your pockets.'

There wasn't much. Some loose *yuan* coins, a wallet with notes and credit cards, a pack of Camel, a Zippo, a handkerchief, a couple of taxi receipts and a bunch of keys. Then, on Xia's instruction, his father's old Rolex watch was added to the pile.

Without a word a second plain-clothes officer, clearly also wearing a suit from Inspector Xia's inadequate tailor, noted each item on a pad before dropping it into a polythene bag.

'Can I keep the cigarettes?'

Xia's eyes narrowed. 'Smoking is bad for you. This is a good chance to give it up.'

Dancer noticed that the policeman's own cigarette was still firmly affixed to the corner of his mouth. 'Ever thought of following your own advice, Inspector?'

'I am not the prisoner,' he replied pointedly.

'So what am I charged with?'

'That will depend.' He shoved the list of possessions across the table. 'Sign your receipt.'

Dancer saw no point in objecting. 'Depend on what?' he asked as he scribbled.

Xia waited until the other policeman took the bag and left the two of them alone in the room. 'It depends on the answers to my questions.'

'Okay, try me.'

The inspector took his time, lighting a new cigarette from the butt of the old before stubbing it into a tin lid on the table. 'Who is that Chinese woman you were with?'

'You know who she is. Miss Cheung Lily Mei-ling.'

'A silver bullet? A whore?'

Dancer was unmoved. 'She is the personal assistant of my business partner, Mr Wang Hu, who is the assistant deputy of the Civil Aviation Administration. We'd all just had supper together, but then you know that already, don't you?'

That low growl again. 'You don't know *what* I know, Mr Dancer.'

'I know one of your officers followed me to the Rising Moon restaurant and sat there stuffing his face at the Bureau's expense.'

Xia ignored that. 'So why are you in a taxi with Miss Cheung?'

Again Dancer found himself talking to the hat brim. 'I was dropping her off at her home on my way to mine.'

'You are taking her to your home to insult her,' he hissed accusingly.

The American was growing tired of this. 'To have *sex* with her, you mean? Copulation! Intercourse! Screw her! Now who's insulting the lady?'

His eyes appeared again momentarily behind the uplifted trilby. 'Using filthy American expressions like that just compounds the insult, Mr Dancer.'

'According to you, Inspector, I was taking her to *my home* to insult her. Therefore I was guilty of nothing.'

'So you admit it was your *intention* to insult her.'

'I admit no such thing.'

'Then how do we know you haven't already insulted her in the car and were planning to insult her again at your home?'

'You don't,' Dancer snapped back. 'But your arresting officers will confirm that the lady was wearing her underwear when we were stopped, so it's not very likely, is it?'

There was a brief silence while tobacco smoke billowed out from beneath the trilby. 'There are other insults. The taxi driver says you were – fondling her person.'

'Then he's a liar.' Dancer leaned across the table and peered under the brim until he could hold Xia's gaze. 'I've had enough of this stupidity. I'm answering no more questions until you contact the American Embassy and I have their legal representative present here. Alternatively you can contact Mr Wang Hu of the CAAC, who will confirm everything I have told you. Right, Inspector, that's *it*!' He leaned back in his chair and folded his arms.

Xia had lost face and considered his reaction for several moments before standing up. 'You will stay here until we complete our inquiries, Mr Dancer. Do make use of the bed, it'll be some time.'

Dancer did not respond, but sat with arms still folded,

staring defiantly at the mirror. Only when the door slammed and the bolts grated home, did he turn around.

Shit, he thought, just what game are they playing at? They knew who he was, who Lily Cheung was, so what was the point of putting on the frighteners? Because that was what it seemed. But for what purpose?

He stood up and stretched his legs. The cell was airless, his clothes were damp and there was no light switch on the inside. He took a long deep breath.

Be calm, be like the river, be like the wind, go with the flow. He dropped down on to the straw-filled mattress, stretched out and closed his eyes. Many years ago in Viet Nam he'd learned the soldier's art of catnapping. Fear didn't need to keep you awake because the body knows that the easiest place to escape fear is in your dreams.

His head hardly seemed to have hit the mattress when he heard the noise of the cell door opening. However, he knew he'd been asleep some time because in his first seconds of wakening he could still remember elements of the long dream. Of being naked in a vast flat terrain scattered with small boulders. Behind him was a slimy-scaled dragon, its breath scorching the skin on his back. Before him, dotted across the landscape like chess pieces were hundreds of men standing stationary. Each wore a grey mackintosh and a trilby hat.

'My dear Mr Dancer.'

He cranked open one eye and lifted himself on to one elbow. 'Yes?'

It was not Inspector Xia. The newcomer was a much taller, slimmer figure in an expensively cut mohair suit. 'There appears to have been an error.'

'You can say that again,' Dancer mumbled, rubbing his eyes with the back of his hands. 'And who are you?'

'I am Mr Ting.'

Dancer climbed unsteadily to his feet. Ting was clean-shaven with a fresh and youthful complexion that didn't really go with a face that belonged to a fit man in his early forties. The eyes were smiling kindly behind the gold-rimmed spectacles. Dancer said: 'I can't tell what time it is in here.'

'Of course.' Understanding, his English perfect, with a slightly American East Coast accent. 'It is six o'clock in the morning. Early, I know, but given the choice of sleeping on or leaving, I imagined you'd rather leave.'

Before Dancer could answer, a uniformed Bureau officer came in carrying a tray with teapot, glasses and a small bowl of pork dumplings. He placed it on the table together with Dancer's polythene bag of belongings.

'Join me before you go, Mr Dancer.' The tone behind the invitation was firm. 'Is Jasmine tea all right?'

'Fine,' the American said, taking a seat.'

'Do check your belongings,' Mr Ting suggested as he poured some of the aromatic tea. 'All there?'

It was, except that only two Camel remained from the almost full pack; he lit one. 'So what was this all about?'

Ting smiled stiffly, a small gold glint showing at one side of his mouth. 'We have lost face and must apologise, Mr Dancer. Inspector Xia is old school, does not trust foreigners. I am afraid he acted a little overzealously.'

Dancer exhaled. 'And the lady, Miss Cheung?'

'She has been released without charge.'

'I'm pleased to hear it.' He swallowed some tea and tried one of the dumplings. Not bad. Casually he said: 'So why was I being followed, Mr Ting?'

The man seemed surprised. 'Were you?'

'I think you know that.'

Ting smiled gently. 'If you were, it was routine. The PSB in Beijing is very old-fashioned, but they did act within the law, Mr Dancer. Perhaps you should remember that.'

'Meaning?'

'Had you insulted a female employee of a government organisation, which, of course, you had not, then it could be construed as an act against the state.'

Dancer raised one eyebrow.

Ting added: 'Inspector Xia thought you might be a spy.'

He left it just like that, without clarification. The American had the feeling his reaction was under close, if casual, scrutiny.

'Me?' he said. 'I'm in partnership with Wang Hu.'

'Silly, I know. The inspector had it in his head that you were seducing Miss Cheung to get information about state apparatus.'

'Very silly,' Dancer replied.

'However,' Ting added softly, 'it may be best that you are not seen alone in her company again. Next time I may not be able to intervene on your behalf.' He dabbed his mouth with a paper napkin. 'Enjoy your breakfast, Mr Dancer.'

But before the American could respond, Ting was on his feet and moving deftly towards the door. Dancer's question, 'Just who are you, Mr Ting?' was left trailing in his wake.

Ten minutes later Dancer was standing on the cracked pavement outside the Zhongnanhai compound. Above, a sky of hazy cloud was pressing down and in the distance he heard a low dog's growl of thunder. It was still relatively cool, but he could already feel the humidity closing in.

He decided to walk back to his apartment, taking the opportunity to reflect on the recent flurry of Bureau activity taking an interest in him and other Stonedancer personnel. A couple of weeks earlier he'd mentioned it to Dawson who didn't appear concerned. Apparently increased counter-intelligence activity by the Chinese against 'foreign devils' had been reported by most Western agencies. Diplomats and businessmen alike had come under heightened scrutiny. It was difficult to know, Dawson said, whether it marked an overall shift of attitude or was just a response to nervousness over the Macao conference. The Chinese had become paranoid about security and in situations like that Chicom cadre mentality was that they should be seen to be doing something about it, regardless of whether the actions were relevant or not. Inspector Xia's action in arresting him the previous night was just another example. For the policeman's superior to have apologised suggested they really *did* recognise that they had gone too far this time.

By the time he reached the Hua Thai Apartment Hotel, Dancer had just about convinced himself that it was nothing to worry about. Easier said than done, when you had so much to hide.

As he left the elevator, he'd even found himself chuckling at the memory of Inspector Xia. He pulled out his key-bunch and weighed them in his palm as he approached the apartment door. Lily Cheung. Suddenly he saw her face in his mind's eye, her faltering smile as she stole a glance at him across the restaurant table . . .

The moment he had the key in the lock he knew that something was wrong. Debs's voice was excited in his ear, shrill, but he couldn't quite make out her words. It didn't matter though, because it was obvious soon enough. He'd had visitors.

Four

Iona felt a sick, sinking feeling in the pit of her stomach. 'Is Dancer sure?'

'Certain,' Dawson replied.

They were within the 'electronically secure bubble' in the basement of the US Embassy in Beijing. No outside walls. Double inner walls filled with white noise and lead-lined. It was one of a number of regular meetings that always occurred between British and American intelligence staff. But this one was different, special. Frank Aspen, Assistant Deputy Director of Operations, CIA had flown in on the trans-Pacific redeye.

'Was he compromised?' the man from Langley asked.

Dawson shook his head. 'He's been playing here for a long time, sir. He's gotten things pretty well buttoned. They'd have to be very, very good, and then be very, very lucky.'

'And he reckons that was why the PSB pulled him in?' Iona asked. 'To get his keys and to give them time for a good look.'

'And the woman, this Cheung Mei-ling from the CAAC?'

'She's nothing. Just served as the excuse.'

Iona sucked at her pencil tip; the Americans didn't allow smoking in the 'bubble', so she swapped nicotine for lead poisoning. 'And it was regular Bureau?'

'To arrest him, yes. Inspector Xia.'

'Ah, the poison dwarf, is he still around?'

'Then in the morning Dancer spoke to someone called Ting who said it was all a big mistake.' He glanced up. 'The man's not on my list.'

Iona studied her toothmarks on her pencil. 'Ting's a new

kid on the block, I think.' She glanced sideways at her assistant Suzy Tobin for confirmation. 'About a month ago?'

The long blonde army brat tapped into her laptop, then studied the screen. 'Yep, boss. From routine monitoring of official Chicom sources. A Brigadier Ting Han-chen transferred to the Ministry of State Security – status unknown – from the Beijing College of International Relations.' The establishment was widely known as the main espionage-training centre for MSS recruits.

'What did he do there?' Dawson asked.

'Lecturer on counter-intelligence,' Suzy replied breezily.

Dawson tried not to be distracted by those intense and intelligent powder-blue eyes, or the legs. 'So the Bureau was doing State Security's bidding when it pulled John in.'

'Almost certainly,' Iona replied, 'but there's no need for us to be alarmist. If Ting's a new broom, he'll want to impress – or maybe he's simply new-school efficient. The Stonedancer outfit has been around so long and is so well connected to Chicom circles that it's bound to be given the once-over.'

Dawson agreed. 'No need for us to read too much into it. Of course, it would be nice to know Ting's exact status and function. But my guess is all the security activity reported recently was nothing to do with Chinese nerves over the Macao conference after all. "Hunan"'s news about the Taiwan invasion explains the *real* reason. A doubling of counter-intelligence security would make sense, give all possibles the once-over.'

Aspen considered that for a moment. He liked to be in control and hated it when the tail tried to wag the dog. Aspen was a fiftysomething CIA bulldog who'd been chewing bones since the Bay of Pigs. He kept his spreading waistline in check with workouts and Diet Coke and his hair short as iron filings as though he expected to be called back into the field at any time.

'*If* "Hunan"'s right. The boys at the Navy Yard have

been going back over satellite pictures with a fine tooth-comb, but they're still drawing blanks.' He regarded Dawson with an expression that said he was barking up the wrong tree. 'Of course, they're monitoring the Amphibious Task Force at Shantou. There's been an increase in activity, but our assessment remains that the capability is vastly below what is required to take on Taiwan successfully.'

Dawson regarded his superior for a moment and hardly bothered to hide his disdain. Aspen was only five years younger, but they were generations apart. While the Beijing desk chief was an old hands-on campaigner, never happier than when in the field, Aspen was a greasy pole climber and always had been. Always wanting to be seen first into the office at headquarters in the morning and the last to leave. Obsessed with a clean records sheet which meant making sure others took all the risks. Being seen as a go-getter, which meant being first to adopt new ways, even if older ones were just as good or even better. That was the difference really; while Aspen was struggling to master Windows '99 – so no youngster would have the edge – Dawson would be happy playing with the abacus.

'Satellites are easily fooled, Frank,' Dawson drawled, 'if they don't know what they're looking for.'

Aspen wasn't sure which way his man in Beijing was coming from. 'Meaning?'

'Meaning we and the Brits fooled Nazi air recon before D-day. Building the landing craft in unusual places away from the usual naval facilities.'

'You think that's what the Chinese are doing?' Aspen obviously hadn't considered that himself.

'Sometimes Langley gets so wrapped up in its high technology, it can't see what's staring it in the face.' He said Langley, but both men knew he meant Aspen. 'Humint goes back to biblical times. Nothing to beat it.'

Aspen really wasn't in the mood to have his nose rubbed in it. Okay, so maybe sometimes he forgot just how effective human intelligence could be – the good old-fashioned spy in the enemy camp. But he certainly hadn't forgotten how dangerous and messy it could be too. 'So what have you got?'

'Dancer asked Xin-Bin to make enquiries on behalf of a client who wanted to set up a ferry business. A big order to be placed.'

Aspen still wasn't following. 'So?'

'Five shipyards have recent experience in landing-craft manufacture for the PLA Navy. Four jumped at the chance to tender for the contract.'

'And the other one?'

'They showed no interest at all. In fact they were almost annoyed at being approached.'

Aspen glanced towards the wall map of China. 'Whereabouts are they?'

'At Hangzhou, just south of Shanghai. Maybe you could get one of the birds to take a look.'

'I will,' Aspen replied. 'The Taiwanese haven't taken any persuading – they're paranoid about a Chinese invasion anyway. No, it's our own President who's the problem.'

'So he's been told,' Dawson murmured. 'And what was his reaction?'

'Like we expected. Disbelief. Terry Tan's assured him there's no way Beijing is contemplating such a move and the sun shines out Tan's ass. And State pretty much takes the same view. They want verification.'

'Christ, we're on a four-month rundown and the President wants verification.' Dawson shook his head in disgust. 'I'll send someone into the next Politburo session and steal their battle plans.'

Aspen smiled a thin humourless smile. 'Now that sort of humint really *would* help.'

'So is the President going to sanction any operations?'

A shake of the head. 'Not yet. Both he and the national security adviser were genuinely shocked at the extent of our contingency plans and suddenly alarmed at how keen the Brits are to run with it.'

Iona frowned. 'He couldn't veto the use of Project Deadwater, could he? That's critically important.'

'He can't do that,' Aspen confirmed. 'It's a joint British–US venture and the protocol signed allows both parties to use the hardware either jointly or independently. My reading of the present thinking is that he'd allow deployment of the US Navy crew, but will draw the line at putting US personnel ashore on sovereign foreign soil.'

Iona could scarcely believe what she was hearing. 'He'd risk that? US SEAL and British SBS teams have been working and training together for five years. You can't suddenly pull half of them off the mission.'

Aspen said: 'I'm afraid, Miss Moncrieff, that the President of the USA can do the fuck what he likes. Jeopardising the lives of fighting men is one thing, jeopardising the final glory days of a presidential career is quite another.'

Dawson was in no mood to dwell on the negative; it wasn't his style. 'Let's cross that bridge when we come to it. The point is nothing is going to happen until we've firmed up support from the People's Liberation Army.' He looked pointedly at Iona. 'Back in Macao you said you had something big brewing on that front. If it doesn't boil soon, it'll be too late.'

'It's boiled and simmering nicely, Bill.' She smiled coquettishly before turning to Suzy Tobin. 'When is Edwin's party?'

She didn't need to consult her diary. 'This coming Saturday.'

Dawson frowned. 'What party?'

'Edwin Prufrock's. Anyone who's anyone will be there.'

He saw the setup coming. 'I don't seem to have been invited.'

'Oh dear, Bill, seems you're not moving in the right social circles. Leave it to Suzy, I'm sure she can pull some strings.'

*

108

Dancer took a taxi to the Beijing International, an élite eighteen-hole golf course amid spectacular mountain scenery, some thirty-five kilometres to the north near the Ming Tombs in Changping District.

It was just gone nine when he arrived and the mist was clearing. The tree-studded links were almost deserted as the early players were just finishing their game before setting off to work. Only half a dozen people, retired or on vacation, lingered at the clubhouse.

He went to the check-in desk and spoke to the receptionist. 'Have you seen Wang Hu?'

The woman had watchful eyes and Dancer had long suspected her of being a Bureau informer. 'No, Mr Dancer. You meet him here?'

'I thought so. Looks like he's got the date wrong again.' Alibi established.

He looked around as three young Chinese executive types dressed in plaid trousers and polo shirts walked in off the patio that led to the fairway. They were engaged in heated debate as they passed.

'Yan Tao?'

One of the three, a thin man with an immobile, serious-looking expression on his face, turned. He wore steel-rimmed spectacles and his jet black hair in a sixties rock-star quiff. 'Mr Dancer.'

The American stepped towards him. 'Mr Yan, how good to see you, it has been a long time.'

They shook hands. 'Please call me Tao.'

'And how's your game, Tao?'

A flicker of irritation sufficed as a smile. 'Frustrating as always. Still a twenty handicap. We have just played nine holes.' He introduced his companions. 'These are office colleagues of mine from the Information Office.'

The two men nodded and gave polite little bows as Dancer said: 'Well, that's nine holes more than I'm going to play. My partner hasn't turned up.'

Yan seemed to have only three expressions: serious, very

serious, and extremely serious. Dancer tried to work out which one the media relations officer was wearing as he said: 'I am sorry to hear that. You must be very disappointed.'

'Devastated. The first time I get to play in months.'

One of Yan's office colleagues said: 'You play with your honourable Arnard Parmar friend; you're on holiday, we're not.' He laughed at his joke.

Dancer's eyes lit up. 'That would be nice. Would you?'

Yan shrugged. 'Yes, sure. I need the practice.'

When Yan Tao's colleagues had gone and they were alone, changing in the men's locker room, Dancer said: 'Your news has certainly shaken everyone up.'

Yan's eyes glinted like ball bearings behind his steel-rimmed spectacles. In a measured voice, he said: 'I thought it might. I am only sorry to be the bearer of such tidings.'

Another player came into the locker room. Dancer said: 'Let's get outside where we can talk.'

Their allocated caddy in her yellow shell-suit uniform was a chirpy girl from Changchun called Ning who wore her straw boater at a jaunty angle. She towed the double-bag trolley without complaint and discreetly kept her distance when her male clients were in conversation.

Dancer teed off first. Two hundred and fifty yards down the fairway. Not bad after a quarter-year lay-off. But Yan Tao was fifty yards better and hungry to win.

'Twenty handicap my ass, Tao.'

Yan let slip the faintest hint of a smile.

'How did you find out about it?' Dancer asked as they walked after the balls, Ning trailing behind.

'By accident. I was drafting public relations documents for some major economic and political events later this year which the Party is very excited about.'

Dancer frowned. 'Really? Would I have heard about this?'

'Certainly not.' Yan was adamant. 'To speak of it is enough to be shot for treason.'

'But you are going to tell me?'

For the second time Yan almost smiled, a thin bitter twist to his mouth. 'Because if it isn't stopped now, I fear that only all-out war will stop the Party from achieving its goal of world domination.'

'The PLA still has a long way to go to match the American military,' Dancer pointed out. 'Sheer size isn't everything.'

Yan shook his head. 'The military is only part of the picture, the main thrust is economic. That is what is coming. In four months the Politburo will announce the establishment of the Prosperity Union.'

'What's that?'

Yan's thin smile reappeared. 'That is exactly what I asked, of course. And I am told it will be the formation of the Chinese East Asian Prosperity Union. It will bring together the economic engines of East Asia and the Pacific Rim: Shanghai, Hong Kong, Singapore and Taipei. To overcome the recent recession, they will all pull in harmony on Beijing's track. And force rival Japan to deal with the Middle Kingdom.' He stopped walking as they reached Dancer's ball. 'I didn't understand. I queried Taipei. I said surely Taiwan will never co-operate. That's when I was told Taiwan will have no choice. It will have been invaded twenty-four hours earlier.'

Dancer lined up his club, swung long and easy and watched the ball gather height. 'Well, thanks to you, Tao, that may not happen.'

They walked on. '*May* not?'

'It depends on so many things, so many people. The agent networks, supporters in the military and government. And the leadership – we have to be able to take it out at a stroke.'

Yan stopped, his golf ball at his feet. 'Murder,' he murmured. 'I hadn't really realised what it would mean. Murder, mass murder. I suppose it *is* necessary?'

Dancer nodded; it was a strange sensation discussing the

111

ultimate crime as though it were perfectly legitimate. It was still murder. 'Most of the leadership will be travelling to Hong Kong to open Phase Two of the airport. It may be the opportunity we're looking for, to get them all together. We need inside information.'

The Chinese public relations man took a swing, but his lack of concentration was obvious as the ball veered off track and disappeared into a patch of rough. 'You already have the perfect contact.'

'Who?'

'Wang Hu at the CAAC. He has a special department which handles top VIP travel.'

'Wang is a sleeping partner in my business and is totally corrupt,' Dancer replied. 'He could never be trusted. Something like this would scare him. He'd shop the whole setup to get himself off the hook. I can't risk that. There has to be another way.'

'That is difficult,' Yan said as they began walking again towards the green. 'The VIP travel department is highly classified and uses only well-vetted Party members and I have no dealings with them.'

Dancer reached out and touched the other man's arm. 'I can't tell you how important this is.'

Yan's eyes were steely behind his glasses. 'I know.'

They played three more holes before they spoke again. After sinking his putt at four over par, Yan said: 'There may be someone else in a position to find out what you want to know.'

'Yes?'

'Someone in Wang Hu's department. You've probably met her. His personal assistant, Cheung Lily Mei-ling.' He sounded hesitant.

Dancer nodded. Small world. 'You seem uncertain.'

'Uncertain?' He looked at the American curiously. 'I have no uncertainty about her honesty or her integrity. Or that privately she believes in democracy.'

'But?' Dancer sensed he was holding back.

Yan stared into the middle distance. 'I am uncertain whether I should involve her in this. Endanger her or her family.'

Dancer understood the dilemma all too well. In fact, every time he met someone he thought would be useful to recruit, he had to make a judgement. But that was what being in the spying game was all about. It was like a doctor refusing to have any patients in case one or two became terminally ill. The problem came with the territory. Something Debs had never understood. Anyway, he decided he wouldn't tell Yan he'd already been warned off Lily by the police. This was not the time to alarm him.

'You know how I work, Tao. Very careful.'

Yan nodded. 'But I don't think you truly appreciate what it will be like if things go wrong and you are Chinese. After something as massive as this, whole swathes of society will literally be cut out like a vast cancer. Not just participants like me, but our friends and families. Fellow villagers, neighbours, cousins and children. All will be executed, imprisoned or sent away for re-education. And the stigma will be passed on generation after generation. It is the Chinese way.'

Dancer could sense Yan back-tracking. Every time he referred to Lily Cheung, his tone would lighten and there was an inner brightness in his eyes. She obviously meant a lot to him. 'Why not put it to her and let her decide?'

There was a sadness in his expression. 'I cannot speak to her on a personal level, Mr Dancer.'

'No?'

'She hates me.' He considered the word for a moment. 'No, that is not strong enough. She despises me.'

'Why?'

'I cannot talk about it, but that is how matters are. Lily will have to be approached through her younger brother.'

'Can he be trusted?'

Yan nodded. 'He is in the movement. Ho is very enthusiastic about democracy. A very nice young man, very jolly, but he is a bit wild and enjoys to gamble. That could make him unreliable.'

'Then we must explain how important it is to maintain security. And in the meantime we must improve secure communications between ourselves, because there will be much to discuss and arrange over the next few weeks. Do you have personal computer access at work?'

'Yes, but it is shared.'

'On-line?'

'Yes, but it is strictly monitored.'

Dancer was thinking fast. 'Yes, of course, it would be.'

The Party wouldn't want its media people getting in contact with Chinese exiles abroad who were considered to be dangerous subversives. 'But you are on the telephone at home?'

'Yes.'

'But not with a computer of your own?'

Yan looked embarrassed. 'I am well paid, but not that well paid. Golf is my luxury. I cannot afford such a thing.'

Dancer smiled. 'Trust me, you *can* now. Go to the drop in two days' time. You'll find money and the address of a shop where you will find a second-hand PC, modem and printer for sale.'

The public relations man made no attempt to hide his admiration. 'At a price I *can* afford?'

'A real bargain, so no eyebrows will be raised that you are living beyond your means.' He did not add that the emporium was one of several in major Chinese cities that had been established in recent years by a Hong Kong entrepreneur at the behest of the CIA. The sort of retail bazaar where you might stumble across anything and every-thing from antiques to state-of-the-art computers disguised within tatty soiled cabinets. 'You'll find it preprogrammed to run an encrypted message hidden under e-mail postings.'

'And that's how we will communicate from now on?'

'For the most part. If we need to meet again, we'll make it the airport golf links next time.'

Yan Tao nodded as though having difficulty absorbing all that was being said. 'Mr Dancer, I have dreamed of this day for ten years. Often I never thought it would come.'

'And now it has,' Dancer confirmed, lining up his next shot.

'I feel empty, hollow. Not how I expected. Not excited or elated. It is strange.'

'No, Tao, it's not strange. What you are feeling is fear. That is good. It means you understand the immensity of what we are undertaking and how easily it can go wrong.'

The young man held out his hand, palm down. 'You are right. It is fear, but my hand does not tremble.'

'It will, Tao, it will.'

Party music floated through the Fragrant Hills park on a welcome evening breeze that had picked up as the sun went down.

Dawson could hear it through the open window in the back of Iona's chauffeured Daimler Sovereign saloon long before they arrived at the top of the wooded slope. And now there were tantalising glimpses of half-hidden pavilions, villas and shrines through the trees.

'I've never known anyone with a pad up here,' he murmured in admiration. 'Thought it was only for Politburo members.'

'He doesn't own it, Bill,' Suzy Tobin replied from the front passenger seat, 'someone lends the place to him each summer.'

'Well-connected is our Edwin,' Iona added.

'He must be.'

They pulled into a gravel drive where cars, many of the official Chicom limos and others carrying CD plates, were already packed nose to tail alongside the flowering hibiscus hedge and jammed into the forecourt of the sumptuous pagoda-like villa.

'I'll phone to be picked up,' Iona told the embassy driver

as they climbed out. She looked fetching in the black velvet number, although it had not occurred to her that it acted like a magnet to her cigarette ash. In good spirits, she felt only mildly irritated to note Dawson's gaze on Suzy's rear sheathed in blue satin as she strode up the steps ahead of them.

New Chinese wealth was all here, Dawson could smell it as distinctly as the incense burners on the terrace. See it in the designer suits and fine silks, hear it in the chattering polite small talk as they mounted the steps guarded by two plump stone dragons.

Wearing a slightly grubby alpaca suit that looked as though it had been slept in, their host was greeting each guest like a long-lost friend. A handshake or a kiss to the cheek, a friendly quip, a drink order to the steward and on to the next. He saw Suzy first.

'My dear child, how gorgeous you're looking!' The dark liquid eyes of a hardened drinker nestled in egg-cup pouches of skin and his slightly puffy face had a sheen of perspiration like butter glaze. He was probably in his late fifties, but alcohol and tobacco had eroded his features until he looked a decade older. 'Already you've made an old man very happy.'

When Prufrock kissed her on the lips, Dawson felt an unreasonable irritation that she did not recoil. 'Not so much of the old, Edwin. More life in you than most men half your age.'

'True, true! Now, can I remember what you drink?'

'I'd like the cocktail I had last time I saw you.'

It was a thoroughly dirty laugh. 'Why is it I remember?' he asked, turning to the steward. 'The lady would like a Long Slow Screw Up Against A Wall.'

'Edwin!' Iona admonished. 'Don't you go leading young Suzy astray. She's very impressionable. You know what army brats are like.'

Prufrock winked at Suzy. 'I see you brought your mother with you. Now I'll have to behave myself.'

He kissed Iona on the cheek as she introduced Dawson. 'Have you two met?'

The American accepted the offered hand, his eyes appraising what he saw, analysing and filing away his first impressions for later reference. He'd known the name, but not the face. Had run a check through Langley. Edwin Prufrock, old Asian hand, more British than muffins and marmalade. Been around since time began. Already on the scene before Viet Nam blew up. Had cropped up since in Cambodia, Laos, Indonesia and Burma. Wherever trouble goes, Prufrock is never far behind. Wheeler-dealer with a shadowy reputation. Trading in anything anyone wants to buy. Black market certainly, arms very possibly. Kept at arm's length by British diplomatic missions, but always around somewhere if you looked carefully enough. Like a rat in the night. Therefore few facts known.

An unfair assessment? Possibly, but unlikely.

'Nice to meet you, Mr Prufrock. Heard of you, of course, but I'm not sure we've actually—'

'A couple of times, Mr Dawson, actually.' Prufrock's smile revealed slightly crooked and discoloured teeth. 'Last time was at the Guangzhou Trade Fair. A reception at the Dong Fang Hotel thrown by the Russians, I think. They were trying to launch a new vodka with a dead lizard in each bottle. Frightful stuff. Some marketing whiz kid in Moscow thought the Chinese would go for it big style.'

Dawson found himself being drawn in by Prufrock's infectious good humour. 'A big mistake. I remember the Russians called it Dragon's Breath.'

The Englishman laughed. 'And the Chinese called it Dragon's Piss – behind the Russians' backs, of course.'

'Rude of me not to remember you.'

'Not at all, old chap. I'm a forgettable old sod at the best of times.' He indicated the fresh wave of guests approaching up the drive. 'Forgive me, but duty calls. I'll catch up with you all later on.'

Dawson found himself already reassessing. Prufrock was

clearly at ease with Iona, so maybe the legends surrounding him were ill-deserved, or manufactured to give him more street cred with less reputable Chinese cadres.

Once the hovering stewards had supplied their drinks, Iona appeared to have read his mind: 'Edwin really is one of our secret weapons, Bill. Unofficially, of course. More of a family friend really. Drops into the embassy for a cup of decent tea occasionally and a chinwag. Later on I'd like him to bring you up to speed personally. No need for us to protect our own little pile now. Having too many secrets from each other can be dangerous at this stage of the game, I always think.'

He smiled back at her over the rim of his gin and tonic and knew that she knew that he knew she didn't exactly mean what she said. They'd both been around for too long to change old habits.

They went their separate ways for the next couple of hours, circulating, networking, killing time. All the while Dawson kept one eye on Prufrock, watching his style, his winning way with the Chinese as he picked his way through the complex etiquette, telling the right jokes to the right people, adopting the tactile, brotherly way with the men and knowing which women to shake formally by the hand and which he dared to kiss on the cheek. Never a foot wrong, it seemed. Prufrock was one of Iona's assets that he was grudgingly beginning to envy. How many more like him did she have in her web?

It seemed that almost every contact Dawson had ever had in Beijing was there, somewhere in the room, on the veranda or in the gardens. A hand raised in recognition here, a smile there and a friendly call across the floor. It was like a dying man seeing his life pass before his eyes.

He saw John Dancer who was with Abe Stone and paid them no more or less attention than the other guests. That afternoon Dancer's encrypted e-mail had come through, just to make his day. Details from "Hunan" of Beijing's political follow-up to the snatching back of Taiwan.

Something that, in its way, was more frightening than the planned invasion itself. He knew that was how it would be viewed in DC. Even if it didn't scare the President shitless like it should, it would have Langley, the Pentagon and State climbing up the wall.

The invitation had said cocktails and canapés from eight to ten and in that precise Chinese way that always amazed Dawson, that's exactly what happened. Just as the alcohol, humidity and high-pitched chatter were starting to get to him, it was as though someone had thrown a switch. Suddenly it was time to go.

By five past ten, he found himself alone with the staff who were clearing away empty glasses and dishes as Prufrock bade farewell to the last of his guests. He wandered through to the rear veranda with its extravagant gleaming red-black padaukwood decking and carved balustrades where he found Iona and Suzy enjoying the eddies of breeze that rustled the leaves of the pepper trees in the garden.

'Hi, Bill,' the younger woman called. 'Did you have a good time?'

He gave a tight smile. 'I'm not the greatest party-goer, but sure it was fine.'

'Bill prefers skulking in the shadows,' Iona teased. 'Not one for the bright lights, are you?'

Before he could answer, he heard Prufrock behind him. 'However much you adore 'em, there's always something nice about it when your last guests leave!'

'*We* are your last guests,' Iona pointed out.

'Bah, you know what I mean! Now we can relax.' He flopped into a wicker chair and beckoned a steward to bring a tray of drinks out on to the veranda.

After they'd arrived, Dawson said: 'It's a fine place here.'

Prufrock agreed. 'Wonderful, isn't it? A dear friend lets me stay most summers. Won't let me pay a pennypiece, either.'

Iona could see the envy in Dawson's eyes. 'Then you're one hell of a lucky son, Mr Prufrock.'

'Edwin, please,' the Englishman protested. 'And yes, I am. But then you make your own luck in this world I always say.'

'Well, you've certainly been making your own luck just recently by all accounts. In fact you've been making luck for all of us according to Iona.'

Prufrock sipped at his drink, marshalling his thoughts. 'Well, it wasn't luck. More damn hard work over several years. I've been supplying bits and pieces of military kit for Chicom for some time, mostly to equip élite units within the PLA. Some specialist weaponry and communications equipment, but mostly mundane stuff like decent Arctic sleeping bags, waterproof boots and dried rations that are half-way edible!' He gave an amused chuckle at this. 'Sounds silly, but it's the simple things the PLA don't have a clue about. Or much of a clue where to start looking. And, of course, you have to strike a big first deal. Otherwise they'll only be too happy to rip off a "round eyes" and make counterfeit copies from your samples. Devils will end up selling them back to the Western markets given half a chance – and put the original manufacturers out of business.'

Iona smiled, all too aware of the recurring nightmare tales of businessmen who thought the Chinese market was going to be the answer to their corporate prayers and balance sheets.

'Anyway,' Prufrock continued. 'I did a good deal, taking some rice consignments from PLA farms in part-payment. They liked that. Then I found them a market for making up counterfeit goods in their factories for Hong Kong traders. They liked that even more.'

'Factories?' Dawson asked. 'You mean *laogai*. The PLA's gulag prison factories?'

Prufrock lifted an eyebrow at the interruption. 'If you want to be pedantic, yes. But you're not going to change the way the Chinese run things. The prisoners may as well be making things for my clients as sewing mailbags for the Beijing Post Office, don't you know.'

Dawson had heard all the arguments before, it was always the same. If we don't sell to this or that pariah regime, someone else will. Usually it was the French, Belgians or Swiss. 'I can see you're a realist, Edwin,' he said.

The Englishman rode the sarcasm like a surfer. 'I am, Bill, and the Chinese certainly are. My first deal with these particular people was five years ago and my trade with them has grown two thousand per cent since. The original élite unit commander told his pals running other PLA units and they all wanted a finger in the pie. Then an air force general took an interest.'

Dawson was listening intently. 'Where are these people located?'

'Stuck out in Xingjiang province,' Prufrock answered. 'As you might imagine, they're all pretty pissed off about being stationed there. The PLA's forgotten ones, they call themselves. But no one much interferes and they've all got their own fiefdoms and they're making the most of it.'

Bells were starting to jangle in Dawson's mind. 'Who is this air force commander?'

Prufrock looked pleased with himself. 'General Sun.'

Dawson swallowed hard. 'That's some contact. He's very well connected with the Chiefs-of-Staff.'

'He's also well connected with a pro-capitalist clique,' Prufrock answered smoothly. 'All the military in Xingjiang are very unhappy with Beijing and since our little arrangements started, they've been getting a strong taste for capitalism. Democracy they can take or leave, but their friends believe that democracy will be good for business.'

'What?' Dawson was confused. 'What d'you mean, friends?'

Prufrock sighed impatiently as though dealing with a tiresome child. 'Over a period I began to learn things – that Sun and his cronies had developed ties with their cousins in Hong Kong, Macao and Taiwan to exploit their commercial enterprises.'

Now Dawson understood. 'Snakeheads.'

Prufrock shrugged, he hated labels. To him, talking Triads was like talking drug cartels or the mafia. It meant different things to different people. 'It's a group calling itself the Red Tiger Society. Strongly Taiwan-based, although it's clearly operational all over the Pacific Rim.'

'How is this relevant?' Iona pressed, because it was the first she'd heard of this; Edwin always liked to keep something in reserve.

Prufrock held his glass at arm's length and gently swilled the contents round and round. 'I went on a few benders with Sun and some of the others. Got to know them well. We met up with a few RTS members in Kowloon and in Macao. A few careless words were spoken and I began to form a picture. Learned that the RTS was expanding rapidly on the mainland again and that its leaders were promoting democracy and the market economy.'

Dawson said: 'Because crime thrives under those conditions.'

The Englishman pursed his lips as he appraised the CIA man; more savvy than he'd given him credit for. 'Exactly. They were starting to thrive again as Beijing relaxed its totalitarian stance. Although, of course, they were worried about losing ground after the Hong Kong handover.' He took a sip from his glass. 'Anyway, I realised that Sun and his PLA mates were being converted to our side, in theory at least. Annoyed at being forgotten by Beijing and frustrated because their own free enterprise ventures were hampered by the Chicom regime.'

'So you approached them?' Iona suggested.

Prufrock blinked momentarily as though he scarcely believed his own words. 'Sun first. A joke, then a hint. Got him to do a favour. Gave him a reward. Sucked him in so I had a hold. You know the form. I wasn't really expecting the sheer depth of his resentment.' He paused, not wanting to say too much. 'His family suffered under the Cultural Revolution. Sun's father was a schoolteacher, therefore bourgeois. Usual story. Pupils made him wear a dunce's cap and forced him to make self-criticisms. Then the Red Guard unit did a little re-education of their own, putting the boot in. Died of renal failure, and Sun's mother died a few years later of cancer. Grief, Sun firmly believes.'

'And Sun himself?' Iona asked.

'Tainted by association. You know how it worked. He was a talented young air force pilot, literally a high-flyer, set for rapid promotion. The Red Guards brought him down to earth with a bump. Grounded and sent to Xingjiang for re-education. He never did come back. Probably could have eventually, but my guess is he didn't really want to. Self-imposed exile. Instead he crawled to the top of the heap in Xingjiang without too much interference from Beijing. The Cultural Revolution set his career back a good ten years, he reckons.'

Dawson watched Prufrock carefully, analysing each word and nuance, evaluating what they had within their grasp. 'How far will he go, Edwin?'

Prufrock paused for a moment and frowned deeply, studying his empty glass. 'All the way.'

Iona found that her eyes were on the fan, mesmerised as it gyrated slowly and steadily above their heads. *All the way*. Those words, almost in rhythm with each turn. *All the way*. To the precipice.

Over the years Aspen at Langley and Lansdowne at 'Riverside' had achieved so much. Had sought and found support for a reunited, democratic China from the overseas Chinese. Their ancient – and fabulously rich – private syndicate corporations around the Far East had been persuaded to provide black cash, the covert funds to finance the gearing up of CIA and SIS operations free from financial constraints. That had allowed her and Dawson to crank up their network of dissidents in education, the media and government to such a pitch that, when the moment was right, people would be in a position to seize power and form the 'Interim Government of Democratic China'.

Iona said: 'Well, Bill, our coup with General Sun takes us that much closer.'

To the edge, she thought, but didn't say, but she felt the chill ripple of adrenalin and fear as she looked over.

She turned suddenly to Prufrock. 'Edwin dear, I've got a bit of a head coming on. Your hospitality was too generous.'

The Englishman leered. 'And you're the original girl who can never say no?'

Iona ignored that. 'I need to stretch my legs. Do show me round your delightful garden.'

'Of course, my pleasure,' he said and struggled out of his wicker chair.

As they wandered through the pepper trees, Iona said, 'There is a problem, Edwin.'

'Yes?'

'Our hand is being forced.'

No emotion showed on the face of the old China hand. 'How?'

'Has General Sun said anything about Taiwan recently?'

'Taiwan? No, why should he?'

'No squadrons in his sector been moved south to Fujian province? Maybe in support of military activity against Taiwan?'

'More sabre rattling?' Prufrock shook his head. 'No, and they wouldn't. All Xingjiang's squadrons are needed against the separatists. Why?'

'No sabre rattling this time, Edwin. We've just heard they're going to grab Taiwan.'

This time the mask cracked and Prufrock's sallow complexion paled visibly. 'Rubbish.'

'Within the next few months.'

His colour returned. 'Bah, just Chinese whispers. Been doing the rounds for years.'

'Not this time, Edwin; it's kosher. Impeccable source. And now it's been confirmed by satellite pictures. The invasion fleet of landing craft we thought they didn't have

– it's been constructed secretly in Hangzhou. Hundreds of vessels camouflaged and moored along inland waterways to avoid detection.'

The Englishman shook his head in disbelief, visibly winded by the news. 'So what happens now?'

Iona's voice was low. 'We have to make our move. Whether we like it or not. Whether we think we're ready or not.'

Now Prufrock understood. 'And you need to know if General Sun and his friends will be prepared to put their heads in the dragon's mouth?'

'I don't think that's the best way to put it.'

His eyes were unblinking. 'Don't you, dear lady? And what if General Sun thinks the time is not right, that the leadership is popular after Hong Kong and a palace coup would not carry the people with it? That we should wait?'

There was a glitter in Iona's eyes like sunlight on granite, a look that Prufrock had seen before and that unnerved him. 'Tell Sun that we have no choice but to act now. But when we've got Beijing by the balls, the people's hearts and minds will follow. He's a military man, he'll appreciate that.'

Prufrock didn't reply. He didn't have to, his expression said it all. However long the likes of Iona and Dawson had served in China, they still didn't understand what made it tick and probably never would.

Troy Krowsky and Nick Lake were bonding and had been for some months.

But if anyone had suggested that to them, jokingly or otherwise, the joker had best be able to run fast. Or more likely swim.

Because both were underwater warriors and neither were the sort to give thought or consideration to such liberal, abstract concepts as male-bonding. Yet any psychiatrist would have told them that was exactly what had happened between Krowsky and Lake and their respective teams.

That bonding process had been as painful as it had been remarkable given that they came from totally different social and military cultures. Krowsky's ten men were hand-picked Americans from Naval Special Warfare Group 1 based at Coronado in San Diego, California. They were heavily muscled SEAL – Sea, Air and Land – special operations teams, expert in unconventional warfare. Fit, proud, outgoing and polite, they reckoned to conquer the world before breakfast and the universe some time after lunch. They had no doubt they were the best in the world, deserving the very best equipment which they invariably had.

Lake's men, on the other hand were members of the Special Boat Service, drawn from the ranks of the three British Royal Marine Commandos. They tended to be wiry, less heavily built and on average shorter than their American counterparts. They were watchful, wary and less talkative, but certainly more cynical than the SEALs they operated with. That was probably due to the fact that they'd had more practical experience of live operations, were familiar with political betrayal and cover-ups and of being at the receiving end of the penny-pinching mentality of successive British governments when it came to the Armed Forces.

The first meeting between the two teams – mutual stand-off, silently antagonistic – in a mess hall in this top secret US Navy facility in Hawaii had not been promising. Perhaps typically, it was the Americans who broke the ice and the bonding process began, beginning where all soldiers start to form their blood brotherhood – not under fire on the battlefield but in a downtown bar.

What made the merger easier and concentrated minds on finding similarities rather than differences, was the need for both teams to learn to work with a whole new concept of high-tech underwater warfare that would stretch them all. The SCUBA concept in the curious shape of USS *Manta*.

It was that curious shape that Krowsky and Lake now watched absently from the gantry bridge above the special enclosed submarine pen.

'When was this?' the American asked. He reminded Lake of an ageing hippy with his ginger ringlets, bandanna and Groucho moustache.

'Just before lunch,' Lake replied. 'I was dropping in our latest report to the Vessel Assessment Office when I saw her.'

'Chinese, you say?'

'Oriental-looking, almond rather than slitty eyes.'

Krowsky's mouth twitched. 'But a nice ass.'

'Not one you'd want to kick.'

'But definitely American?'

'Sounded pure blueberry pie to me.'

'What would you know?'

'After serving a year with you lot, more than I want to!'

'And you're sure she's CIA?'

'That's what Marvin in the VAO said and he'd seen the signal.'

Krowsky still wasn't buying. 'Marvin's a wind-up merchant.'

'I know, Troy,' the Englishman replied, 'but I saw her and the blokes in dark suits with her. They didn't look Navy.'

The SEAL shook his head. 'Nick, we've just got back from the exercise and we're all due leave.'

'Yes, and there was a lot of brass aboard the *Theodore Roosevelt* when we hit Tim-Wan island. Maybe someone became seriously impressed.'

But Krowsky was seriously *un*impressed. 'More likely they're a bunch of accountants from the Pentagon come to close us down.'

'HEY, YOU TWO!'

Both men looked down towards the pier alongside the submarine where its skipper stood beside a couple of US Navy officers. 'What is it, Al?' Krowsky called back.

'We're wanted in the Ops Room pronto.' Al Cherrier was the oldest of the three men. At forty, going on fifty with his greying beard and fondness for an old cob pipe, he had a clear ten-year head start, but wasn't one to pull rank.

Within their curious command structure, Captain Cherrier's prime responsibility was for the safety of the submarine and crew and for getting them to their target – and, of course, for the team when they were aboard. Nick Lake was notionally in command of the assault team's activities with Krowsky acting as his 2IC although they both held the rank of lieutenant.

By the time they'd clattered down the gantry steps, Cherrier was waiting for them. He was a tall man, but with a slight stoop developed as a self-conscious teenager who grew faster than his classmates. It was easy to mistake the gaunt, veined cheeks, fathomless grey eyes, and few words as belonging to a taciturn man. But, although he rarely smiled, dry humour would frequently lie behind his words. He was one who thought long and hard before he spoke and rarely wasted words.

'You heard this rumour?' he asked as they began walking towards the exit door to the hardened submarine pen.

Krowsky nodded. 'About the CIA being in town? Sure.'

That threw Cherrier. 'CIA? No, I meant the admiral.'

'Harding?'

'Apparently he flew in by helo an hour ago,' Cherrier confirmed. 'Been in a huddle with Crozier in Ops ever since.'

Nick Lake was thinking fast and not liking what he thought. Vice Admiral Ross Harding, commander of the US 7th Fleet, didn't get out of his bunk for much less than a full-blown war. And here he was flying into their poxy little facility on Hawaii together with some hush-hush dark suits from Langley. All zippered up with Rear Admiral Crozier who had overall responsibility for Project Deadwater. It didn't look good; Krowsky was right, they were being closed down. They were a leftover from the

Cold War and they all knew it. The miracle was that Project Deadwater had survived this long – probably lost deep in the hard drive of some computer in Langley or the Pentagon or Whitehall. Then New Labour had swept to power in London and cleaned out all the junk from the civil servants' cupboards in the Ministry of Defence.

He knew Jim Hudd, a junior defence minister, had been watching the Tim-Wan exercise. In fact, he'd met the man briefly over coffee in the wardroom the next day and had been congratulated on the overall performance of Project Deadwater.

Typical politician, Lake seethed, saying one thing to your face but meaning quite another.

They hit the open air at a brisk pace, crossing the dusty compound under a high, bright Hawaiian sun before reaching the breeze-block offices that held the Ops Centre.

Krowsky nudged Lake, indicating the two US Marines on guard duty by the entrance. That was something new.

One of the Marines stepped forward. 'Restricted entry, sir.'

None of Deadwater's relaxed team liked unnecessary bullshit, the informality of the British SBS members having been especially infectious. Krowsky liked it least of all.

'We've just been summoned by Rear Admiral Crozier, Marine. I'm Krowsky and these are Captain Cherrier and Lieutenant Lake. We *run* this show. Now I don't know who told you two to stand here using up precious oxygen, but why don't you stop wasting my time and get out the fucking way?'

The Marine looked unsure, but stood his ground. 'I'll need to see your IDs.'

Krowsky's face was reddening. 'We don't use IDs round here, because we all fucking well *know* each other.'

Cherrier placed a hand on his shoulder. 'Easy, Troy, the man's just doin' his job.'

At that moment Marvin's head peered round the door. 'Ah, gentlemen, thought I heard the start of a fight. Sorry about that. Things have changed. Admiral Harding was appalled at our state of security.' He smiled pleasantly at the Marine. 'Hence the clockwork soldiers. Gather he doesn't have too much time for Special Forces' methods. C'mon in.'

This time the Marine guards said nothing and just watched resentfully as the three men passed. As they followed Marvin through to the project commander's office, he said in a low voice. 'I *suspect* Admiral Harding was afraid the Langley crowd would think we were too lax and *he'd* get it in the neck.'

'So it is true about Langley being here?' Krowsky asked, clearly impressed.

Marvin grinned widely. 'Trust me,' he said and opened the door.

Crossed battle ensigns and Old Glory were pinned to the far wall and Rear Admiral Crozier sat at the desk in front of them. He looked up as they entered, the tanned face smiling beneath hair as white as a new fall of snow.

His two civilian guests were seated on the corner sofa, drinking coffee. Vice Admiral Harding stood opposite, talking to them, his bulk and demeanour as huge and intimidating as one of the warships he commanded. As his bleak, long-distance eyes homed in on the new arrivals, Crozier came round to the front of his desk to greet them as they snapped to attention and saluted.

'Stand easy, gentlemen,' Crozier said in his usual friendly manner before presenting them to the fleet commander who then took charge of introducing the two civilians.

'This is Frank Aspen,' Harding growled in his usual pitbull manner.

As Aspen offered his hand, he added helpfully: 'I'm Assistant Deputy Director of Operations, Central Intelligence Agency.'

He was a tall, square-shouldered man in his fifties with hair too black to be natural and a pair of angry eyebrows.

They suited the faded photogenic features that could have belonged to any number of ageing TV soap stars. In short, the regular good looks were infinitely forgettable.

That did not apply to his companion, quite the reverse, because although Frank Aspen was the first to speak, it was the woman at his side who drew the men's instant attention.

She stood five foot five in her sensible grey pumps and the matching sensible grey skirt and jacket she wore over a navy silk blouse gave the impression it covered a strong and physically capable body, although the only visible evidence of this was her athletic tanned legs with smoothly muscled calves. Skin, the men noted, not pantihose.

'Janie Walsh,' she said brightly. And it was the accompanying white smile like a sparkling neon sign that they all remembered. That and the laughing tawny eyes framed by hair that fell in waves of jet black satin.

'Operations Executive,' Aspen added, 'of our Chinese Division.'

'Sir?' Krowsky spoke.

A tic of impatience jerked at the corner of Aspen's mouth. 'Miss Walsh runs operations in our Chinese section,' he said as though explaining to a particularly stupid child.

But Walsh seemed to understand the men's confusion. 'And I'm American-Chinese, as you can see. Father from Shanghai, mother from Baltimore.'

Aspen coughed; it always made him uncomfortable when any of his people said a word more than was strictly necessary. 'Do take a seat, gentlemen,' he said, indicating the sofa. 'Would you like to kick off, Admiral?'

Ross Harding grunted, 'Sure,' and fumbled in his top pocket for one of his Havanas. He nodded at Crozier. 'Okay if I smoke?'

At ease now in a floating cloud of aromatic smoke, much to Aspen's obvious disapproval, the admiral of the fleet began to explain: 'As you know, we've been running

Deadwater from here in Hawaii since around 1990. It's a joint US–Royal Navy research project, now chiefly funded by Mr Aspen's department at the CIA. To keep things tidy, this facility falls within the technical jurisdiction of the 7th Fleet and is described *officially* as an experimental seabed retrieval programme – whatever the hell that means. But as you'll all be as aware as I am, I hardly know the hell what goes on here – except when Admiral Crozier here is kind enough to tell me.'

He grinned through the veil of smoke as the project men obligingly smiled back at his little joke. 'Then last month Mr Aspen asked me to set up the exercise at Tim-Wan, and, as you know, that was considered to be a great success.'

Aspen cut in there. 'It persuaded me and my British counterparts that there was a realistic up-coming operational role for the Project to play.'

Nick Lake blinked. Was he hearing right? Had he missed the word close-down? Had he actually heard the expression *operational*? What the hell did the CIA man mean? It almost certainly involved being pitched against the Chinese. Probably teams being put ashore on the Spratleys or other disputed islands to observe and report back to the 7th Fleet. To keep one jump ahead in case Beijing ever got too big for its boots. Yes, that would be it, he was sure.

'The Project is to be deployed,' Aspen continued, 'to put your Discretionary Warfare Team ashore in support of agent networks and subversive guerrilla and intelligence activity on mainland China.'

He'd said it in a rush as if trying to get it all out before someone spotted the deliberate mistake. So fast, in fact, that it took a moment for the submarine commander and the two assault officers to register exactly what was said.

'Sir,' Krowsky said slowly, 'did I just hear you right? Mainland China?'

'You heard right, Lieutenant,' Aspen replied as if it were the most natural thing in the world. 'The People's

Republic of China. Miss Walsh will be the overall Mission Controller.'

The woman smiled a little awkwardly, clearly aware that she hardly looked the part.

'Pardon me,' Al Cherrier drawled, 'but when is all this activity expected to take place?'

Just as soon as you can be deployed, Captain,' Aspen came back swiftly, nodding towards Admiral Harding. 'As part of the 7th Fleet, of course.'

Cherrier's eyes darkened. 'You mean with *immediate* effect?'

'That's what I just said.'

'There are several major mechanical and technical problems that need to be overcome with the submarine.'

Aspen smiled coldly. 'We've had some ten years to sort out teething problems.'

'But just one year as a fully co-ordinated project,' Cherrier corrected. 'And we've been cash starved pending an inquiry into whether the Project should be closed down.'

'Careful,' Admiral Harding cautioned.

Janie Walsh cut in quickly. 'I'm sure we can discuss all that later, Captain.'

Cherrier regarded her coolly for a moment. 'They aren't the sort of problems that talking can put right.'

Walsh felt unnerved by the sheer intensity of the submarine commander's gaze, and recognised the challenge to her authority. She'd have to put her stamp on things sometime; better now before things got out of hand. 'I said later, Captain.'

At that moment the telephone trilled on Crozier's desk. He snatched it up and listened for a second before beckoning Aspen. 'A call for you. Take it on the scrambler.'

'Who is it?'

'Assistant Secretary Katz.'

Aspen pursed his lips. The Deputy Assistant Secretary of Defence for Special Operations. He picked up the handset of the red telephone. 'Hal, what gives?'

The CIA man listened intently. There was no obvious outward reaction to what he heard; he was the consummate poker player even when dealing hands that could mean life or death to others. Only Lake, whose undercover work on the streets of Northern Ireland and Bosnia had taught him the importance of studying body language of potential enemies, noticed the tightening tendrils in Aspen's neck and the shadow that passed across his eyes.

Slowly he replaced the receiver before turning back into the room. 'A bit of a change of plan,' he said without emotion as though he'd been expecting it all along. He looked at Krowsky. 'Lieutenant, I am instructed to inform you that you and your team are to return to your units of origin forthwith.'

The SEAL's mouth dropped. 'Sir?'

Lake looked on, incredulous.

'You heard, Lieutenant. Forthwith – that means with immediate effect.'

Crozier was on his feet. 'Mr Aspen, would you mind telling *me* what the hell is going on? This *is* my project.'

For once Aspen looked abashed, his expression suggesting he'd just swallowed something rather unpleasant. 'I'm sorry, Admiral. I had been sort of expecting it, but it's orders direct from the White House. No American troops are to set foot on sovereign foreign soil.'

Lake frowned. 'We can't operate with half an assault team.'

'What about the crew?' Cherrier asked.

Aspen almost saw the funny side of that. 'No crew, no operation. Full stop. When it was pointed out it's not the crew's function to go ashore, the President relented. He doesn't want a major spat with the Brits. So the US Navy crew stays.' He glanced around and could see that everyone wanted answers. 'Look, we need time to reassess this now.' He looked at Krowsky and Lake. 'Go back and break the news to your respective teams, but keep them separate until the SEAL contingent flies out – hopefully a.m.

134

tomorrow. Krowsky, forget everything you've heard.'

'They've got R and R due,' Crozier said pointedly.

'Thanks, Admiral,' Aspen replied. 'Then tell 'em that's what's happening, Krowsky. All routine. They won't know any different until they return from leave.'

'Sir,' Krowsky acknowledged, moving towards the door, his English companion from the SBS close behind him.

Janie Walsh stepped forward, recognising the disappointment in the American's eyes. 'I'm sorry about this confusion, Lieutenant. I understand your feelings.'

He held her with an angry glare. 'Do you, do you really? Well, I'm *not* disappointed if this is any indication of how efficiently the operation has been organised.'

With that, he brushed past her and out into the corridor. Lake followed, sparing her a sympathetic smile. 'He doesn't mean that. He's just sore.'

Those bright lights sparkled again as she smiled. 'I know, Lieutenant. Tell him I really do understand. My brother is a soldier in the 82nd Airborne.'

Lake shrugged and winked. 'Sure, someone has to be.'

She didn't reply but clearly understood the ceaseless battle of wit and words between different arms in the military. Soldiers were soldiers and navy was navy, and the only time they came together was to castigate the air force. Or to fight any enemy greater than their rivals. And even the possibility of that was doubtful. 'I'll see you tomorrow, Lieutenant.'

He strode out and found Krowsky waiting for him in the sunshine. 'Christ, Nick, can you believe that! What a shambles! How do they expect you to operate on half a team?'

Lake shook his head. 'It seems like a bad dream. I kept expecting Crozier to jump up and say it was all just an exercise.'

'China!' Krowsky was still finding it impossible to grasp the magnitude of what was planned. 'Is that ambitious or what?'

They began walking back together towards the concrete pen. 'Pity they don't think your lot are up to it,' Lake jibed.

Krowsky shuffled to an angry halt. 'I'll tell you something for nothin', Nick. If the President's pulled us out of this little adventure, you can bet your sweet ass that it's because we weren't expected to return. Chew on that awhiles.'

Five

Nick Lake and Al Cherrier broke the news to the British SBS team and the three-man submarine crew the next morning in the mess when they arrived to find that Krowsky's SEALs had already breakfasted and left the camp – without the courtesy of a word of farewell.

Initial bemusement was followed by resentment at the rudeness of their abrupt departure, until the reason was revealed. That left all those remaining with a stunned sense of disbelief.

They were still reeling an hour later when they all filed into the Operations Centre briefing room, where Rear Admiral Crozier waited with the Chinese-American woman called Walsh. As soon as the audience was seated, he introduced her as the CIA's mission controller.

She stepped forward. A little warily, Lake thought, as well she might. He had no doubt she would be aware that fighting men would be naturally resentful at having a woman placed in charge of their fate. It was barely alleviated by the warmth of her smile or her good looks. Smiles and good looks were associated with bars and discos. Smiles and good looks were about wives, sweethearts and one-night leg-overs, not about soldiering.

Nevertheless, she looked smart and businesslike, standing on the rostrum in chino slacks and short-sleeved pilot shirt, with her hair held back off her face in a simple ponytail.

'Hi, guys,' she began brightly. 'I guess you're all as thrown by this as I was two weeks ago when I was called in to head up the operation. I have worked on Far East affairs for some time, but had never been told how extensive our secret operations in China had become. Basically, I now know that these have been aimed at encouraging democracy and the free market economy wherever possible – and discrediting or pressurising the Chinese Communist Party and the People's Liberation Army to reform at every opportunity.' She paused and smiled at the grim, cautious expressions confronting her. 'Now I realise you guys like to keep things informal, so let's keep it that way. Feel free to interrupt and ask questions as we go. Just be sure you call me sir.'

That one just began to crack the ice and earned a couple of reluctant grins. Some of them were warming a little. 'So what *do* we call you— sir?' asked one of the American crew.

'Janie is fine. Miss Walsh if there's brass about.'

Lake raised his hand. 'Ma'am, there's one overriding question—'

'I know, Lieutenant,' she came back swiftly. 'How do we realistically and effectively replace the SEAL element of the team? I admit that has been a big setback, but it appears to have been resolved. The Pentagon's been talking to the Ministry of Defence in London overnight. It's as yet to be confirmed, but it appears that the SEALs will be replaced by members of our British team's brother organisation, the Special Air Service from Hereford.'

If Janie Walsh had been expecting smiles all round, or even a muted cheer, she was in for a bitter disappointment.

Brother organisation? Brown jobs from Hereford? The Army Special Force coming to join the élite amphibious Marine arm of the Royal Navy? She had to be joking. There was no love lost between Lake's men and their better-known counterparts and previous efforts at cross-training had never been too successful.

The SAS scorned the SBS as 'scaleybacks' and regarded them as hamstrung by the backward-looking and conservative sea-going traditions of their masters in the Admiralty. For their part, Lake's men thought themselves equals of the SAS troops. It was common knowledge that few SAS troops had ever passed the Marines' own gruelling underwater or mountaineering courses. And hadn't SBS units fought covertly in Northern Ireland and behind the lines in the Falklands and Bosnia with as much success as their brown-job 'brothers'? But, as Lake would concede, with possibly less flamboyance and more responsibility. He would probably add, with a wry grin, that scaleybacks didn't go blabbing about their exploits in the media.

The collective groan had been muted, but distinctly audible. There was a flicker of concern in Walsh's eyes as she witnessed the involuntary reaction of these Brits who would be under her overall command from now on. At that moment it dawned on her that she did not begin to understand them. What was it George Bernard Shaw had said about two nations divided by a common language? Suddenly they seemed like complete aliens.

But if she had asked Nick Lake then, he could have explained their feelings. For years now his Special Boat Service had been playing second fiddle to the world-famous SAS. They'd been in the Falklands too, in the Gulf and Bosnia and in Northern Ireland, but you never heard mention of that on television or in the papers. The glory boys took it all.

And now everyone in the room knew exactly what was going to happen. Each man was painfully aware that the SAS would muscle in and take control. It would be as inevitable as it was unwanted. What really galled Lake and the others was that it also made damn good sense. 'The Regiment', as its own members rather precociously referred to themselves, was almost four times the size of the Royal Marines' single Special Boat Service, and it came complete with powerful logistical, intelligence and communications backup the like of which the SBS troopers could only dream of. This was all down to one simple reason: in strict terms, the Special Boat Service's remit stopped an arbitrary three miles in from the coast – or as far as generals would allow an admiral to share their part of any war. By contrast, the British Army's SAS could range far and wide on land, air and sea. They could indulge in a wide range of operations, from surveillance and sabotage deep behind enemy lines to hard-hitting surprise commando raids with an effect out of all proportion to their size. And, if that wasn't enough to keep them busy, they also spearheaded the state's continuing drive against terrorism.

While both SAS and SBS operated alongside the Secret Intelligence Service and the Security Service, MI5, the former's links were far more widely established and routinely used. In fact, Hereford had its own mini-intelligence service known irreverently from Cold War days as 'the Kremlin' It enjoyed special bilateral ties with its American counterparts and access to the world's most sophisticated intelligence support apparatus.

Janie Walsh was saying: 'Now I can see you guys can't wait to meet up with your fellow countrymen. Don't think I've ever seen such happy smiling faces.' She beamed at them all, just to let them know she thought she understood. 'And you'll all be anxious to know how many of the rumours going about are true. Well, for one, you are not being sent into China to take on the entire People's Liberation Army – although I'm sure you're capable – or anything as exciting as that.

'The simple fact is that intelligence sources suggest that China is entering a period of political uncertainty and civil unrest. There is a power struggle in Beijing, capitalism has fired the imagination of the people and there is a growing thirst for political freedom. The old guard in the Politburo can't handle this sort of grass-roots sea change and the PLA is split between the different political factions. In addition to these essentially internal problems, there is mounting pressure from outside. An embryonic guerrilla movement is known to exist in Tibet and Muslim separatists are causing major problems in the western province of Xingjiang. In short, the whole stew is reaching boiling point. Our role during this critical period will be to back up forces for democracy in China that have been identified by US and British intelligence in recent years.'

Lake raised a hand. 'Could you expand on that, ma'am?'

'Of course, Lieutenant. There are student and union movements, as well as elements within national and local government and the armed forces, who want to ditch the entire Chinese Communist apparatus for good. After all, it's gone in all but name. There may be benefits for the people in the new capitalist economy, but there are also great uncertainties. The state can no longer guarantee to look after its citizens from the cradle to the grave. Unemployment and poverty are returning. Many people ask why, if this is the case, they should put up with the old fat cats who wallow in corruption and totalitarian power.

'It will be our job to liaise with agents within these groups so that they are ready to act in concert when the *putsch* comes. Meantime, they will need funding and training in communications and, in some cases, the use of weapons. Pro-democracy elements in the People's Liberation Army must be in position to neutralize those units that are not. Television and radio stations will have to be seized. And, of course, a transitional government will have to be formed. In short, that's the plan. Put simply, our job is to make sure it happens with as few screw-ups as possible.'

She concluded, 'Classic overt unconventional warfare, gentlemen, stay in the shadows and help the indigenous get the job done. Theirs will be the public glory. Your actions must be and *will* stay deniable for the foreseeable future.'

This time it was the submarine's skipper, Al Cherrier, who had a question. 'Ma'am, I can't quite figure out the role you have in mind for *Manta* in all of this?'

Walsh smiled. 'Well, Captain, we don't have too many options for getting a skilled sixteen-man team into the People's Republic at short notice. The front-door method is too time-consuming in terms of setting up decent cover stories, and the more obvious back-door methods require

141

physically long routes in through Pakistan or Kazakhstan. Both are fraught with problems.

'But by basing the SCUBA project off the coast, we can ferry in not only our team but all the equipment that will be needed. That way the requirement for false documentation and cover stories is also minimised. You just turn up on the streets of Beijing one morning and no one will be any the wiser.'

She made it all sound like the most natural thing in the world, but Lake's mind was still reeling with the implications and sheer audacity of what was being planned. He hardly absorbed her final words. 'Now we have a lot to do and many preparations to make. It's not going to be easy for any of us, including me. Of all the things I've trained for, operating out of a submarine wasn't one of them, so I hope you boys will look out for me. Because I'm afraid I can't swim.'

Lake didn't know whether to laugh or cry as the meeting broke up in a sudden rush of excited chatter. Al Cherrier caught his eye; he didn't look a happy man. 'I wonder which egomaniac at Langley dreamt this one up,' he grunted. 'It's got all the makings of a first-class goat rope.'

The SBS lieutenant couldn't disagree. 'You can't rush at a massive operation like this.'

He was suddenly aware of a faint waft of Chanel No. 5 before he realised she was behind him. 'Do I hear dissension in the ranks?' Walsh asked breezily.

Lake looked uncomfortable. 'Sorry, ma'am, it wasn't meant for your ears.'

Her smile was disarming. 'I have reservations too, you know, but I'd rather have them all out in the open. Join me for a coffee.' They walked with her to the officers' mess. As they settled in armchairs with cups of what was universally agreed to be the foulest machine-coffee in Hawaii, she turned to Cherrier. 'So what problems do you have, Captain?'

'How long have you got?'

'That bad?'

He grimaced as he blew on his coffee to cool it. 'The problem is we're dealing with state-of-the-art technology. *Manta* was originally a concept vessel – a prototype for trying out new ideas. Some have worked, some haven't. But we're stuck with them whether they do or not because the project's been fairly starved of cash.'

Walsh frowned. 'Is there anything in particular?'

'The computer', Cherrier replied without hesitation, 'and the software. Over ten years it's all been modified and added to piecemeal. We really need to start again from scratch – and, of course, it would cost millions of dollars to put right.'

'How serious is the problem?'

'It's temperamental and prone to crashing. Like the fuel-cell propulsion package, which is fine except it's too temperamental and should have been further developed.'

She nodded her understanding. 'Pretty fundamental stuff, eh? Well, I'll raise the matter with Admiral Crozier and my boss at Langley. Let me have details of that and the sub's other most serious defects. We'll just have to see what can be done.' Then she looked at Lake. 'And you, Lieutenant, what is your main concern?'

He decided there was no point in hedging. 'Breaking up the assault team. We were just starting to mesh well with Krowsky's SEALs and it had taken a year for us to get there. Throwing a new team in the deep end and at short notice – even SAS Boat Troop – is begging for disaster.'

Walsh's expression barely altered, but suddenly he glimpsed another, harder side of the Chinese-American. 'I share your worries, Lieutenant, but we'll just have to make damn sure that disaster doesn't happen. I agree this mission's been thrown together in unseemly haste from this end, but the Chinese networks have been built up over decades. As long as we hold our nerve and do our job to the best of our ability, everything will be fine. And I intend to ensure we do exactly that. Sometimes opportunities come along at the most inopportune moments. If they're not seized, then the moment is lost.'

Something had been niggling at the back of Lake's mind. 'China will still be there next year. So what exactly's going to be lost if we *don't* seize the moment?'

She hesitated. 'It's a question of need to know, Lieutenant, I'm sure you understand that.'

'I understand my men and I and Captain Cherrier's crew are being asked to put our lives at risk in order to seize the moment.'

Walsh held him in a steady gaze. 'Then I'll tell you exactly what will be lost if you are unable to act.' She paused for effect. 'Taiwan.'

John Dancer waited with Yan Tao on the entrance deck of the floating teahouse. It was a garish affair, more like a Buddhist temple than a junk, with its red paint, carved dragons and turned-up roof eaves, and looked totally incongruous in Chaoyang district's bleak residential zone where sixteen-storey tenement blocks marched for ever across the dusty Beijing suburbs.

'He shouldn't be long now,' Yan said. The information officer was looking surprisingly relaxed now that he was away from the government office environment. He wore a short-sleeved shirt with the collar unbuttoned and the tie loose round the neck.

Dancer nodded. He knew No. 6 Beijing District Steel Rivet Factory was only half a mile the other side of Xindong Lu bridge and that the man would be along in a moment. But it didn't stop him feeling exposed and vulnerable. He'd played the game by the rules for so long now that to break them seemed to be inviting disaster. Getting as superstitious as the Chinese, he chided himself, and cupped his hands to light another cigarette. Hadn't he gone through all the usual checks and double checks of his trade to ensure there was no tail? Wasn't Yan openly known as a casual business acquaintance and occasional golfing rival? So there was no real reason why they should not meet and talk innocently at a teahouse. Why shouldn't Yan be asking the American's advice about obtaining a new set of clubs from the States? It was Dancer's own knowledge of what he was doing that was making him nervous, nothing more. But events were moving faster now, and the rules had to be broken or the opportunity would be lost. Did he say broken? No, that was inviting disaster. Just bent a little. He drew heavily on the cigarette. But meeting Cheung Ho, he realised, was bending them quite a lot.

'That's him now,' Yan said.

Ho looked on top of the world, a wide grin plumping up his chubby cheeks as he strode happily along the litter-strewn path that ran beside the arrow-straight section of the inaptly named Bright Horse River where the teahouse was moored in the oily, poisonous green water that flowed sluggishly between its vertical concrete banks.

He'd been gambling again, Dancer guessed, and was on a winning streak. Yan had told him how Ho had picked up the gambling bug once on a visit to the old Happy Valley horse-racing track in Hong Kong. Back on the mainland he was confined to beetle races or betting at mah-jong – and, at work, betting on the daily production figures of the factory.

'Hey!' Yan called out, 'You with your head in the clouds!'

Ho turned, startled. 'Oh? Hi, I didn't see you there. I was miles away. How are you?'

'Fine,' his friend replied. 'I was just going to have some tea. Join me.'

'Sure, why not?' But it wasn't until he had crossed the gangway that he realised that the "round eyes" in the beige tropical suit and fedora was with Yan Tao.

'This is Mr Dancer, an American businessman,' said Yan. 'We sometimes play golf together.'

'Call me John,' Dancer said in Mandarin and offered Ho a cigarette as they followed the information officer to the

145

upper-deck tearooms. 'Tao says you like a bet. Is that why you look so happy?'

As they took their seats at a table partitioned by flimsy bamboo blinds, Ho began pulling wads of *yuan* notes from his pockets, dumping them gleefully on the table. 'I win an accumulator. For three days I guess factory production of rivets correct to nearest one thousand gross. My friend Fang also has a good week, so I say to him double or quits. You understand?'

When Dancer nodded, Ho's grin was in danger of splitting his face in half. 'And I gather you won the toss?' Dancer said

After the waitress in traditional dress took their order, Yan said reproachfully: 'You won't feel so lucky with all that money if you're investigated on suspicion of corruption.'

Ho's face deflated and he turned to Dancer for sympathy. 'I want to be a businessman like you. An entrepreneur. But No. 6 Beijing Rivet Factory hasn't made it on to the open market yet and I doubt it ever will! Who would want it? So I get forty dollar a month. Only if I gamble will I be able to be a capitalist and make big dollar.'

'You won't get rich by gambling,' Yan warned.

Ho shrugged. 'I do OK. Besides, it's not illegal to gamble.'

'But it is illegal to be a subversive,' Yan replied sharply. 'If the Bureau investigate you on corruption, they'll talk to your family, your neighbours, your workmates, your friends. They will learn about the network, about me.'

A nervous smile had formed on Ho's lips and he stole a sideways glance at Dancer. 'I tell no one about anything,' he protested.

'It's all right,' Yan assured. 'Mr Dancer knows about the network, he wants to help us.'

Ho looked horrified. 'He *knows*?'

'He helped me to set it up,' Yan said flatly, and watched Ho's expression of horror turn to one of astonishment. 'He put me in touch with the American Embassy, with people

146

in the West who believe in democracy and who were prepared to assist us. If you are investigated, it could put everything at risk. Me and Mr Dancer included.'

The nervous smile was still on Ho's lips. 'I would tell no one about the network.'

Yan sighed. 'People are not stupid. Your friends or workmates can put two and two together. Many will suspect you are connected.'

'No one would say anything,' Ho insisted.

'Haven't you learned anything from reading about the Cultural Revolution?' Exasperation showed in Yan's eyes. 'We Chinese only ever look out for ourselves. It is bred in us through the lessons of history. If anybody thinks it will get the Bureau off their backs, they will split on you.'

A very astute observation, Dancer thought, and not one he had ever heard a Chinese make before. Only expats had come to the conclusion that after centuries of authoritarian or totalitarian rule, the Chinese had learned to get on with life and mind their own business in order to avoid trouble. China had become a very insular and selfish nation with little interest outside the immediate family or place of work. How else could it have allowed society to tear itself apart in the Mao years when every citizen would shamelessly accuse innocent colleagues at work, neighbours and even members of their own family and willingly join in their persecution? It was all done in order to avoid the same fate themselves and mostly it appeared to have been done without shame or remorse.

'I am sorry, Tao.' Ho hung his head, suddenly feeling ashamed. 'You must think I am very stupid.'

Before his friend could answer, the waitress returned with a tray and glasses of tea. After she had gone, Yan said, 'So no more gambling. In fact absolutely nothing that might draw you to the attention of the authorities. We cannot do anything that might put the network at risk. Not at this important time.'

'Important?' Ho was surprised. 'Is it?'

His friend made light of it, not wanting to give anything away. 'Well, after Hong Kong and soon Macao,' he said vaguely, knowing full well that Ho wouldn't stop to think he was being evasive. Then he changed the subject. 'And how is your sister?'

'Lily is well. Why don't you come round to the flat and see for yourself?'

A shadow seemed to pass over Yan's face and his smile looked a little forced. 'I don't think so.'

Ho shrugged. 'No, maybe not. Tell me, why is it she hates you so much?'

'It's a long story.' And Ho knew then that Yan wasn't about to tell it. Then the subject was changed again. 'I want a small favour. There is something you could do for the movement.'

'Yes?' Ho's eyes blazed with enthusiasm. 'Just say the word.'

Yan smiled. 'Come out for a drink with me and Mr Dancer tonight. I will explain then.'

Ho's eyes widened at the prospect of some intrigue. He loved the thought of a world of secrecy and whispers, of excitement and danger. 'Yes, of course.'

'Shall we meet back here at eight?'

It was agreed and Cheung Ho scooped up his wad of *yuan* before leaving the floating teahouse without a backward glance.

As he walked, passing several optimistic old men casting fishing lines into the Bright Horse's putrid flow, he wondered about his friend Yan Tao and the American called Dancer. Yan was always full of surprises. Once you got to know the high-flyer in the Chicom's Public Information Office, you found that he wasn't quite the po-faced stuffed shirt he appeared. The dark suit, steel-rimmed spectacles and his unbending manner were a veneer. He could smile, though his humour tended to be dust dry and rather clever. Unlike others who had been quickly elevated to positions of influence in the government apparatus, Yan never let it go to his head, never considered himself to be in some way superior to his former university graduate friends. Even friends like Ho, who had messed up his life and climbed no higher up the social ladder than to become a production-line supervisor at No. 6 Beijing District Steel Rivet Factory.

Who, he wondered, would suspect Yan's deep involvement in the democracy movement? Even he had not realised that Yan actually had personal contacts with the Americans – Americans who actually spoke fluent Chinese at that! What sort of Americans could do that? He'd never heard of one before. Maybe the man was a spy. A spy from the CIA. He had heard the Politburo accusations on the radio that the CIA was stirring up trouble and helping the separatists in Xingjiang province, but he had never believed it. And Yan had confirmed it was rubbish. After all, he should know; he probably wrote the script. Now he laughed at the thought that the stranger might be a CIA spy, that Yan might know such people. He would find out tonight. Perhaps the American would want him to blow up No. 6 Beijing District Steel Rivet Factory!

Overcome with mirth, he left the riverside path and climbed up some steps through a line of junipers and willows to the main road that ran parallel to the path. Beyond were the teetering high-rise blocks that had been home to the Cheung family for the past five years.

The stained grey concrete towers had a forlorn, haphazard look about them. In order to create more space, most of the balconies had been closed in using unmatching doors and windows taken from other buildings due for demolition. Air-conditioning units hung like untidy afterthoughts from the outside walls together with the tatty semaphore flags of drying laundry that fluttered in the waning sunlight.

It was typical of the polluted Beijing suburbs, so it never occurred to Ho just how depressing it all was as he walked across the bare, dusty grounds where ubiquitous plastic carrier bags, cigarette packs and drink cans eddied back and forth in the breeze. Besides, his thoughts were now back to how he could best invest his growing accumulation of *yuan*. Having mentally examined all his options, it once again seemed to him that good betting odds still took some beating.

The elevator had not worked since before the Cheungs had moved in, but at least they only lived on the third floor, which was also good because that was as high as the water pressure reached. All those who lived above them had to fetch their supply in buckets. Now, as woks were lit by the occupants of the block in readiness for evening meals, an array of enticing smells wafted through the building, seemingly carried on the sweet notes of a violin.

Ho wrinkled up his nose as he took to the stairs. That was the one thing he had against living in the same flat as his sister Lily. He hated the sound of violins.

'Are you strangling the cat again?' he asked as he entered the living room. The place was neat and clean, but the fabric of the sofa was worn and the rugs on the concrete floor were threadbare. Lily stood in white blouse and baggy black trousers, her hair tumbling down to the violin which she had tucked underneath her chin. Young Bao sat facing her in an upright chair, emulating his mother with the smaller instrument on which Lily herself had learned to play as a child.

She turned and frowned at her younger brother. 'Don't *you* be so rude. You really are a cultural desert, aren't you?'

Ho put both hands to his ears and feigned agony. 'No, I can't stand it with *both* of you at it now!' That made Bao shriek with laughter and Ho grinned at his nephew.

Lily said proudly, 'It's only his second lesson and he's doing very well.'

'Well, I'm glad I'm going out tonight. Two violinists in the house will drive me crazy!'

Lily frowned. 'Out again? You are always going out. You will never save any money.'

He poked his tongue out at her in a friendly way and waved the wad of *yuan* at her; like a small boy, he still enjoyed provoking his sister. 'That's where you are wrong, see.'

Lily knew all about that. 'Gambling again. And all you've won today you will lose tonight.'

'No, that's all behind me now.' He adopted an aloof expression. 'I shall be sorting out my investments. I am going to be an entrepreneur.'

Lily shook her head sadly. Poor Ho's extravagant plans never came to anything.

'Ho!' a voice called suddenly from the kitchen. 'Did you say you are going out?' The diminutive shape of their mother tottered out through the steam, as thick as dry ice clouds at a rock concert. 'You *are* having supper before you go?'

He bent to kiss her. 'Of course, Mother, I wouldn't miss supper for the world.' He'd done that twice before and had never heard the end of it. Mama Cheung had a fearsome tongue for one so small and unassuming. Now satisfied, she disappeared back into the billowing mist to continue her preparations.

'Are you out with friends?' Lily asked casually, as she packed the violins away neatly in a cardboard box.

'With the old university crowd,' he answered, noting how her back arched perceptibly and her face stiffened. 'You could come too. Mama will look after Bao. You should get out more.'

She forced a smile back on to her lips. 'Not tonight. It's been a long day and Mr Wang's a slave-driver.'

'You really should come,' Ho urged again. 'You know some of the gang.'

Lily said stiffly, 'I suppose Yan Tao will be there?'

Ho grinned. 'Sure. Tao's always there. He's good fun really, very witty. Not the stuffed shirt he sometimes seems. He often asks after you.'

Lily ignored that, the very idea of Yan Tao thinking

about her at all made her wince. She didn't want to be anywhere near him, even if it was just in his mind. Perhaps especially not in his mind. 'I'd be obliged if you told him nothing about me.'

'You don't like him very much, do you?'

'That is putting it mildly.' One fine eyebrow arched in emphasis. 'He skulks like a treacherous dog. Yan Tao is not to be trusted. If you had any sense you would have nothing to do with him.'

Ho was perplexed. 'Why do you say that? Why will you never tell me?'

'Because, little brother, it is too painful for me even to think about.'

'But you and your fiancé were once great friends with Yan Tao. You were all at university together.'

There was no softness in those sable eyes now, they froze over with a patina of anger. 'You are exactly right. We were all friends – or so we thought. But we were wrong. Because Yan Tao is why Jin died and why little Bao was born without a father.'

'I don't understand. Jin died in Tiananmen Square, killed by the People's Army.'

Lily said softly: 'You don't have to be the one to pull the trigger in order to kill someone, Ho. You can kill someone just as easily by doing nothing.'

'Is that what happened in Tiananmen Square?'

She didn't answer for a moment, couldn't because the words would have caught in her throat. Her eyes were staring at the simple shrine on the corner table. Two small glass incense-burners, at present unlit, and between them a brass picture frame from which the handsome, unlined face of Jin smiled. But Lily could not focus on it, her mind's eye seeing only the vast concrete stage that had been Tiananmen Square that night in 1989 when the nation's tragedy was played out before a world audience.

Hundreds of tents had covered the flagstones of the open space that was a kilometre long and half as wide again and which, ironically, meant the Gate of Heavenly Peace. Yet that night even Tiananmen had not seemed big enough to contain the tens of thousands of demonstrators hemmed in by the blood-red entrance of the Forbidden City on the north side and Mao's mausoleum to the south, and flanked by the Great Hall of the People and the museums of Revolution and History to the west and east.

In the centre, the three-stepped terraces and stone obelisk of the Monument to the People's Heroes rose like a ship out of a sea of youthful humanity. From it hung the white banner like a sail with its calligraphy in black. Hunger Strike.

She and Jin had travelled by train from Sichuan province to join the protest. Jin already knew Yan, who was an undergraduate in Beijing, because both were prominent in the student union movements. Jin was immediately invited to join the headquarters staff of the rally to work on speeches to be broadcast to the crowds over the Voice of Freedom loudspeaker system. Lily had felt a little left out; she was not politically minded like her fiancé and felt useless and overwhelmed by the awesome events in Tiananmen. That was when she decided to make her own contribution to the protest by joining the growing body of over eight hundred hunger strikers. Jin was horrified at the prospect, but she had ignored his protest.

And it was four days later, when she fainted and was taken to Beijing Medical College, that she discovered she was two months pregnant. Jin was overcome by emotion at the news. He was already awed by the momentous events of the past few days and now he was told he was to have a child by the girl he loved so dearly. It seemed like a wonderful omen for the future of the whole of China. They hugged each other, smiling and crying at the same time.

The next day, having stirred world opinion, the demonstration's leaders called off the mass hunger strike. And barely had they done so than martial law was declared by the government. Then the rumours began – rumours that more than a hundred thousand soldiers of the People's Liberation Army were closing in on the square. Four helicopters hovered permanently, high above the crowds, watching. Tension mounted as rumours multiplied. Throughout Beijing, over half a million people had barricaded the outlying streets, preventing the troops from entering the centre of the city. Everyone tried to stay awake through the night, tremulous with fear. But, when the sun rose, still nothing had happened. For days the stand-off continued.

Yet they all knew that the critical moment was approaching. When her fiancé Jin visited Lily at the hospital with Yan, she had insisted she was well enough to rejoin them and the thousands of others in Tiananmen.

The memory was still so vivid, as if it was yesterday. She wished she could explain to Ho what it had been like to be there.

She said: 'Just before the tanks came, do you know what my Jin said to that friend of yours? He told that skulking dog, Yan, that, as one of the main leaders, *his* safety must come first. That at the first sign of danger he should run into the crowd, hide and go underground until it was safe again.'

'What did Yan say?' Ho asked. 'I bet he refused to run away.'

Lily wondered how her younger brother could be so naïve. 'Not exactly. Yan was never stupid. No, he listened to my Jin all right and borrowed a white coat from one of the hospital doctors. That was when we first heard.'

Ho's eyes widened, reading the look of relived fear in her eyes. 'What happened?'

'At nine o'clock that evening a student came into the hospital, his shirt dripping with blood. "The soldiers are coming," he said. "They are killing and striking everyone in their path. Women, old men and children. A child of three died in my arms." The student could hardly speak for his tears.'

'What did you do?' Ho asked.

'Jin and Yan immediately decided to return to the students' headquarters tent next to the Monument of People's Heroes. To defend the square. Obviously I went with them. But we never got there. Somehow the People's Army had managed to bypass the ring of barricades – some said there are hundreds of secret passages for just such a situation – so we had no warning. There were soldiers everywhere, blocking our route. And now tanks were pushing the barricades aside, grinding students beneath their tracks. I saw a girl student, a friend of mine, try to stop the soldiers. "We aren't rioters!" she protested to one. "We are patriotic! We want only good for our country!"'

'What did he say to that?'

The memory seemed to jolt Lily like a tiny electric shock. 'Say? He said nothing. He just looked at her sort of curiously, then thrust a bayonet into her chest. Just like that, without a word.'

Ho gulped.

Lily said, 'Before I could stop him, Jin ran over to help her. But the soldier just screamed at him and shoved him away. I asked Yan – the friend you think is so wonderful – to go and stop Jin and help my girlfriend. He was in a white coat, the soldiers would think he was a doctor.'

'Yan did not go?' Ho sounded astonished.

Lily shook her head. 'Yan did not go. He left me there and slunk away into the shadows. Just before the soldier shot my Jin in the head. I did not see Yan again for years. Not until after I was rehabilitated.'

At that moment the kitchen door burst open and Mama Cheung appeared like a wizened little genie amid clouds of deliciously aromatic steam. 'Ready, ready, children! Quick, quick. All sit down before it is cold.'

The spell was broken and Lily was thankful for that. But, as she sat through the meal and watched Little Bao eagerly gulping down his noodles, her memory kept returning to her beloved Jin. Seeing in her mind the vast encampment of tents on Tiananmen Square under a cold white moon, a hundred thousand brave and happy young faces, all listening to Beethoven's Ninth Symphony. It was music from another world. Music from the moon. Solemn, inspiring, magnificent. She remembered how Jin had hugged her close and she had snuggled against his chest in the euphoric early days before the soldiers and the tanks came, before her soul was stolen from her.

To this day she couldn't bear listening to the Ninth without feeling a knife blade twisting deep inside her. But thinking about Jin again also reminded her of happier times. Once Ho had gone out, and Bao had been put into his cot in the bedroom she also shared with her mother, Lily again took up her violin. Slow quiet numbers for lovers she played, sweet sounds that would not annoy her neighbours, songs she and Jin had held hands to, and once had made love to.

Mama Cheung fell asleep, snoring with her mouth open. Lily smiled to herself as the old woman seemed to snore in time with her playing.

Then she heard the noise on the steps beyond the door, a scraping of shoes on concrete. She glanced at the cheap plastic wall clock. Ten o'clock. Too early to be Ho. But time she woke her mother and for them both to go to their beds.

The knock on the door made her jump. As Mama Cheung stirred suddenly, Lily put down her violin and crossed the room. It might be a neighbour, maybe complaining about the music. As she threw open the door, she did not anticipate finding Ho standing there, clutching for support at the arm of a slightly embarrassed American.

'I hope I've got the right address,' he said in near perfect Mandarin, 'he's not making much sense.'

Lily's hand flew to her mouth. 'Oh, is he sick? Is it bad?'

John Dancer smiled. 'As sick as someone can be on too much Dragon Seal. It's dire stuff. Can I bring him in?'

He caught the look of consternation in her eyes and

knew she would be unhappy at allowing a Westerner into her humble home. Ho's legs suddenly buckled and Dancer strained to hold him.

'Yes, yes,' she said, stepping aside to allow them through.

Ho started coming round. 'I am fine, I am fine. Let me stand up.'

Now Mama Cheung was fully awake and on her feet. She smiled shyly at Dancer and gave a sort of bobbing cursty before rounding on Ho. 'You bring disgrace on our family, *laoda*,' she berated him, using his family title of 'eldest son'. 'To be drunk so that a total stranger – a foreigner – has to bring you home! What will he think of the Chinese people?'

'Actually, I am not a complete stranger,' Dancer said, intervening before the old woman decided to hit Ho over the head with her wok; she looked quite capable of it. 'I often have a drink with Yan Tao and his group of friends. Ho is one of them.'

As the young man flopped on to the old sofa, Mama Cheung still glared at him. 'He is a disgrace. A no-good.'

'I've never seen him drunk before,' Dancer said. 'I expect it was the bad beer.'

'Bad beer,' Ho repeated absently.

Dancer had seen the flicker of recognition in Lily's eyes as they'd entered, but she had said nothing. No doubt she was ashamed of her brother and, in the Chinese way, ashamed of the cramped family home. He said softly, 'I think we know each other. You are Lily Cheung. We met over supper with your boss, Mr Wang. And shared a taxi.'

She averted her face a fraction, blushing prettily. 'I remember, Mr Dancer. I am in your debt.'

Ho began to giggle. '*Jiejie* Lily, you must make tea for our friend. He has been most kind. It is the least we can do, to show him some hospitality.'

She hesitated. 'If Mr Dancer would like?'

Mama Cheung tut-tutted. 'Quite right. Tea, tea. I will

157

make some while you young people chatter!' She brushed Lily's protest aside and bustled towards the kitchen.

As she disappeared, Ho took his cue and lolled his head sideways on the sofa cushion, feigning sleep, just as he and Dancer had discussed it. Lily looked abashed as the American glanced round the tiny living room. It was dominated by a television set which had pride of place in front of the main wall which was covered with framed photographs of Cheung family relatives and ancestors. In the left hand corner was the shrine to Jin.

'A handsome fellow,' Dancer observed lightly.

For a second her face lit up at his words. 'Yes. That is Jin, the father of my son.'

'I'm sorry.'

'It was long ago,' she said with a tight smile. 'At least he left me with the most precious gift anyone could. Others at Tiananmen were not so lucky.'

'Tiananmen?' He made himself sound surprised. 'That was a terrible business, wicked. It must never happen again.'

'No,' she agreed.

Then he saw what he'd been looking for. An old electrical record player in sixties style red plastic. Next to it was a stack of LP jackets. The top one was Gershwin. In fact, they were all Gershwin, Ho had told him.

'Ah, is your mother a fan?'

'I beg your pardon, Mr Dancer?' Momentarily bewildered and looking stunningly beautiful in the process.

'Gershwin. I love his work.'

Her eyes glittered with pleasure. 'You like his music too? I adore it. Not Mama though. She loves our opera and taught me music as a child.'

'And was that you playing the violin?'

'Yes.' Again the eyes danced as though she'd suddenly found someone to share a great secret with. 'Do you play?'

He grinned at that, the idea genuinely amusing him. 'Me? I'm tone deaf. I just know what I like. Gershwin and violins.'

158

She looked a little disappointed. 'Violins and Gershwin don't mix so well. Gershwin is best for pianos.'

'Of course,' he replied. He and Yan had been desperately trying to remember some Gershwin titles all evening. He could only remember 'Rhapsody in Blue' and 'Fascinating Rhythm', and Yan came up with two others. 'I think "Summertime" is my favourite.'

Just then Mama Cheung bustled in, carrying a tray. 'Tea, tea!' she gibbered in her excited sing-song falsetto. 'And I make some steam dumplings. Quick, quick, eat before it is cold and all ruined!'

As she fussed about, Dancer caught Lily's eye and smiled. It was a courtesy to provide sustenance for an unexpected guest, no matter what the time of day. Later she whispered, 'Mama likes you. She says you are the first barbarian – oh, forgive me, she means foreign gentleman – ever to come to her home.'

'Your hospitality is much appreciated,' Dancer replied. Then he hesitated for a moment. 'Do you know – I'm getting spare tickets for that concert next week. You know, the Boston Symphony. In return for your kindness, perhaps you would allow me to take you?'

For a moment he saw the look of horror in her eyes. Clearly she couldn't think how to respond to what she took as being openly propositioned by a foreigner and in front of her *mama*. He cursed his phraseology and added quickly: 'I am sure you and Mother Cheung would enjoy it.'

Lily's smile returned instantly and the old woman mumbled happily. It was obviously a long time since she had been invited out for an evening. He may not have won the daughter over yet, but Mama Cheung was in the bag.

Ho, who made a sudden recovery once the outing was agreed, confirmed it with a wink as he later showed their guest to the door. When Dancer returned to his apartment, he immediately switched on his computer and prepared an encoded e-mail for Bill Dawson at the US Embassy.

'Initial contact with "Guizhou" – given codename –

successful. For follow-up, three tickets needed for next week's Boston Symphony Orchestra concert at the People's Hall.' That sent, he switched to his Web browser and keyed Gershwin into the search engine. Half an hour later, he'd accessed everything about the composer he would ever want to know.

He switched off and walked into the living room to pour himself a drink. Debs caught his eye from the mantelpiece.

'What's that?' he could almost hear her asking.

'My homework. A print-out on Gershwin.'

'What are you doing to that poor girl?'

'Taking her to a concert.'

He could hear the magic laugh. 'You fancy her.'

'I only fancy you.'

'But Lily Cheung is living, John, I am not.' A giggle. 'And besides, she fancies you.'

'Rubbish,' he said aloud, feeling suddenly and inexplicably angry with himself.

> *The mountain is moving,*
> *I feel it in my heart.*
> *With no quake or asteroid*
> *To complete the task,*
> *China's children will bend*
> *With bare and bloody hands*
> *To move it stone by stone.*

Fan Xiu Kun could no longer write his words. They'd long ago removed pen and paper from his cell and burned the few books brought in by the rare visitor he was allowed.

In earlier days, he'd have had a pencil stub smuggled in and would scribble lines in a microscopic hand on scraps of paper, like chewing-gum wrappers or can labels that he'd found. He would conceal them in the foreskin of his penis to pass through the guards' searches, then wait until he was at the quarry where the inmates broke rocks from dawn to dusk. When he was granted his one visit to the crude latrine shed on the site, he would transfer the little note of calligraphy to a small plastic container that was buried in the earth behind the bucket. Later, a friend would come and retrieve it.

Eventually, he did not know how, his work would be published – at one time in small volumes smuggled into China from Hong Kong or more lately on sites in the ether which he was told was something called the World Wide Web.

He would learn of this only because the authorities told him it was why the beatings were about to begin again and another round of self-criticism.

But even that was impossible since he'd been incarcerated in his glass cage with only a thin straw mattress and a tin pisspot for company. The light was on permanently day and night and the guards were always watching. After several years, even they had grown bored of mocking him each time he squatted on the pot.

Had a degree of privacy been given back, he doubted he could still hold a pencil with his broken hands or see the words he'd written as his eyesight dimmed. There was no nutrition in a diet of cabbage soup and he could feel his body disintegrating from the inside out as each day went by.

But he had found a way to memorise his words with the help of the woman who came to his cell each evening, passing through the solid glass and invisible to all but him. Only he could see her auburn hair and sky-blue eyes, only he could hear her words and tinkling laughter. For she was a living photograph from his memory, someone whom he could conjure into life at will.

He wondered where she was now, what she was doing. Whether she was aware – just a strange sensation perhaps – when his mind was talking to hers over the miles and over the years since he had last met her.

Apart from being a poet, Fan had been a professor of philosophy at Qinghua University and had long ago learned that nothing in the earthly world was quite as it seemed. He had studied all the great religions of the world and could, at one time at least, quote at random from Laozi, the legendary founder of Taoism, and Kong Zi, known to the world as Confucius.

However, his favourite was the great sage of Ancient Egypt, Hermes the Thrice-Great, for through his works Fan had learned to endure his pain and suffering. Because, as Hermes pointed out, the present did not really exist in any tangible form, only in the smallest microsecond of time. All else was past or had yet to come.

Through such teachings Fan had come to question the nature of existence and the mysteries of life, death and the cosmos. He had gained a fleeting insight into the spirit world and astral planes and other miracles of nature and the power of the mind. He learned that only humans amongst earth's creatures had God's greatest gift and the most terrible curse: the gift of laughter and the certain knowledge they will die. He understood when people saw other humans, what they were actually seeing were reflected images of light. Take away the light and they ceased to exist. All done by mirrors, Fan sometimes mused, but it went a long way to explaining ghosts and spirits, premonitions and apparitions, bizarre but actual occurrences that have puzzled mankind since the dawn of time.

But it mattered little how or why she came to him each evening to lighten his burden, to listen to his words and remember them. And when, as increasingly happened, his disorientated and bewildered mind could not recall the words he had created only the day before, he knew he could rely on her to remind him.

It was his greatest comfort in these ever-darkening days. But it was a comfort that thousands of other political prisoners in China were not lucky enough to share – and would not until they moved the mountain of Communist totalitarianism, stone by stone.

Six

Events were taking on an inexorable momentum of their own which Lieutenant Nick Lake found disturbing when he thought about it. Not that he had time for much in the way of thinking beyond each immediate problem. At any moment he half-expected to get a signal flashed from Admiralty headquarters in Northwood, England: FINEX. Finish of Exercise. But it never came.

What had come were the replacements for Troy Krowsky and his SEALs. They arrived four days later in the shape of eight SAS troopers and a full back-up team who would assist in the preparations. One of their number was a warrant officer from the 'green slime', or Intelligence Corps. He'd already been nicknamed, simply and rather unimaginitively, Slime.

Heading the group was a tall, grey-haired and softly spoken Scots staff sergeant called Dave McVicar.

'Someone told us you need a babysitter. What seems to be your problem?' were his opening words and set the tone.

Lake grinned; he'd met McVicar before. 'There wasn't one until you bunch of wankers walked in.'

McVicar was the best possible choice and Lake felt a vast sense of relief. Some of the SAS new boys seriously believed they were invincible and that could be a real pain while they learned that they weren't. But the Scotsman was old school and had been around since the beginning of time. He must have been close to active service retirement age at forty-five, Lake reckoned, and indeed later learned that McVicar had pushed hard against the CO's inclination to go for someone younger. In the end, experience prevailed.

As soon as they were billeted and their kit stowed, an

assortment of bottles materialised from weighty, stuffed-to-bursting bergens and they settled down with the SBS men and Al Cherrier's submarine crew to discuss the upcoming mission. An interfering US Navy petty officer who tried to enforce the United States 'Right Spirit alcohol-aware program' dry navy rule was told in no uncertain terms that now the SEALs had gone, this SBS/SAS billet was requisitioned on behalf of Her Majesty Queen Elizabeth the Second as an outpost of empire. As such, like any embassy, it was now sovereign British soil and the US Navy could sod off. Cherrier opted to look the other way; he had more pressing problems at hand.

Of the eight new arrivals, four were experienced combat swimmers from Boat Troops. The other four, including McVicar, were Chinese linguists drawn from different squadrons.

'No Chinese speakers left at Hereford,' McVicar said. 'They'll be hard pushed to order a takeaway now.'

'Did anyone brief you what's going on before you left?' Lake asked.

'No. A complete security blackout. We were told it would be exceedingly dangerous, it would involve some underwater work and certain agent-handling procedures. Then, most unusually, we were told individually we could opt out if we wished. So naturally we all signed up. 'Course, we realised that Communist Chinese territory must feature on the agenda somewhere. We thought maybe some recce work in the islands disputed with Beijing.'

Lake gave an uncertain smile. 'Exactly what we thought, and we were wrong.'

When Lake revealed what little he knew about the situation, the new arrivals were as stunned as the others had been.

They had seen little of Janie Walsh, the American-Chinese OpsCom from the CIA, during those first few days. However, it was clear to Lake that she had managed to have the Deadwater Project ring-fenced, so they could get on with their preparations without any outside interference or intrusive visits from empire-builders from Langley or the Pentagon.

The new arrivals had spent the time sorting and checking the 'hamper' of kit and weaponry they had brought with them following an advisory list that had originally been supplied by Lake. This included weapons to be used by the Discretionary Warfare Team in deniable operations and were all Chinese-made versions of Soviet products: AK47s and 74s, Makarov and Tokarev pistols and 60mm mortars. All these were drawn from British Army armouries in the UK, having been captured in Oman and other Middle East conflicts. Amongst the specialist equipment were satcom sets and a wide range of communications equipment for different scenarios, night-vision and GPS navigation aids, radio scanners and portable jammers.

Those who were rusty on combat-swimming techniques planned to undergo a crash refresher course organised by Lake. His plan had been to take USS *Manta* to a remote area of sea beyond the base and familiarise the SAS team with the difficulties of SCUBA operations. This had to be scotched when a group of anonymous white-coated computer technologists turned up to swarm all over the craft, making practical training impossible.

Yet the Discretionary Warfare Team were hardly in a position to complain. Walsh had been as good as her word and had clearly been laying it on the line to her superiors regarding Al Cherrier's fears about the craft's shortcomings.

'Trouble is,' the captain mused to Lake and McVicar, 'you can't solve problems like these by throwing money at them. We're in a hurry and the ship's so small the microchip boys can only work in it one at a time. Doesn't matter how big a budget or priority it's been given.'

At least Walsh had earned herself some much needed Brownie points and was well received the next evening when she turned up unannounced during the mess supper. She looked exhausted from endless meetings at US Pacific Unified Headquarters – dubbed CINCPAC – with a succession of defence intelligence experts flown in at regular intervals from both the United States and Britain for discussions and briefings.

She brought news that they could expect important visitors the following morning.

At 0900 hours sharp, Walsh called Lake and McVicar to the meeting in the facility's conference suite. Al Cherrier was put on stand-by to join them later. He fully appreciated the 'need-to-know' basis of the briefing; if ever *Manta* was discovered and its crew captured by the Chinese, it was imperative that they knew as little about the fine detail of the on-shore operations as possible.

There were only two other people in the suite, both apparently civilians. One was a stoutly built, middle-aged man with cropped thinning hair and pale appraising eyes. The other was a tall woman in a summer dress who carried herself with slightly stooped shoulders. She stood in a cocoon of cigarette smoke of her own creating, looking as though she hadn't had time to wash her hair for days.

'Best we just work on first-name terms,' Walsh said. 'This is Bill from our embassy in Beijing. And this is Iona, his counterpart with the Brits.'

'A fine Scottish name,' McVicar observed as he took her hand.

She smiled back at the tall, quietly spoken soldier who had a seemingly permanent expression of amusement in his eyes. 'And that's a fine Scottish accent. Aberdeen?'

'Close. Peterhead.'

'Shall we kick off?' Bill Dawson suggested, a note of irritation creeping into his voice. 'The sooner Iona and I get back to Beijing the better. As you might imagine, there's a lot going on there right now.'

Iona said: 'Let me give you some background. Western intelligence operations have been going on in China since

166

long before World War Two when, of course, the country was invaded by the Japanese and the OSS and SOE became involved. The Chinese Communists have always been seen as a potential enemy, although perhaps not as immediately threatening as the former Soviet Union.'

'But that assessment got upgraded during the Korean War,' Dawson added. 'After which, we soon found the Chinese had a finger in every bowl of shit around the world. In the mid-fifties one of our agents brought out a high-ranking defector. He had with him a document over a thousand pages long which was the blueprint for chilling Chinese ambition.'

Lake looked quizzical. 'I thought all that yellow peril stuff went out with Fu Manchu and Bulldog Drummond.'

Iona smiled. 'Maybe they gave the Chinese the idea.'

'They've been at it a long time,' Dawson continued. 'Westerners don't understand the Chinese way of looking at things. This Chicom plan of theirs is like the thousand-year-old egg. They'll just work at it for as long as it takes. A lot of people dismissed the defector's report, then years later some had cause to remember. Viet Nam, Cambodia, continually stirring up the whole Far East, then in Africa – always chipping away, mostly by helping the enemies of the West. The latest bag of worms has been providing arms to South American guerrillas and narcos and selling nuclear technology to Iran.

'And, of course, in the Far East they've always had their own agenda. The current ruling Chicom caucus is both aggressive and weak-minded. They live in fear of those they rule. They've seen what's happened in eastern Europe and the former Soviet Union and have no intention of repeating those mistakes in the Middle Kingdom. So the Politburo has set out to claim its post-Marxist legitimacy by promoting vitriolic nationalism instead. All this perceived softening of political and human rights might be swallowed by the politicos on Capitol Hill, but all the changes are cosmetic.'

Iona lit a fresh cigarette from the butt of her first, and added for good measure, 'The present leadership feels cheated by history, you see. The old buffers have chips on their shoulders the size of logs. They know China was once a world power and they're determined it shall be again. For years they lost face over Hong Kong and will never forgive the British for that. And they feel despised by the rest of the world, especially America, who they consider an interfering interloper in their area of influence.'

'But they can see that the tide has turned their way,' Dawson interrupted. 'Without the former USSR to worry about on its western flank, China can turn its attention to dominating the Pacific Rim. We've seen it a hundred times in history. If a nation fears internal unrest – as Beijing does from the Muslims in Xingjiang and growing millions of unemployed from ailing state industries – there is no better way to unify a country than by going to war with those you blame for your troubles. China has a territorial dispute with every goddamn one of its neighbours and, one way or another, it damn well intends to win them. As I understand you've been told, that starts with a planned invasion of Taiwan in under four months' time.'

'Surely they'd be afraid of US military reaction?' Lake suggested.

Dawson's laugh was genuine. 'China's the only country in the world who still targets the US with nukes. The Beijing generals don't think we'd be willing to trade Los Angeles for Taiwan. And I think they could be right.'

Iona said, 'In addition, some factions within the UK and US diplomatic communities have given the impression of supporting the legitimacy of China's claim that Taiwan is a breakaway province. That's encouraged Beijing no end and added to our current dilemma. Besides, the West has too much invested in China to risk losing it all and the Politburo knows that. The Chinese invented chess.'

'And are we to be the pawns?' McVicar asked in a low, grim voice.

Lake glanced sideways at him with disapproval, but then the tall Scotsman never had been much afraid of anything before he was due for retirement, let alone now.

However, Iona Moncrieff just smiled gently. 'No, Dave, our deployment should be seen as part of checkmate if all goes to plan. In chess terms, our opening gambits were made a long time ago.'

Dawson explained, 'At the height of the Viet Nam War, the CIA's head of Clandestine Ops set up a highly secret subsection charged with penetrating the Bamboo Curtain. It was no quick fix, but playing the long game, because that's the only way you'll ever beat China. And it wasn't going to be easy. In those days, the only way for the CIA to get a foot in the door of that closed society was through the OC – the Overseas Chinese.'

'That's where we were able to give a helping hand,' Iona said, 'especially through Hong Kong. There are some fifty-five million OC in the Far East and financially their massive private family corporations dominate the Pacific Rim. Some businesses are a thousand years old, well before Communism was a twinkle in Marx's eye. Their liquid assets alone have been estimated at two trillion dollars.'

A ghost of a smile passed McVicar's lips. 'What's a trillion?'

Iona liked that. Her laugh turned into a congested smoker's cough as she wheezed, 'I don't know, Dave. Several squillions, I suppose!'

Dawson didn't like the jokes and didn't much like what he regarded as the Scotsman's bad attitude. 'The point is, the OC have always been very strong on historical family connections on the mainland, mostly the more prosperous southern provinces, and naturally they were the first heavy investors after the Cultural Revolution. So the OC were our only way in to a closed state. But, because the OC's corporations were as secretive as China itself, we had to start with youngsters. Classic recruitment. Both we and you Brits would have all potentially suitable OC targets screened when they went abroad to study. We'd recruit a fellow student to act as our handler first – interests of national security and all that bull-shit – and to befriend the inevitably lost and lonely OC arrival. 'Course, many of these young handlers realised they already had a leg-up into a career at Langley if they wanted it. I seem to remember Wharton School of Business was a particularly happy hunting ground.'

'In the old days,' Iona explained, 'students from mainland China wouldn't go to American universities, so SIS picked up likely high-flyers in London or Paris or one of the unaligned countries. Basically the same methods.'

'How do you persuade them to work for you?' Lake asked. The inner workings of the intelligence services always fascinated him. 'Blackmail?'

Iona smiled. Why did everyone always think the worst of people in her game? 'Sometimes, Nick, but only if all else fails. As students together, both handler and target would become genuine friends, albeit one of them with an ulterior motive. Most students want freedom and democracy – it's what being a student is all about. The handler encourages that thinking and also steers the target round to his way of thinking about being successful in business. And top of the list is that old adage, It's not what you know, but who. . .'

'We would reinforce this by setting up genuine study courses, emphasising the need to keep track of who's who in foreign government and business and how to utilize this knowledge for commercial benefit. By the time he graduates, the target is thoroughly schooled in noting details about anyone of any influence he meets in mainland China. Wife and kids' names, birthdays, anniversaries, likes and dislikes – and especially whether he appears to have leanings to pro-democracy and free trade.'

'So handler and target keep in touch after university,' Dawson went on. 'The handler puts good business deals the way of his unwitting target. In return the handler asks for some low-grade economic intelligence. He's hooked, but everybody's happy. It takes time to build up the big picture of all the crucial players in Beijing and the provinces, but we've been at it nearly a quarter-century now, so our knowlege is pretty extensive.

'Things accelerated in the early eighties, when China abandoned Maoism. Having identified liberal-minded Party politicos, businessmen and military, we could start getting our handlers and their agents to plug these potential allies into profitable commercial deals. We set up "sterile" front companies and corporations to facilitate this, mostly running out through Hong Kong.'

'What happened after the Tiananmen Square massacre?' Lake asked, but he had already guessed the answer.

'It was the biggest mistake the Politburo ever made. Played right into our hands,' Iona confirmed. 'The student movements in China had grown up organically during the eighties, encouraged and funded through connections with the Overseas Chinese already recruited by the CIA. After the massacre, the leaders went into hiding. Many fled the country and we were waiting for them. By the time the dust settled, links between the West's intelligence agencies, the OC and the student networks were vastly strengthened.'

Dawson leaned forward across the table, his voice low and earnest. 'Since that time, student members of the Tiananmen days have also moved up through the Chicom apparatus. In party politics, the military, business, academia and the media. Those with a burning thirst for revenge are now aged between twenty-nine and thirty-five. Others recruited in the seventies are in their mid-forties and starting to have influence on the levers of power. All these people desire democracy and see clearly the benefits to come from a full-free market economy. It just needs one thing to happen—'

He'd left the sentence hanging. It was an accident, but Lake didn't miss the implication. He glanced across the table at Walsh.

'At an earlier meeting you said intelligence sources

171

suggested that China was about to enter a period of unrest. Did you mean that we are going to be the ones who start it?'

Dawson chuckled. 'Very astute, but nothing quite so dramatic. A lot of Chinese are going to be very unhappy at the idea of an invasion of Taiwan. We believe that may well trigger a political or military coup. If that happens, it'll be your job to see that our agent networks are fully supplied with whatever is required.'

Easy words, Lake thought. Beware easy words. He caught McVicar's eye and could read that expression like a book. Dawson was being more than economical with the truth. But he let it pass, saying, 'So how are we to achieve this?'

The CIA man placed his elbows on the table and slowly interlaced his fingers. 'One of our sterile front companies is a joint-venture courier business in Beijing. It was set up using Overseas Chinese money although it was indirectly a CIA investment. It has since branched into specialist VIP aviation.'

'Handy for our work,' McVicar remarked, seeing the possibilities.

Dawson continued. 'You, Dave, and your three Chinese-speaking buddies go to Beijing through the front door as replacement staff for the courier company, having been recruited in Australia.'

'You act as advance party,' Iona said, looking directly at McVicar, 'assessing with Bill's man on the ground what needs to be done, where and how. Your chaps are fully trained in running agents and the like, even if you are a bit rusty, so you shouldn't find it too daunting. You'll have plenty of expert help at hand. Meanwhile, Nick here and his flippered chums will come in from *Manta* and rendezvous with you on shore. They'll be ferrying in everything from money to communications equipment, arms and explosives.'

Just like that, Lake thought sourly. 'What about cover for

172

shore work?' he asked. He wasn't looking to get shot as a spy or spend the rest of his life in a gulag.

'Let McVicar's boys do the contact work, you just provide backup as and when required, helping out where you can. You'll have passports, stamped visas and return tickets – in fact everything to get you through any routine police or Security Bureau checks. But you'll be covering your own backs, remember that.'

Lake grinned with more humour than he felt. 'You mean we have to shoot our way out of trouble.'

Iona gave one of her disapproving auntie looks. 'That shouldn't be necessary. Just diversion enough for you to get back to your emergency rendezvous and the submarine.'

The meeting was interrupted then by an orderly bringing in coffee and biscuits. 'Let's take five,' Dawson announced. 'Then we'll get Captain Cherrier in here.'

'Where do I find the bog?' McVicar asked innocently.

'You mean heads, landlubber,' Lake corrected. 'Come on, I'll show you.'

As they left the conference suite and entered the passage, Lake muttered, 'Pretty awesome stuff, eh? I feel like I've just stepped into a Clancy novel.'

McVicar grunted. 'Well, if you mean fantasy time, you're right there. This is Bay of Pigs stuff. Sending exploding cigars to Castro and trying to poison Nasser's couscous.'

'What?'

The seasoned SAS veteran smiled grimly. 'If only half of what we were told in there is true, you and I are going to be in a good position to screw up big time. It's going to be the biggest international political shake-up of modern times – and the biggest gamble.'

'I guess so,' Lake murmured thoughtfully. 'And that Yank, Bill, was holding back on something. Not sure what, though.'

They paused outside the door to the heads. 'Maybe it's something to do with making omelettes and breaking eggs.'

'How d'you mean?'

'To be sure of installing a new regime, you first have to remove the old one. So something else big is going down that we're not being told about.' He pushed at the door. 'And I've a sneaking feeling it may be illegal.'

Dawson pointed at the main map, one of several pinned to the cork wall of the conference suite together with various nautical charts. On that small scale it looked deceptively like a small bay just east of Beijing. In fact, it was some five hundred kilometres long and half as wide at its widest point. 'What do you know about the Bohai, Captain?'

Al Cherrier's hooded eyes blinked in slow motion to register his disapproval of the CIA man's opening question. There was no earthly reason why he should know the first thing about the Bohai. So was Dawson just trying to show off or show him up? But, as it happened, he'd been poring long and hard over charts of all Chinese territorial waters for days now. Slowly, he removed the curled Paterson pipe from his mouth.

'The Gulf of Bohai is home to the seaport of Tiajin. It serves Beijing, so it has to be the most important in northern China. There are three harbours, running north to south: Hangu, Tanggu-Xingang and Dagang. The coast is low, flat and bleak. Composed of ancient river sediment. In fact, the whole Bohai Gulf has a major problem with silt, mud and sand – all brought down by the Huanghe and Changjiang rivers. They've created an inaccessible, shallow shoreline that's constantly shifting. Deepest waters are only a hundred feet. There are constant dredging operations going on.'

'You've done your homework,' Dawson said, sounding a little surprised.

Cherrier's eyes narrowed. 'It's what I'm paid for.'

Janie Walsh frowned. 'So the Bohai Gulf must be a submariner's nightmare?'

The submarine captain regarded her thoughtfully for a

moment, his face as inscrutable as that of a sphinx. 'Yes, but *Manta*'s specially designed for "littoral operations" – close inshore work. Under a hundred feet is shallower than I'd choose, but there are some possible compensating benefits.'

'Like what?' Dawson pressed.

'Like not getting depth-charged by the Honourable Chinese Navy,' Cherrier drawled in reply. 'They are never going to believe a submarine crew would be stupid enough to be operating in those conditions, so they won't look. And if they do, they'll not get a fix. Best they could hope for would be an eyeball, but my guess is you won't see shit in that silty water.'

'So sandy seabed conditions are ideal for *Manta*?' Iona asked. 'Bedding-in, someone told me.'

Cherrier allowed himself a faint smile. 'Yeah, to a degree. Better than rocks, but you can have too much of a good thing. Silt can clog water jets, jam intakes – there's nothing that stuff can't do if you get unlucky. Then there's the question of salinity.'

Iona smiled. 'You didn't say *sanity*, did you, Captain?'

He caught her mood. 'Perhaps I should have. The salinity of the water affects a submarine's buoyancy, and its ability not to be heard. A place like the Gulf of Bohai is going to be a right mishmash of unpredictable warm and cold water currents. On the outside you've got the cold waters of the Yellow Sea and from inland major freshwater rivers. Controlling buoyancy in under a hundred feet of water will be –' He searched for the word – '*interesting*.'

'Isn't that all controlled by computer?' Iona asked.

Cherrier was clearly impressed with her grasp of detail. 'Yes, a computer maintains the buoyancy, autopilot and fire-control systems. But how reliable is it? The initial program was installed over ten years ago and it was pretty primitive. It's being updated, yet again, but my guess is it'll still be full of glitches. The whole package needs to be redesigned from scratch, which will cost more bucks than so far anyone in the Pentagon's been willing to spend.'

'And time, Captain, which we definitely do not have.'

Meanwhile, Dawson was assessing on the hoof, anxious to be clear in his own mind that they had a runner that *would* run and not crash at the first hurdle. 'So, are you telling me, Captain, that you could get this son on station to function in the way it's been designed to?'

'In wartime conditions, I'd say there was a slightly better than fifty-fifty chance.'

Dawson frowned: he didn't like that. 'Wartime, Captain? What exactly are you saying?'

Cherrier's eyelids lowered a fraction, and his voice was gravely quiet. 'As there isn't a war on, I'd say fifty-fifty odds for mission success is pretty piss poor. Especially when you consider the consequences for the crew and combat-swimmer team. Death in combat or capture, plus the political consequences.'

'Others make such decisions, Captain,' Dawson came back curtly. 'All you've got to decide is whether or not you'd refuse orders to proceed with such a mission?'

Lake and McVicar glanced at each other, then at Cherrier. Janie Walsh looked distinctly uncomfortable, while Iona Moncrieff merely sat with an amused half-smile on her face.

As the silence began to stretch out, Dawson gave a low chuckle, trying to defuse the tension – his own tension, he realised, winding himself up like a spring until he thought it might snap. 'Of course, Captain, a refusal in these circumstances wouldn't reflect on your future career.'

Cherrier knew damn well it would, of course. He doubted that even one of USS *Manta's* previous commanders could have taken over without a prolonged refresher course and additional sea-trials. And no skipper, no mission. He said slowly, 'I've never refused orders in my life before, Bill. I'm not about to start now.'

'And you, Nick?' Walsh intervened brightly, clearly trying to lift the mood of gloom that had begun to settle around the table. 'What worries do you have?'

Lake looked at the map and the rows of satellite photographs of the shoreline. Just a taster, there'd be more to come as they refined their plans. 'Heavy sea traffic to the port is good to get *Manta* on station unnoticed – using a heavy, noisy ship for cover – but obviously the chances of our being spotted are greatly increased. And that shifting shoreline sounds a nightmare. It means all beach recces will have to be done very close to the time of landing. Otherwise disorientation could be a major problem. I take it the three port harbours are heavily industrialised?'

Walsh nodded. 'Xingang – or New Harbour – has sixty-two berths. Handles containers, coal, oil, grain and salt. A three million-tonne annual throughput. It's big. The whole of Tianjin municipality is industrialised, right the way back to Beijing.'

'Which is how far by road?'

'A new highway was opened in '93. One forty kilometres take around ninety minutes.'

He noticed the facts were at her fingertips; she referred to no papers. 'Transport?'

Dawson cut in. 'We're working on that. Something unobtrusive with a trusted Chinese driver.' He allowed himself a smile. 'Janie here suggests a manure truck. Something to deter any searches by the traffic police or Security Bureau.'

Lake lifted one eyebrow. 'Glad someone's got a sense of humour.' He studied the notes he had made on the pad in front of him. 'I don't fancy landing in a busy port area. Besides which, it would create problems for the transport. No doubt our transport will need all sorts of passes and official stamps to get into the port area.'

'That's my view too,' Walsh came back briskly. 'I've been looking for a suitable beach area in close proximity to a road, but mostly the coast is windswept salt flats and marsh nearby. Anyway, I've marked some possibilities. We can refine our options later.'

Lake was drawn by her efficiency, and the way she wore

177

her reading specs perched on the tip of her button nose. She reminded him vaguely of his first teacher at infant school. He could just remember that far back.

Dawson cut in; he seemed in a hurry. 'We can do the crosses and dots as we go, but that will do for now, except for the chain of command and communication links.'

Iona said, 'Now that the SAS is involved, all satellite communications will be direct through Regiment headquarters in Hereford. From there it'll be copied to SIS and Langley.' She saw that Dawson was about to protest. 'Sorry, Bill, but with SAS involvement, Downing Street insists. Hereford has vast experience of controlling covert ops worldwide and that way it can't get cut out by military commanders with gung-ho egos bigger than their brains.'

'And command?' Lake asked.

Dawson glanced at Iona. 'As agreed?' She nodded and he looked at Walsh. 'Janie has OpsCom – overall command of the operation. You will do your damnedest to see she gets what she wants, but she'll listen to sound military advice from you. She in turn will be taking orders and advice from me and other intelligence personnel on the ground. Naturally, Captain Cherrier has the final say on submarine operations. Likewise Nick on all beach and amphibious operations, and McVicar on land.' He rose from his seat. 'Right, thank you all. If this all goes right, you'll have played a key part in some of the most momentous events in modern world history.'

Dave McVicar grinned, but his eyes were as hard as steel. 'And if it goes wrong, we're dead. Right? Which is why you pulled the SEAL team off.'

Dawson laughed awkwardly, giving the impression he thought it was a joke. 'No, of course not.'

'Oh, that's all right then,' McVicar replied. He winked at Nick Lake as he turned away to leave.

Since the briefing by Bill Dawson and Iona Moncrieff at the Project Deadwater facility in Honolulu, the

Discretionary Warfare Team had been totally immersed in training, preparation and planning.

Representatives from both the CIA, US naval and British military intelligence had flown in to give in-depth briefings on the 'Area of Operations', complete with maps and satellite reconnaissance photography, as well as the disposition of hostile forces of the People's Liberation Army, including the PLA Navy and Air Force.

Lake and McVicar oversaw preparations for alternative plans for deployment, including a programme of training modules for the Chinese dissidents with the underground network.

These covered weapons training, which first involved a refresher and familiarisation session for the Team itself, and demolitions. The experts put together a module explaining about basic explosives, including home-made, special charges and their placement. Likewise, the Team's medics prepared to teach first aid while also making ready medical packs for individuals and the large Team pack for almost every eventuality. Finally they prepared brief lectures on the use of various forms of communications and escape-and-evasion techniques.

Meanwhile the Team's signallers established and tested communications between all the players and set up a direct link to HQ Hereford. Frequencies were issued together with emergency frequencies and the agreed sequence of calls. Finally a special 'brief' was given to all by the Signals personnel supporting the operation.

After informal and wide-ranging successive 'Chinese parlia-ments' – especially aptly named in the circumstances – plans were refined for their own cover stories and their general *modus operandi* in liaison with Janie Walsh.

However, she was deliberately excluded when the Team came to making its own 'actions on' emergency escape-and-evasion plans for an alternative exfiltration route out of China if they or the submarine became seriously compromised or betrayed during the operation. These would be set up directly with the Secret Intelligence Service back in London, which would set up the necessary escape ratlines to a neighbouring country. Everything boxed and separate, even between allies.

Once all that was in place, they were free to hone their own specialist skills. McVicar and the three other linguists attended regular brush-up classes with instructors provided by the CIA. That was when they weren't on refresher subaqua courses set up by Nick Lake operating from a 'borrowed' American submarine, as *Manta* was still in a state of electronic refit, or brushing up on agent-handling and contact drills for which another training module was being prepared for members of the Chinese underground movement on the mainland.

Two weeks later, when *Manta* was at last available, they would enter the final phase, using it and its state-of-the-art inflatable assault craft for rehearsing beach recce and landing and patrol skills on nearby shorelines. Personal weapons would be tested and zeroed on the camp firing range before the final preparations, which included personal searches for any compromising material, wedding rings or letters that might have been inadvertently overlooked.

Only then would Slime join the US 7th Fleet, fully conversant with exactly what the Team would do in any given circumstances.

It was late afternoon when Abe Stone burst through the door of Dancer's office like it wasn't even there. 'John, what the hell do you mean by firing those four guys?' he demanded.

His friend looked up with a start. 'God, Abe! You scared the hell. . .'

'Are we partners or not, dammit?' Stone cut in. 'If not, just do me the courtesy of letting me know if you want to run the whole show yourself.'

Dancer put down his pen; he'd been expecting this. 'You

were on holiday. I didn't want to disturb you for something so trivial.'

Stone shook his head; he couldn't believe he was hearing this. 'Trivial? You fire four of my boys with top Harvard qualifications—'

'Paper qualifications aren't everything, Abe. Those four were getting sloppy with their paperwork, and two of them had bad time-keeping.'

'You can talk,' Stone came back defiantly.

'I'm the boss,' Dancer replied evenly. 'I'm allowed to be late.'

'So I see. Well, I'm not happy about it and nor are the staff. I had one of them phone me at home. What the hell is it with you just lately, John? You don't seem to be behaving rationally. How the hell are we expected to cope without . . .'

'I've hired four new people,' Dancer countered quickly. 'Excellent people a recruitment agency picked up for me in Australia.'

Stone looked aghast. 'Not Aussies!'

'All English actually.'

The operations director smacked his forehead hard with his palm. 'Even worse!'

'They all speak fluent Mandarin.'

'I should hope they bloody do.' His friend was exasperated. 'And I suppose it was also too trivial to ask my opinion about replacement staff?'

Dancer glanced at his watch and rose to his feet. 'Look, Abe, I've got to go now.'

'Go? Why go? I'm in the middle of a fuckin' great row.' His wild dark eyebrows met in a demonic frown. 'And I can't do that by myself. I might even be working up to walking out on you.'

'I've got tickets for a concert,' Dancer said, picking up his jacket from the chairback, 'and I'm running late.'

'Concert, concert? I don't believe I'm hearing this.'

Dancer made a decision. 'Abe, I've got to go. Walk with

me for a few minutes. There's something I need to tell you. About the staff replacements.'

Stone was in no mood to be sweet-talked. 'I suppose I should feel honoured.'

But Dancer didn't answer, just beckoned his partner to follow him down the stairs and on to the street teeming with citizens of Beijing returning home from work.

'Something's not right,' Stone said as he strode alongside Dancer. 'I sense something hasn't been right for weeks. Is there something I should know? Surely we're not going bankrupt. Hell, I am a partner!'

'I know, Abe,' Dancer replied quietly. 'Trouble is, you're not the only partner.'

Stone frowned. 'You mean Wang? You've got trouble with Wang?'

Dancer shook his head. 'No more than usual. No, I mean FII.'

'Feng Interglobal Investments, the Hong Kong outfit? The ones who put up the money for you to get started here?'

'The very same.'

'They're happy with their returns?'

'More than happy, Abe. Just as they have been with other investments. Like Air America.'

Stone shuffled to a halt, the blood draining rapidly from his florid face. 'Don't wind me up, John. Not on this one.'

'It's no wind-up. Feng Interglobal is Langley. Or part-Langley, or somehow connected with Langley. It's one of several front companies they originally used to penetrate the bamboo curtain. There's some link-up with Chinese financiers in Taipei.'

'Jesus.' Stone's wrath flared up again. 'You shitty bastard. You know how I felt about them. And you've let me work for them again for all these years.'

'Sorry, Abe.' He gave a wry smile. 'They *needed* you and knew you wouldn't play ball. As they like to say, a little deception never hurt anyone.'

182

'Huh,' Abe grunted. 'So nothing's changed. So what's going on?'

'Something big's coming up and we're going to be part of it.'

'Count me out,' Stone retorted.

'That's exactly what I am doing, Abe. The business is going to be involved in it – hence the personnel changes – and there could be risks. Better you don't know and leave the country. I'll buy you out.'

Stone stood and glared around at the jostling crowds and grid-locked traffic, his fists clenched in impotent rage. 'The hell you will, Dancer! I've spent all these years building up the business, unscrewing the messes you've made, sorting out your admin. Anyone ever tell you what a lousy fuckin' businessman you are?'

'You mostly.'

'And I suppose ExecFlight is part of it.' It was becoming clearer by the second. 'That's why you kept me out of it. Xin-Bin's in on it?'

'Yes, but not his brother. He hates Wang as much as you do.'

'Not possible.' Stone began walking again, slowly coming to terms with what he'd learned; perhaps he'd even partly suspected once or twice. Now he was trying to work it out. 'I suppose it's connected with the democracy movement – setting up agent networks?'

'You know better than to ask, Abe. If I told you, I'd have to kill you.'

'Yeah, sure.'

'I mean what I say. I'll buy you out, see you're all right. We needed someone good and you were the best. I couldn't have managed it without you and I won't forget that. I'll see to it you make a handsome profit.'

Stone clamped a cigar between his teeth. 'If you couldn't have managed without me then, you certainly can't now. Someone's got to run the business.' He paused at the pavement. 'Pretend I didn't ask and you didn't tell me. I'll ask no more awkward questions. Give me some time and I might even forget what a sneaky, underhanded bastard you turned out to be. And if Langley's actually doing something to repay the pricks for Tiananmen, then I might even forgive the CIA too.'

Dancer grinned, relieved, and shook the big man's offered hand. 'You're a pal, Abe.'

'I'm a fool – especially if the Bureau suspect something.'

'I think that was just routine.'

'You hope.'

'I hope.'

'And the concert? Sixties rock, I suppose.'

'The Boston Symphony.'

Stone grimaced. 'Then she must be worth it.'

There was a slight spring in Stone's step, Dancer noticed as his partner walked away, and he wondered if maybe Abe was just a little tickled to be part of the old business once again. Not that he'd ever admit it, of course.

Their conversation had made him late and by the time he reached the concert hall on Beixinghaujie there were only minutes to spare. He found Lily and Mama Cheung in the lobby standing below the rows of portraits of famous composers.

'So sorry I'm late,' he began.

'She thinks you do not come,' babbled Mama Cheung, looking resplendent in a willow-green tunic top and her grey hair neatly bunned with a pearl-headed pin. 'I tell her you a gentleman. All Americanos are gentlemen. You come, you come, I say.'

Lily blushed. 'Please, Mama, don't say such things!'

He noticed she wore a plain pleated skirt and black blouse and he wondered if she was deliberately dressing down for the occasion, not wanting to give him any wrong ideas.

The old woman was still chortling. 'She says you will not be able to get the tickets. You will lose face and so will not turn up.'

184

'Mama!'

'But I say no. Americano is a man with plenty old friends, good *guanxi* —'

Dancer made an exaggerated expression of disappointment. 'Actually, I am afraid—' He waited until he saw Lily's sudden crestfallen look before he produced the tickets from his pocket with a flourish. 'Dah-dah!'

They all laughed then hurried into the vast thousand-seater auditorium just as the orchestra was striking up.

'When?'

Brigadier Ting Han-chen was lounging in his leather swivel chair, carefully polishing the lenses of his gold-rimmed spectacles. His smart, pale grey suit, shot with a gleam of silver thread, was in marked contrast to the dress of the short Bureau detective who stood before his desk.

Xia resembled a stuffed duffle bag. As always he wore his oversized grey raincoat because he liked the air of menace he thought it gave him. It was also why his face usually gleamed with perspiration and his wife complained about the state of his shirt collars. His only concession to being in the exalted presence of a Ministry of State Security commander was to remove his inevitable trilby.

'Last week,' Xia answered. 'He met the Cheung woman at the concert hall.'

'Alone?'

For a second Xia appeared reluctant to reply. 'No, with her mother.'

'Well, at least he heeded my warning not to be seen alone with her.' Ting casually picked up the heavy cardboard file from his desk and weighed it in his hand. It was stuffed to bursting. Some fifteen years of intelligence reports. If he bothered to look for long enough, he'd probably find out what Dancer ate for breakfast and his inside leg measurement. 'I think we've wasted enough time on him, Inspector. None of my predecessors has found anything on him or the company. We can no longer afford to waste time and effort on such fruitless projects. If we don't become efficient and cut back costs, we'll be privatised, and then where will we all be?'

Xia looked disgruntled, an expression that appeared quite at home on his warty, squashed face. 'He could be spying on the Civil Aviation Administration. Stealing commercial secrets.'

'I've *no doubt* he'll pick up any commercial information he can, Inspector. It is *what* businessmen do! They have also been known to chase after women. Tell me, when did his wife die?'

'Four years ago.'

'Then that's your answer.' He examined the official Party membership photograph of Lily Cheung and compared it to the one taken in the lobby of the concert hall. 'Her ID picture doesn't do her justice. A handsome woman. So, unless you have other grounds?'

Xia seemed agitated. 'People cannot just meet up at a concert without some prearrangement.'

This was getting tiresome, Ting thought. 'So?'

'Since you ordered the security check, he is followed everywhere by my people and his office and home phones are tapped, yet somehow he arranged to meet her.'

A frown creased Ting's disconcertingly boyish and unlined face. 'Do your men never slip up, Inspector? None of us is perfect.'

Xia seethed inside, his face reddening. The brigadier wondered idly if, had he been wearing it, the obviously suppressed anger would be enough to blow the inspector's trilby ten feet in the air. The mental picture made him smile as Xia replied, 'My department only loses someone if someone deliberately tries to lose them. Why should Dancer want to do that?'

'Perhaps because he doesn't want your people following him when he goes out courting his ladylove.' Ting was becoming irked. 'Now, let's forget about John Dancer. There are new projects opening every day with Americans and Europeans. My researchers have drawn up a list of people whose backgrounds could link them with intelligence agencies. Our masters will not forgive us if we allow anyone to slip through the net during the next eight weeks.'

Until the big operation, Xia thought. The one everyone whispered about, but no one was certain about. The retaking of Taiwan for the People's Republic of China.

Even so, Xia still smelt a rat somewhere in the odd relationship between the American and the Chinese woman. And he'd already established that neither Dancer nor any Cheung family member was even on the concert hall's mailing list. Getting hold of concert tickets in Beijing was an art form in itself, let alone getting three seats together for the same performance on the same day.

Why was it that he wasn't surprised when she told him she came from Sichuan province, over in the west where China bordered on Tibet?

The Sichuanese were renowned for their spirit of independence. And the women had a reputation for being feisty and flirty, although Dancer supposed that might be wishful thinking, somehow linked to the famously hot and spicy cuisine that came from the province.

He had been mildly disappointed at the concert to find Lily Cheung conducting herself in the traditional reserved manner expected of a Chinese woman in male company. She had dutifully lowered her eyelids when he looked at her and answered his grins with a faint and polite smile. By contrast, Mama Cheung had no such reservations about laughing and shrieking and generally getting on with her life regardless of the disapproving glances of others.

But over the snack supper he had bought for them at one of the big hotels, he noticed Lily's mask slipped now and then. Her smile had begun appearing regularly, until at last it became almost permanent. Her conversation had been animated and frequently she would lapse naturally into near-perfect English as they joked and laughed. She had studied the language at Sichuan University and was still an avid listener to Beijing Radio's *Follow Me!* programme for teaching English to Chinese.

When he had judged the time was right, Dancer had casually suggested they all have a picnic together the following weekend. Lily could practise her English on him all she liked and perhaps little Bao could be persuaded to try out the few expressions his mother had taught him. If there was a hint of hesitation in Lily's voice, Mama Cheung had no such reservations as she worked her way through another bottle of Pearl River lager.

He met them at the gates of Ritan Park, laden with gifts. There was an amazingly complex red dragon kite for Bao, two Gershwin tapes for Lily and a bottle of Napoleon brandy for Mama. In return, the old woman had prepared a mountain of Sichuan specialities in a wicker shopping basket. The park was full of secret little nooks and crannies and half-hidden pagodas. They found a bench in a jasmine-covered alcove and claimed it for themselves. Soon the mesmeric tones of Marti Webb singing 'But Not For Me' were swirling around them from Dancer's cassette player as they spread the banquet and opened fizzy pop and chilled beers.

Later Dancer helped Bao get his kite aloft, then left him with his grandmother to give instructions and returned to the alcove where Lily had been sitting watching them.

'You are good with children, John.' She was smiling and he thought she looked more relaxed than he had ever seen her before. 'You and your wife did not have children?'

'No, Debs had a medical condition. But it was the only small flaw in our marriage.'

'I feel that you loved her very much.'

He smiled awkwardly; he didn't feel comfortable talking about Debs to those who had not known her. Unless they'd known her, they wouldn't begin to understand how he felt, how he couldn't let go – even now, four years on.

She saw the look in his eyes and gave an apologetic little shrug of her shoulders. 'I am sorry to ask. I have upset you.'

'No. It's fine,' he replied and thought how much more like a Sichuan she seemed now that they were alone and she was getting to know him better. 'Anyway, it's easy to get on with kids when they're good-tempered and fun like Bao.'

Lily giggled, 'You wouldn't say that if you'd heard him call you a "big nose" the day we see you doing *t'ai chi*.'

He touched the offending part of his anatomy. 'Well, maybe he has a point.'

'He takes after his father. Jin was always full of fun, always happy.'

'It must have been difficult for you. After Tiananmen, after Jin's death.'

For a moment the light went out in her eyes, then returned, reminding him momentarily of a guttering candle as her mind reached back to the happy times. 'Yes, it was hard.' She paused, remembering. 'The problem was not letting anyone know I was pregnant. If the authorities knew, they'd have made me have an abortion. That is the rule in China.'

'So what happened?'

'After Tiananmen I return to my university in Sichuan, but I am arrested there with other students who went to Beijing. We are sentenced to "re-education". I ask if I can serve my sentence at my home village because I need the support of Mama. But because I was the girlfriend of one of the local leaders, I am sent to a remote peasant co-operative farm in Gansu province. I wear baggy clothes and tell everyone I am getting fat because I eat too much after all the fresh air and hard work.'

'Did they believe you?'

She gave a shy smile. 'Yes. I tell only two girlfriends who became very close to me. They too had been at Tiananmen and wanted to hit back at the system. One of them had the idea for me to have the baby in a pigsty. We set it up with fresh hay bales. It was clean and dry and warm. So that is where he was born. Like the Christian baby Jesus in the stable almost.'

'But you were found out?'

'It was inevitable, I suppose. I tried to raise Bao secretly in the pigsty, helped by my friends, but we were discovered in a few days. The cadre leaders were furious and condemned me. At meal times I was made to stand wearing a placard saying that I was—' her voice dropped and he could see the moisture gathering in her eyes '—a whore and a bad and irresponsible citizen. . .'

'That's terrible,' he said hoarsely. 'As bad as in the Cultural Revolution.'

She shrugged. 'I could cope with that, but not with losing Bao. The local officials wanted me fined and sterilised and Bao put in an orphanage. I protested but they would not listen. But at least I managed to smuggle out a letter to my mother who was then living and working in Beijing. The rest of my family were ashamed of me, didn't want to know me.

'Mama came immediately to take care of Bao, but the cadre leaders would have none of it. At least she persuaded them not to have me sterilised, but they doubled my fine instead. It is *still* being deducted from my wages each month.'

Dancer said, 'But you got your son eventually.'

'When my period of "re-education" was officially over, my mother came back for me. This time we seized Bao from the orphanage and jumped on a train for Beijing. Attitudes were more relaxed here and my mother knew a lot of important officials from the old days.'

'Old days?'

'From before the Cultural Revolution. She was a famous concert violinist. Very beautiful. She had many admirers. Of course, she was condemned as a "capitalist roader", like all artists, and was sent far away to work in the fields. But by the time I gave birth to Bao, she had long been rehabilitated and had a good job as a music teacher at an academy. Many of the admirers from her youth had also been reinstated in important government positions.'

'So she used her old connections?'

Lily nodded. '*Guanxi* to get the authorities to allow me to keep Bao and to work here and live with her.'

'And so you've had no more dealings with the democracy movements?'

He saw the fear flash briefly in her eyes. After a slight pause, she said, 'Of course not. And officially such movements no longer exist. If you listen to our leaders, they are no longer justified. But then, we Chinese are well practised in the art of self-deception while deceiving others. Sometimes I think it is the very essence of the Party.'

'And you listen to the leaders?'

Her eyes were very wide, very clear and just inches from his own. 'Of course. I have even joined the Party and whenever there is a problem in my life, I ask the Party for guidance on anything and everything. That is what they like.'

He saw it then, just for a second. A glint of steel in her eyes, forged out of pain and bitter experience. Then the moment passed and her face lightened as she turned to see Mama Cheung and her grandson walking back towards them.

'You do this for Bao?' he asked.

'Yes. It took many years for me to be fully rehabilitated and at last to get a good job – even if it means working for Mr Wang. This is essential if Bao is to have any kind of a future.'

Dancer knew what she meant. In China it had always been a habit to visit the sins of the parents on the offspring, and the Party was no different from previous rulers. In fact, it was probably far worse.

The American also saw the first opportunity to plant a seed. He murmured, just loud enough for her to hear, 'Do you think there can *ever* be a real future for Bao, for any of today's kids, while this Communist Government is still in power?'

She looked at him strangely for a moment, but did not reply.

Somehow he knew she was thinking of Tiananmen.

Seven

You've got your answer,' Edwin Prufrock said, as if he'd just tasted something unpleasant. 'General Sun and his friends have agreed to put their heads in the dragon's mouth for us.'

He sat with Iona Moncrieff in the secure room – windowless, lead-lined and screened with white noise – within the British Embassy in Beijing. The army brat was there too, taking notes for her boss. Suzy Tobin observed that Prufrock had hardly glanced at her legs and hadn't offered one lewd comment. He was clearly tense.

'But?' Iona asked. 'What's the snag?'

Discoloured teeth showed an awkward smile. 'Perceptive of you.'

Suzy laughed. 'Hardly, Edwin, it's written all over your face.'

Another uneasy smile. 'That obvious, eh? Well, it's not a snag exactly. General Sun said he had no idea the PLA is planning to invade Taiwan, but then it wouldn't involve his air-force squadrons in Xingjiang. They've got their hands full with the Muslim separatists. He was shocked, of course. Realised we now have to do something fast.'

Iona frowned, impatient at Prufrock's hedging. 'And?'

'Well, Sun's on board, of course. But he wasn't really expecting to have to make a move yet. He thought he'd have another year or so at least to prepare things. He says to move against the Politburo now could be dangerous for him and his fellow generals. It's more likely to go wrong and they'd all be executed.'

'So he's refusing to co-operate?'

Prufrock smiled thinly and used his crumpled panama as

a fan to cool his face. 'No, but let us say his clique's help comes with a condition attached.'

'A price tag?'

'A condition, not a cost. I don't think HMG will be disappointed. The Chicom Air Force MiGs are falling to bits and Beijing's currently running a replacement deal with Moscow. Sun wants our guarantee that the new 'Interim Government' will cancel the existing contract and replace it with a deal with the new EuroSpace consortium.'

Now Iona understood. 'You work for EuroSpace, Edwin. So was it Sun's idea or yours?'

His smile was angelic as he shrugged. 'Does it matter? He's interested in the new cheaper version of the Euro-fighter. It would be built in China under licence by a new joint venture with EuroSpace.'

'You've spoken to them already?'

'One had to take soundings.'

'And General Sun gets a cut of the deal?' Suzy asked.

'You know the form, Your Prettiness. Back-door business.'

Iona leaned forward. 'And your percentage?'

'The usual. I'm afraid New Labour's left a bit of a hole in my private pension plan.'

'Very droll, Edwin.' But she was smiling; this would be the first deal in China's brave new world, and, ironically, was going to be just as bent as those under the old regime. Nevertheless, she could not see the Treasury or the Department of Trade complaining. 'I think I can say that congratulations are in order.'

Suzy Tobin wasn't so sure. 'So why the long face earlier?'

'Ah, well, Your Prettiness,' Prufrock replied, searching for the right words, 'there is one other little thing.' Suddenly Iona could feel something bad coming. 'He wants it agreed in advance with the Americans, the Taiwanese and the Overseas Chinese that he becomes head of the new air force.'

Iona shut her eyes.

Prufrock carried on quickly, 'He's a good man, experienced, fair.'

Iona's eyes opened again. 'General Sun's also up to his ears and over his head with the Triads.'

'Only *we* know that. We also know we're not going to pull this off without Triad help.' He spoke impatiently. 'You lot are all so goddamn self-righteous and keen to kick the Commies out, you've got to realise that there's going to be a downside somewhere along the line. One helluva downside, in fact.'

The Scotswoman's eyes narrowed. 'And you don't think China *deserves* democracy after all this time, Edwin?'

Prufrock gave a dry chuckle and fumbled for his cigarettes. 'The Chinese don't give a stuff about democracy, never have. It's not in their nature, their history or their culture. The average peasant is never happier than when he's being told exactly what to do and then left alone to get on with it. Emperors or Chairman Mao, it's all the same to Mr Wong. Anything for the quiet life, just so long as he's got food in his belly and clothes on his back.'

'There should be more to life than that,' Suzy said defensively.

'Says you.' There was a leer back on his face for the first time. 'China's like an ants' nest, they've got it all worked out over thousands of years. Everyone knows their place. Then you come along and can't resist poking your stick in it. Already state industries are collapsing everywhere, unemployment is soaring for the first time since the Long March, and the food shortages are beginning. All since the West started interfering. The path to democracy for China is the path to anarchy and starvation and the Politburo know it. They've seen it happen in the former Soviet Union and eastern Europe. They want to follow the Gorbachev path, slowly, slowly. You can't change overnight.'

Iona was losing patience. 'They are planning to take Taiwan, Edwin.'

'So what? It's part of China. You and Bill Dawson were planning to do all this eventually anyway. Beijing's just forced your hand.'

'I didn't know you cared so much,' Iona said, not bothering to disguise the sarcasm in her voice.

'I don't. I'll make money whether China stays the same or fractures into civil war.'

'It won't necessarily do that.'

He smiled widely. 'No? Watch this space. Now, is there anything else before I go?'

Iona realised that after her carping about General Sun's involvement with the Triads earlier, this was going to sound just as hypocritical as it was. 'According to one of your earlier reports, Edwin, the Red Tiger Society runs various smuggling routes into and out of China.'

Prufrock nodded cautiously. 'Sure, they do.'

'Including sea routes out of the Tianjin port area, I believe?'

'Yes, mostly the RTS supplies the black market in North Korea. Government officials there still like their little luxuries.'

'What sort of boats do they use?'

Prufrock blinked, surprised. 'No idea, I'm afraid. I could find out.'

Iona consulted the piece of paper in front of her. 'Our American friends are looking for a friendly Chinese skipper.'

'Then I must see what I can do.'

Inspector Xia was hunched over his desk in shirtsleeves and red braces, waiting for the phone call.

He looked uncomfortable as he smoked and worked his way through the ticket list from the concert hall; what he really needed was a taller chair or a lower desk.

The tickets had been issued to three different people on three different dates during the month prior to the concert. When he had asked the manager at the ticket office if anyone had been in contact and offered money to get three seats next to each other for the Boston Symphony Orchestra, she had denied it. In fact she had screamed her protest of innocence at him. How dare he suggest she was corrupt, that she would take bribes!

But when the bluster failed and she found herself in one of Xia's cramped and sunless cells with its smell of mildew and pisspots, she soon softened her tone. Gently, he suggested she had done no wrong in helping someone who wanted three seats together at a certain performance – even if she had accepted a few *yuan* in return for her trouble. Clearly relieved, she then admitted that a black market ticket tout, whom she had come to know over the years, had telephoned her one day. She had met him at lunchtime and exchanged the names and telephone numbers of people who had three seats side by side. A couple and a single man.

The next day the tout phoned back. He said the couple had been pleased to give up their tickets for twice the value, but the single man was a professor of music and refused to coopererate. So the ticket-office manager gave the tout the name and telephone number of the people sitting on the other side of the couple. Apparently, they played ball because the tout didn't phone back again.

'And the name of the tout?' Xia had asked.

The ticket-office manager had looked relieved to be able to unburden herself. 'Mr Lou.'

'Thank you,' Xia had said, and promptly charged her with corruption anyway.

The telephone on his desk bleeped and he reached out for the receiver. It was one of his junior officers, phoning from the apartment of Mr Lou. The ticket tout had just returned to his home and found the Bureau police waiting for him.

Xia picked at the wart on the side of his nose as he listened intently. Lou was singing like a canary. He had 'sold on' the three tickets to a long-standing customer

197

called Qin. Mr Qin often wanted tickets in a hurry for VIPs who were visiting Beijing.

Slowly and thoughtfully, Inspector Xia replaced the handset on the cradle. Mr Qin was a Chinese national on the household administration staff of the Embassy of the United States.

'Mike' Jiang and his Merc were made for each other. Both were big, muscled and expensive. Silver-grey suit to match silver-grey paintwork and Ray-ban shades to go with the smoked-glass windows.

He came to pick up Edwin Prufrock from the Englishman's borrowed villa in the Fragrant Hills Park. With him were two burly minders in flapping suits that could have secreted an arsenal of weaponry. Prufrock suspected that they did.

Jiang was friendly, a ready smile on the large-boned face that had been pitted by acne in his youth. 'General Sun tells me you maybe want to buy some fish.'

Prufrock smiled thinly. 'If that's what the general says, old son, who am I to argue?'

They reached the car, the door already held open by one of the minders. It smelled of leather and vanilla air-freshener. Jiang pointed at the cigarette burning between Prufrock's fingers, smiled and wagged his head.

Shit, Prufrock thought as he mashed the half-smoked cigarette underfoot, I'm travelling with the one man in China who doesn't smoke. And he certainly wasn't going to argue with a top honcho from the Red Tiger Society.

His bottom had scarcely sunk into the soft upholstery than the Merc powered away down the drive before turning east towards the coast.

The journey took eighty minutes. During that time Mike Jiang hardly stopped talking, mostly about heavy metal pop music of which he seemed to have an encyclopaedic knowledge and which filled the confines of the car. The quadraphonic speakers blasted it out with such energy that

Prufrock felt his heart bouncing on its tendons in his chest. As he talked, Jiang happily slapped a drumbeat on his knee with the flat of his hand as the car sped them smoothly through the grey industrial sprawl of Tianjin towards the port area. All around were rusting factory-compound fences, electricity pylons, industrial plants and smokestacks heedlessly belching their pollution into a leaden sky.

At some point, Prufrock wasn't exactly sure where, they'd swung south towards the more rural outskirts and the river that ran inland from the Gulf of Bohai. Paved road gave way to pitted laterite track or dry-crusted earth just waiting for rain to turn it into a squelching quagmire. There were horse-drawn carts now as well as battered pickups and the housing was low and primitive.

Thankfully the last CD had finished and Prufrock's hearing was beginning to return as Jiang beamed at him and said: 'I understand these fish you want have two legs and little flippers.' He laughed at his own joke, letting Prufrock know that he knew. 'General Sun says these are Special Forces guys from Taiwan, yes? They're recce commandos, I guess. I've seen some of those guys; we hire them in Taipei. They're real hot.'

Prufrock grunted. He supposed Sun had to give some sort of explanation. 'Not quite. These are mercenaries, Europeans. Taiwan must be able to deny all involvement.'

Jiang nodded and peered out of the window as they drove through countryside by the river's edge. The soil was poor and salty, leaving trees stunted and spindly and vegetation thin. 'Yeah, that makes sense. They're smart boys in Taiwan. Once they're running this place, there'll be no stopping us. The Red Tiger's got so many deals lined up, I can't tell you.'

'I'm delighted to hear it. Perhaps I can help. We must meet for supper one evening. See if we can't put some business each other's way.'

Jiang inclined his head graciously. 'I should like that, *lao*.'

They were now entering a village of mostly dilapidated two-storey buildings. Old men in threadbare Mao tunics from a previous age which refused to wear out hung around in doorways, smoking and watching. Nets were strung out along the concrete riverside quay where fishermen sat crossed-legged, making repairs. Skulking dogs advanced on wicker baskets of fish, only to be repelled by fat, rosy-cheeked children with stones. The Merc pulled up outside a bar.

Panic suddenly filled Prufrock; he'd never been so directly involved in this sort of thing before. 'You can trust the captain?'

Mike Jiang looked surprised. 'Of course.'

'How can you be sure? Maybe one of the crew members is a Bureau informer.'

Now Jiang looked pained. 'You are dealing with the RTS, *lao*. If anyone betrays us they do not only lose their life, but also that of their wife, children, parents, nephews, nieces. Betray us and your family tree is sawn off at the ground.'

Prufrock fingered his collar. 'Silly question.'

Careful not to leave his briefcase in the car, he followed Jiang and his minders into the bar. It was filled with dense smoke, excited voices and the rattle of mah-jong ivory. Captain Song Yuan-hua looked up from the circle of players highlit by the overhead bulb. Prufrock saw immediately that he was Fu Manchu incarnate. A slim man in his sixties with a bald head sprinkled with liver spots and a drooping silver goatee and moustache. He sucked impassively on a churchwarden pipe, the narrowed cat's eyes missing nothing as he indicated to the fisherman next to him to play for him during his absence.

'Captain Song,' Jiang said. 'This is Mr Prufrock from England. The businessman who is interested in buying fish from us. A contract with restaurants in Beijing.'

Song just nodded. He knew it was a pack of lies, so why speak? Prufrock could read the Chinese like a book.

They followed the fisherman outside. The *Hong*, or *Rainbow*, was moored to a small pier that jutted into the oily dark water a little farther up the quayside. She was a forty-foot, timber, junk-type trawler with a blunt bow and stern, and nets hung to dry from her mast. Prufrock was aware of the boards creaking as he stepped cautiously aboard. The only crew member was a young fisherman in shorts and T-shirt who was mopping down the deck.

'That's the fish-holding tank,' Mike Jiang said, ducking beneath the tarpaulin cover. He pointed amidships at the two oakum-caulked timber bulkheads that divided the boat and the gap between filled with salt water. 'Penalties for smuggling to North Korea are very severe. So we drop contraband in shallow water for them to pick up. It's also the way we sometimes pick up refugees.'

'I'm sorry?' Prufrock didn't understand.

Jiang smiled and spoke to Captain Song, who in turn spoke to the crewman. Without hesitation, he dropped the mop and scrambled down into the water which came up to his waist. He took a deep breath, then leaned forward, reaching down to the floor of the tank until he was completely submerged. Prufrock could see the straining muscles in his arms as the crewman appeared to be grasping some sort of ring-pull.. Then something – a hatchcover – came free against the water pressure in the tank. Through the clear liquid in the tank, the dark flow of the river could be distinguished in the gaping hole.

'Operates like a diving bell,' Jiang said helpfully. 'The level in the holding tank will be equal to the water level on the outside of the hull.'

'And a frogman could come into the boat through that hatch?'

'Of course,' Jiang answered. 'It's the only way. TJ is one of the busiest seaport areas in the world. On land or on ship, there is always some bugger watching. This way, nothing is seen. I think this might suit your purpose very well.'

Prufrock was feeling queasy at the slight rise and fall of the *Hong*. 'Yes, I really think it might.'

Captain Song looked on without comment. He'd seen it all before. As had his father, and his grandfather before him.

John Dancer's suggestion that they visit the Longqing Gorge proved to be an inspiration.

Lily had heard of the beauty spot in Yanqing County, but had never been there, unlike Mama Cheung who had been as a child and waxed lyrical at the memory. Dancer arranged for a decent taxi and he made the two-hour journey with the family the next weekend.

On arrival at the parking lot, crammed with taxis and 'dragon' trams, his hopes for a quiet day of rural tranquillity were rudely shattered. They joined the mass of Chinese tourists climbing the uphill road to the ticket area while trying to dodge the buses that raced recklessly up and down. Vendors yelled at them from the pavement, trying to sell their dried fruits, sunflower seeds and thousand-year-old eggs.

There were more hawkers at the top using more modern marketing techniques to sell their straw hats and stuffed toys, blasting the eardrums of the long-suffering ticket queues through powered megaphones. A huge metal dragon, painted in red, yellow and blue wound up the mountainside towards the dam. Inside was an elaborate multilevel escalator which had Bao screeching with delight.

It was little better at the top where the crowds dispersed onto the flotilla of moored tour boats, each flying its own colourful banner enhanced by calligraphy or with the hammer-and-sickle emblem. They took a double-decker ferry, enduring the canned Chinese commentary which produced a series of oohs and aaahs from the awestruck passengers as they passed red-painted carvings, pavilions and temples half-hidden in the hillsides of the gorge.

It had become hot and languorous by the time they

landed at the picnic area for lunch and most visitors were seeking relief beneath the table umbrellas or in any other shady spot. After another of Mama Cheung's gourmet spreads, Dancer and Lily left the old woman snoozing peacefully in the shade of a willow tree and went for a walk with Bao beside the reservoir. This picturesque Chinese gorge, with trees and wild flowers clinging to its eroded vertical cliffsides, was the perfect setting for Lily, the American thought absently. Under a colourful paper parasol, her shiny black hair spilled like ink to the straps of her white summer frock that floated round her tanned legs as she walked with easy grace along the water's edge.

Bao begged them to hire one of the little boats and it naturally fell to Dancer to do the rowing. He struggled with heavy oars of unequal length which made for a very drunken course that both Lily and little Bao found hilariously amusing. Their giggling laughter rippled across the green tranquillity of the water as he played along and feigned exhaustion.

In fact, he hardly needed to play-act. Despite being in shirt-sleeves and shaded by his fedora's wide brim, he was almost unbearably hot. When at last he pulled into the dappled shadow of some willows, Bao was curled up fast asleep in the bow.

'So much for the fearsome and fearless pirate captain,' Lily said, placing her parasol over the boy's head.

Dancer lit a cigarette. 'He's a fine lad. I'd have been proud to have had a son like Bao.'

That made Lily smile and she gave a pleased little hunch of her shoulders. 'I am very lucky, I think. I just hope he does not grow up to be influenced by Ho.'

'You mean his gambling?'

'Yes, that and everything else. He is always full of mischief.'

'You mean fun. Everyone seems to like Ho.'

'But I'm afraid he will get himself into trouble.' She frowned. 'Ho says he has stopped gambling, but he has become very secretive. He is always out. He says he wants to make his fortune, but I'm afraid he will be tempted. . .'

'Tempted?'

'To do illegal business. He sees too much of that crawling lizard.' She saw the confusion in his eyes. 'I mean Yan Tao.'

'Yan is Party.'

Her eyes clouded momentarily. 'They are the worst. They think they can get away with it. And usually they do. I would never trust Yan Tao.'

Dancer saw his opportunity then. He couldn't let the moment pass for they were beginning to run out of time. But first he glanced at Bao, curled up with his thumb in his mouth. Then he said softly, 'Lily, I know why you don't trust Yan. In fact, I know why you *hate* him. But I also know that you are wrong.'

He could see the anger darkening her pupils. 'You were not at Tiananmen. You did not see him let the soldiers kill my Jin.'

'Yes, Lily, the *soldiers* killed Jin, not Yan.'

She stared into his eyes, imploring him to understand; there was a tortured look in her eyes. 'You do not understand. Yan was dressed like a doctor in a white coat. If he had intervened, the soldiers would have listened to him. They would have let Jin go.'

Dancer nodded. 'That's possible, Lily, but unlikely given the mood of the soldiers that night. And actually I *was* in the area and I saw what was going on. And I know why Yan didn't intervene, couldn't intervene.'

'What do you mean?'

He looked out over the shimmering turquoise waters. 'You know that Yan was high up in the student movement in those days?'

Her voice was hesitant. 'Of course.'

'Well, what you can't have known is that when the three of you left the hospital to make your way to Tiananmen that night, Yan had just been given a complete computer

204

list of the names and addresses of every member of the democracy movement in China. Not just students, but workers and intellectuals. Even those supporters in government and the PLA.'

'I don't understand.'

'If he had interfered between Jin and that soldier, he'd almost certainly have been arrested, if not shot. That list would have been found by the authorities. As it is, you know how bad it was – the executions, the persecution and the witch-hunts – people like you imprisoned or sent for re-education.' He looked at her steadily. 'Then just imagine if that list had been found.'

She was confused, jumbled thoughts filling her head. 'But – how do you know all this?'

He took a deep breath. If this went wrong now, God knows what he'd do. He might even have to kill her. Shoving the thought from his mind, he said, 'Because Yan was collecting the list for me.'

Her mouth dropped. 'For *you*?' Then she began to laugh, a laugh edged with barely restrained hysteria. 'Why should he do that?'

'Because China has friends in the West. Supporters who want to help the country find democracy and free speech.'

Suddenly she looked pale and frightened and put her hands to her ears and closed her eyes. 'No, no, I do not want to hear this! This is dangerous talk!'

He waited, waited several moments, in fact, until she opened her eyes again like a scared animal checking that the coast was clear. He smiled and, as she lowered her palms from her ears, took them in his own. 'Yes, Lily, it is dangerous talk. But it has to be done for the freedom of the next generation. For children like Bao.'

That went home and she blinked at him. After a pause, she whispered, 'You said Yan had the list for you?'

'For me, for the American Government. Washington has always supported the democracy movement.'

'Yes?'

'Secretly, of course. Otherwise lives would be put at risk.'

'And this was Yan's work?'

Dancer nodded. 'It still is. That's why he hesitated to intervene that night. He was paralysed in a moment of indecision, only to see his best friend die. And with him, part of Yan died too, I think. He was a changed man after that. Or perhaps the boy just became a man. It can happen that way.'

She sat in silence, her eyes squinting against the brightness reflected off the water, as if searching for some answer. At last she said in a low voice, 'If what you say is true, then I have treated Yan very badly.'

He tried to comfort her. 'You weren't to know. I think he was deeply hurt when you cut him out of your life, but he understood. Sadly he could not tell you.'

'But you are telling me, John. Why?'

He chose his words carefully. 'Because the democracy movement is about to be reborn, to flower again.'

'How can you know this?' She found it hard to get her mind round what was staring her in the face. 'You are an American spy?'

'I'm just a businessman, Lily, who has grown to love China and the Chinese people.' He felt bad that he could lie so easily, especially to a creature as sweet and innocent as the young woman in front of him. 'I just want to help out however I can. If I'm working for anyone, I am working for Taiwan.'

'Taiwan?' That threw her.

'They are the ones behind the new democracy movement. America is just helping out where it can. Taiwan is coming home to the motherland, but first the old Communist Party leadership must go.'

Since the early eighties, it had been Langley's ploy to run the Chinese networks on a semi-'false flag' basis, giving the impression that the tail was wagging the dog and not the other way round. Hiding the reality that, in fact,

Washington was running things and dragging the Taiwan regime, sometimes kicking and screaming, behind it. Because the truth was that Chinese nationalism and the desire for reunification ran as deep in the people's psyche as did their resentment of America. Whereas potential revolutionaries – even students – might baulk at doing anything to assist US interference in the internal affairs of China, to help Taiwan rid all the Chinese people of their totalitarian yoke and rejoin a prosperous and democratic mainland was more than justified.

Dancer was sure that was exactly what was going through Lily's mind as she stared out over the shimmering water, her eyes drawn by the wheeling aerobatics of two gulls high above the gorge.

At last she murmured, almost to herself, 'It's what Jin always wanted.'

'Then, at last, his wish *could* come true, but . . .' He paused, until she turned towards him, puzzled by the incomplete sentence. 'But it can only happen with *your* help.'

She hadn't been expecting that. '*My* help? It is nothing to do with me.'

'It is, Lily, because you are the only person Yan knows who has access to the movements and travel arrangements of the Politburo.'

Her mouth dropped open in stunned disbelief, but she recovered quickly. 'That is secret information.'

He had to persuade her now. Resorting to blackmail or physical threats against her or her son would have to be a last resort and it wasn't the way he liked doing things anyway. 'You'd be doing this for Bao's future, Lily. And for Jin's memory.'

Her eyes narrowed. 'You did not know him.'

'No, and I am sorry I didn't, because he was a very honourable and brave young man. Yan has told me all about him. Don't let the father of your son have died for nothing.'

She looked at him like a trapped animal, tears gathering on her eyelashes. 'You are using cruel words to persuade me.'

He met her accusing stare without blinking. 'Yes, Lily, I am. Because I have to persuade you for the future of the whole of China. Such an opportunity is rare, so we must seize it now. We need to know the Politburo's travel arrangements for the opening of Phase Two of Hong Kong Airport.'

'Why?' she began to say, but her next words died on her tongue and her eyes clouded as she looked at him. 'No, you can't be thinking. . .'

'It has to be done, Lily. There is no other way.'

She shook her head.

He said firmly, 'It is retribution. Justice for the butchers of Tiananmen.'

The truth of his words reached her with the sudden clarity of ice water. She opened her mouth to speak, then changed her mind. Bao was beginning to stir, rubbing his eyes with the backs of his hands. Her smile was involuntary as she looked at her son and Dancer guessed she was thinking of Jin. Then she looked at him again directly.

'Ho has been seeing a lot of Yan lately. As I told you, he is often out and quiet about what he's doing. Very unlike him. Is he involved?'

Dancer nodded.

She was looking at Bao again as he opened his eyes against the late afternoon sun angling in under the willow fronds. 'It will be dangerous?'

'Not if you're careful. I'll tell you what to do. But, of course, there is always a risk.'

Lily Cheung looked out over the exquisite rock formations and canyons of the gorge. 'That is what my Jin always said. And so did Yan. Yan said once, I remember, that a nation got the government it deserved. I remember his words over the loudspeakers, echoing through Tiananmen during the hunger strike. To have a new, brave government, then we ourselves would have to be brave.'

Dancer felt a great weight suddenly lifted from his shoulders. 'Time we got back,' he said, and slid the oars into the water.

Yan Tao awoke with a jolt, disorientated. The light had flickered on and he could feel the rocking tremors of the earthquake all around him.

Even before he could fumble for the steel-rimmed glasses beneath his pillow his nightmare had melted away, only to be replaced by the horrors of reality. Martial music blasted over the speakers into the Hard Sleeper carriage and an irritable female attendant was snatching blankets and sheets from the tiers of bunks even before the bleary-eyed passengers were awake.

Then suddenly the dormitory corridor was filled with dangling bare legs and half-dressed Chinese were hawking and lighting up as they scrambled to find their top clothes. Experience had told them they would have little time before the unrelenting advance of the slopping-out brigade. Pinched-faced cleaners with mops and buckets mercilessly flooded the floor with the gallons of water needed to wash away the accumulated detritus of chicken bones, melon rinds and nutshells.

While Yan waited on his top bunk until the deluge had subsided, he peered out at the passing landscape. It was not yet five, and in the pre-dawn light it was only just possible to see the rolling prairie of sorghum and the occasional walled village of Gansu province.

Not long now, he told himself. He felt a strange conflict of emotions boiling up inside him. Fear and trepidation along with the excitement and anticipation of taking the first step. 'First step'. Funny that. Gong Li Zhong always used to say that even the longest journey had to start with the first step. Gong claimed Confucius had said it, but Yan wasn't convinced, not least because Gong always was a joker.

And Gong Li Zhong was the man he was on his way to see.

Gong had been a fellow student at Tiananmen and a close friend, and was now the commercial director of a large factory complex. But what nobody, apart from Yan and a handful of others, knew was that Gong also ran Gansu province's underground dissident movement.

It was a year since they had last met and Yan was looking forward to seeing his old friend again. And especially looking forward to the man's reaction to the news he was bringing with him.

By the time he'd washed, dressed and got himself a glass of tea from the samovar at the end of the carriage, the train was approaching his destination. Dawn had finally broken greyly over the narrow valley of the Yellow River into which Lanzhou's stark industrial landscape had been squeezed. Low mountains, pock-marked with quarries, seemed to keep out the daylight and keep in the sulphurous smog created by the city's ever-smoking factory chimneys.

From the moment he stepped down off the train into the gloomy station, the polluted air caught in Yan's throat and he found himself coughing. He took a Number 7 bus two stops to the grim Sino-Stalinist edifice of the Lanzhou Hotel on the Xiguan traffic circle.

Barely had he entered his draughty, high-ceilinged bedroom and removed his coat than the ancient telephone rang rudely at his bedside. It was Gong, waiting in reception with a chauffeured Lexus limousine.

'You're looking well!' Yan greeted his old friend, and meant it. Gong was always smiling. He had a round, unlined and happy face that always reminded Yan of the pictures of the sun that children draw, with laughing eyes and wide grins. Yan fingered the collar of the man's smart suit, feeling the material. 'And doing all right for yourself, I see.'

'I can't complain. Business is good. I'll tell you all about it over a long good meal. There is a new restaurant just opened.'

Yan lowered his voice. 'I need to talk with you somewhere private first.'

'Sure,' Gong said, and told the driver to take them to the White Pagoda Hill on the north bank of the river.

The steep slopes of the park were terraced and the two friends were able to talk without being overheard as they strolled along the woodland walkways.

'So how are things really?' Yan asked.

Gong lit a cigarette. 'Hell. The factory's thriving, of course. But that just makes it worse. Westerners come over in increasing numbers. They don't see the prison entrance, of course. They're taken through the east factory gate. They just swallow everything they're told. So gullible.'

'Maybe it suits them to believe.'

'I don't know. They don't read Chinese and the cadres assure them these are genuine factories. No prison worker is going to open his mouth to tell them differently and get another twenty years of re-education for his pains!'

'So it's as bad as ever.'

'In some ways it gets worse. All the prison-factory managers around here are making a fortune with orders pouring in for the cheap labour goods.' He gave Yan a tight and bitter smile. 'That's hardly an incentive to reduce the workforce, is it? Unless, of course, more body organs are wanted. A man's kidneys are worth more than his labour nowadays, that's for sure.'

'The demand's still growing?' Yan asked, appalled. He'd even had to write a denial story for the consumption of the international media a month earlier, whilst knowing full well it was true.

'As the wealthy cadres grow, so does the demand for transplant operations. Only last week three doctors flew in on a military helicopter. They selected a suitable life prisoner, anaesthetised him, cut him open and chopped out his kidneys. They were put in an ice-box and flown out to Xining immediately. Some sick Party fat cat, I understand.'

Yan winced. 'And the prisoner?'

Gong shrugged. 'They stitched him up and had him executed the next morning.' He stubbed out his cigarette angrily underfoot. 'Had to do it quickly, of course, before he went and died on them. I fear the demand from Hong Kong and abroad will turn this into a major industry. Organ-farming in the gulags, I ask you! Even I wouldn't have thought it would come to this. Still, life has it's compensations. I have a lovely family, a fine house, an excellent salary and bonuses. All I have to do is learn not to hate myself for being part of it. And believe me, that is not easy.'

Yan put a consoling arm around his friend's shoulder. 'Guilt is the last thing you should feel. If you hadn't deliberately got a job in the black heart of this system, how could we have properly prised open its evil secrets. Thanks to your reports we've been able to tell the world what's been going on in the *laogai*.'

'Then I am just glad it has done some good – even if it still goes on.'

'Not for much longer,' Yan said. 'The time *has* come.'

Gong's eyes narrowed suspiciously. 'You are kidding me.'

'No, that's why I've come to see you, old friend. The Politburo and the PLA are getting ready to seize Taiwan this autumn, but Taiwan has got wind of it. Through the CIA, I expect. Taiwan plans a pre-emptive strike, and we must be ready.'

The grin on Gong's face was so wide, it threatened to split it like a melon. 'I can hardly believe that I am hearing these words.'

'Well, you are. Now tell me, how is the state of the movement in Gansu?'

Gong fumbled in his pocket for his cigarette pack; he needed something to quell the sudden surge of nervous tension. 'I think it is good. All the original people date back to Tiananmen – I think you met most of them at one time or another. Anyway, they have been carefully schooled to have no more than four people in a cell. Some cells are run by former students who are now university professors. There are other cells in the local authorities, the PLA and business. What will you want us to do?'

Yan hedged, it was too early to give too much away. 'I don't know the details yet. Something momentous will happen in a couple of months' time – again I'm not sure what. But maybe a coup by elements of the PLA. At that time the students must take to the streets and the workers must go on strike.'

Gong grinned. 'No problem there.'

'But the People's Liberation Army must not respond to any request from Beijing to crush dissidents.'

His friend shrugged, unsure. 'I have some junior PLA officers on board, but the old-timers are enjoying the good life. So are the police.'

'Then the young officers will have to seize the initiative and take control.'

Gong nodded. 'Sure, but they may not have many people willing to follow.'

It was Yan's turn to smile. 'Oh, I think they will. The inmates of your gulag will not need to be asked twice, I think. Just mention kidneys to them.'

For a moment his friend stared at him, then the two of them began laughing, laughing so heartily that they appeared in danger of choking and dying of it. Passers-by turned their heads.

Yan handed Gong a small wad of business cards. 'Start using this courier company. It's run by John, the American you met. Any excuse you can think of. When you contact the other networks, tell them what I've told you. They too should use the company wherever possible.'

His friend frowned. 'I'm not sure I understand.'

'Taiwan can't manage this alone. It is using European mercenaries through this company. They will talk to you about what has to be done, what you require most urgently. Meanwhile, list the things you think will have to be done locally here immediately following any coup in Beijing. They will give you training and equipment for what you need.'

Gong smiled again, never happier since the heady early days of Tiananmen when they thought China was theirs. 'I already know what needs to be done.'

'Good.' Yan watched his friend's face keenly. 'I'm pressing the button now. How long before you can get to Xining?'

He meant he was lighting the touchpaper and the long-planned chain reaction would begin. Gong Li Zhong would go to the capital of adjoining Qinghai province and alert the leader there. He in turn would go to Sichuan, and so on until the entire Chinese underground was primed and ready.

'That's no problem. I have an excuse to fly there tomorrow on business.'

The relief showed on Yan's face. Suddenly he actually believed that this was going to work.

'Don't you think that poor creature's suffered enough without involving her in this?'

Dancer knew exactly what Debs was saying, could see it in her eyes. 'It's the job, and it's why I'm here. It's why you were here too. We both cared.'

'Cared too much, perhaps,' said those carefree eyes. 'Doesn't do to care in our lines of business.'

She was right there, he thought, and turned away from the mantelpiece before pouring another slug of bourbon into his tumbler and wandering over to the open window.

It was raining outside, the city wet and shiny in a hundred hues of grey and blue, thunder rumbling low and lightning fizzing and spitting somewhere in the night sky beyond the Forbidden City. He watched the crisscrossing trails of car headlamps for a moment and listened to the steady drip of rainwater accompanying another Gershwin melody on the CD. He hadn't really realised how much he'd liked Gershwin until recently. Since the time he'd taken Ho back to Lily Cheung's flat, it seemed he'd played nothing else.

But was it just the music, he wondered, or because he could see her more clearly in his mind's eye when it was playing? Could capture the serious look in those sable eyes and their sudden transformation when she would unexpectedly smile in a way that made him catch his breath.

'I'll make sure she's in no danger,' he murmured beneath his breath.

'I know that, John,' Debs's words came back. 'Because I think she's becoming special to you and I'm pleased for you. It's time you let go.'

He turned suddenly, feeling the black anger rising like a thick treacle of bile. 'NO-O-O-O!' he screamed into the night.

It had been like a flash flood, almost coming from nowhere, taking him by surprise. And it hadn't been like that for a long time now. As it subsided slowly, ebbing away like a tide, he found that his hands were trembling.

The doorbell rang. He looked round; he was not expecting anyone. After roughly wiping his eyes on the back of his hand, he crossed the living room and checked the spyhole into the corridor. She was wearing a blue mackintosh and clear plastic rainhood.

He threw open the door. 'Lily, what are you doing here?'

Her eyes were wide and anxious. 'Can I come in please, John?'

'Of course.' He stepped aside, smiling. 'It's great to see you. Can I take your coat?'

He shut the door and followed her into the living room where she looked around as she shrugged the mackintosh from her shoulders. 'It is a nice place you have. It is so *big*. You are very lucky. . .' Then that sudden little smile as she recognised the tune. 'Ah, you are listening to our Mr Gershwin again.'

'I knew you were coming.'

215

Her eyes widened as she untied the rainhood and removed it. 'You didn't.'

'But of course,' he teased, noting that she looked fetching with her hair pinned up to reveal little elfin ears.

She realised he was joking then, and laughed. 'You are making fun of me.' She hit him playfully on the shoulder with her balled fist. 'You are a wicked man!'

'Ouch. And *you* are Mama Cheung's daughter and no mistake. Daughter of the she-dragon.'

Lily giggled and put her hand to her mouth. 'You mustn't say things like that. It is not respectful.'

'I know, and I'm only joking. Guess I'm just pleased to see you, *whatever* your reason for coming.'

And as he spoke the words he saw the light dull in her eyes. 'I could not wait until the weekend. I thought I must come straightaway.'

Irrationally, Dancer felt a sudden stab of apprehension in his chest. 'What's wrong?'

She shook her head. 'No, nothing is wrong. But I thought you would need to know immediately. It is about the airport opening in Hong Kong.'

'Yes?' he said, keeping the tension from his voice.

'Mr Wang gives me a document for the VIP Section today. Casually asks me to type it up. Inside there are the travel arrangements for the members of the Politburo.' She began fishing in her handbag. 'I wrote down all the facts for you.'

Dancer could barely believe what he was hearing and was speechless as he accepted the sheet of paper with its exquisitely neat calligraphy in black ink. His eyes skipped over the details. 'Two aircraft,' he murmured, then grinned mischievously, 'and my dear friend Wang will be travelling with the government party in one of them. This is brilliant!'

'You are pleased?'

'Delighted.'

'Have you seen Yan Tao?'

'Not yet.'

'When you do, please tell him I am sorry. Sorry for the way I have treated him, have thought about him.' She gave a sheepish smile. 'Tell him I do *this* for him.'

Dancer smiled. 'Not for me?'

She beamed and giggled. 'Of course, for you too!' She waved her arms in an uncharacteristically happy and abandoned way. 'And for *all* of Mother China I do this too!'

Her laughter was infectious. 'We must have a drink to celebrate. You like American whiskey?'

She wrinkled her nose. 'No, I don't like whiskey or gin. Do you have a beer?'

'Sure,' he said and went to fetch a can of *Yanjing* from the fridge.

When he returned, he found her sitting on the floor by the music centre. 'So many cassettes and CDs, John! I have never seen so many.'

'They're mostly Debs's,' he replied, handing her the glass and perching himself on the edge of the sofa beside her. 'She loved her music, especially Country.'

Lily tilted her head to one side. 'I like Country too. Not for the music, but for the words. They are so sad, they make me cry.'

He laughed. 'Then we should both stick to Gershwin.'

'He makes me cry too. I think I like sad music.'

Suddenly, on impulse, he said, 'I like to see you smile.'

She seemed surprised. 'Do you? Why?'

He shrugged. 'Because it cheers me up. You know, like sunshine. I don't like to see you looking sad.'

'Am I looking sad now?' She watching him intently, her eyes just a few inches from his.

'No.'

'That is good,' she said softly, 'because I do not feel sad. In fact, I think there is a time, a long time when I feel sad all the time. Maybe ever since Jin died. . . Then only this morning Mama Cheung says that I look happy. And I

217

realised then that I have not been sad now for some while. Several weeks in fact.' She hesitated and smiled. 'Since you bring Ho back home that time. Even if it was a trick to get to speak to me.'

'Do you forgive me?'

She turned her head away. 'I don't know. I will think about it.' She reached over to the music centre and pushed the play button. 'The music has stopped. Without music we cannot dance.'

'Dance?'

'Everyone in China dances.'

The glib words 'I don't' were on the tip of his tongue when he changed his mind. The ballroom craze had had the Chinese in its thrall for several years now. Everyone danced with anyone whenever there was the opportunity. Men and women together, women with women when there were no men, and men with men when women were in short supply. He had even seen soldiers of the PLA dancing rather stiffly together, so that all onlookers would know that their relationship was perfectly kosher.

As Marti Webb's voice floated 'Embraceable You' from the speakers, suddenly dancing with Lily Cheung didn't seem such a bad idea.

From the corner of his eye he caught Debs watching them. 'Go on!'

Lily was already on her feet, smiling at his reluctance as she held out her hand. And he wondered how anyone could look so beautiful in simple black silk slacks and white blouse.

'Come, Mr Dancer, or I think you cannot dance at all! It is just a waltz.'

He smiled. 'You may have to make do with a shuffle. It's been so long, I've forgotten how.'

As he reached for her, she said, 'No one forgets how to dance. It is not possible.'

And he knew she was right as he stepped forward, placing his right hand on her waist and taking her offered palm in his left. Her hand was barely the weight of a small bird in his and she seemed to float effortlessly with him when he moved, as though her feet weren't actually on the ground. Through the thin material of her blouse, his fingertips could feel the cool movement of her body, the lean flesh and light bones of her ribcage.

The music swirled around them in counterpatterns of its own, as he gently spun and turned her to the rhythm, while all the time watching her watching him. Without speaking they knew it was a game, he stepping one way and then the other, trying to catch her out, to wrong-foot her. But her eyes never left his, just narrowed a fraction every time he nearly succeeded, daring him to try again.

They kept on dancing, not noticing that the music had stopped. She said softly, 'Thank you for making me feel so happy.' Then a giggle. 'Or maybe it is the beer. I am not so used to drink.'

'Does the reason matter?' he asked. 'Everyone deserves some happiness. You must grab it when you can.'

That seemed to hit a chord and her eyes lit up as she seemed to play the words over in her mind. 'That is very true, a very wise thing to say.' He found then that both his hands had slipped to her waist and almost without his realising it, her forearms had come to rest on his shoulders, her fingertips toying with his hair. 'You must think I am very brazen. I don't know what Mama would think of me.'

He had to grin at that; he could just see it. 'As a young woman, I don't think Mama Cheung would have had a moment's hesitation about dancing with a man who took her fancy, do you?'

She laughed. 'Even Mama would not dance like *this*, so close. Even I never have. But I have seen them in our new Beijing society, the young girls. It is all so different now. Sometimes it changes so fast that it frightens me.'

'I think the whole world is changing too fast,' he said with feeling, 'and in truth it frightens us all.'

They were no longer moving, both sensing it. She looked

up into his eyes, trying to read what was passing through his mind, what he really felt about her. 'I am frightened now,' she said. 'Hold me.' Then her eyes widened a fraction as his mouth came down on hers and he continued watching in fascinated close-up as her eyelids fluttered momentarily, like settling butterflies.

When they opened again, she took a step back, slightly out of breath. He thought she seemed a little unsteady on her feet. She gestured to the half-open door behind her. 'This is your bedroom?'

He nodded, unsure what to say or do, not wanting to rush anything. Not wanting to say anything to cause offence, not to mention compromising whatever operation might lie ahead.

Then, to his surprise, she took his hand and led him slowly through the door. She said nothing for a few moments, just smiled shyly, then motioned him to sit on the edge of the bed. She took both his hands in hers and stood in front of him. 'I am confused, John. I do not know if I am doing the right thing. This is difficult for Chinese women. I do not know Western ways and I do not want to give offence.'

He realised the drink had given her courage, emboldened her. 'What do you want?' he asked hoarsely.

She smiled self-consciously. 'To give myself. To you. If you want it too?'

'Very much.'

'I think we have both been without love for a long time. Too long.' Gently she moved towards him until her palms came to rest on his shoulders. 'It is many years since – you know, with Jin. And I was very young and did not really know what, how to . . .'

He took one of her hands from his shoulder and kissed it, running his tongue between her fingers. 'Don't think about it, just do whatever you want. Whatever comes naturally.'

She regarded him thoughtfully for a moment. Then she

said softly, remembering, 'I had a great-aunt once. She had been the concubine of a rich merchant in Chengdu. I never knew her, but she kept a secret diary. I discovered it in an old trunk when I was about fifteen. I was shocked at what she had written, all the details of what she did.' She gave a rueful smile. 'What she did and how she did it, has always fascinated me. They say that concubines are the best lovers. Let me be like my great-aunt.'

He smiled awkwardly. 'Whatever.'

He awoke with a start. She'd left the crumpled sheet beside him empty and smelling faintly of jasmine. Outside it was still raining and his watch said it had just turned midnight. He realised then it was probably the noise of her closing the front door that had disturbed him.

Then the bell rang. Had she forgotten something? Or had she decided she would stay till dawn after all?

He grinned in anticipation as he pulled on his dressing gown and noticed the orchid she had taken from the flower arrangement in the living room and placed on the pillow next to his.

'Mr Dancer?' He had not been expecting the tall Scotsman with the greying hair and soft brogue. 'Just arrived, so I thought I'd best touch base. In case, you know. . . Name's McVicar. One of your replacement staff.'

Eight

'Two aircraft,' Dancer said, 'VIP-configured 'Boeing 737-500s. Sent from the CAAC to the PLA Air Force for transporting anyone who's anyone in the Party.'

He was talking in the specially secured suite set aside at Yakuska, the US Navy facility adjoining Yokohama harbour in Japan. As soon as he'd received the news from Lily Cheung, he had set up the meeting.

Of the five other people seated around the table, he knew only Bill Dawson well. Less familiar, because of his lofty perch in the service, was Dawson's boss, Frank Aspen out of Langley. Also Iona Moncrieff from the British Embassy in Beijing, to whom he'd occasionally spoken on the telephone as a bona fide customer of his courier company. Lastly, there were two people who were complete strangers to him. They were a young Chinese-American woman called Janie Walsh, who worked for Aspen, and a slim Englishman with blond hair, heavy glasses and a baby face. Piers Lansdowne, Dancer was told, was Secret Intelligence Service from Vauxhall Cross – known as 'Riverside' – in London.

'I think we can safely assume that the Politburo members will be fairly split between the two aircraft,' Aspen said. 'Usual government and corporate security strategy in case of accidents.'

His glib use of the term 'accidents', with no sense of irony, left Dancer feeling momentarily uncomfortable, wondering if all in the room were acting with the same motive of bringing justice and freedom to the Chinese people that he had persuaded himself justified what they were contemplating.

'Those passengers will include Wang from the Civil

Aviation Administration,' Dawson pointed out, 'and, of course, his personal assistant, Agent "Guizhou".'

'So, one of our assets now has *actual* access to the aircraft,' Aspen realised. 'That's great news, John. Well done. Now our people just have to work out the technicalities. Meanwhile, let's have Bill give us an overview and update.'

Dawson spread his arms out on the desk and knotted together the fingers of both hands as he looked up at the watching faces. 'The current situation is this. In approximately eight weeks' time – immediately following the opening of Phase Two of Hong Kong Airport – the People's Republic is going to seize Taiwan. Simultaneously Beijing will announce a joint commercial prosperity union of Hong Kong, Singapore, Taipei and Shanghai under Chicom's political control.'

'That'll isolate Japan and virtually destroy all future Western influence in East Asia,' Aspen interjected helpfully.

'Of course,' Dawson continued, 'Washington and London have long supported anti-Communist dissident elements in China, but after Tiananmen our involvement with them deepened considerably, basically in training, running and funding the setup of agent networks. For obvious reasons, this is mostly done in Taiwan's name with Uncle Sam playing Santa's helper.

'There are various dissident movements outside official government and military circles – students, workers, business and the media – and one of our agents is at the top of the pyramid, so to speak. When Chicom's plans for Taiwan came to light during his work in the Public Information Office, he told us immediately and begged us to do something.'

Aspen couldn't resist another intervention. 'And that suited us fine, of course, because it was what we hoped to do sometime anyway. It just tightened the time-frame and concentrated minds.'

Dawson continued, 'Our problem is making sure that, when the old Politburo is taken out, the good guys are in the right position to take their place. Like all totalitarian states, China has a helluva problem with natural political succession. Power is centralised and jealously guarded. Likely successors to the Old Guard are carefully indoctrinated and groomed to carry on as before. But, while Number One Honcho is living, he doesn't want a clear-cut Number Two recognised who might then try and usurp him. So after Number One, the real power is spread throughout the Party hierarchy and the Chicom military.'

For the first time, Piers Lansdowne interrupted. 'So what's your point, Bill?'

Across the table from him, Iona noticed the icy glitter in Dawson's eyes and it made her uneasy as he replied. 'It means we have to decide where to make the incision. We cut out the Politburo on its way to Hong Kong, fine. But then we have to ask ourselves about the second layer of Party leadership. And then the military. What do we do about the PLA? Do we take out the military leadership too?'

Dancer said, 'We have to be careful there. Some elements in the Chinese military are going to be very hostile to an invasion of Taiwan. The PLA's General Staff, its General Political Department and the Beijing Military Region is *full* of our potential allies. They haven't forgiven the Party for forcing them to do the dirty work at Tiananmen.'

Piers agreed. 'The PLA sent a letter to the *People's Daily* just a few days before the massacre. Said the PLA belonged to the people and would not confront them. Swore they would not enter the city. They subsequently lost a lot of face with the population.'

'And many will see the invasion of Taiwan as another unwelcome instruction to kill more ethnic Chinese,' Dancer added.

'Don't bank on it!' Aspen intervened. 'You're talking

military men here. There's no way they're going to view well-trained Kuomintang troops in the same light as unarmed Chinese students. To them the Taiwanese are betrayers and traitors. If the Politburo is offering the generals the chance of a lifetime to play soldiers and go conquer the Far East for Beijing, my betting is they'll be up for it.'

'So what are you suggesting?' Dancer asked.

Aspen didn't hesitate. 'We take them out. A big bang. Not just the political and military leadership, but also the second echelon. That way there'll just be minor functionaries and no one left to organise resistance when General Sun flies into Beijing. I suggest we have a pre-recorded TV and radio broadcast claiming the attacks have been mounted in a coup attempt by elements of the 'old guard' PLA against economic change. Sun is hailed as the people's saviour to restore law and order and pledges to hunt down the perpetrators.'

Iona Moncrieff said, 'We know the Politburo is flying to Hong Kong, Frank, but we can't guarantee getting the military leadership together in one place.'

'Oh, I think we can,' Aspen countered. 'We know that while all eyes are on Hong Kong Airport, the invasion fleet will make its move. That means most of the main strategic planning staff will have to be at PLA Headquarters in Beijing. So we just have to take out that and Communist Party Headquarters simultaneously.'

Piers frowned. 'These are hellish big targets, Frank. You can't just go lobbing in a couple of nukes.'

Aspen's eyes focused on the young Englishman. 'I'm perfectly aware of that. But we now have something else that can do the job. A Soviet-developed SBER device.'

'What?' Iona asked irritably. She loathed the military's passion for jargonspeak and acronyms.

Dawson smiled. 'Frank means that highly pure rare-earth element. What the media has coined as "Red Mercury".'

225

'I thought that was all supposed to be a hoax?'

'All black propaganda and story spoilers between East and West,' Dawson replied. 'The stuff's for real all right and is packed into a SBER, or Structural Bond Energy Release device. We've made them now as well as the Israelis. So has *your* Ministry of Defence.'

'Really?' She glanced pointedly at Piers Lansdowne. '*They* never tell us anything.'

The Englishman gave a shrug of helplessness. 'Not my department either, I'm afraid. All I know is our Global Issues Department is busy monitoring proliferation of the stuff, trying to prevent it falling into the hands of terrorists or pariah states like Iraq.'

'So what's so special about it?' she asked.

'Let's just say two kilos of the stuff give you a ten-kiloton explosion,' Aspen said. 'With no fallout. That's a five hundred-yard radius of total destruction and another five of varying blast area.'

Dawson was warming to the idea fast. 'And two kilos with firing circuit would fit in the average briefcase.'

Aspen saw he had an ally. 'They could be triggered any way we liked, even by satellite link. Ideal stuff for cutting the heads off governments.'

Dancer was horrified. 'We're not at war with China, Frank. We've no justification for that type of action.'

The CIA man bridled at that. 'Don't go all wishy-washy on us, John. We're reacting to a request from Chinese dissidents themselves, don't forget.'

'But they haven't asked us to use mass-destruction weapons on their leadership,' Dancer countered, 'and I don't suppose you've got plans to discuss it with them first, have you?'

Aspen said, 'Don't talk wet. You know the score. First, these people in the Chicom leadership are the butchers of Tiananmen, so we needn't lose any sleep over our justification or the ethics. And second, if we don't make our incision deep into the second echelon of government and the military, the bigger the chance of the wrong people seizing power or even widespread civil war.'

'That's going to happen anyway,' Dawson chipped in, 'at least at local level in some areas. Local Chicom warlords are going to vie for power and control. But if we play our hand right, it'll all be over in three months or less.'

Dancer had been listening carefully and understood the arguments. He also knew what no one else around the table wanted to admit. That they were all taking a blind dive on this. It was possibly the most audacious and dangerous power-broking gamble ever played in history and it was clear no one had a clue what the outcome would be. It might all go as planned or China could convulse and tear itself apart in bloody conflict or . . . the permutations were endless and didn't bear examination.

He said, 'I can see the logic of what you want to do, but the plan will stand a better chance if we can ensure our natural sympathisers survive. I've spent years cultivating some of them.'

Aspen was listening at last and nodding. 'Find some subterfuge to get them out before the big bang. Sure, it would make sense. You and Bill give it some thought. Also how we might get the SBERs into position to minimise collateral damage and innocent casualties.'

Iona waved her pencil in the air, describing vague circles. 'These Red Mercury jobies, aren't they going to suggest Western involvement in all this? Could prove rather embarrassing.'

But the boy Lansdowne was already ahead of the game, already gigabytes ahead of her in his thinking. 'I think we can lay a false trail there. A few years back, Russia's General Lebed admitted on television that over a hundred briefcase-sized SBERs had gone missing from his government's arsenals. We know they're in the hands of one of the Russian mafias who are looking for a market.'

Iona saw it then, catching up fast. 'So we buy from them so the big bangs have a Russian signature on them.'

Piers nodded. 'We then feed out a story in intelligence circles that it was all down to our friendly Chinese Triads buying off their Russian mafia neighbours.'

Aspen grinned. 'I like it. So the Politburo gets blown out of the sky on its way to Hong Kong and simultaneous explosions take out Chicom Party and PLA Headquarters. During the shambles and confusion, General Sun flies in to take control and restore order. Our agent, "Hunan", is well placed in the Public Information Office to smooth the way and get him on air, having had his own people seize all television and radio studios. Sun will blame Triads conspiring with anti-reformers for the killings and bombings.' He was waving his hands about expansively now, getting into the mood of it. 'Saying how wicked it all was. How we will mourn our beloved leaders. But, when all's said and done, maybe some good can come out of this. More freedom for the people, more independence, renewed friendship with Taiwan. Then he announces the new Interim Government of Democratic China.'

Dawson was clearly sharing Aspen's vision. 'We'll have our agent networks organise spontaneous rallies of students and workers across China, demanding freedom and change. But we must ensure the country is totally paralysed for several days—'

'I'm on to that,' Aspen cut in. He glanced across at Janie Walsh who had sat watching and listening in silence until now. 'Perhaps you'd like to give us your conclusions. Miss Walsh, by the way, is ops commander of Joint Discretionary Warfare Unit One aboard *Manta*.'

The Chinese-American gave a distinctly nervous smile although her voice was firm and carried a natural authority. Dancer guessed she knew her stuff, but just wasn't happy making presentations in public to seasoned vets like Aspen.

'My office has studied this thoroughly,' she began, 'and we think we can create a virtual land transport breakdown by use of four more carefully placed SBERs. These are, in fact, also current US nuclear strike targets.' She rose from her chair and took two paces back to the map of China pinned to a cork noticeboard on the wall. 'One device at the road and rail hub where it crosses the Hwang Ho, or Yellow River, at Zhengzhou and Jinan, plus the road and rail hubs on the Yangtze River at Nanjin and Wuhan. This will effectively split the whole country into three. It'll take weeks or even months to repair everything. It'll certainly prevent land forces preparing to invade Taiwan from being turned back on Beijing, which has to be a major consideration.'

'What about air power around Beijing?' Piers asked. 'That's worrying me. We want General Sun and his squadrons to be able to fly in unmolested from Xingjiang. With the Politburo down and major explosions all round Beijing, the Chicom Air Force and air defence boys are going to be pretty jittery.'

'I don't envisage that will be a problem, Mr Lansdowne,' Walsh replied smoothly. 'We already know from Mr Dancer that some northern squadrons are being moved south in support of the invasion of Taiwan. Only depleted squadrons will remain around Beijing. Only units in Xingjiang province, with its hands full against the separatists, are at full strength and will no doubt be welcomed when General Sun radios Beijing offering assistance. Once Sun's squadrons land, they'll take out any PLA Air Force resistance they meet.' She smiled briefly. 'That's crucial, because it gives us air power to crush any dissident PLA units surviving on the ground.'

Glancing round the secure conference room, it seemed to Dancer as if it was all a dream. Or perhaps a nightmare. He might pinch himself and find that it was. But this was something towards which he and Debs had worked for years – each in his and her different way – and now that the dream was about to be realised, he suddenly couldn't help wondering if, just possibly, they'd got it wrong.

Frank Aspen looked satisfied. 'So, Miss Walsh, when are you hoping that the Deadwater Deep project will finally justify itself –' he enjoyed the teasing irony '– and deploy in *Manta*?'

Her smile showed a confidence that John Dancer didn't quite think was reflected in her eyes. 'Sir, we are hoping within the next forty-eight to seventy-two hours.'

Lieutenant Nick Lake watched Janie Walsh as she lowered herself down from the main access-and-escape hatch into the empty steel cylinder of the swimmers' compartment which would later have to be flooded before anyone could exit the submerged submarine.

She'd come a long way in six weeks. In her camo trousers and green vest, it was easy for Lake to see how she'd been working to build her upper body strength, the muscle contours clearly defined now around her forearms, biceps and shoulders. Strictly speaking there had been no need; she was CIA and a noncombatant, and she had her work cut out with countless planning meetings and intelligence briefings. But she had insisted on joining Lake and his men and *Manta*'s four-man crew for their early morning runs and evening sessions in the gym. Moreover, she had grabbed every available opportunity to complete a crash diving course, although she could still barely swim in the conventional sense, despite Lake's best efforts to teach her.

That attitude had done her credibility a lot of good and won her some grudging admiration although none of her male colleagues was going to admit it. After all, she was still a spook, which to any veteran fighting man was the second lowest thing that crawled – a politician, of course, being the lowest.

But it wasn't just a physical difference in Walsh that Lake had noted. He remembered the very first time she had climbed into the access hatch, down the short, three-foot shaft between the inner and outer hulls and into the cramped swimmers' compartment. There had been alarm in her eyes and he could actually smell the fear on her as she was shown around the vessel.

Twice she had asked how many people were expected to operate on board as though she hadn't believed the answer the first time. Due to the severe space limitations, the 'linking corridor' between the control room and aft engine room was reduced to a mere tunnel that ran beneath the swimmers' compartment, necessitating a crawl on hands and knees. When she'd emerged at the other end, Walsh was perspiring heavily and her shirt had been stained with sweat. Lake realised then that, although she said nothing, she was suffering from claustrophobia.

But in the last few days, he had noticed how completely at home she had become in *Manta*'s restricted bowels – about as close to the experience of actually living inside a medium-sized whale as Lake could imagine. Only the previous evening the Deadwater Project director, Rear Admiral Crozier had confided to him the secret of Janie Walsh's remarkable transformation. She'd gone to his office, told him of her problem and of her determination to overcome it. Could he help with her plan? Crozier had looked around the Hawaiian base and found the perfect answer: a stack of three-foot-diameter concrete drainage pipes that were waiting to be laid. From then on, one of these became her billet. Walsh moved in with her bedding, a stove and Tilleylamp, plus various makeshift bits of furniture and other home comforts to enable her to spend all her rest, research and study time there.

Looking at the confident way she moved now, it had clearly done the trick. She noticed him as she swung her kitbag on to her shoulder. 'Hi, Nick, all set and raring to go?'

'Can't wait, boss,' he replied and wondered if he really meant it.

Then Walsh was gone, in through the hatch to the control room and into the for'ard crew quarters beyond. More kitbags and bergens were thudding down into the compartment, followed by their owners – a total of eleven combat swimmers from the SBS and SAS, plus a multitude of personal weaponry, some of it made in China and acquired by British military intelligence.

As the hatch was finally locked, it struck Lake how bizarre the set-up must look to the sailors of the US Navy's 21,000-ton submarine tender *Canopus*. It was from her deck that *Manta*, covered with huge tarpaulins the colour of the sub to protect it from prying eyes overhead, had been lowered by crane on to the upper casing of the SSBN nuclear submarine moored alongside. Strapped together with steel hawsers and explosive release bolts, they resembled a gigantic manta ray copulating with a great blue whale under a bed sheet.

The flotilla of US 7th Fleet ships was actually on station eighty miles south-west of the South Korean coast in the Yellow Sea. They were waiting for a signal that the Chilean-registered merchant ship, the *Estrella Fugaz*, was approaching a position ten miles farther out in deep water on her way north into the Gulf of Bohai and the Tianjin port district which serviced the overland route to Beijing. Her master had already radioed the Chinese authorities there to report that the ship was experiencing engine difficulties and, as a precaution, would be making slow headway.

In fact, the *Estrella Fugaz* had been chartered by a front company for Chile's national intelligence agency following a request from London; her master was a former commander in the Chilean Navy.

As Lake left the swimmers' compartment and followed the others through to the crew's quarters, the submarine began to tremble and they were aware of the sudden and unnerving sound of water rushing over the hull outside.

'Here we go, everyone,' Al Cherrier reported laconically.

Their mother submarine, the Ohio-class *Rhode Island*, was casting off from the support tender *Canopus* and beginning slowly to fill her ballast tanks. It was a tricky operation demanding considerable skill. Such a small boat as *Manta* might normally have been carried on a 'dry dock shelter' fitted to the SSBN's aft deck, but the side 'wings' that created the space-age flying saucer look gave her an overall beam of forty-five feet. This meant she was much too large and attracted considerable pulling pressure on the steel hawsers as the mother sub dived, leaving only the near-invisible tarpaulins on the surface as the only testimony to its having been there at all.

Slowly, slowly they became aware that they were going down.

'Fifty feet,' intoned the sonar operator, reading off the echo depth-sounder. 'Fifty-five, sixty, sixty-three . . .'

Manta was heading out to the deeper waters of the Yellow Sea, converging with the *Estrella Fugaz*'s predicted course, still at no more than eight knots because of the pressure on the hawsers. Even so, the crew could hear them rubbing gently against the anachoic tiles. Although no one said, it was an unnerving sound, seeming to emphasise the relative frailty and vulnerability of the craft, not least because everyone was aware that the approaches to the Gulf of Bohai were closely monitored by the Chinese Navy using patrol boats out of the parallel port of Quingdao. Ironically, everyone on the team would be happier when they were away from the protection of the mother sub and on their own, knowing that then the chances of detection would be minimal.

It was another seventeen and a half hours at eight knots before Al Cherrier informed them that they were approaching the rendezvous point with the *Estrella Fugaz*. There was nothing for the skipper to do, the *Rhode Island*'s crew would have made the satcom link with the commander 7th Fleet on burst-transmission and received back positive identification of the Chilean container ship and its exact position before swinging slowly round on a north-north-west bearing, settling at a depth of six fathoms below the twin screws of the *Estrella Fugaz*. The tension ebbed noticeably now they knew they were safely screened from the ears of Chinese Navy's sonar operators by the noise above them.

Now twenty-five hours of excruciating boredom lay ahead until they reached the Laotieshan Shuidao strait opposite Lüshun, formerly Port Arthur, at the mouth of the Gulf of Bohai.

To keep himself occupied, Lake had checked and rechecked his personal kit as well as the weapons and general stores and equipment they had on board. The stuff was everywhere, there wasn't a spare centimetre of space not filled with something for the mission. The situation wasn't helped by the fact that, being the first run-in, they had a full complement of men and gear. Once some members and a lot of kit had gone ashore, the situation would improve dramatically.

He returned to the for'ard crew quarters to find they resembled conditions in a slave ship: everyone squeezed up tight to share the cots or the aisle of narrow deck space between them. Lake managed to find himself a precarious seat, resting one buttock on the edge of a cot mattress. The young SBS swimmer next to him looked up from the paperback in his hand. 'Sorry, boss, I can't move up any more.'

'No problem. Didn't mean to disturb your reading, Dougie.'

Dougie Squires gave a tight smile. He was pipe-cleaner thin and tall with a wiry strength that belied his boyish looks. His eyes were dark and looked perpetually worried. 'That's all right, boss. I've been reading, but I haven't taken in a word. I hate submarines at the best of times, but this one's like living in a beer can.'

'Without the beer.'

Squires's smile deepened. 'Yeah. And without a bloody smoke either.'

Lake understood. 'Can't risk it with so much pure oxygen being carried.'

'Still a bummer, boss. Can't wait to get out. I always fancied visiting China. Never guessed it might be like this.'

'Worried?'

The man considered for a moment. 'Only if we get caught. I mean, they'd be within their rights to shoot us for spying.'

'The Chinese generally don't go round harassing tourists, Dougie,' Lake said and hoped he sounded convincing. 'Stick to our golden rules. Have a camera round your neck and your kiss-me-quick hat. Don't break rules and regulations or answer back to the police and you'll be okay.'

'I can't even manage that back home.'

'Your ID will stand up to scrutiny. If things start going pear-shaped, all the escape plans are in place.'

Squires nodded. 'Yeah. It's just that I've never done anything like this before.'

'Sure,' Lake replied, and didn't have the heart to say that neither had he.

Lake was sitting in a Chinese restaurant in his home town of Poole in Dorset when all the waiters suddenly stopped what they were doing and pointed at him, shouting 'Impostor! Impostor!' Then the floor began to tremble and he awoke with a start. *Manta*'s motor had kicked into play.

All around him, his fellow SBS and SAS swimmers were sitting in a tense, frozen tableau, eyes upward. All reading and card-playing had stopped. The silence was so total he could hear the distinct thud of his own heartbeat.

Al Cherrier's voice drifted in through the hatch from the control room. 'Stand by release charges. Stand by, stand by.'

Explosive bolts would release the hawsers strapping *Manta* to the mother sub.

Without a rise in tone or a hint of the tension he must have felt, Cherrier said, 'Fire release charges!'

Virtually but not quite simultaneously, the six small, muffled detonations blew in a ripple and the retaining hawsers fell away. They all felt the slight wobble of movement as *Manta*'s flank wings took up the strain. The water level in the compensation tank was automatically adjusted by the central computer and the stealth submarine's single rotor began its hushed spin as the *Rhode Island* dived away beneath them.

The huge SSBN would begin a long slow turn to take it back to international waters, while *Manta*'s crew now took control of its own destiny, closing up tighter beneath the Chilean merchantman. From its bridge the captain rang down to the engine room to halve the speed. That reduction would allow *Manta* to keep up and remain on station as the *Estrella Fugaz* steered a course to take it into one of the main dredged shipping lanes marked by buoys on either side.

'Depth reducing,' reported Hinks, the black Louisiana sonar operator. 'Two-thirty feet, twenty, fifteen, ten.' His eyes were fixed on the depth-sounding screen which showed a representative cross section of the shallowing bottom of the Yellow Sea as they entered the mouth of the Gulf of Bohai. 'Levelling out now at two hundred feet, one-seventy-five, one-eighty. In shipping channel, confirmed. Now depth averaging one-seventy feet. Variations seem minor, so recently dredged.'

In the semicircular control suite, Al Cherrier was on the joystick at the helm console. This showed a variety of dials and digital displays relating to the submarine's attitude: depth gauges, rudder and planes indicators, speedometer and shaft rev-counter, plus the gyro compass repeat showing the true course. The information was supplemented by a recent addition, a 'Visual Attitude' monitor to one side of the helm console which showed a computer-graphic cross-sectioned symbol of *Manta* with its distinctive X-configurated diving planes and rudder, indicating visually both the angle of the submarine's stabilisation and its depth in relation to the seabed – as suggested by the depth sounder and the seabed-mapping sonar – and the surface.

The second 'new toy' was another monitor below the

first which showed the 'Operational Overview' – a composite picture of the area in computer graphics. These were based on satellite maps and conventional shipping charts married to and sometimes overridden by input from *Manta*'s own active seabed-mapping scanners. It was vital to upgrade the navigational data constantly in areas like the Gulf of Bohai where the shallow bottom was constantly shifting and silting up until the next Chinese dredging operation.

On the 'OO' monitor, Cherrier could see both the computer-graphic map and the pulsing symbol representing the submarine's position as it passed slowly through the northern sector of the Laotieshan Shuidao strait, south of former Port Arthur. *Manta*'s position was established by the computer's calculations of speed and direction since the last confirmed navigational fix by the Global Positioning System satellite link. Any unlikely error would be corrected the next time the submarine rose to periscope depth to take another fix.

Streams of icons representing shipping, picked up by *Manta*'s state-of-the-art sonars, could be seen inching steadily back and forth along the marked sea lanes to the harbours of the Tianjin port area.

Outside those lanes could be seen the unhurried crisscrossing courses of various coastguard cutters and patrol boats of the Chinese Northern Fleet.

All quiet, Cherrier thought. Everything going to plan. 'Switching to autopilot,' he told the navigator and sonar operator and relaxed back in his leather chair.

Forty hours later, it was nine o'clock in the evening and *Manta* was still in the shipping lane, now just twenty miles out from the bustling industrialised port area of Tianjin.

All resting crew and members of Discretionary Warfare Team One had been roused three hours earlier in good time for changing into rubber wet suits, last-minute checks to weapons and equipment and to eat before the start of the

237

mission. The cramped and limited galley facilities – just hot and cold drinking-water taps, a small work surface and two microwave ovens – were sufficient for the Team members to have the crucial brew and to heat up dehydrated combat rations. This time, however, there were extra spam-and-pickle 'wedges' to fortify those going ashore in the first wave. On the sort of mission-profiles originally envisaged, it had been anticipated that assault teams would usually spend most of their time on land where they would be fed by friendly agents. There was little spare storage capacity left after stacking rations for the four-man crew for thirty days, plus the standard additional fifty per cent.

Lake held a final briefing in the crew quarters. 'Red Team goes ashore. That's me with five other SBs, plus Miss Walsh. Blue Team – that's four SAS – are backup for us tonight and will go ashore tomorrow, if all goes to plan. Red boards the junk and Blue waits alongside until it gets the "All Okay" from Red. If it doesn't get our okay, it means our Triad mafia friends are trying something on. If that happens, you board and take them out. They won't be expecting you, so you should have the element of surprise. Obviously we would abort after that.'

There was the usual last-minute round of questions, but most problems had already been resolved so the briefing was completed some half-an-hour before Al Cherrier's instruction for 'Full silent running', was passed to them. Nick Lake moved into the red-lit control room and found himself beside Walsh; she was leaning against the steel bulkhead with her arms folded, watching the crew at the suite.

'Okay, boss?' he asked in a whisper.

She pulled a tight smile. 'Scared, if I'm honest.'

He gave a grin that was intended to be reassuring. 'We blokes aren't honest, boss. We're merely *apprehensive*.'

'You mean full of bullshit,' she muttered.

He nodded.

Suddenly they were aware of the deck canting. At the helm console, Cherrier was shifting the joystick and engaging the rudder and one each of the fore-and-aft hydroplanes so that the craft peeled away like an aircraft going into a gentle, swooping dive. They realised that now they were leaving the safe cover of the *Estrella Fugaz*'s noisy engines. The submarine was gliding silently away from the dredged shipping lane, slipping between the tethered buoys that marked the channel.

'Seabed depth one-seventy feet,' Hinks murmured, reading off the seabed-mapping sonar. 'One-fifty, one-thirty, one-ten, one hundred, ninety, eighty. Eighty and holding.'

The temperature in the confines of the control room seemed to soar. The tension was suddenly palpable, hanging in the air like undischarged electricity. Each member of the crew and the Team could see it in his or her mind's eye. Could visualise the undulating silt beds of the Gulf beneath them, ever shifting to form and re-form as the mighty currents of the great Chinese rivers emptied into the sea. Imagined *Manta*'s ghostly form drifting through the murky depths like a spaceship in an underwater universe.

'Seventy-five,' Hinks cut back in suddenly.

Cherrier glanced at the sonar operator beside him, the captain's eyes gimlet-hard in his gaunt face.

Hinks said, 'Seventy,m sixty-five– Shit!' A red lamp began pulsing rapidly beside the monitor, a visual warning aid. 'Sixty, fifty-five feet—'

'Slowing to one knot max,' Cherrier snapped.

The sonar operator said, 'Fifty.'

Lake shut his eyes. *Manta*'s full draught was nineteen feet. That meant there were barely thirty feet to spare. According to the 'Visual Attitude' monitor beside Cherrier's console, about twenty below them and ten above. He edged the joystick back and Lake watched breathlessly as the submarine's cross-section symbol rose a fraction until it was exactly half-way between bottom and surface.

Cherrier tapped an impatient tattoo on the console with the fingers of his left hand as he waited for the red lines to take shape on the monitor. These underwater contour lines were feeding through as the discreet high-frequency echo-sounder interrogated the seabed. It used random bursts of sound at irregular intervals so as not to alert any enemy sonar operators.

'Silt mound ahead, sir,' Hinks advised. 'Depth drops to twenty-five feet. Suggest starboard steer, bottom falling away. I'm registering seventy, seventy-five—'

'Roger that,' Cherrier acknowledged. 'Steering three four zero. Speed remaining at one knot.'

Lake noticed that Walsh had turned away, no longer able to look. He said nothing, because there was nothing to say. Cherrier was doing his job, and shortly they'd be in position. He had plenty to think about, because then it would be his turn.

'Property of the People's Liberation Army,' Edwin Prufrock said, and swallowed the last of the whiskey from the tumbler in his hand.

Dave McVicar took the stubby automatic pistol from John Dancer and weighed it in his palm. 'A type Fifty-Nine.'

'Copy of the Sov's nine milly Makarov,' Taffy, the short, ginger-haired Welsh man, agreed, checking the magazine of his own weapon. 'Bog standard. Dependable. Did a refresher on them before we left Honolulu.'

Dancer had been impressed with the professionalism and cool humour of the company's four replacement staff members from Britain. Immediately he felt at home in their company, reminded of his own days in Special Forces which seemed so long ago now.

'No complaints then?' Prufrock said and peered out of the window which gave a clear view of the drive up to the villa in Fragrant Hills Park.

The Welshman smiled. 'These'll do the business if push comes to shove.'

Prufrock looked horrified. 'I most certainly hope it won't. You'll get no trouble from the police and Mike Jiang is a personal friend.'

McVicar raised an eyebrow. 'He's also a Red Tiger mobster.'

A disapproving sort of smile twitched on Prufrock's lips. 'That *is* a very delicate way of putting it. But entrepreneur or mobster, as you put it, Mike can be trusted.'

'We don't trust anyone,' Taffy said flatly.

Prufrock regarded the two SAS men for a moment. 'And so whose bright idea was it to team up a Scotsman and a Welshman?'

Only the eyes showed the humour behind McVicar's stern expression. 'I don't know. Must have been an Englishman. Whoever it was, I'll kill him if I ever find out.'

'I do believe you mean it,' Prufrock rejoined, sharing the joke. Then a movement outside caught his eye. 'Here's Mike Jiang's car now.'

Heavy metal music blasted out from the vehicle as the man bounded out of his car and strode towards the villa, his minders trotting to keep up. As always, Jiang's broad face was all acne and smiles as he swept aside his Raybans and shook hands with the strangers.

'Glad to be of assistance to you fellows,' he said in absurdly good English, before turning to Prufrock. 'Aren't you going to introduce me, Edwin?'

'Just first names,' Dancer said, and glanced at McVicar. 'Okay?'

The SAS man nodded.

So it was John, Dave and Taffy. And, however much Mike Jiang jovially prodded and queried on the journey into the Beijing suburbs, that was as much as he learned about the three men before they arrived at their destination.

The stink of fish hit them as soon as they stepped out of the car in the lorry-park beside a dilapidated warehouse. Through the huge open doors, they could see the workers in white coats and wellington boots, sorting fish at the long grading tables and packing the produce into ice crates. Jiang beckoned them to a side door that led to the administration office. They followed him along a corridor into a sectioned-off garage area at the far side of the building which housed an ancient truck with peeling blue paint.

'This is our secure area – away from legitimate business,' Jiang explained. 'We supply fresh fish to many hotels and restaurants. Much coming and going.' Then he tapped the side of the truck's cargo body just behind the cab. 'This is false section. Just two feet deep. There are four seats, facing sideways.'

Dancer nodded. 'Okay, let's give it a whirl.'

One of Jiang's minders scrambled on to the back of the truck and negotiated his way past the empty crates and bundle of netting. A concealed door was opened up in what appeared to be the wooden planked end of the cargo body. The secret compartment was barely the width of a man's shoulders and four plank seats bridged the gap so that the first man in had to climb over two of the seats before reaching his own. It was extremely claustrophobic, smelly and pitch dark.

'They might have managed some cushions for those seats,' McVicar observed.

Taffy grinned to himself and said: 'We're supposed to be the toughest fuckers in the world, John. You can see how the standards have slipped.'

But McVicar was unrepentant. 'Any fool can be uncomfortable.'

And after the ninety-minute journey, Dancer had to agree with him. Constant bumping over uneven and pot-holed roads had left their bruised backsides on fire. The last time he'd been that uncomfortable had been during a riding vacation in Nevada with Debs. And the situation did not improve as they reached the rutted unpaved tracks along the riverside. The American climbed to his feet and peered through the small removable observation slit in the side of the cargo body. 'We're at the village now.'

They felt the truck slow and the driver shift the gears. Then the momentum changed direction as they reversed up to the edge of the concrete quay and the engine stopped. In the silence that followed, they heard the rear roller door being raised and a hushed voice in Mandarin ask about police or customs presence. Another voice assured that all was clear. Moments later the false compartment door was opened and they were dazzled by torchlight. A bare-footed fisherman in shorts and singlet shone the beam at a pile of clothing on the floor.

'Put these on before you go on boat,' he told them.

Sorting out the bizarre fashion parade by torchlight and finding something that even vaguely fitted would no doubt one day be the source of hilarious reminiscences in the mess at Hereford, but no one was remotely amused this evening. They all just wanted to reach the relative security of the fishing junk.

However, Dancer saw the wisdom of the precaution. These villagers, who had supplemented their meagre income by smuggling for years, knew how to see and hear nothing and to keep their mouths shut. But if a stranger, a zealous official or even a curious child chanced by, then the entire mission could be compromised. Now, in the comings and goings on the gloomy, lamp-lit quay, they were just a few more fishermen going about their work.

With shoulders stooped and heads bowed, each man picked up a couple of empty crates and carried them off the back of the truck to the gunwale of the moored junk, following the fisherman to the lower covered deck. There, Captain Song Xiu Kun waited for them, the light from the oil lamp glistening on his bald head and drooping silver goatee and moustache. He watched impassively as they tramped down the steps, puffing on some evil-smelling substance in his old churchwarden pipe.

Dancer recognised him from Prufrock's description and

offered his hand. 'Captain Song? I am Mr John.'

The man accepted the handshake with a slight inclination of the head. He had no time to waste on pleasantries with a foreign devil.

'We must cast off now if we are to make the rendezvous on time,' he grunted. 'Make yourself comfortable. There will be some tea later when we are under way.'

Making themselves comfortable meant finding themselves seats on the upturned crates they'd brought aboard, while the four unsavoury-looking crewmen busied themselves under Song's impassive eye. The ancient diesel grumbled into life in a cloud of fumes and the boat began to tremble gently like a living thing. Lines were released and the *Hong* was gripped by the current, moving slowly out into midstream. The engine noise increased along with its speed as the old fishing junk headed for the Gulf of Bohai twenty miles downstream.

'Periscope depth,' reported the fourth crew who had taken over the helm console. Every man was competent in the other's skills.

Al Cherrier sat at the 'optronics relay screen' in the control suite. 'Stand by warner clearance!'

With a hiss, the hydraulically assisted electronics-warfare 'warning-mast' rose up from the slight humped 'fin' on the top deck above and broke through the surface of the water. In barely five seconds it had identified every active radar frequency within range before descending back down into *Manta*'s hull. Within seconds the automatic analysis was complete and displayed on one of the auxiliary monitors. The radars and their most usually associated sources were listed and sorted in priority order, beginning with fire-control radars for weapons systems, then general air-to-surface and surface-to-surface search radars.

There was a long list of maritime civilian radars, topped by three printed in red. Two of those were Chinese coastal radars and the third bore the NATO designation: '*Square Tie – associated with Hegu, Houjian and Houxin Classes (some variations)*.'

'Fast-missile attack craft,' Cherrier confirmed aloud.

'The *Hegus* are bloody fast,' Nick Lake said, moving to the captain's side. 'We had a play with one owned by the Bangladeshi Navy a couple of years back. Seriously impressive.'

Cherrier murmured, 'But happily not our concern. This one's heading out into the strait, minding her own business. And she has no real anti-sub potential.'

Janie Walsh had joined them. 'Unlike the *Hainan* class?' she asked.

Cherrier raised an eyebrow. 'Becoming quite a naval expert, aren't we?'

'A girl has to do her best, Skipper,' she rejoined.

The captain looked back at the screen. 'I'll really get worried when I see a Pot Head or Skin Head radar on the screen. That's what the anti-sub *Hainan*s use and there are around a hundred operating in Chinese waters. Packed with mortars and depth charges.' He swivelled his chair to face the optronics screen. 'Safe enough for a look-see. Stand by optronics mast!'

The operation took only marginally longer than the previous EW warner search. The telescopic optronics mast rose like a car aerial above the waves, revolved rapidly and descended back into the hull. 'Take her down to forty feet,' Cherrier ordered.

Now the video-tape image recorded from the low-light level TV camera in the optronics system could be studied in slow motion to ensure nothing was missed. Cherrier quickly identified a tanker, a container ship and an old tramp – and the low silhouette of the *Hegu* class missile boat barely visible in the distance.

But that wasn't what he was looking for. The captain moved slowly round the panoramic view on the screen until he was facing the river mouth. And there she was. Just a dark smudge against the green background, two feeble glows representing the port and starboard lights. The fishing boat *Hong*.

'There she is!' he announced. 'On time and on target. Okay, Hinks, give me a seabed reading.'

'Eighty-five feet, Skipper.'

'Right. Take her down, real gently.'

The tension rose, the submarine silent except for the faint hum of the fuel-cell.

'Forty feet–Thirty–'

Everyone could visualise the seabed looming. Suddenly it felt very hot, very confined.

'Twenty feet–fifteen.'

'Slow now,' Cherrier snapped. 'Hold around ten and catch a stopped trim.'

'Between eight and nine,' Hinks reported. 'We have neutral buoyancy.'

Cherrier nodded. They were hovering horizontally in the water, just feet above the silt bed. 'Flood Q-tank.'

'Aye, aye, sir.'

The ripple of water was drowned out by a fierce hissing gurgle as the valves opened in the Q-tank to allow in half-a-ton of seawater. Slowly the deck began to cant. Everyone held their breath. The impact was soft, barely noticeable as the Q-tank had the effect of anchoring *Manta* to the bottom.

Cherrier looked up at the anxious faces; for once he was smiling. 'Gentlemen – lady – welcome to the People's Republic of China.'

'Well done, Al,' Nick Lake said, slapping his back and turning to the group of figures clad in black rubber. 'Right, lads, time to go!'

The tall, reedy figure of Dougie Squires was first through the hatch into the swimmers' compartment, followed by the others. Within minutes flippers and face masks were on and the A5800 closed-circuit mixed gas rebreather rigs from Carleton Technologies slipped into position.

Designed for special operations, the electronically controlled rigs provided over six hours' 'bubbleless' operation time while emitting low magnetic and acoustic signatures.

This first rendezvous party included Lake, Squires and a big SBS veteran known as Grunt, who was a man of few, if choice, words. Janie Walsh would stay back with a four-man SBS support team which would lurk beside the *Hong* until the first three were safely aboard and gave a confirming signal. Only then would Walsh be allowed to join them. Her swimming had much improved, but she would still require an underwater 'escort' just to be on the safe side.

For this part of the operation, the support team needed no heavier weapon than the US Navy Model 22 Type 0. Made in stainless steel for a saltwater environment, the silenced 9 mm pistol had been specially developed for the SEALs by Smith and Wesson. It was affectionately known as the 'Hush Puppy' for its efficiency at dispatching guard dogs. Other Chinese-made weapons, which would be used once ashore, were carefully wrapped in special waterproof packs.

With everything set, Lake secured the hatch to the control room and signalled to flood the compartment. Immediately it began to fill and Lake felt the familiar surge of adrenalin as the water level rose rapidly. He could just see Walsh's eyes, large and fearful through the glass of her mask. He grinned at her reassuringly and gave her the divers' universal 'O' signal with thumb and forefinger. All okay, nothing to worry about. She had just nodded and returned the gesture when the saltwater swirled and bubbled up over her head.

Seconds later the pressure was equalised and he watched as Squires swam up to the main access hatch overhead and eased it open. Then, one by one, they floated out after him into the murky liquid universe. Grunt stayed with Walsh, attaching her to a steel handhold on the hull with a clasp and line while the rest of the team approached the aft equipment hold. Hydraulic doors opened to reveal a storage compartment some three feet deep between the *Manta*'s outer shell and her inner titanium pressure hull.

Inside was a top-secret SBS inflatable stealth submersible which the men had nicknamed Phantom. Fifteen feet long and eight feet wide, it had originally been developed for dropping from a C130 Hercules for anti-narcotics raids at sea. Coated with anti-radar paint, it was designed to carry ten-plus combat swimmers, sitting one behind the other, horseback style, in two rows at up to fifty knots on the surface, powered by low-noise water-jet engines. In the same mode, it could 'snort' just below the surface with only the swimmers' heads above the water.

For this initial deployment, however, Phantom would be running fully submerged on the two 24-volt electric pod motors set on either side of the rubber bow. But first the team semi-inflated a conventional Gemini inflatable and lashed in all the gear that would be going ashore. This would be towed behind like an underwater sledge.

As soon as Phantom was clear of the hatch and the sledge attached, Grunt helped Walsh to her seat while everyone else took up their positions. Then Lake started the electric motors and they began to move slowly away from the submarine. The *Hong* should now be in position just two miles away.

Dancer hadn't felt comfortable with Captain Song and his crew. It was some sort of sixth sense, and he suspected McVicar and Taffy had noticed it too. The fishing junk's skipper remained watchful and said little. The four crewmen had shared green tea with them, laughing and asking many questions in the usual Chinese manner. But somehow they were a little *too* friendly. Not quite what you expected of Triad gangsters.

Once or twice, when they were out of earshot, Dancer had seen them huddled together whispering amongst themselves and with Song.

Dancer decided he was worrying unduly and pushed the nagging concern from his mind. Instead, he hunched in his quilted anorak against the nagging wind, cold even in the summer in the bleak and open area around the Gulf, and watched the distant aurora of lights from the port and the huge shadows of merchantmen passing in the night down the deep-water channels.

McVicar glanced at his watch. Almost 2300 hours. Zulu time, in theatre. Then he consulted the hand-held Magellan NAV 1000M receiver linking him with the United States' satellite global-positioning system that was accurate to within sixteen metres. He'd been regularly checking their position and course for the two hours since they'd left the riverside village.

'Song knows his stuff,' he murmured. 'Spot on. Let's go see him.'

Dancer and Taffy followed the Scots SAS man down the steps into the lower hold where Song and his crew were standing and talking beside the fish-holding tank.

'Captain, we are now in position,' McVicar said in fluent Mandarin. 'Can you put down a drag anchor?'

Song nodded and sent one of his men to do the job. With another crew member at the helm, there were now two others standing beside their skipper.

Song addressed Dancer. 'You have the money?'

'Used dollars, as we agreed,' the American replied and turned to McVicar who was standing next to him. 'Would you do the honours, Dave?'

McVicar reached inside the Mao jacket and under his own shirt to release the money belt he wore round his waist. He unzipped it and pulled out one of several rolls of notes.

Captain Song's face remained a mask as the Scotsman handed over one of them, but Dancer caught the look in the eyes of the two crewmen as they realised just how much money this stranger was carrying.

One of them said quickly, 'This is dangerous business. We can get shot for spying.'

Dancer's eyes narrowed. 'This is China, friend, you can get shot for smuggling.'

There was an abrupt silence as the rattle of the old diesel engine died away and they could hear the boat's creaking timbers. Suddenly the helmsman and the anchorman joined them in the hold. One was sporting a wicked-looking descaling knife and the other an iron grappling hook.

Another of the seamen became agitated. 'Too dangerous! You not pay enough. It costs more to deal with spies. This is treason!'

Dancer ignored him and faced Song. 'Had this planned all along, didn't you?'

For the first time there was a hint of a smile on the thin lips as the skipper removed the long churchwarden and gave a little shrug. 'What can I do? I am faced with mutiny. My men are afraid. More risk, more money. I have no option but to go along with it.'

'And if we don't?'

Song shrugged. 'These are interesting waters. Shifting sands, never still. Ships that sink are rarely found. Neither are their crews.'

As if his message wasn't plain enough, the helmsman took a step forward.

Nine

Taffy had seen it coming. He had surreptitiously taken a backward step, then another to put more distance between himself and the fishermen.

'We have a deal,' Dancer insisted, but the man with the descaling knife didn't seem to be hearing. He just continued forward towards McVicar with a menacing half-smile on his face and his free hand outstretched for the money belt.

As the tip of the blade reached the Scotsman's chest, he made his move. His left hand came up under the knife-man's wrist with the speed of a striking adder, knocking it aside. Then his fingers closed around the forearm while his whole body stepped across in front of the seaman. As the heel of his right foot hooked behind the other's lower leg, his right palm slammed into the offered shoulder, throwing the man totally off balance.

He went backwards over McVicar's foot, but didn't hit the deck because the Scotsman still had hold of his forearm. McVicar brought his knee up quickly and hard against the fisherman's elbow joint. The squeal of pain and the sound of tearing ligaments were simultaneous. The descaling knife spun away into a coil of ropes.

The other seaman stepped forward, his grappling iron raised.

'DOWN!' Taffy screamed.

Instantly McVicar hit the deck, dragging Dancer down after him. For a moment the American was confused until he saw that Taffy had drawn his Fifty-Nine automatic and wanted a clear field of fire.

'DROP IT!' the Welshman ordered in Mandarin.

The second seaman froze, his eyes darting from Taffy to

Captain Song and back again. There was no expression on the skipper's face as he considered for a moment, then slowly shook his head. The seaman let the grappling hook fall to the deck.

Dancer rolled away from under the muzzle of Taffy's gun and climbed to his feet. 'That was a big mistake, Song,' he said grimly. 'I don't think Mike Jiang's going to be too pleased to hear about your attempt at extortion.'

Song tilted his head to one side. 'It was wrong of my men, I agree. But there is no need to involve Mr Jiang.'

'On the contrary, Captain, there's every reason. We had a deal and you tried to break it.'

For the first time fear showed on Song's face. Dancer could see it in his eyes. 'Please, it will not happen again. I promise you there will be no more problem, no more trouble.'

Dancer glanced at McVicar and the SAS man gave a slight inclination of his head. They both knew it would take time to find and set up a similar operation with another skipper. Time they did not have. Hopefully, Song and his cronies had learned their lesson.

'Try anything like that again,' Dancer warned, 'and Jiang is the first to know. That's just cost you ten per cent of your fee for the first trip. And now we have a change of rules. Nothing more up front. You get paid only after you complete each trip. Agreed?'

A tic of anger flickered at the corner of the captain's right eye, but nothing else indicated his deep loss of face.

'Agreed?' Dancer repeated. 'We haven't got all night.'

Song found his voice. 'Agreed,' he said hoarsely.

Taffy waved the Fifty-Nine. 'Then get a friggin' move on. Get that sodding hatch open or our people will think they've got the wrong boat.'

Song snapped an order at the crewman who had wielded the grappling iron. The man glared at Dancer for a moment, then kicked off his sandals and scrambled up over the pitched timber planks of the fish-holding tank. He reached some three feet under the water until his hands located the ring-pull, then heaved open the circular hatch. A flurry of froth and bubbles broke the surface of the tank as the water rose to equal the level outside the hull.

McVicar checked his watch. Dancer and Taffy looked on anxiously. The crewman in the tank stood nervously with the water now reaching his waist, not knowing quite what to expect.

Then suddenly, without warning, the first one arrived. For just a second they glimpsed the dark shape taking rapid form somewhere below the hull. Then it was there, shooting up through the hatch into the tank and bursting from the surface in an explosion of water and foam. An alien in dripping black rubber and a single glistening eye. The crewman in the tank took a backward step in surprise until he remembered his job and reached forward to help the new arrival find his footing.

The tall, thin combat swimmer floundered forward, walking awkwardly in his fins until he was able to grab the side of the tank and rip the mask and breathing apparatus from his face. It was Dougie Squires and he wasn't smiling as he recognised McVicar. 'Took your time opening the fuckin' hatch, didn't you? I've been round the hull half-a-dozen times.'

McVicar just smiled one of the lazy, patronising smiles he reserved specially for scaleybacks. 'Sorry, mate. Just a little local difficulty with the natives. Made a slight miscalculation on their abacus.'

As Squires hauled himself out of the tank he noticed the injured crewman nursing his arm, then saw the automatic in Taffy's hand. 'Do we have an abort?' he asked anxiously.

The Scotsman shook his head. 'No, we all understand each other perfectly now.'

Having weighed up the situation, Squires leaned back over the tank and fired the laser pulse signal from his wristset back down the hatch where the others awaited the all clear. For some reason best known to the SBS, which

McVicar had never figured, their high-tech underwater communications were known as 'trongles and bongles'.

A minute later, a second undersea creature shot up into the holding tank – this time Nick Lake. As soon as he'd found his footing and pulled off his mask, he turned back to the hatch as the next swimmer emerged, floundering and reaching out frantically for help. Lake hauled the diminutive figure clear of the hatch as her bulky escort also emerged in the shape of the monosyllabic Grunt.

For the first time Dancer saw surprise register on Captain Song's face as Janie Walsh pulled off her mask and rubber hood and shook her hair free. Then he smiled. 'So it is true after all,' Song said. 'You *do* come from Taiwan.'

They never did learn what Song and his crew had originally thought they were *actually* up to, but the atmosphere changed tangibly from the moment the Chinese-American arrived on board. The backup team, who had been standing by in case of trouble, began ferrying up waterproofed equipment from the 'sledge' to the hatch of the *Hong*'s hull. Apart from personal kit, it comprised weaponry, explosives, radios, and considerable amounts of US dollars. When the transfer was complete, the backup team returned to *Manta*, the junk weighed anchor, and put out her nets for half-an-hour's fishing. With a small catch in the holding tank, Song was happy enough and ordered the helmsman to head back to the estuary and the village.

Meanwhile the shore party stripped off their wet suits and put on the one change of clothes they had brought with them. There were plenty of clothes shops in Beijing where they could stock up their wardrobe as necessary. Walsh looked fetching in jeans and a white angora rollneck as she clutched her mug of hot green tea which she attempted to drink through chattering teeth.

'Never been so damn cold in all my life,' she admitted. 'I can't stop shaking.'

'Probably nerves,' Lake added helpfully.

'Never fancied the job you guys do,' Dancer said. 'I did

some in training in the Viet Nam days and that was enough.'

'Who were you with? Green Berets?' Lake asked.

Dancer nodded.

Lake grinned, relieved that they'd made it this far and that Dancer wasn't some desk-bound spook who got everything out of manuals and had never been at the sharp end. That they all seemed to be rubbing along well together was a bonus. 'Nice to know you're one of us.'

'It was a long time ago.'

McVicar added reassuringly, 'But some things don't change, John.'

It was then that they became aware of bright light stabbing in under the top deck tarpaulin and heard the metallic voice over the bullhorn drifting across the water.

'Coastguard,' the helmsman called down.

'Shit,' Walsh said.

Dancer took control. 'Go to the bow section. Move it!' And he followed the others aft, past the holding tank to the for'ard anchor compartment.

It was larger than need be and Song used it for concealing contraband. A skilful village carpenter had crafted the wooden bulkhead so that the planks could be removed one by one to gain access. Two of the crewmen were already pulling them out as the shore-party scrambled in and sat on the pile of kit they'd already stored there.

'HEAVE TO, WE'RE COMING ABOARD!' bellowed the voice from the Chinese coastguard cutter.

The *Hong*'s diesel cut to a low burble and they could again hear the slap of the sea against the hull and the creaking of the fishing boat's timbers. The crewmen had just replaced the last of the bulkhead planks when the officer stepped over the gunwale.

Behind the bulkhead, guns were drawn as Dancer watched through the narrow gap between two planks. Tension added to the claustrophobic sensation in the confines of the compartment, everybody sweating and

255

waiting. But the Chinese officer seemed to have little real interest in what illegal cargo the *Hong* was or was not carrying. He took Captain Song to one side, out of earshot of the crew and exchanged a few quiet words. Then both men laughed conspiratorially and Song produced a bottle of *maotai* spirit and two glasses from a cupboard. They raised their glasses in a toast that Dancer couldn't quite catch. Then he thought something was exchanged, perhaps a small packet, but it was gloomy in the lantern light and he couldn't be certain.

The officer turned and clattered back up the steps to the top deck, jumped the gap back to his own vessel and called up to its helmsman. The coastguard cutter peeled off and disappeared into the night.

'A bribe?' Lake asked Dancer.

'Almost certainly. Police and customs are bound to know about old lags like Song. His family have been smugglers for generations.'

Lake grinned. 'Good. I can't stand dealing with amateurs.'

The remainder of the trip proved uneventful. The junk reached the village quay at just past midnight and tied up. A thin, sour-faced fisheries inspection official was waiting for them, but Captain Song told him they wouldn't unload the catch until first light – everyone was too exhausted. It seemed to be common practice because the official accepted it without demur. The skipper and his crew disappeared into the darkened, deserted village and an edgy silence settled over the scene.

Until three o'clock it remained unbroken. Then McVicar and Taffy, who were on stag, heard the distant lumbering of a truck and alerted the others. Everyone pulled on something from the collection of peasant clothes, flat caps and Mao suits and quilted anoraks, and waited. Finally the lorry's lights came into view along the riverside track, before the ancient vehicle negotiated a three-point turn and backed up to the junk. The roll-up back rattled open and a Chinese man in his twenties beckoned to them urgently. McVicar and Taffy looked out, armed and alert, while the others ferried equipment from the junk to the truck, then followed themselves. In just ninety minutes they would be in Mike Jiang's fish warehouse in Beijing – at the very heart of Communist China.

The SAS backup team, returning to the *Manta* after the successful rendezvous with the junk, reported a rapid build-up of silt around the submarine's nose where it touched the seabed.

Al Cherrier discussed the problem with the crew. Obviously their position was too close to the river estuary and there was a very real risk of their getting trapped in the silt or even buried by it. There was also a chance it could clog the propellers in the forward thruster shaft. Relocation was the only answer and should, anyway, be only a minor inconvenience. When accomplished, they would rise to periscope depth and fire a millisecond signal burst to be relayed by satellite to SAS headquarters in Hereford, who would in turn send back exact details of the *Manta*'s new position by satcom to the shore party in Beijing in time for the next rendezvous.

Cherrier made his decision. 'Blow the Q tank,' he ordered Hinks, who threw the switch which would empty the half-ton weight of water keeping them on the bottom.

'Roger that, Skip,' Hinks confirmed.

Cherrier checked the fuel-cell indicators to be sure that there was nothing amiss with the temperamental system.

A red light flashed above Hinks's console. 'Oh, shit.'

'What is it?'

Hinks studied the computer monitors. 'Outlet valve malfunction. Must have silted up.'

Cherrier scowled at the screen as if it was running a personal vendetta against him. Silt in the outlet valve! He hadn't foreseen that one. And if they couldn't blow the seawater out of the Q-tank, they'd be stuck nose-down and arse-up in the Gulf of Bohai for eternity.

It was a worrying half-hour while four SAS divers were deployed outside with shovels to dig away the silt build-up until they could reach the outlet valve. Simple enough in theory, but in practice it was an exhausting exercise, as no sooner had they dug an area clear, than the current pushed more silt back into the hole. It was two steps forward and one step back.

If Cherrier hadn't made the decision when he did, it could have been the other way round and they'd never have managed to get out. When the shovel blade revealed the outlet valve they immediately felt the passing rush of water as pumped air cleared the tank. The great bulk of *Manta* began to shift and Cherrier juggled with the controls to achieve neutral buoyancy, keeping the craft hovering above them while they swam back up to the access hatch.

'These waters are a bloody nightmare,' Hinks murmured, as the monitor showed that everyone was back on board and the outside hatch shut. The swimmers' compartment began to pump out.

Cherrier smiled grimly and slapped Hinks on the shoulder. 'C'mon, I know you wouldn't want it any other way.'

The captain activated the forward port and starboard rear thrusters to turn *Manta* round in her own length, then notched up the fuel-cell output to achieve two knots and made away from the estuary. The sonar was showing up the crazy contours and dramatic variations of the seabed on the 'Visual Attitude' screen. It was like never-ending rows of underwater mountain ranges in miniature which shifted formation even as they watched. Hinks intoned the depth readings in confirmation as Cherrier used the joystick to steer the submarine through the subterranean valleys and mountain passes, keeping them at equal distance between the bottom and the surface. It was a hideous arcade Nintendo game. Each touch on the control was translated by the computer into a set of instructions sent to the main aft propeller, the appropriate control surfaces or thruster motors. The plethora of blinking icons and running numerals on the screens showed the vast complexity and difficulty of operating in these waters.

'I don't like this, Skipper,' Hinks said.

'The computer certainly doesn't,' Cherrier agreed, his beetle brows furrowing. 'Look at the buoyancy indicator. It's going haywire.'

Hinks nodded. 'It must be salinity changes. River water mixing with salt.' They both knew it affected the submarine's buoyancy and the computer was programmed to adjust to every fluctuation. And here, it seemed, there was a fluctuation every few feet.

Suddenly the computer made a whirring sound of protest. Then the screens went blank. 'Goddammit, she's crashed! Switch to backup!'

Hinks had half-anticipated and was already on to it. Three of the monitors flickered back on, but the 'Visual Attitude' screen remained stubbornly off.

Cherrier called the electrical engineer, Manson, on the intercom. 'Have a look-see at this fucker, will you? Looks like some sort of overload.'

The young, sandy-haired sailor from Illinois was out of his cot and through the hatch from the crew quarters in seconds as if he'd been anticipating the call. His birth had virtually coincided with that of the modern computer and his father had worked on them with NASA. Manson understood binary logic far more easily than he did the thinking process of the human mind, especially one like Cherrier's.

But, by the time he reached the control suite, his captain was drawing sweat as he cut their speed to two knots and tried to adjust their depth manually. All he had to go on was Hinks's continuing sonar read-out. Without the backup of the 'Visual Attitude' screen graphics, it was a nightmare.

'Thirty-three feet, thirty, twenty-seven. This ain't healthy, Skipper.'

Cherrier glanced at Manson who had the machine open and was peering in. 'Any joy?'

'I'll need twenty minutes, half-an-hour.'

Hinks said, 'Twenty-five feet!'

The captain again switched on the port and starboard side thrusters to turn *Manta* on her own axis and head back the way they'd come. He wiped the back of his hand across his brow. That had been close.

Then, barely three minutes later, it was closer still.

'Thirty feet again!' Hinks called. 'And closing fast. Twenty-five, twenty-one. Oh, shit!'

Cherrier had run out of options. 'STAND BY! STAND BY! EMERGENCY SURFACE!'

They were now running at periscope depth, but the seabed was rising fast to meet them. There was no time to take a visual check. Cherrier threw the lever to blow the main ballast tanks.

Manta broke the surface like a great blue whale. The fourth crew member, a Puerto Rican called Sanchez, raised the optronics mast while Cherrier trimmed the submarine down until she rested on her wings and punched the button marked 'Conceal Spray'. Immediately three hundred small nozzles, which were set around the perimeter of the craft, fired off recirculated seawater to create a wall of spray.

Hinks studied the 'Plan Position Indicator' screen as the passive bow and flank array sonars picked up the sounds of vessels in the area. 'We're in luck, Skipper. The shipping lanes are virtually empty – nothing for us to worry about. But there is something small about half-a-mile astern. Oh, shit, and she's interrogating with her surface radar. Square Tie. So Navy or coastguard.'

'What depth reading are we getting?' Cherrier demanded.

'Better. Forty feet.'

'Thank God for that.' He threw the intercom switch. 'Stand by! Dive! Dive! Dive!'

260

The ballast tank valves opened, allowing the seawater to pour in, and within seconds *Manta* had slipped silently back beneath the waves.

Cherrier turned to Manson. 'How you doing?'

'Getting there, Skipper.' He sounded confident. 'But I need to do some reformatting to get around the problem. I'll need a couple of hours, I'm afraid.'

That didn't please Cherrier, but there wasn't much he could do about it.

Hinks leaned forward. 'One of the main shipping lanes is just a quarter-mile ahead, Skipper. It's no less than thirty-five feet depth all the way. In the dredged channel we could lie doggo for as long as it takes.'

Cherrier smiled grimly. 'Good idea. Let's do it.'

Commander Hua was feeling tired and bored. There was nothing much to see from the bridge of the coastguard cutter at this time of night. Just the sea and sky and land mass in varying densities of black, broken only by a rash of pinprick lights marking distant Tianjin and the occasional shadow of a passing merchantman.

He was nearing the end of a long shift and the stiff drink aboard the fishing junk with that old rascal Song had dulled his senses. Increasingly he found himself stifling yawns.

'I'm going on deck to get some air,' he announced to his Number Two.

Once outside, he found that the breeze, with its snap of ozone, cleared his head in seconds. The only sound, as he grasped the handrail and stared out across the Gulf, was the hum of the twin inboards and the slap of seawater being parted by the cutter's prow.

He was not long off retirement now and he knew he was going to miss these quiet moments alone with his innermost thoughts and the spirits of the sea. It was something his wife would never understand. He was staring, unfocused, into the middle distance and had it not been for the quarter-moon shedding a gentle sheen over the water, he would have missed it. A sudden flurry of bubbles and foam some half a mile off the cutter's beam, then the emergence of the shiny blue-black creature. Too large for a dolphin. A whale of some kind? He swallowed hard. That was no whale, it was man-made. He could see the row of viewing ports around the slightly raised fin section and then something that resembled a strange sort of periscope. Periscope? The thoughts tumbled through his mind in a split second. It was like no submarine that he had ever seen. More like the popular conception of a flying saucer. Another fleeting thought – surely it couldn't be a crashed aeroplane?

Then a most remarkable thing happened. Even as he watched, the strange craft was enveloped in mist and melted away before his eyes. He shook his head, squeezed his eyes shut for a moment, then opened them again. What the hell had Song put in that drink earlier? No, no, he told himself, he had not imagined it.

Turning on his heel, he clambered back up the ladder and on to the bridge. He stode across to the radar operator. 'There is a vessel off our starboard bow. Bearing about three-one-zero. What have you?'

But the operator was already shaking his head. 'I think you are mistaken, sir. There's only that large container ship in the marked channel.'

'Well, it was quite *small*.'

'No, sir, see for yourself.'

Hua turned to the sonar operator. 'Have you heard anything?'

An ingratiating and nervous smile. 'Er, no, sir.'

'Try active.'

'Yes, sir.'

Hua listened intently, still sure he was right and that the young crewmen had missed it. But gradually his expectations died away. The pinging sonar signal hit nothing, did not bounce back.

'What did you think it was, sir?'

The commander shrugged. 'Not sure. Perhaps a submarine. Less than half-a-mile away.'

'A sub in these waters?' The sonarman sounded incredulous. 'I'd have picked that up, sir.'

Hua smiled awkwardly. 'Yes, of course.'

He turned away, now faced with a quandary. Did he believe in himself and his years of experience or risk ridicule – or even worse – from his superiors?

The fish truck reached Mike Jiang's warehouse on the outskirts of Beijing without incident before first light. It was a hive of activity, staff already arrived and dressed in white overalls and green wellington boots, ready to deal with the steady stream of trucks arriving with the night's catches from fishing ports and harbours all over Tianjin. But while all the other trucks went into the main area, no one noticed one battered blue vehicle turn into the specially secured section.

With stiff and aching limbs, Dancer and the rest of the shore party climbed down from the tailgate. Big Mike Jiang himself was in the reception committee, wearing his usual big smile and for once casual in jeans and a stylish cashmere sweater. With him were his minders and the two other SAS men who had replaced Stonedancer staff. No one said, but everyone knew they were the insurance in case any members of the Red Tiger Society decided to play silly buggers.

But, in fact, Jiang seemed to be thoroughly enjoying himself as a plotter and schemer to overthrow the Communist rulers who had been the bane of his criminal activities for so long. He insisted on shaking hands with all the new arrivals.

As soon as everyone had changed back from their Chinese peasant clothes, Dancer said: 'It's safest to leave here on foot. Then you can walk, take a cab or the metro to the office. It's highly unlikely any of us will be followed

263

but, if you are, at least this way you can identify Bureau or Security Ministry watchers and shake them off.' He smiled. 'To be honest, they're not much good.'

They slipped out of the warehouse office one by one onto the pavements filling with rush-hour workers, the new arrivals teaming up with those who already knew their way around. Within an hour, each couple or small group had arrived at the secure compound gates of the ExecFlight offices.

Abe Stone had been as good as his word and had thrown his full weight behind the operation, seeming to have genuinely forgiven Dancer for his earlier deception. The big man's organisational ability had been invaluable in arranging to house and feed eight or more illegal guests in secret for as long as it took. Remarkably he'd even managed to bury the hatchet with Xin-Bin rather than *in* him, although he never actually got around to admitting that he'd been wrong to be paranoid about Wang's younger brother.

The top floor of the building had always been Dancer's and Xin-Bin's private domain, sealed off by a steel door with punch-code entry. There they could make phone calls, write reports, send faxes and e-mails, photocopy stolen or 'borrowed' documents without any fear of discovery, while the day-to-day running of the company was conducted downstairs on the ground floor by the regular staff. Now their spacious secure offices had been transformed into a cross between a barracks and a military headquarters. Stone had arranged for half-a-dozen work stations to be installed with PCs and telephones for the SAS and SBS teams to work from. There was a new conference table and a meeting room had been cork-tiled to take the dozens of large-scale maps and satellite photographs that had come out of Langley in diplomatic bags via the US Embassy.

For weeks Iona Moncrieff had been sending out Suzy Tobin to try and acquire items on the SAS's seemingly endless shopping list. They included every telephone and business directory available; bus, train, airline and ferry timetables; every published guidebook on China as well as confidential SIS reports on the disposition of police and military units, the make-up of the Chicom Government and relevant departments.

In terms of hard practicalities, collapsible cots and metal lockers now filled two other offices and a third served as a makeshift mess. But, as it was now stacked with groceries, there was only room for three easy chairs and a small coffee table. The tiny kitchen was woefully inadequate despite the installation of a large refrigerator and two microwave ovens.

There was only one way up to the secure floor, but four ways out. Roll-up escape ladders had been secured by one window at the back and at each side of the building should they ever be raided by Bureau police, the Security Ministry or the PLA.

By midday, the new arrivals had sorted out their sleeping arrangements, stowed their kit and had something to eat. Dancer then called a meeting and everyone gathered round the conference table.

'Guess this is your official welcome to Beijing,' he began. 'I suggest those who've just arrived spend the afternoon doing a bit of sight-seeing and orientation. After a good night's sleep you can set about things in earnest tomorrow. Frankly I don't expect you'll have any trouble from the police, the Bureau boys or anyone else. But I suggest you always move around in twos, just in case. Those of you who arrived last night only have second-class backdrops, I understand. Passports, tourist visas and air tickets, et cetera. You've each been supplied with a key card from the hotel you're supposed to be staying at in Beijing. Of course, as you don't actually exist, the hotel will never have heard of you.'

Janie Walsh cut in. 'But it should be enough to satisfy any zealous official that you're a genuine tourist. Frankly, questions are more likely to be asked in remoter regions and even then only out of the cities. But then we'll try to avoid sending you anywhere like that. Remember it is a capital offence to have forged documents. If it looks as if you're being seriously suspected, then bug out.'

'Do whatever's necessary, then straight down your private escape line into Pakistan,' McVicar advised.

Dancer said: 'The four of you who have replaced my staff should get the results of your medicals in the next couple of days. Then you'll get your full genuine z-visa for working.'

'The medical was a hoot,' McVicar recalled. 'The doc actually asks you if you are sane.'

'And what did you reply?' Nick Lake asked with a deliberate air of innocence.

Dancer continued, 'Now, your function will be to contact the agent networks in each province that the American and British Governments have helped establish over many years. Xin-Bin and I have met many of the leaders personally and have guided them all in forming their networks into secure four- or six-person cells with cut-outs. And this has mostly been achieved. I think the leadership is implicitly trustworthy. If it wasn't, this operation would almost certainly have been blown by now. But, of course, we can't take anything for granted.'

Walsh added: 'Our job is to meet each network leader and get his assessment of what needs to be done on D-day to ensure that particular province's local military is neutralised and that the democracy movement takes control. We then assess and make recommendations, and arrange for instruction to be given to small training cadres who will pass those skills on down the network. Mostly it'll be agent handling and contact drills, safe rendezvous procedures and target reconnaissance.'

Dancer then explained how he hoped it would all work. 'What we're trying to avoid is a civil war and bloody conflict tearing the country apart. We know there's going to be an attempt made by an internal group of well-placed Chinese within the democracy movement to seize power. That'll all happen here in Beijing. In effect, the head of the Chicom octopus will be cut off. The media will be commandeered and broadcasts made announcing a new interim government pledged to democracy and the free market economy. Key military leaders will announce their support. The networks will be organising mass street demonstrations of students and workers. Hopefully, that'll persuade any old diehards that a fight isn't worth the effort.' He indicated the main wall map. 'But as you know, China is vast. And the effectiveness of the coup will vary from province to province. In some regions, there is bound to be resistance.'

Walsh cut in: 'That's why we want the networks to identify hardline Chicom political and military leaders who are unlikely to be persuaded so that network members can take the necessary pre-emptive action. Hence, you'll be giving them some training in home-made explosives and demolitions as well as weapons training.'

Once more, Nick Lake had the feeling that they weren't being given the full picture. He and McVicar had discussed it privately on several occasions now and both had concluded that the Americans were holding back on the full extent of CIA involvement. Lake decided to chance rocking the boat.

He raised his hand and directed his question at Walsh. 'Do we know yet exactly *how* these Chinese dissidents are planning to topple the Politburo?'

Her returning smile was a little frosty. 'No, Nick, we still don't. But if we did, it still wouldn't be sensible for the whole team to know. I'm sure I don't have to spell it out.'

McVicar grinned at him across the table. *Nice try, laddie*, Lake could almost hear him say.

Brigadier Ting Han-chen, his hands clasped behind his back, stood staring out of the window of his office in the Ministry of State Security.

He spoke to the reflected image of the squat Bureau detective in the glass.

'Inspector Xia, two weeks ago, I ordered you to forget about the John Dancer business. It would appear that you deliberately disobeyed my instructions.'

Ungrateful serpent, Xia thought. But he said, with as much humility as he could muster, 'I apologise for that, but I did continue the investigation in my *own* time, during my lunch periods. I hope that you think the result justifies my actions.'

Ting turned back into his office and Xia was surprised to see that the brigadier did not appear to be at all angry. In fact, he had a hint of a smile on his face. 'Yes, indeed, Inspector, I do. You were right and I was wrong. It is unusual to see such selfless zeal and independence of mind in the counter-intelligence services.'

Suddenly Xia felt filled with pride and twice his real height. 'Thank you, sir.'

'So you are telling me that you have traced the man who bought the tickets that Dancer used when taking Lily Cheung and her mother to the symphony concert.' Ting glanced at his notes. 'A Mr Qin. And this Mr Qin is a Chinese national on the household administration staff of the United States Embassy.'

Xia nodded. 'He has worked there for many years. He is popular with the Americans because he is a bit of a fixer. He knows his way around many of the problems foreign devils have in China, has many contacts – including ticket touts.'

'And you arrested him?'

'No, just a quiet word. Made him sweat a little. He said he did not know who in the embassy the tickets had been for. He offered to find out if he could.'

'And now he has.' Ting considered the name written on his pad and mouthed it slowly like a bad taste. 'William James Dawson.'

'CIA,' Xia added with enthusiasm. 'Everyone knows that.'

'Indeed. The question is why should Bill Dawson supply symphony tickets to John Dancer?'

Xia's eyes glittered, as always sensing conspiracy lurking round every corner. 'Exactly my thought, sir!'

Ting smiled. 'Of course, it is just possible that Dancer is a friend of Dawson and he was just doing him a favour. Getting tickets at short notice so that he can woo Lily Cheung.'

Xia pulled a face at the prospect of such a simple solution. 'We know Dawson and Dancer are acquaintances in business. As Dawson's cover is commercial attaché, it would be surprising if they were not. But they are not exactly friends. They are not in the habit of contacting each other socially. When they last attended the same party – thrown by that British businessman, Mr Prufrock – it was reported to me that they barely acknowledged each other.'

The brigadier nodded his understanding. 'Not the behaviour of two people who then do big favours for each other? I take your point.'

'And *what* does John Dancer want with the Cheung woman? Is it to have carnal knowledge of her or something more sinister? I think I should speak with her.'

Ting looked once more at the photograph taken by Xia's men in the lobby of the concert hall. The elfin face and pert nose, the black hair and bright eyes. 'No, Inspector, leave that to my people. But, in the meantime, you may reinstate your surveillance of Mr Dancer and his company – at least until the big operation is over with – just to be on the safe side.'

Xia nodded, turned and left, replacing his trilby hat as he went through the door,

Alone in his office, Ting regarded the photograph of Lily Cheung and gently ran the little finger of his right hand along the line of her cheek. He could almost imagine he saw her flinch. He smiled and put the file aside and drew out another from his in-tray.

It had been routinely copied from PLA Naval

Intelligence following a coastguard's reported sighting of a submarine in the Gulf of Bohai the previous night. The PLA Navy had confirmed that it had no submarines of its own operating in that area at the time. Neither did it have any vessels that matched the unusual design.

In view of the sensitivity of the 'current situation' – Ting knew they meant the coming invasion of Taiwan – the Navy intended to follow up with increased patrols and take various other precautionary measures.

Ting yawned.

In the afternoon, most of the new arrivals were out on the streets, familiarising themselves with the layout of Beijing and shopping for additional clothing items to the one change they had been able to bring in by submarine.

Their absence allowed Dancer and Xin-Bin to run through their secret video library for material that might be needed to 'persuade' certain reluctant key Chicom figures to co-operate with the new regime in the weeks to come. Blackmail was a useful weapon, but Dancer only ever used it as a last resort. It was always better to have a willing ally than a resentful one.

Most of the tapes had been recorded on ExecFlight aircraft by using hidden radio microphones and micro-lenses that delivered pictures to the secret camera by way of a fibre optic link. These were tapes of private conversations between individual Chicom political or military heavyweights when they thought it was safe to talk and exchange confidences or personal views in the ultimate privacy of a hired VIP jet. They were plied with good food and plenty of wine to help them drop their guard.

On other occasions, when either Dancer or Xin-Bin felt they had developed a rapport and trust with an individual, they would ask leading questions in a casual manner. The answers would often tell them whether the individual was a likely ally or enemy when the big day eventually came – if, of course, it ever did.

Dancer was fast-forwarding his third video tape on the player when Xin-Bin came in from the adjoining office.

'Sorry to disturb, Mr John. I have something here I think you should see.' He looked worried.

The American accepted the offered tape, kicked out the one he was playing and replaced it with the one from Xin-Bin. 'Who's on this?'

'It is of General Sun of the PLA Air Force in Xingjiang. Mostly it had been taped over because I didn't think it was any good to us. It was last year when my wife was having our youngest. I am afraid my concentration was not too good. This is all that is left. When I saw it, I realised you should know.'

Dancer smiled. 'Don't worry, I'm sure there's no harm done.' He pressed the play-button, lay back in his chair and lit a Camel as he watched.

The white blur slowly came into grainy focus. It was black and white and the picture of the aircraft cabin trembled slightly. The view was looking down on the two men relaxing in sumptuous leather armchairs on either side of a walnut table laden with a variety of bottles of spirits and glasses. Despite the fuzzy picture and the fact that he was wearing civilian clothes, General Sun was clearly distinguishable. He was a tall man with slightly Mongolian features and thick black hair raked straight back off his face and tortoiseshell spectacles with lenses so thick it seemed unlikely that he could ever have actually been a pilot in the air force.

The man he was talking to wasn't immediately identifiable as he had his back to the camera. However, there was no doubt that he was European and Dancer could see he was perspiring slightly, even though he'd already removed his crumpled jacket and hung it over the chairback.

'*So I would become chief of the new Chinese Air Force?*' Sun was asking. The voice sounded tinny and disembodied, the microphone a little too far away.

'*I'll get the agreement of Taiwan,*' replied the European.

'*And a secret protocol will be signed to that effect.*'

Thoughtfully, Sun relaxed back in his chair. '*And the aircraft deal is part of the package.*'

'*To be absolutely honest, General, it* is *Britain's interest in the package.*' Then he realised he may have been a little *too* 'honest' for Chinese sensibilities. '*And, of course, we will want all key military commanders in the New China to be pro-democracy and of the highest calibre to serve the greatest nation on earth.*'

Sun raised one quizzical eyebrow. '*You are most flattering.*'

'*Your first action on appointment will be to cancel the Russian contract to replace your MiGs. You then sign the agreement with the new Eurospace consortium via our joint company in Taiwan to build the modified cheaper version of the Eurofighter under licence.*'

'*One per cent of the deal to you and two point five to me?*'

'*That's what I recommend. Any higher and questions could be raised in Brussels.*'

'*And the new aircraft factory complex will be built by Mike Jiang's construction company?*'

'*Sure, if that's what you want. I suppose that way there will be plenty more opportunities for you and your friends.*'

General Sun was smiling now like a big kid with a lollipop. '*We have a deal.*'

The other man lifted his glass. '*A toast. Let's drink to it. To partners in—*'

Crime, Dancer thought.

'*Profit!*' said Sun.

Then the European turned his head. Edwin Prufrock was laughing.

Ten

Iona Moncrieff slipped from the bed, pulled on her dressing gown and lit a cigarette before looking out of the window. The sky over Yokohama was as grey and dull as the barrack buildings in the US Navy facility beside the harbour. Only the uniform rectangles of grass offered a splash of colour and even they were yellowing at the end of a long hot summer.

She watched two gulls swooping overhead and felt depressed by their plaintive calls. They were heralding the autumn, she thought bleakly. And winter would be following close behind. Perhaps even closer than she realised.

'Majesty?' The voice from behind her in the shadow was husky with sleep.

Iona turned and smiled. 'Who else, Bill?' Dawson was surfacing from the turmoil of sheets, the heavy body hair on his chest and shoulders reminding her of a floundering walrus. 'Who *else* do you sleep with nowadays?'

He was orientated now, propped on one elbow. 'I'm yours alone, Majesty. Just forgot where I was. Thought I'd died and gone to heaven.'

'Sweet.'

'Besides, you leave me too exhausted even to think about anyone else.'

'Nonsense. You can take all I've got to give. You're my oak tree.'

Dawson grinned and hauled his legs off the bed. 'I fell asleep before you could give me *anything* last night,' he reminded. 'Sorry about that.'

'Love means. . .' she chided.

He was running his big hands over his grizzled scalp. 'Truth is, your oak tree's been feeling fairly damned wind-blown the last few weeks. This business is kickin' the shit out of me.'

'Overthrowing governments is exhausting stuff,' she agreed with feeling. For weeks now it had been a nonstop treadmill of research, organisation and meetings, including almost weekly flights to Japan to give progress reports to Aspen of the CIA and Piers Lansdowne from London. At least she had the compensation of a few snatched hours with Dawson. 'Couldn't you ask for more support, more backup?'

Dawson looked up at her as though she was mad. 'And let assholes like Aspen think I can't handle it? I retire next year. This is my big one. My chance to show these Johnny-come-latelies how it's done.'

'Oh, I think you'll do that all right.' She glanced at her watch, then stubbed out her cigarette in the ashtray. 'Time I got back to my room. Don't want any nasty gossip.'

'Stay for coffee.' He reached for the bedside cabinet and turned on the machine.

'I really shouldn't. Why do you Americans have to have breakfast meetings?'

'Aspen likes them because he thinks it makes him seem butch.'

'Just uncivilised. Like having to watch you and Aspen pour that ghastly maple syrup stuff over your waffles. Besides, my brain doesn't function before ten.'

Dawson's grin was lascivious. 'I'm pleased to report the rest of you functions okay first thing. That's when I'm at my best.'

'I know. And you can stop playing tents. I'm seriously impressed.'

He cocked one eyebrow. 'Seriously enough to marry me?'

She frowned and looked momentarily distracted. 'Your dick's impressive, Bill. Not so your sense of humour.' To emphasise the point and to show how cool she was, she flipped a straggle of hair from her forehead. It promptly fell straight back down.

'It's not humour, Majesty. It's my serious side. Remember how we talked about it in Macao?'

She turned back to the window and fumbled hurriedly in her dressing gown pocket for her cigarette pack. 'We were joking.'

He rose from the bed and crossed the floor to where she stood, encircling her from behind in his arms. 'Sure, we *were* joking. Then I got to thinking.'

Iona ignored the arms around her waist and lit up. 'Men shouldn't think. They don't do it very well.'

'You said if you'd been the second Mrs Dawson, three and four wouldn't have got a look in.' He kissed her ear. 'Well, I can't afford any more alimony, so I'd better get it right.'

'That's a pretty romantic proposition coming from you, Bill.' She said it with her usual measured calmness, but inside she felt a small fist of excitement growing in her chest. 'Let me think about it for a few years.'

'Hell, woman!' His anger erupted suddenly and he spun her round to face him. 'What is it with you? What happened to all this impetuosity of old age stuff we talked about in Macao? Neither of us is getting any younger. We should seize the moment.' He stopped suddenly, realising that she couldn't answer because he was holding her arms and she had a cigarette clenched between her lips. He released her. 'And take that goddamn thing out your mouth!'

She removed it and slowly blew a perfect smoke-ring.

'Well?' he demanded.

Iona indicated the coffee-maker behind him. 'Water's boiling.'

'What?'

'Here, let me,' she said, brushing him aside. 'Why is it men can't do more than one thing at a time? Including thinking and pouring coffee.'

He said nothing more until she'd poured two cups and handed him one. 'Are you going to give me an answer?'

She sipped her coffee and peered at him over the rim of the cup. 'You're serious, aren't you?'

Dawson had stopped playing games. 'Yes. The thought of retiring scares the shit out of me. Just the idea of spending the rest of my days in God's waiting room in some Florida condo surrounded by blue-rinse matrons . . .' He didn't have to spell it out. 'You'd be my insurance policy. You've already said we're a team. As a team we'd be hell-raisers. Together we could grow old disgracefully.'

She chuckled. 'Ah, I get the idea. Sky-diving, white-water rafting, bungee jumping – that sort of thing?'

That fazed him momentarily. 'Er, sure, if that's what you want?'

For a moment she regarded him in silence. 'It may come as a surprise to you, Bill,' she said seriously, 'but I'm not ready to retire yet either.'

He pursed his lips thoughtfully, then grinned. ''Course not. But marry me anyway. I'll wait for you. I was thinking of buying a beach place on Cape Cod. Fishing will soon pass the time.'

A smile had begun to light her entire face and a comfortable inner warmth began spreading through her. 'I don't darn socks and I don't iron.'

'So you'll think about it?'

'The army brat told me to play hard to get.'

'What does that ten-foot blonde bimbo know about anything?'

'Judging by the number of men chasing her, quite a bit.' She looked at Dawson directly, only her eyes letting him know she was really flattered and was now just playing games. 'I will think about it. When all this business is over and we've got our feet back on the ground. Okay?'

He looked like a fisherman who knew he had one hooked. It was just a matter of time before he reeled her in. 'Okay.'

She drained her coffee. 'Now I really must fly. See you at breakfast.'

As she reached the door, he said: 'By the way, how's General Sun?'

'Sun?' She turned. 'Sun is fine, according to Edwin.'

'Ah, yes, Edwin Prufrock.' There was an enigmatic smile on the American's lips. 'He's got General Sun well tied up, has he?'

Iona frowned. 'You know he has, Bill. Sun is a key player in this and he knows it. So does Edwin and so do I. I assure you there is no chance of him going wobbly on us.'

'Sure, Majesty, just checking.' His smile widened. 'And don't forget. I'll be waiting.'

When the door shut he stood staring at it for several moments. So John Dancer's information was correct, he could read it in her voice. Its pitch a fraction too high as she tried to overcome her momentary panic. The witch! He almost said it aloud, but he was still smiling as he thought it.

She'd known that Washington was planning to sell their new F22 superfighter to the new regime in Beijing as soon as it was in place. And quietly she'd gone behind the Americans' back to secure some deal with General Sun and Prufrock that cut them out. Well, lady, by now you should know better than to mess with me, he thought as he began to shave and shower.

Twenty minutes later he had joined Iona Moncrieff and Frank Aspen in a secluded corner of the officers' mess. She had been watching the CIA man pouring liquid calories on to his waffles with undisguised contempt and seemed relieved when Dawson settled for scambled eggs and smoked salmon. Iona herself made do with large helpings of caffeine and nicotine.

Aspen was in overdrive, bringing Iona up to date between gulps of orange juice and mouthfuls of waffle. 'Tel Aviv owes me a few favours, so the Mossad got us the SBERs from the Soviets, just to confuse the trail. Flew 'em to Cyprus where the RAF flew them to Northolt in UK and a switch to USAF which flew them to Honolulu. They're now aboard the 7th Fleet, ready for a rendezvous with *Manta*.'

'Remind me,' Iona said. 'These are the briefcase bombs that use Red Mercury, yes? What does SBER stand for again?'

Aspen had it at his fingertips. 'Structural Bond Energy Release device.'

Iona gave a wan smile. 'Wish I hadn't asked.'

'I'm more concerned with what we use on the Politburo aircraft,' Dawson said, having listened in silence as he demolished his eggs and salmon.

'Progress there, too,' Aspen assured. 'The labs at Langley have been testing two types of bomb – triggered either by an altimeter at a given height or one fitted with a global-positioning-system device that can be fired by satellite signal. Then there's the question of liquid or solid explosive. It all depends on what is most likely to get through Chinese security. And, surrounding such a high-profile Politburo visit, that's gonna be a tough cookie to crack.'

The conversation continued after breakfast when they adjourned to the secure offices that had been set aside for the purpose. The topics were far-ranging, from how Discretionary Warfare Team One's progress was going in contacting various agent networks on the ground and how anticipated problems were being solved. And also how to solve new ones that were arising on a day-to-day basis.

The meeting finished just before lunch when Iona and Dawson were due to take different flights and different routes back to Beijing. The American lingered after his hoped-to-be fiancée had departed.

'Thought I might join you for lunch, Frank.'

Aspen didn't like being put upon. 'Eat rabbit food, do you?'

'Pardon me?' Dawson wasn't following.

'A one-mile swim at my health club, then a sushi and salad at their restaurant. Still interested?'

An uncertain smile. 'Sure, why not?'

'You can't smoke those filthy cigars there.'

'With what I'm gonna tell you, Frank, you'll want to buy me a box of the best Habanos.'

Aspen was scathing. 'I doubt that, Bill. So anyway, shoot.'

Just to spite the man from Langley, Dawson pulled his leather cigar case from the inside pocket of his jacket. 'What if I told you the Brits have gone behind our backs to do a deal with General Sun to buy the new Eurofighter?'

Aspen gaped. 'They wouldn't. They know we have the F22 lined up for China.'

'But they have the in with General Sun. We don't.' He put a match to his cigar. 'It's all been arranged through that slippery mother Prufrock.'

The man from Langley understood. 'So we're talking deals and kickbacks and the like?'

'Sun's going to have no incentive to drop the deal.' Dawson blew lightly on the glowing tip of his cigar. 'Unless, of course . . .'

Aspen's eyes narrowed. 'Perhaps I'll skip the health club. We could lunch and you can tell me what you're thinking.'

'Your tab?'

'My tab.'

From the train, Dancer watched the passing Yellow River scenery without absorbing much of what he saw. His mind was full of a million and one other things. And when he'd considered each of the problems in turn, his mind would inevitably return to thoughts of Lily Cheung.

Somehow, he'd never really thought it would all work out like this. He hadn't anticipated Frank Aspen's 'big picture' concept of planting two massive bombs to take out Chicom's secondary military and political leadership. They wouldn't be able to avoid collateral damage and there would inevitably be some innocent civilian deaths and casualties. Could the ends really justify such means? It didn't bear thinking about. Then Lily. He hadn't anticipated his feelings for her. Now he found himself placing her in danger. And not just Lily herself, of course. If things went wrong, little Bao and even old Mama Cheung would feel the Party's wrath. Having worked towards this moment for so long, he suddenly found himself having doubts. Could Edwin Prufrock have been right? That really, deep down, the Chinese weren't that bothered about democracy, human rights and the market economy? And if so, could it be sensibly argued that they would never miss what they had never had?

Debs would have pooh-poohed all that; an idealist when it came to questions of freedom versus tyranny. But for once, Dancer was beginning to wonder.

On top of all that, Aspen and his cronies at Langley had no real idea how it would all pan out, and he wondered if they really cared. Would it matter much to them if China was convulsed with civil war for a year or two before things settled down? He could just see some smart-ass at State doing computer projections on how much more money the US could make with an extensive rebuilding programme. American corporations would muscle in with their financial clout until they literally owned half of China.

Suddenly the train began to slow and out in the corridor passengers were carrying their cases towards the doors. Seated opposite him, Janie Walsh wiped some grime from the window and tried to peer forward along the track as it curved towards a grey industrialised skyline where numerous columns of sulphurous smoke leached into the clear blue sky.

'I think this must be Lanzhou,' she said.

Dancer dragged his mind back to the present. 'Sure. Just a few minutes now.'

His confirmation seemed to register subliminally with McVicar and Taffy who were both cat-napping on the seats on either side of the door to the corridor. Immediately they began to stir.

Walsh giggled. 'I don't know how they do it. Sleep at the drop of a hat.'

'Soldiers learn to eat and sleep when they can,' Dancer said. ' I used to be quite good at it myself.'

'But not now?'

He smiled thinly. 'Too much to think about.'

'I know,' she said with feeling. 'Can't remember how long since I last got a good night's sleep.' She looked back out of the window. 'I wonder what Gong Li Zhong will be like.'

'He's the best. Gong and Yan are good friends and they've been working for this for a long time.'

In fact, it had been shortly after Yan Tao's visit to the prison-factory complex outside Lanzhou town that Dancer had received a call from Gong asking for a quotation for some courier work. Contact had been made. An exchange of letters followed in which Dancer offered for his company to mount a seminar for Gong and 'other key business colleagues'. The subject would be *Using Courier Services to Enhance Efficiency and Profit*. The venue a secure block within Gong's complex. Invitation was to be strictly ticket only.

When the train pulled into the station they were met personally by Gong and two chauffeur-driven Lexus limos. He was a plump and apparently happy man in an expensively tailored suit. His welcome was effusive and he directed his chauffeurs to load up the party's luggage before driving them to their hotel. Not once did Gong let the pretence slip that they were meeting for the first time and Dancer felt steadily more confident about the man's trustworthiness and efficiency.

'The delegates are at another hotel,' he explained lightly, letting Dancer know that he wanted no risk of chance encounters after the formal seminar sessions. 'They are mostly people I have known personally since my university days. Some are now in business, some in local government. They come from several different provinces, but all feel they have much to learn about business efficiency.'

Dancer took that on board. Meaning that all had at one time been connected with the dissident movements at the time of Tiananmen, and now they were all key players within the underground networks – some here in Gansu province, but others from farther afield who were able to wangle the time off to attend. 'Anyone from the PLA?' he asked innocently.

'Some have expressed an interest, but we had to limit numbers,' Gong replied glibly.

Meaning, Dancer realised, that Gong reasoned that letting his PLA contacts attend might draw unnecessary and unwanted attention to the seminar.

Gong then left them to settle in for the night at their hotel and returned at nine the next morning with the two limos to take them to the gulag. They loaded the usual paraphernalia of seminars, including an overhead projector, a collapsible screen and assorted locked steel filing boxes. It all looked genuine, down to the professionally prepared presentation folders that would be handed out to all those who attended. They would provide the basis for a succession of codes to be used between the networks during the run-up to D-day.

Gong travelled in the first car with Dancer and Janie Walsh. 'Feel free to talk,' he said. 'Both these drivers are members of the movement. Our complex is fifteen miles out of town. There is the prison chief who calls the place a *laogai* camp – 'reform through labour' – and the commercial director, me. I refer to it as the factory or the farm. As pretence, we will take you through the east gate which is for the benefit of foreign businessmen. The camp has been a profit centre since the mid-eighties. We are a self-sufficient farm and sell the best of that produce as well as running five different factories and a stone quarry.'

'How many prisoners are there?' Walsh asked.

'Around five thousand.' Gong gave an unhappy smile. 'And about ten per cent of those are political prisoners.

People who said the wrong thing at the wrong time. In the re-education camps, the prisoners are not even convicted criminals. It is just that the Chicom cadres think they have a bad attitude. Often these people are serving no fixed term. It could be three years or eternity. They are not always told.'

Walsh shook her head. 'That's terrible. We hear these stories in the States, but we're never sure if they're an exaggeration.'

'I'm afraid it is no exaggeration although, of course, it is strenuously denied by Beijing and businessmen defending forced slave labour. Fifty million people have passed through the camps since the Communists took power in 1949. Today there are over one thousand *laogai* and perhaps seven million prisoners. Probably around a million of those held on political charges or for re-education.'

They were now well clear of Lanzhou's grimy industrial sprawl and into open fields of corn and vegetables. A warning sign, reading '*Laogai* Camps Ahead', indicated a roadblock mounted by uniformed Bureau police who recognised Gong and boredly waved him through.

'All this farmland belongs to the prison,' Gong said sadly. 'The good stuff goes to market and the rotten stuff to feed the prisoners. Supervised gangs of prisoners come out to work the fields.'

They crested a hill and now they could see a cluster of high-walled compounds in the distance, each topped with electrified wire and overlooked by watch towers. Five minutes later they drove past another sign – Cherry Tree Valley Products Factory – and a pair of tall steel doors.

'This is where prisoners come when they are too sick or weak to continue with hard labour,' Gong explained. 'And they know what will happen to them if they dare speak to any visiting foreign devil.'

The gates swung open. 'What do you make here?' Walsh asked.

'This plant is labour-intensive. Hand-made stuff like jewellery and artificial flowers. Another one makes fireworks and we are developing electronics production lines.' He gave another misleadingly jokey smile. 'But, of course, we still break up rocks at the quarry.'

They drove into a dusty quadrangle flanked by ugly two-storey blockhouses and pulled up alongside an old yellow bus. The second Lexus with McVicar and Taffy joined them.

'We brought our people up from town earlier,' Gong explained, climbing out. 'My drivers will guard the conference room. It is where we entertain Western businessmen and make our presentations. Everyone knows better than to interrupt us there.'

They began unloading and carrying the equipment up a short flight of steps to the complex's administration building. Beside the door to the conference room was a sign giving the seminar details and the words Do Not Disturb, which Gong's drivers would reinforce. Inside, seven men and one woman waited, standing respectfully in line and looking as decidedly apprehensive as Dancer felt. No doubt everyone, on both sides, dreaded that this would turn out to be some sort of State Security counter-intelligence trap or a 'sting' operation to catch political insurgents.

Janie Walsh quickly set the tone by shaking hands and introducing herself as acting on behalf of the Taiwanese Government which was backing political moves by mainland dissidents in view of Beijing's imminent invasion plans. McVicar and Taffy were professional mercenaries hired by Taipei to help out.

Still the Chinese looked apprehensive and it was really only when McVicar and Taffy also spoke in fluent Mandarin that they showed signs of relaxing. The two SAS men had considerable experience in putting total strangers at ease in training situations and before long there were even a few smiles and laughs shared between them. But mostly the student revolutionaries concentrated in deadly earnest, hanging on every word the soldiers spoke and scribbling furiously in their notebooks.

Over the three-day period of the seminar, they would first concentrate on basic training in standard PLA fire-arms so that they would be able to pick up any weapon that came to hand and use it efficiently. Actual target practice was, however, out of the question. There would be small courses on basic navigation, personal survival and first aid. Considerably more time was spent on running cells and keeping them secure within the network, including contact and rendezvous drills to shake off any Chicom tails and to prevent them walking into traps. How to set up secure meetings and pass secret messages to each other via dead drops was also explained along with various methods of target reconnaissance.

The final phase was teaching techniques in assassination, approach, subterfuge, distraction and escape, plus how to use explosives and, if necessary, how to make them from available materials. Quantities of plastic explosive and various electronic components, including detonators, closed circuit boards and tilt-switches made in Taiwan, had been brought ashore from *Manta*, together with plans adapted, but different, from those perfected by the terrorist Provisional IRA in Northern Ireland over the years. Simple but effective. The lessons would finish with advice on locations for demolition explosives for the maximum effect on various targets: bridges, power and telephone lines, rail tracks and culverts under roads.

While Gong Li Zhong attended some of the lectures, he also spent much time with Walsh and Dancer discussing how to handle affairs on D-day within Gansu province itself. A list of key local figures was drawn up and divided into two: those believed to want to stay loyal to Chicom and those who would support the new regime. They included local mayors, dignitaries and party officials, police and PLA, as well as men of influence such as businessmen like Gong and respected professional people like doctors and teachers.

Dancer guessed that, in fact, after the initial shock of the earth-shattering news from Beijing, most Chinese would remain circumspect and pragmatic. Experience had taught the working cadres to see which way the wind was blowing and to bend that way.

The local police and PLA garrisons would most probably take their lead from headquarters in Beijing, so much would depend on how events had turned out there. If success wasn't as complete as planned, surviving hostile police or PLA commanders might order troops and tanks on to the streets, guarding key installations and crossroads. Just ordinary confusion might cause the same result.

Either way, Gong was already working with the local student dissidents and factory-worker groups to take to the streets – if necessary to confront police and troops peacefully with flowers and chants for democracy and freedom. Already people were stockpiling all the necessary materials for placards, posters and banners following local whispered rumours that they should prepare for big demonstrations coming soon.

Hundreds of thousands of leaflets had been secretly printed on the prison's own press and stockpiled in secure storerooms. One of Gong's old student friends ran the local radio station and had privately agreed he would tell his employees to stand aside without protest when Gong's insurgents arrived at their premises. Of other newspaper editors and local administrators, he was not so sure.

'Once it is clear that new leaders are in control in Beijing, anyone still resisting in the authorities here will be asked to co-operate with us,' Gong said. For once the cheerful face was dark with menace. 'If they do not, I am afraid they will have to be physically eliminated. That is one reason why your training here will be so important.'

Dancer swallowed hard. Such scenarios were being planned all over China now and it was a terrifying thought, especially as he would be largely responsible for its outcome, however successful or however bloody it turned out to be.

Walsh warned: 'The worst of alternative outcomes would be uncertainty about who is in control in Beijing. Many a coup has failed because the right people weren't in the right place at the right time, for whatever reason. There are no guarantees in this game and you can't anticipate *everything*. And you can't account for the unaccountable.'

Gong had clearly been considering that. 'If uncertainty lasts, I am personally prepared for that. I think all my colleagues are. We will resist, whatever the consequences. There would be power struggles all over China, not just here.'

'What would you do?' Walsh asked.

The *laogai* commercial director considered for a moment. 'I know some police and PLA units will be at least neutral. Even if they would not turn against their brothers in other units, they will give us access to weaponry. And if not, we will seize it. I am prepared to release the prisoners in those circumstances.'

Dancer frowned. 'Won't the prison chief have something to say about that?'

Gong gave a tight smile. 'That man is evil, a ferocious despot. He will be the first to die.'

Walsh caught Dancer's eye, imagining for the first time what he had been thinking for days now. She said: 'And you will set the prisoners against any PLA resistance?'

He nodded. 'We will have weapons and explosives. If it becomes necessary we will blow up telephone communications with Beijing, attack road and rail links to prevent reinforcements. If we are attacked by a greater force, we shall not hold ground.' He looked at the window and indicated the low mountains that edged the Yellow River valley. 'We shall take to the hills. If it was the only good thing Chairman Mao ever did, it was to teach the Chinese how to fight guerrilla warfare. Some of us have not forgotten.'

Dancer was impressed with Gong's quiet determination

and felt his recent misgivings ebb back a little. He just wondered how many others out there shared his vision. And his courage.

Walsh then explained that more critical supplies would be on their way to help with the local insurrection plans. They included short-range personal communications and radio scanners that would allow Gong's insurgents to listen into Chicom communications. Of course, she didn't mention that they were coming in by submarine. Or that for weeks now the combined SBS and SAS team on *Manta* had been ferrying in loads on Captain Song's fishing boat, escorted by Nick Lake and Dougie Squires.

'I have a very special gift for you,' she said finally, placing her briefcase on the table. Flipping open the lid, she lifted out what looked like a laptop computer, except for the punch-button receiver on the left of it.

'What is that?' Gong asked.

'An AST satellite phone. It weighs five pounds and can also handle fax and e-mail. This one's fitted with a scrambler device and I'll leave you with a special computer program for super-encrypting any e-mail you want to send. It'll keep you in contact with us and with the resistance head in each province.'

Gong's mouth just dropped. Then he regained his composure. Here was a happy man who, at that moment, could not have been happier. And it made Janie Walsh feel that all her efforts so far had been worthwhile.

However, Dancer had left the final part of his mission until the last day. For one, he didn't want word of what had happened to get about while he was still there and it happily coincided with the prison chief's trip to a conference in Shanghai.

'It is not wise for you to meet Fan Xiu Kun in his cell,' Gong said as they sat in his private office. 'Things have changed. He is now in a cell with two glass walls. The light is kept on permanently and there is no privacy from the guards. It is all different since your wife came.'

Dancer flinched as if he'd been physically struck. 'I'm sorry.'

Walsh was puzzled. 'Your wife? I didn't realise you were married.'

He nodded. It was rare for him to come straight out and tell people Debs was dead. If he said nothing, it sort of reinforced the illusion that she was still alive, around somewhere. 'She was a journalist. And a fully paid-up member of PEN and Amnesty – a passionate believer in personal freedom and civil liberty. When I came here and met Gong for the first time, I learned that the famous poet and protester Fan Xiu Kun was being held here. When I told Debs, she insisted that I try and set up an interview with him for her.'

Walsh frowned. 'Surely not with Langley's approval?'

Dancer allowed himself a smile. 'No way. It was breaking all the rules. But Gong here and Fan himself thought it was a great idea. To this day, Dawson and Aspen don't know the source of the interview. Debs got it splashed in half the newspapers round the world.'

Walsh inclined her head, impressed. 'Your secret is safe with me.'

'Unfortunately, it seems Fan paid a heavy price.'

Gong confirmed his worst fears. 'The prison chief was furious when he learned about the interview. Of course, he didn't realise that Mrs Dancer had actually interviewed Fan. Naturally, he and his superiors assumed it had just been smuggled out as statements and dressed up as an interview. But that was bad enough. The prison boss's own privileges stopped and even he had to go through a period of self-criticism. When it was over, he took it out on Fan himself.'

'That's terrible,' Walsh said.

Gong shrugged. 'That's China.'

Dancer said, 'Are you sure Fan will agree to see me?'

The commercial director looked momentarily surprised. 'I've already asked him. My two drivers are bringing him over now.'

Walsh was concerned. 'Won't the guards think that strange?'

Gong shook his head. 'Fan may be due for some rehabilitation. Hard labour is now proving difficult for him. If he's reformed enough, he may be allowed to work in one of my factories. That is why I've asked to see him.'

Even as he finished speaking, there was a brisk knock at the door before it immediately swung open. It took a moment for Dancer to realise that it was actually Fan Xiu Kun standing there.

The American was shocked at what he saw. It was only four years since he'd last seen Fan, but he hardly recognised the man who stood before him now. The tall, once proud figure was hunched in the scruffy blue prison fatigues. His hair was grey and tufty, shorn with scissors by the guards and he clearly hadn't been allowed to wash or shave for weeks. The smell was foul. But worst of all, were Fan's eyes. They appeared to have shrunk back into the sockets of his skull and were ringed by the dark skin of the habitual insomniac. The sharpness of expression that Dancer remembered was gone, the eyes themselves now dull and unfocused, the whites discoloured like broken egg yolks. Fan was only in his fifties, but now he looked like an old man.

Gong rose respectfully from his desk and indicated the spare chair. 'Please be seated, Mr Fan. There is an old friend to see you.'

The prisoner squinted at Dancer and he clutched the desk edge as he lowered himself into the chair. 'Mr John?'

Dancer smiled, offering his hand. 'Hi, Xiu, it's good to see you again.'

Fan nodded warily, but did not smile. The skin of his hand was rough against the American's palm. 'I am afraid I don't see so well any more.' Then he added vaguely, 'I think it's the diet.'

'A cigarette?'

Dancer offered his pack of Camel and Fan plucked one

out delicately with his thumb and forefinger. The slender artistic hands were flayed and calloused from breaking rocks to build a new mountain road. When Dancer provided the light, the prisoner relaxed a little and leaned back against his chair. He then seemed to register Walsh for the first time, and inclined his head in polite acknowledgement. 'Mrs John is not with you, I see.'

'No, this is Miss Jane. I am afraid Deborah – Mrs John – is dead.'

Fan stared at him, a wild expression in his eyes. Then he looked down at the cigarette burning between his fingers and said nothing for several moments. When he spoke, his voice was cracked and low. 'When did this happen?'

'Four years ago.'

Fan frowned, thinking hard, but his brain was now slow and ponderous. 'The year she interviewed me?'

'About nine months later.'

Walsh glanced sideways at Dancer, curious as to what he was going to say.

'She'd written a series of damning stories about China, including the interview with you. The government threatened to withdraw her visa and the Bureau started harassing her, following her everywhere. She was frequently taken in for questioning.'

Walsh frowned. 'Why didn't they just throw her out?'

'They wanted good relations with the US and knew ejecting big-name journalists didn't go down well in DC. I think Beijing wanted to drive her out. But before that happened, fate took a hand.'

Fan was staring closely at him again. 'If you can bear to tell me, I should like to know.'

Dancer felt awkward, but believed he at least owed it to the man. 'She had set off in a taxi for a secret meeting with someone in the democracy movement. Soon she realised they'd picked up an unmarked police tail. She handed a wad of *yuan* to her driver and asked him to try and lose the following car. It was night and it was raining. There was a head-on collision with a car travelling with no lights on.'

Walsh gave a small gasp. She knew so many drivers in China did that and for the life of her still couldn't understand why.

'I am very sorry,' Fan said gravely. 'Mrs John did more for me, more for the people of China than anyone else I have ever met.'

Gong nodded soberly. 'It seems that both of you paid the price for her courage.'

Walsh leaned towards Fan. She wanted to grasp those ruined hands in her own, to comfort him. But she knew he would not like that. In China a man could do that, but not a woman who was a stranger. 'Are things very bad for you here, Mr Fan?'

'It is not so bad now. Now that I'm too crippled to hold a hammer – or, more important to me, a pen. After Mrs John's articles appeared, I had to start all over again with the sessions of self-criticism and political correction. My food, visits by my family and my sleep have been severely rationed ever since.'

Gong added with disgust, 'The prison chief even moved common criminals into Fan's cell with the promise of early release if they made a good job of beating him up. Well, they did that all right. Stamped on his writing hand and kicked him on the floor. They damaged his spine and now he has kidney problems.'

Fan stubbed out his cigarette in the ashtray and shook his head. 'Don't go on so. I don't want these good people to think that it wasn't worth it. You cannot move mountains without people getting hurt. Pain is just pain. The real hurt is not being allowed to write my poetry.'

'I've read all your work,' Walsh interjected quickly, and for the first time Fan smiled.

'I'm honoured, young lady.'

'It's wonderful,' she added, 'and I think that soon the people will be able to hear the master recite his own words once again.'

A strange expression crept over Fan's features. 'What exactly do you mean? Is there a plan for my release?'

Gong intervened, wringing his hands together as he tried to find the right words. 'What Miss Jane is trying to say, Xiu, is that there are some political developments afoot. We have come to learn that disillusioned elements within the Party and the PLA are to mount a coup in Beijing with the backing of Taiwan. They intend to turn China into a full socialist democracy and they have contacted Mr John with a message for you.'

Dark anger flashed suddenly in Fan's eyes. 'Don't do this. Don't say these things. I don't believe you. Why are you saying these things?'

Dancer said quietly, 'It's true, Xiu. And there is more. When it happens they want to invite you to become the first life President of the New Democratic China.'

Gong leaned forward eagerly. 'What do you say, old friend?'

But Fan Xiu Kun wasn't saying anything. He couldn't. Because there was a lump the size of a fist in his throat and two tears were slowly clearing a path through the grime on his cheeks.

Dancer reached out and placed his hand on Fan's. If only Debs could have witnessed this moment.

Lily Cheung finished typing the revisions to the schedule on her PC, then slipped in a floppy disk and made a copy. She then punched out the disk and placed it in the steel tabletop case with the combination-lock in which all information regarding Politburo travel arrangements was routinely filed.

She glanced at her watch. The visitor had been in with her boss for over an hour. Mr Wang, or the 'Old Rogue' as she now usually thought of him, had seemed unusually apprehensive when the man had turned up unannounced. She didn't know why, because the visitor was polite and suave and charming. But there was a certain look in his eyes that unsettled her. Because she didn't know why the man wanted to talk to Wang, she had no idea how long they might be.

She scolded herself for being so scared. It would only take a second or two, and even if someone saw her doing it, it would mean nothing to them. Still, it didn't stop her heart racing or the clammy sensation on her palms. Her decision made, she took the spare floppy disk, pressed it into the computer and made another copy of the schedule. As soon as it was finished, she extracted it and stood up, facing away from the office door. Hurriedly she fumbled to lift her cardigan and pull out her skirt band before plunging the disk down into the safety of her underpants.

The telephone buzzed angrily and her heart nearly left her body. The shock left her breathless as she answered the call.

It was Wang and he sounded annoyed. 'Come up to my office immediately.'

'Yes, sir. Shall I bring the revised schedule?'

He obviously didn't want to be bothered with such diversions. 'Oh, I suppose so. Now, hurry.'

As usual, she quickly checked that her clothes were tidy and her hair in place before crossing the mausoleum-like lobby and up the wide stone staircase to Wang's lofty office. She knocked and entered, her heels snapping on the tiles and the walk to her boss's desk seeming endless under the intense gaze of the two men. Neither was smiling as they watched her approach and suddenly she felt a stab of apprehension.

'The schedule, sir.'

'Put it down, Miss Cheung.'

The stranger smiled, the eyes friendly behind the gold-rimmed spectacles, and she suddenly felt more at ease. 'That's a big document. Must have kept you busy.'

The voice was mellow and she realised he was just making conversation. She said, 'The schedule for the opening of Phase Two.'

He nodded his understanding. 'Hong Kong Airport. A wonderful achievement. Have you seen it?'

'No, sir, I've never been to Hong Kong,' she replied, returning his smile.

'Never been outside China, in fact, is that right?'

Suddenly she felt the shadow pass over her.

Wang said: 'This is Brigadier Ting Han-chen of the *Chi Pao k'o* section, Ministry of State Security.' In fact, rather than the MSS, he used the popular generic term *Te Wu* or 'secret agency'. Lily's eyes widened and her stomach seemed to shrivel into a tight ball as Wang leaned across his immense desk. 'Is it true you've been going out with my business partner, Mr Dancer?' he demanded.

Ting raised his right hand. 'Please, Mr Wang, I am asking the questions. Now, do you have a room where Miss Cheung and I can talk in private?'

The assistant deputy director looked distracted. 'There is the small meeting room.'

Lily straightened her back, trying to put on a brave face, but immediately felt the secreted disk dig into her flesh as she moved. God, she hoped it didn't show. 'I'll take you, sir,' she offered brightly.

The brigadier inclined his head. 'You're most kind.' He turned to Wang. 'Thank you again for your time.'

A smile flickered briefly like a dying electric bulb on Wang's face as he watched them walk away.

There were no windows in the meeting room which clearly hadn't been used for years. Wang much preferred the ostentatious conference hall with its massive mahogany table to the sixties plastic wood and steel-legged furniture here.

Ting trawled a finger through the dust on the tabletop.

'It's dirty in here,' Lily said awkwardly.

'Sit down.' The softness had gone from Ting's voice and Lily obeyed instantly as though someone had chopped her behind the knees. The brigadier remained standing. 'How long have you known Mr Dancer?'

She frowned, trying to recall. 'I have known him by sight maybe two years, since I came to work for Mr Wang. He visits every so often. Mr Wang and he are in partnership.'

'But now, Miss Cheung, you know him *more* than just by sight?'

It felt strange, saying words she'd rehearsed for so long, having always feared that some day someone would ask her questions. 'We share a love of music, that is all. Gershwin in particular.'

'And you play the violin.'

Lily felt her heart flutter. 'How . . . ?' she began, then stopped. Stupid question. Everyone in their apartment block had family members who worked at the Civil Aviation Administration; the Party liked to have people who worked together live together so that everyone knew everyone else's business. Not least the Party neighbourhood committee.

'When I look at your file, I see that a "round eyes" was reported as visiting your flat a few months ago. He brought home your brother, Ho, who'd had too much to drink.' Ting's eyes seemed to bore into her skull. 'Someone told your neighbourhood committee that they thought he was American. Was that Mr Dancer?'

There was no point in denying it. 'Yes.'

'But you'd met to speak with each other before then, hadn't you?'

She wondered how much he knew, and how much was bluff. It was too dangerous to risk an outright lie. 'I attended a business dinner with Mr Wang and Mr Dancer to take notes of their discussion.' She hesitated, wondering how to put it. 'Mr Wang developed a headache, so Mr Dancer was taking me home in his taxi. That was when we were stopped by police.'

Ting nodded. 'I know. I interviewed Mr Dancer at the time.'

That surprised her. She said, 'We were both arrested, but we were not charged.'

'But you were warned, weren't you?'

Fear rushed through her. 'I'm sorry?'

The brigadier brushed a patch of dust from the table and sat on its edge, bringing his face closer to hers. 'You were warned not to go out alone with him again.'

'I didn't. He only brought Ho home that night.'

'But you've ignored that warning ever since.'

'Sir, I have not!' she retorted indignantly, hoping she hadn't overdone it. 'On no occasion have I been alone with Mr Dancer. I have always been chaperoned by my mother. I have told you, it is all most respectable. We share a love of music, that is all.'

Ting nodded slowly as if believing her. 'It is true that no one has reported seeing you alone with the American. You may or may not be aware, but the Public Security Bureau has been keeping an eye on you.'

She feigned surprise, but Dancer had warned her it was likely. 'I'm being watched! That is horrible!'

'It is the Bureau's duty to monitor those who have dealings with foreigners. But, of course, they try to be discreet.' He sounded bored, as though tired of explaining the obvious. Then he added, 'They really are very good, the Bureau men. Yet recently they seem to be losing track of you with surprising regularity.'

She shrugged. Dancer had taught her all those tricks of his trade. 'I can't help that.'

Ting held her gaze, looking so intently into her eyes that she could swear he could see into her mind. She felt perspiration gather in the small of her back. Then Ting smiled and she felt the knot of tension loosen in her neck. 'No, of course not. But you should be aware that Mr Dancer is an American and as such must be treated with caution.'

She turned her head sharply in the brigadiers's direction. 'You mean with the usual Chinese xenophobia?' she demanded.

Immediately she shut her eyes as she realised what she'd

said, realised the stupidity of saying what she really thought.

'Not a clever remark,' Ting said quietly. 'If China sometimes appears xenophobic to young people, it is because experience has taught us to be careful about foreigners. You should be aware that Mr Dancer could be using you to discover secrets about the authorities.'

She gulped. That one hit home. 'I don't know any secrets.'

'Young lady, everybody knows *something* that others do not. That knowledge is a secret to those who do not know.'

'But he's never asked any questions about work. We only talk about music.'

'Ah, yes.' He seemed to accept that. 'And not long after Mr Dancer brought home your brother drunk, you went to a concert, did you not? The Boston Symphony?'

Lily nodded. 'With my mother.'

'Three tickets. Together and at short notice.'

She shrugged. 'Yes, I suppose. . .'

'Didn't that surprise you? Tickets are notoriously hard to get.'

'I expect he had connections.'

'Did he say how he got them?' She shook her head. 'Did you ask?'

'No, I didn't know him well then. It would have been impolite.'

Ting let a silence form between them. 'Has he ever mentioned another American by the name of Dawson? Bill Dawson? He works at the American Embassy.'

'I don't believe so.'

'Cheung Mei-ling, you really are a trusting and naïve young woman,' the brigadier said. 'Such qualities of innocence can place someone unwittingly in danger. Now I could forbid you to see this American at all, chaperoned or not. Certainly your boss, Mr Wang, has been unhappy to learn of your personal relationship with Dancer. Indeed he offered to recommend you be sent away for re-education.'

Lily's eyes widened, dreading what Brigadier Ting was going to say next.

He smiled gently. 'I persuaded him that would be a little rash, especially if you promised not to see Mr Dancer privately again. . .' He left the words hanging as he studied her face and her body language, and saw the brief moment when the cloud of disappointment passed over her eyes. 'Now we can *tell* Wang that, to keep him happy. But, in fact, I am thinking you may be of more service to the motherland if you retain your respectable relationship with Mr Dancer. But instead of being so naïve, you could *ask* a few more questions.'

She looked confused. 'Questions? Like what?'

Ting shrugged. 'Like who *did* get his tickets? Then ask *who* is this Bill Dawson? Ask if you could go to an embassy party? Say you'd like to meet more Americans. Improve your excellent English. Ask about his business. In short, Miss Cheung, find out things that *we* would like to know.'

'Spy on Mr Dancer?' Her expression changed to one of horror. 'Oh, I couldn't do that!'

Ting lifted an eyebrow. 'Oh, I think you could, Miss Cheung. I've been looking at your record files and I see you have a rather unpatriotic past. Not to mention immoral. Now this business of going out with foreigners. All this from one who is a Party member and works in government. Some might say you are unrepentant of your past. That, indeed, you are *still* in need of re-education, if not reform. If it were to come to the attention of the Eighth . . .'

She knew what he meant. The Security Ministry's Eighth Bureau, the people who ran the *laogai* gulags. The terror was back inside her. 'But you *know* I've done nothing wrong!'

His sympathetic smile was cold. 'These people have a saying that goes back a long, long way, Where there is a will to condemn, there is evidence.' And if there is evidence, they may even consider you unfit to be a mother.'

'Bao?' Aghast.

'Don't distress yourself.' He waited until she'd plucked a handkerchief from her cuff and dabbed at her tearful eyes. 'So, will you ask questions of Mr Dancer and let me know the answers? That is all I ask.'

After a silent pause, she nodded slowly.

He smiled and leaned towards her, running the fore-finger of his right hand lightly along the contour of her cheek, just as he had done to her file photograph in his office. And just as he'd imagined she would, she flinched now at his touch. He was aware of his sexuality stirring as he said: 'You really are very pretty, Lily, and with such wonderful English you could go far with my help. We'll talk again after lunch. And I'll give you a list of things I want you to find out about Mr Dancer and who he knows at the American Embassy. You can go now.'

Her voice was a whisper as she stood. 'Thank you, sir.'

Ting studied the sway of her hips as she moved towards the door and left. He prided himself on knowing when people were lying and when they were telling the truth. Tone of voice, expression in the eyes, body language – all these things.

And he didn't trust Cheung Mei-ling an inch.

Eleven

'Something's definitely up,' Janie Walsh said.

Since her visit to the gulag at Gansu with Dancer, she had been away for a week. Together with Nick Lake and Dougie Squires, she had returned to the *Manta* and left the Gulf of Bohai to link up with the US 7th Fleet in international waters. Walsh and the team had returned with the SBER devices and the two bombs that they hoped would blow the Politburo's aircraft from the sky. As soon as the gear had been safely secured at the ExecFlight offices, she had made her way across town to bring Dancer up to date at the Stonedancer Courier premises.

He poured her some coffee as she continued: 'The PLA Navy have been placing minefields outside the Gulf shipping lanes and patrol boats are everywhere. It was pretty hairy at times, I can tell you.'

'Is this in case they think Washington will retaliate after they've taken Taiwan?' Dancer asked.

Walsh nodded. 'Well, that's the theory according to US Navy Intelligence. The Chinese have got various facilities they'd want to protect. So it would seem a sensible precaution. More worrying is the presence of patrol boats.'

'Same reason, surely?'

'No. These are *Hainan* class. Dedicated anti-submarine. They're not normally seen around the Gulf because it's not deemed suitable for underwater ops.' She looked thoughtful. 'Al Cherrier – he's the skipper – thinks the Chinese may have got a sighting of *Manta* some weeks ago when we first deployed. The main computer crashed and they had to do an emergency surface.'

'I suppose that *could* explain it.'

She finished her coffee. 'To be honest, John, I hate that

contraption, I really do. I just wish, if all this comes off, I'll be able to leave Beijing by the front door. Get *flown* out by the new government.'

He understood. The idea of submarines had never appealed to him either. 'Perhaps you will.'

She grinned, liking his easy manner. 'I won't hold my breath.' Looking at the wall clock she said, 'It's past six. Suppose you don't fancy a drink?'

'Why not?' He glanced at his desk. 'If I stay here, Abe will make me sign cheques.'

'He's a big fella.'

Dancer grabbed his jacket and fedora from the hook behind the door. 'He's a beast.'

She laughed. 'I can believe it. Most of the staff seem terrified of him.'

'He's all bark really. And I couldn't run this operation without him.' They paused at Abe Stone's office door to find him on the telephone behind a pile of dispatch documents stamped 'Urgent'. 'Somehow, I don't think he'll be joining us.'

They walked together down the stairway and out into the street. It had all the usual hustle and bustle of rush hour, but the sky was cloud-covered and there was a marked coolness in the air.

'I detect a touch of autumn.'

She fell into step beside him. 'What's Beijing like in winter?'

He laughed. 'Dire. Bleak and grey. And when the wind blows down from Mongolia, the cold really does seep into your bones.'

Walsh gave an involuntary shudder.

'JOHN!'

The voice came from behind him and they both turned. Lily Cheung was standing, wearing her navy business suit under an open grey trenchcoat, and holding her son's hand. She looked distinctly fraught.

For a moment he was mortified; this wasn't in their game

plan. But he forced a smile and said easily, 'Lily, what a lovely surprise. And little Bao. What are you doing here?'

Lily glanced nervously at Walsh. 'I had to speak with you.'

Dancer saw her hesitation. 'That's all right. Janie is American and a good friend.'

'Yes?' She hadn't been expecting that and her expression changed, as though suddenly seeing Walsh as a different sort of threat.

He added: 'We'll go back to my place. Have a drink.'

'I am sorry,' Lily said. 'I know I shouldn't come to you like this.'

'No problem,' Dancer waved down a passing taxi. 'Don't say anything until we get there.'

As Lily and Bao climbed into the cab, Walsh held back. 'Do you think I should—?'

Dancer beckoned her. 'Sure, why not?'

The journey was cramped, hot and noisy in the taxi that had blown its exhaust, and took for ever. When they arrived at his apartment at the Hua Thai, Dancer first found some lemonade for Bao and settled him in the kitchen with an illustrated book on Chinese fables that had belonged to Debs. Then, with the youngster thoroughly absorbed, he made an electronic bug-sweep with a portable scanner before returning to the living room with three beers.

'So what has happened?' he asked Lily.

She toyed nervously with her glass, not drinking. 'A man from the *Te Wu* came to Mr Wang's office. His name is Brigadier Ting Han-chen. He is asking questions about me and you.'

Dancer frowned. 'Ting Han-chen?'

Walsh said: 'Isn't that the man who apologised to you after your arrest?'

He raised an eyebrow in astonishment; it was an impressive piece of instant recall for someone so fresh to the Beijing scene. He nodded and turned back to Lily. 'What sort of questions was he asking?'

303

She shrugged, finding it difficult to talk of such matters in front of another woman. 'Like why do we meet? Are you trying to find secrets from me about the CAAC? I say, No, no! That's not true. I am always chaperoned by Mama and we meet to talk about music.'

Something about the way she said it made Walsh glance sideways at Dancer. He had a boyish grin on his face. 'That's true enough.'

'He is suspicious because lately I have been giving the slip to the secret policemen that follow me.'

Walsh turned to Dancer for an explanation.

'I taught Lily a bit of tradecraft, so it would be safe for us to meet,' Dancer told her. 'Obviously we can't discuss things in front of her mother.'

Lily added: 'But mostly Brigadier Ting goes on about the concert tickets you bought. He says that you got them from the American Embassy. And he asks me if you know a man called Bill Dawson?'

Walsh's jaw dropped. 'Holy cow! And what did you say?'

'The truth. I have never heard of that person.'

Dancer said, 'I expect he was just trawling. But if he's ordered you to sever your connections with me again, it could make life more complicated.'

Walsh added: 'And coming here could have been a risk.'

'No, no,' Lily said quickly. 'He didn't say that. In fact, the opposite. That's why I had to come and see you. I don't know what to do. Brigadier Ting *wants* me to go out with you. He wants me to find out things about you and the American Embassy!'

For a moment Dancer stared at her in disbelief, then burst out laughing.

Anger flickered in Walsh's eyes. 'It's not funny, John.'

He managed to bring his mirth under control. 'Ting wants Lily to spy on me. That's very funny.'

'I don't know what to do,' Lily said, the desperation plain in her voice.

Walsh was picking over the implications. 'It means State

304

Security *is* still interested in you. That is not good news. If they're suspicious.'

Dancer shook his head. 'If they had anything concrete, they'd be down on me like a ton of bricks. They aren't that subtle or patient when it comes to counter-espionage. I'd be out on the next plane.'

'Don't you think you're being a bit complacent?'

He lit a cigarette before replying. 'I'm being practical and realistic. There are just two weeks to go and every-thing's looking good. All we've got to do is hold our nerve. Ting trying to turn Lily plays right into our hands as events reach a conclusion. Now we can meet as often as we need to with Ting's blessing.'

Walsh clearly still wasn't convinced.

Lily then reached for her handbag. 'By the way, I have something for you.' She extracted an envelope and handed it to him. 'A floppy disk. It is a copy of the revised schedule for the Politburo visit to Hong Kong.'

'Brilliant.'

'You are still scheduled to travel with your boss?' Walsh asked.

Lily frowned. She hadn't realised this pretty stranger would know so much about what she and Dancer had discussed. For one silly moment she wondered if the Chinese-American had been listening in to their pillow talk. Absurd, but – it was a stupid thought and she pushed it from her mind. 'Yes, Politburo will be divided between the two aircraft. Mr Wang and I will be on the plane with the Central Committee chairman.'

Dancer had been mulling over the problem for weeks and discussed it thoroughly with both Walsh and McVicar. Finally they'd stumbled on a solution and the necessary equipment had come in, courtesy of *Manta*.

'And you still think you will be left alone with his luggage?'

She laughed bitterly. 'Whenever we travel on business, it's the same. He strides off being all important and I'm left to push the trolley with all our luggage. He is an arrogant beast.'

Walsh did a double-take, but said nothing.

Dancer said: 'Would it be possible for you to get off the aircraft once Wang was on board?'

Lily shrugged. 'I suppose so. It would be easy to hang back and say I have a headache and fever. Wang hates being near sick people. He won't even let me in his office if he learns Bao caught a cold from school . . .' Her voice petered off as she suddenly realised what she was saying. Her eyes widened in horror. 'Not Wang? Oh, no. I can't do that.'

'I'm sorry,' Dancer said firmly, 'but there is no other way.'

Walsh broke in forcefully. 'Wang sums up all that is evil about the Communist Party and the country. It's a choice between him and the New China.'

It was the first time he'd ever seen Lily flare with anger, eyes tearing into Walsh's.

'What would *you* know? You are not Chinese, you are American! You come here with your arrogance and your wealth and your wicked plots. You think you know it all, but you know nothing.'

'I'm sorry,' Walsh said and reached for Lily's arm, but the Chinese girl pulled back.

'It's not easy, Lily,' Dancer said soothingly. 'It will take great courage.'

Lily had her fingers interlaced on her lap in a fierce knot and stared hard at them, her lower lip crumpled. 'And what happens if things go wrong? What will happen to me and Bao and to Mama Cheung?'

Walsh said: 'There is nothing to go wrong.'

Lily spared her a withering glance.

Dancer said: 'Basically Janie's right. There's little real danger. But if things didn't go as planned, you and your son would be out of the country within twenty-four hours.'

'Please don't treat me like a fool, John.' Lily had

regained a little of her composure. 'This is a totalitarian state. There are uniformed or plain-clothes police in every street. Over a million of them. If there was an emergency, I wouldn't get half a mile. *You* would not even get *that* far.'

'There are plans. This is a professional operation. A submarine off the coast. I can't go into details, but you and your family *could* have a new life in America if you wanted it.'

'Mama?' It was Bao, standing at the kitchen door, a pout of concern on his lips. 'Why do these people make you angry?'

Lily forced a smile and rubbed the tear-damp skin beneath her eyes. 'It's nothing, little one. Just grown-up talk. We must go now. Thank John for the lemonade.' She stood up and moved towards the door, ignoring Walsh. When Dancer followed to let them out, she said: 'I am sorry if I was rude.'

He smiled: 'It's a tense time. It takes a lot of courage to do what you're going to do.'

'I *am* going to, aren't I?'

A nod. 'For Bao and his father. And for Yan Tao.'

'And for you.'

Hidden from Walsh behind the door, he kissed the tip of her nose. 'I must see you again in the next few days,' he whispered.

'Lunch-time would be best.'

'Friday?'

'Yes. And next time, *she* won't be here?'

'She won't be here.'

Slowly he closed the door.

Walsh said: 'You shouldn't have mentioned *Manta*.'

'She was going wobbly,' Dancer replied, lighting a cigarette. 'Poor kid needed reassurance.'

'It was careless and unnecessary.' Walsh really wasn't pleased. 'Besides, I think you've been giving *more* than enough reassurance.'

He frowned. 'Meaning what?'

'These meetings you've been having alone together. I hope you haven't been . . .' She allowed the implication to hang like a ripe fruit. He couldn't miss it. 'Don't foul this up for me, John. I won't stand for it. You know the rules. Don't compromise yourself or others.'

That irked him. She irked him, period.

'I've been in this game a long time.'

She moved towards the door. 'Too long perhaps.' As she stepped through, she added: 'I'll see you tomorrow.' The door slammed shut.

Two blocks away, Lily and Bao were waiting for a bus to take them home. She felt her son tug her sleeve. 'Is a submarine an underwater boat, Mama?'

'What? Er, yes.'

'I thought so.'

The operation had begun to develop a momentum of its own. Two-man SAS or SBS teams were for ever coming and going, returning to the secure office at ExecFlight for a debrief by Dancer and Walsh, then setting up the next job before disappearing again for several days. McVicar's first job with Taffy had been to check out feasibility of the British Special Force's own private escape route out of the country if everything went wrong.

The Scotsman didn't offer details to Dancer and Dancer knew better than to ask. He guessed Iona Moncrieff would have devised the escape ratline in liaison with the Secret Intelligence Service in London and thought that the route would probably be westward to Xingjiang province and over the remote mountain passes of the Karakoram range on one of the old smuggling runs to Pakistan. In fact, the same fundamental route, but going in the opposite direction, that the CIA had been using to supply weapons to the anti-Chinese Flames of Aktu separatists in Xinjiang. However, he guessed that Moncrieff would be making use of Edwin Prufrock's contacts with Mike Jiang and the Red Tiger Society Triad.

Of the twenty-one provinces of China and the five 'autonomous regions', Dancer's efforts in recent years had been mostly targeted against those in the northern half of the country. The southern provinces were more prosperous, with historical ties to the Overseas Chinese in the rest of Asia and would be unlikely to resist a new pro-democratic and market-driven government. And Xingjiang, Tibet and Inner Mongolia were sure things if they were offered their independence.

McVicar's teams had now contacted and provided initial training to all the pro-democracy movements loosely controlled by Yan Tao as well as individuals recruited by Dancer, Dawson and Moncrieff over the years. It was indeed a formidable network. Now the Discretionary Warfare Team concentrated on deficiencies it had discovered, spending more time with groups that had shortcomings. Weak local leadership was identified and others were encouraged to take over.

More time was being spent manning communications and servicing requests for additional training, equipment or money. Mostly, hardly surprisingly, it was for the latter. They all knew that some people had very quickly seen that they were on to a good thing.

Nothing was made in the media of the growing rash of local assassinations throughout China. The victims were generally diehard Chicom cadre members in the regional police, administration or judiciary who were certain to resist change and were in a position to do so. The murders usually appeared to be the work of street thugs, the method usually a beating-up or the fire-bombing of a house or car. Individually, a killing might be seen as a random mugging or a revenge attack by criminals. There was nothing to suggest that it formed an orchestrated plan carried out by members of the Red Tiger Society following payment and instructions delivered by Iona Moncrieff and sanctioned by both SIS and the CIA.

Dancer was unhappy about his own contribution to the

lists, but had convinced himself it was something that had to be done. He wasn't sure Debs would have seen it that way. There had been feedback of a small ripple of concern permeating the higher echelons of the Communist Party. But any blame for the rise in violence was being placed on inevitable changes in society under the growing influence of capitalism. It was a convenient and smug assumption that Dawson had rightly predicted the Party would make, so obscuring the reality of what was happening from itself.

However, Dancer tried not to dwell on the silent assassination campaign and on the day following Lily Cheung's delivery of the revised schedule, he began working through the passenger lists of the two aircraft that would be taking the Politburo to Hong Kong Airport.

They had devised a solution to the problem of getting a concealed explosive device on board the first aircraft by using Lily, but not the second. Now he had the passenger lists, he prayed he'd find a name he recognised. He breathed a sigh of relief, seeing several at a glance. But then, on consideration, none was likely to volunteer. All were career politicians and would have to be blackmailed or coerced into co-operation.

But then he caught sight of another name, right at the bottom of the list. The most familiar of all. Yan Tao had recently been promoted and his name had been added to the Politburo's senior media relations team. As Dancer hadn't heard from him, it was quite likely that Yan didn't yet know himself.

Dancer gave the good news to Walsh.

'Will Yan play ball?' she asked.

'He's one of the most courageous men I've ever met.'

She nodded. 'He must be. It would be good to meet him.'

'I'm sure you will some day soon.' Dancer looked back at the computer screen. 'Lily can let Wang take the first bomb on board, but Yan himself will have to place the second. Then he'll need an excuse to get off the aircraft at the eleventh hour.'

'You know, John,' Walsh said with a grin, 'I'm just *certain* he'll think of something.'

Just then the telephone rang on Dancer's desk; it was Wang from the Civil Aviation Administration.

'Hello, Hu, old friend,' Dancer greeted him.

But Wang wasn't in his usual jovial mood, demanding an urgent meeting. When Dancer asked what about, the man became evasive. Nevertheless, the idea of a lunch with the assistant deputy had appeal for once. They agreed to meet at twelve thirty at a hotel restaurant.

Walsh smiled when she heard about the lunch and immediately went to fetch one of the waterproof packages she had brought ashore from *Manta*. Other team members gathered round, fascinated by what she extracted.

It was certainly a very handsome instrument of death. A beautiful, hand-stitched attaché case in burgundy calfskin with gold-plated fitments and red silk lining. Carefully, she lifted the lid. Behind it was a concertina compartment to take documents, and others were already filled with pocket calculators, pens and pencils and a matching leather drinking flask. The base was mostly taken up with a laptop computer.

'SX-2 sheet explosive,' she explained. 'Four ounces of it around the edge of the case under the lining. Non-detectable.'

'How's it triggered?' McVicar asked.

'The laptop works, but it doubles as the control unit. Inside, the components include a global-positioning device which can be monitored via satellite and will be triggered remotely by radio signal from a secret Agency facility when the aircraft is, say, half-way between Beijing and Hong Kong.'

'And the det?'

'The detonator is in one of the three jackplug ports for accessories at the back of the laptop. When triggered by the satellite signal, it fires straight through the lining into the explosive sheet.'

McVicar laughed. 'Brilliant. James Bond eat yer heart out!'

'Wang will have one,' Dancer said, picking up the case, 'and I'll give the second one to Yan. I'll get this one monogrammed on my way to lunch.'

Walsh's smile was dazzling. 'Good idea. I really don't want Wang getting it mixed up with someone else's.'

Wang, as usual, was already seated, Buddha-like, at the restaurant table when Dancer entered. He waved his napkin to attract attention, but made no attempt to smile as the American sat down opposite him.

'John, I am very disappointed in you. You have taken advantage of an old friend.'

Dancer frowned. 'I have?'

The deputy assistant director nodded and his lower lip quivered as though he was on the edge of tears. He seemed genuinely upset. 'Behind my back you have been going out with a member of my personal staff. Namely one Cheung Mei-ling.'

'Oh, you mean Lily?' Dancer laughed.

Wang scowled. 'Look at my face, John. Am I laughing? I introduced you that time at the restaurant and now I learn from the Ministry of State Security that you then started going out with her regularly.'

'And her mother.'

'What?' He looked taken aback.

'Lily, her mother and I share a love of music. Especially violin and the work of George Gershwin. I discovered that talking to her when you – er – fell asleep that first night. Ask her yourself.'

Wang looked as though he'd swallowed a gobstopper. 'I can't.'

'Of course you can. She'll confirm our meetings have been purely platonic. For heaven's sake, Hu, she is almost young enough to be my daughter.'

'No, no. I can't ask her because I've fired her.'

The words slammed into Dancer like a boxer landing a punch. He caught his breath.

'You've what?'

'I had her sent home. I didn't want to set eyes on her again. She betrayed me.'

This was the biggest possible disaster imaginable. Without Lily in the CAAC, their plans lay in ruins. Desperately, he tried to retrieve the situation. 'No, Hu, you just *thought* she'd betrayed you. Contact her, give her her job back.'

He shook his fat head miserably. 'She will think I'm a fool. I will lose too much face. The director and the deputy director will sneer behind my back.'

Dancer reached across the table and placed his hand reassuringly over Wang's. 'Old friend, you will not lose face in Lily's eyes, I promise you that. In private she's confided to me that she holds you in great affection.'

Wang blinked and stared at Dancer. 'She has a strange way of showing it. I'd like to believe you, but I think you are mistaken.'

'They were *her* words, Wang, not mine.'

'But the director and the deputy . . .'

Dancer smiled. 'They don't have Lily's eyes or her sparkling smile.'

That surprised Wang. 'You have seen her smile? She doesn't smile much at work.'

'She smiles when she talks about you.' He chided himself for going too far. God, surely Wang wouldn't believe that?

'Really?'

'She'd be so pleased if you asked her back, I'm sure.'

Wang pondered that one, then slowly ran the tip of his tongue over his lips. 'And *grateful*, I should think.' Suddenly his usual insincere smile returned. 'Thank you for that, old friend. I shall heed your advice and send a message to her home, telling her she is forgiven.'

'Let's celebrate with a really good bottle of wine,' Dancer suggested.

Wang picked up the menu. 'Suddenly my appetite has returned.'

'There's something else, Hu.'

'Yes?'

'We talked a little while ago about the percentage you are paid from us. Well, Abe and I have been thinking it over and have decided you have a point. Let's talk about an increase. From, say, in a month's time.'

This really was Wang's day, and he smiled broadly. 'That is most kind.'

'Nonsense. We haven't shown you nearly enough gratitude for what you have done for us over the years. And as an interim gesture of our good will, here is a little gift.'

Wang's mouth fell open as the exquisite burgundy leather attaché case was placed on the table. And when Dancer opened it to reveal the laptop computer, Wang gave a little squeak of delight. 'Old friend, that is truly wonderful.' For once in his life, the man appeared genuine. 'It will go everywhere with me and I shall treasure it always.'

'And your favourite brandy is in the flask.'

'It is all too much.'

Dancer lifted his wine glass. 'Let's toast.'

'Indeed, old friend. To a long and happy life!'

Brigadier Ting watched Dancer leave the restaurant from the back of an unmarked car which was being driven by Inspector Xia from the Bureau. The Chinese counter-intelligence officer saw the American climb on to his bicycle and pedal nonchalantly into the stream of frenetic traffic.

A few minutes later Wang Hu emerged carrying a burgundy leather briefcase, the same one that Dancer had carried in two hours earlier. The assistant deputy director surveyed the teeming street scene and caught Ting's wave. He waddled across the busy street, opened the rear door of the car and fell into the seat beside the brigadier who recoiled from the smell of alcohol.

'Well?'

Wang smiled. 'Pretty much as you predicted. You should have seen his face when I told him I'd fired her. Said how Lily had confided to him how much she cared about me, that sort of thing. Said I really should give her her job back. Huh, he must think I'm a fool.'

The brigadier made no comment. If he hadn't warned Wang what to expect, he wondered if the man's ego wouldn't have allowed him to swallow it hook, line and sinker.

'I'm sure you'll find her in your debt,' he said, and had little doubt that Wang would exploit that to the full. Sexual harassment by a boss was not something that most Chinese women felt they had much right to complain about. If they did, they didn't usually get very far.

'I'll send a messenger round to her home this afternoon.'

Ting nodded. 'But he may not find her in. If I am any judge, she will want to tell the American she's been fired as soon as possible. She will want his advice.'

Wang considered that for a moment. Then a thought occurred to him. 'Do you think what they said is true? That they don't have carnal knowledge of each other?'

'Probably,' Ting said. He didn't want Wang going all emotional on him again. And he didn't tell Lily's boss that he really didn't care if Dancer and the girl *were* indulging in carnal knowledge.

'I'm sure you're right,' Wang said, finally convincing himself.

The brigadier indicated the briefcase. 'Very smart. A present from Dancer?'

Wang opened his mouth to deny it, then changed his mind. 'Er, yes. A gift of thanks for the help I have given his company over the years.'

'Quite so. May I?' Ting helped himself, placed it on his lap and released the lid. 'A computer, as well. Indeed, Mr Dancer must think highly of you. Tell me, can you use these things?'

The huge shoulders gave a shrug. 'I'm getting there. It's got the latest Windows. I'll have Lily give me some private lessons.'

Ting just smiled and closed the case, handing it back. 'Of course you will.' He gestured towards the door. 'Now, if you'll excuse me, I have to get on.'

As soon as the assistant deputy director had manoeuvred his great bulk out of the car, Xia drove away at speed. Ting found it an unnerving experience because, even with two cushions on his seat, Xia could barely see over the dash. To anyone travelling towards him, Ting guessed it must have seemed even more bizarre – a car being driven by a trilby hat.

The brigadier was still musing over this when they arrived opposite the Stonedancer courier office. 'Ah!'

'You were right, sir,' Xia said.

Through gaps in the traffic, he caught the flickering image of Lily Cheung like a scene in an old movie pacing nervously up and down on the sidewalk opposite. The early autumn sun was painting everyone and everything in a gentle wash of amber light.

Ting lit a cigarette and exhaled thoughtfully. 'Cheung Mei-ling thinks we trust her. So maybe she'll get careless. And if Dancer is CIA, will he be able to resist feeding her misinformation for me? The game of bluff and double bluff.'

That was far too complex for Xia. 'I'd arrest the lot of them,' came the hoarse whisper from beneath the trilby, 'and throw them out!'

'That's not the way to learn anything. The trick is to give people enough rope to hang themselves. To show us exactly what the Americans are up to.' He paused for a moment's thought. 'At least, I cannot see that Dancer's interest in Lily Cheung has any bearing whatsoever on forthcoming – er – events in Taiwan.'

'I've heard it'll be next week,' Xia said conspiratorially.

Ting gave him a withering look. 'A word to the wise,

Inspector. Close your ears to such tittle-tattle. To repeat it could cost you your life.' He looked back across the street at Lily who was glancing at her wristwatch. 'No, if Dancer's connected with Dawson, then he's either a CIA agent or just a John Doe doing his bit. But, whichever, I think this is a matter of industrial rather than military espionage.'

'That's still serious,' Xia said, his brow furrowing. 'Ah, here he comes now. One of my men is following.'

Ting looked ahead to see Dancer cycling towards them on the opposite side of the street, saddlebags stuffed with groceries.

'Let's get out of here then, Inspector, and let your man get on with the job.'

As the unmarked car pulled away, Dancer saw Lily waiting and half-dismounted, cruising the last few yards balanced on one pedal. 'Hi, Lily! How are you?'

Her anxious expression turned to one of puzzlement. 'You don't seem surprised to see me.'

'I was half-expecting you.'

She was bemused. 'Why?'

'Because you've been fired.'

'How do you know?' Amazed.

'Because I've just had lunch with Wang.'

Lily shook her head miserably and hung her head in shame. 'I am so sorry. I have let you down. Let everybody down.'

He reached out and tilted her chin. 'No, you haven't. I had a long chat with Wang over lunch. Persuaded him that you and I are friends, like – like brother and sister. Now he wants you back. In fact, he's sending a messenger around to you now.'

She looked astounded. 'No!'

'Yes, but let's not stand here talking. Let's walk back to my place. Were you followed?'

'I don't think so. But, like you said, now I do not try to lose any tail.' She said it so seriously and naturally that it made him smile. 'And I didn't make it obvious I was looking.'

He nodded. 'Now they're on to us, we just make like we've nothing to hide.'

After checking with Abe Stone and signing a couple of letters, he left with Lily for his flat. They walked steadily, making light conversation that avoided what they really wanted to talk about. When they reached his apartment hotel, the officer of the People's Armed Police on the door nodded in sullen acknowledgement as they entered. Used to handling such situations, on her very first visit Lily had said she worked for the CAAC and was seeing Dancer on business. She always took her battered document case whenever she went to see him. No doubt this visit too would be duly noted and end up on someone's desk. Xia's or Ting's, it didn't really matter.

As soon as they were inside, he checked his routinely laid giveaways that someone had been in the apartment, then used the portable electronic scanner to sweep the room for bugs.

Lily watched with concern. 'The government *really* does hide secret microphones?'

'Really,' Dancer confirmed, now satisfied that no one had been in during his absence. 'Especially in hotels and offices used by us foreign devils.'

'Of course, ordinary Chinese hear occasional stories, but we never know the truth. I see now why you are always so careful where we talk and what is said.'

He smiled and put the scanner in the drawer. 'Well, here's something I don't care who hears – I've missed you.'

His words caught her by surprise and brought a flush of colour to her cheeks. Her returning smile was involuntary as she reached to take his outstretched hand. 'And I have missed you so much too, John.'

He crushed his mouth down on to hers and felt the gentle, probing flutter of her tongue on his lips. They clung

318

tightly to each other for several moments before drawing back, both slightly breathless.

'When this is over,' he said, 'we'll have all the time in the world together.'

'And you will take me and Bao to America?'

'If that's what you want.'

'And Mama Cheung?'

He grinned. 'I'm not so sure about that.' And they both laughed. 'You could all visit and see if you really would like it. Or stay here or live somewhere that is more of a compromise, like Hong Kong.'

She frowned. 'Live? You mean live together as a family?'

He realised his mistake, rushing and taking things for granted. 'Would you like that?'

'I don't know.' She looked flustered. 'It is all too quick, too soon. I am Chinese and you are American. That is a very big difference. I realised that when I saw your friend Janie.'

'My working colleague,' Dancer corrected, remembering the way Lily had regarded the CIA case officer.

Lily nodded her understanding. 'I gave my heart to Jin many years ago. It will be difficult to give what is his to someone else. Even you.'

Dancer shook his head, understanding. 'Your love for your fiancé will never die, Lily. And I wouldn't want the love that is his. I could never replace him, I know that. I feel the same about my wife. You need time for a new love to grow – we both do.'

She smiled shyly. 'You understand. Thank you.' She glanced away as though looking at him distracted her from finding the right words. ' I do love you, John, but I don't yet know how much. And at the moment I am too afraid to think properly, to know how I truly feel. My thoughts are only of what is about to happen.'

That made him feel guilty. He'd been in this game for years. To Lily Cheung it was new and raw and terrifying. 'You're being very brave, and I'm being very selfish.'

'Half of me was relieved when I was told Wang had fired me.' She gave him a shame-faced glance. 'But then I thought I'd let everyone down. Bao, Jin and you. And, of course, Yan Tao. He was in the office yesterday and I saw how he looked at me. I realised suddenly how much hurt I have caused him over the years. So I smiled at him. For the first time since Jin's death in Tiananmen.'

Dancer was curious. 'And what was Yan's reaction?'

She gave a little giggle. 'He just looked shocked, but you know how po-faced he can be. But later, just as he left the office, he glanced at me quickly and smiled back. He reminded me of a shy schoolboy.'

With a crush on the teacher, Dancer thought, but said instead: 'The only way I could persuade Wang to take you back was to tell him he was mistaken. That in private to me you've said you hold him in great affection.'

Lily stared. 'You said *what*? I cannot believe you said that! He will make my life a misery if he thinks that.'

'I'm sorry – I didn't have too many options.' But she turned abruptly away from him until he took hold of her shoulders and gently turned her back. 'Lily, we are only talking about a week. Seven days, that's all. I'm sure you can stall Wang and play hard to get for seven days.'

'Seven days,' she echoed. She dragged her gaze away from Dancer and stared at the floor as though thinking of something for the first time. 'Seven days. In seven days Wang Hu will be with his ancestors. In seven days I will have killed him.'

'Not you, Lily. Me. I'll have killed him.'

'And I'll have helped you. Let you. I will be as guilty.'

Dancer said: 'If there'd been any other way, anyone else in a position to help – I feel terrible about asking you to do this.'

She forced a smile. 'I think not as terrible as I do.'

When Lily Cheung returned home, a message was indeed waiting for her from Wang. Somewhat pompously phrased, it said that after careful consultation with his superiors, the assistant deputy director had decided to allow his personal assistant to keep her appointment. But under certain conditions and for a trial period. She was commanded to be back at the office when it opened the next morning.

As it happened, Wang was charm itself. An overbearing sort of charm, Lily had to admit, but charm nevertheless. She knew the reason – Dancer had told Wang she found her boss's rudeness and sexual innuendos difficult to handle. If he was polite and gentlemanly for a few days, he might see quite a change in her as she became more confident.

She was for the moment relieved to see a reformed Wang. Then he gave her the good news that he was soon to be promoted to deputy director and she too would be elevated to become his personal assistant. She would enjoy a higher salary and possibly better accommodation for her family. But 'additional responsibilities' would come with her new job. She would have to work some evenings regularly and make business trips away with him, often overnight.

So, Wang hadn't changed at all. But, nevertheless, she agreed with enthusiasm, knowing Wang's promotion would come too late to save his life. But she'd already walked unwittingly into his trap. With his new position would come the perk of a holiday home in the beach resort of Beidaihe on the Gulf of Bohai. He intended to visit and inspect it the next day with his soon-to-be promoted personal assistant. It was unspoken, but clear that if she refused to accompany him, she would not be reinstated.

So she shrugged and smiled and agreed. But as soon as she returned to her office, she went to work on the telephone, booking separate rooms for them in separate hotels in Beidaihe.

Lily did not mention this to Wang during the five-hour train journey the next day, nor during the taxi ride along the coast road below the pine-covered hills. Now and then through the trees, they would glimpse one of the elegant hideaways of the *nouvelle bourgeoisie* of the Party, modern or traditional pagoda villas and sometimes vulgar replicas of Spanish, Indian or Swiss architecture that looked hideously out of place. The end of the season was approaching, but there were still plenty of holidaymakers about in short-sleeved shirts and shorts or summer frocks. The tide was out and dozens of shell-hunters and kelp-collectors had descended on the vast sand flats.

'Smell that!' Wang said, winding down his window. 'Ozone and salt! It's why there are so many sanatoriums here for the cadres. All the top people come here. They say Jiang Quing has a villa here.'

'It is lovely,' she agreed.

Apart from the villas, there were hotels that belonged to individual work units. The Coal Workers' Hotel, the National Traffic Bureau Hotel and the Air Force Hotel. Closed to private guests, they would remain vacant throughout the season until there was a sudden rush to accommodate some conference or seminar.

At last the taxi turned off up a long leafy track which opened onto a lawn on which stood a neo-classical villa complete with Athenian columns.

Inside, it was impressive and very dusty, the furniture covered in linen sheets. Wang was full of himself, overawed as he explored each room, clearly amazed at the extent of his good fortune. High picture windows slid open on to a huge verandah with a stone parapet that offered a breathtaking view over the sparkling waters of the gulf.

'Your wife will love it here,' Lily murmured.

Wang gave a sly smirk. 'Don't think I'll let her know about this place. A man needs somewhere to be alone – with his thoughts.' And Wang being Wang he couldn't resist adding, 'Or his concubine.'

She pretended not to hear. 'I'm feeling rather tired. I must rest soon.'

322

The deputy director designate stepped closer and whispered hoarsely in her ear. 'Well, we know where the bedrooms are.'

'Oh, I've booked us hotels,' she said, feigning surprise. 'This place will be lovely when it's been thoroughly cleaned. We can't stay in this filth. In fact, I organised the taxi to come back here in . . .'

Her words were cut short by the sound of a car horn.

For a moment she thought Wang's huge bulk might explode with suppressed anger. But then he just seemed to give up and deflate with resignation as she smiled sweetly and headed for the front door. 'You're at the hotel on the beachfront, befitting your new position, sir. I'm at a little guesthouse for the workers.'

The school headmistress showed the man into her office.

'Would this be suitable, Brigadier? You're welcome to use it.'

Brigadier Ting Han-chen inclined his head graciously. 'You are most kind. I don't imagine this will take very long.'

'I have asked his teacher to bring him. They'll be here in a minute.'

When she left the room, Ting decided against sitting at her desk. Too formal, too intimidating. Instead he lowered himself into one of two armchairs that stood on either side of a low lacquered table. He had just settled himself when there was a knock at the door.

It swung open, revealing a middle-aged female teacher with a rather stern expression on her face, her hair drawn back into a bun. Her hands rested on the shoulders of the small, chubby boy who stood in front of her.

'Sir, I am Li Mei,' she announced. 'This is Cheung Bao.'

Ting smiled and extended his hand towards the boy. 'Hello, Bao. Is it okay if I call you Bao? I am Uncle Han.'

Bao looked dubious, and pulled back. 'I do not have an Uncle Han.'

'You're smart,' Ting laughed. 'Not a real uncle, more of a family friend. Come and sit on this chair.'

The boy was still reluctant to move.

'Miss Li can stay with us if you prefer.'

The schoolteacher smiled reassuringly at him as Bao looked up. 'Do what Mr Ting says. He only wants a few words with you.'

Bao edged forward and climbed into the spare armchair while Miss Li waited by the door, looking straight ahead like a sentry, pretending not to listen. Ting offered the boy a paper bag of boiled sweets.

'A candy? Different flavours. I like lemon best. The yellow ones.'

The boy hesitantly helped himself and unwrapped the cellophane.

'Like I say, Bao, I am a family friend. I am interested to know how well you're doing at school. I take an interest in all the children of the family.' Ting was making it up as he went along, 'getting into character' as actors called it. 'I expect that's because I have no children of my own.'

Miss Li gave the man an odd sideways glance; the headmistress had said he was from the police. Ting saw the look of suspicion and smiled reassuringly. 'And tell me, what sort of a pupil is little Bao?'

She thought for a moment. 'He is very bright, but he lacks concentration. He is a bit of a dreamer, always with his head in the clouds. A vivid imagination. That is probably because he does not have many friends. He comes from a family that does not have a very good history. Bao himself is a bastard. The other children learn this and poke fun at him.'

'I see,' Ting said, turning back to the boy. 'What do you like best at school?'

'Calligraphy and poetry,' Bao answered without hesitation.

'And at home?'

'Playing the violin. I'm not very good yet.'

'Ah, yes, your mother and grandmother play. Now tell me, do you know where your mother works?'

Bao frowned. 'Of course. At the Civil Aviation Administration.'

'And who she works for?'

'Mr Wang,' Bao replied promptly, then thought for a moment before adding, 'He's an old rogue.'

'Bao!' Miss Li scolded. 'Respect for your elders, if you please!'

Ting hid his smile. 'And have you any idea what your mother is working on at the moment?'

The boy pulled a face and shook his head; it was a stupid question. He wasn't remotely interested and, bored, he began to pluck at the material of the armchair with a thumb and forefinger.

Ting tried another tack. 'Do you know any Americans?'

Bao gave an eager smile and nodded. 'Uncle John. He is a friend of Mama.'

'And do you like him?'

'Oh, yes. He's my best friend.'

'Really, and why is that?'

'Because he gets me things. He bought me a wonderful kite. Better than anyone else has in my year. He also shows me tricks in baseball. I *love* baseball! *And* Uncle John is going to take Mama and me to America one day.'

'Is he now? And do he and your mother talk much about her work? Does he ask her questions?'

A vehement shake of the head. 'No. They talk about music and about history – before I was born. About Tiananmen Square.'

'What about Tiananmen Square?'

Bao played absently with the loose thread from the chair. 'When the government killed lots of unarmed children.'

It just tripped glibly off the boy's tongue without a moment's thought. Miss Li looked horrified.

'So,' Ting said, 'that's what they talk about. They tell you these things?'

He shook his head. 'No, but sometimes I overhear when I am in bed but not asleep.'

'But you never overhear this Mr John asking your mama about her work?'

'Not that I remember.'

Ting could see this wasn't going anywhere. It was a bit of a long shot, anyway. 'Okay, Bao, Miss Li can take you back to your classroom now.'

The boy didn't like that. 'Oh, do I have to?'

Ting laughed. His own memories of school were not fond. 'You really don't like school, do you?'

'Oh no, I do like it, but I will enjoy it better in America.'

The brigadier shook his head sadly. 'I don't want to disappoint you, but you should knuckle down to your schoolwork here. You and your mother are *not* going to America. You would not be granted permission.'

'Yes, we are!' Bao insisted. 'We can always go by underwater boat and then no one can stop us.'

'Underwater boat?'

Bao nodded. 'A submarine. Mr John said there was a secret underwater boat that will take us all away. To America.'

Ting laughed and glanced up at Miss Li. She shrugged. 'I told you he was a dreamer.'

'And you certainly didn't exaggerate.'

But as he strolled out of the school building, shielding his eyes against the light, he vaguely remembered the report that had crossed his desk from Naval Intelligence weeks earlier. Then he shook his head. No, the American had probably been telling the boy stories about all the modern US movie folk heroes. The Sly Stallones and the Arnie Schwarzeneggers. Stealth aircraft and secret submarines.

Yet, as he climbed into the back seat of the car, he still felt unsettled.

Twelve

Edwin Prufrock sank comfortably back into soft leather between Iona Moncrieff and the army brat, as the Daimler Sovereign swept out of the embassy compound on its way to the Fragrant Hills Park.

'Who cares if China fragments?' he was saying. 'It would almost certainly be a good thing.'

Suzy Tobin winced. 'Think what civil war would mean, Edwin. All that death and blood and destruction.'

'Ah, Your Loveliness has such a sweet but innocent nature.' Prufrock rather enjoyed setting out to shock. He'd always found it rather a good way to flirt. 'Some bloodshed is regrettably necessary for countries to sort themselves out politically. The English and American Civil Wars, the French and Russian Revolutions, the Third Reich and, of course, the more recent examples of former Yugoslavia, Chechnya and Georgia. History proves it.'

'So why would it be *good* for China?' Iona asked, unconvinced by his argument.

'Because fragmented independent nations achieve more than vast totalitarian blocks,' Prufrock replied without hesitation, warming to his subject. 'Before the Ming Dynasty the Chinese had invented printing, the compass and gunpowder. During and since Ming, nothing. Culture, technology and the economic competition were stifled under unified rule. That's why, historically, we've been so lucky in Europe.'

Neither woman could quite follow his logic. 'How d'you mean *lucky*, Edwin?' Suzy asked.

'Because Europe is divided up naturally by various mountain ranges, peninsulas and offshore islands, we've developed a rich diversity of competing cultures. Whereas poor old Mr Wong on the Number Seven tram finds himself in a huge lumpen superstate united with his neighbours by rivers and canal systems and no natural barriers.'

Now Iona saw what he was driving at. 'So you can see Xingjiang province hiving off as a separate Muslim state, Tibetan independence, of course, and possibly Inner Mongolia?'

Prufrock nodded. 'And probably another divide – between north and south China. All of which would be good for competition.'

Suzy Tobin was there too. 'You mean good for Edwin Prufrock's business.'

He grinned at her, showing nicotine-stained teeth. 'You're a sharp one, Your Prettiness. Of course, you're right. Better to sell to five smaller nation states than one huge one. Better for peace and stability in the area too.'

Iona thought that was a moot point. She knew Bill Dawson and Frank Aspen at Langley favoured a united but peaceable China in preference to a feuding, fragmented one. They both believed that, for good or ill, the country would function more naturally as one giant monolithic state. By contrast, Piers Lansdowne's view was closer to Prufrock's – that if a free-market economy was introduced too fast, it would create massive unemployment and food shortages resulting in civil unrest which could not be easily contained within a single democracy.

She said pointedly, 'As it is, Edwin, I'm more than pleased to be selling the Eurofighter 2A to one big China rather than five little ones.'

The Englishman grinned; there could be no disagreement about that. 'Ground-floor business,' he said. 'It'll be the first and last time, though. Mark my words, in future all the competition in the world will be beating a path to General Sun's door. He'll be spoiled for choice.'

'And palm-greasers,' Suzy added.

'Talking of Sun,' Iona said, 'I trust he's expecting us?'

Prufrock shook his head. 'No, I didn't want to go into explanations over the phone. Better you just join me as a guest for afternoon tea like you often do and we apparently meet General Sun by chance.'

'Is that where you first met Sun?' Suzy asked. 'At the villa?'

'Couple of years back. We're both friends of the minister who owns it. We'd both been lent a room at the same time. Sun and I got talking, got on. Fate, really.'

'What's he doing in Beijing now?'

'There's been a running series of military planning sessions at PLA headquarters for days,' Prufrock replied. 'Chinese whispers I'm hearing give the impression it's all tied up with the Hong Kong Airport Phase Two opening – or the seizure of Taiwan, by any other name. I understand some PLA Air Force squadrons in northern China are flying south to stiffen invasion ground-attack units there. The Politburo's fully aware that there could be a major clash with the US 7th Fleet. So, in turn, it would make sense for some of General Sun's aircraft from Xingjiang to replace depleted squadrons around Beijing.'

Iona felt suddenly chill as she heard his words, spoken so casually without a hint of what they could mean in terms of life and death hanging in the balance for thousands of armed forces personnel. If she and Dawson were to get this wrong, or to foul up in any of the millions of little ways that suddenly seemed possible, they would carry the burden of guilt to their graves. She peered out of the window, her mind not registering the drab western suburbs flashing by. Instead she saw herself with Dawson on an autumnal Cape Cod beach, under grey scudding cloud with wind tugging at their clothes as they walked arm in arm along the shoreline with all the innocence of adolescent lovers.

Retirement? Marriage? Suddenly she felt weary. After this lot, another sort of life suddenly had immense appeal. A life with Bill, her rock and her strength. They were still young enough to enjoy their remaining years, to squeeze the most out of life and to have some adventures together.

It occurred to her then that she'd already made up her mind. She'd tell him next time they met. She would be the fourth Mrs Dawson. Mrs Iona Dawson. There was a smile on her lips as she imagined it.

'Here we are, boss,' said Suzy, the voice cutting into her thoughts.

There was an official black car parked outside. It was probably an Audi, but it was hard to be certain because the chauffeur had removed the collectable chrome emblems before the street thieves got to them. As Prufrock had his own key, they walked straight in.

General Sun was in the lounge engaged in earnest conversation with half-a-dozen uniformed PLA Air Force officers who sat around a low table spread with glasses of tea. He was easily recognisable: tall for a Chinese with broad shoulders and rather Mongolian features, the heavily hooded eyes behind thick-lensed spectacles, being the most pronounced.

Sun appeared startled. 'Edwin, old friend, I thought you were out all afternoon,' he said in Mandarin.

'Change of plan, General,' Prufrock replied easily. 'These are two good friends of mine from the British Embassy. Miss Moncrieff, second secretary, and her assistant Miss Tobin. Leading lights in Sino-Anglo trade. Don't know what I'd do without them.'

Iona picked up the quick look of understanding in Sun's eyes as Prufrock mentioned the word 'trade', but then she felt unaccountably uneasy at the look which followed it. General Sun smiled at her as he shook hands, but she detected no real warmth in his greeting.

'I should like to stop and talk, Miss Moncrieff, but my colleagues and I were about to go to Beijing for a little sightseeing. We have been posted out in Xingjiang for many years.'

Prufrock slipped an overfriendly arm around Sun's shoulders and steered him to one side. 'You can spare fifteen minutes, General. I was going to show the ladies round the garden. I'm sure they'd appreciate your company.'

A polite tic of a smile pulsed briefly on Sun's face. 'As you wish, old friend.'

After explaining the delay to his fellow air force officers, the general followed Prufrock and the two women into the grounds. Only a few roses remained in flower, the other shrubs already drooping and losing their leaves at the approach of the colder months. There was a chill edge to the soft breeze that had come south across the northern steppes.

'This is just a precaution, General,' Prufrock said, once they were away from the villa. 'I have my suspicions about one or two of the villa staff here. It would be surprising if at least one wasn't a Bureau informer. And I felt it important that you meet the lady who will be ultimately responsible for your exalted position in the New China – and, of course, take this opportunity to establish our new Aerospace business with Mike Jiang.'

General Sun inclined his head towards Iona. 'It is an honour to meet you, madam.'

She smiled in return and motioned towards an alcove seat surrounded by winter jasmine that was yet to flower. 'I shall try not to keep you, General, but we need to have a few minutes of official business.' She lifted her briefcase with its combination locks.

'I don't understand.' Sun looked flustered.

'Nothing to worry about.' Prufrock smiled reassuringly. 'I know it's all been agreed, but we do need your signature on a written contract. Post-dated, of course, for two weeks hence.'

The general looked alarmed. 'That is too dangerous. If it was found—'

Prufrock shook his head. 'No danger, I assure you. The contract goes straight back with Miss Moncrieff in the embassy car and will leave Beijing Airport tonight in a diplomatic pouch.'

Still the Air Force commander wasn't happy. 'Whatever happened to the legendary honour of the English, not to mention that of the Chinese?'

A somewhat oily smile broke on Prufrock's face. 'In my humble experience, General, honour is something of a moveable feast. If deals are not signed and sealed, then memories can be short after ambitions have been achieved.'

The Chinese commander sighed and sat beside Iona on the bench seat as she opened the briefcase on her lap. 'Oh, very well,' he said with resignation.

She extracted a thin sheaf of papers and handed it to him to peruse. 'Please read it and check you are happy and all is in order. Just initial each page and sign at the end. Edwin will do the same and I shall sign as witness. A British Government trade minister will countersign once the document is back in London.'

Sun read over the Chinese translation of the English, then pursed his lips and looked up at Prufrock. 'The requirement for three thousand Eurofighters over ten years to replace our own interceptor and ground-attack aircraft was a very early figure, old friend. It did not take into account that we were replacing ancient technology with the very latest. We would be replacing quantity with quality.'

Prufrock's expression had frozen and his skin was suddenly as ghostly pale as an opera mask. 'We went through all this, discussed it thoroughly.'

Sun shrugged sympathetically. 'We did, but my fellow officers had not at that time. Now it has been discussed very thoroughly and in detail among ourselves. We are concerned that the Eurofighter's capabilities are not yet proven and in the past European projects, like Tornado, have left something to be desired.'

Iona swallowed hard, not believing what she was hearing. 'Exactly *what* are you saying, General?'

He smiled gently. 'Don't worry, nothing has changed. It is just that my colleagues and I feel we owe it to the New

Democratic China to be cautious. Not to commit ourselves to too much, too soon. Our understanding remains, but the contract must be modified. We have since revised the numbers we will initially require.'

Prufrock had difficulty in forcing out the words. 'And what is that exactly?'

'We will purchase one hundred over an initial three-year period for evaluation, twenty each the first two years with training packages and logistic support, then the remaining sixty in year three?'

The Englishman almost had apoplexy. 'What!' he exploded.

Sun added quickly: 'And we will purchase direct from Europe, not build here under licence. At least not until we are satisfied with the outcome of performance trials and your ability to support the programme. I am sure you understand how it is?'

For a moment Prufrock was speechless as he saw the greatest financial opportunity of his life slip through his fingers like so much sand. No consortium with Sun and Jiang meant he was left with a percentage commission on a miserable hundred aircraft. He'd done better trade in counterfeit medicines.

The general was on his feet, eager for a quick getaway before Prufrock recovered from the shock. 'By all means redraft the contract and bring it back to me here this evening after our sightseeing tour. I will be more than pleased to sign it then.' He bowed to the ladies stiffly from the waist, turned on his heel and was gone.

'I'm sorry, Edwin,' Iona said as Prufrock sank down on the bench beside her. 'That's a terrible shock. It'll be bad enough for the DTI, but I know how much it meant to you.' She touched his arm.

Prufrock gave a little twist of a smile. 'You win some, you lose some,' he said stoically. 'Trouble is, I'm getting a bit long in the tooth to keep on losing. Time's getting short to make it big time. That deal was going to be my pension.'

Suzy slipped her arm round his shoulder and gave him a little hug. 'You'll crack it, Edwin. No one can keep you down for long. You always bounce back.'

He grinned appreciatively and roughly rubbed away the moisture that had gathered beneath his eyes. 'Such words of comfort, Prettiness. I only wish I had half the faith you have in me.'

They heard the doors of Sun's car slam and the engine start. Iona stood. 'We'd best get back, Edwin, and get the contract redrafted. We're running out of time and I want Sun to sign tonight. And I don't want to see you lose what little you've got left.'

He nodded numbly, but didn't bother to reply, just remained seated with his elbows resting on his knees and his hands knotted together in quiet desperation. It wasn't until he heard the Daimler start up that he began to emerge from his trance. Wearily he hoisted himself to his feet and plodded back along the rose-edged path and up the steps to the verandah.

Inside, he found that the servants hadn't yet cleared away the glasses that Sun and the others had been using. He slumped down on a sofa and fished in his pocket for his cigarettes. There was only one left in the packet and it was bent, the paper torn. It just wasn't his day. Then he saw the red pack of *Zhonghua* and plastic Bic lighter, and reached for them. He was in luck; one left. As he plucked it out a small screwed-up ball of paper fell out with scraps of cellophane.

Absently Prufrock lit his cigarette and unrolled the little square of paper. It was covered in dozens of mathematical calculations in a neat, microscopic hand. Mildly curious, he fished a pair of grubby half-moon reading specs from his breast pocket, rubbed them with his handkerchief and placed them on his nose. Various figures leapt out at him. Three thousand. Two hundred. Twenty million and a dollar sign. Equivalent in *yuan*. The letters EF, and then F22 with a tick beside it.

He frowned. F22? Wasn't that the designation of the new generation American multi-operation aircraft? He couldn't be sure.

Then he noticed two figures at the bottom of the page, both circled. The first was one billion dollars with the initials E.P. beside it. His initials. The second figure said five billion dollars. Beside that was a name. W. Dawson and a tick.

Suddenly Prufrock knew, suddenly he felt nauseous. Typical! The fucking Yanks had gone behind his back and outbid him in a deal with Sun. And Sun – the honourable Chinese bastard – had thrown him the sop of a hundred, hell, twenty Eurofighters and a worthless promise of jam tomorrow. Sun's friggin' face-saver. But as Prufrock and everyone else knew, tomorrow was sodding never-never land!

Lily felt dreadful. She had barely slept all night, only drifting in and out of consciousness in the last hours before it was time to get up.

She avoided the mirror, instead tidying her hair by feel and slipping a band round it in a ponytail. Wang didn't like ponytails; he said they were undignified. Also Wang would no doubt berate her for not wearing make-up. But then Wang didn't matter, because tomorrow was what John Dancer called 'D-day' and tomorrow Wang would be dead. And then it really *did* matter, because that was why she couldn't sleep. Because, for all his bad ways, she didn't want the old rogue dead, smashed to death in an air crash.

She kissed Mama Cheung goodbye and left with Bao, dropping him off at school before continuing on to the office. Once there, she buried herself in her work. Or at least she tried. But she found she could not make head nor tail of anything she read and everything she typed on to her PC was littered with errors. It was all so unlike her.

All she could see before her eyes was the airliner and Wang squeezed into his seat, that familiar smug grin of contentment on his face as the hostess kowtowed and refilled his glass. Her boss sharing crude jokes with his fellow passengers and giving no thought to the burgundy briefcase in the locker above his head. Then the bright white light, the pulsing core of the explosion seemed to lance her eyeballs. It was so real in her mind it hurt. Would Wang die in an instant? In the air or when he hit the ground?

Tears began to roll down her cheeks. Why are you making me do this, John? Why, why, why?

She sniffed heavily, straightened her back. No, be sensible. As he had told her, she wasn't actually doing anything. All she had to do was do nothing apart from making sure Wang didn't forget his briefcase. Even then, Dancer wasn't *making* her do anything. She was doing it for little Bao's future, for her dead fiancé's dream of freedom, and for the cruel silence she had so stupidly and ignorantly imposed on Yan Tao for all those years. The deep hurt he had nursed without a word behind that cold, unblinking gaze of his. After his best friend's death, his mind had been as numb with guilt as her heart was black with anger, and she hadn't even begun to realise it.

Poor Tao.

A tear fell onto her keyboard. She pushed back her chair, stood up and walked to the ornate gold mirror over the dusty marble fireplace with its neo-classic columns. What a fright she looked! Eyes sunken and prickly, the natural honey tone of her skin darkened like grey parchment. She dabbed at the moisture on her cheeks with a tissue.

'You are looking tired.'

She looked past her reflection as the voice spoke. Yan Tao stood behind her in the high doorway of her office. He was smartly dressed in suit and tie as always, his steel-rimmed spectacles still giving his face that hard and distant look.

'I did not sleep well.'

'I understand. Neither did I. You've been crying?'

She turned to face him directly. She found it hard to say the words. 'Will he feel much pain?'

Yan frowned. 'Who?'

'Wang. Will he know he is going to die?'

Yan glanced behind him, checked there was no one there, then shut the door. He took a tentative step towards her. 'No, Lily, he will not know. And he will not feel anything. The moment the bomb goes off, pressurisation will be lost. Loss of consciousness will be virtually instant.'

She nodded, seeming to understand. 'Then it will not be so bad.'

Yan stepped nearer and tentatively reached out to her. With his forefinger, he gently raised her chin so that she looked directly at him. 'Have courage, little one, do not waver,' he murmured.

She forced a smile. 'I will not.'

He too smiled then, a rare sight which transformed his face. It was strange, Lily thought, to see Yan Tao with eyes alight.

He said, 'Tomorrow will be a momentous day for the Middle Kingdom.' He used the old-fashioned term for China. 'A day when our ancestors in the heavens will rejoice for the sake of the Motherland.'

Her smile faded. 'You have no doubts?'

'Any doubts I ever had, I lost when they killed your Jin at Tiananmen.'

She nodded, understood. 'Mr Dancer told me – you should have said.'

Yan looked embarrassed. 'I couldn't speak of such things.' Another smile flickered on his face. 'And you were not listening to me then.'

The pain of the memory was plain to see. 'I am truly sorry, Yan. I have been wicked. Somehow I will make it up to you.'

'You already have.'

'Yes?'

'By doing what you are going to do tomorrow. It is an honour that we will be doing it together. Together for Jin.'

She saw then that tears were welling in his eyes and he was trying desperately to hold them back. Her hand reached out and brushed his cheek. 'Dear Tao.'

It was too much. The dam burst and he couldn't help himself. Ten years of guilt and sorrow and pain came flooding out and he sobbed like a child as she ran her hand soothingly over the back of his head and neck until his head rested on her shoulder and she could feel his glossy black hair against her cheek. Absently she thought how unlike Dancer's his skin smelled. Yan's skin smelled faintly of dust, sorghum and sandalwood. Of China.

He straightened up, regaining control, and stepped back. 'I'm sorry.'

She smiled. 'Don't be.' And kissed him quickly on the cheek. 'For years I thought you were a robot. Ho said you weren't, but I never believed him. Now I know you're human after all.'

'Oh, I promise you I am that.'

Suddenly there was something she felt she had to know. On impulse, she asked, 'You have never married?'

'No.'

'Why?'

He shrugged, averting his head. 'Does it matter? I had this work to do. There was no time for other things.'

'Have you been afraid?' she asked.

'Sometimes. Not always.'

Her eyes travelled back to the mirror where she barely recognised the haunted expression on her face. 'I am frightened, Tao. Frightened about tomorrow, about what will happen.'

He took her wrists in his hands and gathered them together, turning her round to face him again. 'You know I will be at Beijing Airport tomorrow too?'

She looked up into his eyes and nodded. 'On the other plane.'

338

'I will look out for you, make sure you're all right. We can leave the airport together.'

Her smile returned, a little uncertainly. 'But not holding hands.'

'No,' he laughed, 'we had better not do that.'

Then the ancient telephone rang like an old ambulance bell. It was Wang, demanding his letters for signing because he wanted to be away early to pack.

'You'll be taking that lovely new briefcase with you, sir?' she asked lightly.

She could imagine Wang's expansive grin. 'Think it'll impress the director, eh?'

'It most certainly will.'

But somehow it didn't seem at all funny to Lily as she pulled on her coat later that afternoon and made her way along the gloss-painted corridors and out of the building with all the other assistants and secretaries and onto the teeming streets. The autumn air was chiller than ever today and from the overcast sky came a steady, slow drip of raindrops.

She nearly didn't turn her head when she heard the beep of the car horn. Then she thought it might be Dancer. John had said he wanted to see her the night before D-day, but had decided it would be safer if he didn't. After all, another twenty-four hours and they could spend as long as they liked together.

Inspector Xia sat in the driver's seat, smoke trailing from under the brim of his hat. Brigadier Ting Han-chen threw open the rear door and beckoned her across. Reluctantly she peered inside the car.

'I can't stop. I have to collect my son from school.'

'I'll give you a lift. Get in.' The voice was smooth as groundnut oil.

'I really can't put you to any trouble.'

'No trouble. It's your son that I wanted to talk about.'

For a second icewater seemed to form in her gut. 'Oh?' She stumbled into the car, closing the door behind her at his request.

As the car pulled away, Ting said: 'I saw your son the other day. I spoke to him at school. Did he tell you?'

She shook her head.

He looked out of the window at the other cars grinding along in the traffic jam with them. 'Tell me, Lily, are you political?' he said.

'No, not really.'

'But you belong to the Party?'

'Yes.' She hesitated, 'But I do not really understand politics.'

'And you have no views?'

'No, there is no need. If I'm not sure about something, or what to do or how to act, I seek advice from the Party.'

She was tripping out the textbook answer all dissenters learned during their 're-education' process and they both knew it. Ting turned his head from the window and looked at her directly. 'And you have no views about the events at Tiananmen?'

Lily shook her head. 'It's so long ago, I've forgotten. It is the past. I never talk about it.'

'You've talked about it to the American in front of Bao. The boy seems to have got the idea that unarmed students were massacred by the People's Liberation Army. Most unfortunate.'

She tried to think clearly, tried not to panic. 'Is that what he said? I'm sorry. Mr Dancer talks about it sometimes. He was in the area when it happened. I gather Americans have a fixation about it.'

Ting acknowledged this with a grunt. 'And has he asked anything more about your work?'

She felt a little happier now, on safer ground because she'd gone over it with Dancer. 'Well, I have noticed since you talked to me that he asks about his company's competitors sometimes. Not often, just now and again.'

'What sort of questions?'

'About contracts and how much they're worth. What

tenders they have put in.'

'And what do you tell him?'

She looked aghast. 'Nothing, sir! That is confidential. My boss would not want me talking about such things.'

A bland smile. 'Of course, you haven't.' Then a thoughtful pause. 'And has he asked you anything about tomorrow? I understand you're flying to Hong Kong with Mr Wang.'

It was as though a steel dart had pierced her heart. She could swear she felt it stop dead in her chest and she was sure Ting heard her catch her breath. 'Yes, to the airport opening. But Mr Dancer hasn't asked me about it specifically.'

Ting's forehead creased into a frown. 'And has he mentioned Taiwan at all?'

Her acting was getting better now, her confidence restored. 'Our province? No, why should he?'

The brigadier shrugged. 'Like their fixation with Tiananmen, Americans also have a fixation that China is about to seize back Taiwan.'

Lily thought for a moment. 'If we did, we would be within our rights. Taiwan rightly belongs to the motherland.'

Ting regarded her for a moment. 'I thought you weren't political?'

Then he lit a cigarette and left her dangling, knowing she was getting too smart and that Ting knew it and that he could smell the sweat of fear on her. 'I'm not, I. . .'

'And he's promised to take you away with him? To America?'

She shrugged, making light of it. 'It's just talk. Trying to impress me.'

'By submarine?'

The blood drained from her face. 'What?'

'By secret submarine. That's what Bao said.'

'What nonsense.'

'That's what I thought.' He leaned forward and spoke to Xia. 'Pull in here, Inspector.'

Lily looked out. Bao's school was just across the street.

341

'You can walk from here?'

'Yes, yes,' she gasped. 'Thank you for the lift.'

'We'll talk again. Maybe next week.'

'Yes, yes, sir. Thank you.'

And she was gone, slamming the door, running across the damp pavement.

Smoke billowed from beneath the brim of Xia's hat. 'She's hiding something, that one,' he rasped in his low whisper. 'The fear smells on her so much I thought she'd shit herself.'

A tic flickered at the corner of Ting's mouth. Xia's crudity had hit a nerve with him, and it wasn't altogether unpleasant. 'Language, Inspector.'

'No offence. But she's hiding something and it's to do with the American.'

'You're still convinced he's a spy, aren't you?'

'Just a private view.'

'Although you found nothing in those earlier raids on his apartment and his office?'

Xia shrugged. 'It could just mean he's good. He's up to something. And over the past two weeks most of his American staff have left the country on vacation. Whatever happened to holiday rotas? It must leave them seriously understaffed.'

Ting nodded his understanding. 'You've asked yourself why? If something was going on, they'd want more people here, not fewer.'

'All I can come up with is the coincidence, the timing. Most of his American staff have left just before Hong Kong Airport Phase Two opens.' He didn't add just before Taiwan is seized back. 'I still don't know exactly why.'

The brigadier's mind was turning over and over, but getting nowhere. Still the nagging worry remained. 'I agree with you about the girl. She was hiding something. You get to know these things.'

'And she'll be travelling with Wang tomorrow. On a top-security Politburo flight.'

Suddenly he realised what Xia was suggesting. But it was too preposterous for words. In no way was the timid Cheung Mei-ling assassin material. Xia's obession was getting seriously out of hand.

Then something clicked in his mind, like a switch being thrown and an electronic pulse linking the present to one of the trillion pictures filed in his memory. But not too deep. This picture was quite recent. His visit to Wang's office at the CAAC. Lily Cheung walking in with the detailed list of the VIP flights. Was that the connection he'd been looking for? The missing piece of the jigsaw? He still wasn't convinced. But nevertheless, one should never take chances, not with the Politburo at least. Never. 'We will have her watched tomorrow, Inspector. Closely.'

The atmosphere in the secure ops room within the ExecFlight offices had become electric with tension by midday. Tomorrow was D-day and no one could believe that something wasn't going to go wrong. It was just a question of when and where and how seriously?

Dancer knew that the democracy movements *had* to have been penetrated by the Chinese security services to some extent. Dammit, there were domestic spies in every street reporting back to the Party neighbourhood committees. No chance then that some informers hadn't got mixed up with the democracy movements, by accident or design. And given the size of China, they could probably be numbered in hundreds rather than dozens.

The viability of their plans over the next crucial twenty-four hours would depend on the strength of the cell-system security Yan Tao had developed over the years. But any chain was only as strong as its weakest link. The other hope was that Chinese internal security suffered in the way of all totalitarian regimes. It became simply subsumed in the masses of irrelevant data collated for the sake of collating with no real purpose. That made the system creakingly inefficient and frequently prevented intelligence officers from seeing the wood for the trees.

Nevertheless, they had been taking no chances in these final days. In case things went wrong, getaway cars were kept in the compound car park with full petrol tanks. There were always a couple of armed SAS or SBS men on watch at the office windows and two more in a parked car on the street outside, on the lookout for any suspicious police or security activity developing. Essential kit was packed, ready for grabbing on the way out should someone press the button. High explosives and fire-bomb attachments were rigged around the building, designed to bring it down and turn the rubble into a blazing inferno to destroy any evidence if they had to leave in a hurry.

'Embuggerance factor, we call it,' McVicar said laconically. 'If something can go wrong, it will. But just not how you anticipated.'

Dancer grinned. 'I just love you Brits' delicate turn of phrase. In the Green Berets they used to call it Murphy's Law.'

The Scotsman shook his head with mock disapproval. 'That's racist talk. Besides, it's been superseded by McVicar's Law.'

'And just what does McVicar's Law state?' Dancer asked.

'That Murphy is an optimist.'

Janie Walsh wandered in from the communications suite. Her white pilot shirt and beige chinos were fresh and ironed, but she herself looked decidedly tired and crumpled.

'I've had no calls for over an hour,' she sighed. Even the quick flash of her now famous smile seemed weary. 'Guess it's the calm before the storm.'

'This time tomorrow,' McVicar said pointedly.

'We'll be in the middle of it,' Dancer said. 'The biggest political sea change in the world's history.'

Walsh said, 'Is Abe getting a flight out later today?'

Dancer looked awkward. 'That's what he said.'

344

She picked up the tone in his voice. 'But?'

'I don't think he means it. He feels part of all this now. I think he wants to see it through.'

Walsh nodded, understanding. 'But if anything goes wrong and your company is implicated, there'll be nothing we can do for him.'

'He knows that. Abe's an old hand.'

'Sure he is.' She glanced around the room at the drawn faces of the SAS and SBS men who had worked so tirelessly under her control for the past weeks. Now the fatigue was really beginning to show. 'Anything outstanding?'

'All done,' McVicar confirmed.

'Then let's go for a wrap,' she decided. 'Just me, John and Dave will stay on here to monitor events. I want the rest of you out of the country when the balloon goes up tomorrow. Signal *Manta* into position for an RV between twelve and one tonight. Mike Jiang's people are ready with transport. Take away all the communications equipment except my own satcom phone in case of a last-minute emergency. Remove all the demolitions stuff around this building, all your personal gear and anything else incriminating. Take it all back to the sub.'

'That's a lot of kit, chief,' Taffy said.

'Then throw it off Captain Song's boat once you're out in the Gulf. Just make sure this place is so clean it squeaks. If we're not compromised, my people would like to continue using this setup as cover.' She gave a mischievous grin. 'We're not going to stop spying on the New China just 'cos we become friends.'

McVicar glanced around at the tired but smiling faces of the team that had meshed so surprisingly well together. As businessmen, they had travelled the length and breadth of the country to contact dissident groups, delivering and collecting, reconnoitring and instructing. There had been some tense moments and a few close shaves including one shooting incident with a police patrol in distant Yunnan province, after which the two SAS soldiers had managed to lose their pursuers. But mostly it had run smoothly right under the noses of the Chinese authorities. Fifteen years of an increasingly open society had lessened xenophobia and paranoia to a point where such a mission by professionals had become possible. He was proud of them.

Walsh seemed to read his mind. 'I'd like to thank you all for a job well done. I admit when I first met you I wasn't sure I could cope with such a bunch of scruffs who hated each other.' She grinned as she added, 'Even more than they clearly hated me.'

McVicar laughed. 'Nonsense, Janie. It was our common hatred of you and all things American that bound us together. Even to the extent of working with this bunch of web-footed scaleybacks.'

'Thanks anyway, boys. I hope we'll meet up sometime for a debrief and a beer. But if not, I won't forget you. God bless.'

'Aw, gee shucks,' mimicked Taffy, 'the Chief's goin' all blueberry pie on us.'

'Don't push your luck,' McVicar cut in. 'Let's get cracking. We've a lot to do.'

Dancer said quietly to Walsh, 'They love you really.'

She grinned at him. 'I know. It's just that Brit humour takes a bit of getting used to. They don't seem to take anything or anyone seriously.'

He'd learned that lesson long ago in Viet Nam on joint ops with SAS men on exchange tours with the US Army. 'They just hide it well.'

'They sure do.' She was looking more relaxed as the team began dispersing. 'What about you, John? There's nothing else for you to do here. Why don't you get off home and unwind. It's going to be a long, hard day tomorrow. I'll phone if anything breaks. What I wouldn't give for a long soak in a hot tub.'

Dancer grinned. 'You angling for an invitation?'

'Pardon me?'

He laughed. 'Drop over this evening. You're welcome to

use my bathroom.'

The neon light was back, teeth dazzling in the perfect almond face. 'I might just take you up on that,' she said, then added in a mock Chinese accent, 'Most Honourable Gentleman.'

He winked. 'Don't count on it.'

But when he got back to his apartment, he couldn't sleep. He closed the shutters and lay on the bed in his shirt and trousers, hands behind his head on the pillow. Although his eyes were shut, a jumble of images filled his head, each fighting for attention, then fading away to be replaced by others. He saw Lily walking alongside Wang Hu on the tarmac of Beijing Airport, the burgundy briefcase swinging in his hand, saw a close up of Yan Tao's face, the eyes inscrutable behind the sheen of his spectacles, then the Politburo aircraft taking off for Hong Kong. A clock was ticking. He found himself waiting for the bang, but was aware only of the everyday noise of Beijing's traffic permeating the window from outside.

He must have dozed once, because he remembered seeing Lily's face drift across his vision, in and out of focus. She looked troubled, her eyes clouded. He knew she was scared. But then she wasn't Lily any more. There was a subtle change in shape, a metamorphosis as she became Janie Walsh, her bright smile lifting his spirits and her laugh like tinkling water in a fountain.

Then she looked serious, staring directly at him. She opened her mouth and the words came out: 'This is wrong, Johnny. They're not doing this for China, they're doing it for themselves.'

With a shock he realised the voice did not belong to Walsh. It was Debs speaking.

He awoke with a jolt as though an electric current had passed through him and in a cold sweat. The bedside clock said five. Must have dozed for five minutes at the most, he thought.

Trust Debs. Trust her to make him doubt himself. Trust her to question the morality of it all. Trust her to make him think. He hadn't heard from her for several weeks now – there had been no quiet words whispering around inside his skull. He'd have thought he'd have missed their comfort, but strangely he hadn't. And now, the day before . . . Bad timing, my love, because there's nothing I can do about it now.

He sat up, swung his legs off the bed and stood up. Crossing to the door, he entered the living room. He went straight to the drinks cabinet and poured a shot of bourbon and took his pack of cigarettes from the mantelpiece. Debs's picture caught his eye. What an amazing photograph that had been. A quick, barely focused snap taken in Gansu province on the day she'd interviewed Fan Xiu Kun. But when it was processed, he quickly realised that, for him at least, there was a magical quality about it. It exuded vitality, happiness, lit up her eyes and smile. Yet viewed in a certain light, he could sometimes detect an underlying sadness – almost as if, even then, she sensed that their life together had only a short time left to run.

'I see dark clouds moving over China. You must be careful, Johnny. One day we will be reunited but, pray God, not yet . . .'

The voice in his head faded into silence. He turned away, angry with himself for listening. Debs was wrong. Some politicians in Washington and London might have dubious ulterior motives, but what he was doing was surely right? For the likes of Lily and little Bao, for Yan Tao, for Xin-Bin and those who had suffered like Fan Xiu Kun. It was all very well saying leave it to the Chinese to sort out their own destiny, but that way things might *never* change. Was it wrong to give them a helping hand, even if some innocent lives would inevitably be sacrificed?

He thought he knew Debs's answer to that. They were manipulating and interfering in the fate of a nation that wasn't theirs.

He threw open the shutters and looked out of the window. He couldn't take all that moral philosophical stuff. He couldn't really understand it when Debs was alive, and he certainly couldn't now. His was a simple soldier's view. Pretty much black and white. If you questioned everything in this game, nothing would ever get done.

Quite deliberately he ignored Debs's words, pushed them to the back of his mind and instead ran over the events of the past two months.

He lit a Camel, forced himself to loosen up, and leaned forward on the sill, watching humanity passing back and forth and crisscrossing in the streets below. A vast, living tapestry of Chinese life.

He noticed someone – probably a man, but it was too difficult to tell from that distance – wearing a red shirt. He was moving against a tide of people wearing duller shades – blues and greens and grey. Then the man stopped on the sidewalk and spoke briefly to someone before moving on.

That was how it had been for weeks now. One man passing unnoticed in the Chinese crowds. Stopping and talking and then moving on, the word spreading.

It had been radiating out like the ripples from a stone thrown into water.

One man from each cell in the underground democracy movements secretly contacting one from another. And then another, and then another. Identity codewords exchanged. Sometimes just bringing a message or an order from the ruling committee or simply giving the time and place of another rendezvous, sometimes handing over cash, or a telephone pager, or arms, or explosives, or scanners for listening in to local police and PLA radio traffic, or sometimes bringing along a stranger who had newly acquired knowledge to impart about explosives, about secret communications, about weapons handling, about the art of following others and preventing others following you, about the tactics and psychology of facing down the apparatus-of-state in a confrontation.

The wary Chinese citizens lecturing these small and hastily convened groups were usually men. But sometimes they were women, mostly young, usually over twenty-five and under forty and always they were educated, had belonged to the student movements of the late eighties. Each was cautious about what he or she said or what questions they answered. Each wore the haunted expession of people who knew that to be caught saying what they were saying or doing what they were doing, would mean death. And because they all had families and friends, who would suffer miserably from the inevitable swathe of arrests, executions, torture and indeterminate prison sentences that would follow. One or two might admit they'd been taught this or that new skill by a fellow Chinese, a stranger who had been introduced to them. Only if one was able to pass up the linking chain of teacher and pupil, teacher and pupil would one eventually find someone who had been taught by a 'foreign devil', a white-skinned mercenary believed to have been hired by a political faction from Taiwan.

There were many whispers and much speculation about exactly what was happening. As no one was told for sure, most guessed that a group within the Politburo or the Party or the People's Liberation Army was about to launch a coup or *putsch*. That they were supported by their Chinese cousins in Taiwan or even the Taipei Government itself. All the talk was of democracy and civil liberties. Those who feared that mass unemployment would follow the collapse of the Communist Party were assured by their peers that investment would flood in from the Overseas Chinese con-glomerates and the Western nations. There would be jobs for all, the optimists believed.

And that belief in the future for a New China gave them the courage and energy to keep going as they met furtively to plan and plot late into the night exactly what they would do in their town or city on the day that the people's insurrection began. Under guidance filtering down from Yan Tao, who in turn had been advised by John Dancer and psychological warfare experts out of Langley, placards and banners with appropriate slogans had been made and stored, Tannoys and public-address systems at schools and theatres earmarked for immediate seizure and quantities of artificial flowers diverted from factories and hoarded. These would decorate any vehicles used by the democracy movement and by marching supporters who would offer them in gestures of goodwill and peace to any police or soldiers who confronted them.

These were the television images of passive revolution that the CIA was keen should be seen quickly throughout China and around the world. To this end, both the United States and Britain's intelligence services had conspired to lure the major networks to have news teams in Beijing and Shanghai during the week of the planned coup, on the pretext of covering a trade fair which usefully coincided.

At the moment confirmation was received that the two aircraft carrying the Chinese Politburo had crashed, killing all on board, an unstoppable chain of events would begin. From the secure ExecFlight suite, Janie Walsh would use an encrypted satellite telephone link to Langley which would in turn instruct a satellite signal to trigger the six SBER devices secreted in China. The first two sub-nuclear explosions would simultaneously take out both the Communist Party and PLA headquarters buildings in Beijing before any key players could move to seize power for themselves. These bombs, concealed in suitcases, would be taken in by young officers who were also trusted members of Yan Tao's secret network.

Four more SBER devices were due to explode at the road and rail hubs formed on the Yellow River at Zhengzhou and Jinan and on the Yangtze River at Nanjin and Wuhan. They would go off the night following the Beijing bombings in the small hours of the morning to avoid civilian casualties. The effect would be to divide the country into three zones and snarl up road and rail transportation for several months, which would serve to frustrate any attempt at mass troop movements by any surviving rival factions wanting to grab power for themselves.

These bombs were now in place. Over the past two weeks, McVicar had organised four-man joint SAS/SBS teams to visit each of the target areas by road or rail under the guise of executives doing genuine business on behalf of Stonedancer Couriers or ExecFlight, using Dancer's local Chinese contacts. During these visits, the businessmen would naturally visit local places of interest and innocently take photographs of one another against backgrounds that were of interest to them. Retiring to their hotel rooms for the night, they would plot and amend their earlier plans made following the study of satellite surveillance photographs.

Once the best positioning site for the SBER had been reaffirmed, the unit would go tactical, changing into black overalls and balaclavas before slipping away from the hotel and making their way surreptitiously to the target area where the device would be concealed. The missions were naturally heart-stoppingly tense, but were really little different from hundreds of similar exercises and active missions in Northern Ireland or Bosnia. Shadows were shadows the world over and you got used to living in them.

Meanwhile, on D-day in Beijing, news of the Politburo plane crashes and explosions at both Party and military headquarters would stun the remaining survivors within the apparatus of government. These would be the crucial minutes and hours when all would be won or lost, when all the chesspieces must be in the right place.

And one of the most important pieces was General Sun. He and his coterie of fellow dissident officers would be in the air, also flying to Hong Kong, but not on the Politburo aircraft. As soon as there was news of the disaster, Sun would order the pilot of his aircraft to turn and head back to Beijing. By the time it landed, it was likely that he would be one of the most senior and certainly the most ambitious military commander surviving.

An even more pivotal figure was Yan Tao himself. Knowing what was about to happen, he would be poised outside the Public Information Office with half-a-dozen of Mike Jiang's armed henchmen from the Red Tiger Society. As soon as the air crash was confirmed, Yan had to establish himself as the mouthpiece of the new interim government. Some of his superiors would have perished in the crash and others would be temporarily stranded in Hong Kong; the remaining senior chiefs would be in the Office headquarters. Yan was to march in with the RTS thugs, who would seize them and take them away. Now in command of the Office, Yan would issue a number of sequential, pre-prepared statements hour by hour, to the Xinhau News Agency head office in Beijing. These would be redistributed automatically without question to the national press, the major domestic radio station, Central People's Broadcasting, and the Chinese Central and Beijing TV news programmes. In addition, the agency routinely distributed bulletins to its local branches in each province and army unit to reach every provincial and local newspaper and radio station throughout China.

That was the beauty of such a centralised news system. The Office was government and therefore its statements went unchallenged as Party policy and within the hour would be circulated on radio and television and in the press by the end of the day.

Yan Tao's first bulletin, already drafted and printed, reported briefly that all members of the Politburo were dead following an air crash in Jiangxi province. It was not yet known whether it was the result of a mid-air collision between the two aircraft or the result of foul play. The people were asked to remain calm and to stay in their homes or places of work and treat it as a normal day. Police and PLA units should continue normal duties until instructions were received from Beijing.

Half an hour later, the second bulletin would be

released, acknowledging two massive car bombs, one each at the Communist Party and PLA headquarters. It confirmed that there were several hundred dead and injured. This was believed to be the work of a secret 'Anti-Reform and Anti-Democracy' group within the ruling authorities and the military. However, they would not be allowed to deter the government on its march towards greater democracy, better human rights and a healthy free market economy.

Ordinary Chinese hearing this over the radio might raise a quizzical eyebrow. Democracy was a word seldom heard in government broadcasts, and the term 'human rights' almost unknown. But they would no doubt have been reassured by the promise that the perpetrators of these evil deeds would be hunted down and punished.

The following two hours would be crucial as General Sun and his fellow officers arrived in Beijing, where they would find absolute chaos and no doubt a few stunned survivors from the former political and military hierarchy. He would drive immediately to the Public Information Office to meet with Yan Tao and a handful of his key followers, including a few like-minded politicians and military officers who had been persuaded to change their plans for the day and so missed the bombings.

It was anticipated that General Sun would be able to assume command with no opposition from others present. If that occurred, the presence of armed RTS men would ensure such opposition was short-lived until élite and trusted PLA troops could be assigned to protect the new leadership.

Sun's first act would be to order all military units gathering for the taking of Taiwan to stand down with immediate effect.

Then the general would make his broadcast, now fully prepared, announcing plans for the huge state funeral of the leadership and promising that the murderous 'Anti-Reformers' – an expression that would inevitably and increasingly be seen as meaning the Communist Party – would not be allowed to intimidate the people of China.

He himself would temporarily assume the role of Prime Minister and form an Interim Democratic Government until proper multiparty elections could be held, it was hoped, within the year. He would immediately have the much-loved folk hero, dissenter and poet Fan Xin Kun released from prison and invite him to become the first President of the New China in order to oversee the transition of the country to full democracy. The people would be asked – in the oddly formal style of Chinese political language – to take to the streets in celebration of the triumph of the 'New Democrats' over the old 'Anti-Reformers'.

On hearing the broadcast, small local core groups of activists throughout China would mobilise and lead a march to local high schools and universities, carrying prepared placards and calling on the students to join them. As the crowds gathered in size like a rolling snowball, they would visit factories and offices to swell their numbers.

Then would come the biggest test when they marched on the local police and PLA barracks. Most commanders would presumably follow the lead coming down from Beijing. But some, like local Communist Party dignitaries who now saw themselves labelled 'Anti-Reformers', would see the sudden political changes in the distant capital as a threat to their position, status and future. Local mayors and politicians might form alliances with local soldiers or police to form armed fiefdoms. And, if that's the way things went, Yan Tao's dissident members would have to act firmly and decisively, putting into practice the lessons taught by McVicar and Lake's teams before the country broke down in regionalised anarchy. But, with luck, such situations would be rare.

Then, as the dust settled, events would move swiftly, orchestrated by forward planning at Langley in consultation with London. As the previous regime's intentions to invade Taiwan would inevitably become public knowledge, General Sun would quickly admit this to them, but lay the blame at the door of the 'Anti-Reformers' in the old Communist Party – the same people who had tried to stop progress by blowing up the Politburo aircraft and bombing Party and PLA headquarters. Police would be asked to find the culprits and would eventually come up with very little evidence, except the discovery that some of the SBER bombs had been purchased illegally from one of the Russian mafias. It would all fit – old-fashioned Chicom diehards in league with their former Soviet cronies.

Meanwhile General Sun would announce Chinese withdrawal from Tibet and offer increased autonomy to separatists in Xingjiang and Inner Mongolia. Political overtures would be made to Taiwan in an attempt to heal old wounds. A rash of new political parties would inevitably spring up. The largest would be secretly funded by the CIA and have General Sun at its head.

But before the election was held, probably in a year's time, Taiwan would rejoin mainland China. The jubilation among the people would be such that Sun's party would have a landslide victory. And no one would much notice or care that Sun had become head of the Air Force and his Interim Government had placed many commercial orders with the West – not least to replace its ageing fighter aircraft.

Debs certainly wouldn't approve of that, but, hell, that was the way the world worked.

Just then his doorbell rang. That would be Jamie Walsh. Dancer felt his pulse quicken, and smiled.

Brigadier Ting Han-chen was about to leave his office when the call came through on the priority red telephone.

He dropped his raincoat over the back of his chair and reached for the handset.

It was a Ministry of State Security colonel calling from local offices in the town of Wuhan on the Yangtze River.

He was gabbling, overexcited, and Ting had to make him repeat his story several times before he could make sense of it.

A local man had been out walking with his dog along the river bank in the early hours of that morning. When they were passing under a major rail bridge, the dog started digging and unearthed what turned out to be some sort of suitcase. But the man was puzzled by its strange technological contents with wires and dials and took it to the local police. PLA scientists were called in and had been examining it all day.

Initial reports said it appeared to be something known as an SBER – a very high explosive utilizing a material popularly known as 'Red Mercury'.

As it was radio-controlled, there was as yet no way of telling how long it had been there, who had put it there, or when it was intended to be used, or indeed whether plans to use it had been abandoned. Cyrillic lettering on certain parts suggested that it was of Russian manufacture.

When Ting finally hung up, he felt distinctly uncomfortable. He glanced down at the calendar on his desk. Tomorrow marked the opening of Phase Two of Hong Kong Airport and within the next forty-eight hours the full might of the Chinese People's Liberation Army was due to be unleashed against Taiwan.

Thirteen

Bill Dawson was running late, but he didn't care.

He was on an adrenalin high. Under twelve hours to go and he could almost feel the stuff coursing round his system, fizzing and bubbling like champagne. He felt ten years younger, maybe more. There was a spring in his step and his feet scarcely seemed to be touching the pavement. This was a far better lift than you got from a *ganja* roll-up back in Viet Nam or a snort of white lady in the politicians' men's room in DC. He was fast-moving, alert and ready for anything. Invincible.

The call from Iona Moncrieff was the perfect end to the working day. Her suggestion to meet up for a drink and a meal solved the problem of how the hell he was going to get to sleep that night. In Iona's company, that wouldn't be a problem. She'd always been one of the boys when it came to a night on the town; she could drink most of them, probably even him, under the table if she had a mind. They'd burn the midnight oil over a bottle of brandy. Reminiscing a lot and laughing even more. Now that things had moved on they might even, he thought, snuggle up as they waited for the dawn light to break over Beijing.

When he arrived at their rendezvous point outside the Jixiang theatre, she was already waiting outside. Dressed in a familiar drab, belted raincoat and her hair in desperate need of a shampoo, she was looking anxiously about her. Another cigarette butt joined the growing collection at her feet. How lost, almost vulnerable she looked.

'Hi, Majesty.'

She turned, only a twitch of a smile to greet him. 'Ah, there you are! Ratfink! What time do you call this?'

'Busy at the office, would you believe?' Just a touch of sarcasm.

'Do I take that as an apology?'

He frowned; her smile still hadn't broken through. 'In the apology game tonight, are we?'

'You certainly are.'

'Well, I'll do my best seeing as you've asked me out.'

She shook her head. 'Oh, no, Bill, most definitely not. I invited you to take *me* out. This is your shout and no mistake. C'mon, my liver's been standing here doing cold turkey for an hour. And make it expensive.'

He grinned. 'Why not? Hopefully there's a lot to celebrate.'

She glowered. 'Well, it seems *you* certainly have,'

'What sort of food do you fancy?'

'French.'

But they ended up having a gigantic Texas spare-rib barbecue at the Great Wall Sheraton as Dawson had intended all along.

Too scared of what he might hear about his marriage offer, he avoided asking her directly what was wrong until they were on coffees.

She viewed him darkly. 'So you *really* don't know?'

'Swear I don't, Majesty.'

She lit a cigarette, thinking about her words. 'How can I put this? Why should I marry a two-faced, conniving, cheating, uncouth motherfucker like you?'

'Ah, I've obviously upset you.'

'And you can't think how?'

He grinned broadly, beginning to enjoy the game.

'One moment you ask me to marry you and the next thing I know, you've gone behind my back and Edwin's and unstitched a deal with General Sun that took us an age to set up.'

'Oh, that?'

'Yes, Bill, that.'

'It's called free enterprise, it's what America is all about.'

'Where I come from it's called stabbing your friend in the back.'

'Which is why we're the only superpower left in the world and Britain has become a province of Europe.' He leaned forward with a grin of boyish triumph on his face. 'C'mon, Majesty, this is a competitive game and you and I are the best players east of Suez. You'd have expected nothing less of me. And I know damn well you'd have done the same if the positions had been reversed.'

'Do you? I seem to remember something about us being a team back in Macao.'

'Well, yeah. To a point. But I'm not retired *just* yet.' He realised he hadn't yet won her over. Suddenly his blue eyes clouded with concern. 'Does that mean you're turning me down?'

She nursed her coffee cup and frowned at the dregs. 'Poor Edwin. He was utterly crushed when he found out.'

'I'm not plannin' to marry Edwin fuckin' Prufrock.'

A bitter half-smile jerked at the corner of her mouth. 'No, I guess I've got that honour all to myself.' She looked back at him. 'Had to go and ruin the big day, didn't you?'

'So it is a no?'

Her hand reached across the table and clasped his large fist. 'No, you old grizzly bear, it's not a yes and it's not a no. But it *will* be if you pull any more stunts like that.'

He winked. 'Ah, yes, and talking of cunning stunts . . .'

'I mean it, Bill. I've got a lot of love to give and a lot of time to make up.'

He placed his other hand over hers and squeezed fiercely. 'I know. From now on we're a team. No more tricks. I'm sorry.'

'Dear Bill, I do believe that really was an apology.' Then her smile broke through at last.

Edwin Prufrock bowed graciously in response to the polite kowtow of the middle-aged secretary. She was a handsome woman, although not much given to smiling, and the severely pinned-back hair seemed to emphasise the seriousness with which she regarded her position.

She was old school and Prufrock had no doubt she ran General Peng Zhi Yong's diary like clockwork and protected him fiercely from the everyday ravages of Chinese political life.

But then Peng would appreciate that, because Peng was old school too. In his late seventies, Prufrock thought, judging by the yellowing parchment skin, the snow-white hair and stooped shoulders. Legend had it that, as a young teenager in the early 1930s, the senior PLA Air Force general had fought alongside his father with the Communist peasants in Mao Zedong's Long March south against Chiang Kai-Shek's *Kuomintang* nationalist government forces.

After witnessing the horrors of the enemy's extermination campaigns and their eventual defeat and flight to Formosa – later to become Taiwan – with all of China's gold reserves, Peng became a fervent and lifelong supporter of Communism, as well as one of the youngest pilots in the air force of the Workers' and Peasants' Red Army.

But then Prufrock didn't mind old school. Wasn't he old school himself? Sometimes he found himself aching for old times. Old standards and old values. Like Peng's old-fashioned reception area with its dusty pot plants, wicker chairs and black-lacquered cabinets inlaid with mother-of-pearl.

How Prufrock hated the austere banality of Beijing's modern architecture compared with the startling neo-classic Western styles of old Shanghai, even if they were cheap copies of 1930s Paris and New York. A time warp perhaps, but it was where Prufrock felt at home. The feel of marble underfoot and mahogany panels to the touch. Gold taps in the gents and tea served on a silver tray. When people still bothered to put on a tie before dinner, when there was still order, respect and politeness. God, how he hated tourist pollution and what it had done to the Far

East, his personal Orient. Nowadays the wrong people had the money to travel.

He waved the brim of his hat to cool himself down and loosened his tie a fraction. Although, he had to admit, maybe air conditioning in Peng's old-fashioned reception area wouldn't go amiss.

A bell rang stridently on the receptionist's desk, startling him.

'The General is able to see you now,' the secretary announced. 'I'll show you in.'

Prufrock shuffled to his feet and followed her in. It was as old-fashioned as the reception area, dark panelling and heavy brocade curtains conspiring to keep the light level low. On one wall were rows of framed pictures of aircraft, from old stringbags that Prufrock didn't recognise to World War Two P-51s, early MiGs to China's first home-produced Shenyang version of the Soviet MiG 19.

Peng himself was dwarfed behind the huge leather-topped desk, complete with nibbed calligraphy pens and gold-plated inkwells. Prufrock could have sworn the old boy had shrunk.

Peng's smile was as genuine as ever when he struggled from his seat and reached across the desk to shake Prufrock's hand. 'It is good to see you, Edwin. It's been a long time. I thought you had deserted me.'

Prufrock's cheeks coloured a fraction. 'One gets so busy, you know how it is. Time seems to slip through one's fingers.'

Peng regarded him for a second, his eyes a little dim, as though he were trying to see through mist. 'It is not just that I am no longer of any help to your business?'

'Perish the thought.'

The general chuckled, a light frothy sound, as he sat down again and pushed a cigarette case towards Prufrock across the desktop. 'I am teasing. But it's true. When you get to my age, the youngsters say how much they respect your wisdom, then take care to promote you so high there

362

is no more work for you to do. I am one of the most senior officers in the PLA Air Force, but, in truth, I probably have the least authority.'

'Does that mean you're not going to Hong Kong Airport tomorrow?'

The old man's eyes twinkled. 'Certainly not! I am told I am much too important to attend. Someone of immense experience must hold the fort here in Beijing.' There was another chuckle as he offered Prufrock a light, then attended to his own cigarette with a series of little sucks that sounded like kisses. 'Of course, the truth is they are afraid I'll keel over on the podium and China will lose face in front of the world's television cameras.' He seemed to think the idea of this hilariously funny.

'I am sorry, General. To me it seems such a waste of your years, your wisdom and talent.'

Peng shrugged. 'Maybe, old friend, but the truth is today's aircraft baffle me. I haven't flown for forty years. I like to see propellers turning in front of my eyes and see all the little wires pulling the flaps. I like to know what's keeping me up there. I don't trust all this electronic stuff.' He nodded for a moment as though agreeing with his own words. 'But I will admit I miss not having more real respect and more influence on decisions.'

'Like your replacement fighter programme.'

He nodded. 'Yes, that. They listen to me politely, but – the Politburo is leaning towards Moscow, you know. But I do not trust the Russians. They are quick to screw you when it suits them and they can no longer be trusted to deliver on time. Their aero industry is in a mess. And everyone knows their technology is crap compared with the Americans'.'

Prufrock saw his opening. 'Or the British.'

Peng nodded. 'Or the British. But no one is matching the Russian price.'

The Englishman paused for just long enough to have Peng's absolute attention. 'I can.'

'I do not understand, old friend.'

'The Eurofighter. I can match the Russians' deal. China gets better technology for the same price.' He had a clincher, knowing the Politburo's paranoia about the rising tide of unemployment. 'And you get to make it here under licence.'

He saw Peng's eyes widen. 'I am not being a good Chinese. But then barter was never my style. I admit it is a very attractive proposition. Usual trade credits and offsets, of course?'

Prufrock nodded. 'And a percentage for yourself, of course.'

Irritation flickered in the old man's eyes. 'I am Communist, Edwin. We do not believe in back-door business.'

Not much, Prufrock thought. Why the hell did Peng think he stayed in China? But he said, 'I know. But you will have earned it, and you can donate it to the Party or invest it in business for your heirs. It will be your choice.'

Peng thought about that for a moment. 'But why are you telling all this to me?'

'Because I think you deserve better from the Politburo. This deal will restore your authority, your due respect.' He didn't add that, despite his modesty, the old man still knew better than most how to manipulate and wield the levers of power and which strings to pull.

'I fear it may take more than that.'

Prufrock examined the tip of his cigarette and blew gently on it until it glowed. 'I can give you more than that. The British Government is making this special offer to China because its intelligence services have discovered a plot in place to assassinate the Politburo and install a new government in Beijing. It's a plot by radical reformers, all funded by the United States and the CIA.'

Peng froze and looked suddenly so pale that Prufrock feared for a moment that the shock had proved too much for him. But then the old man smiled. 'For a moment I thought you were serious.'

'I was. I mean, I am.'

A nod. 'Yes, perhaps you are. Forgive me, but the Ministry of State Security comes out with such claims several times a year. In fact, whenever they want more funding or to distract the politicians' attention from something else. It never comes to anything.'

'Oh, believe me, General, this one will.' Prufrock leaned forward. 'If I tell you that the Americans know about the Politburo's plans to take Taiwan in the next few days.'

Peng pursed his lips. This was awkward territory for him.

The Englishman followed up. 'I'm not asking you to confirm it. The Americans *know* about it. So do the British.'

'Ah, so.' He seemed lost in thought for a moment. 'That may explain it.'

'I'm sorry?'

'The Americans' 7th Fleet on manoeuvres in the South China Sea and reinforced by a carrier task group from 3rd Fleet with 6th in the Mediterranean reported to be on stand-by to pass through Suez to the Indian Ocean.' The old boy's brain still hummed like a computer, facts at his fingertips. He'd been in this game a long time. 'All this and yet they have issued no public warning to us, issued no private diplomatic threats.'

'Now you know why,' Prufrock said with a slight feeling of triumph. 'It's because Washington wants to give no hint it knows what China's plans are for fear that will lead to the discovery of its own plot. The Americans expect Beijing to be rather distracted tomorrow, too distracted to continue with the invasion plans. But, of course, the US fleets have to be in position as a contingency.'

Peng looked startled, having latched on to one key word. 'Tomorrow?'

'It has to be, General. Otherwise the Americans will have run out of time.'

The old man leaned forward. 'How is it to be done, Edwin? How can it be stopped?'

'The Politburo will be grateful to Britain?'

'But, of course.' Clearly it was a strange question.

Prufrock raised an eyebrow. 'Grateful enough to sign a protocol of intent to purchase the Eurofighter? Say, one thousand over five years and a further two thousand within ten years?'

Peng drew back, a mask of hostility now covering his face. He was being backed into a corner and didn't much like it. 'Within fifteen.'

Prufrock smiled. 'Agreed, General. I have the documents with me. I'll just amend the figures.' He picked up his attaché case from the floor, set it on his lap and sprung the clasps with his thumbs. Then he looked up. 'Oh, and one small thing. Before I tell you what I know, you must stand down your invasion fleet. The one supposedly making for the Hong Kong Airport celebrations.'

There was a brittle silence between the two men for a moment, then Peng's frothy little laugh burst out. 'We really must play chess sometime soon, old friend. While there is still life left in this old body.'

Relief flooded through Prufrock and he smiled widely as he felt the perspiration dripping from his forehead and on to the draft contract on his lap. 'I'd really like that.'

'It will be a pleasure to stop the Taiwan invasion. The Politburo will now have no realistic choice. I have been dead against it; it is not the way forward. But no one listens to me.'

'They will now.'

'I will contact an acquaintance in the Ministry of State Security first. A man called Ting. He's supposed to be very good.'

'Of course,' Prufrock said, 'this is an American operation, so we don't know everything. But hopefully enough to get it stopped.'

Prufrock leaned back in his chair. Never did to screw one's own. Not cricket. Let the Yanks take the blame and the freedom movement carry the can.

'God, that feels better.' Janie came out of the bathroom, still drying her hair. Dancer's borrowed terry-towelling robe swamped her.

He looked up from the armchair where he sat reading that morning's newspaper with a drink in his hand. 'Glad to be of service.'

She tossed her hair from side to side, testing the dampness. 'I'm surprised you can concentrate to read. I'm a bag of jitters.'

'I've just read the same article three times and I still don't know what it's about.'

'I guess you've been involved in stuff like this before?'

'A long time ago.' He lit a cigarette. 'But never quite like this. Not as big.'

Then she recalled that the smile and laughing blue eyes which had secretly fascinated her ever since their first meeting had been missing that evening. 'Are you worried about something, John?'

'What am I *not* worried about?'

'Lily?'

'Lily, sure. And Yan Tao. They'll be at risk.' He hesitated. 'Others won't be so lucky. Some good friends.'

'I don't understand.'

'A drink?' He was on his feet and walking across to the cupboard.

'Have you got vodka? And orange juice? Not too strong.'

His smile returned. 'Keeping a clear head?'

She gave a tight little laugh. 'I thought it best.' Then she accepted the glass. 'What did you mean? Good friends?'

'I was looking over the passenger lists for the Politburo flights. There are quite a few names I recognise. People who might well be on our side if we gave them the chance. But we can't risk warning them.' He drew heavily on his cigarette, taking comfort from it. 'It's the same with the two headquarters bombs. We've managed to get some of our likely allies away from the place on some pretext or other. But by no means all.'

'I know, it's tough, especially for you.' She touched his arm. 'They're mostly just names to me.'

'Not so easy when you've known them so long.'

She studied him closely for a moment. 'You love the Chinese, don't you?'

He tried to look cynical. 'For my sins. It can get you that way if you stay here too long.'

'And have you been here too long?'

'Probably. But then there's nothing for me to go back to the States for.'

'And Lily Cheung is here?' An edge of reproach had crept into her voice.

He caught her drift, caught the questioning in her eyes. 'For the moment.'

Walsh nodded towards the photograph on the mantelpiece. 'And your wife.'

His voice was a whisper. 'Debs will always be here. In spirit. I don't know if I'd hear her voice back in the States.'

She thought she understood. 'And that frightens you?'

He gulped the last of the whiskey in his glass. 'You know, when she first died, after the first few weeks I found I couldn't picture her face. Old photographs only worked when I was actually looking at them. Then I found that one. It seemed to speak to me. But not quite. That was the most lonely feeeling in the world. Seeing her there but not hearing what she was trying to say.'

'I can imagine.' She felt his sadness. 'But you hear her now?'

'Sometimes. Stupid really, but the only record of her talking was the old answerphone tape. Just our number and some sort of quip, but you could hear the sparkle, the mischief in her voice. I must have played it over a million times. Still do sometimes, late at night.'

'She must have been a lovely lady.'

He nodded. 'Oh, she was.' His voice was wavering. He checked the emotion. 'And I don't think she'd approve of

368

what we're doing. Certainly not of the sacrifice of innocent people in the bombings.'

'And what do *you* think?' she asked softly.

He poured out another drink for himself, but Walsh shook her head. 'I tell myself that the end justifies the means. That we must do it thoroughly or not at all.' Debs had fixed him again with a look of disapproval. 'That's what she'd say. Then not at all.'

'We've done our best to minimise victims, John. But if you want to know whether it is worth a few innocent lives to free China, you should speak to my dad. He grew up under Mao and lived through the Cultural Revolution. When the Red Guards made people dig up grass and flowerbeds with their bare hands because gardens were bourgeois. When there was chaos when they reversed the rules for traffic lights because red couldn't possibly mean stop, it had to mean go forward. Sure, those times have gone, but the Party still runs the show. That's what my Dad would tell you.'

Dancer gave a wan smile. 'Unfortunately, it's not his voice I keep hearing in my head.'

Walsh shrugged. She said softly: 'Maybe you should stop listening to it. Maybe you should listen to Lily instead. Hasn't she said she'd like to go to the States?'

He nodded. 'To visit, but she's apprehensive. China is her country and her culture.'

'Are you in love with her?' The words were out before she could stop herself, her eyes wide and candid.

There was a slight hesitation. 'Yes. At least that's what it feels like. For the first time since Debs died.'

'And Lily loves you?'

'She says she does.'

She sensed there was something else. 'But?'

'Perhaps she only thinks she does. Just a feeling I've got.' He gave a sheepish smile. 'Hell, why am I telling you this? What's the first unwritten law in spook school. Never tell control your personal secrets, otherwise they'll use it as a stick to beat you.'

Walsh's smile flickered awkwardly. 'Sometimes I wish I wasn't, but I'm a woman first and control second. Not quite what Langley likes, but hell.' She gave a little shrug of her slender shoulders buried under a mountain of terry towelling. 'I'm glad you felt you could share it with me.'

'Thanks for listening.'

They stood, not talking, looking at each other for just a few seconds too long. Walsh touched her hair. 'It's almost dry. I'd better be getting back. Thanks for the loan of your tub.'

Ten minutes later she had dressed and was gone, back to the secure suite at the ExecFlight office. And the moment the front door of the apartment closed behind her, Dancer thought how empty the place felt. He poured another drink, promising himself it would be his last that night, and put a CD on. Of course, he could only seem to find Gershwin lately. The smile came involuntarily to his lips as he thought of Lily, remembering how they had danced here on this very spot, her step so light her feet seemed to float above the floor, her waist so narrow and supple that her body seemed almost ethereal.

In bed together he had never once really felt her weight against him. Hers was a butterfly touch, a sort of loving spirit that wafted around him like a silken veil. Her body so delicate and somehow virginal. So different from Walsh whom he had accidentally glimpsed through a double reflection in the mantelpiece mirror and an opened wardrobe door as she stepped into the shower. Of similar height, but a more athletic build, the light had caught the muscled contours of her limbs.

Lily and Janie Walsh were two sides of the same coin. The two faces of China separated by a generation. Chinese Chinese and American Chinese. Both members of the same tribe, yet divided by their cultures. The old and the new. The shy and deferential and the confident and outgoing. One mentally tormented and imprisoned by her own people; one happy and truly free.

370

Yang and Yin, he mused, and swallowed the last of the whiskey. Tomorrow could change all that.

Lily Cheung awoke in a cold sweat. It was still dark outside but after a disturbed night of shallow fitful dozing, she knew she would not get back to sleep.

She got up, checked that Bao was curled up and content with his thumb in his mouth in the bed next to hers, pulled a dressing gown over her nightdress and went into the kitchen. Her stomach churned with apprehension and the very thought of breakfast made her feel sick. She made some herbal tea and, nursing the cup in her hands, looked out of the window as the steely dawn light began to draw the ugly sprawl of urban Beijing out of the shadows.

It was overcast, the clouds murky and oppressive and a fine drizzle fell. Was today really the day, she asked herself silently? Or was she just dreaming that this was what it would be like, as she had dreamed it so many times over the past few weeks? What was it Mama Cheung always used to say when she was a child? Pinch yourself and see if it is real.

But Lily didn't need to pinch herself. She knew full well that this was the day and it was all too real.

Turning her head a fraction, she could see the line of workers' concrete apartment blocks spread out towards Beijing centre. Alongside were the skeletal steel power pylons, the tangled strings of telephone cable and the canal, all disappearing towards the capital. That was where everything was happening. Where it would happen today.

Where John Dancer would be waking in his flat. The flat where he had made love to her so gently and considerately on several occasions now. He seemed to sense it was not easy for her, that she was crossing both a mental and cultural divide. He had been patient and tolerant, careful to find out what she liked and what she didn't. Only at the end, before he climaxed into her and she contracted in response, did he dig his fingernails into her so hard that it

371

had scored her flesh, leaving behind a hairline of blood. Arching her neck, she had reached up to kiss his forehead. She smiled now at the memory. How she had kissed him to tell him it was all right, that she enjoyed feeling the pain of his passion for her.

Suddenly sl.. heard his voice. 'Good morning, lotus blossom. There's no need to be afraid.' The words were so loud and clear in her head, teasing her the way he did, that she could almost believe he was in the room.

Now she knew he was also awake. That he had slept badly too despite drinking heavily. She'd noticed that about him. How often he drank when it got late into the night, as if he knew the memories that haunted him wouldn't go until the dawn.

'I'm not afraid, John.' Her voice, talking to her own ghostly reflection in the window glass, was barely audible. 'I know you'll look after me.'

Twenty minutes later, she was washed, dressed in a grey two-piece business suit and had pinned up her hair with a tortoiseshell clip. Mama Cheung emerged blearily from the bedroom and observed her daughter's small grip and document case. 'You look very smart, daughter, I'm proud of you. Enjoy yourself in Hong Kong.'

Lily forced a smile. 'I will, Mama.'

'And watch that old rogue Wang. Make sure he doesn't try his old tricks while he's away from his wife.'

'I don't think Wang will give me any trouble in Hong Kong.' She kissed her mother on the cheek. 'Thank you for looking after Bao while I'm gone.'

'Isn't that what mothers are for?'

They laughed together until the toot of a horn outside announced that the car had arrived to take Lily to Wang's house and on to the airport. On her way to the front door, she passed Jin's shrine and hesitated. His photograph looked up at her and she said quietly: 'This is your day, Jin. Today I do what I do for you. Tomorrow your spirit will be free.'

'Lily?' Her mother asked. 'Are you all right?'

'Never better, Mama,' she smiled broadly. 'I'll see you in a few days. 'Bye.'

It was a relief as the door slammed shut behind her. Now she was on her own; no more distractions. She took a deep breath to steady herself and started down the concrete steps to the lobby. The pool driver glowered at her, although she'd hardly kept him waiting. He clearly didn't think much of running round after a woman and certainly not one who was not one of the cadre élites. In return she treated him with frosty disdain, so they both understood each other perfectly.

Wang was waiting with two enormous suitcases at the gateway in the high wall that surrounded his smart house in the inner suburbs. You'd have thought he was going away for months, Lily mused, not just a few days. In fact, he would be going away for much, much longer than he realised.

It was something of a circus when they arrived at the airport. Red carpets were already laid outside the Beijing terminal building in anticipation of the arrival of the Politburo motorcade. Crash barriers kept rubbernecks at bay and there was a special media pen with a rostrum at the back for TV news crews and an array of flash photographers under colourful golf umbrellas at the front, all hoping for some shots of big names in the run-up to the rolling coverage of the Hong Kong Airport opening.

Their car pulled up outside the VIP entrance guarded by armed police. The driver put on a show of lifting the luggage on to a trolley, which Wang told Lily to look after while he waved at the crowds and at the popping flashguns of the cameras. It was crazy, Lily thought, because no one would have a clue who he was. Plain-clothes security men with walkie-talkies and heavy shapes bulging in their armpits shrieked excitedly at Wang, telling him to get a move on. The Politburo and its entourage was at the airport approaches.

Wang walked on imperiously, still waving, and indicated to Lily to follow him inside. She struggled, pushing with all her might to get the trolley moving. It weighed a ton with Wang's two bulging cases, her own grip and document case and, balanced precariously on the top, the burgundy leather briefcase. Lily's gaze was fixed on it, terrified it would fall, not knowing what might happen if it did. Suddenly the trolley veered sideways. She was struggling now – and sweating.

'Here, let me help.'

She turned. It was Yan Tao. He inclined his head courteously, his eyes hidden by the myriad rainspecks on the lenses of his steel-rimmed glasses.

'That's most kind.' She noticed he was carrying a sports-bag and a briefcase identical to Wang's. He found a place for his bag on the trolley and handed her the briefcase.

They walked on together in silence and joined a short queue in front of a special VIP desk where staff were checking names and issuing specially numbered security lapel badges. 'Cheung Mei-ling,' Lily said. 'I'm travelling with Wang Hu of the CAAC.'

The security clerk nodded, ticked her name and handed her a badge. 'Wear this at all times to and from Hong Kong. Follow the signs for Aircraft A.'

She hung back until Yan joined her. He smiled quickly. 'I'm Aircraft B.' Meaning so far, so good.

They were approaching the special security check for the VIP flights to Hong Kong, a knot of people forming by the metal-detector arch and the X-ray machine. Yan took his briefcase back from Lily and glanced at his watch. As he did so, his mobile telephone rang and relief showed on his face as he pulled it from his pocket. 'Hello. What? Yes, I see.' He beckoned to another member of the Public Information Office who was also in the queue. 'I understand. Goodbye.'

The other press relations officer was an older man with a mean, pinched face. 'What is it, Yan Tao?'

'That was the office. I've got to go back. There's some problem with clearance for tomorrow's speeches. I'll have to get a later flight, but would you mind taking my luggage on for me. Something less to worry about.'

A small sportsbag and a briefcase: it wasn't much to ask. The other man didn't look the sort who liked doing anyone favours and he hesitated.

'I'd be so grateful,' Yan pressed. 'I will owe you a favour.'

'A big one,' the other man replied without a smile.

Yan thanked him and rejoined Lily. 'Actually, that was John on the phone. He said to tell you good luck. I'll be outside at the taxi rank.'

Then he was gone.

The queue was shortening, Wang's huge key ring, fancy cigarette case and lighter, and fresh-breath spray were now sending the metal detector into a frenzy of buzzing. Security men rushed forward to frisk him and empty out his pockets. Lily's heart fluttered in her chest like a small bird.

'Hello, Lily.' She jumped and turned. It was Brigadier Ting Han-chen. He smiled. 'I didn't mean to startle you. May I?'

Stupidly, Lily was too shocked to say anything as Ting took the briefcase from the top of the trolley and placed it on the rubber conveyer belt of the X-ray machine. He added her small grip, then struggled with Wang's huge cases.

'You're most kind,' she said at last.

Ting was just getting his breath back. 'Your boss likes to travel light, I see.'

She forced a smile. 'He doesn't like to wear the same suit to more than one reception.'

'No doubt one of his ancestors was a former Emperor of China.'

Part hysteria and part genuine amusement at visualising Wang in such a role made Lily giggle and blush. 'I don't think so.'

375

'Enjoy Hong Kong, Lily. We will speak again on your return.'

She nodded and on reflex gave a sort of bobbing curtsy.

A voice shouted from the television screen behind the X-ray machine. 'Whose is this?'

The security man was holding up the burgundy briefcase. Lily's heart stopped, literally. She was aware of two or three beats missing before it kicked in again. There was no option but for her to hold up her hand.

'Come through,' ordered the official.

Lily pushed forward through the metal-detector arch. The buzzer didn't go and on the other side she found that the man had the briefcase open on a trestle table where suspicious luggage was being checked. 'This is your briefcase?'

'Actually it belongs to my boss, Wang Hu, Assistant Deputy Director of the CAAC.'

The official wasn't impressed as he lifted out a sheaf of documents to expose the laptop computer that sat snugly in its special compartment. 'We have to check all electrical goods.'

'Yes?'

'In case they are concealed bombs.'

For a moment she thought she was going to throw up there and then. 'Oh?'

He lifted out the offending laptop and scrutinised it carefully from several angles, then switched it on. The screen flickered into life and the icons of the program manager appeared. Seemingly satisfied, he snapped it off and tried to force it back into its compartment.

'Wrong way,' she breathed.

It snapped back into place, the documents were returned, the lid shut and the official lost interest. Lily picked it up and went to the end of the conveyer belt where baggage handlers were loading all the VIPs' luggage on to large trolley cages. Wang was looking anxiously about him.

'Ah, Lily, *there* you are!'

'Yes, sir. And here is your briefcase.' She held it out for him.

He looked irritated. 'Yes, yes, of course it's my briefcase. Now bring it along, will you. We'll be boarding in a moment.'

'No, sir, you don't understand. I've got a migraine, a head like thunder. It will explode at any moment.'

Wang pursed his lips in exasperation. 'I see. Well, hurry up and you can go to sleep on the aircraft. You'll soon be fine.'

She shook her head vehemently. 'No, not when it's like this. It hurts too much to sleep. I have to lie down in a dark room. It could be a day before it passes.'

'What are you suggesting?'

'I'm saying, sir, that I have to go home. Now.' Again she thrust his briefcase at him and this time he accepted it.

Picking up her grip, she smiled briefly and turned, walking away as fast as she could without actually running. She was frantic, her pulse racing and the rush of blood loud in her ears as she pushed her way against the flow of the crowd. There were several hundred VIP passengers, selected from the ruling cadres to join the Politburo in Hong Kong because they had a function to perform or as a reward for their loyalty or efficiency. There was a scattering of PLA uniforms with their pancake caps to be seen amongst dull civilian suits. She recognised the face of one of them from the newspapers. His name was General Sun, a senior air force commander from Xingjiang province. He was laughing and joking with some fellow officers as he passed and it reminded her that, apart from the two Politburo aircraft, there were several military transports on the tarmac which would also be making the journey to Hong Kong.

She was breathless by the time she reached the exit. There, the police were holding back a growing crowd of onlookers as the first limousine in the Politburo cavalcade pulled up by the red carpet. Quickly she veered away, seeking out the taxi rank, feeling that all eyes were on her.

Then she spotted Yan Tao, standing on tiptoe as he searched for her over the heads of the crowd. Suddenly he recognised her, waved and beckoned eagerly for her to hurry. She ducked and weaved until she reached him. Already he had a taxi door open and she scrambled in. He followed quickly and the taxi pulled away.

For a moment she and Yan looked at each other in disbelieving silence. Both began to shake their heads and smile. At what they'd done, at what they'd got away with. And, without thinking, fell into each other's arms. Hugging for a moment, Lily then quite deliberately kissed Yan on the lips.

She pulled back and smiled, her eyes alight. 'That's to say sorry. For how I've wronged you, and to thank you for giving me courage today.'

Neither had looked back. If they had, they might have seen Brigadier Ting Han-chen push his way through the taxi queue to the edge of the pavement.

'Damn! Did you see who was with her?'

There was no reply, so he turned round. The diminutive Inspector Xia was trying to keep up, wheezing furiously and sweltering in his raincoat and trilby hat.

Ting repeated his question.

'I don't know his name, but I recognised him. He works for the Public Information Office.'

Ting nodded. Now it all made sense.

Abe Stone dumped the bottle unceremoniously on the table in the secure suite. 'Moët and Chandon '85. Does fizzy wine improve with age?'

'I'm sure it does,' Janie Walsh said with a tense smile. 'Which is more than can be said for Langley's old-timers, Abe. You told John you were leaving on a flight yesterday.'

'I lied. Didn't want to miss the party.'

'It's a bit premature for a party.'

Dancer glanced at the wall clock. 'Coming up to twelve

noon. The Politburo flights were delayed forty-five minutes, so we should know soon enough. The time-frame for them reaching the triggering location over Jiangxi has another seven or eight minutes to run. If we don't hear by then, we *know* something's gone wrong.'

'Sod it,' McVicar said. 'Let's open the bubbly anyway. I'm parched.'

'Yeah, sod it,' Stone agreed, 'why not? If things *do* go pear-shaped, we'll *never* get to drink it.'

Seconds later the cork popped, narrowly missing Walsh and bouncing off the ceiling to titters of nervous laughter. A stream of white bubbles frothed out in its wake. 'Lousy shot,' she chided. 'Is that why you left Langley?'

Stone gave a bittersweet smile. 'Bit more serious than that, young 'un,' he said darkly and steered the neck of the bottle in the direction of her glass. 'And I wasn't pushed. I jumped.'

'Oops,' she said. 'Obviously a sensitive spot.'

'I'll tell you about it sometime.' He turned to Dancer. 'So no hitches at the airport this morning?'

'Apparently not. Yan Tao phoned in earlier. He went with Lily by taxi to pick up her son from school and dropped them at the railway station. In another couple of hours, Lily and Little Bao will be at Beidaihe.'

Stone frowned. 'The coast resort? Why there?'

'Wang's got a new holiday home there and Lily's got a key. He was hoping to set up a love nest with her. It's the safest place we could think of, well away from the action. Meanwhile, Yan's with some of Mike Jiang's snakeheads outside the Public Information Office.'

His partner nodded with considered approval. 'All sounds tickety-boo.'

The 'receive' indicator light on McVicar's portable MEL sky-wave set began blinking.

'Incoming,' he announced coolly.

All eyes turned to watch as he sat down and began working the keyboard. The 'burst transmission' had been bounced across the stratosphere from SAS headquarters in Hereford, the signal electronically encrypted and squeezed into a split second's worth of sending time in the 1.5 to 40 MHz frequency band which was received by a length of aerial wire spooled out in the office loft space.

McVicar keyed in the instructions to expand the signal and decode, then waited for what seemed a very long few seconds before the words displayed on the small screen. He read it out aloud as the others gathered around. 'Green X-Ray to Yellow Alpha One. Confirmation received from our cousins as follows. One gift received at party time. Repeat, one gift received at party time. Awaiting news update. Meanwhile prepare to leave the party pending further instructions. Advise latest from your end and your view of action to take.'

'Shit!' Walsh said.

'What the hell does all that mean?' Dancer asked.

The CIA controller said, 'The National Security Agency can only confirm that one of the two aircraft bombs has gone off at the confirmed GPS position over Jiangxi. Of course, it doesn't mean the second one *hasn't* gone off, just that it's not confirmed.'

'We've been ordered to prepare for a mission abort,' McVicar added, 'pending clarification of the situation.'

Dancer was stunned. He just could not bring himself to believe it had gone wrong like this. Just typical if it was the high-tech stuff that had dropped them in it from a great height. And if just one bomb had gone off, what the hell did it mean? Immediately he thought of Wang and, perversely, hoped the old bastard had survived. But if the report was right, at least half the Politburo members had survived. But which ones? Old Chicom hardliners or more modern reformists? Probably a mix. This was going to be a horrible mess now and no mistake.

The whole underground movement poised on hold. The poet Fan Xiu Kun about to be released from his tormentors in the gulag after fifteen years – all for nothing.

And now they would be in grave danger as the state apparatus began its inevitable knee-jerk reaction. Immediately he thought of Lily and little Bao sitting on the train to Beidaihe, oblivious of the catastrophe that was about to unfold.

'What the hell do we do now?' Abe Stone asked.

'Finish that friggin' champagne,' was McVicar's considered reply.

Fourteen

'Turn the radio on,' Walsh said. 'See if there's anything on the news.'

As Stone obliged, Dancer crossed the room to the desk that served as their communications centre. Next to McVicar's sky-wave link with Hereford sat the GMP2000 portable satellite phone. Since identical sets had been distributed to each of the provincial heads of the freedom movement, the system was now their secure communications link in-country.

Dancer tapped Yan Tao's number into the keypad on the handset. At the other end, the press officer snatched up his handset almost immediately. '*Red Zero Foxtrot.*'

'Yellow Alpha One here,' Dancer confirmed. 'Are you in position?'

'*Of course.*' Terse. Meaning he was sitting in an RTS Triad van opposite the Public Information Office with half-a-dozen of Mike Jiang's armed thugs. '*What's happening? Cars have been arriving here. Some of my superiors who were supposed to be flying to Hong Kong have returned.*'

Dammit, Dancer cursed. 'Only one briefcase went off. At least that's what we think.'

Yan said quickly: '*Let me go into my office and find out what is going on. I can walk in alone as if nothing has happened. Play the innocent. Then get back to you.*'

'Definitely not,' Dancer snapped. 'If you're caught, you'll compromise the entire movement.'

Yan sounded desperate. '*And what will that matter?*'

'Because you can fight another day.' The silence was brittle with no response from the Chinese leader. 'Do you hear me?'

'*I hear you.*'

'Get Jiang's men to drive you immediately to the safe house. Meet up with Lily and stay put until you're contacted.'

A pause, then, *'Yes, I understand.'*

Dancer hung up. In the background he could hear the discordant strains of Chinese opera coming from the radio as Stone tried to tune in a station.

'What did Yan say?' Walsh asked.

'People from the aircraft have been returning to the Public Information Office. I've told him to pull out to the fall-back RV. He's one unhappy bunny.'

'Then it sounds like the NSA is right. Just one bomb went off.'

Abe Stone waved from the other side of the room. 'Quiet! It's a newsflash!' He turned up the volume as the anxious faces turned in his direction.

The voice of the announcer was very solemn. *'It is our sad duty to report the news of a tragic air crash in the Luoxiao mountains in Jiangxi province. The military transport aircraft was carrying senior Liberation Army commanders to take part in the celebrations for the opening of Phase Two of Hong Kong Airport. The accident took place on a remote hillside and it is not yet possible to confirm if there are any survivors. One of the passengers is believed to have been much respected PLA Air Force commander, General Sun Lihua. Members of the Politburo, now in Hong Kong themselves, have promised a top-level investigation into the cause of the crash. We will bring more news as soon as it is available.'* It cut abruptly back into the plaintive wail of operatic voices.

'Christ,' Walsh said. 'General Sun.'

Dancer stared at the radio set, simply not believing. 'How the hell did that happen? They called it a military transport, not a VIP Boeing . . . and Sun wasn't to be on one of the Boeings anyway.'

'Remember we were talking about embuggerance,' McVicar said. 'If something can go wrong it will – but in a way you least expect.'

Walsh shook her head. 'Well, it makes my decision easier. Signal HQ, give them the news and tell them I recommend an immediate abort and exfil.'

'Aye, boss.' The Scotsman turned back to the sky-wave to encrypt a suitable message.

The CIA controller looked at Dancer. 'We don't know how much the Chinese have uncovered, John, but we must assume the whole operation is compromised until we hear differently. I'm pulling out with Dave within the hour. We'll get Mike Jiang's RTS snakeheads to run us down to Captain Song's village and arrange to link up with *Manta* tonight. Meanwhile, can you take a train and meet up with Lily and Yan Tao at Wang's holiday villa? Do some baby-sitting, hold their hands. I'll get Jiang to have transport provided for you tomorrow to get down to Song for a rendezvous with *Manta* tomorrow night.'

Dancer frowned. 'Yan might not want to go. He can be pretty stubborn.'

Anger flashed in Walsh's eyes. 'Then persuade him. We need to preserve his knowledge and his membership lists so we can try again in the future. He can serve his country better now from the outside than from within. My orders are not to leave him behind. Do whatever it takes.'

It was a chilling throwaway remark, especially coming from Walsh. Langley knew almost as much about Yan's movement as Yan did, so Yan was expendable. In fact, now he was a liability. Dancer caught the expression on Abe Stone's face and he could read it like a book. *Remember Laos. Those bastards never change.*

But Dancer just said, 'What about Abe?'

'Abe shouldn't be here,' she replied tersely. 'He should have left yesterday.'

Everyone knew what she meant; it wasn't the CIA's problem. Official.

Stone stood up suddenly. 'I don't take orders from you, Janie, or those motherfuckers at Langley. I've helped out because John's a pal. I don't want your thanks. Which is just as well, because I don't think I'm gonna get any.' He snatched his tatty straw trilby from the table and moved towards the door.

Dancer was on his feet. 'Hang on, Abe. You can stick with me.'

'John,' Walsh called after him, 'don't be stupid.'

He turned. 'Abe helped us out when he didn't have to. Now, either he's pulled out with the team or else he and I will take our own chances. Maybe overland to Pakistan.'

She could imagine Frank Aspen's apoplexy at being told that. 'I don't think my boss would be very happy.' The smile fizzed and sparkled briefly. 'Operational decision. Abe can pull out with you.' She took a Chinese-made automatic from the table. 'Here, you'll want this.'

'No, Janie, if I ever need to use that, I'll already be so deep in the shit I'll never get out.'

She regarded him in silence for a moment, then nodded. 'Your decision. We'll be gone from here shortly. If you need to contact me, go through Bill at the embassy, okay?'

'Okay.'

Her smile returned. 'Good luck.'

'Yeah.' A reluctant, lazy half-grin appeared on Dancer's lips as he picked up the portable satellite case. 'Break a leg.'

He turned and pushed through the door. Stone was waiting on the other side. 'Bad move getting involved with those bastards, John.'

Dancer hesitated on the steps. 'Too late to tell me that. Twenty-five years too late.'

'Xin-Bin's at the airport with an ExecFlight plane waiting.'

'What?' Dancer had been out of touch with the day-to-day running of their commercial business. 'I didn't think we had anything running today.'

'We don't.' Stone jerked a thumb over his shoulder. 'But I half-expected Langley would dump on me when it suited. This used to be my game too. So I made my own arrangements just in case. Planned to fly with Xin-Bin to one of the western provinces, then take a hike to the border. So now you can forget the train to Wang's villa. We can take the plane.'

'What would I do without you?'

'Be in the admin mess you were in when I first joined you.'

Dancer grinned. 'You love paperwork, Abe. I hate it.'

'And I hate wasting half my life sleeping, son, but it's gotta be done.' They stepped out into the street. 'Do you think there's any real chance the Chinese will be on to the connection with us?'

'Personally, I doubt it,' Dancer answered. 'There's been a tragic plane crash, that's all. Even if there's clear evidence of sabotage, there's no reason for them to be looking for a bomb on the second aircraft that landed without incident. They're not to know the second briefcase malfunctioned. Even if they decide to go through all the luggage on the second plane for suspect devices, it's well disguised. It would take experts days to inspect every item of baggage and its contents. And only Wang's briefcase could lead them to us. And as yet, we don't even know if it was Wang's aircraft that went down.'

Stone grimaced. 'That would be some compensation for this. Get Wang off our backs.'

'You are a sweet-natured ol' softie really, aren't you?' Dancer laughed as his partner scowled. 'I need to go to my apartment on the way to the airport. Collect a few things.'

'Okay. But we take a taxi. You're not getting me on a bloody bicycle.'

Wang Hu sat miserably on the straw-stuffed mattress on the cell floor and hugged his knees. He rocked slowly back and forth, wailing quietly to himself.

The secret police, or whoever they were, had stripped him naked, shone a torch up his arse and prodded about a bit before handing him threadbare prison fatigues and removing the laces from his shoes. That had been two hours ago – or was it three? – when they'd first dragged him here from the airport and dumped him in this cell with its damp-stained concrete walls and stink of enamel pisspots. What was worse was that no one would tell him what he was supposed to have done wrong. All he knew was that it was something to do with his smart burgundy briefcase which had been seized by security men at the airport just before his arrest.

Door bolts were suddenly shoved back and the metal door groaned open on unoiled hinges. 'C'mon, Fat Wang!' called one of the two guards who entered. 'On your feet. You're not out of trouble yet!'

Wang was quaking so much he had to be helped up and supported as they walked down corridors of discoloured white bathhouse tiles under the fitful blink of fluorescent tubes. The stale air still smelled of the cabbage soup that had been served up earlier.

After passing through several open-barred gates that divided the corridors into sections, they entered what appeared to be an administration area. Police officers in both uniforms and civilian clothes hung around their grey metal desks chatting, smoking or drinking tea. One or two were typing reports on to ancient typewriters and another had his nose buried in a lurid comic. No doubt one of the new sex-and-violence magazines flooding the country of late, thought Wang, and no doubt confiscated and then resold by the obscene publications squad.

'You're wanted for an interview,' one of his guards said. 'Don't worry, we've had no orders to execute you yet.'

The other man laughed as Wang groaned, 'Very amusing.'

They arrived at yet another anonymous grey steel door. Inside was another concrete floor strewn with cigarette ends and candy wrappers and more glazed tile walls. Additionally, there was a table with a fake wooden top in plastic and a couple of tubular steel chairs. Wang recognised the man in a very smart grey suit and gold-rimmed spectacles who stood smoking, waiting for him. Brigadier Ting Han-chen. Momentarily his spirits lifted, but the man did not smile and appeared deep in thought as Wang's arrival distracted him.

'Ah, yes, Wang Hu. Please sit down.'

The hapless prisoner had no option as the two guards virtually threw him into the spare chair which looked in danger of buckling under his weight.

'You seemed in a bit of a daze at the time of your arrest at the airport, Wang.' The interviewer regarded him through a cloud of tobacco smoke. 'We've searched your house and found many items of interest. Lists of what appear to be the contraband goods we discovered there will be passed on to the anti-corruption police. No doubt they will want to question you in due course. But, in the meantime, we must continue to investigate your involvement in this conspiracy.'

Wang didn't really understand. 'What conspiracy?'

Ting put out his cigarette in an old jam-jar lid that served as an ashtray. 'Let me explain. Last night we received intelligence that there was a CIA plot afoot to plant bombs aboard two aircraft carrying our honorable leaders to Hong Kong. It was to coincide with a general uprising of the public and an attempt by senior military dissidents to seize power.' Wang's eyes bulged in wonder at how close he himself had come to death and then horror as he realised he was now in the shadow of the gallows. Ting took his time, lighting a fresh cigarette. 'Our source had no details. So through the night the VIP aircraft were stripped and searched for bombs. Nothing was found. It was decided that someone must be smuggling them aboard in the luggage this morning. Again we found nothing, until it caught my attention that two people were leaving the airport at almost the same time. Yan Tao of the Public Information Office and your personal assistant Cheung Mei-ling.'

'Lily? Yes, she had a migraine.'

'That's what she told you.' Why did Ting's smile unsettle him so much, Wang wondered? 'That's when we discovered the two briefcases. Yours and the one belonging to Mr Yan that he had left with a fellow passenger before departing. Our bomb-disposal experts examined it and found the laptop contained what is called a global positioning device and a detonator. Special explosive was sealed in the frame. It went through security totally undetected.'

Wang was astounded once again. 'The bomb was in my briefcase? I had no idea! Oh, by the souls of my ancestors, you must believe me!'

Ting said, 'Well, we know how the briefcase came into your possession, don't we?'

Panic showed in Wang's eyes. 'Yes, you know it was given to me by that American, John Dancer, my business partner.'

'And your business partner is obviously a CIA agent.'

The brigadier smiled; he rather liked seeing people sweat with fear. He was fascinated by how it diminished them.

'I had no idea the briefcase contained a bomb. Or that the American was, I suppose, a spy.'

Another smile from Ting. 'Well, Wang Hu, it's true I'm told you are more interested in receiving money from Dancer's company than actually earning it.'

'I want nothing more to do with that company, believe me!'

'Oh, I do. But what about your brother, Xin-Bin? I believe he actually works in the company?'

'Yes, you should speak to him.'

'I intend to. But first things first. You told me Dancer gave you the briefcase as a business gift.'

'Yes, in thanks for all I have done for him.' Wang looked sheepish. 'At least that's what he told me. Obviously it was for a different reason.'

'Obviously,' Ting agreed. 'Even you, Wang Hu, would not be stupid enough to blow yourself up.'

Wang was about to protest when he realised what the

brigadier had just admitted. 'There, you see, how can I be part of this conspiracy? I should be released immediately.'

Ting gave him a withering glare. 'Don't take me for a fool, Wang. I think you were involved in this conspiracy all right. You'd be in a position to become a very rich man if China abandoned Communism. But you didn't realise you were being double-crossed and used by the Americans. Perhaps you just didn't realise Dancer was duping you into becoming a human bomb.'

'That's nonsense.'

Ting pressed on like a tank; nothing was going to deter him now. 'I think you were in on this with your brother, with Dancer, with Yan Tao and with Cheung Mei-ling!'

'No, it's not true.'

'Where is Lily Cheung now?'

Wang had begun to snivel. 'I don't know. At her home.'

'The police have called. She isn't there. And she collected her son from school. We have brought her mother in for questioning, but so far she denies everything.'

'Well, *I* don't know where she is,' Wang sobbed, anger and frustration overcoming him.

'Somebody told me you have been allocated a holiday home. To go with your new post. Is this true?'

'Yes, a villa on the coast. In the resort of Beidaihe. Why?'

'Do you have keys?'

'Yes, why?' Wang repeated.

'Because it will have to be searched for evidence of your involvement in this conspiracy.' He handed Wang a pen. 'Write down the address.'

'How long will your investigation go on?' Wang asked plaintively as he scribbled. 'After all, you foiled the foreign devils' plot, didn't you?'

Ting leaned forward until his face was mere inches from the miserable not-so-soon-to-be deputy director. 'Oh, of course, I'm forgetting you do not know.'

'Know what?'

'That mysteriously your briefcase found its way on to a

military aircraft carrying General Sun who was involved in your conspiracy. It blew up where you intended the Politburo's planes should crash.'

Wang was aghast. 'How could that happen?'

'I hoped you might volunteer to tell me. So, you see, my inquiries will go on for as long as it takes to unearth the truth. Until I've spoken to everyone who has ever had the remotest connection with you. And that's before I think of letting the anti-corruption police get their hands on you.' He went to the door and called the guards. 'Take him back to his cell.'

The brigadier watched him disappear down the corridor. He almost felt sorry for Wang; the man's life would never be the same again. Almost sorry, but not quite. Wang might be innocent, but Wang was also the ideal fall guy. Eventually he would be charged with blowing up General Sun's plane. An inspired and neat conclusion really, and personally approved by that canny old-timer, General Peng of the PLA Air Force, who had uncovered the plot.

Feeling quite pleased with himself, Ting walked across to a table where four police officers were playing rummy while they ate their lunch from a takeaway bag of steamed meat balls and dumplings. One of them wore a wide-brimmed trilby.

The inspector looked up, and placed his hand of cards on the table. 'Sir?'

'Xia, it seems you were right about the American all along. I want him arrested and everyone who works for him brought in for questioning.'

The squat detective was on his feet in an instant. 'I'll send units to both his offices and his apartment. He won't get far.'

'Is there an airport at Beidaihe?'

'The resort? No, but nearby at Qinhuangdao.'

'Fine,' Ting said. 'Book us on a flight this afternoon. Have the senior Bureau policeman there to meet us when we land.'

Frank Aspen from Langley was waiting impatiently with Dawson outside the monkey house at Beijing Zoo. He had his hands thrust deep in his overcoat pockets and his collar turned up against the marrow-chilling air blowing down from the distant Mongolian steppes.

He stamped his feet to warm them and stared gloomily at a group of children who were laughing as they poked sticks through the bars at the golden monkeys from Sichuan. 'I suppose the Brits can't tell us fuck all. They never can.'

Bear with a sore head, thought Dawson. Aspen always was when the shit hit the fan and it was coming in his direction. The man was looking for a scapegoat, he knew. 'The Brits've got their own assets, Frank, their own resources. Besides, like you, the boy Lansdowne's in town to keep an eye on things. He may be able to shed some light.'

Aspen grunted. 'My hunch is Dancer's the only one who can do that. And there's no way anyone from the embassy's going to contact him now.' It was an unnecessary thing to say. They all knew the rule: illegal activity always kept well distanced from the official and diplomatic, especially when things were going wrong. Denial, denial, denial. That was the only rule in the game. Even the British and American Embassies weren't communicating on the subject, in code or otherwise. There must be nothing to give the Chinese Communists any evidence to justify expelling diplomats. They could think the hell what they liked as long as they couldn't prove anything.

So now it was down to chance encounters while feeding the ducks together in the park. Or a visit to the zoo.

'Here they are now,' Dawson said.

Iona Moncrieff in a long black overcoat that reached her ankles was almost as tall as Lansdowne, whose only concession to the cold was his old Eton scarf wrapped round his neck and stuffed between the lapels of his suit jacket. They walked together, engaged in earnest conversation, their hair tossed and matted by the nagging wind.

Iona appeared to notice the Americans only at the last moment. 'Hello, Bill. Nice surprise. Think you both know Piers Lansdowne?' It was all an act, of course, for any Security snoop who might be loitering close by, but it irked Dawson to see his opposite number seeming so cool about the disaster that had befallen them.

Aspen clearly felt the same. 'Does anyone know what the hell's going on?'

'Too early to tell,' Iona replied. 'Let's walk. It's too cold to stand around.'

No one was arguing and they moved off slowly in a ragged line abreast, hunched against the raw chill. Eyes began to water in the wind.

Iona said, 'The last signal I received from McVicar via Hereford was that Lily Cheung and Yan Tao had cleared the airport. She's safely on a train to Beidaihe with her son and Yan was outside the Public Information Office when the news broke.'

Lansdowne added: 'He was ordered to abort and join Lily at Wang's villa. Dancer's planning to join them and help them out of the country. That was the last decision before Walsh closed down the ops centre. She and McVicar are with Captain Song's people now. They'll rendezvous with *Manta* tonight.'

'And Dancer and the others?'

Iona answered. 'Tomorrow night, if all goes to plan.'

'At least our crisis management seems up to speed,' Aspen observed bitterly. 'Which is more than can be said for the rest of this monumental fuck-up. How the hell did they get wind of General Sun's role in all this? He was your man, so it must be a leak from your side.'

Iona stopped beside a cage containing moth-eaten Tibetan donkeys. Her eyes fixed on the man from Langley. 'Balderdash, Frank. There's no *must* about it. Before you start pointing fingers, I don't think Sun was exclusively *our* man any more, d'you?' She turned to Dawson. 'In fact, I heard he'd become more *yours* than ours.'

Dawson hardly looked shamefaced; in fact his expression was rather smug. 'Sorry, Majesty. All's fair in love, war and business.'

'Don't know what you're talking about,' Aspen protested, starting to walk off.

The others quickened their pace to keep up with him and Lansdowne smiled. 'A small matter of a fighter aircraft contract with the new regime.'

Aspen waved that aside. He had all the oily skills of a politician when it came to ducking a challenge. 'It's all irrelevant now. Sun's just so much strawberry jam and we have to work out what the hell to do about it. We've still got two SBERs sitting in Party and PLA headquarters . . .'

'You mean you hope we have,' Lansdowne interrupted. 'There's no way of telling if they've been found.'

Aspen came back hard. 'Except by letting them off.'

Iona shook her head. 'We can't possibly do that now.'

'No?' Aspen's eyes seemed lit with evangelical fire. 'Hong Kong Airport opens today and we've got the Chinese invasion fleet approaching Taiwan. I think two SBERs sitting in Beijing might just come in useful right now.'

'Ah,' Lansdowne said, 'then you haven't heard.'

'Heard what, for Chrissakes?'

'The Taiwan invasion's been called off.'

Dawson frowned. 'How the hell do you know?'

Iona answered. 'A source close to the old Party leadership. And it's been confirmed by a Royal Navy reconnaissance aircraft earlier this morning. Landing ships turning back from the Chinese celebration regatta. No doubt the Pentagon will be telling you the same any time now.'

'It's all over,' Lansdowne said with an air of finality. 'It's just a question of damage limitation. How big are our losses and how compromised are the freedom movements?'

'General Sun's the worst loss,' Iona said.

Dawson shook his head. 'There'll be others to replace

him. I'm more concerned that Dancer's operation could have been exposed. That's taken years to build up.'

But Aspen had his own view. 'Dancer's been around too long, Bill. Since his wife died, he's become a burnt-out case. I was planning on cutting him loose anyway. Dump the Stonedancer outfit and set up a fresh front company. It's the information he's provided that counts, not the man himself. We can use that to reinvent something better.'

Dawson shuffled to a halt and glowered at his fellow American. 'Y'know, Frank, you really are the sweetest guy I know. With pals like you, who needs enemies?'

To Aspen it was like water off a duck's back. 'No room for sentiment in this game, Bill.' He was scathing. 'Do I really have to preach to the converted? We've only got one priority now. That's to preserve the integrity of Yan Tao's underground movement. We've got a copy of the membership list and what mustn't happen is for that to fall into Chicom hands. Or Yan, for that matter. Once he's out of the country, we can rest easy. We can try again in a year or two when the situation's right again.'

Even Lansdowne had to agree with that assessment. 'So the next thirty-six hours are crucial.'

'You can trust Dancer,' Dawson said and added pointedly, 'Burnt-out case or not, he'll get Yan Tao out.'

'I hope you're right,' Aspen muttered, glancing at his wristwatch. 'Time we were getting back. Need to keep abreast of developments.'

Dawson turned to Iona. 'Perhaps we should meet at close of play tonight? Compare notes.'

She smiled and understood. 'Good idea. I think we'll both be in need of a drink.'

The Americans left then and she and Lansdowne watched them walking briskly away between the cages. 'What breathtaking arrogance,' she murmured.

'Dawson?'

'Actually, I meant Aspen. Little shite.'

A bored, pacing snow leopard opened its jaws in a

nearby cage. It did not let rip a terrifying roar, but more a hideous wail of frustration and self-pity. The tragic noise reverberated through the stark landscape of concrete paths and steel bars. It could have been the animal's trapped spirit trying to escape. Or the spirit of a trapped nation.

'God, I hate this place,' she said.

Dancer told the taxi driver to drop them a block away from his apartment. 'Just in case,' he said to Stone.

They began walking along the crowded pavement, weaving between the oncoming stream of Chinese. 'I don't think they'll make a connection with us, John.'

'Nor do I, but it all depends where their information's coming from. Better safe than sorry.'

'Sure.'

They reached the corner and turned. Three police cars had slewed to a halt in front of the hotel, left abandoned with their doors wide open as the officers had raced to seal the place off. A couple of uniformed policemen in dark glasses stood by the vehicles. They looked decidedly edgy as they cradled sub-machine-guns in the crook of their arms. As a crowd of gaping onlookers started to form they were ushered angrily away.

'Christ,' Dancer breathed. 'Keep walking!'

Instinctively they swerved in a different direction and their pace quickened to cross the mouth of the intersection and get out of view as soon as possible without drawing attention to themselves. A battered taxi swung round the corner without signalling, narrowly missing Stone. The driver hit his horn, but didn't slow. No one seemed to be paying attention.

Dodging the second stream of cars, trucks and weaving bicycles, they reached the far sidewalk and the cover of the corner building. For several minutes as they continued walking, they expected to hear the sound of a policeman's whistle or a voice shouting after them. Gradually they were overcome by a sense of relief.

'Was there anything incriminating left there?' Stone asked.

Dancer shook his head. 'No, any remaining stuff was dumped in the past few days. It was just a few personal things.'

Stone guessed. 'That photograph of Debs?'

His friend shrugged. 'Maybe it's time I let go.'

'Maybe it is, pal, maybe it is.' He shuffled to a halt and began looking round for a vacant taxi. 'Sooner we get to the airport the better.'

'They're looking for us, Abe. I've got a passport in another name, but they'll just pick you up if you try to board.'

Stone patted his breast pocket. 'Old dogs and old tricks, John. When I offered to help you, I also took a couple of precautions. Like a false passport and getting some gold coin. I've still got some useful friends in Laos. Those guys can forge anything and it doesn't cost a fortune.' Just then a dilapidated taxi pulled up, its rear door kept closed by a loop of string. 'Airport, friend, at the speed of light.'

The scrawny, toothless driver in a grubby old Mao jacket thought that a huge joke and stamped the accelerator to the floor. They took off like a back-firing rocket, pushing their way into the torrent of traffic.

Dancer lit a cigarette, then wiped a streak of grime from the window so that he could see out. He wondered if he was seeing Beijing for the last time and, once more, wondered why he was so fascinated by the place. Why he loved the way the grinding grey monotony of its recent architecture sat at such odds with the Imperial splendour of its past. A land of contradictions, like the people themselves. He thought momentarily of his friends in the morning *t'ai chi* class that he hadn't attended now for several weeks. Mr Ren the butcher, 'Shanghai Joe' the market trader and Mr Liu with his telephone pager. Through them, he'd witnessed the gradual change in Chinese life. The slow, shifting sea change that was closing the gap of centuries faster than anyone would have ever dreamed possible. If he couldn't come back, he knew he would miss them. Miss them, but never forget them. He smiled to himself in his own reflection as he remembered many small and insignificant instances, small gestures of friendship and concern from a people whose culture made it hard for them to show emotion.

'By the way,' Stone said suddenly, his voice breaking into Dancer's thoughts. 'I've split with Ding.'

That was a surprise. 'You never said.'

'You had enough on your plate.'

'I thought you two were made for each other.'

'You said she was a petulant old dragon.'

Dancer smiled. 'Exactly.'

'We'd been falling apart for months. Then she started complaining about all this extra work I've been putting in. I couldn't stand it. She went back to her family last week.'

'And you?'

'If we're finished here, I thought I'd go back to Laos for a while. Take another shot at finding Bambi or Lindy-lou.'

'Is that wise?'

'Probably not.' He thought for a moment. 'You could come too. Chill out awhile. You need the break. Maybe we could set up some business, run a bar.'

Dancer smiled. 'I'll think about it.'

Then the dream dissolved into unnerving reality as the airport terminal came into view. Dancer was aware of his pulse quickening. The taxi pulled in and Stone paid it off while Dancer scanned the scene of scurrying humanity for signs of danger. It could have been his imagination, but there seemed to be more armed police than usual and he could see an armoured car parked near the Arrivals entrance. The crew were sitting relaxed on the turret, smoking and reading newpapers without any apparent concern. Low-profile stuff, a precaution, he decided.

'How's it looking?' Stone asked.

'Okay, I think.' Dancer removed his fedora, rolled it

tightly and stuffed it into the pocket of his linen jacket. That hat was his hallmark; no need to advertise his presence. As a coach party of European tourists walked by, hauling luggage and carrying souvenir pandas, Dancer nodded to his friend and they merged in with the crowd.

Once inside the terminal, they slipped away towards the special VIP gate. Now Dancer's heart was really pounding and he was not surprised to notice Stone, too, was sweating heavily. He felt better when he saw that it was not regular airport security staff checking passports and tickets, but an armed Bureau policeman.

He had a mean youthful face, pitted with acne, and anthracite eyes that showed no emotion. 'Name?'

'Crawford. R. ExecFlight EF106.'

The policeman regarded Dancer with a long, penetrating gaze as though trying to face him down, then consulted his list. He drew a tick beside the name and ushered him through. There was no problem with the security checks, although a mild interest was shown in Dancer's portable satellite phone in its smart aluminium case. As neither man had luggage, they were soon through to the departure lounge where it was a relief to be met by Xin-Bin.

He was smiling nervously. 'Good to see you, boss. I phoned all passengers scheduled for this flight and cancelled. You have it all to yourselves. The pilot is waiting.'

'No problems?'

Xin-Bin shook his head. 'Not really. There is much confusion and security personnel are squabbling over who does what. Some police were asking after you and Mr Stone earlier, but they went off.'

'I think we're just ahead of the game,' Stone said. 'There'd been a police raid on John's apartment—'

Xin-Bin cut back in, 'Then the sooner you are airborne the better.'

Dancer said, 'I wish you could come with us.'

'No, I have my wife and child to look after. I'll go back

to the office now. I'll be okay, I'm the innocent party. I cannot be blamed for the actions of my foreign devil bosses. I expect my brother Wang will have some grand idea about taking over your business.' He gave a sheepish smile. 'Despite his evil and corrupt ways, I am pleased his life was spared. I just hope he doesn't make mine a misery.'

Dancer shook the young man's hand. 'Thanks for all you've done.'

'No, sir. It has been my honour to have worked with you. And to have known your late wife. She was a wonderful lady.'

Xin-Bin's words had been unexpected and hit a chord with Dancer, his reply sticking in his throat. He just nodded and smiled his thanks.

Then it was Abe's turn. For once his voice was slightly croaky and Dancer guessed he was remembering the thousand and one run-ins he'd had with Xin-Bin before he knew what the man was really doing. 'Good luck, son, to you and your family.'

And then they turned away and through the swing doors to where the ExecFlight jet waited, whining savagely as the pilot ran up the engines. It was starting to sleet.

Lily Cheung had heard the news on the train to Beidaihe with little Bao.

The announcer on someone's transistor radio was relating how General Sun and other illustrious revolutionary heroes had died in an air crash. It puzzled her, because Sun had not been due to travel on either of the Politburo aircraft. . . Then she heard that the Politburo were speaking from Hong Kong. That was when she knew something had gone profoundly wrong.

What was worse was not knowing *exactly* what. There was no one she could ask and no one she could phone. Her instructions were simply to get to Wang's villa and wait. If everything had gone to plan, Dancer would have sent for her when it was safe. In the unlikely event of anything going wrong, someone would soon contact her and tell her what to do.

She just hoped someone would come and tell her soon because she was now very scared. The worst moment had been walking up the drive of Wang's villa, inserting the key in the door and boldly marching in. She half-expected Wang himself to be sitting there. Or servants – a cleaner or gardener perhaps. But there was no one. The shutters were closed and dust sheets still covered the furniture. The air was musty and there was a deathly silence. Being there felt almost like an act of desecration, as though this was, in some way, Wang's tomb.

At the back of the villa, she opened the shutters at one window to let in some light, then found an alcove that wasn't overlooked from the outside. She scattered silk cushions on the floor and sat there with Bao and opened the bag of little foil food parcels she'd bought at the railway station stall.

There were fried noodles and vegetables, boiled dumplings and fried bean curd in oyster sauce. It was tepid and tasteless.

Bao tested some with the wooden chopsticks provided in the bag and spat it out. 'This is horrible.'

Lily smiled sympathetically. 'I know. It's not very nice, but it's all there is. Eat up what you can.'

'I can't, I'll be sick.'

'Please try, for your mama.'

He shrugged and tried again. He ate a few mouthfuls in silence then pushed it away. 'Why do we have to sit on the floor? I'm tired, isn't there a bedroom?'

'There is, but, well, we shouldn't really be here.'

'Why not?'

'This place belongs to a friend. He doesn't know we're here.'

Bao looked thoughtfully at his food. 'Well, if he's a friend he won't mind.'

'You don't understand.'

He looked directly at his mother and could see how drawn and worried she was. 'We're running away, aren't we? That's why you don't want anyone to know we're here?'

She looked down into his big, dark innocent eyes and knew she couldn't lie. 'Yes, darling, I'm afraid we are.'

'Why? What have we done wrong?'

She leaned forward and kissed the top of his head. 'You have done nothing wrong, my sweet, and neither have I. But I have done some things to help life become better for the people in our country. Some officials in the Party do not approve.'

'Bad people?'

How could she explain? 'Some, yes. People who do not understand. People who do not believe in freedom.'

'What is freedom?'

She shrugged and looked around the spacious and sumptuously appointed lounge for inspiration. 'When you can decide to do whatever you want to do, whenever you want to do it.'

He looked puzzled. 'Not like school.'

She laughed. 'No, not like school.'

He caught her mood, pleased to have brought a smile to his mother's face. 'Freedom sounds good to me.' Then he became serious again. 'How long do we hide from the bad people?'

'Until our friends come to help us. Not long.'

'Uncle John?'

She was surprised by his perception. 'Maybe he will come here. Maybe someone else.'

Suddenly the boy's eyes were bright with anticipation. 'He takes us to America? To Disneyland?'

'Maybe, some time.'

'And we go by undersea boat, by submarine?'

'I don't know what is arranged.' She certainly hoped not; the very idea terrified her. 'We will be told soon.'

That seemed to satisfy Bao. Tiredness after the long journey began to overcome him and he snuggled up alongside his mother on the cushions. Soon he was sound asleep. Lily's head began to nod.

Tap-tap. Tap-tap.

She was blind, could see nothing. Knew nothing. Could hear nothing, except the tap of her white stick.

Tap-tap. Tap-tap.

In an instant she was awake, Bao stirring and rubbing his eyes. It took a moment to orientate herself, to remember where she was.

Tap-tap. There it was again.

It seemed to be coming from somewhere in the room, beyond the alcove. She climbed on to all fours and crawled across the cushions. Then she peered cautiously round the corner of the wall.

Tap-tap.

There it was! She half-screamed, half-gasped. The face was pressed up against the window, ugly and distorted, peering in at her.

Tap-tap! Fierce now, trying to get her attention.

She pulled back inside the alcove. Only then did she realise and lean forward again.

'Lily, quick! Open up!'

She swallowed hard and breathed again. 'Tao?' Then she was on her feet, rushing across the marble floor to where Yan Tao stood outside the window. She struggled with the lock then slid it open.

For a moment she stared at him, speechless, tears forming in her eyes. He held out his hands to her and she fell against him, sobbing into his chest. 'I am so, so glad to see you,' she said. 'Please help us.'

'We'd better go inside. It won't do to be seen here.'

She wiped her eyes and sniffed back any further tears and showed him in, relocking the patio window. 'Do you know what went wrong?'

'Not exactly, nobody does. But they must have discovered the briefcases. Dancer aborted everything and told me to come here to meet you. I caught the first available train. He will join us as soon as he can and arrange for us to leave the country. I understand the Americans have a reliable escape route.' He smiled to reassure her. 'So you should not be afraid. They are very professional.'

Bao's voice piped up nervously from the alcove. 'Who is it, Mama?'

Lily smiled. 'It's a very dear friend. Uncle Tao. You've met him once or twice before. He was a friend of your daddy.'

The little boy emerged from the shadow and looked up, pleased to see his mother looking relieved and happy. 'I am very pleased to meet you again, Uncle.'

That was when they heard the sound of the car crunching up the gravel drive. Lily stiffened. Yan caught her worried glance, then turned and moved swiftly to the front of the villa, opening one of the shutters a fraction.

The car had stopped some way short. He could just see its front wing at the bend in the drive. Then, through gaps in the hedge, he caught fleeting glimpses of plain-clothes and uniformed policemen being directed left and right, disappearing into the gardens. Others were moving stealthily up the drive towards the villa.

Yan pulled back, pressing the shutter closed. He looked deathly pale.

'What is it?' Lily asked.

'The police, coming here.'

She stared, 'No, it can't be.' Instinctively she gathered Bao to her.

'We must get out of here.' He looked left and right, unable to think, his mind paralysed.

Lily shook her head. 'No, Tao, *you* must get out of here. You are the one they mustn't catch. Technically, I've done nothing wrong, John explained that to me. I've just been duped and used by the Americans.' She saw that he was hesitating. 'Go now. Out through the back. The garden is big, you will be able to escape. I will stall them. Please, GO! GO NOW!'

He placed his hands on her shoulders and looked solemnly into those large dark eyes imploring him to go. 'I love you, Lily. I always have and I always will.'

She shook her head in anguish, wanting him to stay, begging him to go. And she felt the raw flame of emotion in her chest and throat so that she barely heard her own words. 'And I love you, Yan Tao.'

He'd heard what he needed to hear. Quickly he kissed her on the mouth and then was gone. Slipping open the rear window, he stepped out on to the patio. Steps fell away to a sloping garden of lawns and shrubs, dotted with exotic trees. He jumped down to ground level in a single bound, landing awkwardly on the grass. He cursed, regained his balance and looked around. He'd make for a thick patch of ornamental grass and use it for cover. He started to run as fast as he could. Legs pounding and his heart thumping as he sprinted like an athlete, his chest out and his head held high. Nearly there, nearly there. Running for the finishing tape.

It was then that the man stepped unexpectedly out from behind a bush in front of him. He was just a blur to Yan, who skidded to avoid him. His soles slipped on the damp grass and he tumbled, rolling over several times before he came to a halt.

Winded, he looked up.

The face with the gold-rimmed spectacles was smiling gently down over the stubby barrel of an automatic pistol.

'What an unexpected pleasure,' said Brigadier Ting Han-chen.

Fifteen

It was a strange feeling, being on the last ExecFlight flight out of Beijing.

John Dancer and Abe Stone had sat in the facing leather armchairs looking out of the ports at the familiar receding grey mass of the city below. Neither man spoke until the layers of cloud closed in and finally hid it from view. So much had happened over so many years. And now all that had also come to an end.

'And this, too, will pass,' Stone murmured.

Dancer looked across at his friend.

'Old Chinese saying,' Stone explained helpfully.

'Meaning nothing stays the same for ever?'

Stone nodded and looked back through the window at the sullen floor of cloud below them. 'Think Xin-Bin will be okay now we're going?'

Dancer lit a cigarette as he considered his reply. 'I think he might be in for some tough questioning by the police, but there's nothing to incriminate him. We took all the secret cameras and recording stuff out of the the aircraft weeks ago. Everything else is circumstantial. We take the can.'

Stone gave an uneven smile. 'The wicked old CIA.'

Dancer grinned back at his friend. 'So you're always telling me.' It helped to crack a joke, however bad. He exhaled a cloud of smoke, feeling his taut nerves start to relax a little. Then he added, 'Xin-Bin is sure Wang will look after him, probably anxious to get his hands on the business.'

His partner nodded; he could well believe that. 'And what happens when we meet up with Yan and the Cheung woman at Wang's villa?'

'The Brits have got some connection with the Red Tiger Society. The RTS snakeheads will organise transport for us to one of the Tianjin fishing villages on the river. Then it's out to sea.'

Stone looked dubious. 'Don't like mixing with Triads. Can't trust the bastards.'

Dancer smiled thinly, remembering their earlier problems. 'I've seen the operation first-hand. We understand each other. It's okay.'

'Sure. If you say so.'

Their conversation had lapsed then, each man alone with his thoughts and his memories. It was time to think of the past, finally to put it in perspective, because the future was still too far away even to contemplate.

It was late afternoon when they touched down at the nearest airport to the resort of Beidaihe. A cold wind moaned across the concrete strip and they hunched against it, scurrying for the shelter of the Arrivals lounge in the Qinhuangdao terminal building. There was a military passenger jet parked close by and a gathering of PLA and police officers standing around, smoking and looking bored. Dancer and Stone ignored them and walked on through with all the nonchalance they could muster. An official checked their tickets and passports and entered their names in a log, but he showed no enthusiasm for the job and even less interest in them.

Stone grinned as they strode across the near-deserted concourse. 'Last hurdle. Thank God for that, I had a nasty feeling.'

'Let's find a cab,' Dancer said. He was anxious to be with Lily again.

But it was not that easy. The vacation season was over and most hotels and facilities along the nearby coast would be closed until the following summer. Only seamen made their way to and from the ice-free port of Qinhuangdao and they travelled cheaply by rail or bus. So there were few passengers at the air terminal and no taxis.

It was half-an-hour before one trundled noisily down the road. The driver had a greasy, unwashed-looking face and a fat mouth into which he continuously stuffed the contents of the bag of dumplings on his lap. He appeared jovial, but smiled too much, suggesting it was a veneer hiding a short temper. When Dancer gave him the address of the villa, he nodded his acknowledgement but, of course, when they reached the resort itself, he didn't have a clue where it was. As always, Dancer had taken the precaution of bringing a sketch of the route, although the driver kept overriding the instructions he was given. After several losses of temper and heated exchanges, they were finally on the right track and moving through secluded wooded hills where ruling cadre elites had their hideaway holiday homes.

Stone leaned forward from the back seat to get a better view. 'Trouble ahead.'

Half-a-dozen police cars were pulled over at the side of the road where a tree-lined drive led away up to the hills.

'Dammit!' Dancer hissed. 'That's Wang's place.'

'What happens now?'

'Change of plan.' Dancer snapped at the driver in Mandarin. 'Drive on.'

'But this is your villa!' protested the driver. 'I *know*, I see from your map!'

'I don't care. Drive on!'

The man shrugged, stuffed another dumpling in his mouth and stared hard at the police activity as he drove past. 'Someone is in big trouble with the cops. All the fat cats live here. Someone's been caught with his fingers in the people's money pot,' he chortled. 'Serve them right. They should cut off his head.'

'They probably will,' Stone muttered, distracted as he looked back. 'They're bringing someone out.'

'Pull over!' Dancer ordered.

'You told me to drive on,' the driver protested.

'Just do it!'

The brakes squealed. 'Is it your friends in trouble with the cops? Hey, are you in trouble with the cops?'

'No, we're not,' Dancer retorted.

The taxi came to a halt as the worn brake-pads finally bit. 'If you're in trouble, I want nothing to do with you.'

'Just shut up,' Dancer ordered and pulled a wad of *yuan* notes from his pocket. 'Do what I say and all this is yours, no questions asked. Okay?'

The driver stared at the notes as if they were another bag of his favourite dumplings, then shrugged happily. 'Sure, whatever you crazy foreign devils say.' He added chirpily, 'My father was a capitalist roader and I travel the same road.'

'They're bringing out a woman,' Stone reported. 'Ah, and a small boy.'

Dancer turned to look out of the smeary rear window.

'Christ! It must be Lily and her son.'

'I wonder if Yan Tao has got there yet.' Then he swallowed hard. 'Oh, no. I think that's him.'

Dancer had a clearer view as the arrests were completed and the prisoners ushered into the waiting police cars. There was no doubt about it. Lily, little Bao and Yan Tao. Doors slammed and the first of the vehicles pulled away, coming down the road towards them. The first flashed past and he caught a glimpse of Lily in the back seat. She looked pale and bewildered, hugging the boy to her. Dancer felt an almost irresistible urge to call out, to shout some word of comfort. Then a second car shot by, and then a third.

'That face,' he murmured. 'I know that face.'

Stone glanced at him. 'Yeah?'

'I'm sure. It was Brigadier Ting Han-chen.'

'I'm sorry, John. There's nothing we can do.'

Dancer ignored him and leaned forward towards the driver. 'Follow those cars.'

'Are you mad?' Stone protested.

'Probably, but I've got to know where they're taking them.' He prodded the driver. 'Go on, if you want this money. And don't get too close.'

The taxi juddered forward and pulled out. It was with some effort that the dilapidated vehicle managed to keep the speeding convoy in sight as it hurtled back along the coast road towards the ugly industrial port area of Qinhuangdao. On the outskirts it turned off on to a side road through a fairly remote area of scrub and rough woodland. They lost sight of the last car over the brow of a hill. When they crested it a few minutes later, the scene was spread out before them. A mile ahead they could see the low concrete block buildings behind a compound of high electrified fencing with watchtowers erected at intervals. Half-way down the road the convoy had halted at a roadblock.

'Stop now,' Dancer ordered. 'Now!'

The driver jumped at the anger in the American's voice and the taxi slithered to a standstill. 'I am right,' the man said.

'What do you mean? What is that place?'

Blood had drained from the taximan's face. 'It is out of bounds to the public. Around here they call it the Dragon's Nest.'

'What?'

'Some say it is a prison. Others say it is the local headquarters of the Public Security Bureau. It is rumoured that is where they take smugglers and people who try to leave the country from the port.'

'The local interrogation centre?' Stone suggested.

The driver was beginning to tremble. 'They say people who go there never return.'

Dancer made his decision. 'Okay, reverse up back over the hill, then turn round.'

For once the driver was more than happy to oblige.

'What next?' Stone asked.

'I've seen enough,' Dancer answered. 'I've got to let Bill know what's happened. Take instructions.'

Stone looked uncomfortable. 'He'll probably say there's nothing we can do now. Langley will want to wash their hands of the situation.'

Dancer gave him a withering look. 'I hope to God you're wrong.'

'What about chummy here? As soon as he drops us off, he might go straight to the cops.'

'So do you want to cut his throat, or shall I?'

Stone looked affronted. 'Don't take it out on me, John. This is your party.'

Dancer forced a ragged sort of smile. 'Sorry, Abe. You're right. But I don't think Charlie Chan here will want to get involved. Especially if it means explaining away the money we've given him. I think we can get away with it and let him live.'

'You're going soft as noodles.' Stone's grin looked a little forced. 'Maybe we both are.'

Dancer told the driver to take them into the centre of the Qinhuangdao port area and twenty minutes later he dropped them off outside the Seamen's Club. He grinned widely as Dancer handed over the wad of notes. 'This is private business,' the American reminded him. 'No one else's. Understood? If you talk, the police will ask where you got the money.'

'Don't worry, I speak to no one. Not even my wife.' His grin was in danger of breaking his face in half. 'Especially not my wife.'

And then he was gone, his taxi backfiring rudely down the road. As soon as it turned the corner, Dancer and Stone began legging it as fast as they could without drawing attention to themselves. After a short distance, they reached the main supply road to the docks and were able to flag down a Number Two bus to take them to the railway station. There they picked up a taxi to the other nearby coastal town of Shanhaiguan. In sharp contrast to the port, the ancient walled fortress town was picturesque and attracted some tourist interest as it marked the point where the Great Wall met the sea.

It was dusk when they paid the taxi off at the East Gate and went on foot to seek out a clean, but basic backstreet hotel. They were shown to a largish twin-bedded room with bare floorboards and rough-rendered walls. As soon as the porter left, Dancer sat on the bed and opened up his case with the GMP2000 satellite phone and called the American Embassy in Beijing asking to speak to the commercial attaché. Moments later, he recognised Bill Dawson's voice on the line.

'Sorry to disturb you at this time,' Dancer said quickly. 'You don't know me. The name's Crawford and I'm a businessman.'

The sharp intake of breath was just audible. Ralph Crawford was the name in Dancer's false passport. Dawson recovered quickly, no hint of concern in his voice. 'How do, Mr Crawford? What seems to be the problem?'

'I was due to meet two important Chinese business contacts up here in Qinhuangdao, but they had to cancel at the last moment. I know where they are and wondered what you thought would be the best way to contact them? You know, local etiquette, loss of face and all that. Could your people help?'

Dawson's voice didn't betray the anxiety he must be feeling. 'We can try. Do you have an address for where they are?'

'Not exactly. It's a factory on the southern outskirts of Qinhuangdao. Owned by a certain Mr Ting, I believe.'

A brief pause followed. 'Might I know this particular Mr Ting?'

'Yes. I myself met him earlier this year in Beijing.'

Now a solemnity had crept into Dawson's voice. 'I understand. Let me look into this and I'll get back to you soonest.'

'Your office will have this number. I can be reached all night.' Dancer replaced the handset in the case and looked up at Stone. 'Expect that's just about made his day.'

'Expect it has.' Stone moved towards the door. 'I'll go get us some vi't'als and a bottle of hooch.'

Dancer gave a weary smile. 'It's going to be a long night.'

When Dancer's call came through, Dawson had been about to leave the embassy for his prearranged drink with Iona Moncrieff. Aspen had already left the building with the US Ambassador for a cocktail party at the Japanese Embassy; Dawson thought about leaving an urgent message for him to make contact, then changed his mind. He'd talk it over with Iona, get a plan of action clearer in his own mind first.

He was feeling slightly breathless when he arrived at the favoured British haunt of the Pig and Whistle pub on the ground floor of the Holiday Inn Lido and was mildly irritated to see that Iona already had company. Her tall blonde assistant, Suzy Tobin, was seated next to her and Piers Lansdowne was bringing their drinks from the bar.

The Englishman spotted him immediately. 'Hello, Bill, what'll it be?'

'Something strong and warming,' came the immediate reply. 'Stiff bourbon on the rocks.'

Lansdowne nodded. 'We'll leave you and Iona in peace in a few minutes. Suzy's going to introduce me to the delights of the playwright Gao Zingjian. Do you know his work? Rather avant-garde.'

Dawson shook his head, feeling irritable. Who in the fuck went to Chinese theatre unless it was a means to getting a leg over Iona's scrumptiously cool assistant? Fuck Lansdowne for knowing just how to pull her, which line to cast. He slumped down at the table, feeling defeated all round, as Lansdowne returned to the bar.

'You look exhausted, Bill,' Iona said, touching his forearm.

No point in beating about the bush, he decided. 'I've just had some bad news. John went to meet Guizhoe and Hunan.' He used their code names. 'At the villa.'

Concern clouded Iona's face. 'I know that.'

He lowered his voice. 'John found they'd been picked up.' He avoided the term arrested. 'Ting's got them in for questioning.'

'Good God.'

Lansdowne rejoined them with Dawson's bourbon. 'Not sure I caught that. Ting's got hold of them? Where?'

'A security facility south of Qinhuangdao. I've checked and we've got it listed as Security Ministry property. Suspected local headquarters and interrogation centre.'

Suzy grimaced. 'Not nice.'

'It won't be for our two friends once they start pulling fingernails out. Or whatever it is that sort do nowadays.'

'What does Aspen say?' Iona asked.

'Frank doesn't know yet, but I can guess.'

So could Iona. 'Go let 'em hang?'

Dawson took a hard swig at his glass, emptying half in one swallow. 'Aspen's a career spook. He doesn't give a shit about China or any other place. This was a big ambitious project and in the event it hasn't come off as planned. So what? He'll still get top marks for effort. Doing anything about our friends would just complicate things. Make them messy. Leave well alone.'

Lansdowne frowned. 'It's a bloody shame, Bill. Apart from the human tragedy – no doubt it'll be life sentences or execution for them both – there'll be the inevitable crushing of the freedom movement. Hundreds could die.'

Anger sparked like a loose wire in Dawson's head. 'Tell me somethin' I don't know,' he snapped.

The Englishman's voice softened. 'Trouble is, Bill, I don't see what we *can* do.'

Dawson glared across the table with undisguised hostility. 'Guess you haven't been around too much in hot war zones, have you, son?' Iona was taken aback by his rudeness as he added, 'Guess you missed out on Viet Nam and Cambodia and all that shit.'

Lansdowne said nothing, just watched the American steadily, waiting for him to finish.

The CIA station chief gave an awkward smile. 'Sorry, unfair. But in hot wars you do what has to be done. Simple as that.'

'And what has to be done here?' Lansdowne's voice was low.

'See if a breakout's possible. Before Ting manages to make them talk.'

Iona's eyebrows almost took off; Lansdowne blinked hard. 'You're not serious?'

'It can be done. It's been done before. We've got an ideal unit in place to carry it off.'

'But not regardless of casualties.'

'No,' Dawson agreed, 'but we're not the best ones to assess that. They are.'

'So what exactly are you recommending?'

'Infil the DW team. Or ask them if it's feasible. And if it is, put them ashore for a close recce and assessment. Let them go in and decide what to do and how?'

Suzy's brain cells were working overtime as usual. As quick as a flash, she said, 'And what's Aspen's reaction going to be to that?'

Dawson didn't answer, he didn't have to. Iona felt so proud of him at that moment. Proud of his gung-ho, can-do courage that hadn't diminished with the years. Beneath the gruff exterior, he was still the handsome, courageous young lieutenant who'd stolen her heart all those years before. Still a battered hero. A bit flawed perhaps, but a hero nonetheless. She said tentatively, 'Aspen can only react *if* he knows. This *could* be an operational decision. Made between Dancer and Janie Walsh. It's not as if our people haven't been on the mainland all these weeks. Nothing's so different.'

'At least for a recce,' Lansdowne murmured, half to himself.

Dawson was clearly surprised at the reaction. 'You'd run with that?'

'If the team agrees, they can at least take a shufty.' The Englishman gave a boyish grin. 'If it'll make you happy.'

'It'll make Dancer happy. Not just to save everything

we've all worked for. I think the woman, Cheung, is pretty special to him. I'm grateful, Piers.'

'Then I'd best be off and get some things sorted,' Lansdowne said, turning to Suzy Tobin. 'Sorry, I'll have to pass on the play.'

For a second or two, Dawson felt perversely pleased at having torpedoed the young Englishman's amorous intentions – until she replied, 'That's fine, Piers. I've a couple of chums who'd love the tickets. I could come back to the office and give you a hand.'

'That's most kind of you,' Lansdowne replied with a knowing smile and rose to his feet. 'Drop round to our embassy later, Bill. We can dot some 'i's and cross some 't's. See how we can best pull this off.'

They watched Lansdowne leave with his arm held loosely around Suzy's waist. Not too tight, just a polite and gentlemanly guiding touch as they threaded through the growing crowd of after-work drinkers.

'Envious?' Iona asked.

The American tore his eyes away and back to her. 'Of him? 'Course, not.'

'Of them. All that youth and beauty.'

'When I've got you, Majesty?' He raised his glass to her. 'Thanks for backing me.'

She raised one eyebrow. 'Why do you want to do it, Bill? Take the chance and risk Frank Aspen's wrath? Maybe your President's too?'

'Does it matter?'

'To me it does.'

Dawson stared down at his drink. 'John Dancer and I go back a long way. We've been working at this project for so many years. It even cost John his wife and that devastated him. Then Lily came on the scene and I've noticed the change in him. Seen the light come back in his eyes. I know how he'll feel about her arrest. Totally crushed. Knowing him, he might even try something off his own bat, and that would be a disaster. So I owe it to him. To him, Majesty, not the likes of Aspen.'

She was touched. 'That's very noble, Bill. And so like you. You're my rock.'

'What?'

Iona touched his forearm. 'Just what a husband should be. A rock in a stormy sea.'

He was half-amused, half-embarrassed by that. Trying to steer away from the subject he said absently, 'I was surprised the boy Lansdowne went along with it though. Don't think of him as front-line material, more a lounge lizard on the diplomatic circuit.'

'I've told you before, Bill, you're wrong about Piers. All that stuff you were saying about hot war zones, about him having missed out on Viet Nam and Cambodia.'

'Yeah?'

'He was undercover in Bosnia, behind the lines.'

Dawson absorbed that, nodded slowly, beginning to understand the nature of the beast.

'It's up to us,' Walsh said to Captain Cherrier. 'What d'you think about it?'

She stood with Dave McVicar and Nick Lake beside the control suite, dressed in army camo trousers and a sweat-damp green singlet with a can of iced Coke in her hand. Even a constant supply of the stuff had failed to bring relief from the stuffy heat of the submarine.

Cherrier was looking his age, she decided. No, *more* than his age. For eight solid weeks *Manta* and its crew had been on duty, either on station off Tianjian or shuttling back and forth on occasions to join the 7th Fleet in international waters for replen or urgent makeshift repairs. Day after day of lying doggo on the seabed or running the gauntlet of the newly laid minefields and PLA Navy patrols.

The submarine had been back in the turbulent shallows of the Gulf of Bohai for the past two weeks in the crucial run-up period to D-day. Bodies were listless, muscles were cramped and tempers were sorely frayed. *Manta* might be designed for such prolonged periods of inactivity, but human beings weren't. Walsh noticed that Cherrier's once neat beard had grown wild and long, streaked with white like a badger, and reminding her of Jules Verne's Captain Nemo, commander of the *Nautilus*. Or, she thought with a private smile, even old King Neptune himself.

As usual, the old cob pipe, unlit and empty, was clamped between his teeth. 'You know the score, Janie, I don't have to tell you. The fuel-cell efficiency is reducing and needs a complete recharge which can't be done at sea. So we no longer have the performance we had when we started. And the system needs a complete overhaul. We've got high-pressure couplings springing leaks daily.'

'And the computer still crashing?' she asked.

He gave a half-smile. 'So regular you can almost set your watch by it.'

She understood what he was saying. 'And that's before we look at the state of the crew, right?'

There was no need for him to answer that; they both knew it. 'Commanding *Manta*'s starting to feel like flying a World War One stringbag. Maybe a comparison with the Russians' Mira space station would be more accurate. High tech held together with bits of string and sticky tape.' He looked reflective. 'Don't get me wrong. This has proved the best trial of her strengths and weaknesses. But she is just a prototype and it shows. I can ask her to do what you want, but I can't guarantee she'll be able to.'

It was hard for Walsh to make up her own mind. 'But she'll try?'

Cherrier nodded. 'Well, I'm sure the crew will.' He glanced up at McVicar and Lake. 'And your team?'

'They're up for it.'

He almost smiled. 'I thought they might be. So what exactly do you want to do?'

A chart had been pegged out on an adjoining table. Walsh studied it for a moment. 'We'll need to travel north off the coast. Past the port of Tianjin some one sixty miles and position ourselves just south of Qinhuangdao.' She looked directly at Cherrier. 'We could do that in around sixteen hours, couldn't we?'

He shook his head. 'Sorry, Janie. Like I've said, the fuel cell's power is running down. I can't get more than ten knots out of her any more.'

Manson, the electrical engineer, was tapping a calculation into a keyboard. He said, 'The faster we go, the less the range and speed available for the rest of the mission.' The resulting figures flashed up on the screen. 'Right, well there's our answer. We can make eight knots to the target area. That'll give us reserves enough to return to international waters at ten knots steady.' He looked at Walsh and shrugged. 'But that's with no leeway, ma'am, and no room for error.'

Cherrier straightened his back, decision made. 'Then I think the sooner we get going the better. Prepare for departure in fifteen minutes.'

And exactly as the console clock registered the quarter-hour, the fuel-cell motor began its faint hum and Cherrier ordered the ballast in the tank to be blown. Slowly they felt *Manta* break free of the bottom and the canting deck begin to level as neutral buoyancy was established. Then the sensation of motion was almost imperceptible as the side-thrusters turned her on her own axis and she headed north. Just one last task to perform on her journey home.

It was just after dawn when Dancer's satellite phone purred into life and the irritating sound pushed its way into his haunted dreams. He threw off the covers, swung his legs to the floor and reached for the handset of the machine that he'd placed on the bedside table.

''Morning, Mr Crawford,' Dawson's voice sounded confident but a little weary. 'I've been looking into the problem of your two missing Chinese business contacts. I'm sending someone to help out, if that's possible. Old friends, Jane and Dave. Don't know if you remember them? They'll be arriving by their usual mode of transport, so will need some directions from you.'

As Dancer listened, relief surging through him, Stone's bulk was stirring in the bed opposite. The big blunt face peered out from under the bedclothes as he watched Dancer stare for an indication of the news.

'When are they going to arrive?' Dancer asked.

'If all goes to plan,' Dawson replied, 'around ten tonight. You'll be there to meet them, of course?'

'Of course,' Dancer replied. 'And I'll let you have the directions later today.'

'That's fine. By the way, a set of wheels will be with you later this morning.'

Dancer grinned. However much he'd loathed Dawson at times, he had to admit the old bastard came through when the chips were down. Finally he hung up and lit a cigarette.

'We're in with a chance, Abe.'

'Good news, son. Guess we've got our work cut out for the rest of the day.'

'I think we have.'

As it was, they had to wait until ten before they could begin. That was when the transport arrived. The Chinese driver of a black Ford Galaxy people-mover pulled up at the kerbside in front of their hotel. The passenger door opened and down stepped a familiar figure in a crumpled linen suit and panama, carrying a malacca cane.

'My dear Mr Dancer,' Edwin Prufrock said, 'where *did* you find this place? Not in any Michelin Guide, I'll warrant. Had the dickens own job finding it.'

'Humble but clean,' Dancer rejoined, just pleased to see a set of wheels.

'And a bar, I trust. I'm parched.'

There was no gin, so Prufrock drenched the local firewater with tonic and the juice of half a lemon. 'Wasn't easy getting the wheels,' he confided after a long swallow. 'My friend Mike Jiang – he of the RTS – has gone a bit wobbly on us since yesterday. Didn't want to co-operate, but I've a couple of big deals going through with him, so he had to oblige eventually. I thought you might want to keep his driver. Less suspicious than two "round eyes" wandering about by themselves.'

That made sense to Dancer. 'We'll keep him with us in daylight, but dump him tonight. Book him into another hotel and give him a few *yuan* for a meal, some booze and a woman to take his mind off things.'

Prufrock smiled. 'We fellas are so predictable the world over, aren't we? Creatures of such simple basic needs.' He drained the glass and pulled a face. 'So what do you want to do?'

'Take a leisurely look along the coast,' Dancer replied. 'Can you come up with a decent story for the driver?'

The Englishman shrugged. 'Easy enough. You're Americans planning to invest in a new holiday hotel complex?'

Abe grunted; he instinctively disliked Prufrock. 'That'll do fine.'

After Prufrock had explained the fictional situation to the driver, they found him a hotel room nearby before they all went in the Galaxy to the station where they dropped the Englishman off, before continuing to the coast. They began cruising the road south from Qinhuangdao towards Beidaihe.

In fact, it didn't take them long to stumble across exactly what they wanted. Just a mile east of the state security facility, where Lily and Yan Tao were being held, the road crossed two river bridges in quick succession. Both rivers flowed east for another couple of hundred metres before emptying into a small saltwater bay.

Dancer told the driver to pull over, then he and Stone wandered down to the shared rivermouth. It was mostly hidden from view by wind-stunted trees and a few spindly shrubs that had managed to put down roots in the thin sandy soil. There were a few low dunes and clumps of grass and on the meagre strand of beach, local fishermen were casting nets.

Abe Stone regarded the scene with the eye of an old professional. 'What d'ya reckon, John?'

Dancer lit a cigarette, cupping the old Zippo against the offshore breeze. 'This is probably as good as it gets.'

At ten that night the unearthly black shape passed slowly and silently like a shadow over the undulating silt beds off the coast of Qinhuangdao. Only the faintest ripple of disturbed water flowed over the sleek tear-drop form, propelled by an unseen, noiseless energy that a passing patrol boat of the Chinese PLA Navy failed to detect.

The submarine's speed diminished until it had come to a hovering standstill, suspended in neutral buoyancy feet above the bottom. Then, inch by inch, the hull lowered until the rounded nose nuzzled into the soft sand as water rushed into the Q-tank to provide anchorage.

Barely had the beast come to rest than the circular aperture of the main hatch slid open on the top of the rounded deck and a strange dark apparition appeared. It floated out and upward in a thin trailing wake of disturbed water. Another followed. Then another and another. In all, six alien creatures, seemingly half-man, half-reptile. While four of them began opening the outer storage compartment that held the Phantom stealth submersible, two others kicked their way towards the opaque ceiling above.

They witnessed the increasing pool of brightness above their heads as it lit the transparent indigo fluid, picking up the stark white fluorescence of the breaking wavecaps. The light was all-engulfing, like a near-death experience as the surface rushed down on them.

McVicar and Lake burst up into the open sea of the Gulf almost simultaneously. On reflex, both men paddled themselves round immediately, peering through the droplets on their facemasks to check for danger and to orientate themselves.

There was a three-quarter moon and a sky of stars which gave the Gulf waters a gleam like dark satin. But towards the Strait and the open sea, everything bled into blackness pitted only by the distant navigation lights of a merchantman. In the other direction, the shoreline of China was faintly visible as a charcoal smudge along the horizon. To their right an amber aurora in the lower sky marked the port town of Qinhuangdao.

Satisfied that there was no danger and nothing to compromise the continuance of the mission, the two combat swimmers disappeared again below the surface.

By the time they returned to the location of the submarine, the rest of the team had secured all their kit in waterproof bags inside the fifteen-foot Phantom submersible. Lake took the front seat at the helm wheel on the craft's left-hand side and kicked the twin 24-volt electric motor pods into play.

They surged gently forward, fully submerged, towards the coast on a compass-bearing to take them to the rendezvous point at the mouth of the two small rivers. For a further twenty minutes, the open-topped, semi-rigid inflatable was propelled silently forward until Lake took it up to 'snorting' depth. Only their line of masked heads and the water jet's breathing tube broke clear of the surface as they continued towards the shore and the blinking green light of Dancer's makeshift signal torch.

McVicar scoured the waterline through the nightsight of his M16 assault rifle, then swung back until he picked up the American's form standing alone on the narrow strip of shingle. 'There's John,' he confirmed. 'All looks clear. Let's go for it.'

Finally, the Phantom surfaced and hove to a few yards from the shore. Four of the combat swimmers held the craft steady with paddles and McVicar covered with his M16 while Lake slid over the side. It was deeper than he'd anticipated, the sea suddenly up to his chest. He cursed silently and forced himself forward against the pressure of the water, wading ashore with his rifle at the ready.

He didn't waste words, but hunkered down beside the crouching American. 'Sitrep, John?'

'Everything's okay,' Dancer replied. 'There's no one in this bay. Watch out for the railway bridge just up the river and a roadbridge beyond that. Abe's waiting there with a vehicle.'

Lake nodded his understanding and beckoned the others to come ashore. McVicar, Dougie Squires and Taff struggled through the water with heavy waterproofed bags of personal equipment and dumped them on the shingle. Meanwhile the remaining two SBS swimmers kept station in the Phantom.

'Guess you've used these before,' Lake said, handing Dancer his M16. 'Be a pal and keep guard while we change.'

It was strange, Dancer thought, having the half-forgotten feel of a rifle in his hands again after so many years. Remembering the days when his life had depended on it. Almost a friend. He pushed the memory from his mind, crouched down beside the nearest dune and watched for any sign of someone approaching.

Within five minutes the four combat swimmers had stripped off their Phibian closed-circuit breathing apparatus and rubber wet suits and pulled on boots and black denim fatigues to which they added specially designed combat vests and belt orders. Lake threw a separate bag down in the sand beside Dancer. 'Some kit there for you too, John. Reckon it's your size.'

Dancer smiled at the careful thought and preparation someone had been giving this hastily prepared operation. 'I'll change later.'

The temporarily unwanted scuba kit was consigned to the waterproof bags which Taffy and Squires then ferried back to the Phantom and returned.

'We plan to be back here at 0300,' Lake told Dancer. 'The Phantom lads will give us till 0330, then try the agreed fall-back RV just up the coast. If there's a no-show, they'll pull out and try again tomorrow at 0100 hours. After that it'll be Walsh's decision what action to take.' He checked that everyone was ready. 'Right, let's go.'

Dancer led the way back along the river bank and under the arch of the railway bridge. He then took a well-trodden footpath that climbed steeply up the right-hand embankment of a road bridge that spanned the river some hundred metres beyond. There was little traffic on the road, just the occasional rattling lorry or moped whining through the night, but they kept to the cover of rough scrub on the verge until they reached the spot where the Ford Galaxy had pulled off the road.

When he threw open the driver's door, Dancer was startled to find no one there. Then Abe Stone's voice came from the bush behind him.

'I'd be a sitting target to stay in there,' he growled, brushing the dead grass and leaves from his trousers.

'As sharp as ever,' Dancer teased with a grin. 'Nice to see you haven't lost your cutting edge.'

Lake and the others threw their kit into the back and followed in after it; Dancer climbed into the passenger seat beside Stone as the big man started the Galaxy and turned on to the road.

It was only a short distance to the unmarked track that led towards the Security Ministry facility where Lily Cheung, Bao, and Yan Tao had been taken. Stone slowed to reduce the sound of their approach and killed the headlights some hundred metres short of the crest of the hill. He then steered off the laterite track on to a level area of rough grass and kept going until the vehicle was hidden in fairly dense shrubbery a few metres farther on.

Dancer shone a torch on the sketch map of the area he had drawn earlier that day. 'Not exactly to scale, I'm afraid. But here's the track and this is the crest of the hill ahead. A mile beyond is the camp. Typical barracks layout by the look of it, with watchtowers and high fences. But before you get there, about half-way along, there's a roadblock with armed police.'

'That's the usual Chinese setup, isn't it?' McVicar said.

'Yes. Just to deter nosy local officials or foreigners, journalists, anyone using the road. Peasants can usually wander round the perimeter areas without too much hassle from guards.'

Lake checked his watch. It was eleven thirty already. 'Let's press on. Take a look-see from the top of the hill, then we'll take a close recce. Okay?' He flipped open a khaki daysack. 'I think the two of you should use these now. It's getting to the stage when you won't be able to talk yourself out of trouble any more.'

'Smart kit,' Stone said admiringly, accepting the automatic pistol with its dimpled screw-on silencer.

'Yeah, sexy,' Lake said. 'Heckler & Koch's Mark 23. US Special Forces have dropped nine milly calibre and gone back to the ol' .45 after the Gulf War experience. This bugger's the size of the Israeli Desert Eagle, but the polymer frame makes it a fraction of the weight.'

Dancer pulled on his set of black denims while the four British soldiers buckled up their belt orders, which included sleeping-bag rolls and collapsible entrenching tools. Then Stone stayed behind with the vehicle while Dancer led them stealthily up to the crest and into a shallow depression in the ground from where they had a view of the camp spread out below them.

As the American had warned, there was a roadblock a half-mile distant. In the glow of a hurricane lamp they could see a handful of soldiers lounging around while one of them rustled up some supper on a small wok over a wood fire. Beyond, the camp was identified by the darker outline shapes of the barrack blocks and lights in some of the windows. A dog yapped as the moon came out from behind a cloud.

McVicar turned to Lake and exchanged a few words before he spoke to Dancer. 'We're going to take a closer look, do a circuit.' He glanced at his watch. 'It's midnight now, I reckon two hours should do it. Would you stay here and keep watch?'

'No problem.'

McVicar dug out a pair of Bofors night-vision binoculars from one of his custom-made kidney pouches and a small radio handset. 'That's a MEL Caracol; just press the "send" tit if you want to speak to us. It's an automatic frequency-hopper, so there's no risk of compromise. If we're not back, RV with the Phantom at the river mouth and bring them up to speed. Okay?'

Dancer nodded. 'And give you covering fire if you need it?'

McVicar grinned. 'Fuck me, John, you are the optimist. But thanks anyway.' Then he and the other three pulled night-vision monocular goggles over their heads. 'Aye, I know we look like one-eyed aliens, but, apart from seeing in the dark, we can pick out the invisible aiming laser beam on our rifles and handguns.'

'Wonders of modern science – a bit different from my day.'

Lake's parting shot was, 'They'll be replacing us with robots next. We can run the next war sitting in front of the telly with a six-pack of lager.'

Then all four were gone, melting into the shadows, moving in a fast and effortless leopard crawl until they vanished completely. Within seconds the night had closed in around Dancer and he shivered. Somewhere, far away, an owl hooted mournfully. Slowly he was attuning to nature, gradually becoming aware of the breeze rustling in the grass. And, for the first time, could just distinguish the distant sound of the Chinese troops laughing by the roadblock. It was going to be a long cold wait, he decided. He wished to hell he had something warmer to wear. And wished to hell he could light one of the Camels from the pack in his pocket. He grimaced, remembering Viet Nam. Dammit, he had always hated being a soldier.

The seconds dragged by into minutes, the minutes stretching into an hour with agonising slowness. His mind wandered, visualising McVicar and Lake, Squires and Taff, creeping around the base and wondering what was going on inside. What was happening to Lily and Yan Tao? Were they using Bao to break her? Had either or both broken down at the first threat of violence? Were members of the freedom movement being swept up by a security dragnet throughout China even as he lay there helpless? He had no real idea what interrogation techniques the Chinese might use. Certainly threats and intimidation and probably beatings. But as for truth drugs or pulling out fingernails . . . ? And he didn't want to know. He just hoped Lily and Yan would be able to play for time. But then, why should they? They had no idea that help might be at hand, although that was by no means yet decided. Action might still be refused, or forbidden by the politicians in London or Washington. And whether or not it was leaked to them would be down to one person only – the operational commander, Janie Walsh.

After an hour and a half, the cold had crept into his bones. He ached all over and his ears felt like ice. His concentration was going and his head began to nod. That was when he heard it.

Instantly he was awake again, the adrenalin coursing through him and his heart thudding.

A vehicle was grinding up the track to his right, out of sight beyond some light scrub. He heard the gears change down as it crested the hill and continued down the other side towards the camp. Reaching for the Bofors night-vision binoculars, he fumbled with numb hands to bring the vehicle into focus as it emerged from behind the scrub. It was an ageing 4 × 4 truck in PLA green with a canvas top and now it was rolling easily towards the roadblock. The two Chinese troopers on watch shifted themselves from the warm comfort of their roadside shack and ambled out on to the track, sub-machine-guns on straps hanging carelessly from their shoulders.

The truck creaked to a halt and the driver leaned out of his window, exchanging a few words with the soldiers. Dancer tried to pick out what they were saying, but the rumble of the vehicle's diesel prevented him from hearing a single word. He swept the binoculars across the back of the truck. A bored-looking soldier had his rifle pointed over the tailgate. There was someone else sitting opposite him, but the man's face was in shadow. Dancer frowned. He wasn't a soldier; he was wearing a white singlet vest. Then one of the roadblock troopers moved to the back and shone a torch up at the tailgate. Just a cursory check, Dancer guessed. The beam lit up the civilian's face.

Dancer swallowed. Was it? Yes, he was certain. It was Cheung Ho, Lily's younger brother.

The barrier was lifted and the troopers waved the truck through. A few minutes later, as the truck approached the main gates of the camp, the fence was suddenly floodlit from the watchtowers. A precaution, Dancer guessed. Then the vehicle drove through. It was too far distant to see what was going on beyond the gates once they closed, but not long after they had gone inside, lights came on in one of the darkened barrack blocks. He made a mental note of which one.

Then a hush fell over the landscape again, the checkpoint soldiers went back to their shack and the camp floodlights went out.

He had another twenty minutes to wait before the recce party reappeared, approaching from behind and scaring the life out of him.

'You trying to give me a heart attack?' Dancer demanded.

McVicar grinned. 'That's not a very friendly welcome for your old mates.'

'How'd it go?'

'Okay, but it's not going to be easy. We're going to have to do some careful planning.'

Dougie Squires and Taffy had taken off their belt orders and unfolded their entrenching spades.

'What's happening?'

'They're digging an OP. We want this place under surveillance from now until a strike goes in – or we pull out – whatever Janie decides. Let's get back to the beach.'

As the two soldiers began digging up squares of turf to be relaid over the observation post when it was complete, Dancer led the way back to the Galaxy and Abe Stone.

Once inside the vehicle, he said, 'I had a bit of a shock while you were out on recce. A truck arrived, with prisoners, I guess. I recognised Lily's brother, Ho.'

McVicar shrugged. 'We shouldn't be too surprised. Once those interrogators get to work . . .' Then he saw the look on Dancer's face. 'Sorry, John. No point dwelling on that aspect of things.'

'We're limited in who we can take,' Lake warned. 'And that's assuming we decide we can achieve anything.'

'What did you find?' Dancer asked, finally lighting up the cigarette he'd been craving for so long.

'The compound's around a half-mile square,' Lake told him. 'There are gates at the rear but they don't appear to be in use and there's an overgrown track that goes off in the direction of the river. There's an eight-foot electrified fence with razor wire all the way round. The guys in the watchtowers have mounted searchlights, but apparently no heavy machine-guns.' Lake didn't refer to any notes as he spoke. 'I counted ten accommodation blocks – concrete and wriggly tin roofs – but couldn't tell what each was used for. Must be a sizable garrison because there were a dozen 4 × 4 trucks plus some jeeps. Probably company strength.'

The Scotsman added, 'And apart from any telephone land lines, they've a fairly sophisticated communications setup judging by all the fancy aerials.'

'We've got to know more,' Lake said. 'That's why we need that OP in place. Dougie and Taffy have got scanners, so they can do some listening in and maybe get some better idea of the scale of the opposition.'

Dancer thought he was detecting more negative vibes than positive ones. 'Do you think there's a chance of pulling something off?'

Lake looked as though he had been asked some sort of devilish trick question. 'Oh, sure, but given the one thing we haven't got. Time. As it is, there's a good chance Lily or Yan will have spilled the beans by the time we go in.'

Dancer didn't want that notion gaining ground. 'They'll only know Yan's *a* player in the underground movement, not that he's at the top. So they might be asking the wrong questions, give him time to bat a few boundaries to keep them running round.'

'You hope,' Lake came back unkindly.

'Yeah, I hope.'

'Then there's transport,' McVicar said. 'We've only got this poxy Galaxy.'

'I've had some thoughts about that,' Lake replied. 'Including how to create an element of surprise.' He turned to Dancer. 'What plans have you got for tomorrow?'

'Plans?' he laughed. 'None. Just to spend the day praying for a goddamn miracle.'

'It might be more practical if you could get this Galaxy sprayed a different colour.'

For the first time, Abe Stone spoke, 'What exactly did you have in mind, son?'

'PLA green. And maybe a bit of livery or sign-writing to make it look genuine.'

Dancer was intrigued. 'We could probably do a yellow star.'

'Ideal,' Lake replied quickly. 'You saw what happened when that truck arrived in the middle of the night. The roadblock guards are half-asleep. It'll be dark and we've got some fluent Mandarin speakers.'

'With Welsh and Scottish accents,' McVicar pointed out.

But Lake was dismissive. 'They're not that bad. If we

can bluff our way through and just get the guards on the gate to open up, then we're halfway there.'

Dancer wasn't so sure, but wasn't going to say so. 'Chicom uniforms would help,' he said encouragingly.

Lake sighed. 'I wish.'

McVicar tapped his watch. 'Time we weren't here, Nick.'

'Sure, I'm getting carried away.' The SBS lieutenant looked at Stone. 'Mind playing taxi again, Abe?

Fifteen minutes later, the Galaxy pulled off the main road beside the river bridge and the team began debussing with their kit.

'Thanks for your help,' Lake said to Dancer. 'Can you make sure you or Abe stay by the satellite phone at all times. *Manta* will communicate with you and our people in Beijing via Hereford. We'll let you know as soon as any decision is made. If this plan goes ahead, I imagine we'll RV with you again here tomorrow, sometime after dark.' He extended his hand. 'What is it you Americans say? And watch yer sweet ass?'

Dancer smiled. 'Something like that. Enjoy your swim.'

And then they were gone like ghosts into the night.

'Takes me back,' Stone murmured wistfully.

'Back too far. We're getting too old for this sort of caper, Abe.'

'Bah, you're still a young buck.'

'I wish.'

'And I wish we could do something more to help,' Stone said, starting the engine. 'I'm feeling like one useless motherfucker, I can tell you.'

Dancer had been thinking. 'There are one or two things we could do.'

Stone let out the clutch and turned on the headlights as the Galaxy bounced over the verge and on to the road. 'All I can think of right now is sleep.'

Sixteen

Janie Walsh listened to the debrief by the shore party with a growing sense of despair.

Nick Lake, Dave McVicar and the others had returned to *Manta* at just gone 0400 hours. They'd barely had time to strip off their wet suits, change into slacks and sweaters and grab some breakfast before Walsh called them into the forward crew quarters.

All thirteen combat swimmers and Al Cherrier were present, to save time and to promote the sort of Chinese Parliament think-tank that she'd come to learn was the British Special Forces' way of doing things. They listened in total silence, some making notes, as Lake reviewed the situation and their findings.

He concluded with: 'I would pinpoint our main problem as transport. We have one Ford Galaxy at our disposal, and that would not even carry the full assault team to the target. Given the tight time-frame, we can't even get assistance from the CIA or SIS in Beijing.'

'Couldn't we commandeer vehicles from a local village on the way in?' suggested the SBS sergeant, Grunt, speaking more words, it seemed, than he had during the entire mission.

McVicar shook his head. 'There isn't a village on an axis between the landing zone and the target. We'd have to detour to one of the river villages some five miles away. Then trying to hot-wire civilian vehicles at night is begging to be discovered. It would be a disaster if alarmed locals told the cops a bunch of foreign devils were running round in the dark nicking cars!'

'There's another consideration,' Walsh pointed out. 'The standard of maintenance of Chinese civilian vehicles is crap. Even if we got them started, there'd be no guarantee they'd be up to the job.'

'I agree,' Lake said. 'Best to make do with what we've got. One element in the Galaxy and another using shanks's pony. It's not far. I'd rather tab it with what I can carry on my back.'

Grunt raised his hand again; this was a world record for him. 'Aren't we missing a trick here? There are trucks in the camp compound. We can use them to get away afterwards.'

'Good point,' McVicar agreed. 'We take what we need and blow away the rest so the PLA can't give chase.'

'So it's only half a problem,' Walsh said thoughtfully. 'We go in with the Galaxy and on foot, then leave with the Galaxy and any other army vehicles available at the camp. It's a bit hit or miss for my liking, but I guess there's no viable alternative.' She turned back to Lake. 'Have you any immediate thoughts how best to mount the assault?'

Lake nodded. 'We haven't had much time to discuss it. But our initial idea is to use the Galaxy to get through the roadblock.' He saw the look of doubt on Walsh's face. 'It'll be dark, we've got fluent Chinese speakers and Dancer's going to get the Galaxy sprayed up in PLA colours.'

'One drawback, Nick, you don't *look* Chinese,' she said flatly.

'No, boss, but *you* do.'

'What?' She hadn't been expecting this. Walsh had always envisaged she'd be running things from *Manta*.

'The PLA have women drivers. You lean out and chat up the guard. The rest of us would be in shadow.'

'I don't have a PLA uniform, Nick, if you hadn't noticed.'

'I didn't say it was perfect.'

She was starting to have serious doubts about this Chinese Parliament approach. 'Go on.'

'Meanwhile, the second half of the team have tabbed round to the far side of the camp with every bit of heavy weaponry they can carry. As the Galaxy gets to the main

434

gates and they're opened, the diversionary attack goes in at the far side of the camp with a big display of fireworks. The Galaxy team take out all the Chinese troops in the area, break out Lily Cheung, her son and Yan Tao and grab the necessary transport before high-tailing it. The rear assault team regroup and get picked up on the route out.'

She still looked sceptical. 'Do we even know where the prisoners are being held?'

Lake shook his head. 'Not yet, but we're hoping the boys in the OP might learn something during the course of today.'

McVicar and the others looked towards Walsh expectantly, anxious to get her reaction. She gave a small sigh. 'I've got to be honest, fellas. It sounds to me like a recipe for a monumental screw-up. I've got to weigh up your lives against two people who may have *already* compromised the Chinese underground movement.'

'Who dares wins,' McVicar pushed. 'We can do it. We've done this sort of stuff before.'

A smile flashed momentarily. 'Yes, I *am* aware of your reputation and I've seen you at work. But there's a danger in your starting to believe your own publicity. I think you're confusing eagerness with readiness.'

The Scotsman winked. 'Ach, we get used to walking on water.'

Lake added, 'We're up for this, boss. Don't abort. Give us some time to work up the plan and see what we get from the OP during the course of tomorrow.'

Walsh could see the sense in that. There was nothing to lose by planning. They could always cancel nearer the time. 'Okay. I'm not optimistic, but I'll review the situation further down the line. Good luck.'

She turned away then, back to the control room, knowing it was best to let the boys get on with it in their own way. Absently, she pulled out one of the flip-down bunks and lay out on the mattress, hands behind her head on the pillow. Aware that she desperately needed sleep, even if just a couple of hours, she tried to clear her brain. But she was haunted by John Dancer, seeing his face in front of her eyes and his expression when she told him she was going to abort the mission, and that he and Abe Stone would have to join them on the submarine, leaving Lily Cheung behind.

Oh God, she thought, he's going to hate me. It didn't occur to her that this was the very last thing she wanted him to do.

Dancer didn't manage to sleep much that night either. He stretched out on the blanket, listening to Stone's intermittent snoring from the adjacent bed and thought about Lily. Time and again he forced the worrying images of her interrogation from his mind and concentrated on what could be done the following day.

He'd drifted off to sleep, it seemed, just minutes before his watch alarm began its eight o'clock bleep. Bleary-eyed, he forced himself to get up and out of bed. He stripped to the waist at the washbasin and sluiced his face and torso with cold water. That would have to do, because neither he nor Stone had shaving kit with them.

His partner began to surface, yawning and coughing himself awake and rubbing the sleep from his eyes. 'Dammit, John, you were right. This is definitely a young man's game.'

'We'll survive.'

Stone grimaced, running his great paws through the matted curls on his head. 'Sure, but for how long?'

Dancer moved towards the door. 'I feel like shit. I need a kick-start, grab some breakfast.'

'You mean tea and nicotine,' he grinned. 'I'll pass and grab a banana later. See you downstairs in ten, okay?'

The hotel had no dining room and Dancer stepped out on to the sidewalk, looking for a teahouse. Then he saw their RTS driver leaning against the parked Galaxy reading a newsapaper.

'Good morning, sir,' the man said politely, folding away the journal. 'Where you want me to drive today?'

'Nowhere today.' He took a wad of *yuan* from his pocket. 'I want you to find a small garage that will respray our vehicle a different colour.'

'Respray?' The man was bewildered. 'You don't like black?'

Dancer smiled. 'I hate it. Here, white is the funeral colour, in my country it's black.'

'What colour you want?'

'A nice green. Natural, peaceful. Good *feng shui*.' He noticed a PLA truck parked a few yards down the street, soldiers loading up with groceries from a stall. 'That colour.'

The driver wrinkled his nose. 'That's army colour.'

'It's also a nice colour. But make sure the garage has it ready by four o'clock this afternoon. No later.'

'There will be no time for paint to dry.'

'Matt paint,' Dancer insisted. 'Not gloss. It'll dry.'

With a shrug the driver agreed and wandered off, shaking his head in wonder at the crazy ways of foreign devils. Dancer then found a nearby breakfast stall, downed a glass of oolong tea and sweet wheat cakes and had just returned to the hotel when Stone emerged. After a brief discussion, they set out on their shopping expedition. They scoured the market for clothes stalls and sought out a variety of military-looking garments, nearly all second-hand. It wasn't difficult. In the old days PLA and peasants' tunics and caps looked almost identical, just different colours. Green for the soldiers and drab blue for the workers. Metal Chinese star badges were also easy to come by. Within an hour they'd amassed a sizeable collection which they took back to their hotel room. Next on the list were a couple of large plastic tubs, washing line and pegs and cold-water dye. Colour, dark green. Sixty minutes later, their room resembled the Chinese laundry of legend, bedecked with lines running to every available fixture and hanging with drying clothes.

While Stone was pegging these out, Dancer went out again in search of a bicycle shop. He found several and bought six machines and a bicycle trailer for cash from the largest of them, arranging with the bemused owner to collect them later. His ad-libbed explanation that he was setting up a bikes-for-rent business for foreign tourists seemed to be accepted at inscrutable face value, although he guessed there'd be a lot of sniggering over the family rice bowl that supper time. He was surprised by his own success, but it had given him a problem he hadn't anticipated. The bicycles were bulky and had to be transported.

Still pondering the problem, he returned to the hotel at midday and made a call by satellite phone which would be quickly relayed to *Manta*. He just hoped that Walsh and the others would appreciate their efforts.

Aboard *Manta*, Nick Lake had opted, with half the team, to crash out and sleep between six and noon while McVicar and the others painstakingly began to put a plan together. Then it would be the turn of McVicar and the others to grab the shuteye and let Lake's boys continue the work until six that evening. They'd then have supper, go over the plan one more time, and put it to Walsh to make the final decision. Given a mission start of midnight, there'd be plenty of time to prepare all the necessary kit and weapons.

Dancer's message, received half-way through the day with grins and much slapping of foreheads, had everyone kicking themselves for not having thought of bicycles as a solution to their transport problem. As Nick Lake pointed out, it took a long-time Chinese resident like Dancer to come up with such an obvious answer.

For her part, Walsh was pleased to learn of the unexpected conjuring up of PLA army uniforms. It made the boys' wilder plan of bluffing their way through to the camp gates suddenly more feasible.

At midday, Lake's team had changed shifts with McVicar's team, who were exhausted, having hammered out the main strategy of the attack and planned rescue. It fell to the refreshed members to revise this, taking account of the latest news from Dancer, to refine the timings and to allocate the most appropriate weapons available to the various elements of the force.

Then, at one o'clock, a signal came through from Taffy and Dougie Squires at the observation post outside the camp that demanded another major rethink.

Walsh broke the news to Lake. 'They've confirmed that more arrests have taken place. Not exactly a wave, but a steady trickle arriving with police escorts. Dougie was actually able to identify a couple of faces he'd met on liaison with the underground network.'

'Sounds like someone's starting to sing.'

'Not necessarily, Nick. It could just be the result of ongoing police enquiries. Over the years the Bureau will have drawn up lists of suspect subversives, even if they've no evidence.'

'Have Taffy and Dougie been able to put figures on it?'

She shrugged. 'Only from those they've seen, and that doesn't include Lily or Yan Tao. But others were out in an exercise yard this morning, including Lily's son and her mother. They're obviously rounding them all up. They're hazarding a figure of twelve to eighteen so far.'

'Sod it. How many more could we squeeze on board here?'

Walsh's expression hardened. 'That's not our mission, Nick.'

Al Cherrier had overheard the conversation. 'And it's not an option, Nick. We carry a maximum load of four crew and sixteen others. For short periods we can add another four. That takes care of Dancer, Stone and the two Chinese prisoners.'

Lake shook his head. 'What's the point of rescuing Lily and Yan if we're leaving other key members behind?'

She regarded him closely. 'You may well ask, Nick. It may be a final argument for aborting the whole mission.

Except, of course, that Yan Tao is the only one who has overall knowledge of the network. If I don't make a decision, then it'll be made for me by our superiors.' She stared up at the overhead deck in search of inspiration and bit her lower lip. 'But I don't want to let John down – or Lily.'

'You met her once?'

Walsh nodded. 'We're different builds, but there's a similarity between us. Not surprising really. Almost a mirror image, I thought, when I saw her. It occurred to me then, had it not been for an accident of history, our roles could have been reversed. Me in China and her coming to my rescue.'

'Never thought of you as sentimental, boss.'

She gave a wry smile. 'Don't tell me you don't still love your teddy bear?'

But Lake didn't respond, because a sudden idea had occurred to him. 'I know *Manta* can't carry a heavier load, but I suppose there isn't a chance of getting hold of any other shipping transport for them?'

Walsh shook her head. Had he taken leave of his senses? 'There's no way the 7th Fleet is going to sail in here, Nick. Get real.'

He grinned. 'No, I had in mind something different. A local fishing boat, perhaps.'

'I really don't think . . .'

'The camp can't be more than three miles from the coast, boss.' He was warming to the idea, barely registering her protest. 'Under cover of dark, they'd be well out in the Gulf before anyone realised what had happened. We could then get the passengers picked up by a tame merchantman in international waters.'

'We don't have time to go finding a fishing boat . . .' Her voice trailed away. Was it possible? It could be worth a try, but they'd have to act fast. 'Okay, Nick, work up a Mark Two variation on the plan, just in case.'

Lake suddenly looked surprised and rather pleased. 'You think it could work?'

'There's just an outside chance. Very outside.' She pulled a tight smile. 'So I hope you're a gambling man.'

'You bet.'

'So what's the hurry, pretty maid?' Prufrock asked.

Suzy Tobin gave her warmest smile. He'd been baited now and she didn't want him wriggling off the hook. 'Can't say, Edwin. She'd kill me if I did. Let's just say it's a matter of life and death.' She leaned forward towards the back of the British Embassy chauffeur. 'Can't you go any faster?'

'Given wings, ma'am, I could fly.'

She grimaced. 'Sorry, I asked for that.'

Prufrock fanned himself with his hat. 'How intriguing this all is. Whose life and whose death, I wonder?'

Mine, Tobin thought, if we don't get out of this traffic jam soon.

And just then there was a minor miracle. Within a quarter-mile the road had mostly cleared and the Daimler Sovereign was sweeping into central Beijing. As soon as the car pulled up outside the British Embassy, Tobin was out and striding towards the entrance, leaving Edwin Prufrock struggling to catch up.

She waited impatiently at the door. 'Do hurry along, Edwin.'

He gasped for breath. 'You really are in danger of turning into an Amazon, m'dear.'

That appealed to her and she grinned. 'Thought you liked your women masterful, Edwin.'

'But, alas, Prettiness, you are not *my* woman.'

She winked. 'You just play your cards right,' and began tapping in her security code to enter through the bullet-proof glass door.

They found Iona Moncrieff pacing the 'secure-bubble' conference room, trailing a stream of smoke in her wake. She looked a wreck. Her grey skirt and jacket with the power pad shoulders looked as if she'd slept in it – which she had – and her hair was spiked with static electricity from constantly running her hands through it. The moment they entered, a smile broke on her face. She hurriedly stubbed out her cigarette in the ashtray and extended her hand to the new arrival. 'My dear Edwin, how good of you to come at such short notice.'

He glanced sideways at Tobin. 'I didn't exactly have much choice. I'm not sure what the dividing line is between an invitation and kidnap, but it was a pretty close-run thing.'

'I'm sorry, Edwin, but things have been fraught since General Sun's plane crashed.'

Prufrock shifted his balance and toyed with the rim of his hat. 'No great loss there.'

Iona frowned. 'I wouldn't say that exactly. Anyway, I thought he was a pal of yours.'

'So did I. But pals don't stab you in the back.'

'You mean the aircraft deal with the Americans?' Suzy asked.

The look on his face said that was exactly what he meant.

'Oh, c'mon, Edwin,' Iona chided, 'that sort of thing goes on all the time in big business.'

'Not in my sort of business it doesn't. I'm old school. My word is my bond and all that. The Chinese have always shared that philosophy. That's why I've done so well with them. I obviously don't find it so easy to forgive treachery as you obviously do.'

She knew he was being ridiculously selective in his memory. There were none more slippery than Prufrock and his corrupt Chinese wheeler-dealer counterparts. 'Meaning what exactly, Edwin?'

'The Americans. Your boyfriend in particular.'

Anger flushed her cheeks. 'Actually, you're referring to my husband-to-be.'

For a moment Prufrock stood in shocked silence as though someone had just physically slapped him in the face. Then he sighed and eyed her steadily. 'Forgive me if I'm ungracious enough not to congratulate you. But at least you can't say you don't know the sort of man you're marrying.'

'Bill was just doing his job, Edwin. Putting America first just like I put Britain first.'

'Well, he certainly screwed us both.' A salacious smile flickered on his lips. 'One way or another.'

'I'm sorry about that, Edwin.' She touched his forearm, wanting him to know he was still considered a friend. 'You can tell him to his face, if that'll help. He'll be here in a moment.'

'What's this all about?'

She looked at him imploringly, aware that she was 'vamping it', as the army brat called it. 'We need your help again.'

'We?'

'Bill and I.' She sighed, resignedly. 'All right, me, Edwin. *I* need your help.'

A buzzer sounded at the door and the Entry Requested sign flashed above it. Suzy Tobin walked across, checked the spyhole, and released the catch.

Although Dawson was wearing a heavy tweed overcoat against the Beijing chill, he looked hot and bothered. 'Ah, Edwin, good to see you.'

Prufrock didn't hide his hostility. 'I'm sure.'

Dawson shrugged off his coat into Suzy's waiting arms. 'Coffee, Bill?' she asked.

'Hot, treble strength and three saccharin,' he replied without thinking.

'Not good for the heart,' she chided.

His returning smile didn't come easily. 'Nor is having Frank Aspen sitting on your shoulder.' He turned back to Prufrock. 'But first things first, Edwin. Has Iona told you we need help?'

'She has, but she hasn't been specific.'

'Well, the specifics are these. Since this operation's gone belly-up, a number of dissidents have been rounded up. They're being held for interrogation at a state security camp down Qinhuangdao way. John Dancer and Abe Stone are in the vicinity and we've a force in place to break out the prisoners and spirit them away.'

'A force? You mean the people from the submarine?'

Dawson shook his head. 'Sorry, Edwin. Can't give details. Need to know and all that.'

'So how can I help?'

'There are going to be more prisoners than we can handle. We need shipping. A junk to get them out into international waters. I was thinking of your contacts through Mike Jiang. Maybe Captain Song or someone like him.'

Prufrock hesitated. 'Mike Jiang is giving us a wide berth at the moment. Doesn't want to be associated with what was going on.'

The American leaned forward. '*Persuade* him.'

'It'll cost.'

'That doesn't matter. I need action and I need it immediately, no questions asked.'

Prufrock smiled and inclined his head as he mentally added a few more noughts to the bill. 'Then it'll cost even more.'

Iona said, 'You can phone from here, Edwin. We've got a secure phone. Suzy will show you how to use it. She has all the details.'

Prufrock shrugged. 'See how it pays to have friends – and to keep them.'

Dawson watched him leave the room with Suzy and then seemed to relax a little. He picked up his coffee from the conference table and drained it in one long swallow. 'God, I needed that.'

She was sympathetic. 'You been up all night too?'

'Yes, most of the time avoiding Aspen. He smells a rat, I'm sure. He knows something's going down, but he's not sure what.'

'What have you told him?'

'That *Manta*'s withdrawing from the Gulf, but there are

some technical problems which are causing a delay. When it's all over, I'll tell him it was a last-minute operational decision between me and Walsh, and there was no time to consult with him or others.'

'He won't believe you,' Iona said. 'But if we all stick to our story, he won't be able to prove otherwise.'

Dawson shook his head. 'I'm not so sure, Majesty. I've had to make a decision now that we're going to have to try and get the junk out of Chinese waters too.'

She was suddenly alarmed. 'What in God's name have you done, Bill?'

'I've had Naval Special Warfare Group put *Manta*'s former SEAL unit on immediate stand-by. If either the sub or the junk gets into trouble with the Chinese, Walsh is going to need outside help. Trouble is, I won't be able to explain that away to Aspen.'

Iona nodded her understanding. It was a wise precaution. 'What could Aspen do to you?'

'I'm gambling that he can't do a lot. I'm retiring anyway. If we get this half right, he may even try to claim the credit.'

'It's still a brave thing for you to have done, sticking your neck out like that.'

He smiled. 'It's hardly brave, Majesty. Not when you consider what Dancer, Walsh and the others are putting themselves through.'

She returned his smile. 'You're still my hero.'

'Your rock, eh?'

'My rock.' There was a slightly wistful look in her eyes. 'The two of us walking on the beach at Cape Cod. Roll on this time next year.'

A few minutes later, Prufrock returned with Suzy. 'You're in luck. Mike Jiang was feeling in a good mood, especially when he knew he could name his own price. Captain Song's junk is out in the Gulf at the moment. Jiang will have him radioed and diverted to help out.'

Iona was overjoyed. 'Brilliant! Edwin, you're a marvel.'

445

The Englishman smiled smugly. 'Can't disagree with you there.'

'I'll have our car take you back. Let me take you downstairs.'

'Thanks, pal,' Dawson called out. 'I owe you.'

Prufrock turned at the door. 'Actually, Bill, no, you don't. Ciao.'

Leaving Dawson behind with Suzy, Iona led the way back down to reception, where she stopped by the glass security door. 'Thanks again, Edwin. We're all most grateful. And I'm *so* sorry about what Bill did and that deal going sour with General Sun. But as it turned out – with the plane crashing – it wouldn't have come off anyway.'

He placed his panama on his head and adjusted the angle. 'Oh, that's right. Knew there was something I meant to tell you. There's a new deal set up to buy the Eurofighter. This time with General Peng Zhi Yong. Similar to last time.'

'Peng?' She was dumbfounded. 'The old boy who's just been promoted to deputy head of the air force?'

'That's him.'

Suddenly the awful truth dawned on her. 'God, Edwin, you didn't? You didn't tell Peng about the plot, did you? Is that what you meant back there? That Bill doesn't owe you.'

Prufrock gave a rather sheepish smile. 'Under the circumstances, I must admit I rather feel that it is now I who owe *him*. 'Bye.'

Lieutenant Troy Krowsky was lying on his barrack cot at the Naval Amphibious Base at Coronado in San Diego reading a battered paperback about business management.

After being hauled off the Deadwater Project nearly four months earlier, when he and his colleagues had been deliberately split up and sent to different SEAL units, he'd decided he'd had enough of the military.

Within the next two months, he'd hit civvie street. And

he'd already decided to hit the sidewalk running. In true SEAL tradition. He certainly had no intention of becoming some backwoodsman or a parking-lot attendant. He planned to make it big time. He was already into a Harvard correspondence course on corporate business and had read stacks of books on the subject.

The only downside was that his head of seventies hippy ringlets and the Groucho moustache would have to go. They just wouldn't fit with the city slicker's suit and tie.

Many a time he'd wondered what had happened to his English oppo, Nick Lake, and the *Manta*'s skipper. But there'd been nothing on the grapevine, not a whisper. Then, a couple of days ago, he'd felt a flutter of excitement when he heard about an airplane crash in China killing some leading military figures. But there was no follow-up to the story on CNN. The Beijing leadership remained in place and it looked like nothing was about to change. So he assumed the whole Project Deadwater mission had, like so many in the world of Special Forces, eventually come to nothing.

So he was curious when his business studies were interrupted by the unannounced arrival of the base adjutant. 'Message for you, Krowsky. You're moving out. Special duties.'

He was surprised. 'Pardon me, sir?'

'A back channel from Rear Admirial Crozier in Hawaii. You're wanted on stand-by for something called Project Deadwater. Be packed with all your kit and in my office in one hour. A special helo is coming to pick up you and other members of your old team.'

Krowsky dropped his paperback and swung his legs off the bed. This sounded interesting. 'No details, sir?'

The adjutant shook his head. 'No further dissemination. So no goodbyes or phone calls to girlfriend, wife or parents.'

As soon as the man had gone, Krowsky began packing as

his mind reeled. Why was he being recalled? Had the mission gone ahead after all? And, if it had, could it now be in some sort of trouble?

By the evening, Dancer and Stone were exhausted but in good spirits. It had been a satisfying day of problem-solving and improvisation.

By mid-afternoon the cold-dyed second-hand clothing had dried over their room's heater and the driver had taken it to a local laundry for ironing. The Galaxy was returned from the spray shop at four; while the shade of paint used wasn't exactly PLA green, it would look close enough in the dark. After several attempts, Dancer had made a passable cardboard stencil of a Chicom star cut from an old packet of cornflour and had purchased a small tin of bright yellow paint in readiness for use later that night. He and Abe had then gone to work with purchased spanners and screwdrivers to unfix all the vehicle's rear seating.

When darkness fell, they drove to some derelict land on the outskirts of the town, opened the doors and dumped all the seats and bracket fittings before returning to the bicycle shop. The owner was waiting, happy at having his best day's business in years and helped them load up the bicycles into the back of the Galaxy.

They then drove back down to the road bridge and pulled over into the same small clearing in the under-growth where they had met the night before.

Dancer had barely killed the lights and switched off the engine when a face smeared in cam-cream appeared at the side window. Dougie Squires was barely recognisable.

He opened the door. 'How goes it?'

'Fine today. No probs.' But Squires's tense face belied his glib words. 'Taff's staying back at the OP till the rest join him. Got a signal about the bikes, by the way. Bleedin' brilliant idea.'

Dancer grinned. 'Glad to be of some use. Have you checked the landing area?'

Squires nodded. 'Slight hiccup there, I'm afraid. Some old sod fishing.'

Now Dancer knew the reason for the man's haunted expression. 'What you going to do?'

'It's an operational decision,' Squires said. 'No one will order me to kill him. Some of our guys have had to murder innocent civilians in the past, but it's bad for the soul. I've never had to do it before.'

'Do you *have* to take him out?' Stone asked.

'If he compromises the mission. But I don't think that need happen. He can stay with the guys guarding the beach. I've got Plasticuffs and he can be gagged – if only I can get to him before he starts screaming blue murder.'

Dancer recalled the layout. The trees at the roadside behind them offered cover down to the beach. 'Is there a way down through there?'

Squires nodded.

'If you go down and get in position behind him, we could distract him. Walk along the beach and have a chat.'

The combat swimmer suddenly looked as though a great weight had been lifted from his mind. 'Forgot you spoke the lingo.'

But Stone was looking concerned. 'I'm not sure that's a bright idea. I don't like the thought of murder any more than you, but as you're not taking the old boy with you, then he's going to be a liability. When he's found, he'll tell the police we left by boat.'

Squires shrugged. 'Then it'll be up to McVicar or Lake – or Janie, I guess, to overrule my decision.' He gave a sheepish grin. 'That's easier for me to live with.'

It was obvious that Stone thought it was a bad decision, but they had no time to hang around discussing the moral ethics any longer. While Squires disappeared into the undergrowth and made his way down to the river mouth, Dancer took the holdall filled with the pseudo PLA uniforms from the Galaxy, then he and Stone began descending the embankment along the footpath to the river. As it levelled out, they could see ahead the hurricane lamp, flickering beside the old fisherman in his quilted jacket and fur cap. He was casting his line out into the water at the river mouth. They waited until they received two clicks from the 'send' button on Squires's radio to let them know he was in position.

Then they began walking slowly towards their target. It wasn't long before the old man picked up the sound of their footsteps on the shingle and turned, suddenly alarmed.

'Who's there?' he demanded, squinting to make out the two dark shapes.

'*Duìbùqǐ*,' Dancer said in a friendly voice. 'We didn't mean to startle you, old man. We're just taking a stroll. How is the fishing?'

The fisherman relaxed and wiped his nose on his sleeve. 'The fish get smarter by the year. Or else it is pollution in the water. I've caught nothing yet. Still, there's plenty of time until the dawn.'

As they drew closer, they could see the dark shadow gliding silently across the strip of beach behind him.

'I haven't fished for years,' Dancer said conversationally, dropping the holdall by his side.

Suddenly the old man frowned as the light from his lamp fell across the two strangers. His mouth dropped. '"Round-eyes"', he murmured in surprise, his alarm returning.

At that moment Squires's forearm swept round the man's throat and dragged him down on to his back. Dancer sprang forward, pushing the silenced .45 pistol in front of his nose. 'One squeak from you and you're dead. Be quiet and you won't get hurt. Understand?'

The old man was almost cross-eyed as he stared in terror at the muzzle and nodded frantically. Stone was helping to get their victim's arms behind his back while Squires slipped the thick Plasticuff loops around his wrists and snapped them tight. Then they lifted the hapless fisherman into the shadows by the dunes. His feet were similarly bound together, a strip of plastic parcel tape wrapped round his mouth and a scrim net scarf used as a blindfold.

'Can you breathe okay?' Dancer asked, and when the man nodded, the American patted him on the back, trying to reassure him he'd come to no harm. 'You're safe now if you just stay there and don't try to move.'

They had barely finished when Squires received the signal from the landing party. He heard Nick Lake's voice in his radio earpiece. '*X-ray to Whisky One, X-ray to Whisky One. Over.*'

'Roger, X-ray, you're clear to land.' Squires turned to Dancer. 'I'm just going back to cover the approaches.'

And, as the SBS man returned to a vantage point farther back along the river, Dancer looked out to sea. Tonight the blue-black water was millpond calm, the tide rippling in without energy. It was almost eerily quiet and he strained to see or hear anything to mark the approach of the landing force. Not a sound, and nothing in the slowly forming and reforming mist that had any recognisable shape. Yet he knew they were out there and he had the awesome and vivid mental image of the combat swimmers emerging one by one, as if from the bowels of the ocean bed, intent on mayhem and destruction.

Then he picked up the first sound, a rippling of water different from the gentle ebb and flow of the tide. Then another and another. A muted *dip-dipping* noise was beginning to have a recognisable rhythm. Paddles. A shadow in the mist began to take on a denser shade of black and a solid form. He was aware that his pulse had quickened and he was holding his breath.

And in the second it took to blink, they were there. First the bulbous hull of rubber stealth craft running silently on its electric engines and resembling some grotesquely bloated sea monster from primeval times, bristling with weapons and men in glistening black confirming visually that the coast was indeed clear. It was followed by three more conventional Gemini dinghies being paddled out of the mist in quick succession. The first two craft carried most of the team, those behind, low in the water under the weight, carried an arsenal of heavy support weaponry. It occurred to Dancer then that it must have taken literally hours of exhausting work to have manhandled it all from *Manta* to the surface and then load it all aboard.

Before the Phantom touched the shoreline, its occupants were out and wading through the shallow water in their rubber wet suits with M16 rifles and heavy-duty Stoner Mark 23 machine-guns at the ready. They fanned out, passing Dancer and Stone without a word to form a defensive arc around the shingle beach.

It took a moment before Dancer could identify Lake and McVicar, and then the markedly smaller figure of Janie Walsh.

Her smile seemed to shine in the dark. 'Hi, John, I had hoped we wouldn't meet again in a while. Still, thanks for all you've done . . .' Her voice trailed away as she noticed the bound, gagged and blindfold figure curled up in the sand. 'Who the hell is that?'

Dougie Squires had been relieved by the new arrivals and had returned. Before Dancer could reply, the SBS marine said, 'A fisherman, boss. It was my decision not to kill him.'

Walsh hesitated, clearly weighing up the risks. All around, the men were beginning to peel off their wet suits.

'I'll slit his throat for you, Dougie,' one SAS trooper offered, adding, 'you big girl's blouse.'

'That's enough,' Walsh snapped. Then to Squires, 'Okay, I'll stick with your decision.' She gave a tight smile. 'After all, he could be a distant cousin of mine.'

Squires looked thankful.

Dancer kicked the holdall by his feet. 'I've got the uniforms. They don't look bad.'

'Excellent.' She turned to the others. 'Clothes here for everyone in Red Team.'

Then, without another word, she began to unzip her own suit, apparently oblivious to those around her and they to her. Dancer and Stone exchanged quick glances and edged discreetly away as Walsh stripped down to an olive drab T-shirt and rather matronly army-issue knickers.

It became clear to Dancer now what was happening. The members of Red Team, who would be travelling with him in the Galaxy, were changing into the makeshift uniforms, the rest into black denim fatigues, combat vests and belt orders.

Walsh noticed him standing, eyes averted. 'You, too, John. Don't be coy. I like a man with a nice pair of buns.'

He grinned at the wind-up. 'A Chippendale I'm not.'

'He's got legs like one of the chairs,' Stone guffawed as Dancer reached for the holdall.

Those who were changed switched with the guard detail to allow them to discard their wet suits and begin the selection of weaponry. The entire procedure was completed within ten minutes.

On Walsh's insistence, Abe Stone was staying behind with White Team, call sign Whisky One, with two SBS men who would hold the beach assembly area secure until the others returned.

'Take care, old son,' Stone said, gripping Dancer's hand firmly. He wasn't normally one to show emotion, but his eyes were moist. 'Remember, we got some new business to set up someplace. A new life.'

'Sure. Back to Laos, eh?'

'There're worse places. Ciao.'

And Dancer fell into step beside Walsh, leading the crocodile of heavily armed men up the footpath towards the waiting Galaxy. While the bicycles and trailer were unloaded, Dancer used the cardboard stencil he'd made earlier to paint a passable yellow star on the front of the vehicle in quick-dry matt paint.

When everyone was ready, Walsh resynchronised watches with Nick Lake and McVicar. She no longer had control of the operation which had passed to McVicar as OpsCom, with Lake acting as his second-in-command. The SAS sergeant would be travelling in the Galaxy with her as part of Red Team.

Meanwhile, Lake commanded the four-man Blue Team, which now prepared to set off independently across country by bicycle to prepare for a diversionary attack at the rear of the interrogation centre.

Two bicycles remained on board when the Galaxy started up ten minutes later with Walsh at the wheel, a green-dyed Mao cap pulled low over her eyes. Following instructions from Dancer, she took the vehicle on to the main road, then after a short distance turned off inland along the track which led to the camp. Just below the crest of the hill, she pulled over to where Taffy was waiting for them. He had just withdrawn from the OP overlooking the camp; all day he had been updating Walsh on board *Manta* by satellite via Hereford.

'Any more news?' she asked him, sliding out of the driving seat.

'Only one thing in the last hour,' Taffy said, and she saw the concern in his eyes. 'I decided I'd take a leisurely scout around closer to that roadblock. Make sure we didn't rush into any nasty surprises tonight.'

'And?'

'I was quite close when a truck arrived with two new prisoners. I couldn't see their faces, but I heard a name mentioned. Fan Xiu Kun.'

She looked crestfallen. 'Oh, no, not the poet. God, as if he hasn't been through enough.'

Dancer was shocked. Somehow Fan's fate had become inextricably linked with all the hopes Debs had ever had for the freeing of China. But before he could react, McVicar said, 'Then it's as well we've got that junk as backup.'

'I hope,' Walsh replied. 'It's going to be touch and go whether it gets here in time.'

'At least,' Dancer said, 'Fan's presence vindicates our

454

going ahead. It was a brave decision and I'm grateful you made it. And I know Debs would have been too.'

Momentarily, Walsh failed to connect the name. 'Sorry? Debs?'

'My wife. She carried a bit of a torch for Fan.'

She smiled. 'Your wife. Of course.' For a moment their eyes met, words unspoken, then she turned away.

Dougie Squires and Taffy pulled the last of the bicycles from the Galaxy and after donning their monocular night-sights and mounting up, they moved off cautiously into the inky darkness. The two men formed Red Two. It was their job to get into position behind the roadblock. Hopefully the ruse with the painted Galaxy and the PLA uniforms would work, allowing Red One to approach the camp and get admitted. But if the roadblock guards became suspicious, the role of Red Two was to take them out from behind as swiftly as possible and, they hoped, silently.

However, if it all went to plan, Red Two would wait until the main attack went in before taking out the roadblock guards, so freeing up the whole team's axis of escape.

The team's call signs matched their designated colours. R for Red became Romeo, B for Blue became Bravo, and it was an anxious twenty-minute wait before Romeo Two's call sign confirmed they were in position. Only seconds later, Bravo One called in. Nick Lake's four-man diversionary team had reached the far side of the camp by bicycle.

'All set,' McVicar told Walsh.

This time her nervous smile lacked sparkle. 'Let's do it, soldier.' And she swung back up into the driver's seat of the Galaxy and started the engine. Everyone scrambled aboard and seconds later Red One was bouncing over the grass on to the track and cresting the hill. Below them lay the black void of the next shallow valley, the sprinkling of lights at the camp resembling stars floating in space. And some-where in between they could see the burning charcoal brazier beside the roadblock. Walsh took a deep breath and put her foot down on the accelerator.

All eyes were fixed ahead on the fitful flicker of flame and the elongated shadows thrown by the figures of the PLA troops standing outside their wooden shack. As they drew closer, the men, in bulky quilted coats and fur caps, could be seen warming themselves by the fire and sipping from tin mugs. One of them saw the Galaxy's headlamps approaching and called out to the officer-in-charge, who emerged from the shack a few moments later.

He looked young, Dancer thought, but also arrogant. The jumped-up son of some cadre official with connections, he guessed.

The roadblock itself was a primitive affair: a collection of concrete-filled oil drums and a weighted, horizontal red-and-white pole resting across two upright posts. On instruction from the officer, one of the soldiers ventured into the middle of the road and raised his right hand, palm out. Walsh eased on the brakes, careful to stop a short distance back so that the Galaxy's interior wasn't illuminated by the brazier's fire. The soldier and the officers began walking towards them.

She knew that Red Two were out there and that all around her hands were reaching for the door handles as weapons were readied – just in case. She took a deep breath, threw open her own door and dropped down to the track. The officer looked surprised, she thought, as she brushed down the dyed tunic top. She had to admit it fitted more snugly than she would have liked.

'Good evening, comrade,' she said, looking up with the brightest smile she could muster.

But the officer obviously put his own self-importance before a pretty woman's smile and frowned at her. 'Who are you, comrade? We're not expecting any more prisoners tonight.'

'Not prisoners, comrade. Rotational troop replacements from Beijing. We're late because we broke down on the road.'

'I have no notification.'

She waved a fax print-out at him. Earlier in the day it had been sent via Dancer's satellite phone from a special forgery unit attached to Langley. It had a facsimile Ministry of State Security letterheading, which had originally been obtained for them by Dancer himself, and a terse letter of explanation written in Chinese. 'To whom it may concern,' she said.

'I should have been notified,' he complained again.

In the Galaxy, Dancer was becoming concerned at the lengthy delay. In guttural peasant Chinese, he called out through the open driver's door, 'Hurry up, comrade commander! We've been on the road all bloody day! We need food and sleep!'

McVicar decided to add some colour. 'And I need a crap! I'm busting!'

Outside, Walsh winced at the voices behind her. The officer shone a torch over her shoulder at the vehicle. All he could see were shapes in uniform and Mao caps and a lot of shadows. She said, 'They're an undisciplined shower.' Her eyes went heavenward in an expression of exasperation. 'But they *are* exhausted. Why don't you phone the camp for confirmation?'

She knew they weren't linked by phone or radio and guessed rightly that the upstart prick wouldn't want to lose face by admitting that his function was not much more than a deterrent to nosy local peasants.

Irritably he indicated to one of his soldiers to raise the pole and said, 'Go on. But next time make sure everyone is properly notified and the camp sends papers to me.'

'Of course,' she said with a sweet smile, 'it's a shambles. You are most kind, comrade.'

With that she saluted smartly, turned on her heel and jumped up into the driver's seat.

'Sweet Jesus,' she murmured and slipped the gear into first.

'Well done, girl,' McVicar said as they moved off. And everyone slunk back down to avoid prying eyes as they passed swiftly through and back on to the open track.

Once the light of the roadblock brazier had receded to a mere flickering speck behind them, she slowed on the handbrake and stopped.

McVicar spoke into his radio. 'Red One to all units. Confirm readiness and all clear. Over.'

White, back at the beach, Blue at the far side of the camp, and Red Two at the roadblock behind them all confirmed.

'Stand by, stand by,' McVicar said, and nodded to Walsh.

Again they moved forward and the eight-foot razor-wired fence with its odious watchtowers and the lighted barrack blocks loomed before them.

Lily Cheung curled into a ball in the corner of her cell like a wounded animal waiting to die. She could not stop the involuntary trembling that had taken control of her body. Every inch of her torso and limbs throbbed with pain from the beatings.

They'd been rough peasant types, no doubt chosen for the job. They had come in after Brigadier Ting Han-chen had become tired of being coaxing and persuasive on and off for twenty-four hours and getting nowhere. Until then he had seemed like the perfect gentleman with his quiet oily voice, cultivated manners and smart suit. Patiently he had taken her through her story time after time after time.

Then, without warning, it was as if something had snapped inside his head. He had called out and the cell door had opened. The soldiers had apparently been waiting, sticks and lengths of hosepipe in their hands. Ting just stood there, watching impassively, as they leered and ripped the skirt from her waist in their first act of humiliation.

They called her all sorts of names. An unpatriotic whore, a silver bullet, an American's poke-hole and a hundred others as the shame and terror washed over her and drowned out their baying voices. Each tried to out-insult his companion. They pulled and tore at her blouse and laughed at the smallness of her breasts, calling her a boy, while another held his nose, saying he could smell her sex like rotten fish. They all laughed at that, even more so when they suddenly realised from the tiny puddle on the concrete floor that she had wet herself in fear.

Then the first blow was struck, a length of hosepipe at her face. Her forearm came up and she went down, half-ducking and half-falling. Then the rain of blows closed in and she curled in a ball, hands protecting her head. Her eyes were tight shut as though if she couldn't see what was happening it wasn't happening.

But it was and it did. For how long she couldn't tell, but it had seemed like for ever, and there were periods when she couldn't remember what had happened, so she reasoned she must have drifted in and out of consciousness during the violent thrashing.

Now she vaguely recalled the voice, Ting's voice, she thought. And suddenly it stopped, just as quickly as it had begun. She heard the men swear and curse at her, the shuffling of their feet followed by the slamming and bolting of the steel door. Then, perversely, the searing heat of the pain returned with a vengeance, surging through her body so that she felt as though she was on fire from the inside out. Worst of all was her feeling of shame. Shame that while she was cowed and thrashed, she had thought only of herself.

Tears trickled down her cheeks as she sniffed miserably and risked opening her eyes. The first thing she saw was the lens of the small closed-circuit TV camera watching her from the corner of the ceiling.

At the end of the corridor outside, Brigadier Ting stood in a room observing the curled, sobbing figure on one of a bank of wall monitors. Beside him was Inspector Xia.

'I wonder if she'll stick to her story now?' the diminutive policeman thought aloud.

Ting chewed on his lower lip. 'Well, it's true she had nothing to do with the briefcase bomb. That was given directly to Wang by the American.'

Xia nodded in thoughtful agreement. 'And, I suppose, there's nothing to prove she didn't have a migraine, as she says, and decided she needed a few days' peace and quiet at Wang's holiday home. After all, he'd given her a key.'

'But then Yan Tao turns up.'

'She claims she wasn't expecting him,' Xia reminded, 'but that he had always fancied her. That he knew she'd be alone at Wang's place and went along to chance his luck just before we arrived.'

'She could be telling the truth,' Ting conceded. 'Which would mean she was just being used. By the American Dancer for sex and as a source of information. And by Yan Tao – for what? Why should he go to see her after he knew the assassination attempt had gone wrong?'

Xia agreed. 'I'd have thought he'd have more important considerations on his plate.'

Ting's eyes moved along the line of monitors. Cheung Ho, in his underpants, sat miserable and ashamed of his abject cowardice on a cell bench, hugging his plump and lacerated body.

'Her brother's been singing like a finch,' Ting said. 'Says Yan Tao is big in the resistance and has given us lots of names, including the poet Fan.'

'That one would say anything to save his life,' Xia said.

Ting nodded. 'But he still insists his sister is innocent.' A half-smile. 'Or is his own sister where he draws the line in his treachery?'

'There you have it,' Xia agreed. He glanced at another monitor showing Yan Tao stretched out on a mattress in his underwear. Mind and body now beyond exhaustion, his bruised and torn frame had clearly seeped blood on to the mattress. Xia did not have Ting's taste for physical interrogation and had turned away when the torturers went to work. But the sound of the screams and the pitiful wails had been too much for him. He had only just managed to leave the cell before throwing up into a fire bucket in the corridor. Despite the barbarous treatment and despite Ting's refusal to allow him medical attention, Yan had remained resolutely silent.

'So how do we break him?' Xia now asked. 'How do we make him tell us what he knows? Already he's lost teeth and, I think, has fractured bones. What more can be done?'

It was exactly what Ting had been asking himself and, as his eyes suddenly returned to Lily Cheung crawling painfully across her cell floor towards the enamel pisspot, he thought he had the answer.

He turned to one of the camp's interrogators. 'Have Yan Tao brought in here.'

The interrogator stifled a yawn. 'In the morning, sir?'

Irritation blazed in Ting's eyes. 'No, *now!* You can sleep when we've broken this cunning dog.'

Xia was confused. 'Why bring him here?'

Ting smiled and inclined his head to one side thoughtfully. 'If Cheung's right and he thinks that much of her. . . Watch the screen.'

When Ting re-entered her cell a few moments later, Lily was just pulling up her pants. But she was now beyond caring, beyond shame.

'How are you, Lily?' he asked in his low, honeyed voice.

She averted her eyes. 'I am hurting,' she muttered, barely audibly.

'Yes?' Almost sounding surprised.

Still she refused to look at him. 'I think my kidneys are damaged.'

'And what makes you say that?

'There is blood in my urine.'

Ting was suddenly bored with her sullen manner. He reached for her chin with his right hand, his fingers like angry, rigid claws as they twisted her face round until her eyes couldn't avoid looking into his. 'Well, that is a shame, isn't it? And all *so* unnecessary. You have no one to blame

461

but yourself. I gave you every opportunity to speak the truth. So, have you learned your lesson? Have you anything more to tell me now? About *exactly* who Yan Tao is in the underground resistance movement? What your own involvement was?' His eyes bored into hers. 'Think about it.'

He gradually released the pressure of his grip until just his forefinger remained. With it he drew a feather-touch stroke along her chin. He could smell the fear on her now and feel the soft down of hair on his fingertip, just as he had imagined it back in his office when he had first seen the file photos of Cheung Mei-ling.

His interest in the texture of her skin and his stirring physical response was so intense that he didn't see the change in her eyes. The seething hatred of the years of institutionalised intimidation, oppression and cruelty boiled up to a volcanic rage. Her eyes were dark with loathing.

The thick gob of spit struck him just below his left eye and he recoiled in shock. 'YOU ARE A DOG TURD!' she screamed.

Instantly, on reflex, he retaliated, striking her hard across the face and sending her reeling across the cell, where she stumbled and fell back on to her mattress, legs splayed.

Ting used a handkerchief to wipe the mess from his face, then forcing a smile to his lips, he said softly, 'Well, Lily Cheung, don't say you weren't given every opportunity.' He paused for a moment and glanced up at the TV camera. 'Tell me, young lady, do you know what an electric cattle prod is?'

She huddled on the mattress, shaking her head, not understanding.

'Well, you're going to find out. And, however much it hurts, I'd like you to smile because you are going to be on television.'

Seventeen

It had been a long time since Dancer had felt fear like this. Gut-wrenching, nauseating fear, so powerful he could hear his heart thudding in his chest, the blood rushing in his ears. He hadn't experienced anything like this since he'd been behind the lines in Viet Nam. The only consolation, as the Galaxy trundled towards the looming wire mesh gates of the camp, was that he knew the feeling would vanish the moment the first shot was fired.

McVicar, the seasoned professional, showed no outward sign of the tension Dancer knew he must be feeling. The Scotsman gave Walsh a reassuring wink and she returned an uncertain smile to let him know it was appreciated.

Suddenly torchlight shone in their direction, momentarily blinding them. The guards were no doubt wondering who the unexpected arrivals were, but as the Galaxy had already passed through the roadblock, they wouldn't be alarmed, probably just annoyed at having their game of mah-jong interrupted.

Walsh pulled up short, applied the handbrake and climbed down. She strode towards the gate and repeated to the guard what she'd told the soldiers at the roadblock. He accepted the faxed message through a gap in the fence.

The man read it and looked perplexed. 'We're not expecting you.'

'I know, I've already been told that. The usual bureaucratic bumbling in Beijing.'

That went down well. Everyone knew about the useless PLA bureaucrats at headquarters.

'I'll have to check with the duty officer, comrade. I don't know where there's room to billet you.'

'Of course,' Walsh replied reasonably. 'But let's get in

first. My men are tired and have been cooped up all day. They need to stretch their legs and take a pee.'

The guard looked uncertain.

Her best neon smile flashed. 'I'd be most grateful to you, comrade.'

That persuaded him. He turned the lock and swung one of the gates open. 'Pull in over there and wait. I won't be long,' he told her.

Walsh called her thanks as she ran back to the Galaxy and climbed in. 'God, for a moment I didn't think . . . '

'Well done,' Dancer said.

As she pulled away, McVicar spoke into his radio. 'Red One to Red Two and Blue One. Stand by, stand by.'

They rolled up to the gates, their headlights picking out the barrack blocks and the neatly parked row of trucks and jeeps.

McVicar said into his radio, 'Go, go, go!'

All five doors of the Galaxy eased open. Half-a-dozen Chinese troops stood around outside the guardhouse, hunched against the cold in their quilted anoraks, idly watching the first soldier relock the gate behind the new arrivals.

Then, suddenly, all eyes slewed round as they heard the abrupt scream of displaced air in the distance, followed almost immediately by three scorching pulses of blinding light in rapid succession. Gasps of surprise were drowned out by the rolling detonations, the first two high in the air as the watchtowers at the rear of the camp disintegrated. The third anti-tank rocket, fired from a disposable LAW launcher, took out the back entry gates, blowing them asunder in a shower of sparks so that they were left hanging uselessly from their torn hinges.

The Chinese soldiers gawped, rooted to the spot as the dying thunder was replaced by a ripple of smaller explosions as Blue Team's grenade-launcher went into action, backed up by a heavy-duty Stoner machine-gun. It sounded like an entire division out there.

At last the startled guards began to react, some reaching for the weapons rack beside the guardhouse door. Eyes widened and mouths dropped as they realised that the soldiers emerging from the Galaxy were armed and were clearly not Chinese. McVicar led the assault, firing his Heckler & Koch sub-machine-gun from the hip. Rounds from the other four SAS men in the Galaxy ripped along the line of soldiers as they tried to leap for cover, only to be cut down and tossed contemptuously aside.

'GRENADE!' another SAS man yelled and hurled the L2A2 in through the guardhouse door. Everyone ducked at the brilliant flux of light as the sides and roof of the wood-and-brick structure blew apart like an exploded diagram, hurtling split planks and broken masonry far and wide over the parking area. Arc lights from the two front watchtowers suddenly came on, picking up the attackers in their dazzling beams. Bullets started peppering the ground around them. The answering fire from McVicar and his men was as fast as it was ferocious. The watchtowers were hosed with sustained automatic fire until the guards' shooting stopped and the lamps were knocked out.

The silence that followed was sudden and stunning.

Then Blue Team's diversionary attack resumed, automatic fire rattling in from the distant slope. McVicar closed in to check the Chinese survivors for signs of life while Dancer drew out his silenced .45 and ran across to the guard who had let them in. The man was lying against the perimeter fence looking dazed as blood dripped from a minor shrapnel wound to his left bicep. Otherwise he appeared to be unhurt.

Dancer grabbed the lapel of his coat. 'Where are the prisoners being held for interrogation?'

The man stared back at him, terrified. It took a couple of moments for him to find his voice. 'Blocks Five and Six.'

Dancer hauled him to his feet. 'Show me! Now!'

As he pushed the man forward, he was joined by Walsh, McVicar and a couple of SAS soldiers. Meanwhile, the remaining two SAS men were checking the parked PLA trucks for ignition keys and diesel in the tanks. If all went to plan, they would be reinforced in a few minutes by Red Two, who by now should have silenced the roadblock duty guard and be cycling back down to the camp's main gate.

Dancer was half-running, pushing the injured guard along in front of him. They were moving through the main drag of the camp, a twenty-foot wide concourse of concrete that ran between two rows of identical brick barrack buildings. Up ahead, several doors had opened and Chinese soldiers and personnel in civilian clothes were pouring out to see what was going on as Blue Team continued their diversion.

Meanwhile, Dancer was counting the number signs on the barrack doors. Finally they'd arrived at Number Five. 'Which one is the woman in?'

The guard was confused, now feeling the effects of blood loss. 'There are two women – one young, one old. Mother and daughter.'

Of course, Dancer realised, Mama Cheung had been taken into custody with the others. 'The daughter.'

'This hut,' replied the guard.

Dancer glanced at his watch. The attack had begun barely two minutes earlier and the entire camp still appeared to be in total confusion. It was just as well because time was of the essence.

With Walsh and the SAS team close behind him, he climbed the concrete steps and inched open the door. Just inside there was a small area for the guard with a hard-backed chair and camp table, then iron bars and a gate separated off a long corridor with steel cell doors leading off both right and left. The guard himself was peering out of a side window at the pyrotechnic display being put on by Blue Team.

On hearing the creaking hinges of the door, the man began to turn. 'Do you know what the hell is going . . . ?'

The two .45 rounds spat viciously and silently from

Dancer's pistol and slammed into the guard's chest within a centimetre of each other. The force of impact threw him back against the bars and he slid to the floor in a crumpled heap.

'Haven't lost your touch,' McVicar observed, following in as the American stooped over the corpse to search for keys.

'It's called self-preservation,' Dancer replied. He detached a ring of keys from the guard's belt and moved swiftly to the gate. Instinctively he tried the largest key first and it fitted. A double twist and it opened on to the still deserted corridor beyond.

Then, just as he stepped inside, two guards emerged from one of the far doors. Slumped between them, with an arm around each of their shoulders, was a prisoner. His blood-streaked body was naked except for a pair of baggy underpants and his head lolled as though he were only half-conscious.

One of the guards saw Dancer and immediately yelled a warning, shrugging the prisoner's arm from his shoulder as he reached for the holster on his belt. The prisoner looked up suddenly and, despite the bruised and battered face, Dancer knew it was Yan Tao. He raised his automatic a fraction, but hesitated. Yan and the guards were bunched together; there was no clear target.

Behind him, McVicar made a snap decision. 'GRENADE!'

'Christ!' Dancer breathed and threw himself to the floor. What the hell was the SAS sergeant playing at? He wasn't able to identify the Haley & Weller multi-burst stun grenade as it sailed over his head.

The first ear-splitting burst of sound filled the corridor and he waited for the hot shards of metal to rip into his body following the blinding flash.

They didn't, but another deafening, disorientating explosion and dazzling pulse of light followed, and another. As the truth dawned, he was vaguely aware of McVicar's heavy boots passing just inches from his head, racing towards the guards and prisoner. Others followed close behind. A 'flash-bang', he now realised. That was what the SAS jokingly called them. Some 160 decibels and several million candelas of light, designed to stun hostage ta'.ers for vital seconds when an attack went in.

As Dancer crawled to his feet, his ears ringing and his vision blurred with the after-image of the searing incandescent light, he could just make out McVicar and his team dispatching the prostrated guards with silenced bullets to the head.

The Scotsman looked back. 'John, Yan's injured. Stay with him while we clear the rest of the cells.' Then he looked beyond the barred gate. 'Janie, keep watch and shoot anyone who tries to come in – and don't hesitate.'

Walsh gave a nervous nod and turned back to the door. Dancer crawled across the floor to where Yan had been propped against a wall.

Yan's face was bloody and bruised, his eyes closed with the blue and yellow swellings on his face. He squinted and tried to force a half-hearted smile. 'Mr John? Is it really you? I never thought I'd see you again.' There were bloody gaps where his front teeth should have been. 'Never live to see you play a decent round.'

The three SAS men were starting to work down the corridor, two covering at each cell door while the third used the bunch of keys to open the locks.

Dancer moved closer to Yan. 'Where's Lily, Tao, do you know?'

He nodded, indicating the far end of the corridor. 'The last cell on the left.'

The last cell. The last one that the SAS team would reach. 'Tao, I must leave you for a moment.'

A nod. 'Yes, you must. I'll be all right for a few minutes.'

The American touched his shoulder and gave a tight smile of reassurance. 'You're a brave man, Tao. And we'll have you and Lily out of here in no time.'

He left then, bounding down the corridor, lifting the .45

automatic as he went. The door wasn't locked, but slightly ajar. The two guards stood with pistols drawn. They were staring directly at him, clearly terrified by the noise they'd just heard in the corridor outside. But Dancer was momentarily distracted by the woman spreadeagled against the wall behind them. It took a moment for him to recognise Lily Cheung, her hair matted and filthy, her arms spread out and secured to pinion rings set on the wall on each side of her. The sight of her bruised body and her bare breasts whipped at his senses. On the floor lay some sort of electrical device attached to a cable. Suddenly he realised what it was. A cattle prod.

That moment's distraction nearly cost him dear. The first guard fired. But it was wild and unaimed, singing past Dancer's ear and sparking off the steel doorframe to spend itself uselessly in the corridor.

'BASTARDS!' Dancer screamed and closed his finger on the trigger of the .45 as the second guard fired back simultaneously.

Dancer was barely aware of the sharp, burning sensation in his left bicep as he watched his opponent curl over under the impact of the round entering his gut. In a half-pirouette, the man appeared to be screwing himself into the ground as he went down with a strangulated cry.

The first guard threw down his weapon and raised his hands. His face was ashen and his eyes wide with terror. 'Don't shoot, don't shoot!' he pleaded in Mandarin.

The American hestitated and regarded the trembling guard for a second as a puddle began to form around the man's feet. Then he raised the pip sight of the .45 and shot him squarely between the eyes. The man's face disintegrated.

There was a gasp from Lily as the guard fell. 'John, John! Oh, thank God. They were going to use that awful thing on me.'

He moved across to her. There were tears of joy in her eyes.

'Oh Lily, Lily, what have they done to you?' Dancer croaked.

She turned her head away abruptly. 'Do not ask. Do not look at me.'

He examined the steel cuff on her wrist. 'Do the guards have the keys?'

She nodded. 'The fat one.'

Moments later, he'd found them and released her. She fell into his arms, sobbing uncontrollably.

McVicar stepped into the room. He looked around, taking it all in. 'You've been busy. How is she?'

Dancer eased her hands from his neck and looked into the sad sable eyes. 'Can you walk?' he asked urgently.

She nodded numbly. 'I think so.'

McVicar said, 'There's a cupboard out here with prison uniforms. I'll get her something to wear.'

A moment later he returned. The black cotton jacket and trousers were the smallest he could find, but they were still several sizes too large and she had to roll up the sleeves and trouser cuffs. When they stepped out into the corridor, they found the SAS team lifting Yan onto one of several collapsible stretchers they had brought with them.

'Oh, my poor Tao!' Lily gasped and stumbled towards him.

McVicar blocked her path. 'Sorry, sweetheart, no time. He's okay. Our medic's given him a shot of morphine. But now we have to scoot.'

'Scoot?' she queried.

'Go,' Dancer explained, as they started walking towards the door. 'We have to get out of here before the garrison realises what's happening.'

A look of horror came over her face. 'Bao and Mama Cheung! You must help them!'

'They're here?'

'In the next block, I think.'

McVicar heard. 'Sorry, John, no time.'

Dancer shook his head. 'I can't leave the boy.'

Walsh said, 'Take Lily and Yan Tao, Dave. I'll go with John.'

McVicar shook his head. 'Breaking your own rules? We can't hang about.'

She looked suddenly angry that he was questioning her word. 'If we miss the first truck, we'll have to take our chances with the junk.'

The Scotsman started to say something, then changed his mind. There was no time to argue. He beckoned to the rest of his team.

Dancer turned to Lily. 'Go with them. I'll get Bao and Mama Cheung and join you in a few minutes.' He saw the hesitation in her eyes. 'Now GO!'

McVicar ushered her forward after the two SAS stretcher-bearers. Dancer just saw her anxious backward glance before she was swallowed up by the night.

'C'mon,' Walsh said, 'we've got work to do.'

Although it had seemed like for ever, they'd actually been in the camp for barely seven or eight minutes. Outside, the darkness on the far side of the camp was still being lit by the tell-tale fireflies of tracer rounds pouring down from Blue Team's onslaught and the occasional crump and flash of an incoming grenade or lightweight mortar round. The few soldiers they could see were half-dressed and crouching behind any available cover. Having turned out of their cots, they were no doubt still drowsy and confused by the unexplained attack.

By contrast, it appeared quiet at the front of the camp, where the SAS team was dealing with trouble as and when required with silenced weapons. But Dancer knew they would only hold the truck park until they'd got what they'd come for: Lily Cheung and Yan Tao. And although expendable Racal jamming devices had been planted to disrupt any Chinese attempt to radio out for help, Blue Team had limited ammunition to maintain their diversion.

They found Block Six deserted. The first room was some type of CCTV monitoring centre, rows of television screens showing various cells. Dancer recognised one with its pinion rings on the wall and the discarded cattle prod on the floor. Perhaps the occupants of this room had witnessed the shoot-out and fled for their lives. He scanned the screens showing the cells from Block Six until he saw her.

'There she is!' Dancer pointed at one of the screens. Mama Cheung sat upright on a hard chair, dressed in a dark prison tunic and with her hair drawn back in a bun. Her expression was impassive, almost aloof, and Dancer thought that she looked quite regal. He guessed she would not give her interrogators an easy time.

A small boy wandered into the frame. 'That's Bao with her,' Walsh observed. 'Thank God they both look okay. You go and get them, John, while I open as many other doors as I can.'

He noted the cell number, Twenty-five, then left for the corridor, snatching keys from a rack outside. This was not a top security block; there were no bars or gates in the way, just steel cell doors. One was open as he passed and it was not as austere as the block where Lily and Yan had been held. These were furnished with proper cots and straw mattresses, wooden chairs and a table.

Walsh was following him down the corridor, unlocking cell doors, as he ran for Twenty-five. As he swung the door open, the old woman looked up apprehensively. She did a quick double take, fazed as she registered who was standing in front of her.

'It's all right, Mama Cheung,' he said, smiling. 'We've come to get you and Bao away from here.'

The boy gawped. 'Uncle John? Is it really you? What's happened? Where's my mama?'

'She's safe now. So are you both, but you must hurry.' He paused. 'Are either of you hurt?'

Mama Cheung was on her feet. 'The crawling snakes had not touched us yet. They said it would be our turn tomorrow.' She reached up and kissed him on the cheek.

'Bao said you would rescue us. Like an old fool, I did not believe him. You are a good man, Mr John.'

He ignored that, urging her and the boy out through the door. The corridor was filled with bewildered-looking Chinese in prison garb. Walsh was trying to persuade them to move out, but they clearly weren't sure what was going on. Suddenly Dancer recognised Lily's younger brother, Ho. He had lost weight, his once plump cheeks were sunken and his eyes had a haunted look. Both his hands were covered in blood-stained lint bandages.

'Ho,' Dancer called. 'What have they done to you?'

The young man turned. 'Mr John! What's happening?'

'We're getting you out of here.'

'We?'

'Me and my friends.'

Ho looked miserable. 'This all *my* fault. All these people are here because of me, because I am a coward. I told them. I am so ashamed.'

'What have they done to you?' Dancer repeated.

Ho looked down at his hands. 'They hammered toothpicks under my nails. I said nothing. But then they threatened to do the same to my eyeballs. I was scared and pissed myself and then I betrayed my friends.' Tears began to course down his cheeks. He seemed incapable of moving; he just stood there with his shoulders heaving as he sobbed.

Mama Cheung stood quite still, looking at her son until he suddenly recognised her.

'You too?' he wailed. 'And Bao? Oh, no, what have I done?'

His mother reached out with both hands and gripped him firmly with one on each shoulder. 'I am proud of you, Number One son. You tried to withstand what no man can endure. It is only since I have been here that I am starting to understand what has been going on. It took courage for you and Lily to be part of this conspiracy.' She glanced sideways at the American. 'But it is Mr John who should be

473

ashamed. Ashamed of putting Lily and her family at such risk.'

At last Walsh was shepherding the prisoners out into the night and Dancer said, 'Come on, there's transport outside. You can talk later.'

Ho sniffed back his tears and allowed his mother to take his hand as well as Bao's as they followed the others.

At the back of the queue at the door, Dancer saw his old friend Gong Li Zhong, the commercial director of the *laogai* prison camp standing in a cell doorway. Gong didn't look his usual jovial self as he talked earnestly with another familiar figure – the hunched and emaciated poet, Fan Xiu Kun.

Gong looked round and saw the American approach. 'Mr John, what in the hell are you doing here? What went wrong? I was arrested and brought here yesterday with Fan.'

'No time to explain now. Just get the hell out with the others. There's a boat to get you out of the country.'

Fan regarded Dancer darkly. 'Clearly the gods did not approve of your plans, Mr John. Perhaps neither did your dead wife.'

Dancer ignored that. 'Please, just go.'

Fan shook his head.

'He insists on staying,' Gong explained.

'I will not leave my country,' Fan confirmed.

'If you stay,' Dancer said, 'they will execute you. If you leave you can fight from abroad where your voice and your poetry will be allowed to be heard.'

'That's what I'm telling him,' Gong said.

Fan gave a resigned sigh. Now they were the only ones left. 'Perhaps you are right. I will be killed. Better to fight on from abroad.' He gave a wan smile. 'And a little creature comfort would not go amiss in my old age.'

Dancer felt relief. He didn't want to abandon dear Fan to his fate. Debs would never have forgiven him for that.

As they stepped outside, Dancer was immediately aware that the Blue Team's onslaught had ended and an uneasy quiet had settled over the camp. It was broken by Chinese troopers calling out to ask each other what they thought. Had the shooting stopped or was it just a lull? Was it safe to move out of cover? What was happening? Where had their brave comrade officers vanished to? What was happening at the camp entrance? Should they go and look?

Fan and Gong could only move slowly because the soles of their feet had been cruelly beaten with lengths of rubber hose. Dancer stifled his impatience as he guided them past the barrack blocks to the vehicle park.

Walsh was waiting anxiously beside a truck full of prisoners, its engine turning over.

'For God's sake hurry, John! Everyone else has gone.' She bit her lip when she saw the state of the two prisoners with him. 'You drive, John, you know the area better than me.'

'Okay.' As willing hands reached down to help Fan and Gong up over the tailgate, Dancer and Walsh hurried to the cab and climbed up. Without turning on the truck's headlights, the American let the clutch out gently and they began moving quietly out of the camp.

Half-a-mile later they reached the roadblock strewn with the corpses of the PLA guard unit. It was an unnerving reminder of Red Two's handiwork. Then Dancer threw the wheel to the right to take them down an unmade track that would eventually lead them to the riverside where he hoped to God he would find the junk moored.

'The line is dead,' the soldier said and replaced the telephone on its cradle.

Brigadier Ting Han-chen stood fuming in the so-called communications centre of the camp's admin block. The operators of the two ancient radio sets could get nothing except hiss and static out of them, they told him. They were sure the signals were being electronically jammed. 'And now the bastards have cut the land lines,' Ting said in disgust.

When the attack from the north of the camp had started ten minutes earlier, he'd rushed out of the monitoring suite in the interrogation block to see what was going on. Like everyone else, he'd dived for cover as lines of tracer poured into the grounds and explosions started going off along the perimeter fence.

After a few heart-stopping minutes, he realised that the spineless officer cadres of the camp garrison had no idea what to do. Ting himself could only think that their attackers were saboteurs from the secret freedom movement intent on releasing his prisoners. Somehow he and his department had failed to move swiftly and tenaciously enough to crush it. But there was no way he was going to allow them to snatch back those who could lead him to its source and its total destruction.

Gathering his courage, he left the safety of a low concrete wall and raced for the admin block. There he found men and officers in the darkened offices crouching low as they peered warily out of windows at the muzzle flashes on the distant rise. Ting screamed at the most senior officer to mount an immediate counter-attack, but the man appeared terrified and explained that his men were camp guards and not trained for aggressive soldiering. In despair, Ting then demanded that he radio or telephone for reinforcements from the nearest garrison of 'real soldiers'.

They had tried, but it was proving impossible.

Then, just as he was deciding what to do next, a new explosion rocked the room. Plaster fell from the walls and pictures crashed to the floor. Window glass shattered. Everyone ducked instinctively, including Ting. God, he thought, this was much closer!

The explosion was immediately followed by another and another.

Then one of the soldiers yelled from a broken window: 'It's the trucks in the front park! They're exploding!'

'Sabotage,' Ting guessed aloud and rushed to the door. Several other soldiers rediscovered their courage and followed him out into the night. The air was thick with smoke and the front of the camp was full of long, dancing shadows cast by the raging pyre of burning vehicles. Only then did he see the corpses of the PLA troops strewn around the area.

'Some of the trucks are missing,' someone said.

Then a PLA trooper, looking pale and shaken, emerged from the shadows. He was clutching his blood-soaked arm.

'I was wounded,' he told Ting sheepishly, 'but I saw what happened. They were foreign devils dressed in Chinese uniforms. They shot the guards on the gate then released some prisoners. They took them away in trucks. I heard some of the prisoners talking about a boat.'

'When did the last truck leave?' Ting demanded.

'Just before these ones blew up.'

Ting stared round at the scene of carnage. 'We must have transport! We must give chase! They mustn't be allowed to get away.'

Another soldier said, 'Comrade Brigadier, there are jeeps garaged in the servicing area. Some of those are working.'

Ting gave a sigh of relief. 'Thank God for that.' He turned to the most senior officer present. 'Get a group of your best men together. Armed to the teeth. And HURRY!'

On the return journey to the river inlet, Taffy drove the Galaxy while McVicar followed in one of the stolen PLA trucks. In the back, Dougie Squires who was one of two fully trained field medics on the team, attended as best he could to Yan Tao while Lily Cheung looked on anxiously. With broken ribs and fractures to one arm and one leg, there was no way the man was going to be able to make an assisted dive to the submarine.

This fact was preying on McVicar's mind as he turned on to the main coastal road and headed towards the bridge. It meant that *Manta* would have to surface to pick them up.

That didn't please him and it certainly wouldn't please Al Cherrier. But then they'd always known that they could be returning with casualties of one sort or another. In fact, he was more vexed at having left Dancer and Janie Walsh behind. Especially her.

She was OpsCom and as such should have known better. It was breaking every rule in the book, written and unwritten. He just prayed to God the Chinese didn't get hold of her. Having seen what they'd done to Lily and Yan, he had little doubt they'd show her absolutely no mercy. At least if the junk *did* manage to make its rendezvous, then she and Dancer stood a good chance of getting away.

But even if they did make it back to link up with the US fleet, he had little doubt her career with the CIA would be over, at least as far as field operations were concerned. Her actions would have persuaded the likes of Frank Aspen from Langley that she was impulsive and emotional to the detriment of the job. In short, Walsh had proven herself a liability.

McVicar consoled himself with the fact that at least his team was aboard the two-vehicle convoy with no casualties. White Team had confirmed by radio that the landing zone was still uncompromised and Nick Lake's diversionary Blue Team should soon be joining them after a hard cross-country cycle ride.

Up ahead, Taffy was steering the Galaxy off the road and into the cover of some shrubs. McVicar pulled the truck in to the kerb. It was too big to hide, but there was no traffic in these early hours of the morning. Everyone scrambled off, Squires helping Lily while two others carried Yan Tao's stretcher. They quickly made their way down the embankment where White Team was waiting for them.

No one was happy to hear they'd been separated from Walsh and Dancer, especially Abe Stone. But at least there was some good news. Fifteen minutes earlier, they'd seen the junk *Hong* come in from the misty sea and begin chugging upriver towards its rendezvous point.

A few minutes later Lake's Blue Team arrived, looking pleased with themselves despite their obvious exhaustion. It wasn't every day they got to play with their fireworks big-time. A signal to rendezvous was then sent to *Manta* and within a few minutes the Phantom and the three Geminis were loaded up with their eighteen passengers and equipment. After a final check that the old fisherman, still trussed and gagged, was comfortable and would survive until daylight, they set off, the soft burble of the Phantom's electric motors accompanying the rhythmic dip of muffled paddles.

Sitting in one of the Geminis, Abe Stone took the bewildered Lily under his wing, introducing himself and being rewarded with a shy smile. She said she'd heard all about him and to be with a friend of Dancer's clearly made her feel happier. He draped a reassuring arm round her shoulders as she sat and shivered in the thin material of her prison fatigues and the rubber dinghy bounced into the first of the swells. She gasped when the cold spray splashed over her.

'Are we going to the submarine John talked about?'

Stone nodded. 'Just a short way out. It won't be long.'

She noticed the collection of scuba gear at their feet and looked petrified. 'I cannot go underwater. I cannot even swim.'

'They would have shown us what to do, held our hands. You *just* have to breathe through the mouthpiece.' He smiled at her look of concern. 'But don't worry. Because Yan Tao is injured, the sub will surface. You might not even get your feet wet.'

She laughed with relief and saw how silly his joke was as another wave broke over them. They were both soaked already.

It seemed like for ever that they edged through the floating tendrils of mist while the deep purple sea lapped and slapped against the dinghy's bow. Lily was now freezing, her teeth chattering and her fear beginning to return. Distant voices drifted from the shore they had left, but it was too far away to distinguish what was being said. She saw the white soldiers around her exchange anxious glances and noticed how their fingers toyed with the gunmetal surface of their rifles as though getting reassurance from their touch.

She didn't really know what to expect next. But when it happened, it caught her by surprise.

In front of her eyes, the slow swell of sea ahead of them began to froth and bubble and form into a scrambled white foam on the dark surface. A blue-black hump appeared like a fat shark. Water poured from it in streams, running over the barnacle-free surface and dripping from the thick Plexiglass visual-observation ports.

As she gasped, one of the SBS men said, 'That's our baby.'

Lily frowned. 'The submarine? But it's so small.'

The man laughed. 'That's just the top fin. The rest of it is underneath us.'

She peered disbelievingly over the side as the helmsman on the Phantom steered the craft into position behind the shallow hump of the conning tower. A small flat deck area was recessed into the aft slope which was fitted with a vertical secondary hatch in the rear of the fin. Only usable when the vessel surfaced, it gave direct access into the control room. She watched in amazement as the hatch opened and an unshaven face appeared. 'Casualties?' the man asked in a distinctly American accent.

One SAS soldier scrambled out of the dinghy and splashed on to the small recessed deck. 'One stretcher case,' he told the crewman.

He and another then manoeuvred Yan's stretcher from the Phantom. She saw that he had been strapped in and realised why when it was her turn to board some minutes later. When she ducked her head to enter the hatch, she found a sheer twelve-foot drop to the deck of the control room below. Turning awkwardly, she managed to get a foot on the ladder and begin a nervous descent.

With relief she reached the bottom and turned round. It was another world. A high-tech world of control consoles and computer screens against a background of astonishingly complex and gleaming pipework that reminded her of the inside of a spaceship she'd once seen at the movies. And it was all drenched in a soft red glow.

Lily could hardly believe she was here with the now familiar faces of McVicar, Lake and Taffy.

Beside them stood a tall man with a beard and an unlit cob pipe in his mouth. He wore a navy baseball cap with the legend USS *Manta* picked out in gold.

He smiled graciously. 'Welcome to our little piece of America, ma'am.'

'There it is!' Walsh said. She couldn't disguise the relief in her voice.

They'd been driving beside the river for several minutes, peering into the headlight beams as they played along the willow trees and lit the quicksilver flow of the water beyond. It had been pitch black with no one around. They had passed one or two peasant dwellings but, thankfully, there were no lights on. Only once a dog had barked angrily at having its sleep disturbed.

Dancer followed her pointing finger. There it was, the swinging light of a lantern. 'I hope you're right.'

Walsh checked her silenced automatic. 'So do I.'

He eased on the brakes and halted. Now they could see the squared-off silhouette of the *Hong* as she shifted serenely at her moorings. Walsh climbed down.

'Soldiers!' someone shouted suddenly from the direction of the junk. The voice was full of alarm.

Walsh suddenly realised the problem. 'No, it's all right!' she called out. 'We have your passengers!'

Three of Captain Song's crew advanced warily, holding up lanterns. She saw that they had guns at the ready. One of them gave a nervous smile. 'You had us going there for a moment,' he said in Mandarin.

'You're lucky you didn't get yourself shot,' said another.

Dancer joined them. 'C'mon, let's stop the chatter. We've no time to waste.'

He returned to the rear of the truck with Walsh and released the tailgate. Still looking bewildered, the prisoners began climbing down. Bao was crying, still traumatised by the sight of the dead PLA troops at the camp gate. He clung to Mama Cheung until she managed to prise his fingers free. Walsh reached up and lifted him down, while Dancer helped the boy's grandmother.

'Don't worry,' Walsh said to the boy. 'We'll soon have you out of here. Be brave. Here is our boat.'

Bao snivelled and wiped his nose with his forearm. 'That's not a submarine.'

'I'm afraid it's the best we could do.'

Ho took his nephew's hand. 'I'll look after him now.'

As the crocodile of prisoners limped towards the junk, the crew watched sullenly. Then the familiar figure with its bald head and silvery Fu Manchu beard appeared from the shadows.

'I'm glad you could help,' Dancer said.

'It was not my idea,' Captain Song answered curtly. 'I am ordered by Jiang of the RTS under pain of punishment.'

'We're still grateful.'

Song waved his hand at the line of prisoners stepping over the junk's gunwales. 'There are too many. We cannot hide all of these in the secret compartment.'

'I know that, but there's no reason for anyone to stop us.'

'You say.' He shook his head vehemently. 'It is no good. I will take half-a-dozen, that is all.'

'Captain, listen to me,' Dancer began.

Walsh stepped forward. 'Yes, Captain, listen to him.' The muzzle of her silenced .45 pressed under Song's chin. 'This deal is non-negotiable. Got it?'

The skipper appeared unfazed and unafraid. 'You would shoot your own countryman?'

'I'm only half-Chinese, Captain,' Walsh replied in a low

voice. 'And it's the American half holding this gun. Don't push your fucking luck.'

For once his eyelids fluttered. He shrugged and turned away, but made no attempt to stop the last of the prisoners boarding.

Dancer grinned. 'You have a certain way with words, Janie. I'm impressed.'

Her returning smile flashed in the gloom. 'You know, I almost impressed myself.'

The moment she and Dancer joined the others, the crew threw the lines ashore and jumped aboard as the current immediately took hold and widened the gap between the hull and the river bank. The junk was showing no lights.

The factory director Gong Li Zhong stood beside Fan Xiu Kun on the deck watching the land recede as they drifted into mid-channel to the burble of the junk's diesel.

'Is this to be my last sight of China?' the poet asked.

'If you had stayed you would have been executed,' Gong repeated. 'This way you can restore your health and live long enough to see China when we try again.'

'Again?'

'Oh, yes. When we reach America you must work with Yan Tao and me. Use the power of your words. We will broadcast to the students of China through the Internet. They've tried to, but even Chicom can't stop that.'

Fan seemed amused. 'My poems on the Internet. I've heard this has been done. You know, that is not something I would ever have imagined.'

'Get below immediately!' a crewman demanded.

Fan stared into the darkness where, a few seconds earlier, he had seen the shapes of the willows. 'Farewell, Motherland.' Then he turned and followed Gong, ducking under the tarpaulin roof to the cargo hold and out of sight.

Brigadier Ting followed the leading PLA troops down the track from the road bridge and along the riverside towards the estuary.

They had left the camp in jeeps that were in the mechanics' garage for servicing and raced down the track, unwittingly passing the unmade road down which Dancer's vehicle had turned for its rendezvous with the junk. When Ting's convoy had reached the deserted main coast road, there was no indication which way to turn. By chance Ting had decided to go right, and in minutes, they saw one of the stolen PLA trucks tucked in at the roadside. Beyond it, they discovered the abandoned Galaxy.

Now his men were in hot pursuit and Ting was soon breathless trying to keep up. The footpath had now descended to the thin strip of beach and ahead he could hear the soldiers' boots crunching on shingle.

Now he knew. The Americans had snatched the prisoners and were attempting to spirit them away by boat.

Ting caught up as the soldiers slowed, approaching cautiously with their firearms ready. They were at the rivermouth here, where the low, wooded coastal hills gave way to dunes and wild grasses. It was deserted. There was no sound but the gentle slap and swish of the tide along the waterline.

He listened intently as he stared out at the misty sea, so empty and peaceful. No sound of a ship's engine, no racing outboards of fleeing assault craft. Just utter tranquillity . . .

Then he heard it; they all heard it. A muffled moaning from somewhere in the darkness behind them.

Soldiers shouted to each other, rifles swung round towards the source of the noise. Half-a-dozen men advanced cautiously.

'It's an old man!' someone called back. 'He's bound and gagged.'

Ting frowned. What the hell—? 'Bring him here! Immediately.'

Seconds later the old man had been hoisted up by two PLA and carried towards Ting, his bound feet dragging behind him. The terrified eyes were wide above the gag. They propped him up until he could stand alone.

'Take that damn gag off him!' Ting demanded, irritated at the soldiers' stupidity. He waited impatiently while the old man stretched his jaw muscles and gathered saliva to speak. 'Who are you?'

The man gulped. 'Sir, I'm but a humble fisherman. I was jumped on by two "round eyes" – American, I think. I was tied up and blindfolded, but it came loose so I could see with one eye. And then . . .' He stared out to sea as though not believing his own words . . . 'then men in rubber suits came ashore.'

Ting frowned. '*Rubber* suits? Are you sure?'

'Yes, yes, sir, please believe me. They had face masks and webbed feet like ducks.' He searched for the word, tried to remember the nature programme he had once seen on television. 'Frogmen, I think they're called. Yes, they were frogmen.'

'And they came back here?'

The fisherman nodded earnestly. 'Yes, yes. They left here a few minutes ago. Well, maybe half-an-hour now. In rubber boats.'

Ting turned away and looked out at the calm sea. Frogmen. Underwater warriors. Bells were ringing in his mind. Lily Cheung's son had related some sort of fantasy story about a submarine. And then there had been rumours from PLA Navy intelligence of a submarine operating off the coast. Rumoured, but never confirmed. Dismissed by experts as impossible in those waters. But if—?

He looked back at the old man. 'How many came ashore?'

The man shrugged. 'Fifteen, twenty maybe.'

'And how many left?'

'About the same.'

Then, Ting thought, they couldn't have taken all his prisoners out by boat. At least not from here. So where the hell had they vanished to?

He called the radio operator over. 'Try headquarters again.'

The soldier looked pained. 'But the signals were jamming.'

Ting regarded the man with disdain. 'How powerful do you think their jammers can be? They were only a light raiding force. Try here.'

As the soldier obliged with his manpack set, his face suddenly lit up. 'You're right, Comrade Brigadier. I'm through!'

'Good. Get me the district head of naval operations.'

'Sir!' replied the soldier.

Ting paced the shingle impatiently, then stood still, the water lapping at his feet, and stared out at the rivermouth.

He nearly missed it. Nearly missed it because it wasn't even showing navigation lights and its engine was throttled right back. It was like a black wraith slipping through the shifting veil of mist. A fishing junk.

'She did *what*?' Al Cherrier demanded. He couldn't believe he was hearing this.

Manta had submerged and was setting a course for home when Nick Lake approached the skipper.

'Dancer refused to leave Lily's son behind,' the SBS lieutenant told him. 'And Janie decided he shouldn't go alone. She went along for backup.'

'She should have sent some of you lot with him, not gone herself.'

McVicar joined them. 'My decision, Al. I command land ops and I wasn't having anyone put at risk for sentimental reasons.'

'It took them too long,' Lake added. 'So I guess they'll be trying to get out with the others on the junk.'

'God preserve us,' Cherrier muttered. He turned to Hinks who was manning the sonar console. 'Got anything on that junk?'

Hinks regarded the circular 'Plan Position Indicator' screen. 'That's probably her, bearing zero nine five. Just leaving the river mouth.' He moved the rollerball beside the keypad until it covered the blip on the PPI screen, then hit the 'enter' button. On the top of the console, the rectangular frequency-analyser sprang into action. He studied the electronic representation of the sound pulses with an expert eye. 'Yep, it's an old diesel. I'll match it up with our record of the *Hong*'s signature.'

They waited impatiently while Hinks tapped in more instructions and watched the numerical display match the sound they were hearing with earlier 'fingerprint' records of the junk's engine noise. 'A hundred per cent match,' he announced.

Cherrier grunted. 'Well, so far so good.'

Lake stared at the console. 'Al, can we keep an eye on her?'

The captain glared. 'My job, Lieutenant, is to get us the hell out of here with all speed, not play nursemaid to some fishing boat and put all our lives at risk.'

'Understood, Al. You're in charge and it's your decision.' He glanced back at the console. 'But with respect, that's not just *some* fishing boat. Janie's hopefully on board and so is Dancer. Not to mention a lot of the other poor buggers we've been trying to help. If they're caught, they'll without a doubt be executed.'

'Not our concern,' Cherrier replied, wrestling with the problem. 'In fact to do otherwise would be to disobey instructions from Langley. In short, when the mission's over, we're to get out and stop for nothing. Period.'

'Your last word?'

'My last word,' Cherrier confirmed. Then his expression softened a fraction. 'But as we're on the same course as the *Hong* and she's got more speed than we have, I guess we'll be within visual of her for a while yet.'

Lake slapped the man on the shoulder. 'You're a pal.'

The captain shook his head. 'Just because you've got the hots for Miss Walsh.'

McVicar laughed. 'Unfortunately, *she's* got the hots for Dancer.'

Lake looked crestfallen. 'You reckon?'

'I reckon. Never mind, let's get our priorities right and let's get some scoff down our necks.'

The 'scoff' was totally bewildering to Lily Cheung as she looked at enormous slices of defrosted bread being passed round together with thick slabs of strong cheese dripping with pickled relish.

Abe Stone sat beside her on a flip-down canvas seat at the side of the control room and watched as she struggled to get her mouth round the gargantuan British sandwich. She looked up, chewing dubiously, with pickle smeared around her mouth.

'Nice, eh?' Stone asked, nodding enthusiastically.

She smiled politely as he reached forward and used his handkerchief to remove a splodge of relish from the tip of her nose. That made her giggle. 'American food?'

'Certainly not.'

Suddenly her smile vanished and she looked away.

'What is it?' Stone asked anxiously.

'We are here joking. How can I do that?' She looked at him imploringly. 'Little Bao should be here too. Eating and laughing with us. I am ashamed to laugh at such a time.'

Stone reached out and patted her hand. 'He'll be okay, you'll see. John will look after him.'

'I cannot eat this.'

'You must. It will keep your strength up.'

The three crewmen manning the control suite had been quiet for some minutes. Then suddenly, Hinks called over to Cherrier who was talking to Lake. 'Hey, Skipper, I'm picking something up.'

The captain looked across. 'What?'

'Bearing two seven eight and moving very fast – around twenty knots. Due across our bow on an interception course with the *Hong*.'

'What is it? Run a check.'

'I am running a check,' Hinks replied, irritated to be told to do what Cherrier must know was second nature to him. 'But I can guess. It's a Chicom coastguard cutter.'

Eighteen

Dancer stirred. He'd drifted off to sleep curled up on some old fish netting in the junk's hold.

'Something's happening,' Walsh said.

He rubbed his eyes and sat up, suddenly aware of the junk's creaking roll in a long, slow swell. The air stank of fish and stale sweat. Outside he could hear an excited exchange in Chinese – first the crew members and then Captain Song's ponderous tones.

Sleeping bodies seemed to be everywhere, huddled together in the cramped conditions.

'What is it?' he asked.

Walsh was trying to catch the crewmen's words. 'Something's spooked them, John, I'm sure of it.'

He climbed to his feet. 'Then let's go look.'

She stood and followed him up the short flight of wooden steps to the aft deck. Song and his crew were standing looking at the tell-tale red and green navigation lights way out in the Gulf. The first thing Dancer noticed was that out here in the open sea, the mist had been blown clear. Visibility was good and the moon and stars were covered by only the thinnest veil of cloud.

He scrambled up alongside Song. 'What is it, Captain?'

The old seadog hardly seemed to notice his presence. 'A patrol boat. Maybe navy, but probably coastguard.'

Dancer remembered the encounter on their very first run-in and felt a sudden sense of relief. 'I recall you have a good relationship with them.'

Song forced his eyes away from the distant pinpricks of light. 'That was then. This is now. There has been an attempted coup, as I am sure you are aware of. Everything will be different now.'

Walsh stepped forward. 'How fast can you go? When you open up your engines?'

The skipper shrugged. 'Ten knots.'

Anger flashed in Walsh's eyes. 'Don't lie to me. Your diesel may be old, but I've been told you can still get a good fifteen to seventeen knots out of this boat.'

Suddenly his eyes bored into hers. 'Sure, but this is a wooden junk with a blunt bow, lady. Fifteen knots and she will start to disintegrate.'

But she wasn't in the mood to be deterred. 'Not immediately. We can try to outrun her. We've got weapons to deter them.'

Song looked at her as though she were a fool. 'And they've got 20mm cannon.'

Walsh shook her head. 'Okay, okay, but let's not sit here and take it without a fight. Let's open up and give her a run for her money. Maybe we can make it to international waters.'

'Forget it,' Song said. 'Just accept your fate.'

Dancer moved forward, his .45 out now. 'No, Song, you accept yours. You've got some of the bravest men in China on board and I'm not including you and your crew. We'll stop if we're forced to, but not before. Give the order for full speed.'

Song's disdainful expression almost included a smile, but not quite. 'This is becoming quite a habit with you and your friends, isn't it?'

But Dancer was unrepentant. 'I'm afraid it is.'

Hinks said, 'The junk's opened up to full power. She's making a break for it.'

Cherrier, Lake and McVicar had gathered behind the sonar operator's chair.

'Can they do it?' McVicar asked.

The captain shook his head. 'Not a chance. That coastguard cutter can make twenty plus knots.'

'If only we could get a team aboard the *Hong*,' Lake said.

'She's five miles off our starboard bow,' Cherrier pointed out. 'Too far ahead for us to get to.'

'We'd need heavy weapons to fend off another ship,' McVicar pointed out. 'And we exhausted all of them at the camp.'

Lake suddenly remembered something. 'That signal yesterday – about Krowsky's mob being put on stand-by.'

Cherrier nodded. 'They were being flown out to the 7th Fleet.' But that was as optimistic as it got. 'Still too far away to reach the *Hong* before that cutter does, I'm afraid.'

Lake stared at the console in desperation. 'We can't let Janie and Dancer fall into Chinese hands.'

McVicar looked grave. 'We don't seem to have much choice.'

A heavy silence fell over the group. Cherrier watched the revolving scan of the PPI screen and sucked thoughtfully on his empty pipe. Suddenly, he leaned down and said in Hinks's ear, 'What's the cutter's projected interception course for the junk?'

'Soon tell you, Skipper.' His hands flitted expertly over the keyboard. The *Hong*'s course and speed, followed by the cutter's course and speed. He pressed 'Display and Enter' and two coloured lines were overlaid on the PPI.

'Ah,' Cherrier said. 'That will take the cutter across our bow at an oblique angle.'

'Yep,' Hinks confirmed. 'In about fifteen minutes' time.'

'Then we have an opportunity.'

Lake didn't follow. 'Opportunity to what?'

'Engage.'

'What? Are you joking?'

Cherrier chewed on his pipe. 'Never been more serious.'

'The Pentagon will never give permission, you know that. Sink a Chinese patrol boat? Never! It would have to be in our own self-defence with no other option.'

'Then we won't ask permission. Operational decision.'

'They'll throw the book at you.'

'Probably. But at least Walsh and Dancer may be alive to give evidence at my court martial.'

Lake regarded Cherrier for a long moment. He'd always rubbed along well enough with the man, but he'd always been somewhat apart from the crew and combat-swimmer teams. A different generation for a start, detached and somewhat taciturn. A man of few words who it was not always easy to warm to. He was certainly not one to take unnecessary risks, which made his sudden decision all the more remarkable and earned Lake's deepest admiration. 'I can't tell you how grateful I am.'

A semblance of a smile hovered on Cherrier's lips. 'You might not be so grateful when the depth charges start falling.'

'But why?'

Cherrier sniffed. 'My father was a sub skipper in World War Two.'

'You never mentioned that.'

'It was something he told me once. I've never forgotten.' And that was it. Cherrier had other things on his mind now. He called over to the Puerto Rican called Sanchez. 'Man the Electronics Warfare console. As soon as we're at periscope depth I want that cutter's radar and radio jammed until it's over. No point in letting the Chinese on the mainland know what's going on.'

'Aye, aye, Skipper.'

He turned to Manson on the joystick at the main console. 'Maintain present speed and course, but bring us up to periscope depth.'

'Sir.'

Cherrier then settled himself at the Fire Control console. At the top, six digital displays showed *Manta*'s own attitude: course, speed, depth, roll, pitch and yaw. Below it was the 'Action Information Organisation' screen, similar to that on the sonar console. The AIO displayed the position of all shipping in the area gleaned from all the submarine's surveillance sources.

He used the keyboard to bring up all the *Manta*'s available weapons and counter-measure choices on the touch-screen above. Both mobile decoys and lightweight torpedoes were housed in the fore-and-aft Magnum system which revolved between the submarine's inner and outer hulls like a giant six-shooter. Then he pressed the touch-screen above the keyboard to activate two Stingray acoustic torpedoes in the for'ard firing-chambers and entered the cross-matched signature of the cutter's engine noise. As he confirmed the setup, everyone was aware of the gentle background grinding noise of oiled steel as the huge cylinder revolved to line up the two Stingrays with the outer firing shutters.

'Confirm periscope depth,' Manson reported.

'Stand by warner clearance on automatic!' Sanchez added and pushed the red button on the Communications and Electronic Warfare console. Immediately the EW warner mast was propelled up through the surface.

Cherrier studied the AIO screen for a moment. The warner mast was picking up no unpleasant surprises, no radar signals from warships or military aircraft. Just the sweep of the cutter's surface searcher matching and confirming the position shown on Hinks's sonar. Cherrier's hand spun the rollerball control until the fire-control cursor was over the cutter's icon. He pressed 'Lock-on'.

'Right, let's take a look-see,' he said. 'Raise optronics mast!'

There was another sigh of hydraulics and the second mast telescoped up to break the surface. Cherrier activated the low-light televison mode and watched as the hazy green picture of the sea's surface flickered into life on the overhead monitor. The lens was splattered with droplets of spray, but the target was unmistakable. A touch of adjustment on the zoom-function brought it into sharper focus. There was no doubt about it, the sleek shape of a Chicom coastguard cutter.

'Begin jamming operation,' Cherrier ordered.

Sanchez confirmed.

Cherrier tapped into the keyboard to bring up co-ordinates and timings for a torpedo intercept. Just under two miles' distant and Stingray travelling at a stunning seventy knots. The countdown appeared on the AIO touch-screen. Sixty seconds to go. . . Fifty. He threw the switch to open both the bow shutters of the torpedo system and primed the warheads.

'Stand by torpedo launch. Stand by, stand by,' he warned.

Thirty seconds, twenty, fifteen, ten, nine, eight, seven. . . four, three, two. . . Fire One.

'Number one tube launched!' He pressed again. Fire Two. 'Number two tube fired. Both tubes cleared!'

The expectation was to hear an immediate explosion but, of course, the torpedoes' electric motors would take a brief interlude to drive the silent and deadly projectiles on their intercept trajectories. A heavy silence fell over the control room, Cherrier's eyes glued to the AIO, everyone else watching the monitor picture relayed from the optronics mast.

Lily Cheung turned to Abe Stone. 'I don't understand. What is happening?'

'A Chinese coastguard patrol boat is trying to stop the junk with John on board. We're going to stop them.' He raised his right hand, two fingers pointing to represent a gun.

'We will shoot them?'

'With torpedoes.'

'Ah.' Now she understood.

The silence dragged on for a seeming eternity. Squires wandered in from the for'ard crew quarters to report on Yan's progress to Lily. 'He's doing fine. I gave him a shot of morphine so I could set the bones, but I think he's coming to now. I'll make some tea and you can take it to him. You'll be a pretty sight for him to wake up to.'

She blushed. 'Thank you.'

'No milk in the tea, I guess?'

Suddenly a blinding core of heat pulsed on the overhead optronics monitor as the first Stingray slammed into the bow section of the coastguard cutter. Momentarily the screen turned white as though recording a nuclear blast. Then the screen pulsed again as the second torpedo found its mark amidships. Another flash and shockwave. The noise of the near-simultaneous detonations followed, awesome and deafening as their power was magnified beneath the waves.

A spontaneous cheer went up from the crew and the combat swimmers gathered at the hatchway to their quarters.

There was nothing on the optronics monitor now, just a dark and empty sea littered with the fitful flames of burning debris and slicks of oil.

Cherrier turned to Sanchez. 'Make a satcom signal to Hereford. Tell them we have torpedoed a coastguard cutter and request the Deadwater stand-by team be dispatched to fishing junk *Hong* soonest to protect from boarders until she can reach international waters. Give her bearing and speed.'

'Aye, aye, Skipper.'

Lake said, 'I wonder what Dancer will make of the big bang?'

'I should hope,' Cherrier said, 'it'll make him one very relieved bunny. Even more so if the 7th can fly Krowsky's mob to the junk by helo before sunrise.'

Iona Moncrieff just had to get out of the claustrophobic atmosphere of the secure ops room in the British Embassy. She'd hung on until four in the morning when she knew that both *Manta* and the fishing junk had cleared the coast. From now on it should be plain sailing. Before she left, she'd phoned Bill Dawson at the American Embassy to double check there were no more complications of which she was unaware.

He sounded pleased with himself. 'It's all running sweet as a nut, Majesty.'

She frowned into the receiver. 'Despite the best efforts of your Janie,' she said pointedly.

'It was all a bit heroic as it turned out.'

'We're not supposed to be in the heroics business, Bill,' she chided.

'I've heard a whisper she's got a thing about Dancer. You know what women in love are like. Impetuous.'

'I'm not.'

'In love?'

'Impetuous. I thought you knew that by now.'

She heard Dawson chuckle at the other end. 'Don't be too hard on her. I thought of inviting her and Suzy Tobin to be your bridesmaids.'

That brought a smile to her lips. 'Those two? No better way to curse our marriage. Look, Bill, Suzy's holding the fort here. I'm knackered. Just slipping home for a shower. You can reach me there if you need me.'

'I need you.'

She ignored that. 'I'll be back in an hour or so.'

'I'm goin' to catnap myself,' he confessed. 'I feel all in. Got a cot in the office. Catch you later, Majesty.'

'Sure thing.' She hesitated before hanging up. 'And, Bill?'

'Yeah?'

'Guess that was one in the eye for Frank Aspen.'

Mention of his chief brought a laugh for once. 'He'll go ape-shit when he hears what we've pulled off. Can't beat us old-timers, eh?'

She was still laughing when she replaced the receiver and told the army brat she was going home to grab a shower. As usual, Suzy Tobin was as unfazed, unflappable and stunning as ever, despite her lack of sleep and hours on duty.

'Sure, boss, if anyone needs beauty sleep, you do.'

'I said shower, not sleep. Any more cheek and I won't let you be my bridesmaid.'

Her eyes widened. 'Really?'

'Bill's idea. Not mine, I assure you.' She turned dramatically on her heel and snatched her coat from the hook. 'Ciao.'

Minutes later she was out on the pavement and making her way to the gates of the embassy compound. It was still dark, but the air was deliciously damp and unusually fresh. She sucked it deeply into her lungs and coughed. Christ, she thought, they didn't like that. Too much of a shock to the system. But at least the tiredness stopped dragging at her eyelids and the feeling of nausea was fast evaporating as she strode the two blocks to her apartment.

The streets of Beijing were coming to life, hordes of workers already cycling to work before dawn and the buses lit up and full to bursting. By the time she had her key in the front door of her apartment, she was cursing her lack of planning as she remembered that none of her clean clothes had been ironed. Out of habit, she turned on the radio, then went to the bathroom, stripped off and ran the hot water. It was cold. But, as an old Scottish public schoolgirl, that was only a mild deterrent. As the water drilled into her flesh she wondered what it would be like to share it with that hairy old American bear. A cold shower and then a hump on fresh linen.

She was still smiling as she towelled off , pulled on a clean bra and briefs and opened the ironing board. Feeling much refreshed she made light work of blouse, jacket and skirt. Then she poured a fresh glass of orange juice from the fridge and settled on the sofa to give herself five minutes with her feet up.

The next thing she knew it was seven thirty when she woke to find that the glass of orange juice had spilled all over her newly ironed skirt. Cursing, she sponged down the stain in the kitchen, threw her coat on and raced for the front door. It had barely closed behind her when the telephone began to trill urgently.

Blissfully unaware, Iona scurried back towards the

embassy through the bustling crowds. It was now daylight and she consoled herself with the fact that at least she felt fresher and more alert after her impromptu sleep and that, if anything serious had occurred, Tobin would have rung her. The worst that could happen would be the army brat's relentless leg-pulling for the rest of the day.

By the time she reached the steps, her pace had slackened somewhat. Old George was on reception and waved as she entered the number in the keypad beside the bullet-proof glass door. She thought absently that the usually cheery Londoner was looking a little glum.

'Sorry to hear the news,' he said.

'What?'

He looked embarrassed. 'Your news.'

Oh God, she thought, what had gone wrong with the operation? So much for embassy security! She gave a tight smile. 'Sure, thanks, George,' she replied and hurried up the stairs.

She burst into the ops room to find it deserted. Suzy's computer was on, but the blonde wasn't at her desk. Iona swept across to her own work station, slipping off her coat as she walked and throwing it at the hook. There was an issue signal sheet propped against her PC keyboard.

She sat and started reading, feeling for the cigarettes and lighter in her handbag.

God Almighty! She couldn't believe it. *Manta* reported torpedoing a Chicom coastguard vessel trying to intercept the fishing junk. Cherrier was requesting Deadwater's SEAL stand-by team be deployed to protect it until it could reach safe waters.

'There you are, boss!'

Iona turned. Suzy Tobin was standing at the door with a plastic beaker of grey sludge coffee from the machine. 'I know, I know, I fell asleep. Don't say a word! Just get me Bill Dawson on the secure line *immediately*!'

Suzy paled. 'You haven't heard? The US Embassy was phoning you at home.'

Iona was growing impatient. 'Heard *what* for God's sake?'

'Bill's dead.'

The shock hit her like a bolt of lightning. It took her breath away. For one split second she thought it was a joke. But then she knew even Suzy wouldn't make a joke like that. She opened her mouth, but she couldn't speak. The emotion suddenly expanded in her chest like a balloon until it physically hurt and was forcing its way up into her throat. She gasped and felt a raw prickling sensation behind her eyeballs.

Suzy put her coffee on the desk and dropped to her knees beside Iona and grabbed the woman's hands tightly in her own. 'I'm *so* sorry, boss.'

'How?' It was a croaked whisper, nothing more.

'They think it was a massive heart attack. He must have died in his sleep. They found him in the cot he used.'

Iona found her hands trembling. 'Oh, Suzy,' she gulped. 'Tell me it isn't true.'

There were tears in the girl's eyes too. 'I wish I could, boss. He was a lovely man.'

'My rock.'

'Pardon?'

'He was my rock. He can't be dead. Not now, not yet. Bill's so—' she caught herself, 'was so strong.'

Suzy nodded. 'It must have been the strain.'

'He said he was feeling tired.'

'At least he died in his sleep. It would have been all over before he knew anything about it.'

Strangely, Iona was finding that the tears weren't coming. She could feel them building like a dam behind her eyes, but they weren't coming. After several long minutes, she asked in all seriousness, 'Do you think he was dreaming about me?'

Suzy smiled. 'I'm sure he would have been. The guys at his embassy said he was always talking about you and the wedding. Boring them stupid.'

499

Iona managed a stifled laugh and the faintest trickle of moisture ran on to her cheek. 'The silly old fool.'

'I think he loved you very much.'

'Do you think so?' Iona blinked. 'Do you really?'

Suzy squeezed Iona's hands tightly. 'I'm sure of it.'

There was a prolonged silence then, neither of them moving, but both staring into the middle distance as though trying to make some sense of it all.

At last Iona murmured, 'I really don't know what to do.'

'I don't think there's anything you can do, boss.' She paused, wondering if it was the right thing to say. 'They'll fly his body back to the States, I guess. Maybe next week. As soon as they get Chinese authority clearance.'

'Yes, I suppose they will.' Ironic that, she mused, under the circumstances.

'I know this is hardly the time, boss, but there are still things to be done and decisions to be made.'

Iona heaved a deep, deep sigh and straightened her back. 'Yes, yes, of course.'

'You've read the signal on your desk?'

'Yes. God, as if we didn't have enough to worry about.'

'I'm afraid there's more. Frank Aspen's been on the phone screaming blue murder. He went into their embassy as soon as he heard about Bill's death. Bill's staff were rather obliged to put him in the picture. Of course, Aspen knew nothing about the rescue attempt from the inter-rogation camp. He had fifty fits. Then the news came in about *Manta* sinking the coastguard cutter.' Suzy released Iona's hands and stood up. 'Of course, they didn't want any blame for Bill's decision to mount the operation. I gather they rather gave the impression it was mostly down to you.'

Iona sniffed heavily and roughly wiped her eyes with the back of her hand. 'Ah, I see. And I suppose Aspen won't know that Bill put Deadwater's old SEAL team on stand-by. Even if he does now,' she tapped the signal, 'he's hardly likely to agree to this request for their deployment.'

At that moment the door opened and Piers Lansdowne entered. He was unshaven and dishevelled, the crumpled slacks and old rugby shirt the nearest things to hand when he'd rushed from his room at the ambassador's residence.

'Came as soon as I heard,' he said. 'Iona, I know how devastated you must feel. It really shook me up. You know, like losing a close friend. God knows how it's hit you.'

She held up her hand. 'Thanks, Piers, but don't say *any* more, I can't bear it.'

'You should go home. Take some leave.'

'I can't, not yet. We've got problems – and Aspen's on my back. I've got to get through today. For Bill's sake as much as anything. He'd want me to do that, expect it.'

Suzy quickly brought him up to date with developments. The eyes behind the heavy spectacles stared hard as he took on board their significance. At last he said: 'I'm sure you're right, Iona. Aspen will want to wash his hands of the whole affair. But the SEAL team is on stand-by under the auspices of Project Deadwater. In other words, back under joint British American control.'

Iona wasn't sure of Lansdowne's point. 'But they were taken off the mission.'

'They were. But, in effect, Bill put them back on. They're under Rear Admiral Crozier's command which in turn is under 7th Fleet control.'

'I suppose,' Iona agreed warily.

'Besides, the SEALs were forbidden to land on sovereign foreign soil. Nothing about stopping them from protecting US citizens – key intelligence personnel at that – on a private boat.'

'But still in Chinese waters.'

He smiled. 'You can't have everything. Their capture would compromise our Chinese operations as much as it would the Americans'. So it's in our own mutual best interests that they be protected. I think I'd be fully entitled to have Ministry of Defence London signal Crozier to make the request for deployment under the standard

Deadwater agreement. After all, Bill had already had them put on stand-by.'

Iona was amazed and it momentarily lifted her spirits. She said thoughtfully, 'No point in mentioning that Bill is dead. Crozier might not get to hear for days, even weeks.'

'Then let's do it.'

The phone rang and Suzy picked it up. After listening for a moment, she turned to Iona. 'It's our switchboard. Aspen again.'

Iona said, 'Ask them to tell him I'm in mourning. Won't be back in the office until next week.'

'And if he asks for me,' Lansdowne added, 'I left for London last night.'

Dancer had spent the rest of the night propped against the timber gunwale on the junk's aft deck, Walsh huddled against him for warmth, sleeping fitfully. He had kept the .45 hidden but handy under the rough woollen blanket he'd been given. All the time his eyes had been on Captain Song and his crewmen who were gathered around the wheel. If he had dozed off for a moment, he had little doubt that the Chinese would attempt to overpower him. And God only knew what might have followed if that had happened. More than likely the crew would have massacred their passengers and thrown their weighted bodies overboard rather than risk returning to explain matters to the less-than-sympathetic Chicom authorities.

The unexpected explosion in the early hours had been a mixed blessing. Song had assumed that the coastguard cutter had hit a mine; he said the PLA Navy had laid several new fields in recent weeks and that one might have come adrift. However, Dancer had noted that it was a double explosion, one following fast after another. Of course, the second could have been fuel tanks or ammunition going off in sympathy. Or it could have been two torpedo strikes.

When he'd suggested this to Walsh, she seemed

astounded. 'Al would never risk that. It would be strictly against orders.'

'Just like you helping me get out Lily's family.'

She'd smiled. 'Ah, but they had been my *own* orders. I'm allowed to break *them*.'

'Maybe we were all born in the wrong age. You, me and Al. We were born for wartime.'

'Don't say that.'

'It's what we're good at.'

'I could have been a nursery nurse.'

'But you're not. You're here now, with me.'

Her smile had flickered uncertainly. 'It sounds silly to say it, but I can't think of a place I'd rather be.'

He'd laughed at that. '*I* can.'

'You know what I mean.'

He really wasn't sure he did. 'Do I?'

'I think so.'

But, if the sinking of the cutter had given them extra time and a lucky break, it was also likely to mean that further retribution was inevitable. If the authorities hadn't been certain about the junk's involvement in the break-out, their suspicions would be roused following the disappearance of the cutter, whether or not they knew about the explosion.

When the cold dawn light came creeping in over the Pacific skies, Song's crew were on the alert. Song's impassive weather-beaten face scanned the grey horizon with eyes narrowed like a cat's. The crew took it in turns with the binoculars, examining each distant shape. Far away, container ships, tankers and rusted merchantmen were plying the dredged shipping lanes to and from the Taijin ports like lines of ducks. Overhead, gulls swooped and called in their wake.

Tea was heated on a gas stove by one of the crew and passed round with cold corn cakes.

Dancer finished his meagre breakfast and climbed to his feet. Above the gunwale, the harsh offshore breeze hit him, snapping at his clothes and tangling his hair. Song stood behind his helmsman, back ramrod-straight and an aloof expression on his face like an emperor, which here on his ship, Dancer reasoned, he normally was – at least when a silenced .45 wasn't pointing at him.

The American stepped towards him. ''Morning.'

Only Song's eyes swivelled in Dancer's direction, with a slight nod of recognition.

'All clear,' Dancer observed unnecessarily.

Song spoke to the horizon. 'You appear to be the cat of nine lives, Yankee. But just how many have you used up?'

Dancer smiled. 'That's the question, all right. I've been asking that since I was knee-high.' He looked up at the vast dome of chill neutral tones, where it was impossible to judge where the grey of the sky merged with the grey of the sea. Spume flew back over the hull as the blunt bow chewed into the waves. 'How long till we reach the straits?' He meant the mouth of the Gulf of Bohai and the straits off old Port Arthur and the start of international waters.

A smile almost made it to Song's face, but not quite. 'Seven hours or so.'

'AIRCRAFT AHOY!' one of the crewmen yelled suddenly.

Dancer turned towards the stern where the man was standing in a padded Mao jacket and a fur cap with its ear flaps down. He lowered his binoculars as the black speck raced towards them, growing menacingly by the second until it resembled a giant bat. Flying at around five thousand feet, he guessed, but not moving quite as fast as he had anticipated. The noise of its engines was slow to come, muted by the wind coming off the sea.

As the lumbering shape and steady drone became clearer, Dancer murmured, 'Turboprops.'

Walsh joined him. 'What is it?'

The wide dark shadow passed directly over them. 'A Harbin SH-F. Maritime patrol.'

Captain Song turned his head. 'Still counting lives, Yankee?'

The aircraft kept on going, its image fading away into the distance.

Dancer forced a smile. 'At least one left.'

The Chinese skipper nodded. 'That is the one you might need.'

It sent a chill through Dancer and Walsh tugged his arm to give some reassurance. And it seemed to work because, although they watched out for another thirty minutes, the aircraft did not reappear.

They returned to the shelter under the gunwale. This time Dancer dozed while Walsh kept vigil.

Later, Dancer wasn't sure what woke him. He thought he felt someone touch his shoulder. As his eyes opened and he became aware of the diesel's throb and the creaking of the junk's timbers, he was surprised that the weather had closed in, coils of mist unravelling over the afterdeck, half-obscuring his vision. He could vaguely make out Song and the helmsman and someone standing in front of them – a female form in some type of translucent summer dress. Immediately he assumed it was Walsh, which he realised was crazy because she surely wouldn't have a dress in her kit. Then he realised she was dozing against his shoulder.

His anger at her laxness flared momentarily until he was distracted by the voice.

'Johnny.'

It was the woman speaking, the mist dispersing slightly as she took a step towards him. Suddenly it was as though she had entered into a pool of sunlight and he could see her clearly now, just feet away from him. The familiar copper ringlets, the laughing blue eyes. He swallowed hard.

'Johnny,' she repeated. 'Save the boy, get him now. It is not his time.'

Debs, he mouthed.

Her words echoed around his head. 'It is not his time.'

He reached out. But as he did, the woman floated away from him, melting back into the mist. Then a breeze eddied in off the sea dispelling the mist and he found himself watching Song and the helmsman beneath a clear and sunny sky.

Walsh said, 'Are you all right, John?'

He looked at her, confused. 'You're not asleep.'

'Of course not. Do I look asleep? Have you been dreaming?'

'Maybe.'

Suddenly one of Song's lookouts began gabbling excitedly and pointing over their stern. Dancer and Walsh turned to look, squinting to see the distant shape in the sky closing in low and fast from the direction of the coast.

'Is it that surveillance plane? Coming back for another look?'

Dancer shook his head and began climbing to his feet. 'Too fast.'

The approaching shadow was already transformed, taking on the distinct and awesome resemblance of a marauding hawk. It was zooming over the water, closing the gap at breathtaking speed. The lookout began shouting in alarm. Now the aircraft was almost upon them, catching up with the junk's trailing wake. There was no doubt now and everyone held their breath. It was a Chinese fighter.

With an ear-splitting shriek, the grey Nanchang Q-5 flashed overhead. It was so low it appeared barely to clear the junk's mast, its hanging genitalia of rocket pods and air-to-air missiles clearly visible. Then it was gone, as fast as it had come, the deafening blast of its afterburners receding across the water as it disappeared towards the distant band of haze that joined the sea and sky.

'First pass,' Dancer said. 'He'll be back.'

'It's gaining height and banking,' Walsh murmured, trying to keep track.

'I'm going to get everyone on deck,' he said and ran towards the tarpaulin.

Scrambling down the wooden steps he found the frightened passengers in the gloom, talking anxiously about the noise overhead. Mama Cheung and Ho were sitting together with Bao.

Dancer grabbed the boy's hand and lifted him to his feet. 'Quick, come with me.' He ushered him towards the steps. 'Up on deck.'

Bao looked puzzled, scared.

'Now!' Dancer hissed. The boy jumped at the anger in the American's voice and scrambled up towards the daylight. Dancer turned back into the hold. '*Everyone* on deck, as fast as you can!'

Without waiting for a reaction, he followed Bao up on to the aft deck and took his hand again.

'You're right,' Walsh said. 'It's coming back.' There was a slight tremor in her voice. 'Surely it won't open fire?'

'I hope not. The pilot might have second thoughts about massacring civilians. They won't stand a chance if they stay below.'

Already the passengers were scrambling up, panicking to get out of the cargo hold.

'But if the pilot sees all these people on board,' Walsh said, 'he'll *know* we're the boat he's looking for.'

Dancer shrugged. 'Damned if we do and damned if we don't.' He turned to Song. 'Where are your life-jackets?'

The captain pointed to some ancient canvas and cork vests tossed carelessly on top of a heap of old netting. 'Just for the crew.'

'Get one for the boy.'

Song hesitated, then picked up one of the life-vests and handed it to Dancer who dropped it over Bao's shoulders. 'Tie up the straps. Quick now!'

There was no time for further discussion. 'Oh, my God!' Walsh gasped. 'Here it comes!'

Half-a-dozen people were now on the afterdeck. He saw Mama Cheung, but not Ho or Gong Li Zhong or the poet Fan. Maybe they were amongst those who were climbing out on to the deck amidships. Beyond the junk's prow he could see the Nanchang entering its shallow dive. He had witnessed the attack attitude of US aircraft too many times in Viet Nam to have any doubt about what was coming next.

The pilot wasn't going to waste his rockets on such a soft and easy target. Dancer saw the stuttering muzzle flashes of the twin 23mm cannon mounted in the wing roots and just caught sight of the tracer rounds kicking up the water in the junk's wake. Then the first rounds struck, chewing into decking and ripping holes in the canvas tarpaulin. Screams filled the air, but it was imposible to know if they were cries of terror or pain as the huge rounds stitched their way towards him. People flung themselves clear as part of the mast collapsed.

Dancer grabbed Bao around the waist and leapt on to the gunwale, yelling to Walsh, 'JUMP!'

He was a second in midair before hitting the water. It was like liquid ice, taking his breath away as he felt himself dropping into the murky depths like a lift in a shaft – he thought his descent would never end. He tried to count the seconds, but his brain refused to function. Then gradually the downward movement slowed. Still clutching Bao with his left arm, he tried to swim upward with his right. After a moment of hovering, the process began to reverse. He stared up at the bizarre distorted mirror above him. It seemed far, far away and his lungs felt as though they were about to explode out of his chest long before he reached it.

Inch by inch the water lightened as he rose to the depth where daylight penetrated. The surface suddenly came at him in a rush. He burst through the waves like a rocket, gulping in the air. After the utter silence, the sudden sound of screaming voices and the roar of the jet's afterburners came as a stunning shock.

He only then became aware that he was still holding Bao in a vice-like grip as the boy began to splutter and cough up ingested seawater. The salt stung Dancer's eyes, but he could see enough. It was a scene of total devastation.

The junk was a floating wreck, smoke billowing raggedly

from its canting hull. Flames raged from the burning lamp fuel, people were on fire, hurling themselves into the sea in desperation. He thought he glimpsed the hunched figure of the poet Fan on the deck, making his way to the side, but the black smoke engulfed him and he fell back into the blazing cargo hold.

All around survivors clung to charred debris and drift-wood – anything that would keep them afloat. Dancer trod water as best he could, trying to keep Bao's head above the surface as he searched for a sign of Walsh. But all he could see were anguished Chinese faces.

'Mr Dancer!' a voice yelled.

'Grandma!' Bao called and took in a mouthful of seawater for his pains.

Mama Cheung was standing on the aft deck, her face white with horror, her arms clutched round her body as though that would give her some kind of protection. 'I cannot swim!' she shouted.

Then the junk's deck canted suddenly and she slid from view. The sea bubbled as air escaped the vessel's hold and it took on more water. Then, quickly and almost majestically, it gave up the unequal struggle and slipped beneath the waves. There was one final hiss of extinguished flames and it was gone, leaving just a wreath of white woodsmoke to mark its grave.

'Christ,' Dancer cried savagely.

And suddenly he realised he'd be following it to the bottom if he didn't find something to cling to. At the moment he wasn't sure if he was keeping Bao afloat or the boy's life-vest was saving him. He glanced around, but there was nothing nearby.

'John! Over here!'

His heart leapt as he recognised Walsh's gasping voice.

He saw the hand wave. She was some way out, clasping something that looked like part of the junk's mast. There was no way he could wave back, but used his free arm to start pushing himself and Bao towards her. His muscles

509

were on fire from the strain, but he persevered with clenched teeth and tried to blot out the excruciating pain from his mind.

It was ten minutes before he was close to her, and realised she'd been frantically kicking to push her makeshift raft nearer.

At last the fingers of his free hand reached out to within an inch of the mast. As they touched, relief surged through him and a weight like lead was lifted. Dancer slipped his arm over the pole, then helped Bao get a grip.

He found Walsh watching him from the other side. 'Thank God you made it,' she said. 'And *thank God* Nick never gave up on me.'

'Nick?' he asked, getting his breath back.

'Nick Lake. Made me learn to swim, the brute.'

And at that moment, as he looked at her laughing eyes and the smile that told him how pleased she was to see him, he thought she was probably the loveliest and most welcome sight he had ever seen.

Al Cherrier had watched the Nanchang's cannons rake the junk on the optronics monitor above the control suite. McVicar and Lake stood behind him, sharing his horror as the massacre took place. Aware that something was going on, Lily Cheung had joined them. She stared at the screen in horrified silence then let out an uncontrollable wail of grief.

Not until the boat had disappeared amid the bobbing heads of the survivors did anybody speak.

'My God!' . . . Lake's voice was hoarse with suppressed fury. 'Who says the Chinese Government has changed?'

'Same old leopard,' McVicar agreed. 'Same old spots.'

Lily was gasping for breath between her sobs. 'Can you see my son? Or my mother and brother? Or Mr John? Any of them?'

Cherrier zoomed in the optronics camera, but at five miles' distance it was impossible to see anything now that the junk had gone. 'Sorry, Lily,' he said. Then added, 'There must be some survivors.'

'It looked to me like several jumped,' Lake said.

'Was Janie one of them?' McVicar wondered. 'Or John? Or any of Lily's family?'

'We must save them!' Lily said anxiously.

McVicar glanced at Lake who shook his head slowly.

The Scotsman said, 'We've already broken the rules, Lily, by attacking that patrol boat. But to surface would be a serious risk to the crew and everyone on board. Yourself included.'

'But my *son*!' Lily pleaded.

'The place is swarming with patrol boats and aircraft,' Lake explained and pointed at the sonar and radar screens on the control suite. 'Just look for yourself.'

However, that meant nothing to Lily. 'You can't just let them die.'

McVicar tried to be patient. 'I don't like it any more than you do, but we only have the capacity to take two more people on board. We'd have to push people off by force.'

Cherrier had said nothing, but had been deep in thought, chewing on his empty pipe. At last he spoke:

'Gentlemen, if I may interrupt you. . . This is *my* part of the operation. If the coast seems clear, I'm prepared to risk surfacing to see what we can do. For a start, we can leave the Geminis for the survivors. If we can locate Janie and John Dancer or Lily's family we'll take them on board. At least some lives would be saved.'

Lake regarded the captain with incredulity.

'I know I speak for my crew,' Cherrier continued, 'but if you and Dave oppose the idea, I shall bow to your wishes.'

McVicar didn't hesitate. 'Let's go for it,' he said quietly.

'I agree,' Lake said. He just wanted to see Walsh's face again.

Cherrier turned to Manson. 'Make for the site of the sinking at maximum knots.'

'Aye, aye, sir.'

'I'm surprised, Al, to be honest,' Lake said.

A rare half-smile broke through the beard. 'Because I'm a taciturn old fucker?'

'Something like that.'

Cherrier nodded. 'Doesn't mean I don't have feelings, Nick.'

'So why?'

'Same reason I had a crack at that patrol boat. Told you my father was a sub skipper in the last war. Well, he told me of the one time he was dived off Singapore just before it fell to the Japs. A Nip destroyer opened up on a fleeing passenger liner. He managed to sink the destroyer, but could do nothing for the damaged liner for fear of other Jap warships in the area. He assumed the Japs would eventually board and take the passengers prisoner and back to Singapore. He later learned he was wrong. The Japs massacred them and scuttled the ship. He never forgave himself for not doing more – although it's hard to see what he could have done. It haunted him until the day he died.'

'How terrible,' Lily said.

'My father didn't have that choice,' Cherrier added. 'Today I have.'

'I don't think the Pentagon would agree,' Lake pointed out. 'Or the Admiralty in London.'

Cherrier's enigmatic smile returned. 'Maybe the three of us just march to the beat of a different drum.'

McVicar nodded. 'Maybe we do.'

But it was to be a further forty-five minutes before they reached the co-ordinates of the junk's last sighting. By that time the survivors, clinging to bits of wreckage, had spread over a wider area. After a final sonar check and radar scan with the warner mast to ensure there was no immediate threat, Cherrier ran up the optronics mast. From inside the submarine, he was able to zoom in on individuals in the water. McVicar, Lake and Lily watched anxiously, trying to put names to faces. Their spirits ebbed. No one could recognise Walsh or Dancer. The Chinese faces looked very

512

similar in those conditions, so no one could identify Mama Cheung, Lily's brother Ho, or the poet Fan. They did, however, pick out the junk's skipper Captain Song and a couple of his crewmen.

Suddenly Cherrier's eyes narrowed. 'What's that, I wonder? Farther out, I think someone's clinging to that piece of driftwood.'

As he zoomed in again, McVicar said, 'Looks like part of the mast.'

'Bao!' Lily screamed. 'It's Bao, I know it!'

A big grin spread on Lake's face. 'Damn me, and that's Walsh. Dancer too. He's got hold of the boy.'

'Steer two-zero-eight,' Cherrier told the helmsman. 'Two knots.'

Everyone waited anxiously as they closed the distance.

'Stand by to surface. Sanchez to the secondary hatch.' He turned to Lake. 'You want to get the Geminis ready?'

Sanchez was up the aluminium ladder to the vertical hatch set in the rear recess of the fin and in position just as it broke the surface. After a quick visual check through the Plexiglass ports, he turned the wheel lock and opened the hatch on to the flat countersunk deck space. He could see Walsh waving furiously and hear her excited shouts.

Sanchez opened the built-in compartment beneath his feet and unrolled a flexi-ladder down one side of the hull. It then took several minutes for Dancer and Walsh to manoeuvre the mast close enough to the monstrous black bulk of the submarine.

For the first time, Bao's face broke into a beaming smile. 'It is the undersea boat. The submarine!' He turned to Dancer. 'I knew you tell the truth! You are my most favourite uncle.'

Walsh laughed as Sanchez descended the ladder to pluck the boy from the water and place him safely on the rungs. By the time Walsh and Dancer had followed to the safety of the recessed deck, the sea around them was suddenly full of survivors swimming frantically towards them.

513

Sanchez spoke into his radio mike. 'Captain, there's a lot of people coming this way'

'*How many?*'

Sanchez gave a quick scan. 'Maybe twenty, probably more.'

Cherrier said, '*Nick and the boys are bringing up the Geminis now.*'

On cue the SBS lieutenant appeared at the hatch and the first dinghy began ballooning as the compressed air from the attached cylinder was released. It was then thrown unceremoniously over the side. Two others followed in rapid succession.

Suddenly Cherrier's voice was terse in Sanchez's ear. '*We're picking up an airborne maritime search radar. Closing fast. We're preparing to dive.*'

A Chinese with a plump face swam to *Manta*'s side and, gasping, reached for the bottom rung of the ladder, only to have it whisked away from his fingertips.

'Sorry, pal,' Sanchez called down. 'Get into one of the dinghies.'

'Please, please,' the swimmer cried, 'I must get to America!'

Sanchez stowed away the ladder and pointed out to sea. 'Then you'd better start rowing. It's that way.'

'*Dive, dive, dive!*' Cherrier's warning rang in the sailor's ear and he ran for the hatch as the sea began swirling up over the hull.

The man in the water swam a few strokes to bring him alongside one of the Geminis. Other Chinese, already on board, helped pull him up. He gasped his thanks and fell back exhausted against the rubber gunwale.

With a heavy heart, he watched the waves breaking over the humped black fin of the submarine as it slid away beneath the waves. A few minutes later he became aware of the sound of approaching aero engines. Four turbos powered the huge and ungainly Harbin amphibian, which reminded him vaguely of a pterodactyl as it droned towards them on dead reckoning.

Suddenly he realised what it was going to do and snatched up a paddle. 'Quick, everyone! Row for your lives!'

Others realised too and there was a frantic thrashing of water as they struggled to put more distance between the Gemini and the spot where the submarine had vanished.

As the noise of the anti-submarine patrol swamped them and the vast shadow passed overhead, they saw them fall like giant excreta from the amphibian's racks. He counted four. The depth charges struck the surface with huge splashes some quarter-mile away. He held his breath, just waiting. They exploded in rapid succession, no doubt at different settings. But the effect was of one long, rippling detonation as the sea erupted in mushrooms of froth and spray. They felt the shock wave of displaced air that lifted the Gemini off the surface and sent it spinning in the air. As it landed again with a slapping thud, the occupants were drenched as seawater rained down on them from the sky.

The Harbin had begun a long slow circle to bring it back on a return course.

Cheung Ho watched as huge black slabs floated to the surface at the spot where the submarine had been. He recognised them as some sort of tiles that had covered the entire hull. Ho just prayed that his sister was not on board.

Nineteen

As the submarine dived, Lily was still hugging her son tightly with one arm as she smiled at Dancer. 'How can I ever thank you enough for saving him?'

'No need,' he said, but noticed that there was a distance between them now. 'I'm afraid I have bad news. Your mother was on the junk when it went down.'

Lily gasped. 'She cannot swim.'

'I'm afraid she's dead.'

Her hand went to her mouth. 'And Ho?'

He shrugged. 'Neither Janie nor I saw him. But there's always hope.'

The stupefying noise and force and closeness of the explosions took everyone by surprise. They felt the deck physically lift beneath their feet and cant to port under the power of the blasts. People were stumbling to keep their balance, others falling. The red lighting flickered ominously and the titanium plates trembled under the awesome pressure.

'Fuck me!' Hinks gasped, his face ashen.

Cherrier was at the helm console, hands on the half-wheel joystick. 'I'm taking her to full ahead,' he said and glanced at the digital depth gauge. 'I've got eighty feet clearance.'

Hinks looked at the seabed-mapping sonar indicator on his console. 'Uneven readings ahead, Skipper. Don't go below sixty.'

'Confirmed,' Cherrier came back. 'Diving to sixty.' He turned to Lake. 'Damage assessment, if you please. All compartments.'

'In hand, Al.' Lake returned.

The SBS team had various secondary roles when the

crew was at full stretch and visual damage assessment was one of them. All hatches had been centrally locked from the control room, but now Dougie and Taff went fore and aft, using a manual override to gain access to each compartment. Clearly, at least one of the bombs, each set to detonate at a different depth, had gone off too close for comfort. There was water seepage in the forward crew quarters and a more serious leak in the aft engine room.

They returned with the bad news which Cherrier acknowledged with his usual calm.

'Well, we can add to that external damage to the starboard hydroplane control – I'm getting a sluggish reaction. And the computer's telling me there are leaks in the fuel cell system. Hardly surprising – it's a bit Heath Robinson with numerous connection joints. Nature of the beast, I'm afraid. But that could mean a danger of carbon dioxide poisoning, as you know. So we'll keep the engine room sealed. Any further entry will be with the use of oxygen masks.'

Lake nodded his understanding. 'So what's the master plan, Al?'

'It's around a twelve-hour run to the Laotieshan Shuidao Straits off Port Arthur. That's where the Chinese will mount their maximum effort as we try to squeeze through the narrow gap. But shortly after that we'll be in international waters where we have a rendezvous planned with elements of the 7th Fleet.

'Meantime,' Cherrier continued, 'I want to get to one of the dredged commercial channels and see if we can't hide behind some merchant vessel's noise. You see, given the closeness of those depth charges, there's every possibility we've lost some of our anachoic tiles from the outer hull.' He gave a tight and weary smile. 'That means we may no longer be as stealthy as we were.'

Then, as though to emphasise his words, Hinks announced suddenly, 'Torpedo attack! Coming at us on active sonar. Bearing three fifty-five degrees. Distance one and a quarter miles and closing at a rate of twenty-five knots. Estimated time of impact –' he watched as the computer flashed up its calculation '– three minutes, twenty seconds.'

'Right up our ass,' Sanchez said. 'It must be getting a reading off us.'

'So we *have* lost tiles,' Cherrier confirmed and gave a small grunt of annoyance as he turned to Manson on the Fire-Control console. 'Prepare aft decoys.'

'Aye, aye, sir,' the man replied, but he was already at work, activating the huge cylindrical Magnum system now starting to revolve to line up two Decoy Ones with the aft firing shutters. The grind of oiled metal was faintly audible as the submarine gave a slight tremor.

'Torpedo ETI sixty seconds.'

'Four Decoy Ones loaded,' intoned Manson.

'Stand by to fire,' Cherrier ordered. 'Fire!'

They all felt the slight jolt as the underwater missiles discharged from the Magnum's aft ports. But they could only visualise each missile dividing into four acoustic submissiles, each generating an electronic echo to confuse the torpedo and offer tempting alternative targets.

'Evasive manoeuvres!' Cherrier warned, pulling the joystick towards him and turning the wheel hard to starboard.

Instantly the *Manta* began to climb sharply, gaining another twenty feet. The damaged rudder reaction was slower, the abrupt ninety-degree turn taking vital seconds. Dancer saw Walsh close her eyes momentarily and knew that, like him, she was bracing herself for the impact.

Then they heard it. A reverberating muffled roar as the torpedo decided it had found its target and struck the decoy. The submarine trembled in the shock wave and again the lights flickered momentarily. Everyone breathed again.

'All clear,' Hinks reported.

'Eject oil decoy,' Cherrier decided.

'Ejecting,' Manson confirmed. He pressed the key to open up the valve of a five-gallon tank located on the top deck between the inner and outer hulls. Dirty black sludge pumped out towards the surface as Cherrier set a new course.

Ten minutes passed with no further attack. Walsh turned to Dancer. 'I think we've done it.'

'Sure,' he said with a smile. But it wasn't what he thought.

Vice Admiral Shi Yushu, commander of the Chicom North Sea Fleet, studied his large-scale wall map in the vast operations centre at PLA Navy headquarters in Qingdao on the coast of the Yellow Sea.

There was a sly smile of satisfaction on his face as he turned to Brigadier Ting Han-chen of the Ministry of State Security who had flown direct by military helicopter from the interrogation centre at Qinhuangdao. 'As you can see, my trap is closing.'

'You're sure the submarine wasn't hit by the torpedo fired by your patrol aircraft? I mean, that oil slick . . .'

Shi shook his head. 'An old submariner's trick, my friend. There was a lot of decoy activity at the time. That's how the submarine managed to escape the net. But the pilot and crew of the amphibian are wily old-timers. They are following its movements.'

'I thought you said they couldn't detect it?'

'Ah yes, that was so. But it may have sustained damage from the depth charges. You see, from what we now know, piecing together earlier intelligence reports, this is a very sophisticated vessel. State-of-the-art. What we call a stealth submarine.' He stroked his chin thoughtfully. 'In fact, Naval Intelligence thinks it may be to do with something the Americans call Project Deadwater in Hawaii. Our people have tried to get close for years, but without much success. The Yankees said it was a deep-recovery rescue submarine, but we weren't convinced.'

'The point, Admiral?' Ting pressed, his patience wearing thin.

'Stealth submarines are covered with special rubberised coatings or tiles to minimise the radiated noise and target echo strength. If the depth charges caused damage, it would explain why our surveillance aircraft has suddenly been able to get a faint reading on its Magnetic Anomaly Detector. And why the torpedo was able to find the target.'

'Then why not continue the attack and blow the thing to smithereens?'

The vice-admiral regarded his guest as though he were a particularly stupid child.

'Because, my friend, the signature is faint and intermittent and the submarine runs in virtually total silence. She is still a very sophisticated and difficult target to identify.'

'So what do you plan to do?'

Shi took a long pointing stick from his desk and jabbed it at the map. 'That's the most recent sighting on almost an exact one eighty-degree bearing. Obviously it is making for one of the deep dredged channels into Tianjin port area. Probably plans to hide behind the skirts of some ship leaving port.'

'So how can you stop her?'

'For a start all ships due to leave Tianjin have been stopped and those that have already left have been ordered to return. Secondly, whatever the submarine does, she has to pass through the Laotieshan Shuidao Straits, barely twenty miles across. With the sort of depth the captain will want, that's reduced to nearer ten. That's where we'll catch her.'

Now Ting could see the significance of all the markers closing in on the straits from all directions.

'Mostly fast anti-submarine patrol boats,' Shi explained. Then she's caught?'

'I think so. And I hope her captain will realise that.'

'And surrender?'

'Maybe. Or lie doggo on the bottom.'

'So then you will destroy it?'

Shi shook his head. 'Oh, no, because I'd very much like to get my hands on that craft intact. I have a Ming Class patrol submarine in the vicinity with naval commando swimmers on board. They will prise open the Yankee sardine tin, be assured of that. With luck you'll get your prisoners back.' He allowed himself a wide smile. 'I expect you'd like that, wouldn't you, my friend?'

For a split second, Ting's mind was filled with the vision of Lily Cheung kneeling defenceless before him. Again he sensed her soft skin beneath his fingertips and could feel her flinch as she looked at him with those pleading sable eyes.

'When will this be?' he asked.

Shi looked at the large clock above the wall map. 'Some time tonight'.

It was now three in the afternoon. 'I should like to see this. Could I be flown to one of the patrol boats in the area?'

'By helicopter? But of course.'

Manta almost felt its way across the undersea landscape like a blind man. Its crew sought the deepest waters in the undulating and ever-shifting shallows, following valleys between mounds of silt until, eventually, they came to the first deep-water channel.

A shipping channel that ran from the Tianjin port area to the Yellow Sea. A shipping channel, but with no ships in it. Al Cherrier cursed, his hope of slipping close to a merchantman now firmly dashed. There was nothing for it but to head for open waters alone. At least now he would have more depth in which to manoeuvre and it would give his crew a chance to unwind and relax their flayed nerves.

Three times they rose to periscope depth and ran up the warner mast for a rapid radar scan. And each time it picked up an air-to-surface search radar which the computer matched with a PLA Navy Harbin maritime surveillance aircraft.

Morning drifted into afternoon, then drifted into evening. Despite the uncomfortable, cramped and claustrophobic conditions, most of the combat swimmers and their passengers managed to get some sleep. The crew themselves didn't quite have that luxury, dividing themselves into two two-man shifts. One pair operated the main helm console and the AIO and sonar consoles between them, while the other couple attempted to snatch some desperately needed sleep.

Dancer had catnapped a little, but it was too hot and airless for him to sleep for long. He'd stripped off his shirt, but he was still sweating. Beside him, Walsh was in a green army singlet, the cutaway sleeves emphasising impressive muscle tone for one so small and distinctly feminine.

She noticed him watching. 'You can't sleep?'

He shook his head. 'I thought you were out to the world.'

'I wish. Had my eyes closed, that's all.' She appeared to be studying him closely. 'If you can't sleep, maybe Lily could do with some company. She doesn't really know anyone else in our team.'

A smile. 'She's still in with Yan Tao, playing nursemaid. She's only got eyes for him now.'

'Really? Are you disappointed?'

'I was. But then I didn't want to admit we really were from two different cultures. East is east, and all that.'

She nodded, trying to understand. 'Guess my parents were very lucky then. What will you do now? When we get out of this?'

Positive thinking, he noted. *When*, not if. 'Well, I can't go back to China. Abe wants us to set up some business in Laos. Maybe run a bar.'

'Sounds fun.' She giggled.

'Then you should join us.'

'No shortage of lap-dancers there.'

'I wasn't thinking of that exactly.' He hesitated. 'What will *you* do?'

Her smile lost some of its brilliance in the ruby glow of the ops room light. 'Lap-dancing might be a real option. I think I've blown my career on this operation. I don't think Frank Aspen ever did like me much. I don't see a future for me in the Agency.'

'I don't think I've ever asked, are you married?'

'Once. For six weeks. I hadn't realised he was *such* a coke-head. It was really sad to see such dependency.' She noticed his expression alter a fraction. 'You look tense. I guess we're all scared. Are you scared?'

He shook his head. 'You just reminded me I'm *dying* for a Camel.'

Walsh almost burst with sudden laughter.

At that moment, Sanchez, who was on the sonar console, turned to Manson at the helm and spoke to him in an earnest, hushed tone. Manson nodded before calling out to Cherrier. The captain was apparently sleeping on one of the bunk cots that hinged down from the bulkhead. 'Skipper, we've started picking up a lot of activity. Think you should take a look.'

It was said that Cherrier had the ability to dognap, seemingly always aware of what was going on despite being sound asleep. True to form, he casually lifted himself up and dropped to the deck. Hinks stirred himself with more obvious effort, forcing himself to follow his commander's lead.

'Sonar's picking up several *Hainan*-class anti-sub patrol boats,' Sanchez said. 'Coming from several directions, but, on their present courses, all headed for the Straits. And they'll all be there well ahead of us.'

Cherrier studied the 'Plan Position Indicator' screen as he dug the cob pipe from his pocket and stuck it firmly between his teeth. 'Going to cut us off at the pass,' he murmured, 'just like in the Westerns. How long before we get to the Straits?'

'About two hours.'

'Then it's going to be an interesting night.'

For the next ten minutes, Cherrier went into a huddle with his crew and Nick Lake, thrashing out a strategy and trying to cover every contingency. When the process was complete *Manta* was taken to periscope depth and the warner mast raised above the surface for just a few seconds. One reason was to reaffirm, locate and identify all active radars operating in the area; it was a bitter disappointment to find the Harbin patrol aircraft still loitering in their vicinity. The other purpose was to send one compressed 'squeeze-box' satellite signal to the operations control centre at Hereford in England.

Cherrier gave their position and the situation that faced them. Any reply should be sent at 2105 hours precisely, when *Manta* would return to periscope depth again to receive.

When it came, the reply lifted their spirits, but not too much. The prearranged flotilla from the US 7th Fleet was just outside Chinese territorial waters with orders to assist a 'disabled rescue submarine'. However, the Navy could do nothing for them unless *Manta* managed to leave Chinese territory under its own power.

Lake decided that all combat swimmers should be fully prepared and kitted out in case an emergency evacuation became necessary. Spare rubber wet suits were issued to the sub's passengers with the exception of Yan Tao and little Bao. Yan couldn't struggle into one with his fractured limbs and there wasn't one that fitted the boy. The entire prospect absolutely petrified Lily despite everyone's attempts to assure her she had to do nothing at all but breathe normally into the mouthpiece of her scuba system. She sat at Yan's bedside, totally unaware of how fetching the soldiers thought she looked in tight black rubber, and sobbed gently.

Manta was approaching the Straits from the north-west as the six patrol boats now spread themselves out across the deep channel some seventeen miles away. At that

524

distance it was unlikely that even their active sonars would detect the submarine's presence, despite the missing tiles.

Cherrier was back at the helm console with Hinks on sonar and Sanchez on fire-control.

'Sealing off all compartments,' the captain advised and activated the central-locking. To Dancer it felt like pulling on a safety belt before a deadly car chase. 'Activate Type Two decoy.'

'What's that?' Dancer asked Lake.

'A small electric torpedo. It has a towed array that replicates our noise – well, louder, I hope – and its fin and control surfaces are enhanced to resemble a full-size submarine.'

'A decoy?'

Lake nodded. 'Trouble is we only have two. Quite expensive bits of kit.'

The giant Magnum cylinder in the bow section turned to bring the firing tube in line with the outer shutter.

Cherrier lined up *Manta* on a 144 degree bearing. 'Fire decoy!'

'Decoy fired!' Sanchez confirmed and the submarine gave a slight but distinct jolt as the torpedo was ejected. 'Travelling at ten knots.'

Lake turned to Dancer. 'We're approaching the Straits and a flotilla of patrol boats. Al's fired the decoy across their bows, out of torpedo range, towards a necklace of small islands that run across the south part of the Straits. With any luck they'll think we're trying to sneak past them in the shallow waters around those islands.'

For five minutes nothing happened. Then Hinks said, 'Ah, something's starting.'

Dancer stepped forward so that he could see the consoles more clearly over the operators' shoulders. He noted the trajectory of the decoy, then saw three of the emblems representing patrol boats gradually start to move, the sound-picture relayed back through *Manta*'s sophisticated passive listening sonars.

'Taken the bait,' Hinks said with satisfaction.

But it was clear that the Chinese naval commander wasn't totally convinced and wasn't going to put all his eggs in one basket. Half his flotilla remained on station while the others gave chase to the decoy.

Cherrier had slowed *Manta* to a near standstill. Now he went to full throttle, pushing them to a full ten knots. While the three patrol boats gave chase, it opened up a gap in the Chinese defence line. Cherrier intended to slip through before it closed again.

Watching the electronic images move across the screen was like viewing some bizarre and deadly arcade game, Dancer thought. It was hard to imagine all this was going on around them. For real.

With seemingly agonising slowness *Manta* was inching towards the gap. It was then that the nearest *Hainan* patrol boat abruptly changed course and began moving towards them.

'She's picked us up,' Hinks decided. 'Either that or the bloody patrol aircraft's got our fix on MAD and radioed the boat.'

'She can't be sure,' Sanchez said, 'or she'd have fired by now.'

Cherrier made his decision. 'Prepare to engage target. Range?'

'Seven miles.'

'Prepare Stingray torpedo. Stand by to fire.'

Again the great forward Magnum revolved into position. 'Torpedo ready,' replied Sanchez. 'Standing by.'

'Fire!'

Again they felt the faint shudder as the Stingray was discharged on its mission.

Sanchez said, 'Target heading this way at twenty knots. Reducing ETI to seven point five minutes.'

Cherrier gave a grim smile of satisfaction. Dancer could see why. The Stingray's Estimated Time of Impact was just seven and a half minutes away. The patrol boat was unwittingly racing to meet the torpedo and its own destruction. It seemed that the patrol boat's sonar operator hadn't picked them up after all.

A tense and solemn silence fell over the control room, broken only by Sanchez counting down every half-minute. Walsh glanced at Dancer, clutching her own arms anxiously as she waited.

Just two minutes to go. On the screen the icon of the Stingray was seen homing unerringly on the approaching boat.

Suddenly Sanchez called out: 'Torpedo incoming! Torpedo incoming!'

'Shit!' Cherrier snapped in a rare display of temper.

Dancer suddenly realised what had happened. The oncoming patrol boat had already fired at them, but at such a distance the *Manta*'s sonars hadn't picked up the torpedo's tiny sound signature immediately. Now it had and he could see the tiny blip flickering across the screen. It was hard to believe it was out there, homing silently in on them. Hard, but not that hard. He seemed to feel a cold hand on the back of his neck.

Now all thoughts of the patrol boat's destruction evaporated. Defence overrode attack. 'Stand by to launch Decoy Ones,' Cherrier ordered.

'Loading,' Sanchez reported, turning the Magnum chamber, lining up with the outer shutters. 'Confirm two loaded.'

'Fire one!'

The first decoy missile was on its way. They watched the two symbols on the screen, moving on a collision course. Then, the decoy divided, emitting noise from each sub-missile as it went off in a different direction.

But the incoming torpedo was in no mood to be distracted; it seemed to know exactly what it was after. *Manta*.

'Stand by second decoy,' Cherrier decided. On the screen it looked as though the torpedo was on top of them. 'Fire!'

The second missile shot from its port and divided almost

immediately. This time the torpedo was tempted, its electronic brain possibly confused by the closeness of *Manta* itself.

It was like an earthquake, the submarine trembling with the force as it was physically pushed sideways in the water by the proximity of the three-hundred kilogram warhead as it went off. The lights flickered and for one awful moment Cherrier thought the computer was going to crash. He willed it to hold on, just as their own torpedo struck the advancing *Hainan* head-on. The low boom of sound reached them above the low purr of *Manta*'s power cell.

Walsh opened her eyes. 'God, I thought we were dead then.'

Dancer took her hand in his and gave it a reassuring squeeze.

She gave a quick smile of appreciation. 'I'm not such a tough guy, you know.'

'I'm beginning to realise.'

Now warning lights were flashing all over the 'Damage Assessment' panel in the control suite. An intercom call came through from the locked crew quarters that the seepage had worsened; Lake donned his breathing apparatus and crawled through the access tunnel to the aft engine room to make a visual inspection there. Meanwhile Cherrier reported that the controls were becoming progressively more sluggish. That suggested further damage to the rudder and hydroplanes as well as some water ingress between the outer and inner hulls.

'Those other two patrol boats,' Sanchez reported. 'They're coming this way. A bit cautious though, now they've seen what happened to that first one.'

Cherrier studied the screen and weighed up the situation. Time was running out. The Chinese patrol-boat commanders assumed they were the hunters, assumed that the submarine was on the run and they were giving chase. They were veering towards the far side of the Straits to cut them off.

Cherrier made his decision. 'Prepare two forward Stingrays.'

'Preparing, Skipper,' Sanchez replied. 'They're our last ones.'

'Then we'd better make them count.' He activated the fore-and-aft side thrusters, bringing the horizontal propeller shafts into play to turn the submarine on her own axis until she faced back into the Gulf. 'Just a short detour.'

Dancer observed the screen with fascination. As the patrol boats began to cut diagonally across the Straits, *Manta* headed back into the Gulf before turning in a wide arc so that the Chinese vessels were about to cross her bows at a distance of some three miles.

Anxious to avoid the attentions of a torpedo homing in on the sound of their active sonars, they were now searching for *Manta* only on passive, an electronically enhanced listening technique.

Both hunters and the hunted were playing the listening game, none wanting to give their position away by interrogating the enemy with active sonar sound pulses. But the patrol boats had a distinct disadvantage because they were inherently noisy. By contrast, even with some anachoic tiles missing, the stealth submarine's sleek teardrop shape and virtually silent running made it almost impossible to detect. The Chinese commanders would be unaware of *Manta* lying invisibly in wait for them to cruise into her sights.

With his hand on the rollerball control, Sanchez deftly moved the cursor on the screen over each target in turn, then keyed the computer to tell him their precise speed and bearing and the projected speed and bearing of the *Manta*'s Stingrays.

'Attack evaluation complete.' Sanchez announced. 'Request firing in forty-five seconds.'

'Fire when ready,' Cherrier confirmed.

Sanchez watched the digital clock. 'Firing both torpedoes – NOW!'

They all felt the faint jolt as compressed air hurtled the Stingrays on their way, for the moment heading towards empty stretches of sea. By the time they'd covered the three miles, the patrol boats should be in exactly the right position. If they altered course or changed speed, they should still be close enough for the torpedoes to home in on the noise of their powerful engines.

Now that the weapons had been unleashed, Cherrier turned his mind to escaping before the other half of the flotilla realised they were chasing a phantom. He brought *Manta*'s nose round to face the gap in the Straits and the beckoning Yellow Sea beyond, and opened up the throttle.

The fuel cell purred as they surged forward to a full ten knots. A few minutes later they heard the two explosions, one close after the other, the joint shock waves rippling through the water until the submarine itself trembled slightly from the rippling force of displaced water.

Hinks grinned. 'Target sonar readings have disappeared, Skipper.'

'Well done, everyone,' Cherrier said flatly. 'Now we're on our way.'

The tension eased noticeably. There were a lot of grins and many silly jokes. The compartment hatches were opened to the relief of everyone locked in the crew quarters. McVicar organised a brew of strong tea; for once even the Americans seemed to relish it as much as the British.

For two hours they cruised on without incident, some even managing to get back to sleep. The sonar console told Cherrier that half the flotilla of patrol boats had given up their chase after the decoy and had returned to rescue surviviors after the remaining three of their number had been sunk. Eventually two resumed their search for *Manta*, but they were now looking too late and thirty miles behind the fleeing submarine.

Cherrier's only serious concern was the leak in the forward crew quarters, which was now quite severe, but at least the pumps were coping adequately.

The US 7th Fleet was now tantalisingly close. That was when Hinks announced without warning, 'I'm picking up a submarine. Engine noise analysis –' he hit the keyboard. '*Ming* class. Diesel electric patrol submarine. One five eighty-four displacement. Dived speed eighteen knots. No active sonar interrogation, so she's listening on passive.'

'Then let's give her something to get excited about,' Cherrier said instantly. 'Load the Second Decoy Two. Action stations!'

Walsh saw that Dancer was studying the sonar screens. 'What's happened?'

'Looks like the *Ming* submarine is the Chinese goalkeeper across the Straits as we enter the Yellow Sea. Al's going to fire a decoy one way –' He watched the line appear in confirmation on the screen, '– south. As the *Ming* jumps that way to catch the ball, we slip through to the north and join the US Fleet.'

Cherrier had to make a careful calculation. The *Ming*'s dived speed was almost twice that of the *Manta*. He waited until the Chinese submarine was twenty miles off before giving the order to fire the decoy. As soon as it had gone, he altered course and aimed for the cluster of sonar icons that represented the welcome committee of the 7th.

Shortly after, the *Ming*'s speed increased and she swung south to give chase to intercept the decoy. A slow smile began to spread over Cherrier's face. She'd taken the bait.

Then, suddenly, after five minutes, Hinks announced, 'Shit, the *Ming*'s slowing. She's turning back. Setting a new course.' He looked across at Cherrier. 'In our direction.'

The captain frowned. 'There's no way she's picked us up. It must be . . .'

'Our old friend, the Harbin?' Hinks suggested.

'It must be.' He pulled back on the joystick. 'We need to know. I'm taking us up to periscope depth . . . Stand by warner mast . . .'

The electronics mast slid upwards to the faintest hiss of hydraulics. Above, the aerial broke the surface for five seconds then vanished again, having surveyed all radar signals and downloaded the results into the computer. Sanchez's hands flew over the keyboard as the analysis appeared on the touch-screen of the AIO.

'There she is, the Harbin maritime recce,' he confirmed. 'Right on our tail. She's got the scent all right.'

The aircraft must have picked up *Manta* on her MAD, Cherrier decided. Because of the lost tiles, the MAD system was able to read the difference between the bared steel hull and the surrounding magnetic field. All he could do was dive deep and go through a series of evasive manoeuvres until they were able to wriggle out of the MAD's limited focus.

Cherrier swung them to port as *Manta* plunged towards the seabed, then he veered suddenly to starboard. The deck canted and everything not tied down went on the slide. It was like a crazy rollercoaster, a theme-park monster ride gone mad. The vessel trembled intermittently as they heard the deep sonic booms of the patrol aircraft's depth charges somewhere in their wake.

Dancer listened intently and saw the fear in Walsh's eyes. The explosions, he thought, sounded fainter. 'I think we've got away with it,' he said.

That was when it happened. The words had scarcely left his lips than the earthquake occurred. At least, that was what it felt like. The noise was awesome, an ear-splitting tremulous roar that completely engulfed them as though they were at its very core. It was like being inside a cathedral bell when the hammer struck. They could actually feel the movement, the cosmic force contemptuously tossing a hundred and ninety tons of submarine skyward like so much flotsam. Crew and passengers, supposedly secure in cots or on seats, went flying. Dancer found himself hurled against the bulkhead, and then felt Walsh's shoulder land painfully in his ribs. Equipment detached itself from mountings and smashed to the deck. Pipework trembled, chiming discordant notes as steel vibrated against steel. The light fluttered, dimmed and went out.

Seconds later, the emergency generator cut in and the red lights blinked back on. The screens did not.

'Oh, fuck!' Hinks swore. 'The computer's crashed.'

'I'm taking over on manual,' Cherrier assured him quickly. The deck was just rocking gently now, *Manta* stabilizing and regaining her composure. He pressed the intercom 'send' button and spoke into his throat mike. 'Damage assessment please.'

Water was now seeping rapidly into both the aft engine room and the crew quarters, the pumps failing to get on top of the torrent.

It was then that everyone became aware of the abrupt silence. The faint and omnipresent background hum-like air-conditioning systems you only realise have been on when they have been turned off, had gone.

Cherrier examined the helm console before him and his heart sank as he watched the revs dial needle sag slowly back in an anticlockwise direction from its original forty rpm. 'Losing power,' he reported solemnly. 'Total engine failure.'

Then the lights went and, for a few horrifying seconds, they were thrown into intense darkness. Again the emergency battery kicked in and the control room was reduced to an eerie crimson twilight. *Manta* was floating, suspended and motionless. Now Cherrier's personal skills took over from the computer to hold her steady.

He glanced at Lake. 'Evacuate the crew quarters, Nick. Advise when done.'

'Sure.'

'What happens now?' asked Hinks. 'We gonna surface?'

Cherrier shook his head. 'I'm not sure if we offered a surrender whether the Chinese would accept it. I don't want to go up until I'm sure.'

'Lie doggo awhile?'

'Maybe. What's our last known GPS position?'

Hinks told him. 'That's with the computer's last update assessment. Pretty much a hundred per cent accurate.'

'That must put us close to international waters?'

'Bloody ironic that.' Hinks looked depressed. 'Barely a half-mile.'

Lake returned with everyone from the forward crew quarters, including Lily and Yan Tao on his stretcher. 'Everyone evacuated, Al,' the SBS officer advised.

Cherrier hit the central-lock button, closing off fore and aft engine compartments. Now the control room was so full of people it resembled a rush-hour subway train.

'What's the plan, Al?' Lake asked.

'I'd like to go to the bottom, Nick. See if we can't lose the Chinese.'

'But?'

'We'd have limited time. The pumps are losing the battle against the leaks. Above a critical point, we'll never get up off the seabed again.'

Lake said, 'If that happened, my lads could run out the remote radio aerial and signal assistance from the 7th Fleet. How far away is it now?'

'Ten miles,' Hinks interjected.

Sanchez said, 'I think it's a bit academic. That *Ming* submarine is dead ahead and still coming. She's interrogating us on active now and we're clean out of torpedoes and decoys.'

'What's her range?'

With the computer down, the figure would be very approximate. 'About one mile.'

'And she hasn't fired?' Cherrier was puzzled. 'Why not, for God's sake?'

Sanchez shrugged. 'Maybe she's not getting a very clear reading off us, still relying on info from the Harbin.'

It was crunch time. 'Okay, Nick,' Cherrier said. 'I'm taking her down, real slow. When we've settled on the bottom, you can take out a team of swimmers and run a wire for the remote radio buoy. I'll put out an SOS, give

534

our position and let the Fleet commander make the decision. At least, Washington can try for an assurance from the Chinese we'll all be arrested and not shot if we evacuate.'

Dancer listened, deeply depressed. 'All that for nothing,' he murmured.

'It won't be good news for Lily and Yan,' Walsh said. 'They *will* be executed or else spend the rest of their lives in a labour camp.'

Abe Stone grunted. 'The Chinese would love to put us all on a show trial and Washington knows it. So don't bet your sweet ass our illustrious President will agree to anything of the sort.'

Walsh smiled grimly. 'Sure, he's more likely to order the US Navy to pull the plug on us themselves.'

'We're a liability now, an embarrassment,' Stone added. 'And that means *expendable*. I've seen it all before.'

Dancer scowled at his friend. 'So what's the bad news?'

They all felt the sensation, like being in a lift in a shaft as the *Manta* floated gently into the deep, Cherrier juggling with the hydroplanes to maintain an equal balance. It seemed to be going on for a very long time. Then, suddenly they felt the soft jarring, a scrape of steel against rock, and then just the teeth-grating sound of the hull grinding against sand.

Cherrier fell back in his chair, mentally drained. 'That's as far as we go, folks,' he announced wearily.

Hinks leaned forward towards his console. 'Say, Captain, that's strange.'

'What?'

'The *Ming* sub's stopped too. About a quarter-mile distant.'

Cherrier jumped at the straw. 'Maybe she's lost us.'

'Maybe,' Hinks agreed optimistically. 'But she's also stopped using her active sonar. She's just listening.'

The captain turned to Lake. 'Not a moment to lose, Nick. Get your boys outside. And be as quiet as you can. If the *Ming* hears the ship's cat squeak, she'll be down on us like a ton of the proverbial brown stuff.'

Dancer felt a surge of hope as he tried to work out what had happened. Perhaps most of *Manta*'s lost tiles, which had given away her position to the enemy's active sonar, were on the bottom of the hull? So when she was lying on the seabed, she could no longer be detected.

He wished he could join the team outside, away from the claustrophobic confines of the submarine. It seemed that the hull and bulkheads were closing in on him with every second that passed. Cherrier was stretching his legs as Dancer approached him. 'Al, would it be out of order for me to watch Nick and the boys from the observation ports?'

The captain understood. 'Confines getting to you?'

'A bit.'

Cherrier indicated the ladder. 'Be my guest. But you won't see much.'

But at least he was escaping the press of bodies by scaling the aluminium ladder as Nick led McVicar, Taffy and Dougie Squires into the combat-swimmers' compartment and locked the hatch behind them before opening the valves for the water to flood in.

Moments later Dancer was able to observe through the Plexiglass ports in the fin as the main hatch opened and the first swimmer emerged like an astronaut in an underwater universe.

It took him back again to his training days during Viet Nam, seeing all the familiar paraphernalia of the diver: rubber wetsuit, like he himself and most on board were now wearing; mask, fins, weightbelt and inflatable stab vests for 'stabilisation' of depth which were incorporated in the closed-circuit Phibian scuba system which gave away no tell-tale bubbles. Nothing quite that fancy back then, of course, and he'd never felt that comfortable in an underwater environment. He'd dived several times since when on holiday with Debs who had always enjoyed exploring reefs. But even now, however technically competent he was, he preferred to keep his feet on dry land.

He watched as all four swimmers gathered round the hatch before beginning to hand-crank open the hatch doors of the aft equipment compartment set in the deck between the inner and outer hulls. In the murky, blue-green water he could just discern the transceiver buoy and the coiled wheel of cable that could be run out for a distance of half-a-mile in any direction. If any Chinese ship was able to pick up the burst transmission and somehow get a fix, they'd still be some way off the mark. Seeing the calm professionalism of Nick's team at work, he actually began to believe they could yet pull it off.

That belief prompted him to think, momentarily, that there might be a future after all. For him and for everyone on *Manta*. Suddenly he imagined himself in the bar in Laos serving beers, Walsh in the kitchen slogging over a wok and Abe Stone sitting at the cash register. A smile crept on to his face. Maybe not such a good idea.

Then, abruptly, his smile froze. In total disbelief, he squinted out into the shifting liquid world with its layers of mist-like sediment, reflected light and blending shades of green and blue and black. Forming and reforming, was he imagining the shapes? Were they coming closer or drifting away? Were they a trick of the moonlight above? Dark spectres, underwater phantoms? The ghosts of long-dead seamen? The bizarre thoughts tumbled through his mind.

Oh shit! Ghosts didn't blow bubbles. Now he could detect fine streams of them floating towards the surface as the figures became more defined. And somehow he knew instinctively these could not be US Navy frogmen.

Then he realised – they had come from beyond the submarine's bow. From the direction of the *Ming*. He began counting, and by the time he'd registered a dozen it dawned suddenly that he was wasting precious seconds.

'AL!' he yelled down into the control room. 'CHINESE SWIMMERS APPROACHING! CAN YOU WARN

NICK! I DON'T THINK HE'S SEEN THEM!'

Cherrier's face stared up at him, mouth agape. 'Oh, my God!' He reached for the laser-comms set to contact Lake's team.

Dancer turned to concentrate on the scene outside. The submarine's combat swimmers continued their preparations around the open storage compartment, engrossed in their work and unaware of the ghostly black figures closing inexorably through the underwater murk. Dancer shouted a warning, had to shout although he knew it was useless. He willed one of them to notice.

Then perhaps Cherrier's laser signal got through because suddenly one of the team – he thought the long, gangling form must be Dougie Squires – began looking round. The man hesitated for a moment as he saw the first of the wave of Chinese frogmen, then frantically began nudging the others. Dancer saw the problem. The team was armed only with fighting knives for close combat.

As Squires pointed at the advancing formation, the lead frogman lifted his harpoon gun and fired. Dancer saw the flash of polished steel and its silvery wake as the barbed dart shot across the watery void. Squires saw it coming and pushed McVicar roughly aside as he himself tried to duck. The action no doubt saved his life, but it didn't save him from the piercing agony as the dart thudded into his thigh. The power of the impact sent him spiralling backwards, tumbling like an astronaut in space. Black clouds billowed from the wound, obscuring him from view.

Now the others were doing the only thing they could – try and meet their attackers head on against hopeless odds. Hands reached feverishly to release the knife scabbards strapped to their ankles. Ambient light glinted on the double-edged, seven-inch blades as the Puma knives were drawn and the three survivors faced the enemy, forming a defensive half-circle around the wounded Squires.

The line of Chinese frogmen drew to a ragged halt, treading water as masked faces turned towards their leader.

He lifted his harpoon gun in signal and, as he did, the water was suddenly filled with streaking lines of barbed steel. They homed in on the little knot of defenders with vicious accuracy, like killer wasps. Suddenly the water was filled with a bubbling turmoil as Lake's team tried to evade the onslaught. Taffy went down, a harpoon embedded in his right shoulder. One ricocheted noisily off McVicar's back cylinder as he ducked. Some studded the *Manta*'s upper casing, quivering from the unspent power of their flight, while others missed completely and zipped away into the surrounding blackness.

Because the harpoon guns were one-shot weapons, the Chinese frogmen were closing in for the kill with knives drawn. As the first two approached, McVicar launched himself at one, diving to one side and curling his body violently round in the water so that he came up behind the man's back. McVicar's left forearm locked around the diver's throat while the Puma in his right cut through the rubber tubes of his enemy's breathing apparatus. Another carving action found the exposed flesh of the man's throat. McVicar jerked the blade hard back, severing the windpipe. With that, he pushed the frogman contemptuously aside and watched him spiral upwards in a streaming vortex of bubbles.

Meanwhile, Lake had lunged straight at the second frogman, parrying the thrust of the Chinese diver's knife with his left forearm. The razor-edge caught the rubber of his wet suit, painlessly slicing deep into his flesh, only the black coil of blood telling him he'd been injured. But he'd opened up the frogman's guard and now lunged with his right arm, the blade of his Puma punching into the man's exposed front. He felt the resistance of the rubber and shoved again with all his strength, forcing it up under the ribcage and into the lungs until it was buried up to the D-guard handgrip. The frogman's mouthpiece fell away in a silent scream. A rush of air bubbled out of his mouth, followed by ribbons of black blood, trailing unhurriedly towards the surface.

Breathing heavily, Lake and McVicar trod water a few metres apart and searched out the rest of the underwater pack. The Chinese were holding back, assessing the situation. About fifteen of them left, Dancer thought as he watched from the submarine. He saw the leader motion to a group farther back and realised then that they had not yet fired their harpoon guns. They would pick off McVicar and Lake first before coming in again. It would be a turkey-shoot.

At that moment Dancer became aware of the strange fluttering light from above, like an old movie film flickering through a projector gate. He hunkered down so that he could see towards the surface. Great rotating shadows were being cast by the three-quarter moon, so that the light of the undersea world began to tremble. It was unsettling, like the vision of a man entering into an epileptic fit.

Even then he did not immediately grasp what was happening, that the giant windmill of flashing light was created by the six-bladed rotors of the hovering Sikorsky Sea Stallions. The brilliant white beams of the helicopters' search-lamps suddenly cut in, boring deep holes of light into the water, seeking out the enemy.

Then they came like human depth bombs. One after another, black heavily weighted shapes plunging down fast through the translucent ceiling in a storm of phosphorescence. Dancer began to count as they descended rapidly like underwater paratroopers. But he became distracted as the Chinese frogmen realised what was happening. Their body language and postures said it all. Some were already turning, not waiting for instructions, swimming back towards the *Ming* submarine, kicking their fins furiously in their panic.

Those closer to the new arrivals did not have the luxury of time and distance. Some drew knives and prepared to make a stand, those still with unfired harpoon guns hurriedly brought them to bear.

But the American combat swimmers were well rehearsed and fast off the mark. A volley of harpoons let rip as soon as they had regrouped after their dive. Their united aim was deadly, sending Chinese frogmen spinning left and right as the bolts found their targets. Bodies tumbled or cartwheeled away as blood pumped out into the growing black fog. In desperation some of the wounded headed straight up to the surface. Seeing that the Americans were making no attempt to follow, the remainder began heading back towards the *Ming*.

Dancer began clambering down into the control room to tell Cherrier and the others what had happened.

Outside, the American combat swimmers divided into teams. One took the badly injured Taffy and Squires up to the surface to be winched aboard one of the hovering Sea Stallions, while another team formed a defensive ring around the *Manta*.

Their leader motioned Nick Lake to go back inside the submarine through the main escape hatch. Minutes later they were floating down into the flooded compartment, resealing the cover above them. As the auxiliary pumps began their work, the water level lowered until, when it was at waist-level, Lake pulled off his mask and examined the cut on his arm. Nothing a dressing wouldn't put right, he decided.

The American leader pulled off his face mask and hood. The wildchild ginger ringlets had gone, but there was no mistaking the familiar drooping moustache above the wide grin.

Lake was amazed. 'Troy, you old bastard! What the fuck are you doing here?'

'Saving your sweet ass, by the look of it,' Krowsky said, laughing. 'Trust you Brits to go messing things up. Lucky you got the US SEALs to get you out the shit!'

Lake took the American's enormous hand. 'Two world wars, Troy, and nothing's changed. We do all the work, then you come in at the end to take all the glory.'

Krowsky roared. 'You ungrateful asshole. Gave up my new job on Wall Street to be here with you bunch of fuckers.'

'Then I wonder who's saved who?'

The last of the water drained away and Lake spun the wheel-lock to open the hatch to the control room. Cherrier and the crew, Dancer and Janie Walsh were waiting as Krowsky followed Lake through.

'Bloody hell,' the American said. 'This is your original sardine-tin. Are you guys overloaded or what?'

Cherrier shook the man's hand. 'Never thought I'd see you again, Troy.'

'Tough tit, eh?' He raised a hand in greeting at the gathering. 'Our top sonar boys have been following events. But now the game's over. I've orders to evacuate everyone pronto. We've got Sea Stallions up top to spirit you all back to the 7th.'

'What about the Chinese?' Dancer asked.

'We've got our Tomcat top-guns up doing loop-the-loop and talking mean.'

'We've got one badly injured with broken limbs,' Cherrier said.

Krowsky was dismissive. 'No problem. Just give him a scuba rig and tie him to a stretcher. We'll take him straight up through the hatch. The helo medics will take care of him.'

'And what about *Manta*?' Cherrier asked.

'You still got the demolition charges rigged?'

The captain nodded solemnly; he'd been expecting this, and it hurt. 'Of course, standing orders. I'll have the circuit checked and set it to fifteen minutes when I go.'

'Sure.'

Krowsky wanted the civilians out first. Two SBS men manhandled Yan Tao's stretcher into the combat swimmers' compartment, then Dancer followed with Abe Stone, Lily and her son. Lake and McVicar came with them to give instruction and moral support. Bao was very stoic and giggling as he put on his mask; it was all just a great adventure.

Lily was terrified.

'I'll stay with you,' Dancer said, 'all the way to the surface. Just keep calm and breathe normally.'

She smiled the smile the Chinese smile when they think they're going to die. 'I know you will look after me, John.' She reached out and touched his hand. 'Thank you for everything you've done.'

'I was just doing my job.'

A frown fractured the smooth surface of her brow, 'Not always, I think – I hope.'

He knew what she meant. 'No, not always.'

'You will always mean a lot to me. Always be close to my heart.'

Dancer understood. The old Chinese proverb. 'And this too will pass?'

'Yes.' Nothing stays the same for ever, they both knew. 'Yan Tao has asked me to marry him when we reach America.'

'I'm pleased. For both of you.'

She held his gaze for a moment, a questioning look in her eyes as though she were trying to make up her mind about something. Then Lake ordered everyone to put their mouthpieces in place and pull their masks down. Water began rushing in and the compartment started to fill.

Al Cherrier was the last to leave, one SBS man waiting to go with him. When the demolition charge was set and the switch thrown, he looked around the control room for the final time. Emotion was thick in his throat. *Manta* had served as his home for many months now. But, more than that, she had been his mistress for several years. She'd been troublesome and cantankerous at times, but in his eyes had never been less than a beauty. And she'd never let him down, not really.

Funny, he thought as he went through the hatch for the last time, how grown men have the ability to fall in love with inanimate lumps of metal. Cars, motorcycles, steam trains. At least, he consoled himself, a submarine was a bit different.

Goodbye, old girl, he mouthed silently, it's been good to know you.

Epilogue

The huge Sea Stallion helicopters came in low, line astern with their rotors throbbing dully in the night air.

Below, through the port, Dancer could see the necklace of deck lights on the USS *Theodore Roosevelt* advancing to meet them. Then something caught his eye out in the Yellow Sea in the direction from which they had come. A sudden flash of white foam amid the black lacquer of the water and a geyser of spray. He didn't hear the rolling boom of the explosion above the din of the helicopter engines, but then he didn't have to. *Manta* was committed to the deep, her final resting place.

Then, suddenly, they were down, the Sea Stallion's wheels thudding on the deck as it rose to meet them on the swell. Moments later the engine noise died away to a whine and the rotors slowed to a standstill before the helicopter's rear loading ramp was lowered. As they stepped out, Dancer realised that they were on one of the aircraft carrier's outer lift sections and already it was beginning to descend to the breathless wheeze of strong hydraulic arms. He guessed the Navy wanted all evidence out of sight before the sun rose and Chinese air patrols attempted to take an interest.

Bao stared around him in total awe. 'Mama, this is the biggest ship in the world! When I grow up I want to be captain of *this* ship!'

Dancer grinned. 'Maybe you will.'

With a great sigh of resignation the lift came to a halt. Dancer recognised the two civilians waiting for them amid the group of senior US Navy officers.

'Am I glad to see you,' Iona Moncrieff said, looking clearly relieved. 'You know Piers Lansdowne.'

The man from 'Riverside' had a wide, boyish grin on his face but was otherwise cool, just raising his right hand in informal greeting. 'At one point we didn't think you were going to make it.'

Dancer laughed, relief rushing through him now like a flood. 'Neither did we.' He glanced around. 'Isn't Bill here?'

Iona took a deep breath. 'I'm sure he is in spirit, John. But I'm afraid Bill's dead. A heart attack.'

'God, no,' Dancer breathed. 'I can hardly believe it. I thought the old bastard was indestructible.'

'So did I.' Flatly.

Abe Stone overheard. 'I was even getting to like him.'

Dancer frowned. 'And no sign of Frank Aspen?'

A faint smile played on Iona's lips. 'If Frank were here, John, then I don't think any of you would be. Bill took the risk and put Krowsky's boys on stand-by to help you out – but without informing Langley or the Pentagon. Once he'd done that, it was just operational detail and Piers and I were able to bypass official channels in Washington.'

'Then I guess we all owe him,' Stone said.

She sighed. 'We'll all miss him.' She straightened her back. 'Anyway, Piers and I just wanted to welcome you back. And to say thank you for all you did – or tried to do. It all took great courage.'

'We're being flown off to Seoul now,' Lansdowne explained. 'Then back to London and Washington for debriefing.'

'We've a wee bit of explaining to do,' she admitted sheepishly. They shook hands then and walked off with Vice Admiral Harding to be shown to their transport and a thrill-of-a-lifetime ride in the rear two seats of a twin-engined Lockheed S-3A Viking anti-submarine jet.

Dancer then noticed the stretcher being carried by two US Navy corpsmen. Yan Tao was laughing as he talked to Lily who walked by his side with little Bao.

'You're looking brighter,' Dancer told Yan as the stretcher-bearers paused so they could talk.

'During that nightmare escape to the surface, I saw my ancestors and they approve of me. I can cope with *anything* now!' He clasped Lily's hand tightly. 'Especially with my wife's help. We have a long fight ahead of us.'

Dancer interrupted. 'Rest now,' he said quietly. With the democracy movement mostly still intact, there'll be other opportunities.'

Yan nodded, his enthusiasm undiminished. 'We are just grateful that you tried. There is an expression in English, I think, it is better to have tried and failed, than never to have tried at all.'

Abe Stone grunted. 'That's Brit-speak,' he said acidly. 'Sure winning ain't everything – it's the *only* thing.'

'Goodbye, Lily,' Dancer said, taking her offered hand. It was as cool and feather-like as he remembered, her eyes dark and full of uncertainty. Somehow he knew what she was thinking and he wondered for how long she would carry her secret torch for him. Not long, he prayed, for Tao's sake. Soon Lily would be distracted by her new life in America with Tao and Bao. Then perhaps another child. Dancer hoped that then the embers of her brief and burning relationship with him would be left untended and fade to just a fond and distant memory.

'We will not forget you, John.' She looked down at her son. 'Will we, Bao?'

He shook his head vehemently. 'You will always be my favourite Uncle John. You will write me many letters?'

'Sure,' Dancer said, but knew even as he spoke the words that he was lying. Some things were best left undone.

He felt a momentary sadness as he watched the stretcher-bearers walk on into the floodlit bowels of the carrier. Everyone had gone now, except Stone and Walsh who stood chatting and laughing at the edge of the lift.

He came up behind and between them, placing an arm around each of their shoulders.

Walsh's smile sparked like a short-circuit. 'I could *murder* some chow!'

'Bacon, eggs and beans,' Stone suggested as they started walking forward together.

'Waffles and maple syrup,' Walsh added.

Dancer said, 'And a bottomless pot of Colombian coffee.'

'We must do American breakfasts at our bar in Laos,' Walsh said.

Stone frowned. 'You know about this?'

'Sure,' she replied breezily. 'John invited me to join your partnership.'

'Is this true?' Stone asked.

Dancer shrugged. 'I think she more or less invited herself. What d'you think?'

'A pretty face won't hurt, I guess.' The idea was growing on him.

She said, 'Maybe we should call it Janie's Bar.'

Now they had reached the ranks of Tomcat interceptors and A-6 Intruder fighters stripped down for servicing under the arc lights.

For some reason, Dancer felt a compulsion to let the other two walk on while he turned back towards the huge open port that led on to the lift where the Sea Stallion still stood alone. It was in silhouette against the sea and a sky that was lightening by the minute as the sun rose in the east.

Her voice was as clear as though she were standing next to him.

'It really is time for me to go now, Johnny. Fan's here. Time for me to let you get on with your life. I'll love you always.'

And the words were drowned out by the demonic roar of afterburners as a Tomcat took off from the deck above.

Momentarily he thought he saw the figure with the copper ringlets and smiling eyes standing on the lift in the same white summer dress, outlined against the Yellow Sea. But even as he thought he focused on the image, it dissolved before his eyes.

Slowly he turned back. Stone had gone on through the bulkhead hatch, but Walsh was waiting for him. As always, there was a smile on her face.

**POCKET
BOOKS**

The new thriller by Terence Strong
President Down

Former intelligence officer and one-time instructor at the
British Army School of Sniping, Phil Mason is struggling to
make ends meet as a private investigator when he's contacted
by his former M15 liaison officer.

The overstretched security service needs all the help it can
get hunting down members of al-Qaeda terror cells in the
UK – and Mason needs the cash.

But in the murky intelligence world of smoke and mirrors,
nothing is what it seems. As a routine surveillance operation
escalates into a full-blown international crisis, Mason must
come to terms with the unthinkable: there must be a traitor
within Britain's security forces.

Entering a desperate race against time to identify and avert a
major terrorist threat, Mason must hastily re-hone his old
counter-sniper skills as he returns to the business he swore
he had left behind forever. The killing game.

'Relentless energy from a man who knows his tradecraft,
survival skills, muzzle velocities and conspiracy theory as
well as anyone in the business' *Guardian*

**ISBN-13: 978-0-7432-8564-3
PRICE £11.99**

**POCKET
BOOKS**

This book and other **Terence Strong** titles are available
from your local bookshop or can be ordered direct
from the publisher.